I0762397

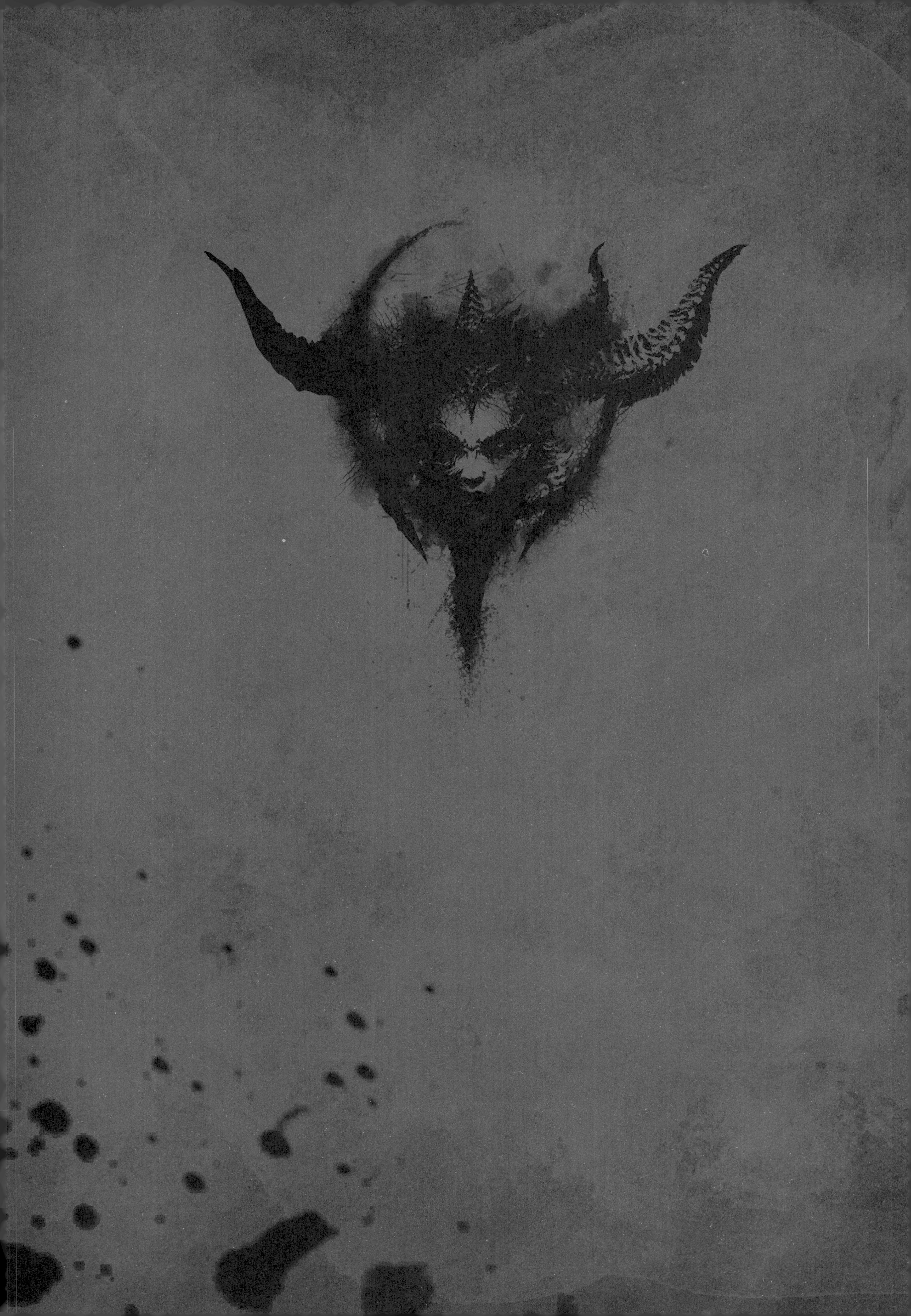

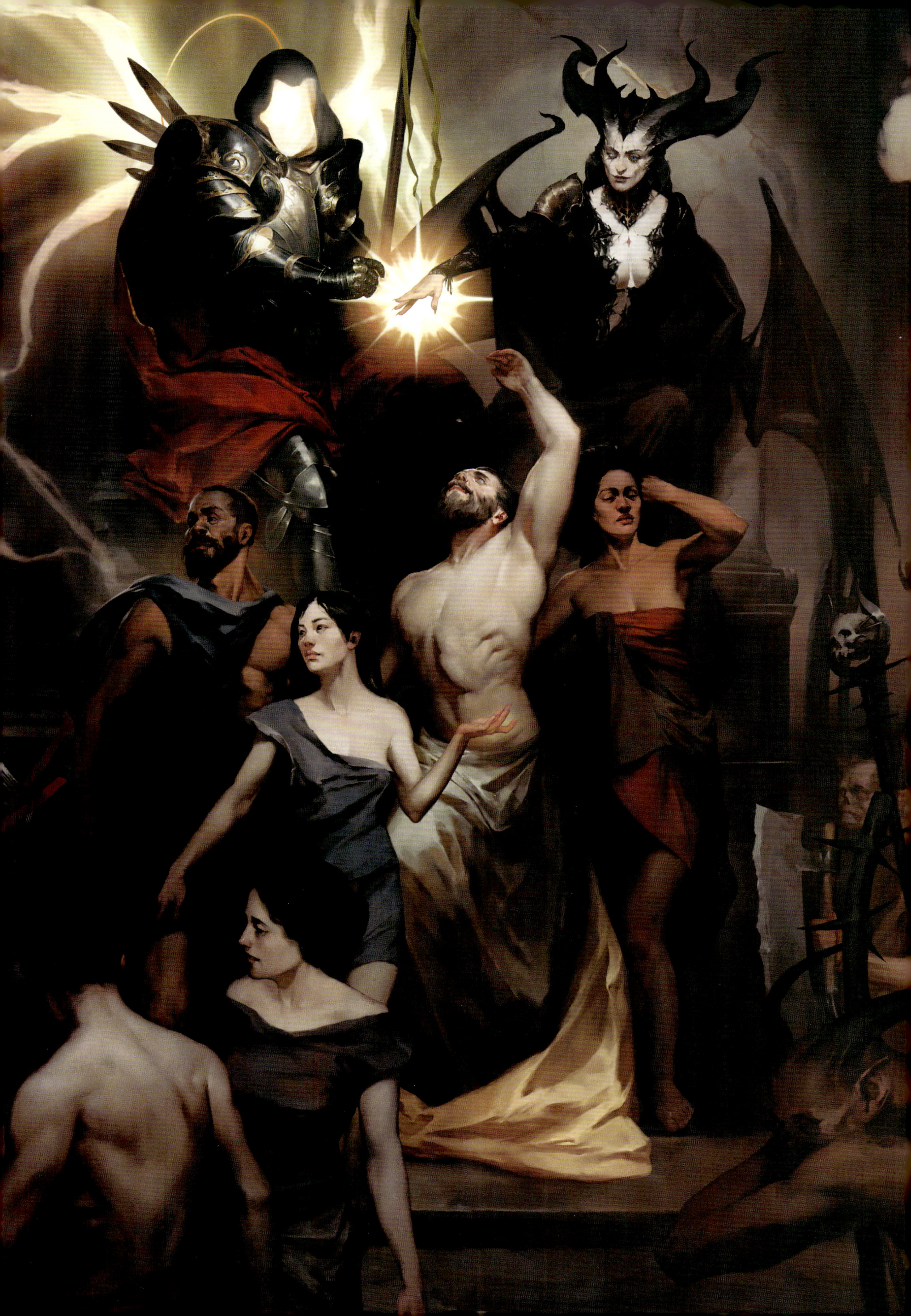

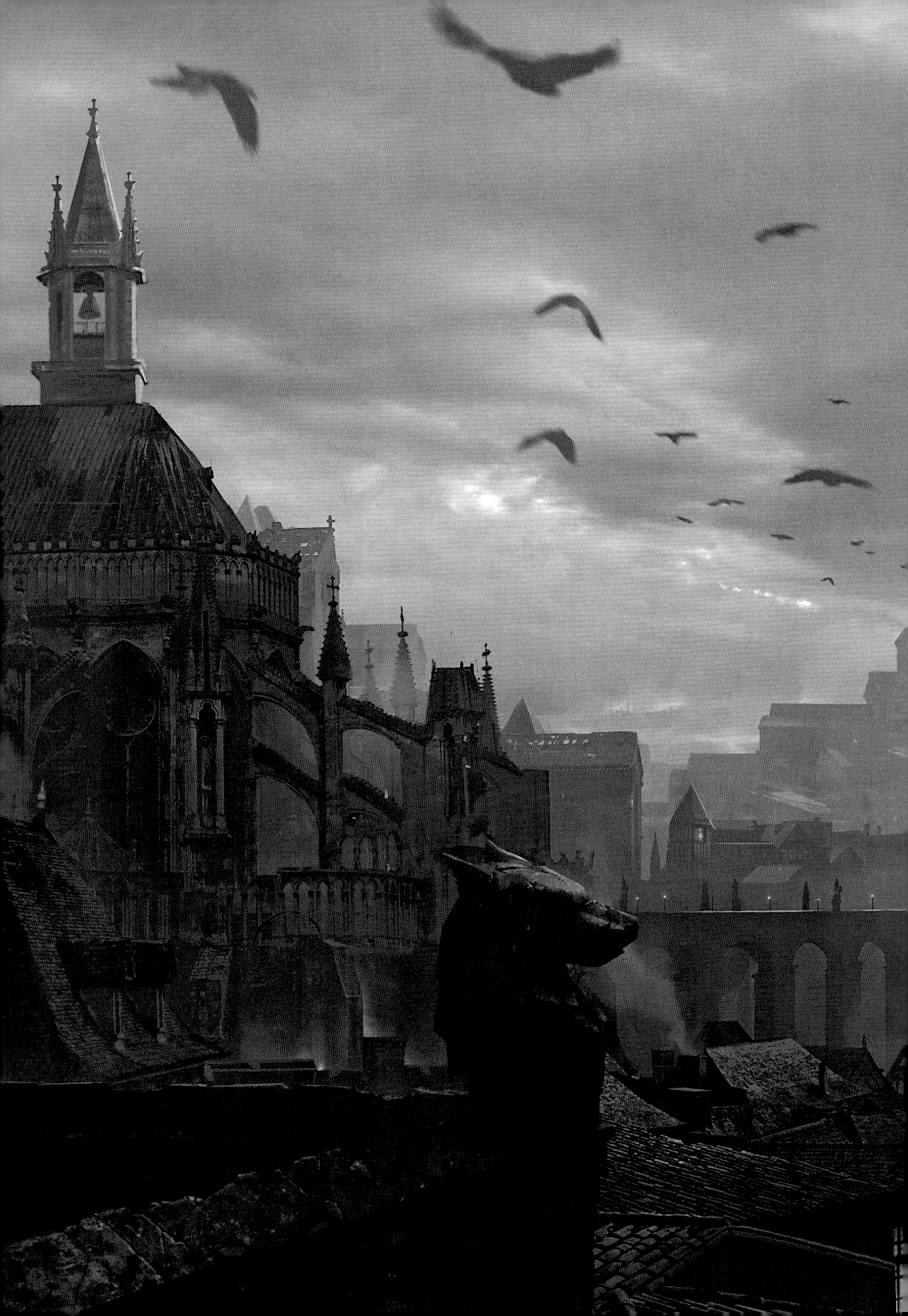

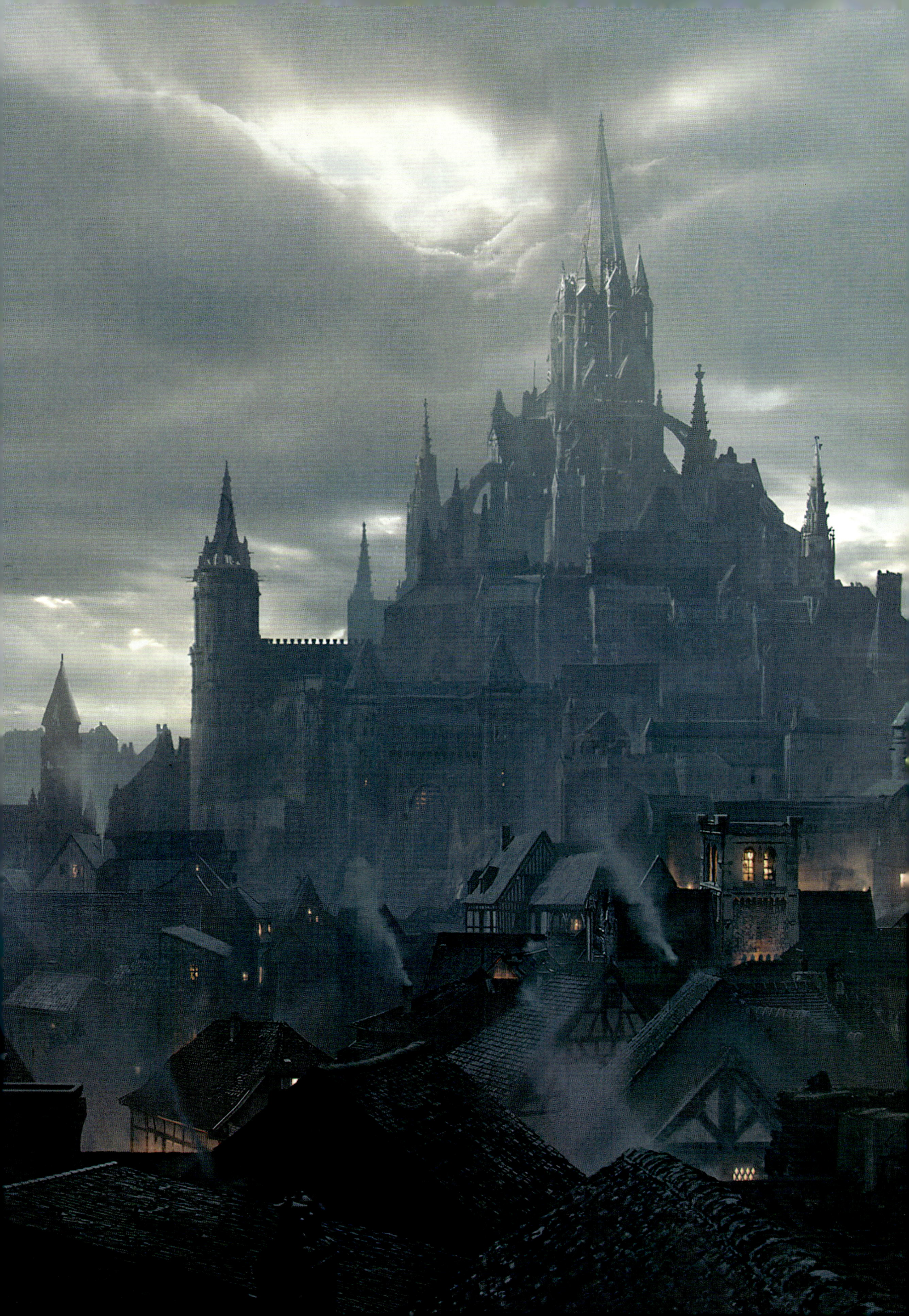

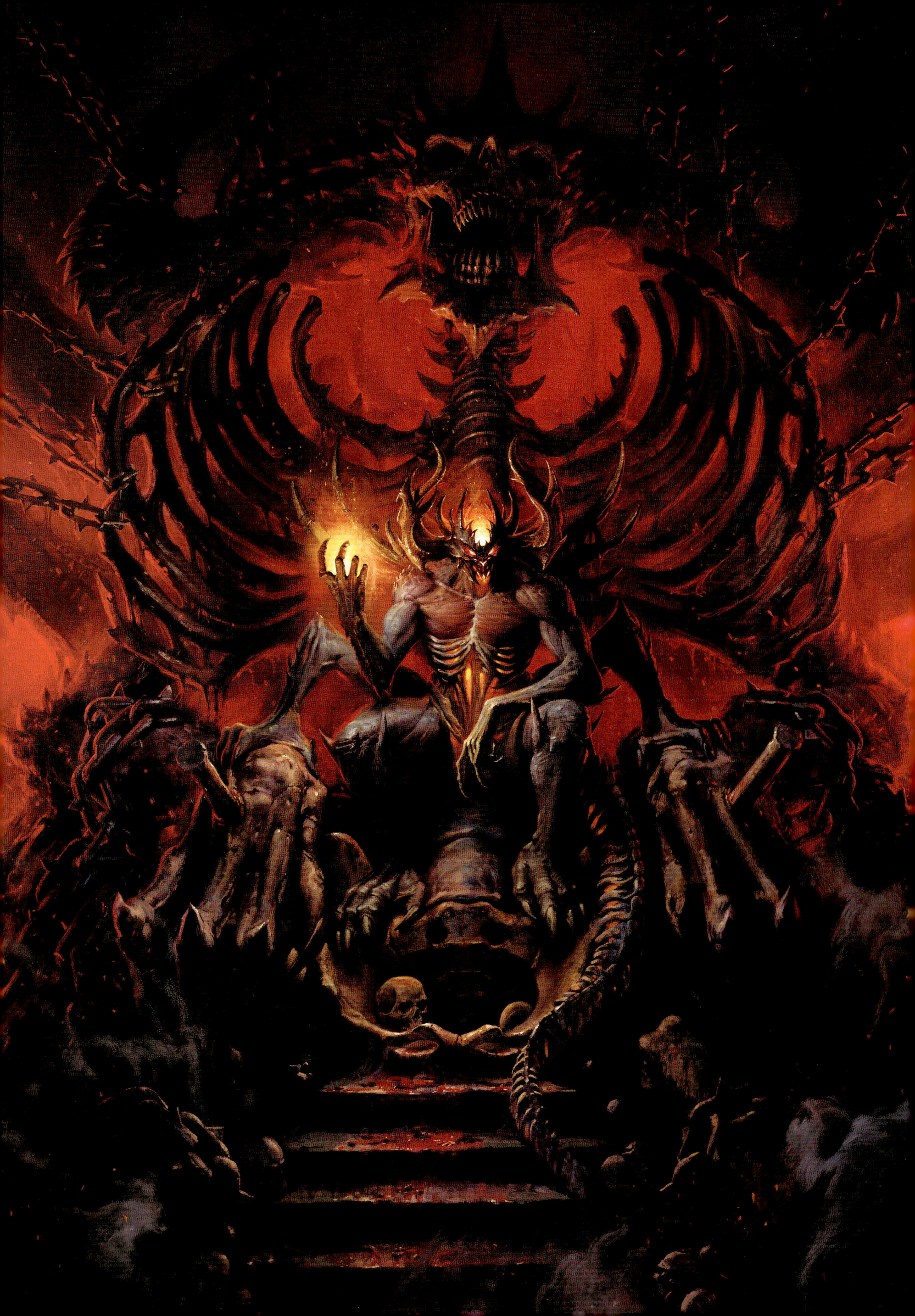

THE ART OF

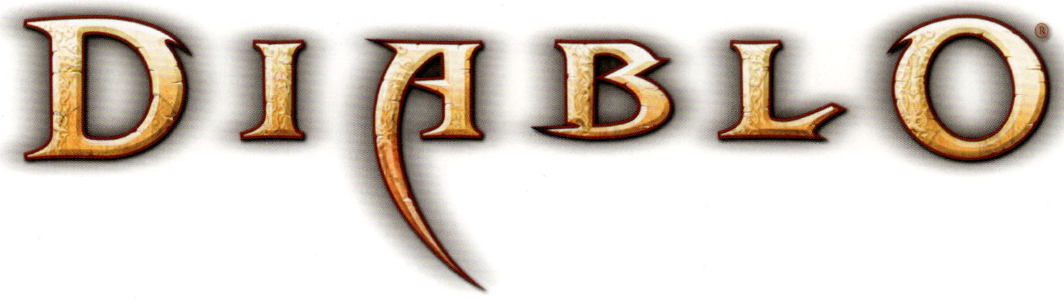

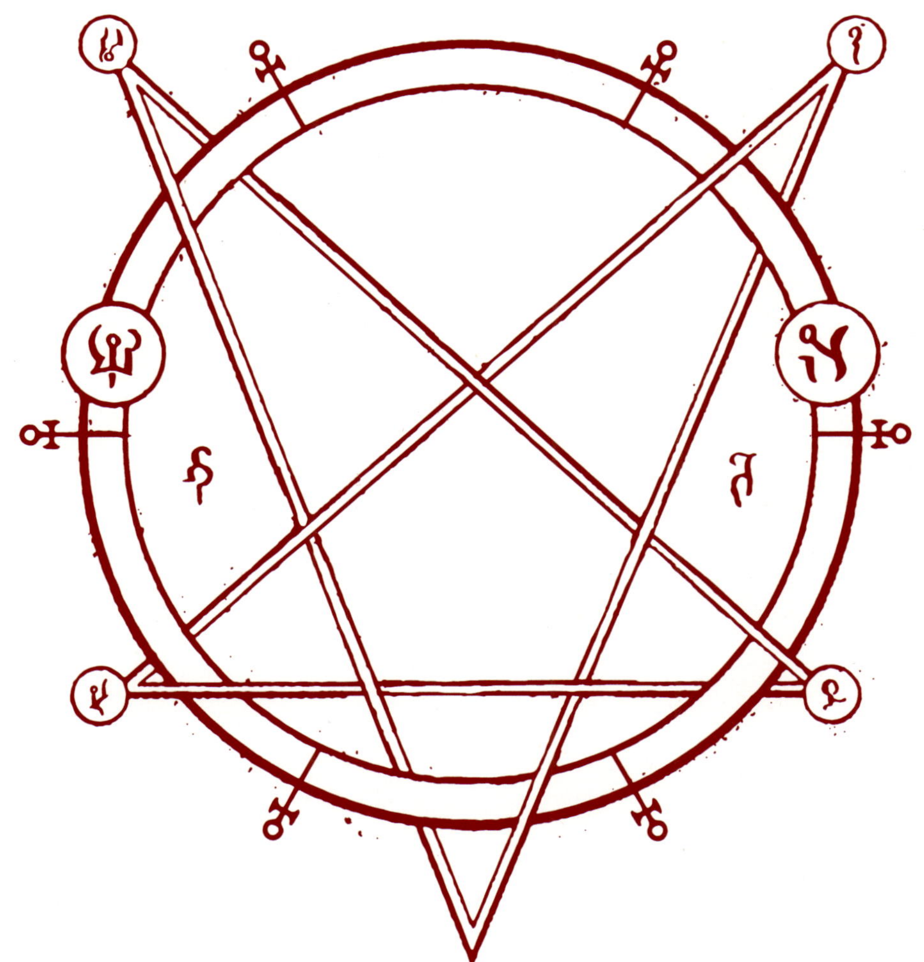

VOLUME II

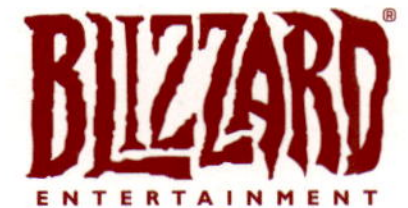

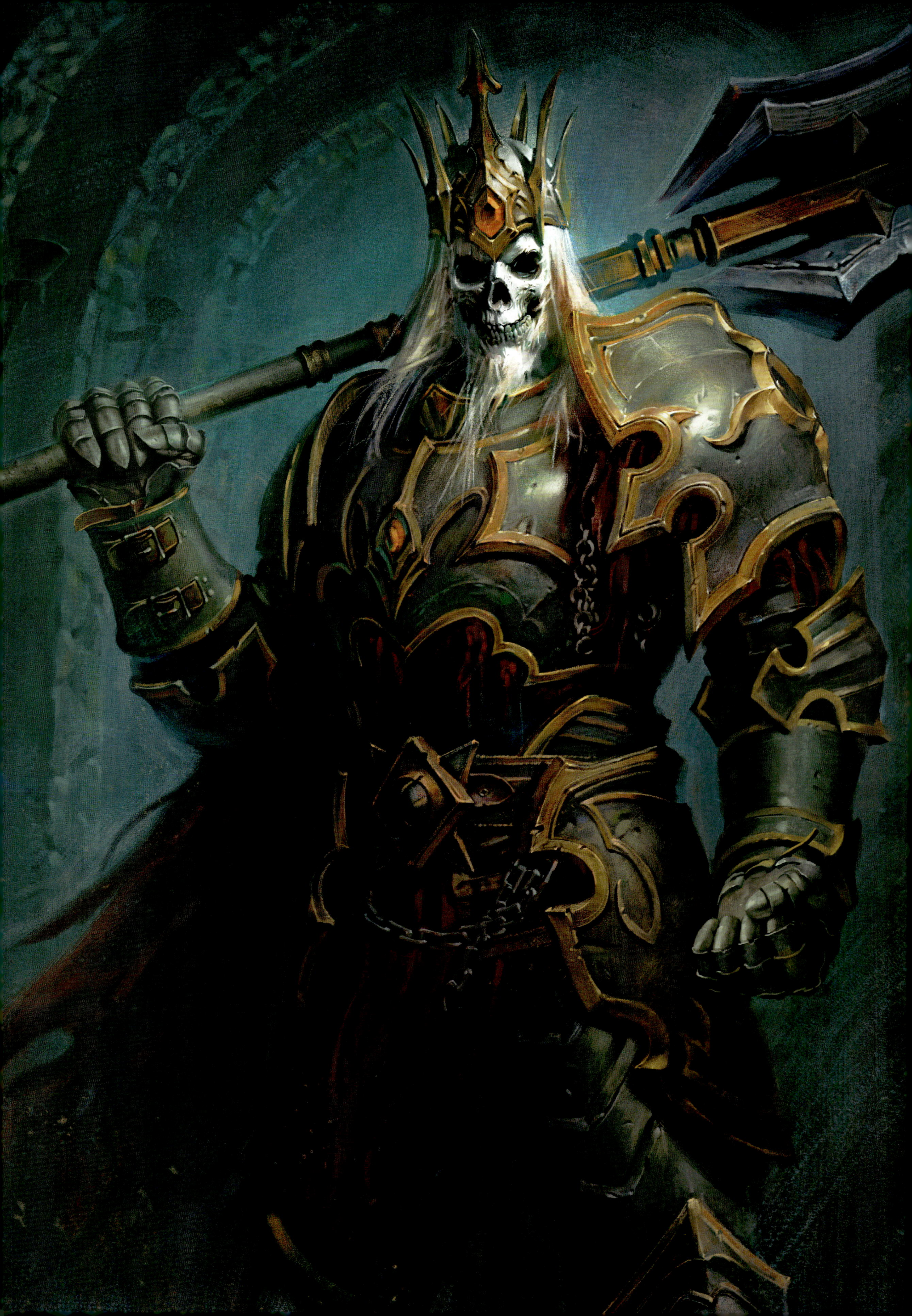

CONTENTS

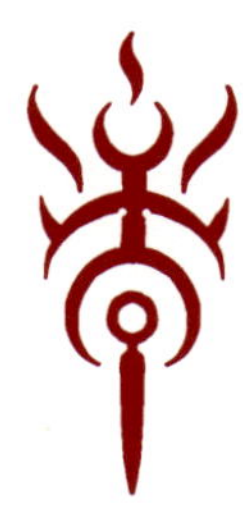

FOREWORD

BY JOHN MUELLER

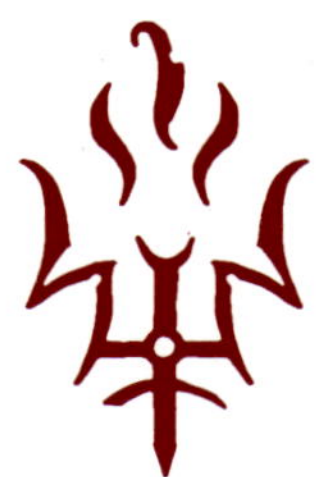

It is an honor to write the foreword for *The Art of Diablo: Volume II*. For over two decades, the world of *Diablo*, Sanctuary, and its denizens have captured the imaginations of millions of gamers worldwide. Its unique blend of dark fantasy, horror, and action has inspired countless artists on their own artistic journeys.

In this book, you will find a stunning collection of artwork that has inspired the creation of three recent releases in the *Diablo* universe: *Diablo II: Resurrected*, *Diablo Immortal,* and *Diablo IV*. From the dark and foreboding dungeons to the twisted landscapes of Hell itself, each piece of art expertly depicts the world and its inhabitants through different lenses, yet still remains undeniably *Diablo*.

The artists featured in this book have poured their dark hearts and souls into each piece, and it shows. Their artwork is a testament to the passion and dedication they have for this revered franchise.

For those of us who are lucky enough to work on *Diablo*, it is a dream come true to have our artwork added to the history and legacy of such a beloved series. Through their art, they have brought to life the characters, creatures, environments, loot, and effects that make the world of *Diablo* so unforgettable.

I am certain that fans of *Diablo*, as well as fans of dark gothic art and fantasy, will be captivated by the incredible artwork contained within this book. It is a true celebration of the creativity and talent of the artists who have contributed to the world of *Diablo*—and a fitting tribute to one of the greatest video game series of all time.

ABOVE Triune Insignia Concept + *Diablo IV* + Fernando Pinilla
OPPOSITE Lilith Early Concept + *Diablo IV* + Igor Sidorenko

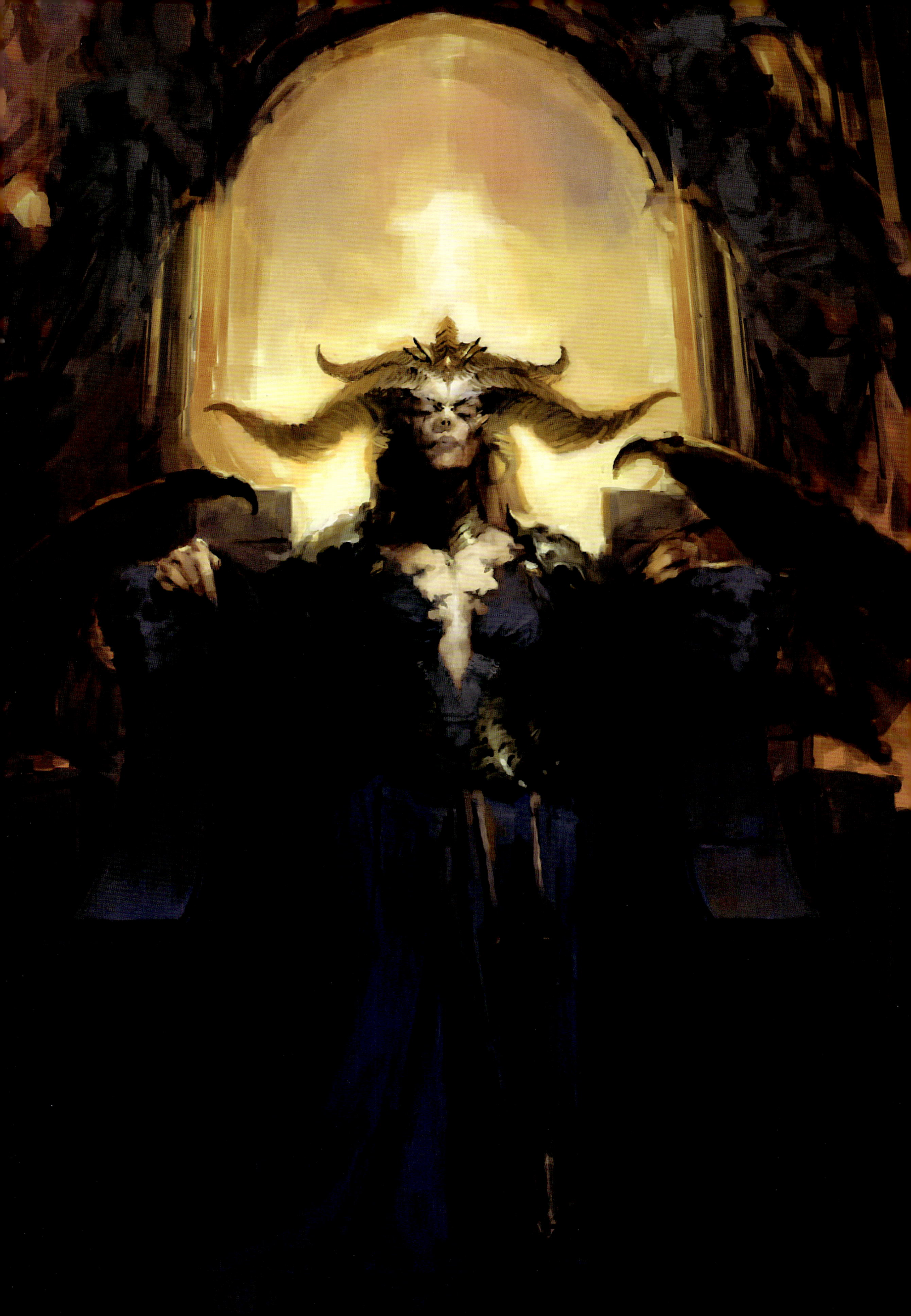

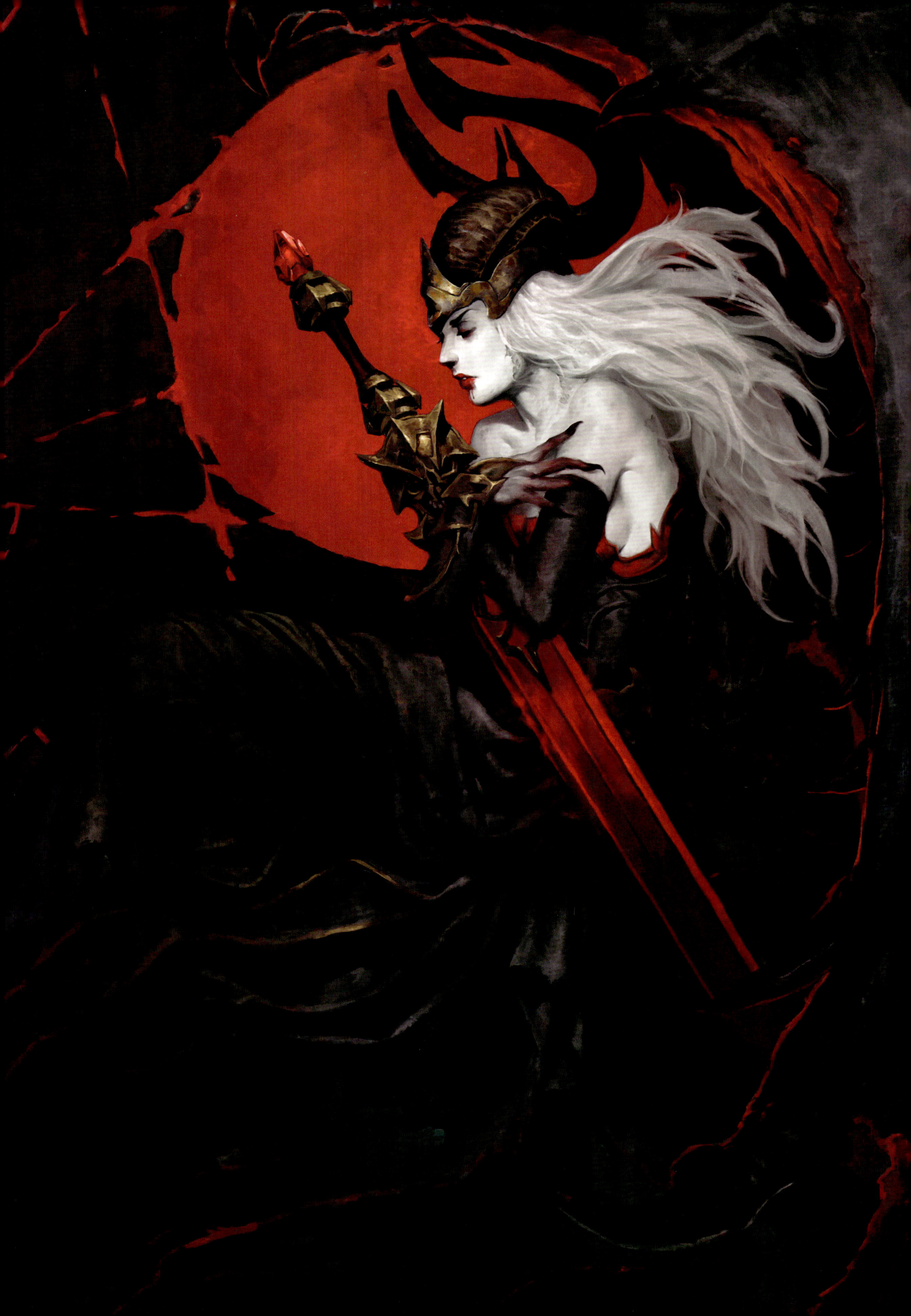

INTRODUCTION

BY ROD FERGUSSON

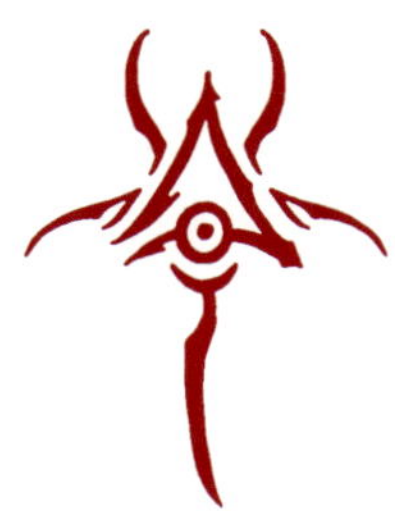

When I first entered Sanctuary, I was alone, armed with just a sword against the darkness . . . but not for long. In 2001 I visited my much older brother in Winnipeg, and we spent an entire sleepless weekend playing *Diablo II* and its newly released expansion, *Lord of Destruction*. We still talk about it to this day; the experience strengthened our bond tremendously.

Fast forward to 2012: launch night for *Diablo III* with my two sons. We arranged our new laptops around the table like some kind of summoning circle then; but in the decade that followed, you could find us ritually setting up three TVs and consoles side by side to play every Christmas break. My journey through Sanctuary may have started small . . . but it grew to mean so much more.

So, when Blizzard offered me the opportunity to head up the series, how could I refuse?

In 2021, we launched *Diablo II: Resurrected*, a full remaster of the classic that defined its genre. This entry renders both the original game as well as the new native 3D version at the same time, switching between them with a simple button press. Our artists were able to create beautiful next generation visuals that felt so faithful to the original, you'd swear it was what the game looked like twenty-one years ago . . . until you swap back to the original 2D sprites to realize just how far we've come.

2022 brought the launch of *Diablo Immortal*, our first mobile game. I still struggle to understand how the team managed to craft such an authentic Diablo experience for mobile. Even on a tiny screen, the work of the artists captures my imagination and transports me back to Sanctuary. . . and now I can do it almost anywhere.

Finally, *Diablo IV* arrived in 2023. Our art style embraced the "return to darkness" aesthetic to its fullest: a Renaissance painting come to life, as if the old masters themselves had guided our development team. The artistic vision is so clear, I find myself pausing after a fight just to take in the beauty of the gothic surroundings.

While I may have been alone when I first entered Sanctuary over 26 years ago, I've found a lot of kindred spirits in family, friends, colleagues, and now teammates, all summoning me back to this epic series. What you hold in your hand is a collection of stunning artwork created by those kindred spirits, and a discussion of the philosophy behind their work; a visual expression of talent, dedication and passion for a world and a series that we all love.

Please enjoy.

ABOVE Triune Insignia Concept + *Diablo IV* + Fernando Pinilla

OPPOSITE The Countess Concept + *Diablo Immortal* + NetEase Art Team

FOLLOWING SPREAD Hall of Ascension Illustration + *Diablo Immortal* + Geunjoo Baik, Yongsoon Park

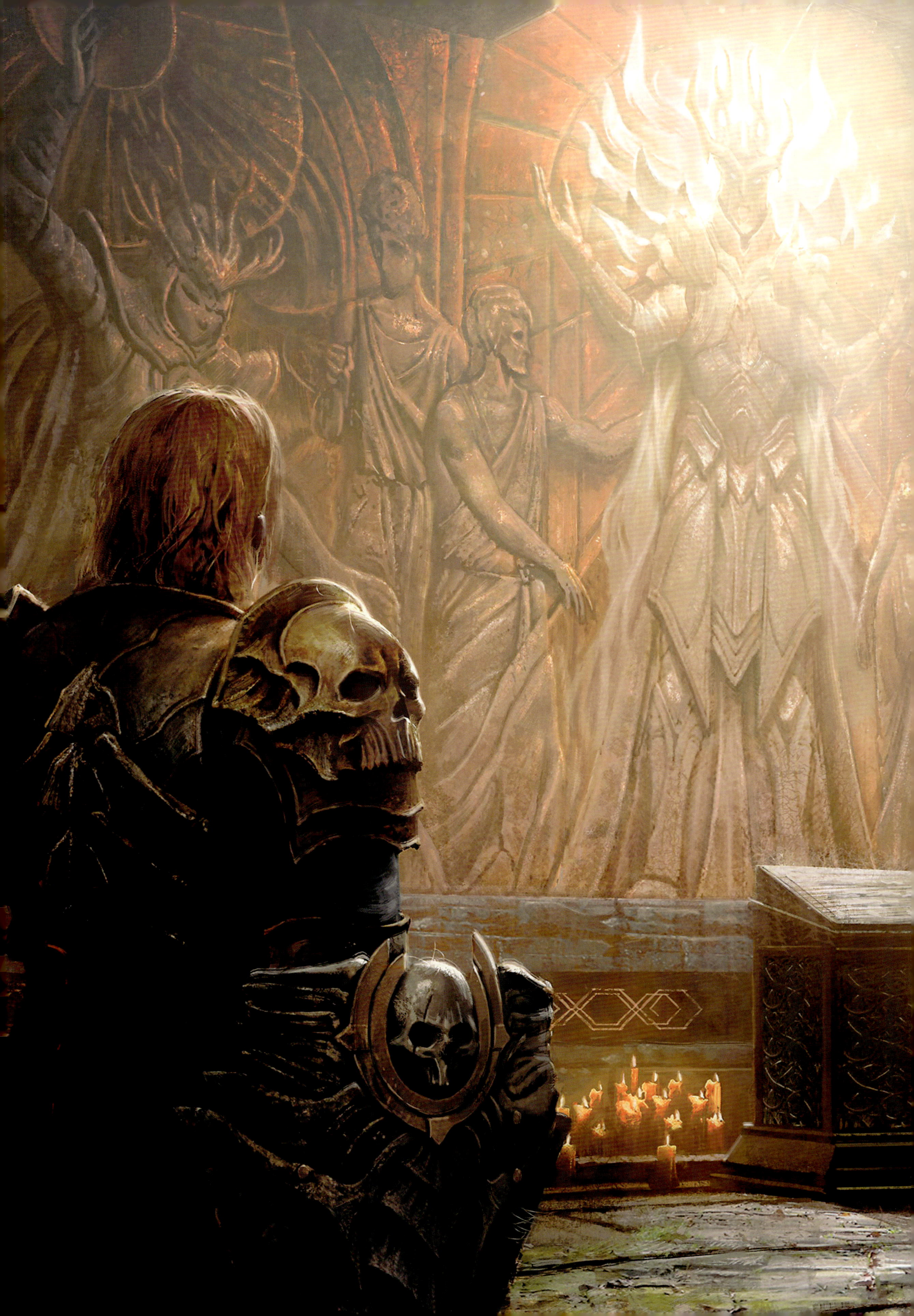

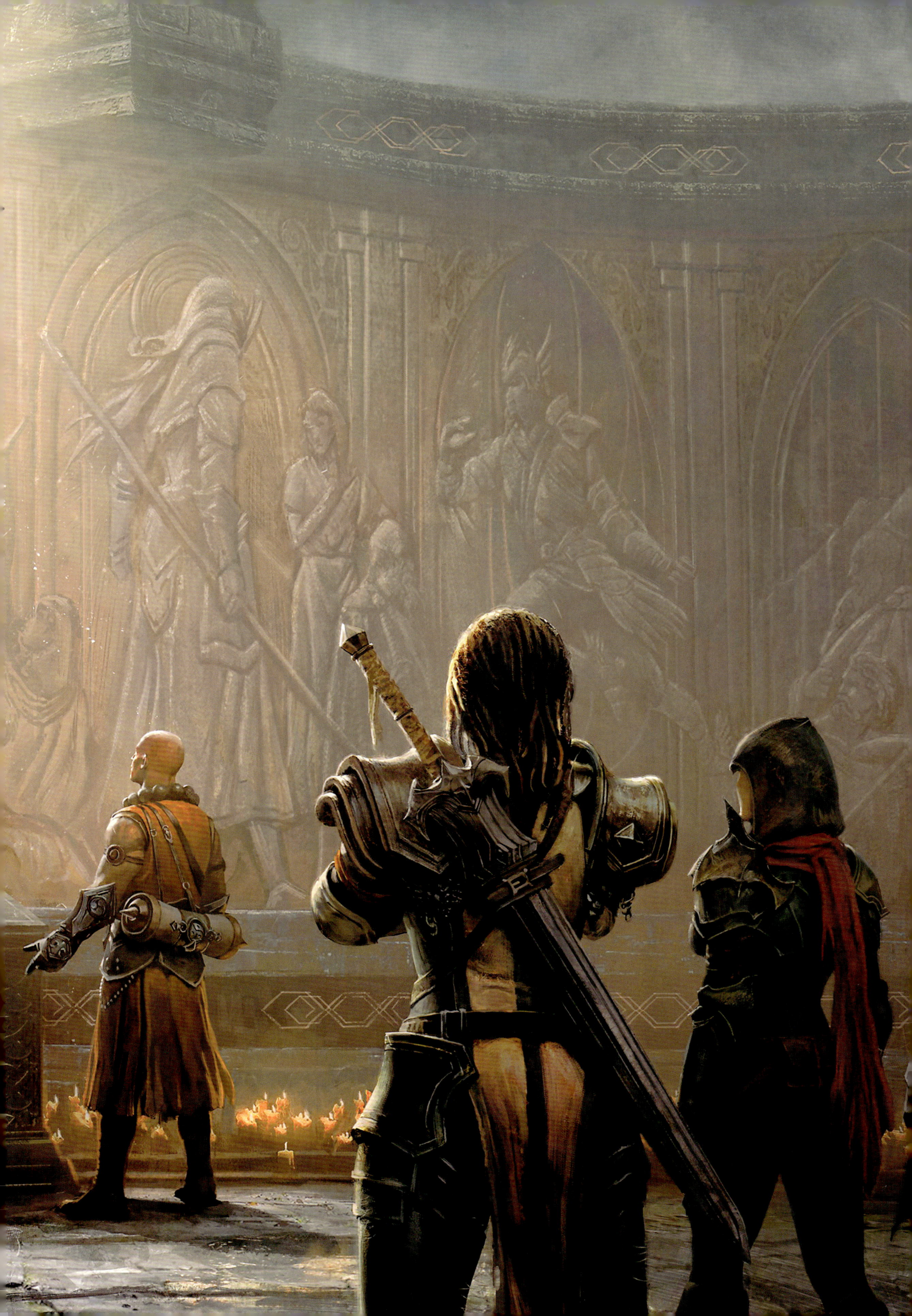

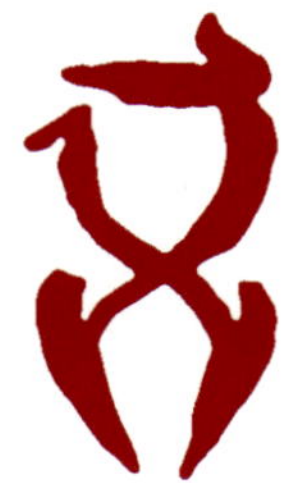

The Art of Diablo, Volume I leads readers into the dark heart of the Diablo universe. It showcases the grim world of Sanctuary, where beleaguered but determined humans fight to survive in the midst of the Eternal Conflict between the Burning Hells and the High Heavens. Its terror-filled pages introduce the characters, loot, creatures, and environments of the *Diablo* franchise, offering up a host of varied artistic styles—from the gritty realism of *Diablo I*, *Diablo II*, and the *Lord of Destruction* expansion to the more painterly high fantasy aesthetic of *Diablo III* and its expansion, *Reaper of Souls*.

The Art of Diablo, Volume II continues the legacy of the first book while focusing on the three latest entries in the franchise.

Diablo II: Resurrected harkens to the game's storied past. Developers took on the mammoth task of updating the beloved installment, deciding early on to convert the original from 2D sprite-based graphics to full 3D. It was a choice that introduced many hurdles but would also reinforce the themes and tones of the classic game.

"Contrast," observes *Diablo II: Resurrected* art director Dustin King. "That's exactly what *Diablo* is; it's a game of contrast. Good versus evil, light versus dark. And we were able to represent that in the 3D space in the conversion."

The remaster also allowed creators to enhance the original game's gritty, detailed style.

"We felt it was important to show that Blizzard fidelity could be pushed further," says character lead Cory Turner. "We really wanted to show that the in-game art could look much closer to the cinematics, and that we could fulfill the desire for this realistic *Diablo*. We wanted to get ahead of that messaging, that the brand was going to come back to the whole dark, gothic feel."

While *Diablo II: Resurrected* elevated and enhanced the gritty detail of its classic namesake, *Diablo Immortal* substituted detail for clarity.

"In *Diablo II* or *Diablo IV*, you might get away with smaller details," says *Diablo Immortal* art director Hunter Schulz. "But for us, it came down to choosing what was most important in the design and distilling that down into what made the most sense, then exaggerating it. Say you're doing a shoulder pad that has a skull on it; maybe it's more simplified with less details and you exaggerate the shape of the skull so that on

ABOVE Horadrim Symbology + *Diablo IV* + Fernando Pinilla

OPPOSITE Hell Portal Concept + *Diablo II: Resurrected* + *Diablo II: Resurrected* Art Team

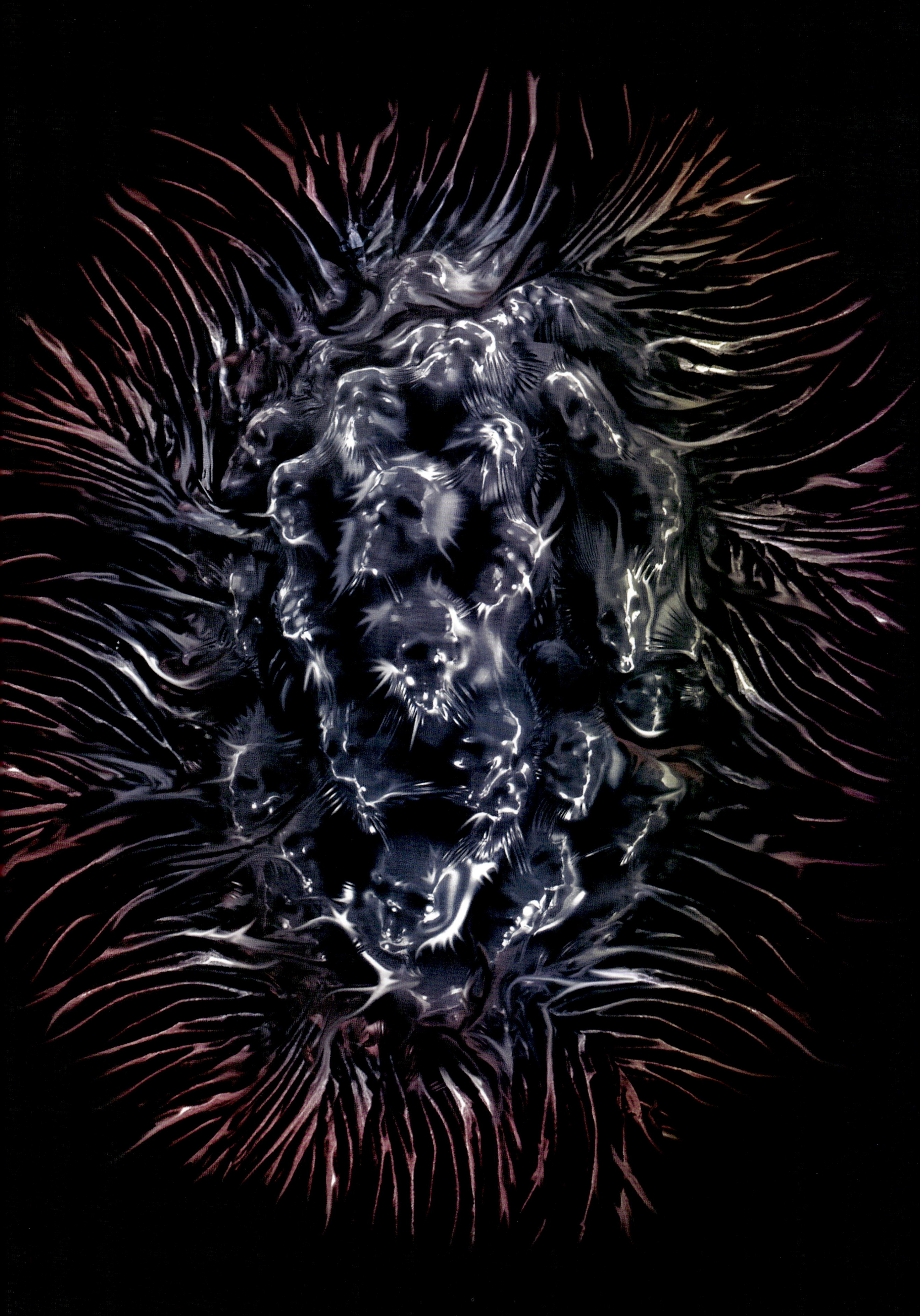

a small screen from the isometric camera view, you're able to recognize it. It's the idea of being *bold* in your design decisions."

Diablo Immortal's story takes place within the twenty-year span between *Diablo II: Lord of Destruction* and *Diablo III* and is centered around the collection of powerful and dangerous Worldstone fragments. The setting allows players to revisit familiar faces such as Deckard Cain and Zoltun Kulle. Importantly, *Diablo Immortal* also offers up an all-new story, characters, and monsters while remaining faithful to the core elements that *Diablo* players love. "There's a limited amount of space on the screen," continues Schulz. "So getting everything to read was paramount. Not just for clear art and to show off cool designs, but also for the gameplay. That was something that had to be fine-tuned because of the limitations of the screen size."

No matter what platform it's played on, *Diablo* is dark and epic. With *Diablo IV*, the scale and scope of the settings, characters, and narrative eclipse anything that has come before.

The storyline for *Diablo III: Reaper of Souls* ended with more than half of Sanctuary's population obliterated by Malthael—the Angel of Death—and his reaper minions. The High Heavens closed the Diamond Gates, leaving Sanctuary to be ravaged by famine and war. And though the Prime Evils—including the biggest bad of all, Diablo himself—remained banished, in a dark fantasy world built on the never-ending conflict between humans, angels, and demons, evil never stays vanquished for long.

While just nine years have passed between the last expansion and the release of *Diablo IV*, fifty years have come and gone in franchise lore. Now, a shadowy figure named Elias has summoned Lilith, the daughter of Prime Evil Mephisto, back into the world . . . and Hell is on its way to Sanctuary once again.

Diablo IV is promoted as a "return to darkness."

"If you think about that statement," says *Diablo* art director John Mueller, "it's like you're returning from somewhere. I think *Diablo III* was a more heroic fantasy, about heroism and

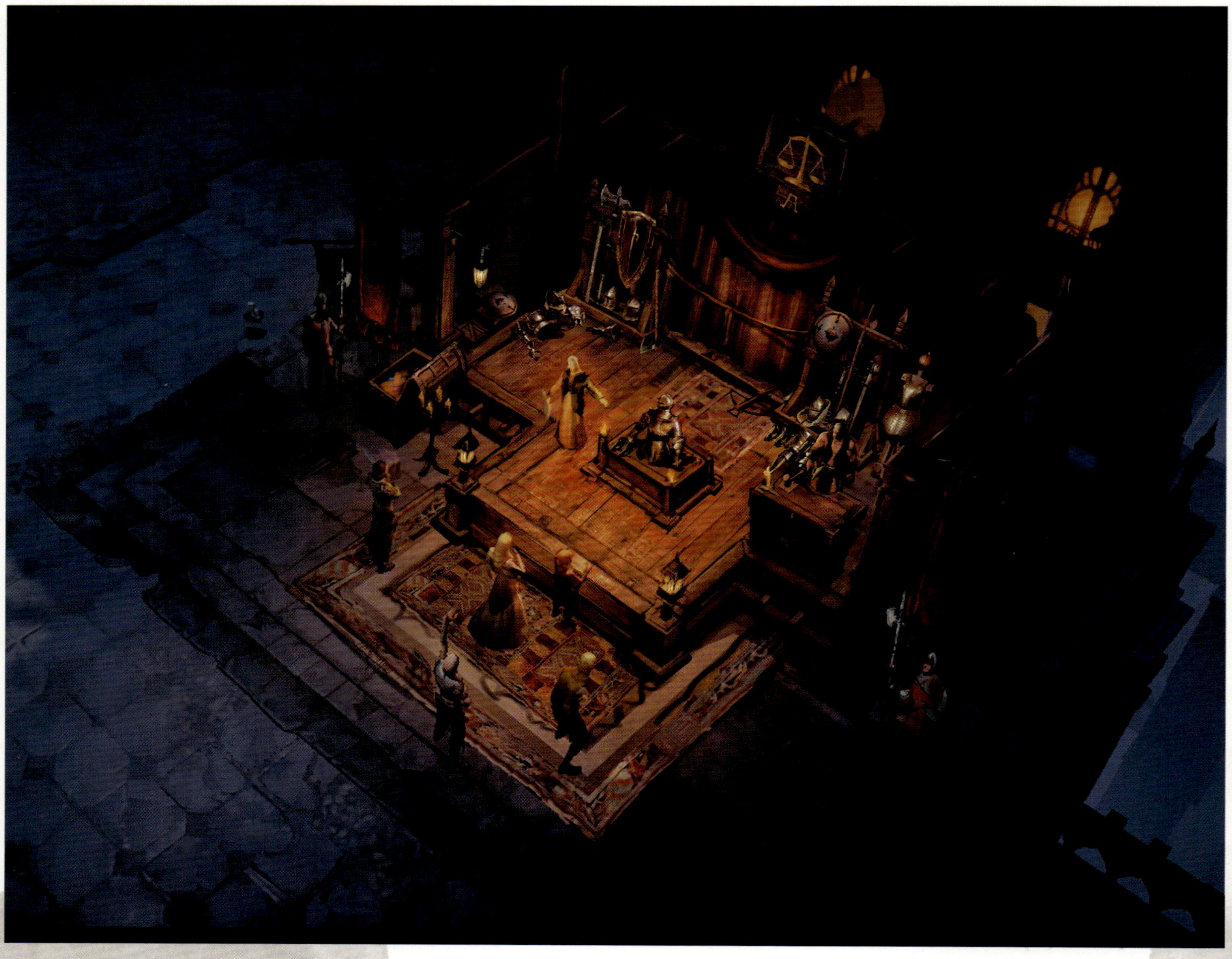

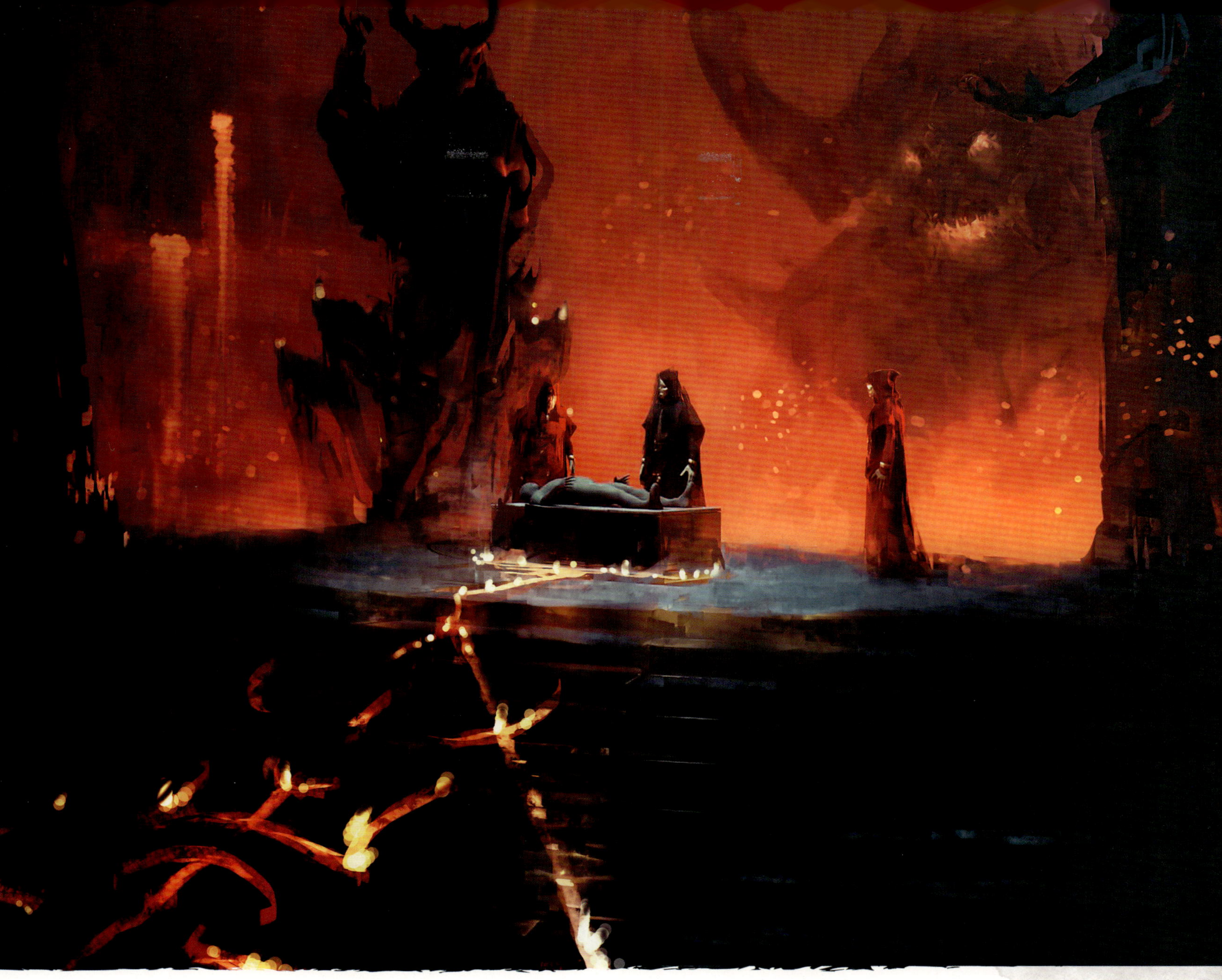

grandiosity, so a return to darkness is more about going back to the roots of *Diablo I* and *II*, which is that broken world in decline."

Diablo IV aims to create a style that is both familiar but also adds its own unique lens through which we view the world of Sanctuary. "It means we're going to bring something new," Mueller explains. "But there's going to be a lot that's familiar."

This is reflected in the game's overall aesthetic, which establishes its own identity while staying true to the *Diablo* legacy. This balance was ultimately accomplished by combining old and new techniques, mixing a traditional painterly look with the latest philosophy, called physically based rendering—a method that is remarkably faithful to real life—for a result that Dustin King describes as "an old master's painting of dark fantasy."

Most exciting of all, for the first time ever in the franchise, Sanctuary is fully explorable as an open world. Beyond dungeons, towns, and cities, gamers will discover a vast array of exciting new locations and environments in a nonlinear experience.

A world of contrast. A broken world. A world in decline. Sanctuary is all of these things. Yet so long as heroes continue answering the call to adventure, it is a world destined to endure.

So welcome, brave traveler! Pick up your torch, grab your sword, and join us once again as we build upon *The Art of Diablo, Volume I* to explore more characters, creatures, items, environments, and classes of the world's greatest action role-playing game: *Diablo*.

"Our game is more vibrant than past *Diablo* games. It's on par with *Diablo III*. If we went with a dark tone with more grays, it does feel appropriate for *Diablo*, but it also makes it harder for the player to understand what they're looking at."
—**HUNTER SCHULZ**, *Diablo Immortal* Art Director

ABOVE Temple of the Triune Illustration + *Diablo IV* + Victor Lee
OPPOSITE Market Concept + *Diablo Immortal* + NetEase Art Team

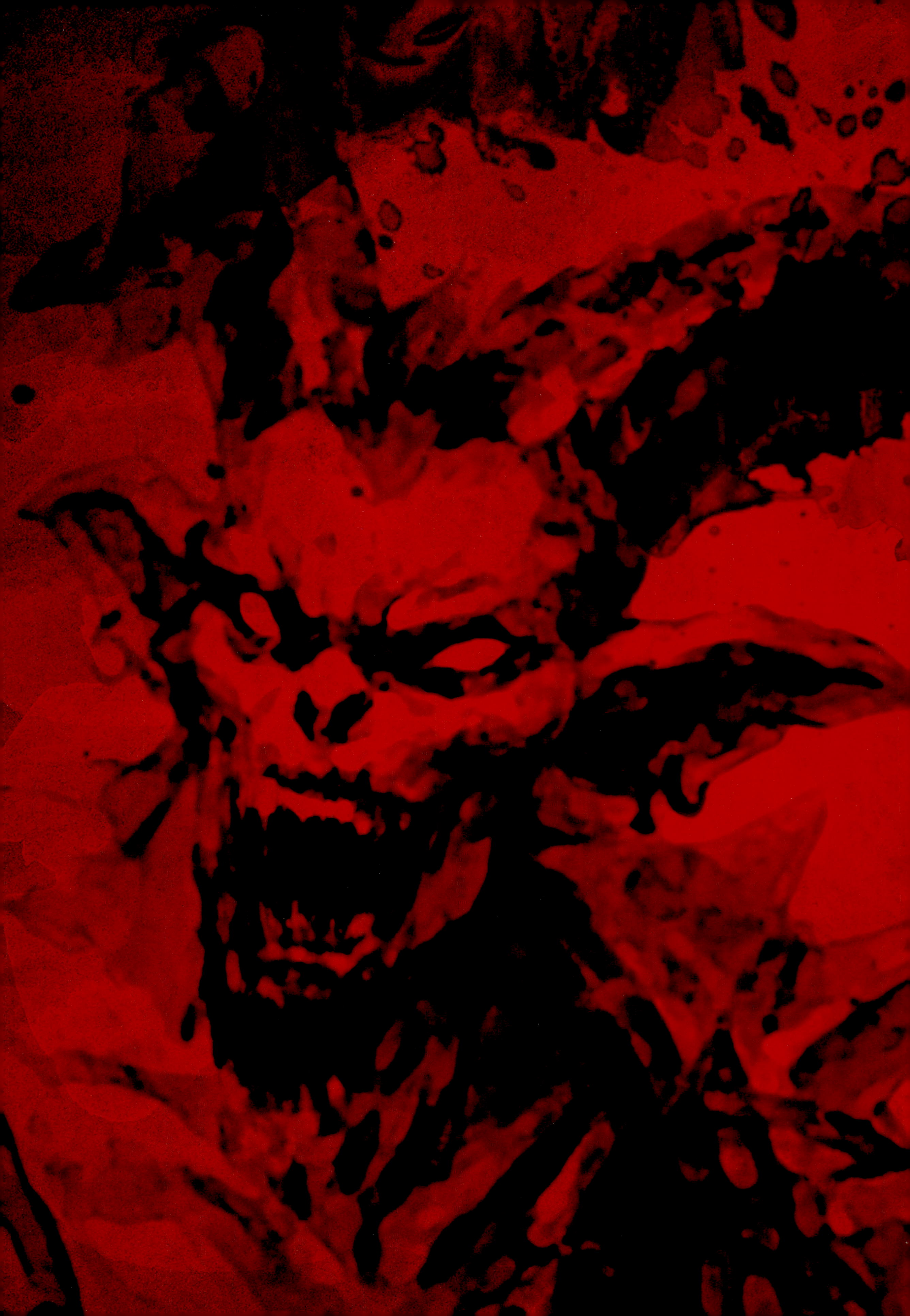

DIABLO II: RESURRECTED

Hell and Back Again

An important decision was made early on in the developmental stages of *Diablo II: Resurrected*, one that would affect the entire project moving forward.

"The project at the time was described as an up-res of *Diablo II*," recalls lead FX artist Evan Mennillo. "The vision of that wasn't clear. Originally, we were just going to take 2D assets and make higher-res 3D assets. I think it was our graphics team who had the wild idea that we should go full 3D—make a 3D engine, make everything from scratch, and re-create assets, because even if you were to up-res, you'd be creating these 3D assets anyway, so why not do it in real time?"

The immediate question was: *How?*

"What we technically did," says lead graphics engineer Kevin Todisco, "was create a layer that sits in between all of the fancy new 3D engine stuff that we wrote and the original game, that could scan everything coming in and say, 'Oh, there was a unit that was just created at this spot in the world.' And then we had a giant relational table that said, 'Okay, for this unit in the original game, it corresponds to this three-dimensional asset; this brand-new thing.'"

"The magic trick," says Evan Mennillo, "is it's *Diablo II*. It's that game you saw twenty years ago that's running underneath all of the graphics. So we had to construct everything to fit on top of that old scaffolding."

This layering of new on top of old provided an incredible mechanic that allows players to toggle between the classic game and the remaster at any point in real time.

So, what did all of this mean for the art? For one thing, the ability to add new content raised the question of just how much new content to add. The team implemented a 70/30 rule. Kevin explains: "The boundary was that 70 percent had to be true to the original game. That left 30 percent to embellish, alter, or flare up for the remaster to make it a fresh and new experience."

"The fans are very partial to the look of a *Diablo* title," says art director Dustin King. "We've seen this all through the history of the franchise, so this was an effort to really please the fans and make sure that we were hitting those notes, the things that they remembered from the original game. And color has always been one of those tough ones with *Diablo*. Everybody wants it dark, dark, dark. But I think with the remaster, we showed, 'Hey, you can use color.' You want your blood to be bright red. You want certain things to *pop*."

In this chapter, we'll learn how developers went about modifying the various elements of *Diablo II*, and we'll discover how the team overcame numerous obstacles to deliver a stunning remaster of this time-honored classic.

Warriors of Fate

ABOVE Ko Rune + John Dee
RIGHT Paladin Concept + T-Rex Lab
BOTTOM Sorceress Concept + Hossein Diba, BOSi, Little Red Zombies
OPPOSITE Paladin Model + Sergey Samuilov, BOSi, Little Red Zombies

Diablo II featured some of the most iconic classes in the franchise: the Amazon, the Barbarian, the Necromancer, the Sorceress, and the Paladin, all of which were later joined by the Druid and the Assassin in the *Lord of Destruction* expansion.

As with everything else in *Diablo II: Resurrected*, the process of re-creating these beloved archetypes involved striking a balance.

"We believed folks had a specific vision of them," says character lead Cory Turner. "There were the small sprites in-game, but also the promotional renders and materials, the paintings and illustrations that went along with the game. There was a good amount of stuff out there that made it clear that we were going to need to provide everyone with what they imagined and remembered but also hit what they wanted in the game."

One area that proved tricky to nail down was the armor. "There's how the characters are dressed and the iconic art, and then there's how they function at a gameplay level," says Turner.

While the armor for, say, a Paladin, had swappable components—boots, gloves, helmets, pants, chest armor, etc.—the customization wasn't the same as *Diablo III* or, as we'll explore later, *Diablo IV*.

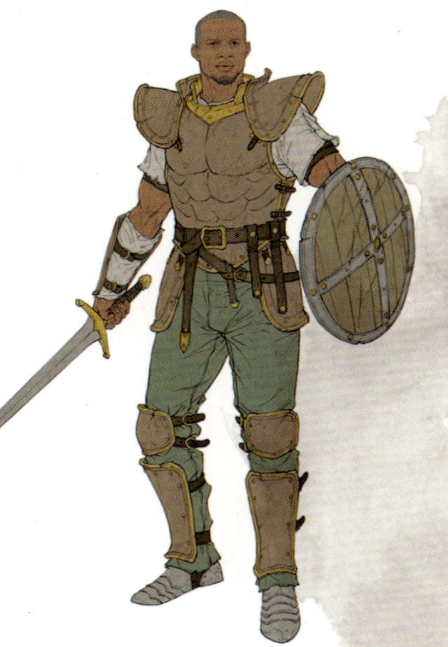

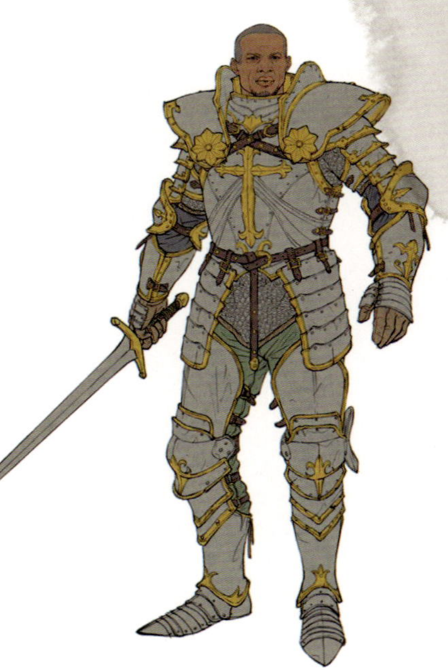

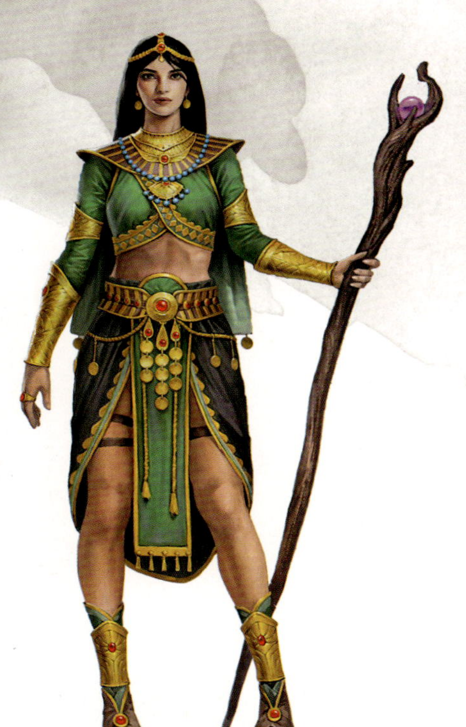

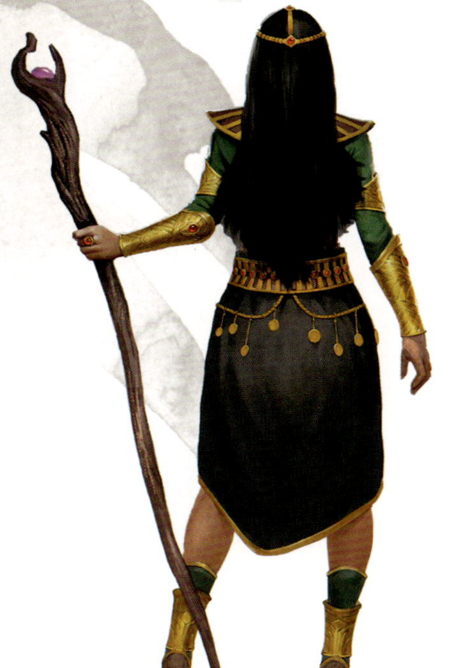

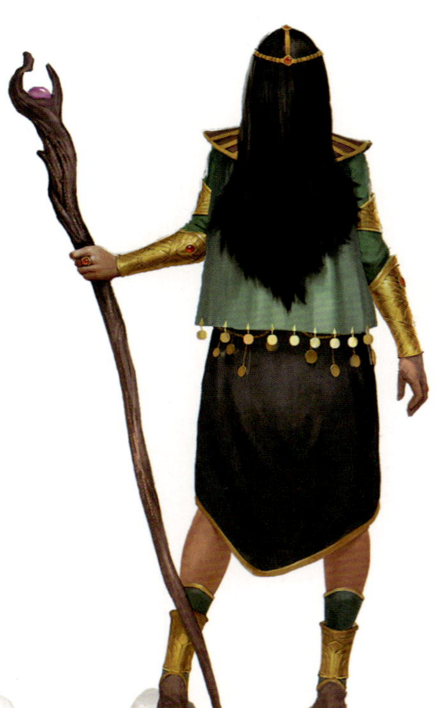

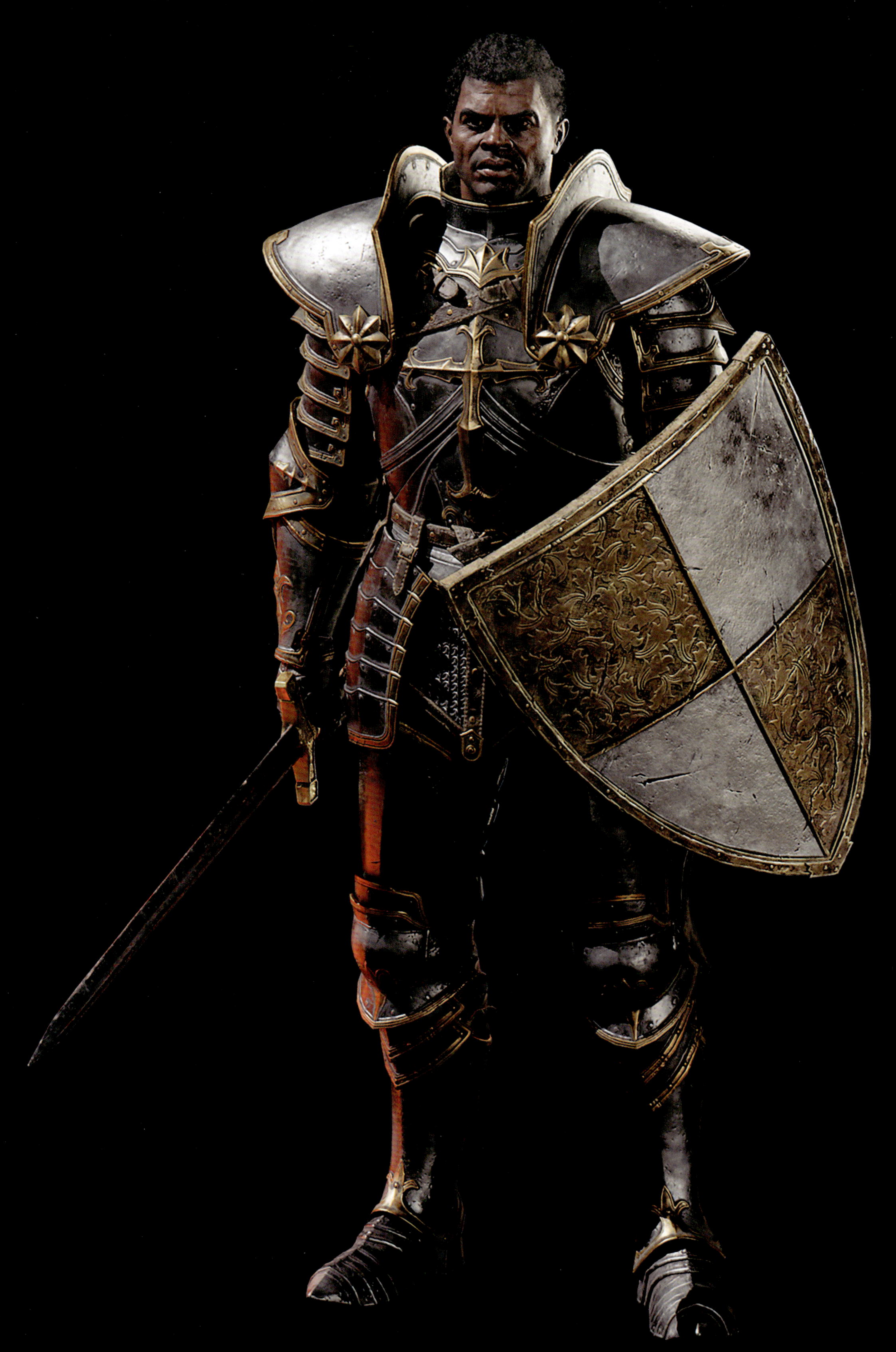

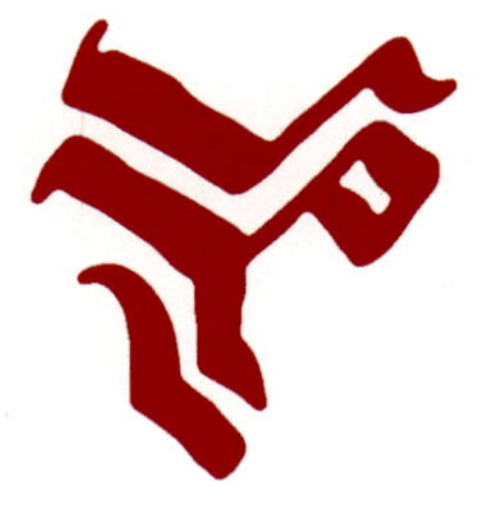

ABOVE Ohm Rune + John Dee

RIGHT Unused Crusader Concept + T-Rex Lab

OPPOSITE Sorceress Illustration + Hossein Diba, BOSi, Little Red Zombies

"We had to make decisions about 'What are the proportions that people expect to see?'" says Turner. "If they put on this armor set, they're expecting to see this much of the green pants and this much of the silver plate armor torso, and we want to balance that visual recollection with what actually looks right so it doesn't look weird and disconnected."

Ultimately, in Turner's words, the balance came down to "What compromises did *Diablo II* make so it would function as a game, and what compromises do we need to make to capture what they did and circle it back around to historical accuracy and kind of complete that circle?"

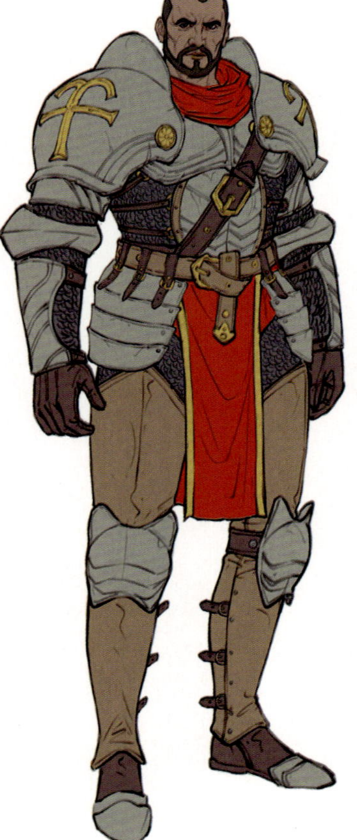

Once those choices were made, a new element of the remaster allowed players to zoom in and view the classes at a greater level of detail than ever before.

Dustin King explains: "We redid the whole front end of the game specifically so people could gear up their characters and really take in and appreciate what we put in there. Now when you're on the front end of the game, it doesn't just launch you from the campfire scene into the game; now you have little act dioramas where characters are placed with all this new gear."

While lighting and color also proved instrumental in bringing the remastered classes to life, the team's early approach of realistic environmental lighting didn't quite hit the mark.

"The Sorceress has that very specific emerald green," says Turner. "And if we made everything feel naturalistic or understated, we weren't going to get that. *Diablo II* has super dramatic light and dark contrast, but it also has really clear and crisp primary colors. So we did a ton of tuning for color."

Because *Diablo II*'s classes are so well known, the team threaded a needle in terms of modifying versus staying faithful to the originals. Case in point: the Barbarian. By the time *Diablo II: Resurrected* was in development, a new and different Barbarian had been featured in *Diablo III*—one whose white beard, long hair, and exaggerated proportions became quite popular among fans.

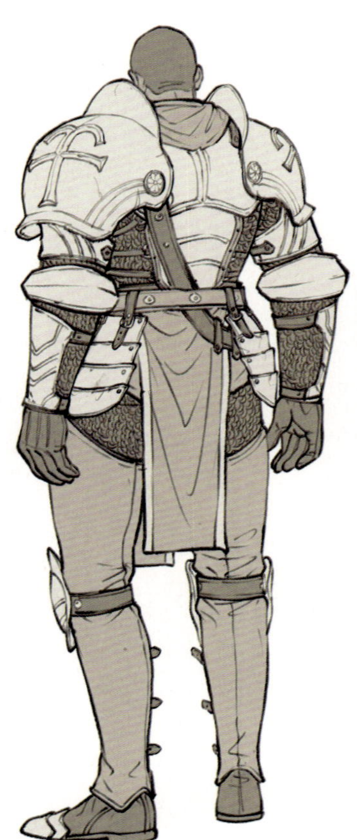

"The thing about the *Diablo II* Barbarian," Turner notes, "is that it's very iconic in the starkness—he's bald, he has no beard, he has that very prominent blue tattoo on the face and down the arm, and it felt like that had gotten pushed to the side over almost two decades."

While early versions of the remaster explored similarities to the *Diablo III* Barbarian, successive iterations led back to the original.

"We decided, 'Let's do the Barbarian from *Diablo II* because there's probably a hunger for that,' and to make it . . . an evolution of the *Diablo II* version into realism," says Turner. "We decided that it doesn't need to be another fantasy type of Barbarian or something from current media. It just needs to be a really well-executed, realistic version of the classic one."

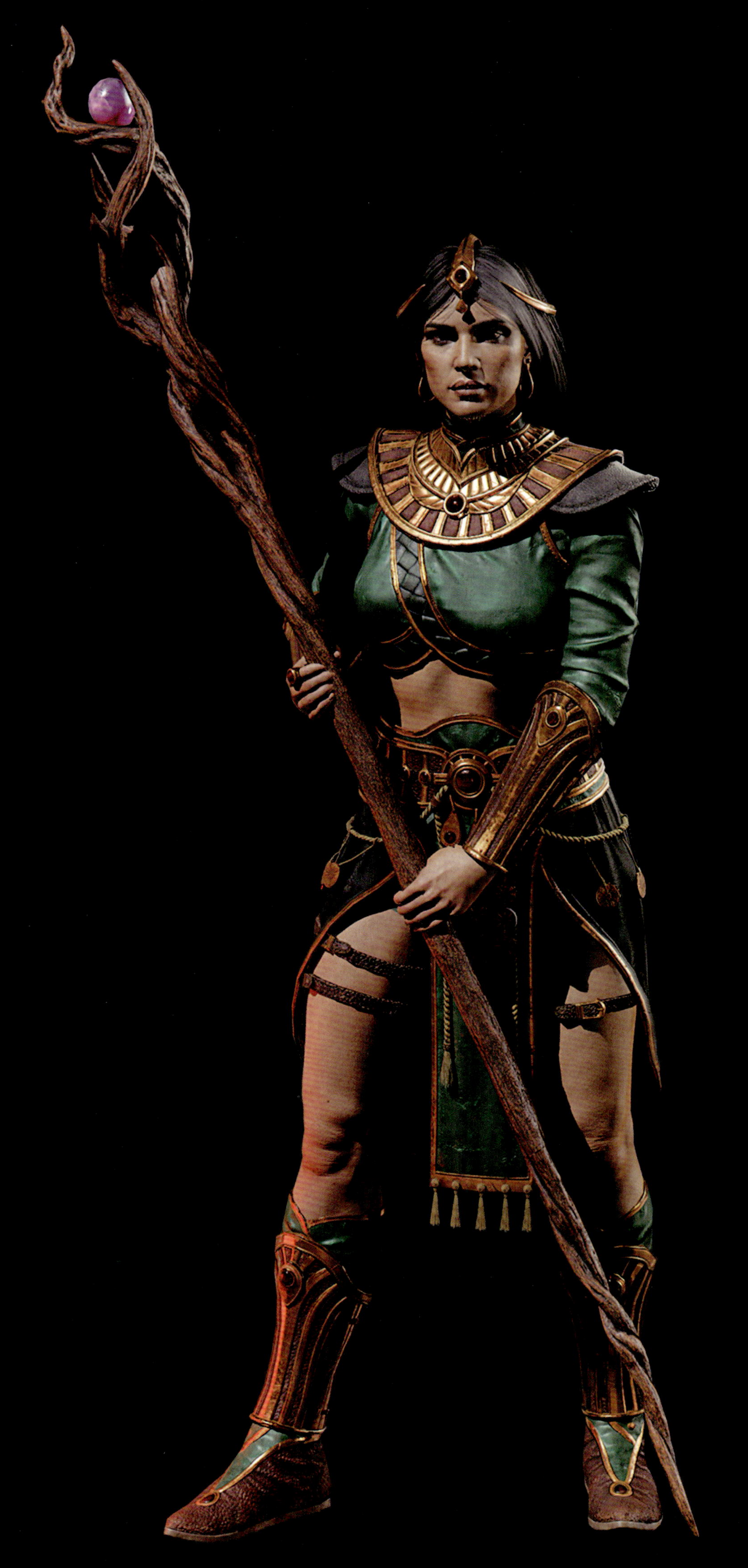

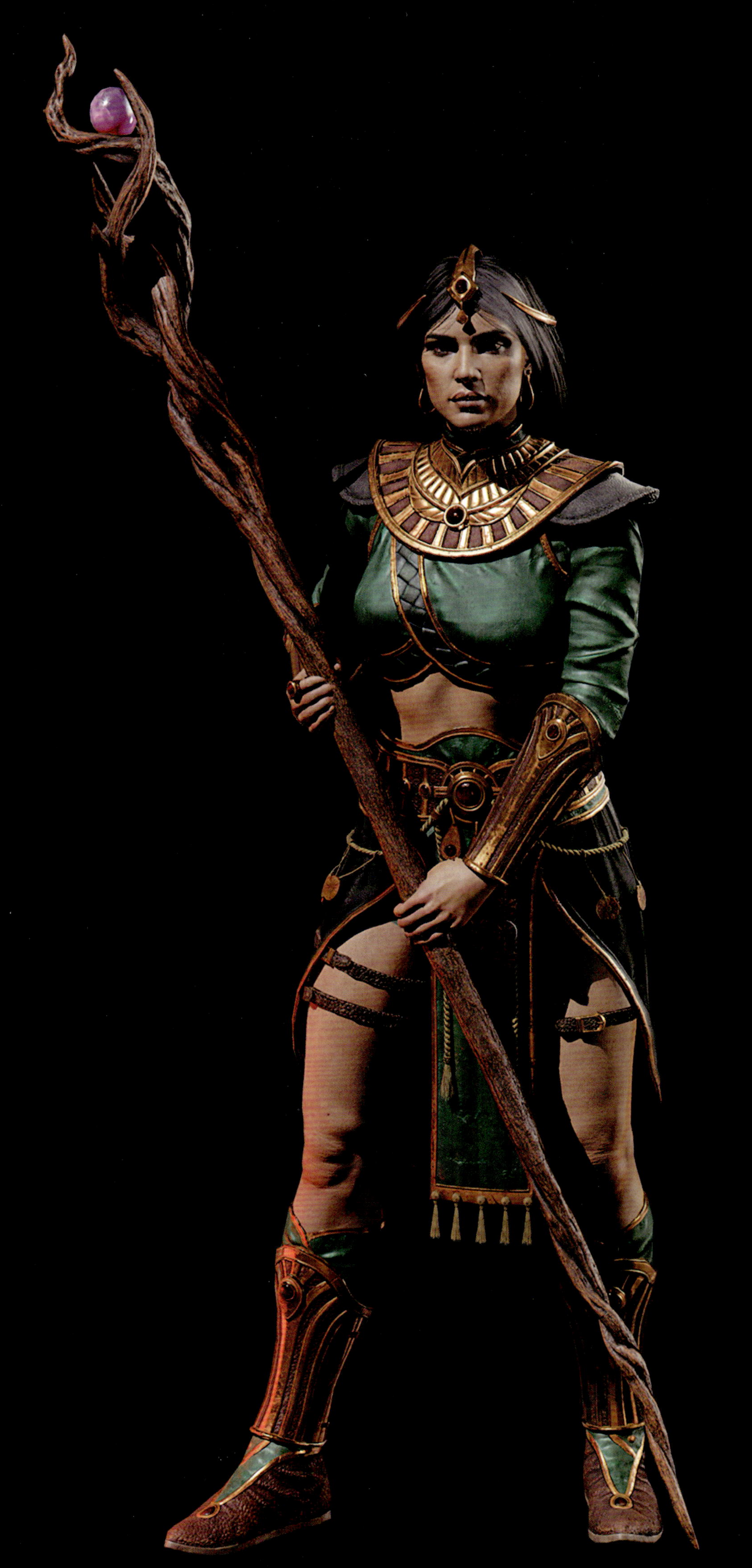

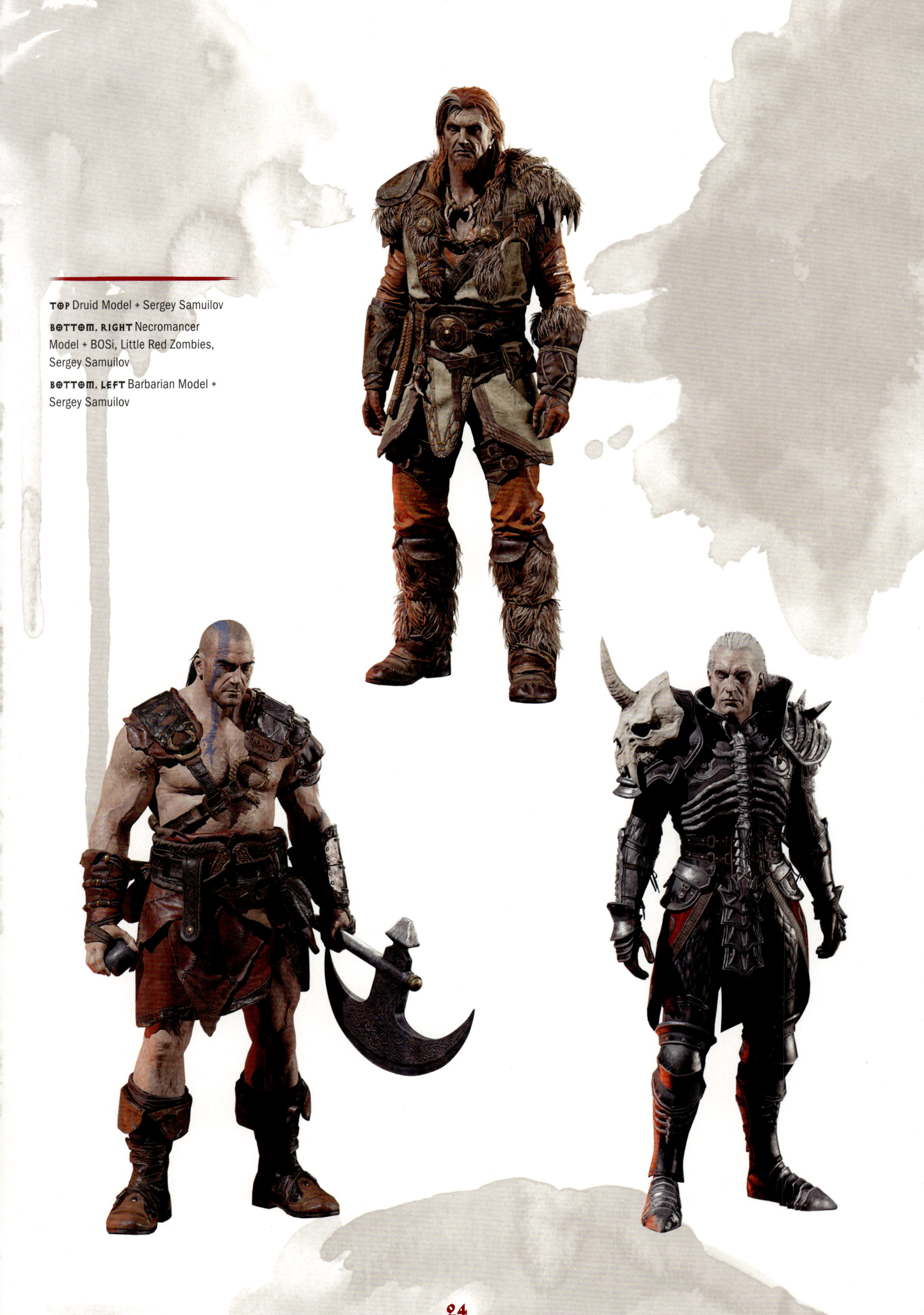

TOP Druid Model + Sergey Samuilov

BOTTOM, RIGHT Necromancer Model + BOSi, Little Red Zombies, Sergey Samuilov

BOTTOM, LEFT Barbarian Model + Sergey Samuilov

LEFT Assassin Model + Hossein Diba, BOSi, Little Red Zombies

RIGHT Amazon Model + Hossein Diba, BOSi, Little Red Zombies

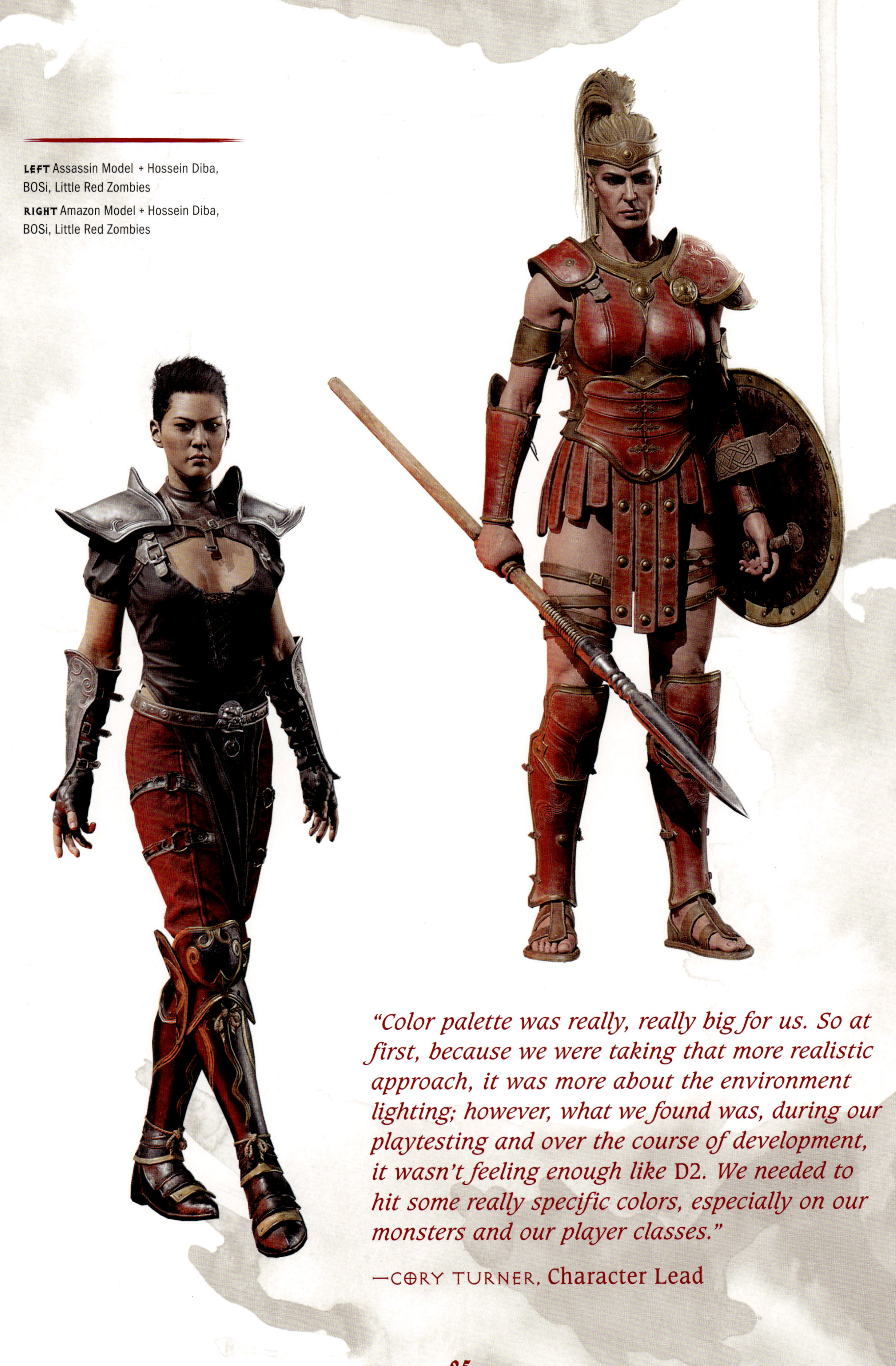

"Color palette was really, really big for us. So at first, because we were taking that more realistic approach, it was more about the environment lighting; however, what we found was, during our playtesting and over the course of development, it wasn't feeling enough like D2. We needed to hit some really specific colors, especially on our monsters and our player classes."

—CORY TURNER, Character Lead

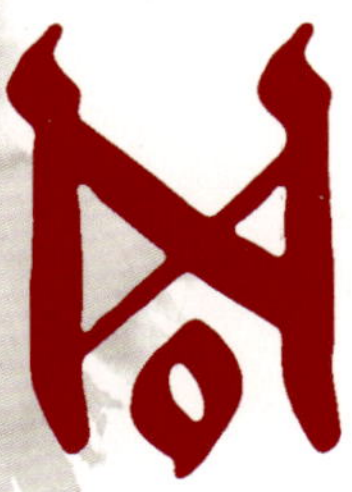

Embracing Icons

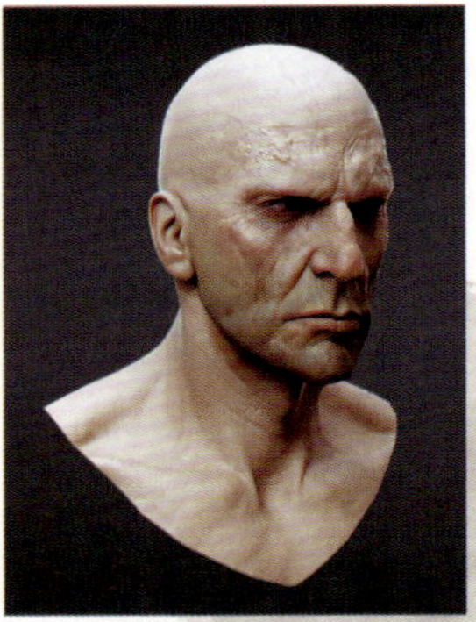

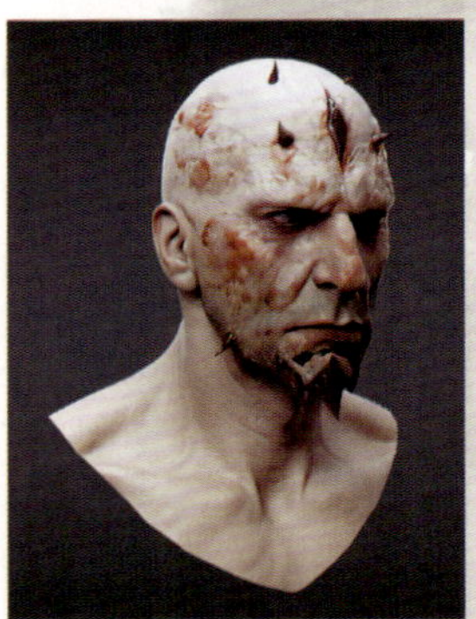

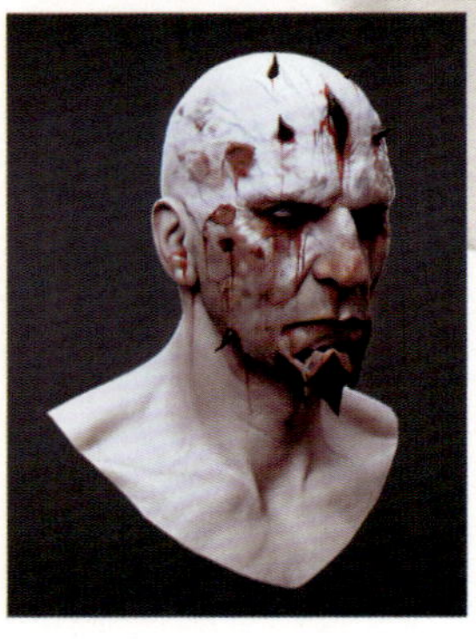

ABOVE Jah Rune + John Dee

RIGHT Dark Wanderer Possession Evolution + Josh Tallman

BOTTOM Baal Illustration + Blizzard Cinematics

OPPOSITE Baal Illustration + Blizzard Cinematics

For many players of *Diablo II*, the characters remain unforgettable. "The way they built the old game was relatively ingenious," says Kevin Todisco. "They made 3D assets for it, but at that time it was a little too early to make a game of this caliber in full 3D. The hardware just wasn't there."

This meant that many of the assets were rendered offline. In the case of a character, frames were rendered from the desired perspective, creating 2D images that were used in-game. Because the images originated as 3D assets, the characters had a 3D look and feel to them. But it wasn't until the creation of a 3D rendering engine for *Diablo II: Resurrected* that the characters became truly three-dimensional. While this breakthrough allowed for much greater detail and dynamic lighting, it introduced challenges as well.

"Mood and shadows and lighting is a really strong part of the *Diablo* identity," explains Cory Turner. "But getting that sense of really pushed shadows, super dark and super light contrasts, and the hope light around the character was challenging. The lighting had to go through many, many passes."

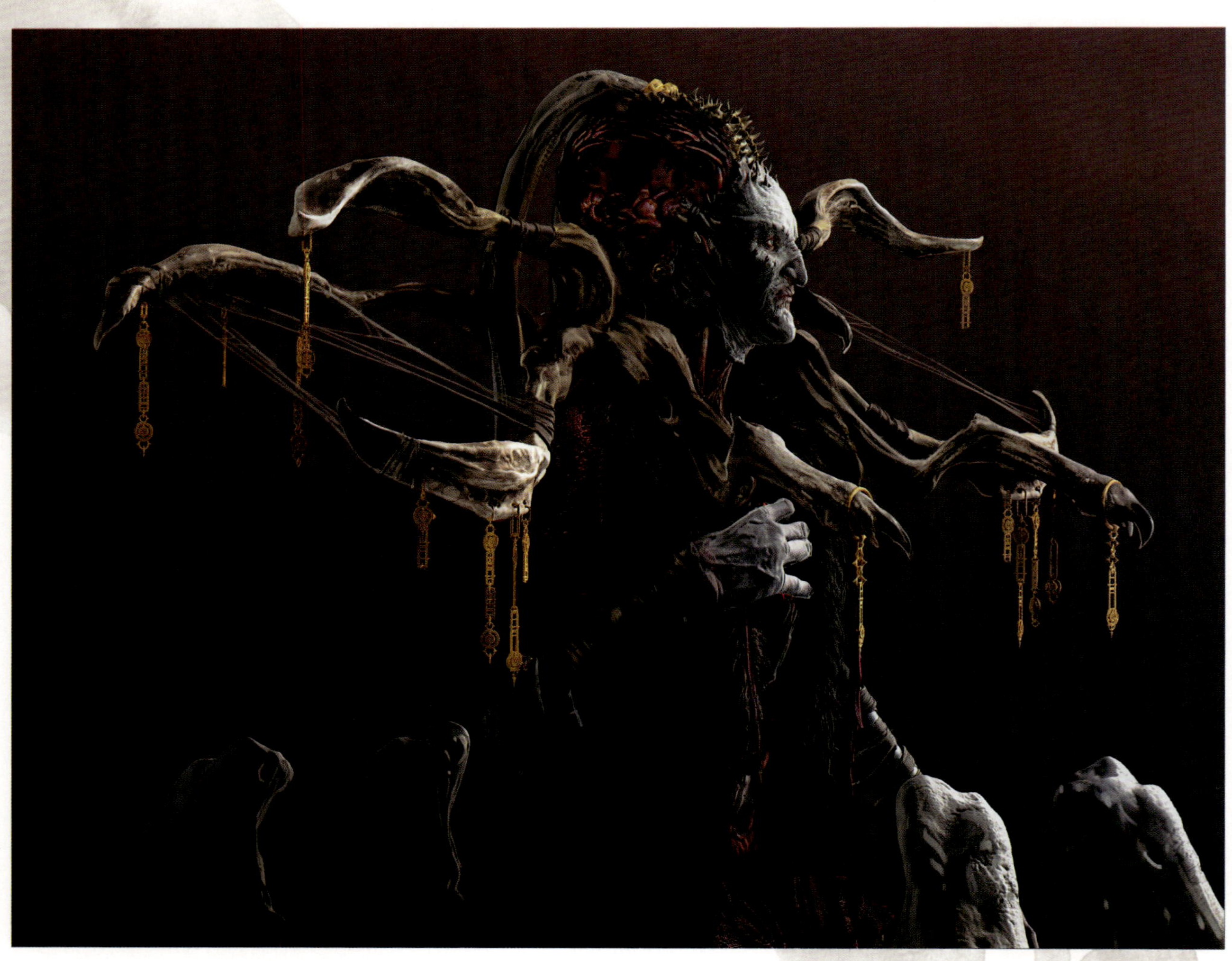

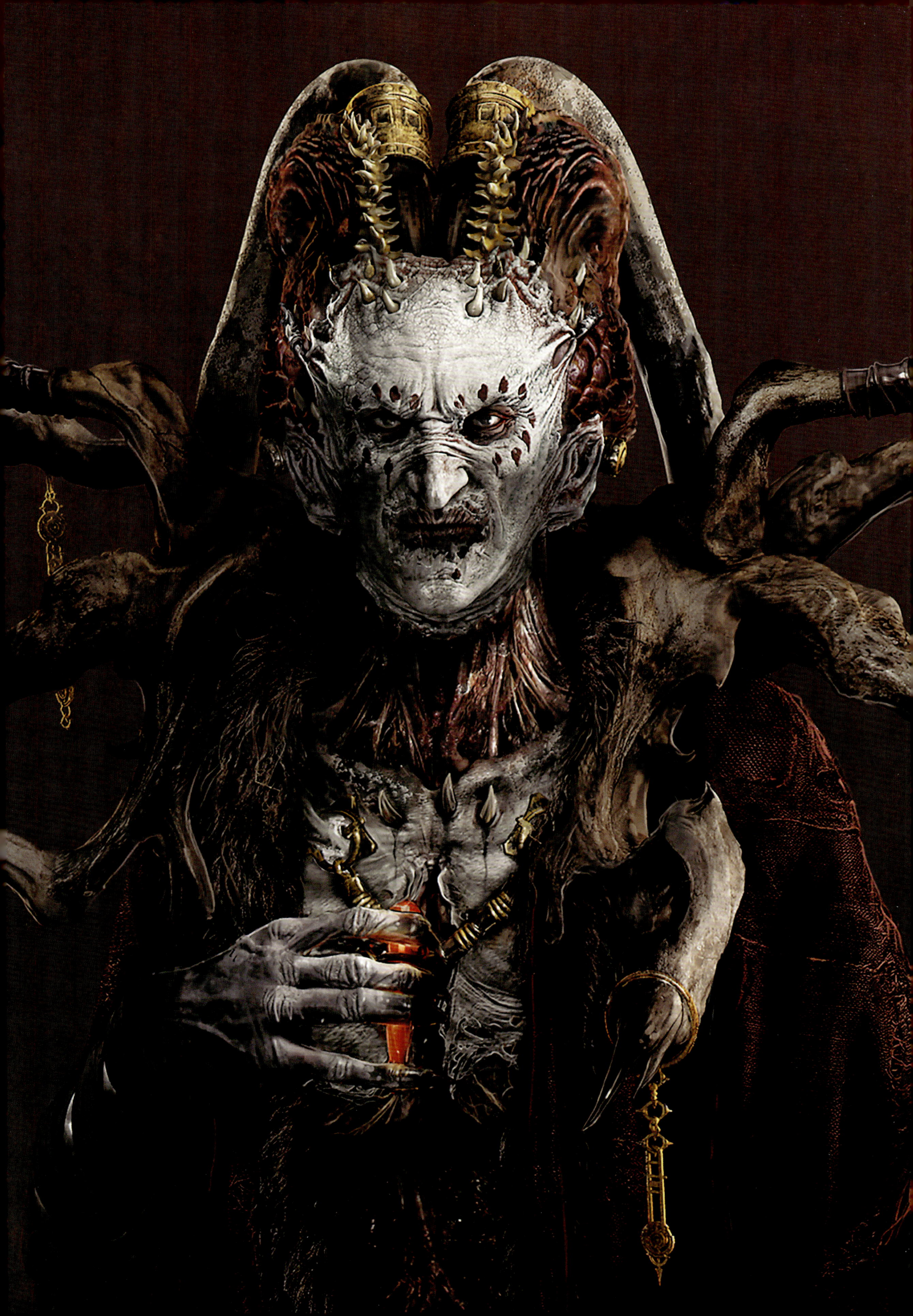

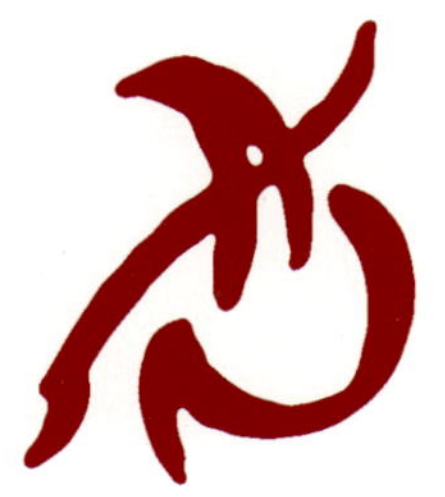

ABOVE Dol Rune + John Dee

RIGHT, TOP Original *Diablo II* Jerhyn Concept + Blizzard Artist

RIGHT, MIDDLE Original *Diablo II* Meshif Concept + Blizzard Artist

BOTTOM, RIGHT Fara Concept + T-Rex Lab

BOTTOM, LEFT Elzix Concept + Vicarious Visions

BELOW Original *Diablo II* Lysander Concept + Blizzard Artist

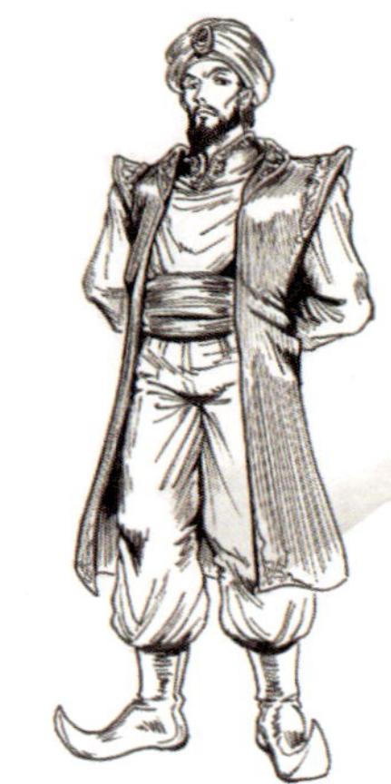

The kind of realistic lighting first used in the remaster did not behave as expected. Characters often blended into the backgrounds.

"If you wanted the character to stand out," Todisco explains, "you needed to start breaking the rules a little bit. So there were a lot of cases where we did that."

Some of these rule-breaking methods consisted of creating custom light rigs for characters, as well as artificially increasing their brightness. Lighting and color often go hand in hand, and *Diablo II: Resurrected* was no exception.

"*Diablo II* is dark both tonally and visually," remarks Dustin King. "It's also really great at using saturated color for very specific purposes. When we first started, everything was brown and muddy and almost *too* real. It didn't feel like *Diablo*. We had to go back and make a diligent effort as artists to extract color wherever it should have been used."

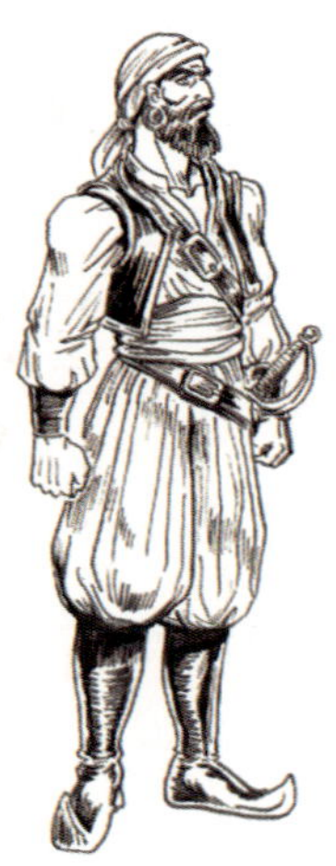

One example where color played a critical role for a character was with fan favorite Charsi.

"Very bright red hair," says Dustin. "Everybody knows her by that hair. That is a good use of color and one where we converted her hair back from a brownish red to a bright, vibrant red."

Another problem introduced by the conversion was clipping. Characters would sometimes stand with their feet inside of rocks or other objects on the ground, something that would *never* happen in the old game.

To remedy this, the team developed a way to "draw" characters to always stand on top of objects on the floor, an optical illusion that only works because of the game's isometric camera angle. "If you tried to do this in a first-person shooter," Kevin Todisco says, "it would break your brain."

All of these efforts led to characters that are highly detailed and clearly readable and, most important of all, faithful to their original, unforgettable predecessors.

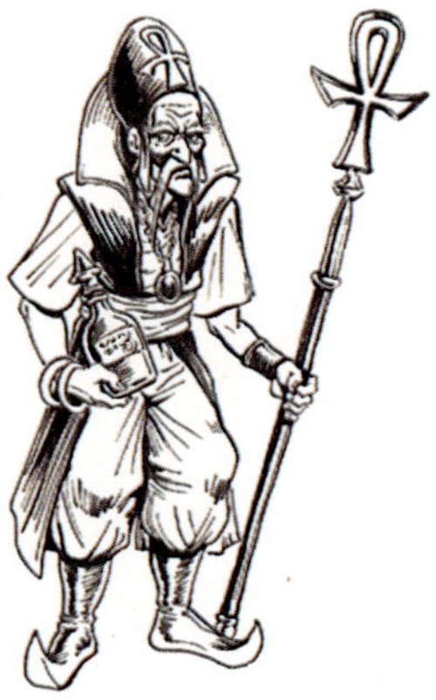

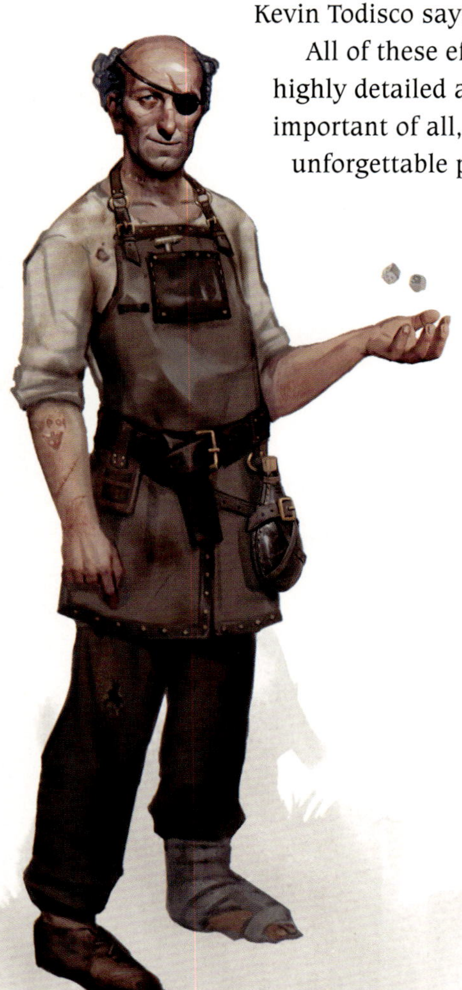

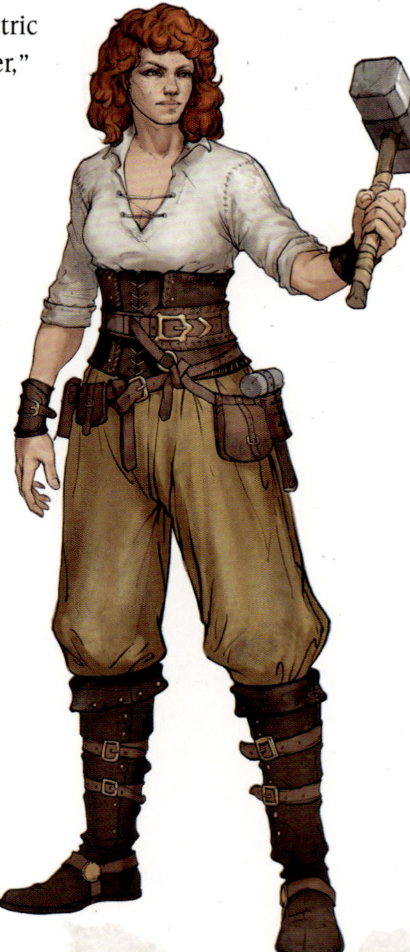

TOP, LEFT Meshif Concept • Vicarious Visions

TOP, MIDDLE Natalya Concept • Vicarious Visions

TOP, RIGHT Flavie Concept • Vicarious Visions

BOTTOM, RIGHT Jerhyn Concept • Vicarious Visions

BOTTOM, LEFT Geglash Concept • Vicarious Visions

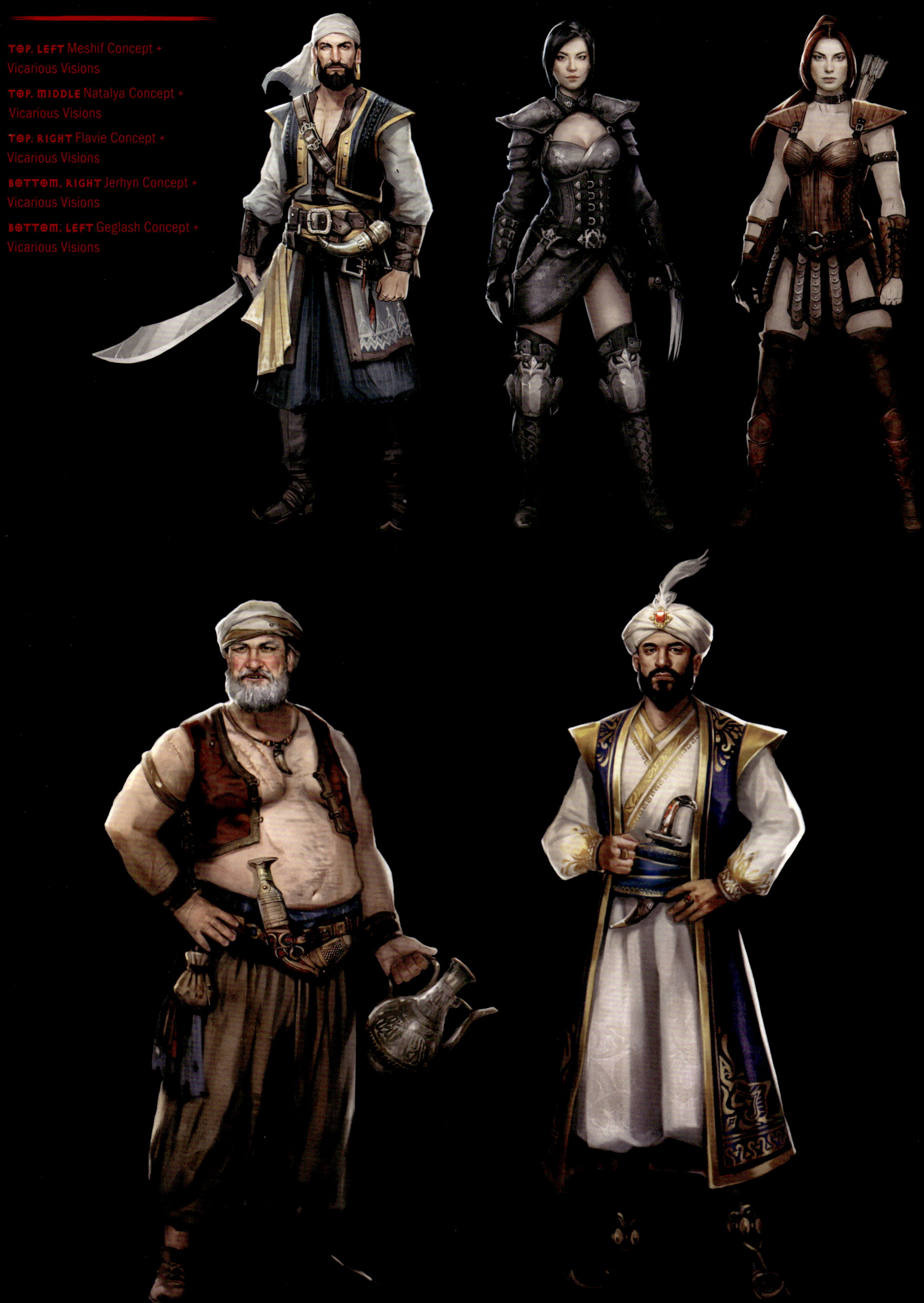

RIGHT Mephisto Concept • Pixel Mafia
BOTTOM Baal Concepts • Pixel Mafia
BELOW, LEFT Diablo Concept • Pixel Mafia

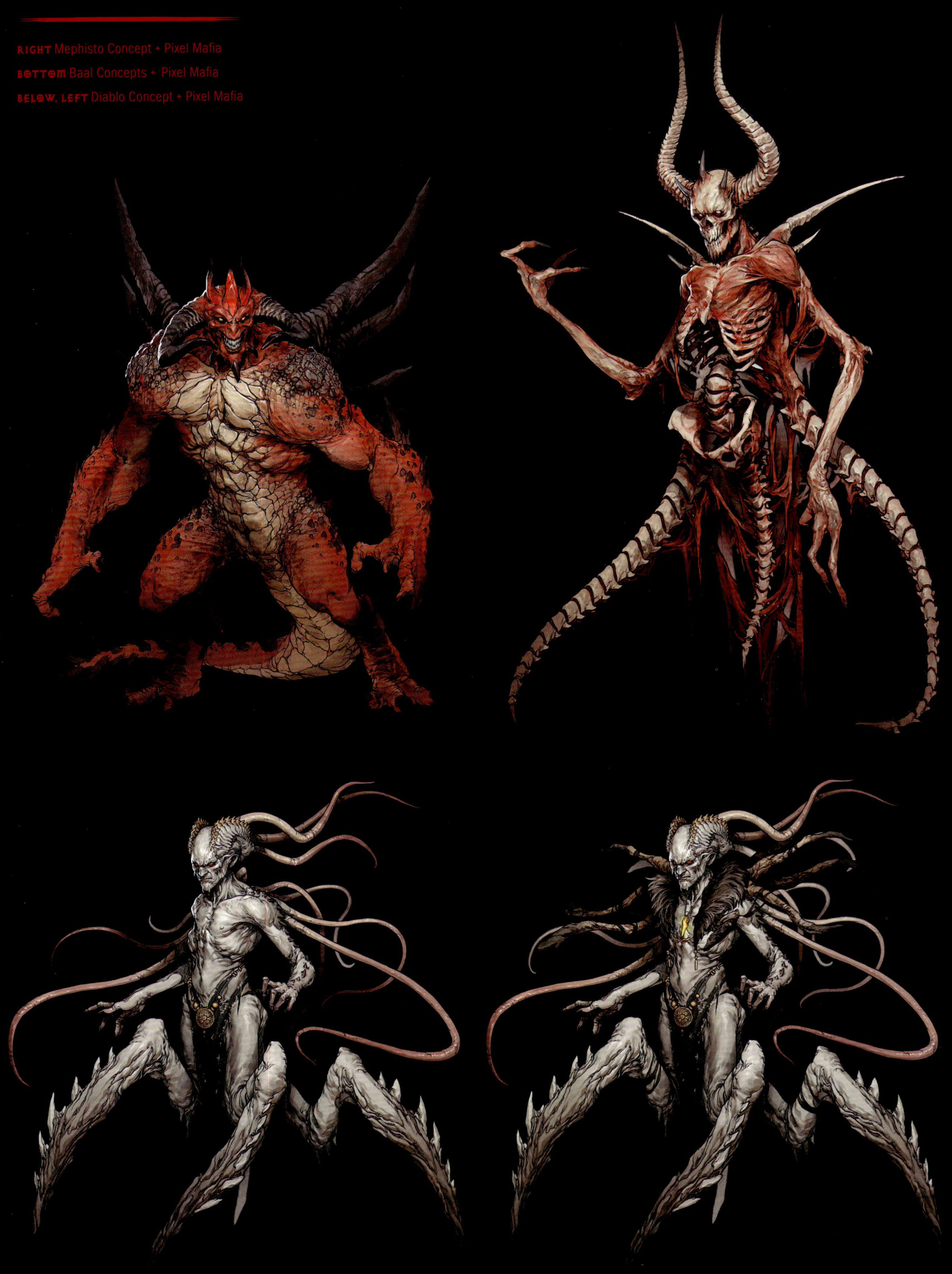

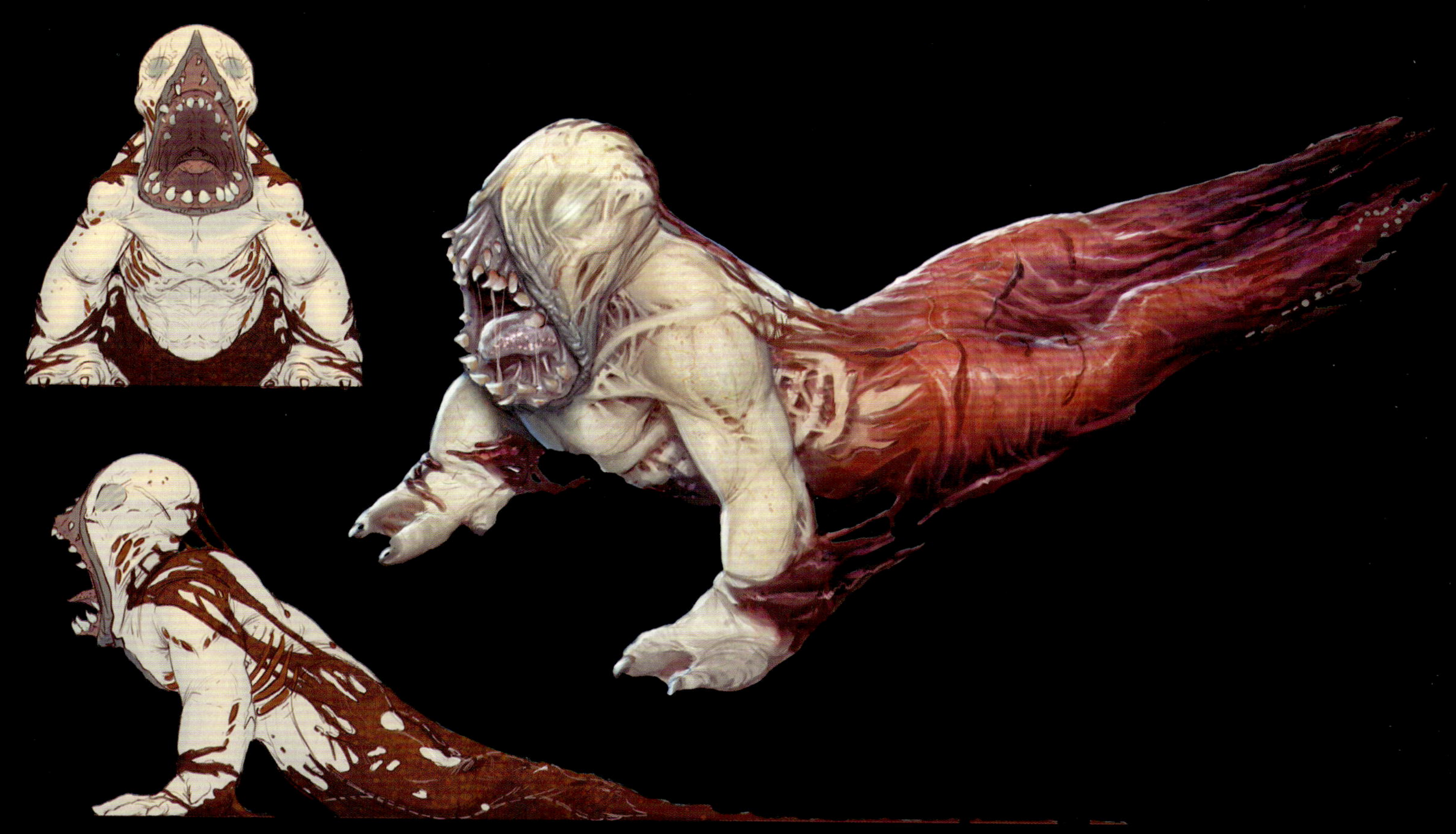

"When you're going from the former game, which was 800 by 600 resolution, on old CRT monitors to 4K monitor size, that increased the real estate on our characters, so we had the opportunity to go back and add in a large amount of detail."

—DUSTIN KING, Art Director

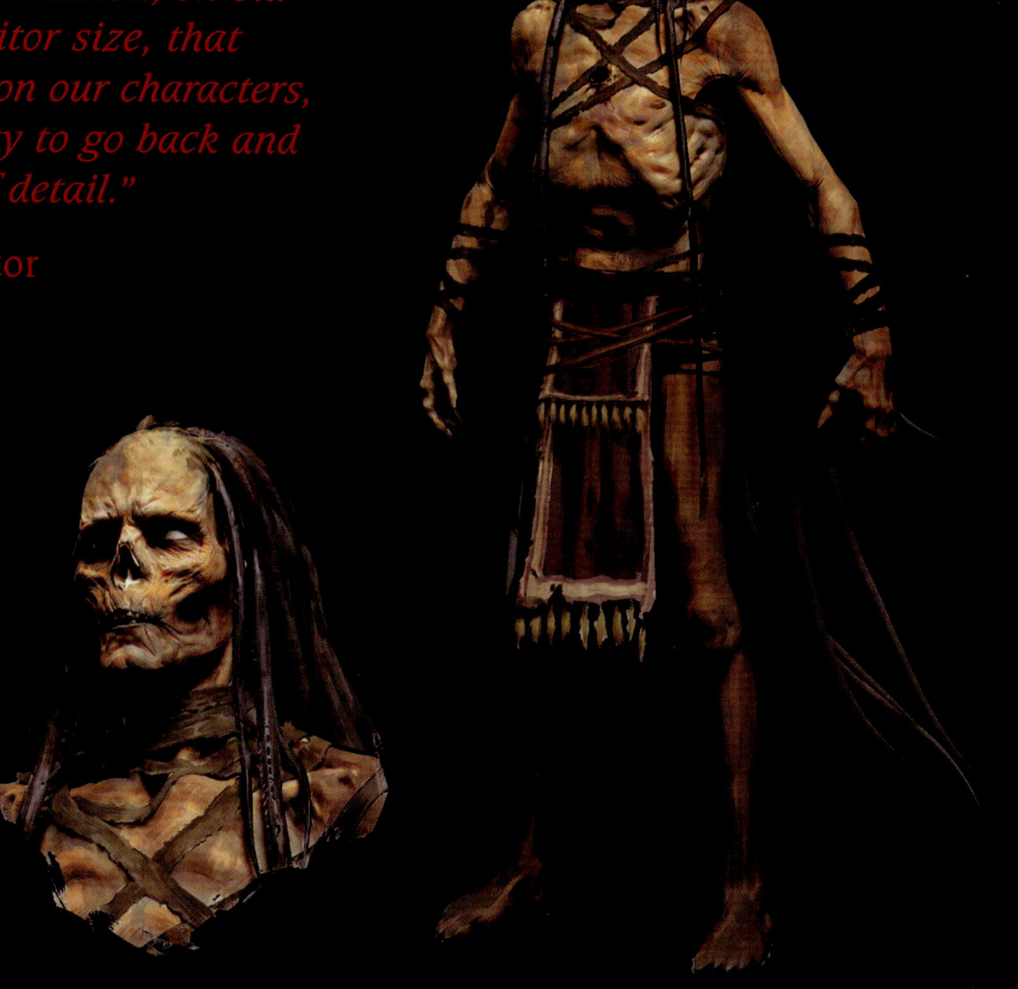

TOP Vile Child Concepts • Danny Williams

BOTTOM Tal Rasha Concepts • Josh Tallman

Denizens of Shadow

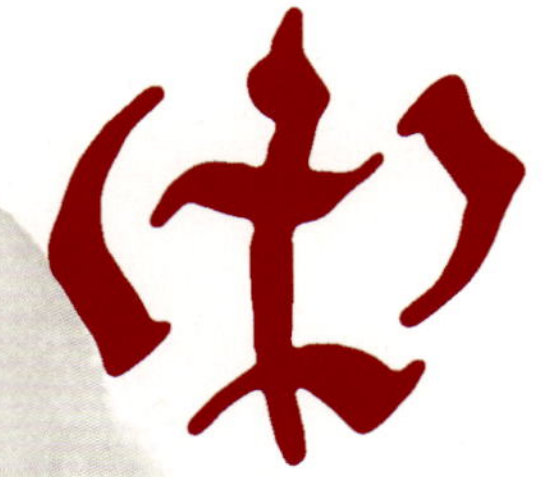

ABOVE Lo Rune + John Dee

RIGHT, TOP Sand Maggot Concept + Pixel Mafia

RIGHT, MIDDLE Dark Elder Concept + Pixel Mafia

BOTTOM Regurgitator Concepts + Danny Williams

BELOW Swarm Bug Concept + Pixel Mafia

OPPOSITE Werewolf Concept + Maxim Verehin

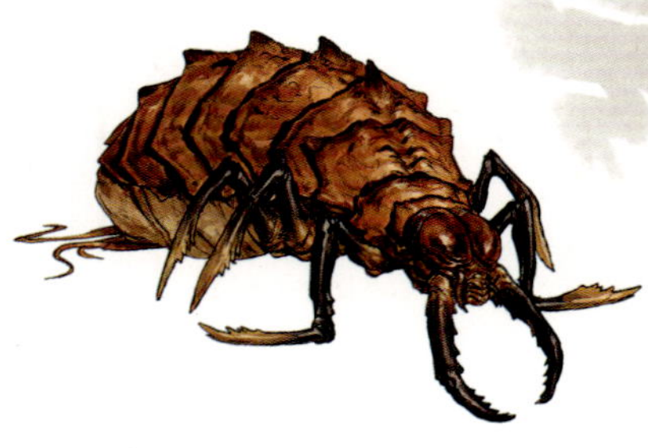

Diablo II was renowned for its horrific creatures: Zombies. Skeletons. Demon bosses. As detailed in the previous chapter, converting the old game from 2D into 3D brought a tremendous increase in detail, something that was especially true for monsters.

"There are a lot of embellishments we were able to accomplish with the realistic renderer," says Kevin Todisco. "Especially when you compare the new stuff to the original 3D assets, some of which we were able to dig up from yesteryear. We found one—the original zombie model they used, a 3D asset out of the '90s. Very low poly, low detail. When you look at a close-up of ours, there's detail all over."

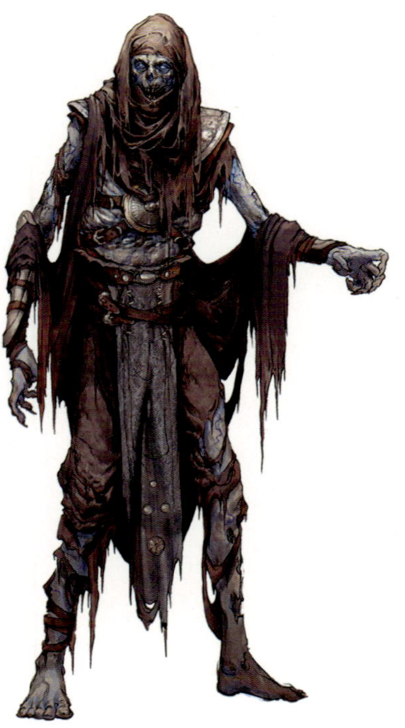

As with characters, the addition of many new facets to creatures meant filling in gaps and occasionally trying to get into the original creators' heads.

"There were times," recalls character lead Cory Turner, "when we didn't have reference material of the original models. The sprites might be three or four colors, so you're zooming in on a cluster of fifteen pixels, trying to interpret 'What was the intent behind those pixels?' You want to figure that out. You want to decode what those original graphics are telling you."

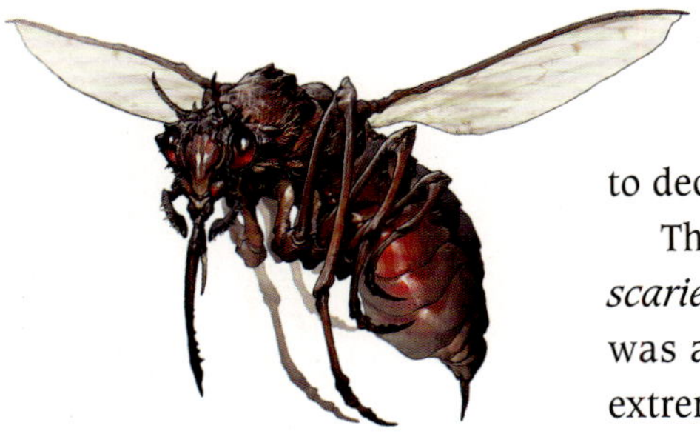

The goal was to make the monsters just as scary—no, *scarier*—than the classic game. Per Dustin King: "*Diablo II* was a very realistic-looking title. Those creatures are extremely detailed and gory. With this version of the game, they became darker and gorier. The biggest takeaway I had with our monsters was that they look like the nightmares you had as a child based on the old game models. Now that they're in 3D, they're terrifying."

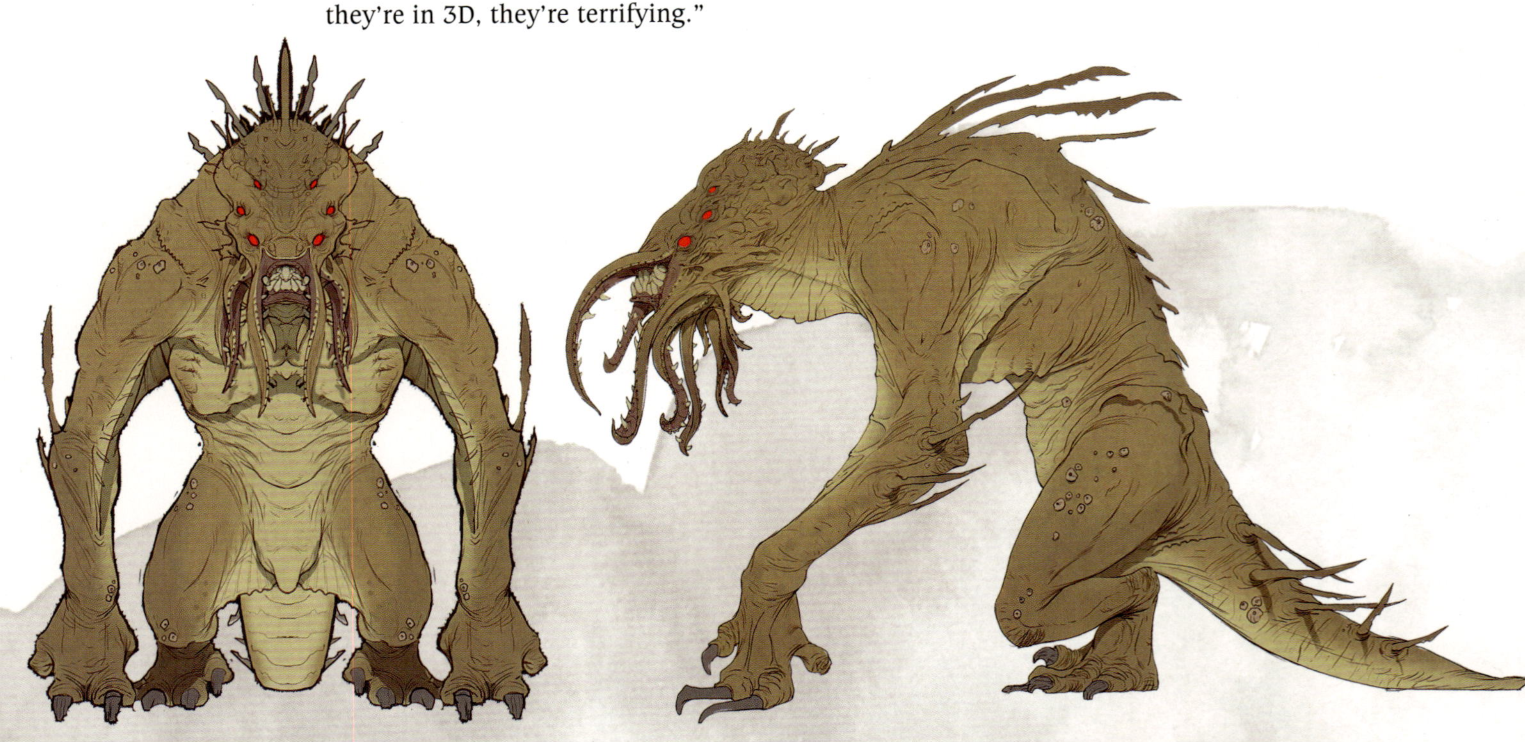

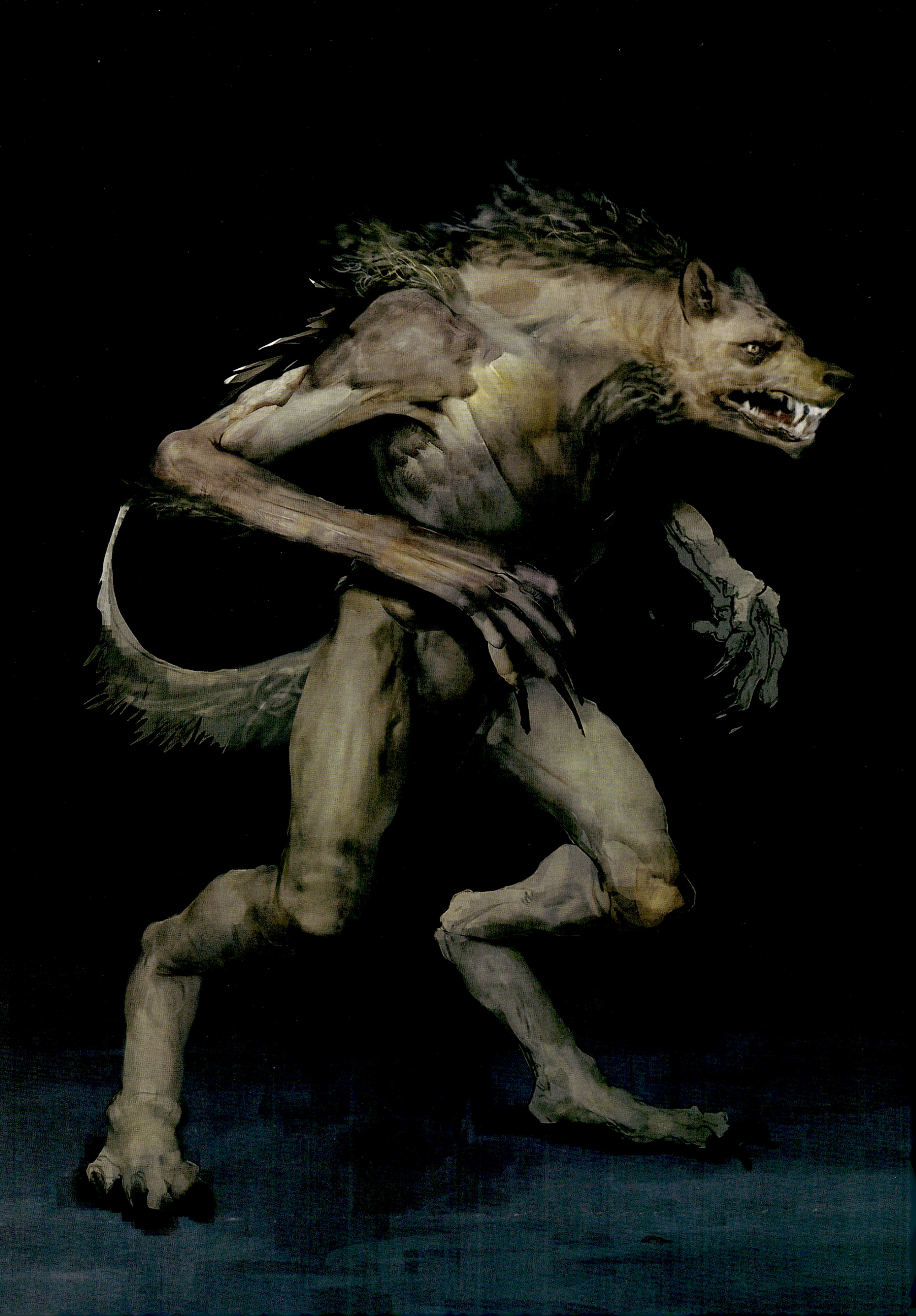

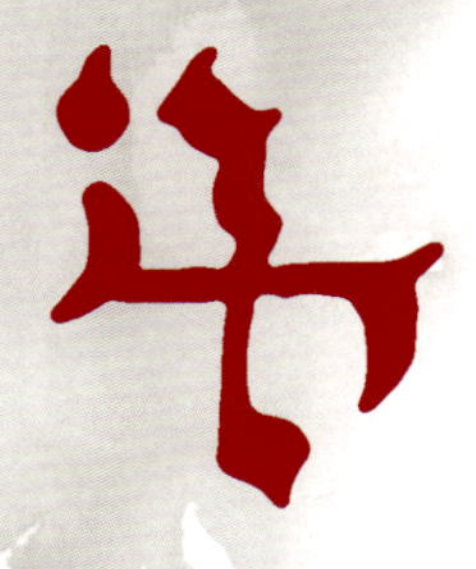

ABOVE Fal Rune + John Dee

RIGHT, TOP & MIDDLE Mummy Concept + Pixel Mafia

BOTTOM, RIGHT & LEFT Demon Concept + Mike Franchina

OPPOSITE, TOP Vulture Demon Concept + Little Red Zombies

OPPOSITE, MIDDLE RIGHT Claw Viper Concept + Pixel Mafia

OPPOSITE, BOTTOM Vile Child Model + Axis Studios

OPPOSITE, MIDDLE LEFT Goatman Model + Maxim Verehin

Of course, those creatures can't be nightmare-inducing if they're too difficult for players to see. A few tricks were used to help creatures leap off the screen.

"There are small things that are cheats," notes Cory Turner. "If the monsters are just lit naturally, they sink into the background, so instead they're kind of cut out and popped out a little bit."

As with everything else in the game, the 70/30 rule was applied.

"We made a commitment," lead exterior artist Jeffrey Lee says, "that if it exists in the old game, then it is our seed of storytelling. Start with that, then extrapolate. We made ourselves disciplined in that way, to link any fancy stuff or creative intuition to the previously established thoughts. If we couldn't find anything in the art, we would look at the lore or the stories of the bosses."

Sometimes, opportunities existed to enhance those stories.

"The first time we did this," continues Lee, "was with Cold Corpse, which was an Act One boss in the Den of Evil. He was just a regular old guy, but we knew that every time he spawns, he spawns in this one preset and in this one location. So we figured if we roughly knew where he is every single time, we could tell a story there. We could set-dress tents and make it look like there was something special about this place. Once we noticed the pattern, we capitalized on that. Every time there was a unique preset where a boss spawned or a big story beat happened, we jumped on that and reasoned we could do all of this additional storytelling."

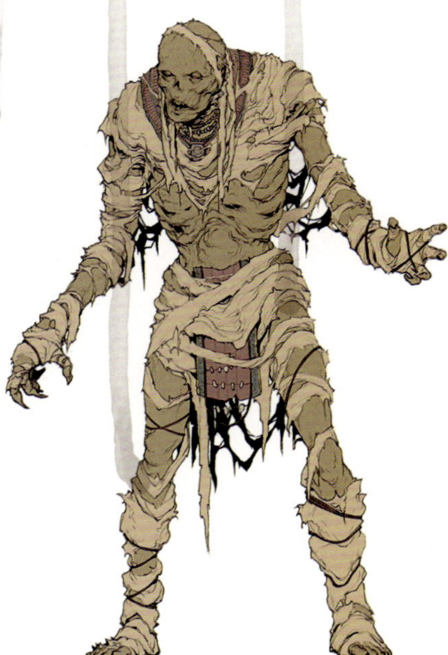

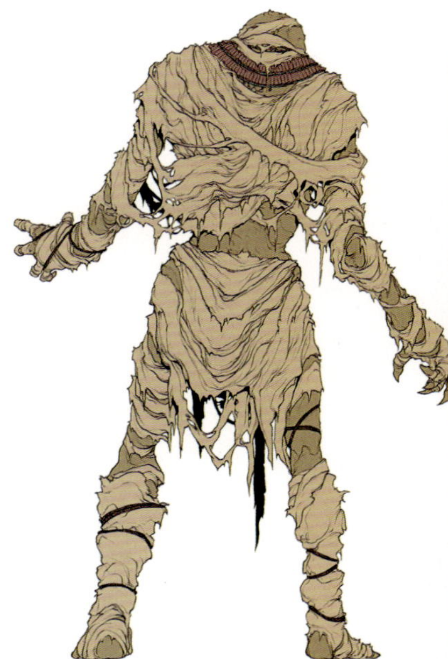

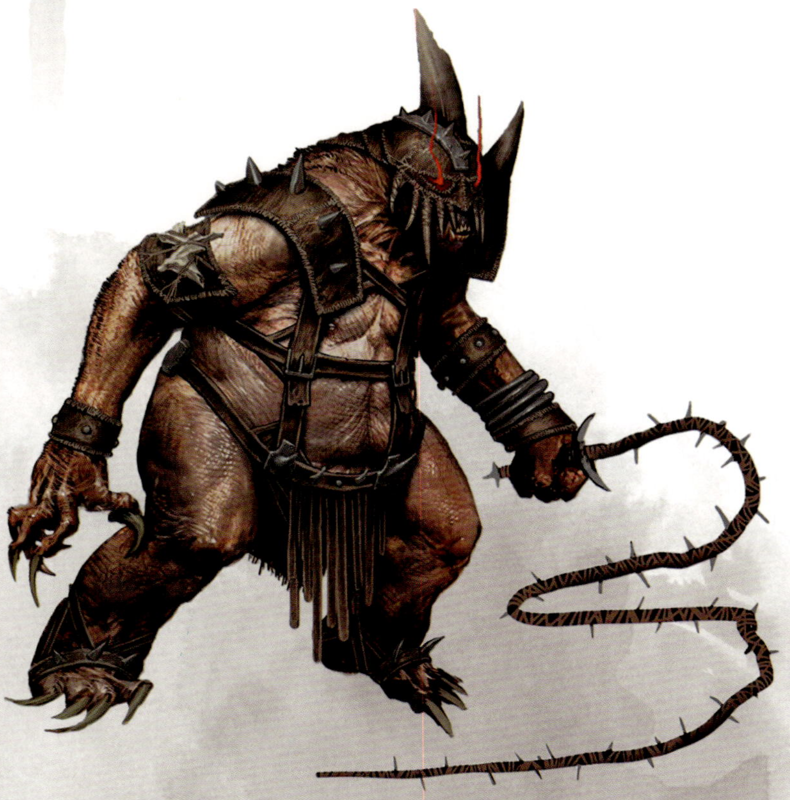

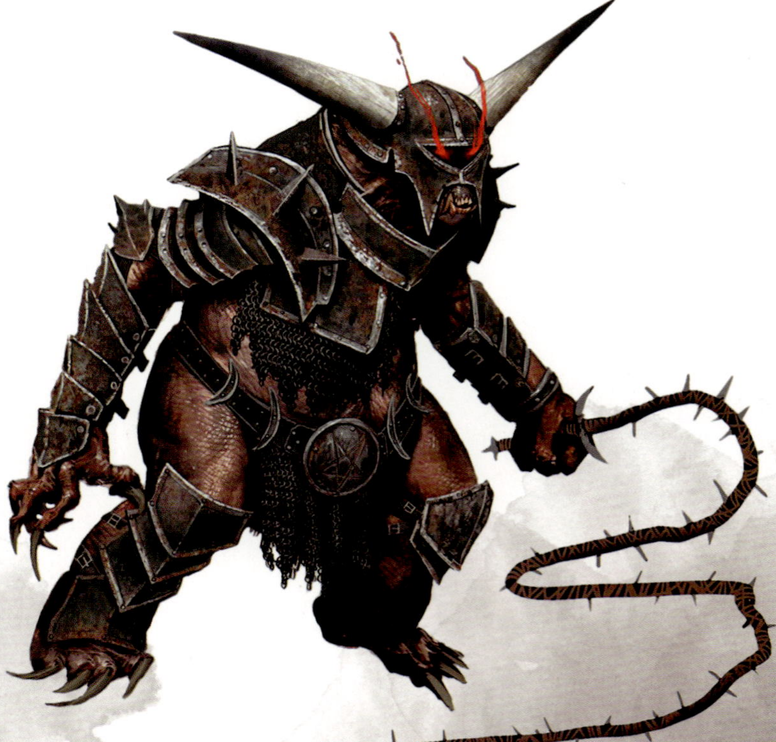

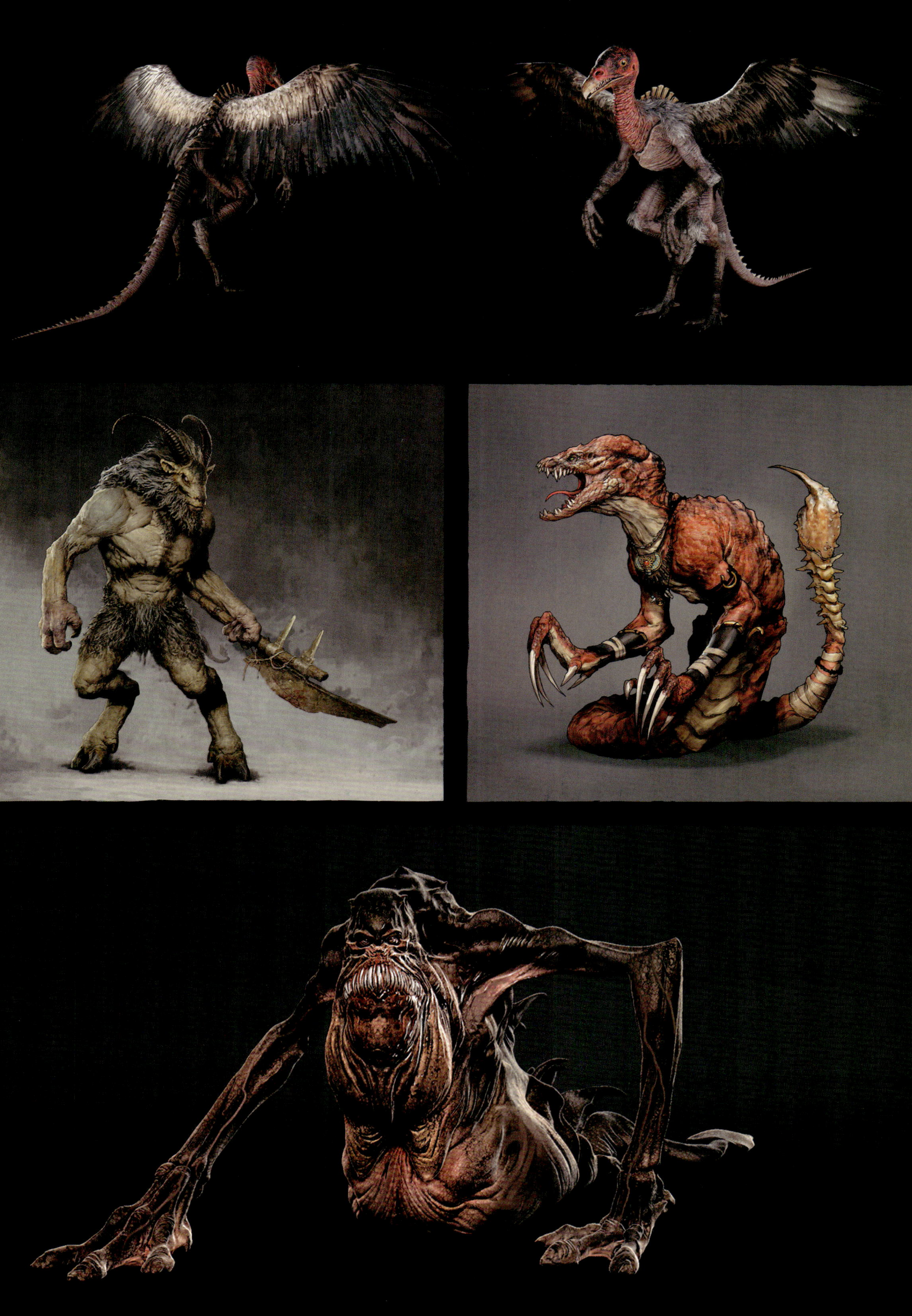

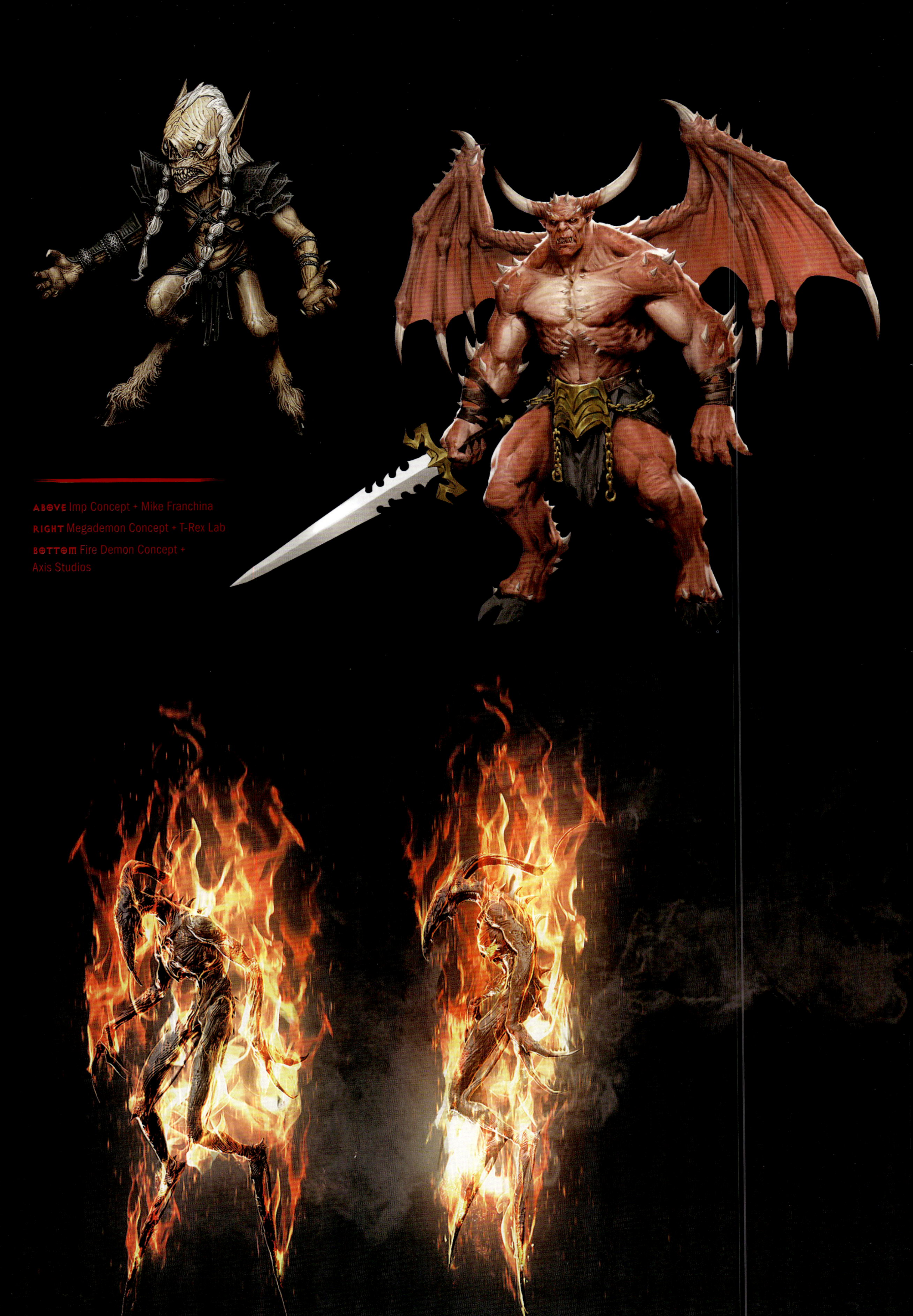

ABOVE Imp Concept • Mike Franchina
RIGHT Megademon Concept • T-Rex Lab
BOTTOM Fire Demon Concept • Axis Studios

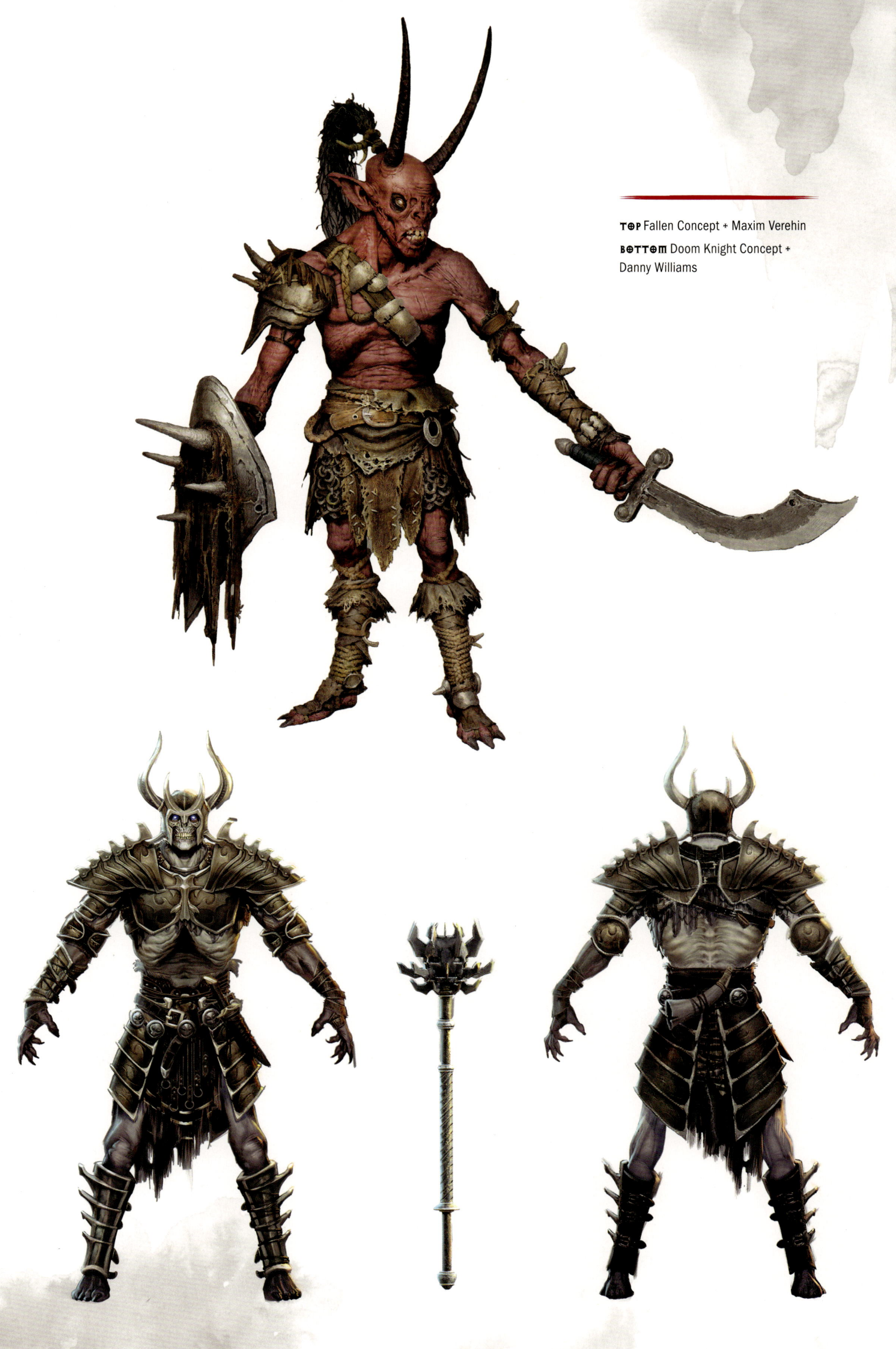

TOP Fallen Concept + Maxim Verehin

BOTTOM Doom Knight Concept + Danny Williams

Strapping Back In

ABOVE Tal Rune + John Dee

RIGHT Kriss Dagger Concept + Maxim Verehin

BELOW, TOP Dirk Dagger Concept + Maxim Verehin

BELOW, MIDDLE Dagger Concept + Maxim Verehin

BELOW, BOTTOM Blade Dagger Concept + Maxim Verehin

OPPOSITE, TOP LEFT Zombie Head Concept + Maxim Verehin

OPPOSITE, TOP MIDDLE Skull Head Concept + Maxim Verehin

OPPOSITE, TOP RIGHT Unraveller Head Concept + Maxim Verehin

OPPOSITE, BOTTOM RIGHT Demon Head Concept + Maxim Verehin

OPPOSITE, BOTTTOM LEFT Preserved Head Concept + Maxim Verehin

Diablo II is all about the loot: armor sets, weapons, jewels, potions, gold, and more. Few thrills compare to the acquiring of rare or unique items. The game's gear had a look and style all its own, but the remaster provided an opportunity for developers to take *Diablo II* items to new heights. For one thing, the team enhanced their level of detail tremendously. With this increased detail came consideration of how some items, armor, and equipment might actually work.

"We made a very hard push on functional realism," says Dustin King. "So if a character has a strap, a buckle, or a loop, it needed to make sense. It couldn't simply be stuck on there. We wanted to make sure that a player could see the detail in their equipment and appreciate it. That is, after all, why someone plays the game: to get the equipment."

Sharp-eyed players may notice something else about items in the game: a fresh look across the board.

"There were a lot of unique weapons in the game that did not have unique models," says Cory Turner. "There are a lot of items that are now no longer just a recolor of something that existed. They are truly unique. While we couldn't give a unique model to every single monster, we could do so with the weapons and the armor."

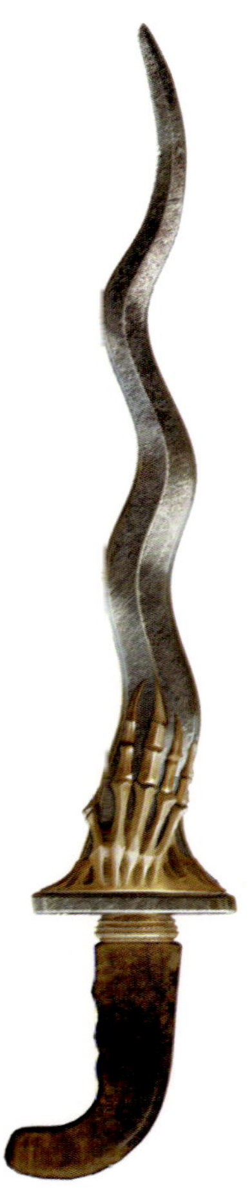

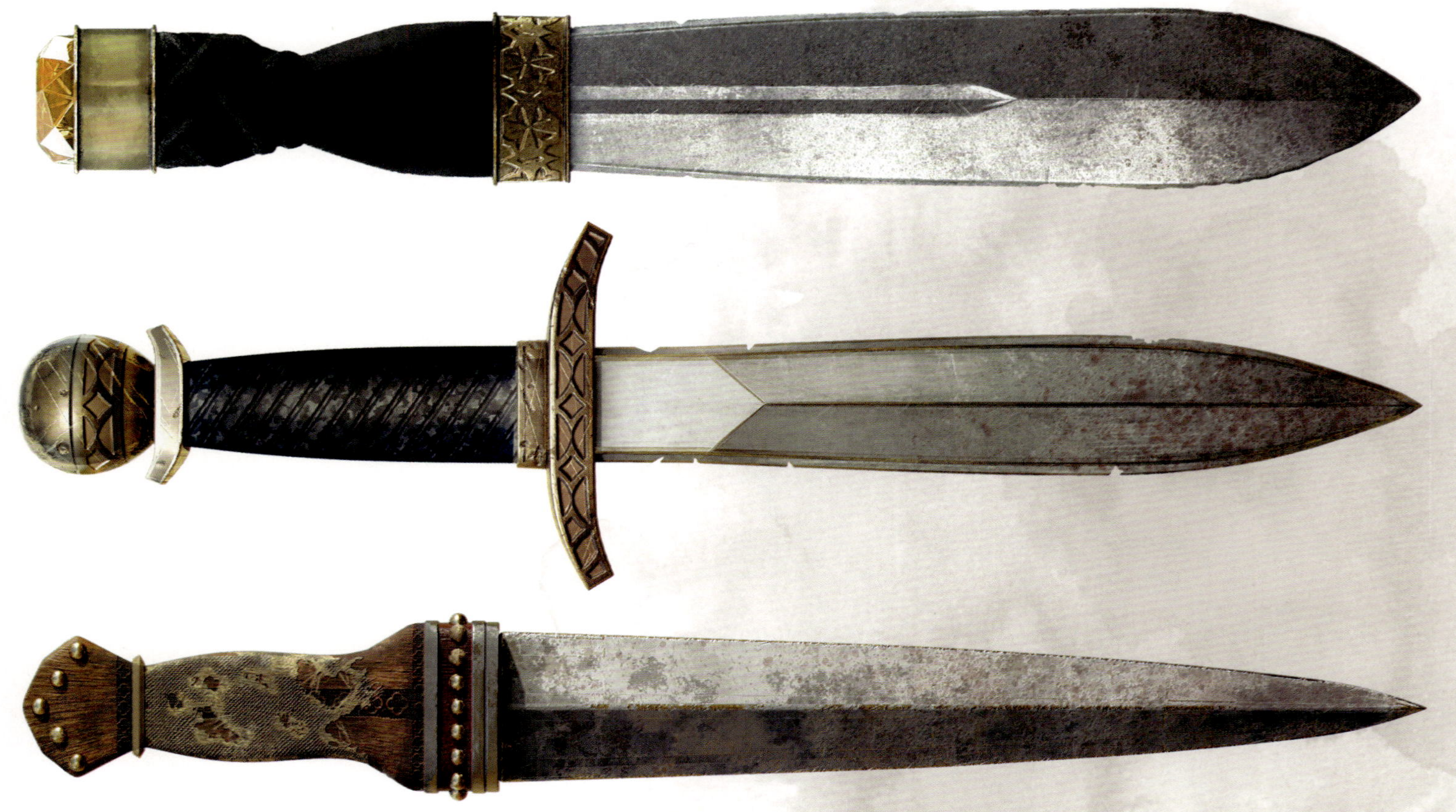

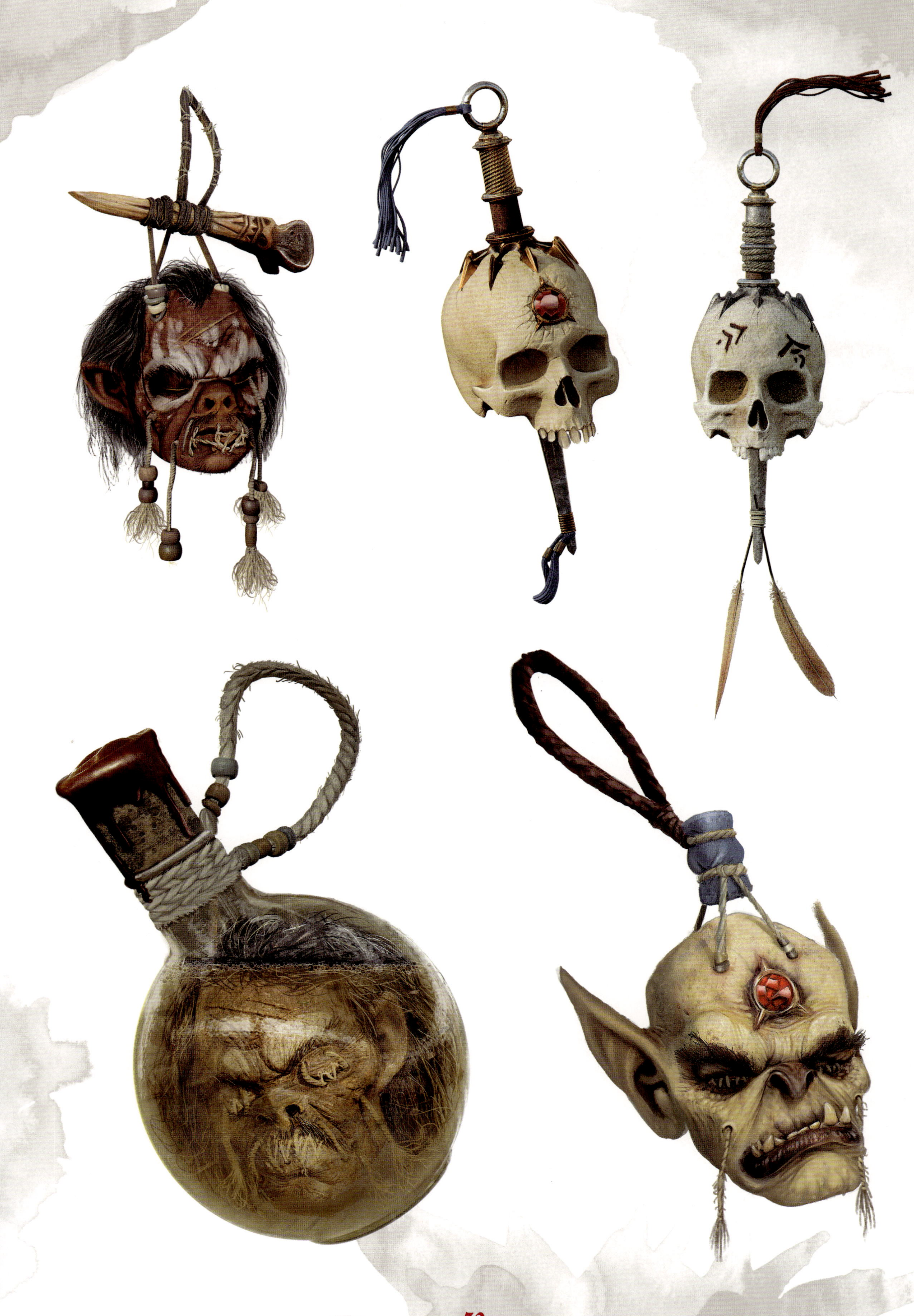

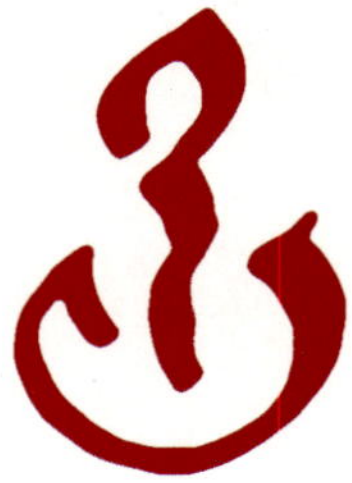

ABOVE Amn Rune ◆ John Dee

RIGHT, TOP Spike Club Concept ◆ Maxim Verehin

BOTTOM, RIGHT Wirt's Leg Club Concept ◆ Maxim Verehin

BOTTOM, LEFT Brainhew Axe Concept ◆ Maxim Verehin

OPPOSITE Weapon ideation ◆ Maxim Verehin

Having highly detailed, unique gear is all well and good, but only if players are able to see the items in order to pick them up. In the same way that characters and creatures blended into the background, loot was sometimes difficult to discern.

"Readability is huge," explains Turner. "So is gameplay. That's Blizzard. We couldn't make it hard for people to play the game simply because we liked how real we got it to look. If players can't play the game, it's moot. We really tried to be mindful of that and not forget the real goal."

Ensuring that loot was clearly visible often fell to the graphics team. Kevin Todisco explains: "Our lighters would go in and make sure that it was always possible to distinguish key elements like items, chests, and monsters from the background so that players could pick them out."

In the end, loot was the component of the original game that *Diablo II: Resurrected* developers were able to make the greatest strides in when it came to new and unique content.

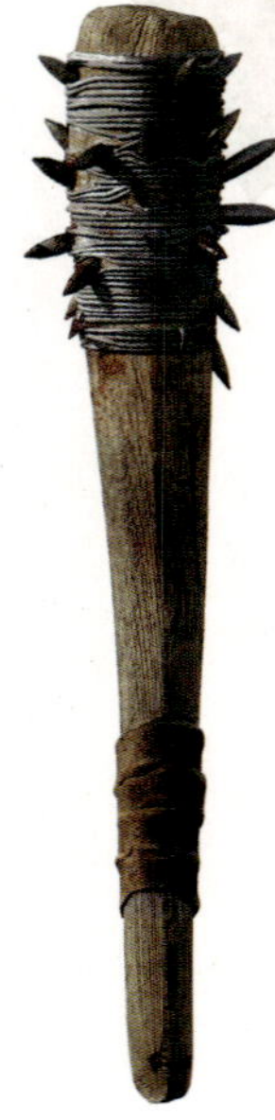

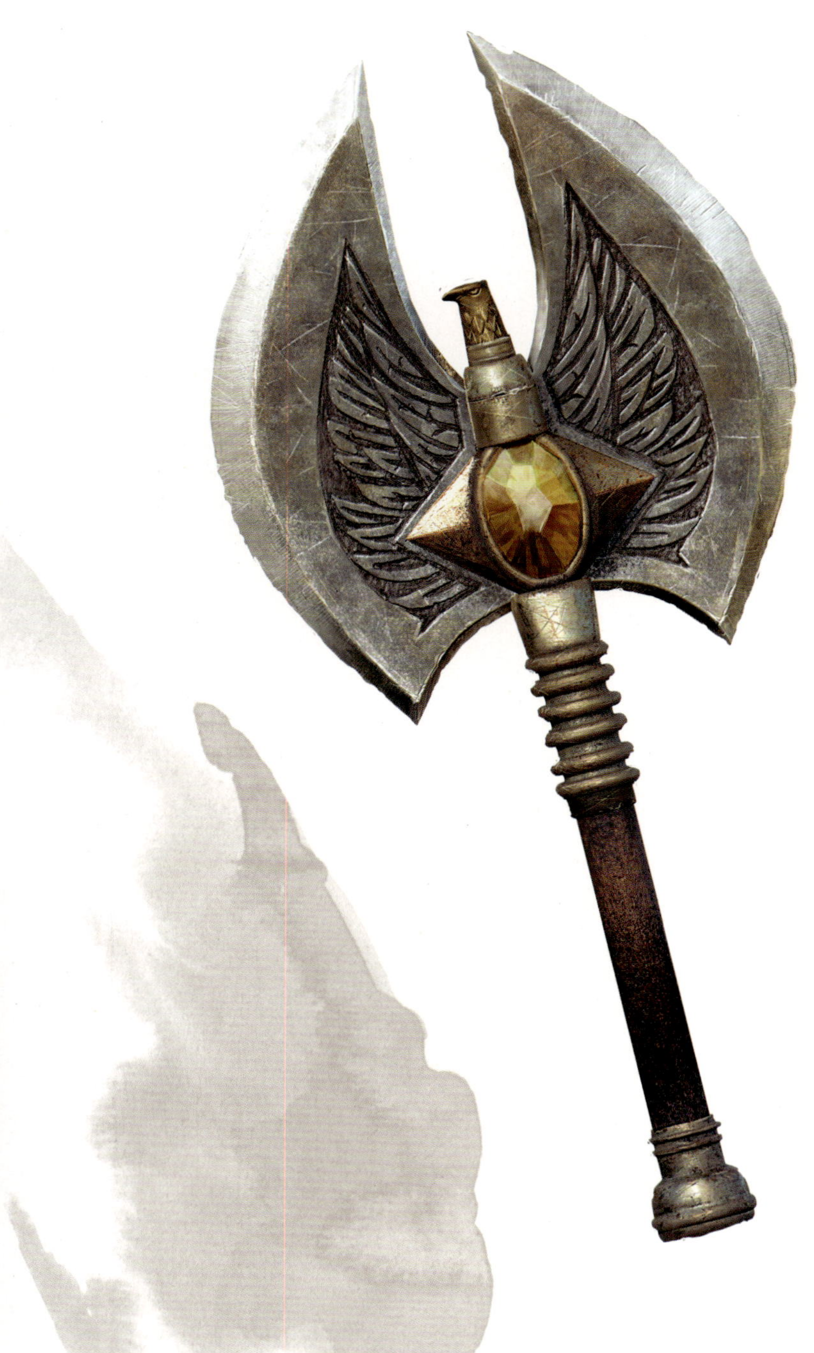

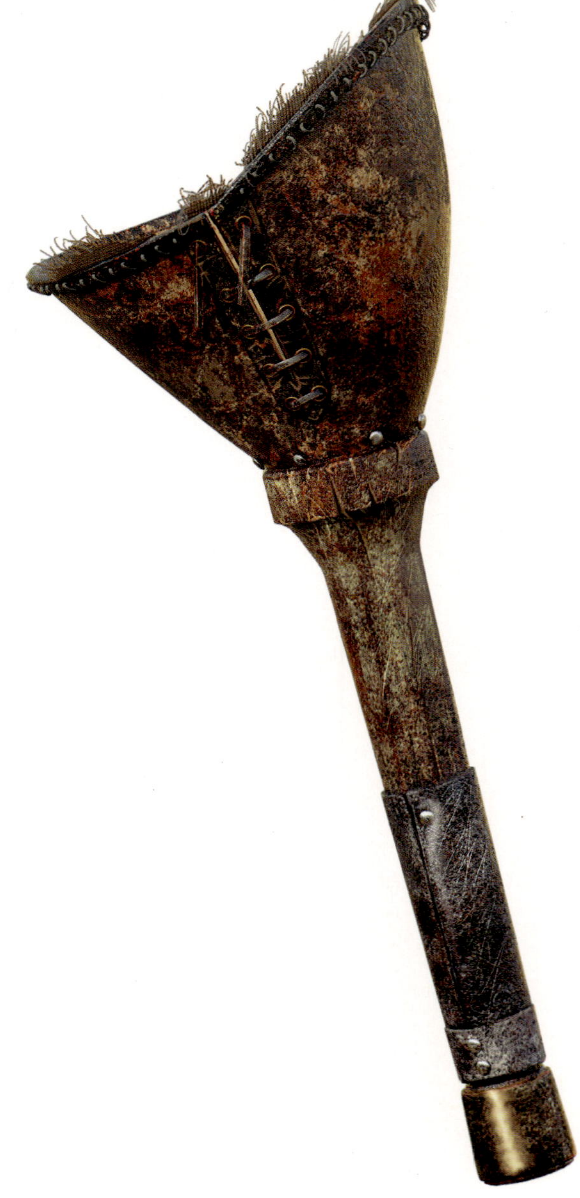

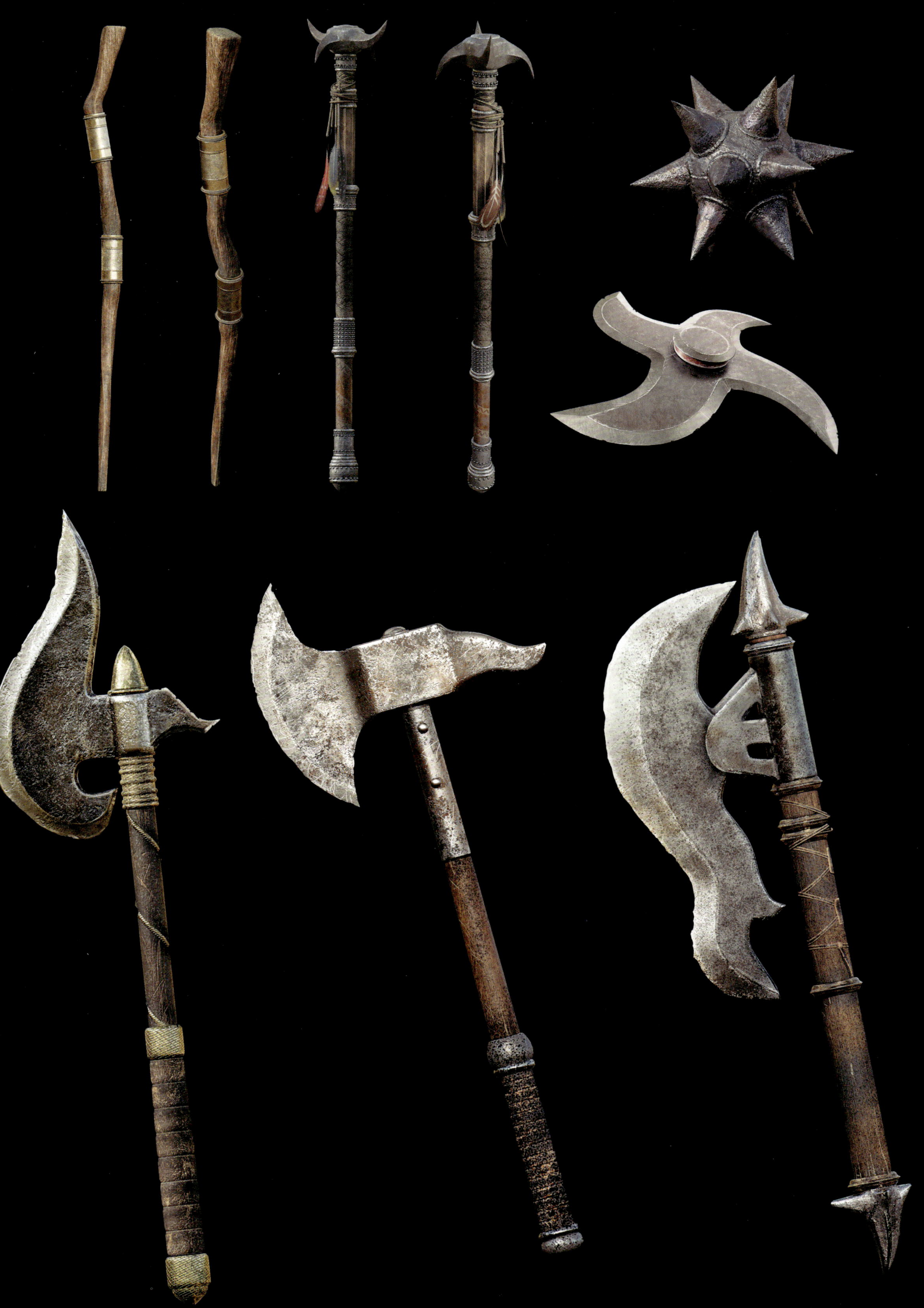

Retracing Footsteps

ABOVE Lo Rune + John Dee

THIS PAGE Original *Diablo II* Concept Sketches + Blizzard Artist

OPPOSITE World Stone Concept + *Diablo II: Resurrected* Art Team

Early on, developers considered doing a more limited 3D conversion of *Diablo II*. An audit of the classic game revealed that for a full upgrade, twenty-six hundred maps would need to be represented in 3D. It was a daunting prospect. Only when the audit proved how much detail could be added by going full 3D would the path ahead become clearer.

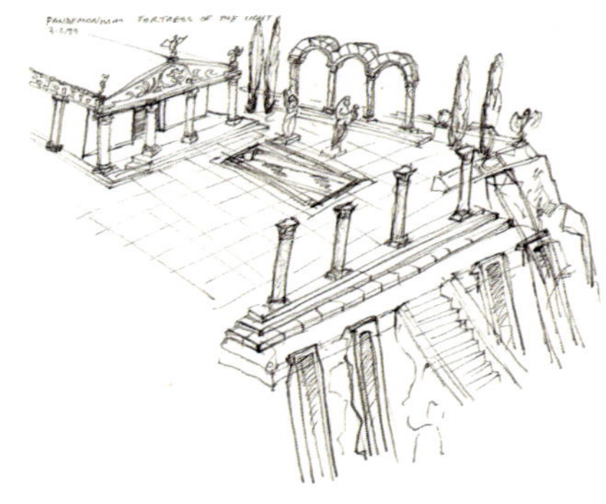

With the help of a new system, developers found multiple methods for reimagining *Diablo II*'s environments. Artists landed on a baseline of tracing over the original tiles with 3D models in a program that mimicked the original game's camera angle. This approach, however, could sometimes cause problems.

Jeffrey Lee explains: "After re-creating some of the environments, we said to ourselves, 'This just looks weird. It looks really wonky. Why is this?' It was because a lot of times, the original artists stitched things together in a way that technically, from a bird's eye perspective, made sense while not physically making sense."

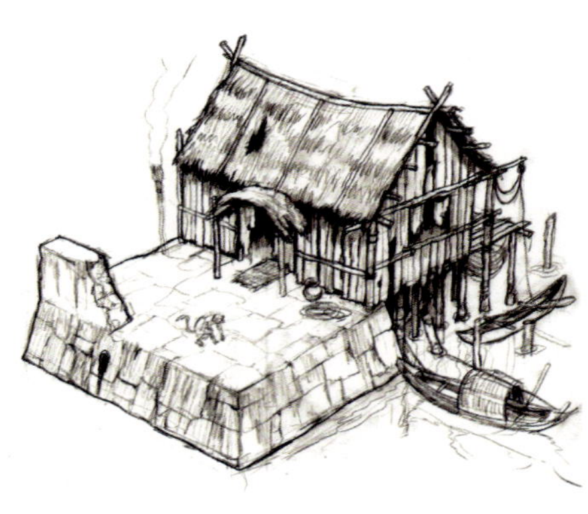

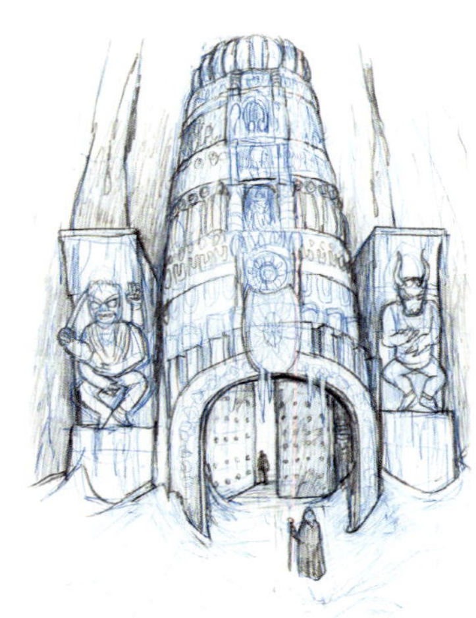

One level where the original developers capitalized on the non–physically bound nature of *Diablo II*'s renderer was the Arcane Sanctuary. "That's where it all went out the window for us," says Lee. "We had to mimic it being seamless while being physically correct. We played with perspective some, and we flattened it in such a way that we got it to work. Much of the challenge was answering: How do you re-create what is essentially an illusion—but in a real way?"

One tool that proved invaluable in aiding the conversion process was the toggle feature from the old game to the new. As Kevin Todisco remarks: "For as much as we said, 'This is a feature for the players,' the ability to go back and forth was needed to make the game. We needed to go back and forth, and ask ourselves, 'How does this look? How does that look?'"

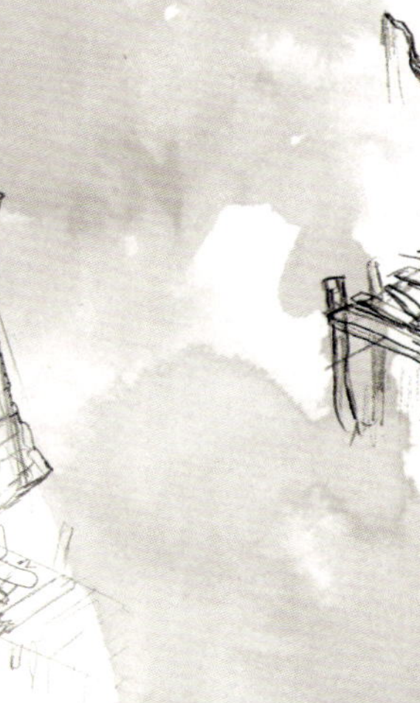

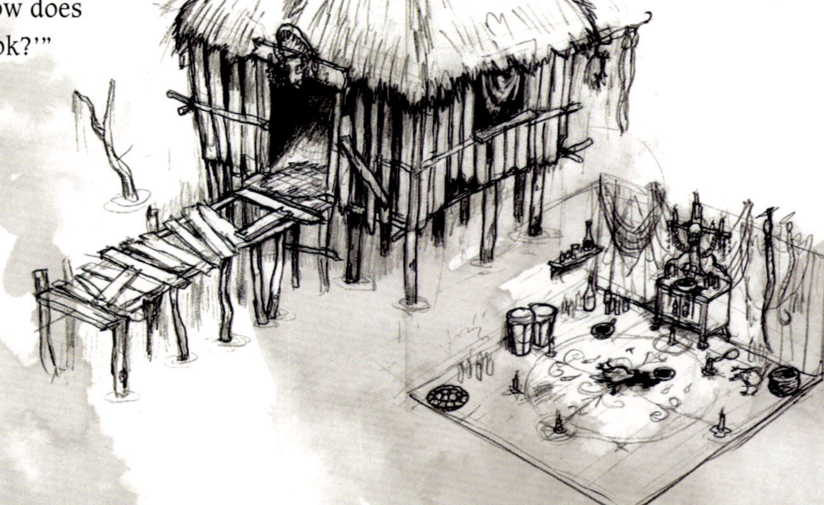

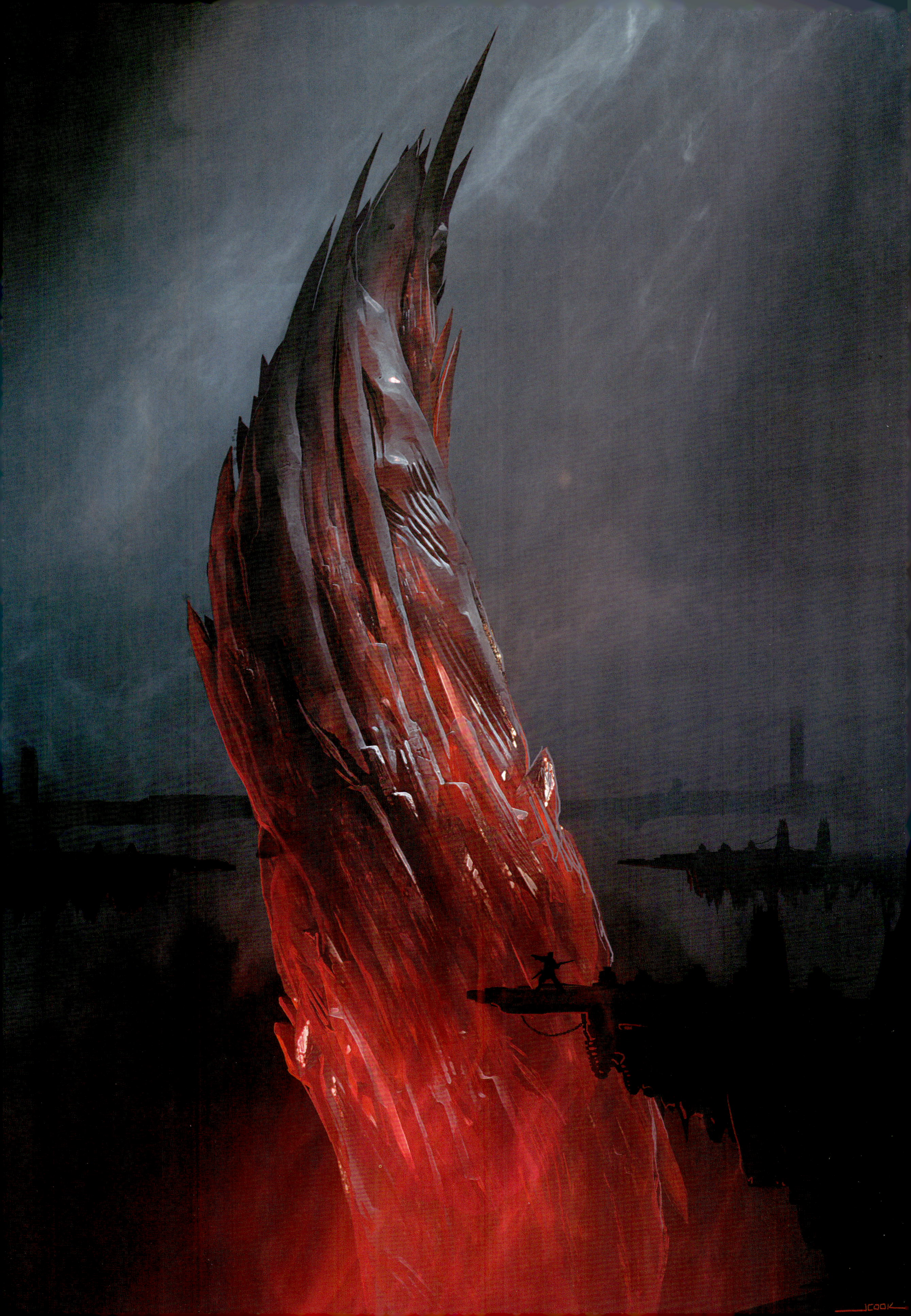
JCOOK

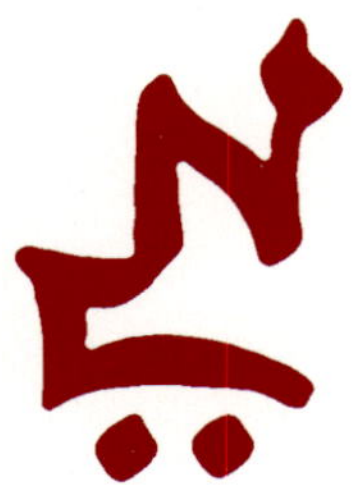

ABOVE Zod Rune + John Dee

RIGHT, TOP Jungle Totem Concept + Pixel Mafia

RIGHT, MIDDLE Travincal Doorway Concept + Pixel Mafia

BOTTOM Baal Litter Concepts + *Diablo II: Resurrected* Art Team

OPPOSITE, TOP Tal Rasha Tomb Concept + *Diablo II: Resurrected* Art Team

OPPOSITE, MIDDLE River of Flame Concept + Gray Rogers

OPPOSITE, BOTTOM Hellgate Concept + *Diablo II: Resurrected* Art Team

With the process established, the art team was able to not just update the old environments but also to create stunning new backgrounds in the select hero screen. "When you selected your character, depending on what act you were in, your character would be standing in front of a vista of the town from that act," says lead visual effects artist Evan Mennillo. "For the first time, you were able to see your character in full armor in this incredible representation of the level."

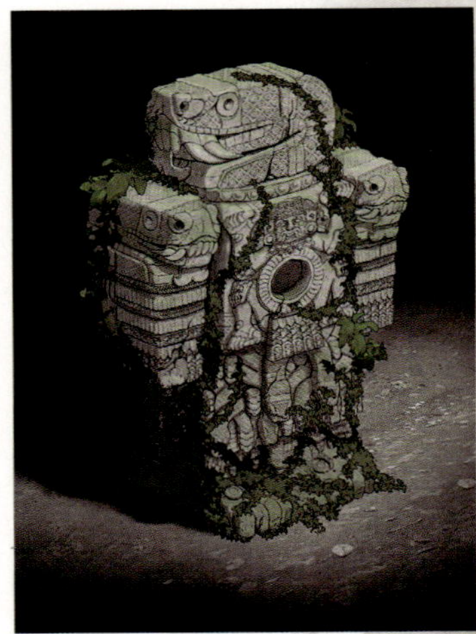

Ultimately, the trickiest element for artists to nail was simply the feel of the environments and, by extension, the overall tone of the game itself. Much of this was conveyed through lighting and color.

"Color palette was a big deal," says Cory Turner. "We wanted to make *Diablo* more real. Yes, *Diablo II* is a dark game. That said, it's also a really colorful game. The monsters are highly saturated. The grass is really saturated. *Diablo III* was colorful in a different way, but *Diablo II* wasn't a desaturated game. There was a lot of discussion around color for the entire duration of the project."

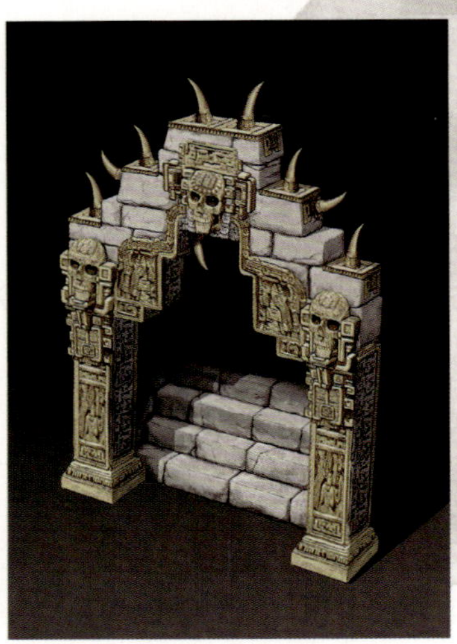

It was a balance that took time to strike.

"The textures were too dark," says Lee. "The lighting was slightly off; it was a little too dramatic, and the overall ambiance didn't feel right. But once we got to the tail end, it started to really take shape. It all finally came together in those last six months."

When all was said and done, it was the reaction of the players that mattered most.

"My biggest satisfaction from this project," says Lee, "was not when people marveled at the graphics. It was when they said, 'This is *Diablo II*,' and they didn't even talk about how it looks; they just played the game. That's how I know we landed in the right spot."

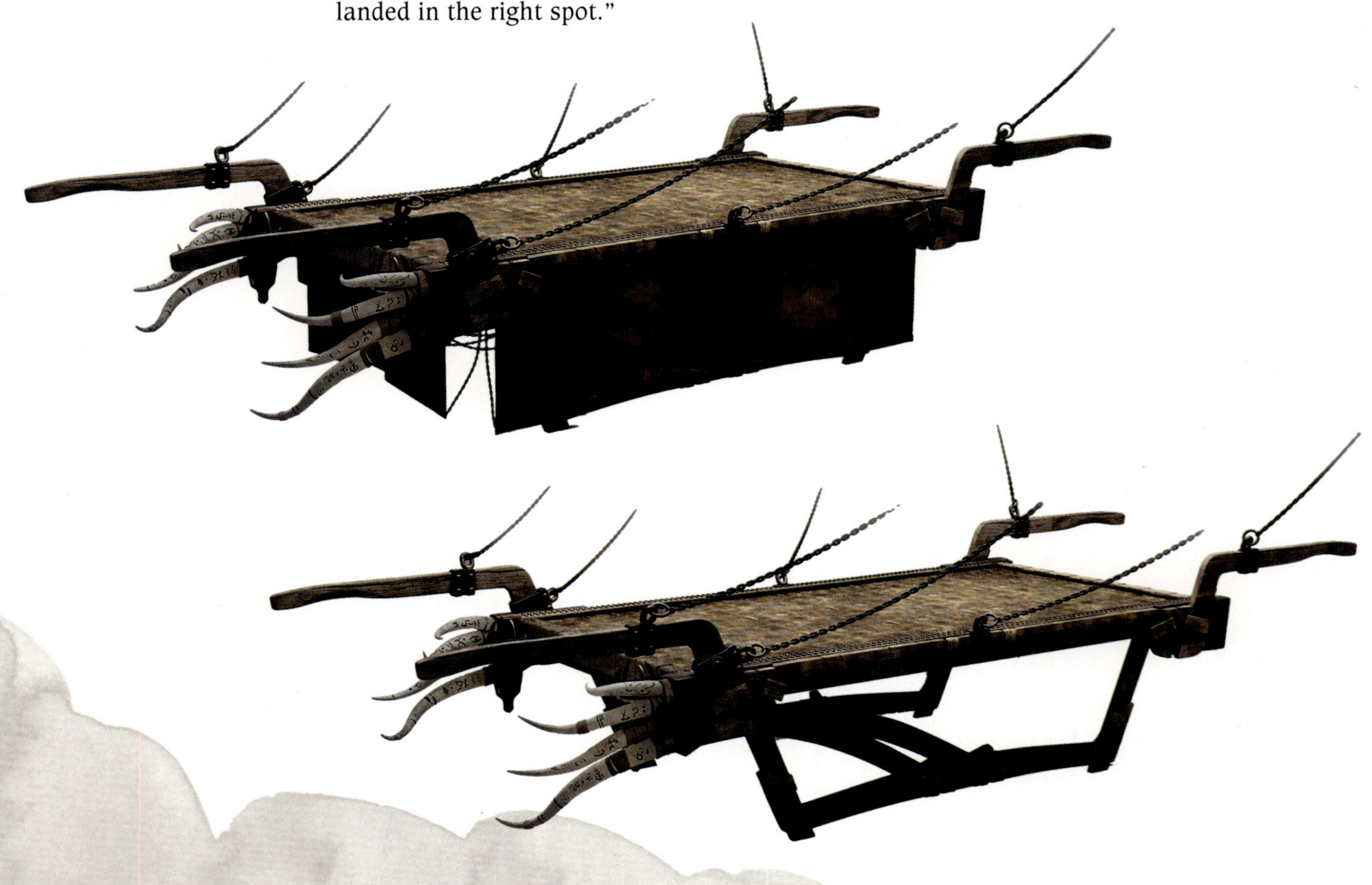

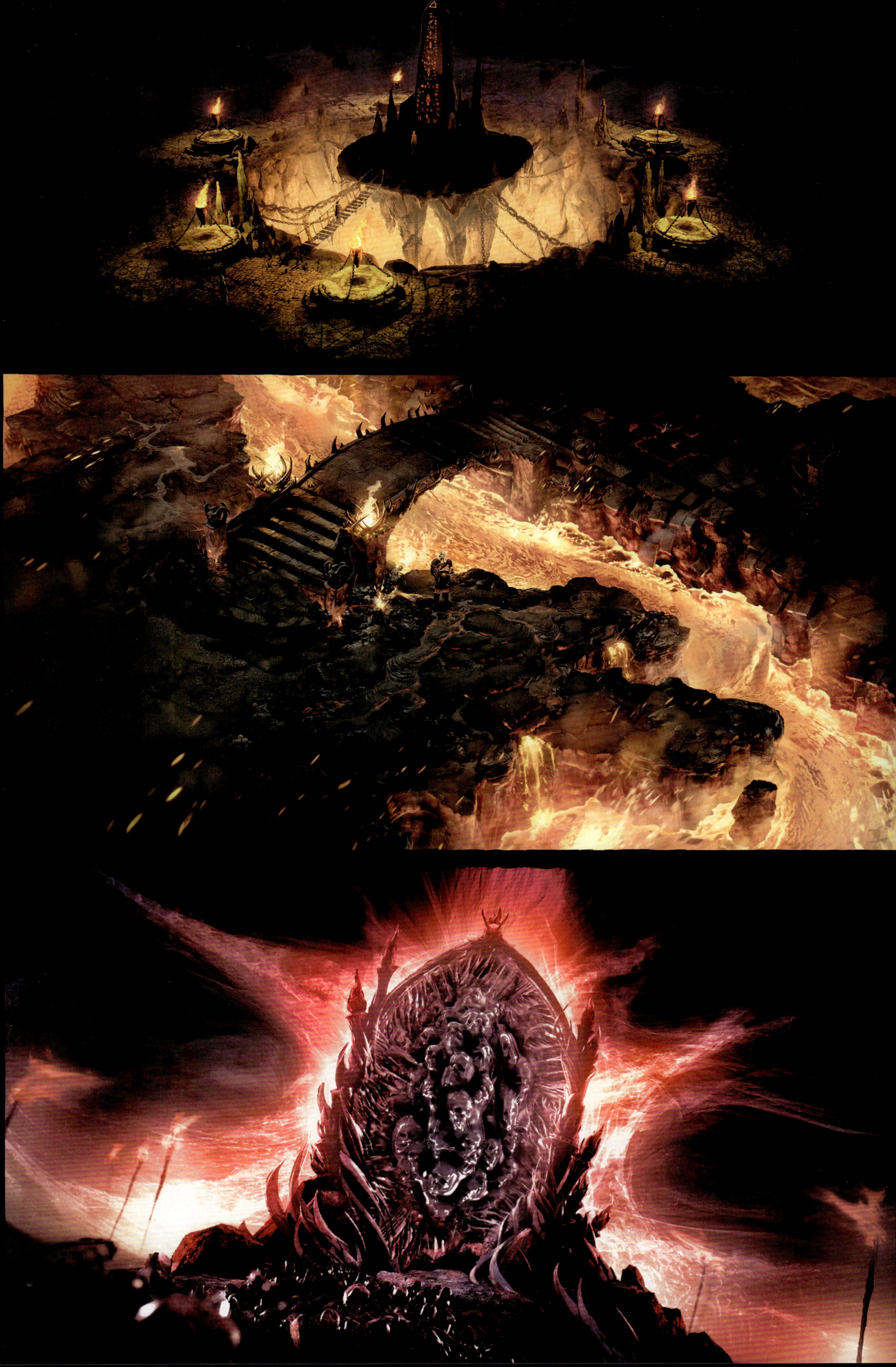

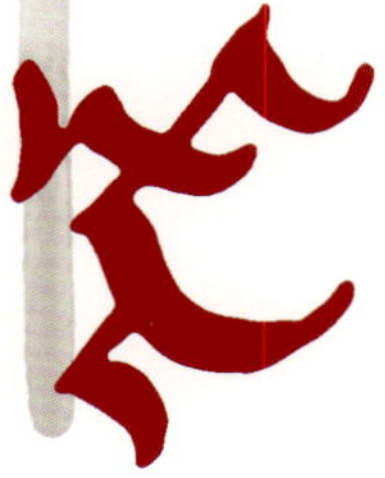

Dark Wanderings

ABOVE Eld Rune + John Dee

BOTTOM Diablo Appears + Blizzard Cinematics

OPPOSITE, TOP Tal Rasha Released + Blizzard Cinematics

OPPOSITE, BOTTOM The Dark Wanderer at fireside + Blizzard Cinematics

From the earliest stages of *Diablo II: Resurrected*'s development, there was a consensus that the original game's cinematics should be remade. It was, however, an undertaking that would come with considerable challenges.

"We were making the game relatively fast," Cory Turner explains, "and it was a huge investment, almost thirty minutes of cinematics. We considered different things, like a storybook style or re-presenting the original cinematics through a freshened-up filter. Ultimately, we decided: 'We need to remake the cinematics.' The question was how to make that happen with all of our resources committed on different projects."

Clear direction was given that the remade content should resemble the source material as closely as possible. This meant redoing the cinematics shot-for-shot with the same camera angles and characters, using original 3D models and sets where possible and digging up the old audio files.

For the opening scene in the cell of Marius—a human caught up in the war between the High Heavens and the Burning Hells—surfaces were retextured and fidelity was improved, but otherwise the set was left relatively unaltered. The updating of Marius himself was more involved, as scrutiny was applied to the old model's proportions.

"The face ratio to the size of the head was wrong," says visual effects supervisor Mike Kelleher. "For all characters we have what's called a gen-person . . . which is just body proportions. We always start with gen-person as our base model for any character, including orcs or protoss. What I think is interesting is that for all of the characters in *Diablo II: Resurrected*, none of that would have worked. It would have actually diminished the characters."

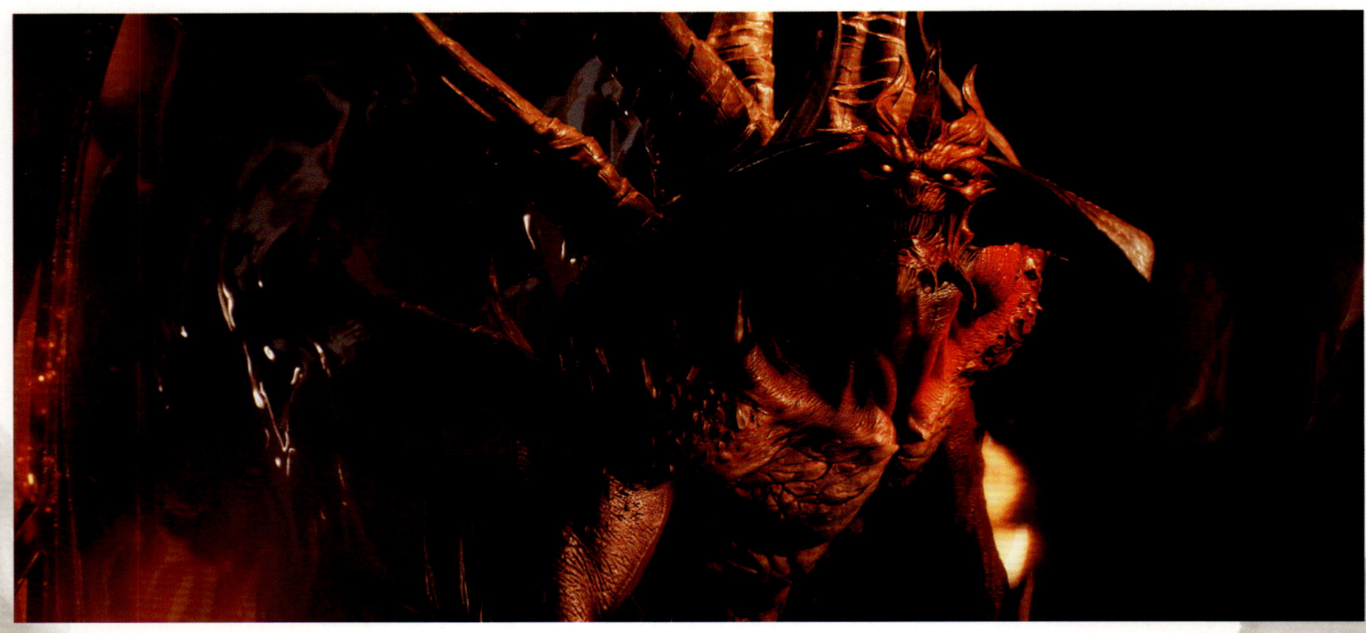

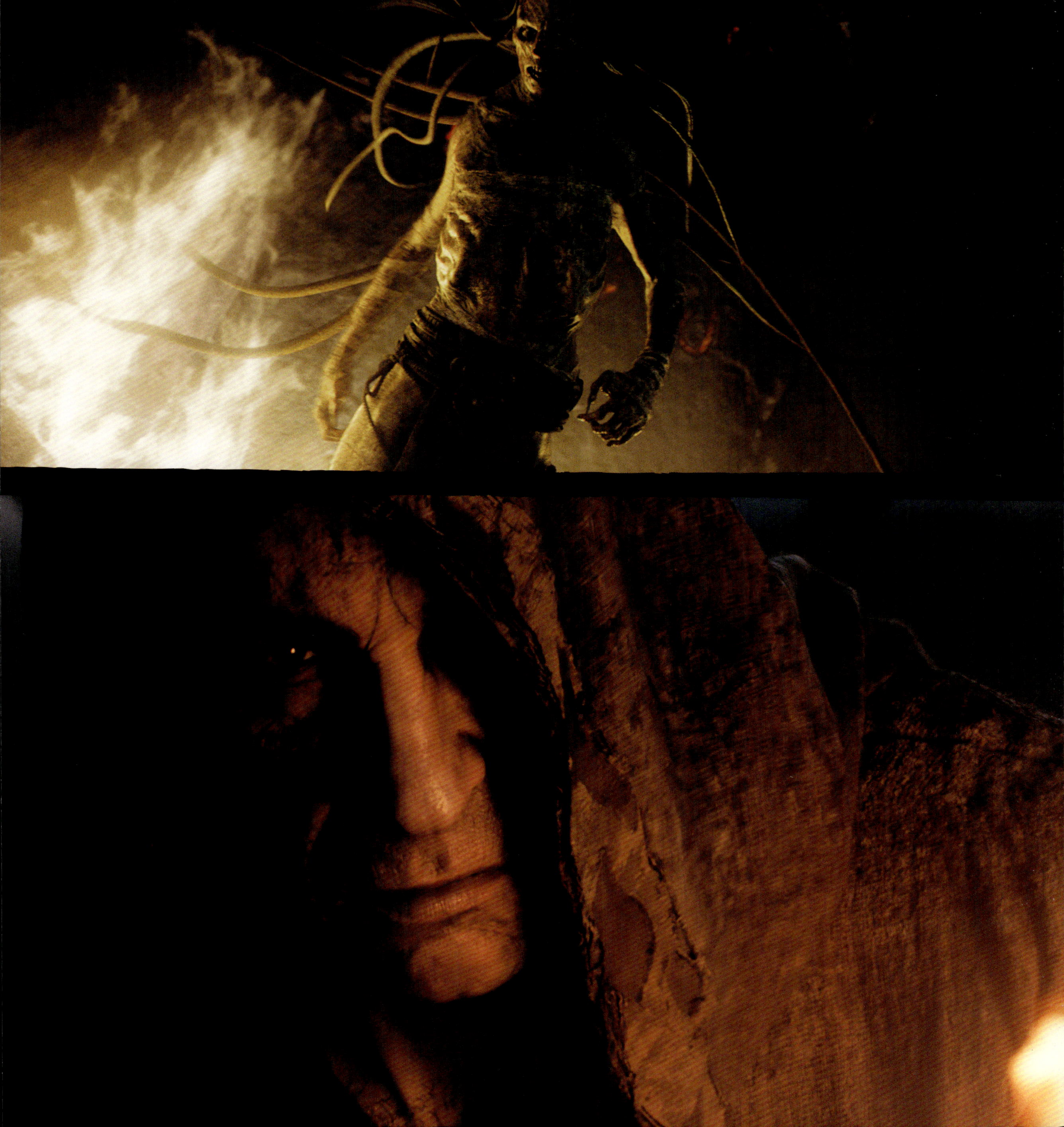

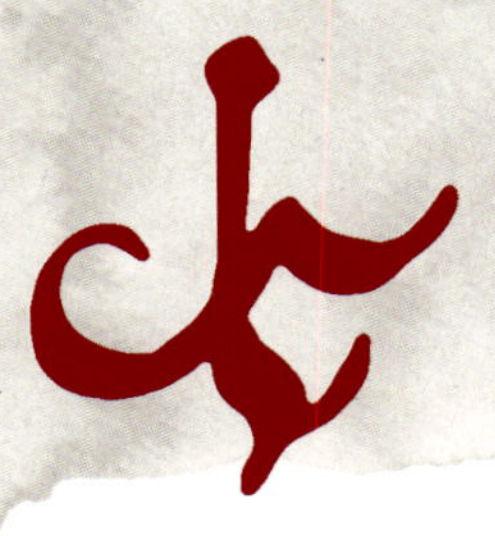

ABOVE Shael Rune + John Dee
RIGHT Marius Concept + Blizzard Cinematics
BELOW Marius Aging Concepts + Blizzard Cinematics
OPPOSITE, TOP Dark Wanderer's Rest + Blizzard Cinematics
OPPOSITE, MIDDLE Marius and the Burning Bridge + Blizzard Cinematics
OPPOSITE, BOTTOM The Hellgate Opened + Blizzard Cinematics

The result was an updated version of Marius that remained faithful to the exaggerated anatomy of the original.

"He is stylized," says Kelleher, "and his proportions may not be considered 'correct,' but I think he works in a way that in some respects I wish we would get back to, just letting ourselves branch out a little further from the tried-and-true method. Don't mess with people's touchstones for their memory."

For one of the biggest sets that was rebuilt, Tal Rasha's tomb, lighting became a main focus. Despite how far technology has come since *Diablo II*'s release, some elements of the lighting that reflected technical limitations of the time were preserved to maintain the tone of the original.

"A lot of modern-day cinematics are going to use fire as light sources," Kelleher continues. "There's a ton of fire in the scene—there are torches and braziers, and the entire set catches fire later on. None of that is really reflected in the lighting in the characters in the original piece; it just wasn't there for the time. And there's something special about the way it looks—especially for Tal Rasha, who has Baal inside of him. It's creepy. We felt that some of the creepiness came from the fact that he isn't lit or that he has shaded areas. The term we used was 'anti-light.' He looked like he was just shying away from light."

Technological advancements did enhance a story-related detail in the sequence that was much more ambiguous in the classic version. Kelleher explains: "I had a lot of people say that in the original it's difficult to tell that there's this ghost that's coming out of Tal Rasha asking for help. Even though it's Baal underneath there, just for the rendering quality, people said, 'Thank you, now I get it.'"

While the team remained faithful to the original cinematics throughout, for the literally explosive finale, the choice was made to go far above and beyond the original shattering of the Worldstone.

"The first one looked a little like wood," Kelleher remarks. "They used every 3D trick back then to have as many particles as possible. Turning that into something that felt bigger than life was a challenge, and it was one of the only places where I felt like, 'Okay, for this one, people are expecting it to be the culmination of their gameplay, and they really want it to be something special.' That Worldstone is almost a half mile tall in 3D space and has almost half a billion pieces that it breaks into."

When all was said and done, the team had re-created the entirety of *Diablo II*'s beloved and now-classic cinematics, all while remaining true to the source material.

"I think that the watchword of 'don't reinvent the wheel' is the way to go," says Kelleher. "These cinematics are now part of people's lives, part of their experience growing up. You don't mess with that, and you certainly can't reinvent it; so if we update it, great, but let the memories be the memories."

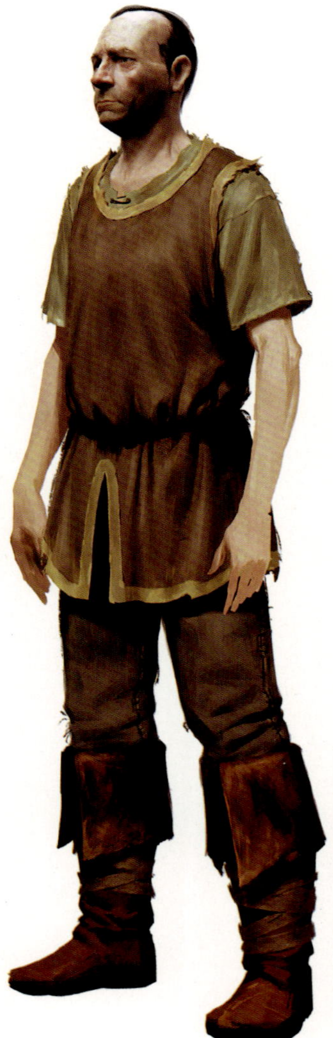

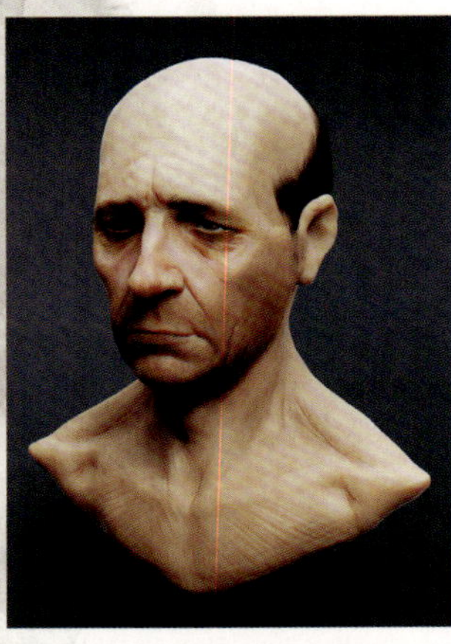

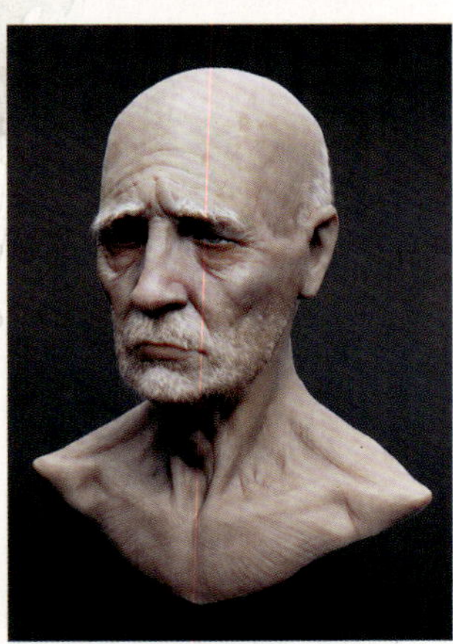

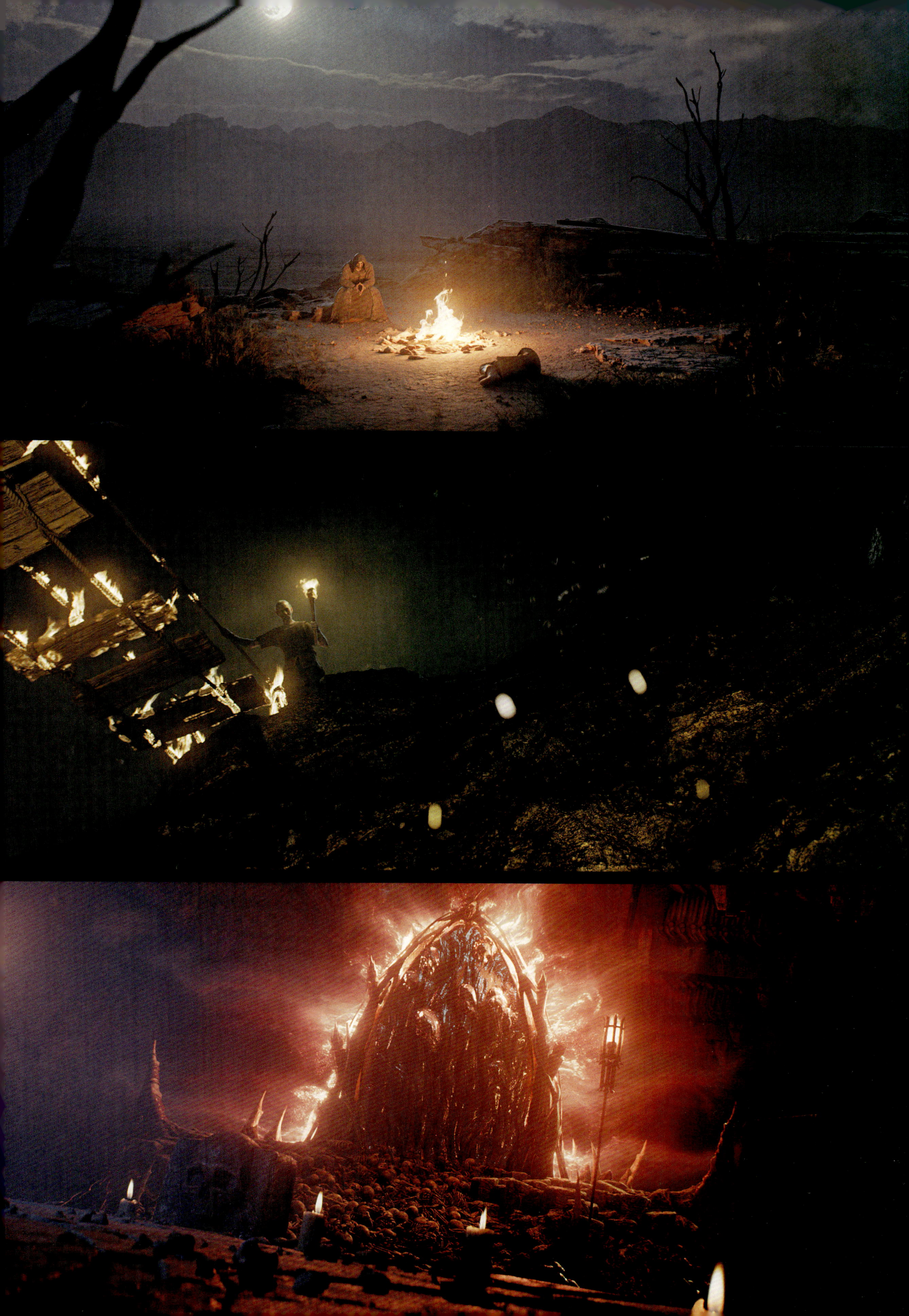

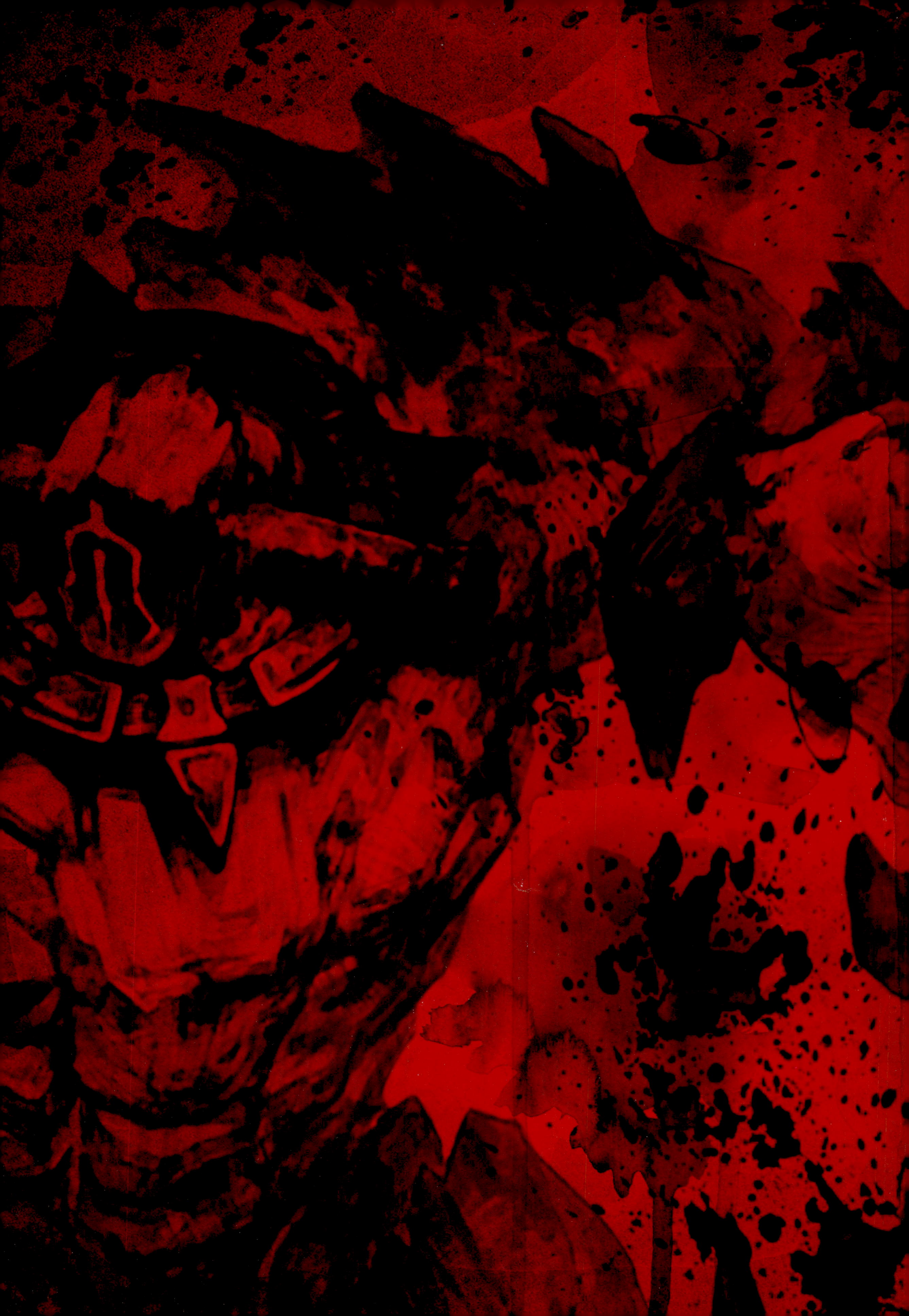

DIABLO IMMORTAL

Shadows of the Past

The storyline of Diablo Immortal is set five years after the events of Diablo II: Lord of Destruction. The Worldstone, the Heart of Creation, has been destroyed by Tyrael following its corruption by the Prime Evil, Baal. The Archangel of Justice, Tyrael, had seemingly died in the ensuing chaos.

This is the backdrop for *Diablo*'s first-ever mobile game: *Diablo Immortal*. Quite often, the priority when developing a new game is to establish a look and feel. For an installment in an ongoing franchise, much of that had already been done. Whereas the goal of *Diablo IV* was to set itself apart from other entries in the series, *Diablo Immortal* embraced what had come before.

"We actually chose it to match more of the style of *Diablo III*," says associate art director Richie Marella. "It's on the lighter side compared to *Diablo IV*. I think it fits with that kind of mobile/arcade aesthetic. It's a matter of not making it look too realistic, and more artistic."

It was imperative for the style to not only be true to the franchise but also a good fit for the small screen size.

"The starting place for this kind of game has to be readability," says art director Hunter Schulz. "That's a challenge. The main premise for the art was to stay true to the *Diablo* lore, the *Diablo* look, to make sure there was a consistent feel and vibe with the other *Diablo* games, and to deliver a *Diablo* experience on mobile. All decisions we made for the art had that goal in mind."

This philosophy behind the art affected everything from backgrounds to user interface (UI).

"The first UI we had was just the globe and a couple buttons," Marella notes. "There were many paint-overs in which we tried to incorporate a little bit of fantasy, a thin layering of details, to indicate this is a gothic UI. There are so many elements that are packed into that screen, which had to balance out so that art had to take a step back. It was really important to have the gameplay first."

Some of the art developed for the UI was repurposed in pop-outs and inventory. This give-and-take continued in the realm of icons.

"At first, the icons were almost screenshots of the effects in the game," adds Marella. "What we had to do was stylize and simplify. For instance, we had to make a fireball in a more graphic way and then add color to it so that the read was flat. Then we started adding a little bit of volume and effects, so it wasn't as bright and busy."

Simple, clean, readable, stylized. But no less exciting. By following a few basic principles, the *Diablo Immortal* development team was able to deliver an epic game on a small screen.

No Rest for the Wicked

ABOVE Kulle Library Rune + NetEase Art Team

RIGHT, TOP Blood Knight Concept Sketch + NetEase Art Team

RIGHT, MIDDLE Blood Knight Portrait Sketches + Geunjoo Baik

BOTTOM, RIGHT & MIDDLE Blood Knight Armor Sketches + NetEase Art Team

BELOW Blood Knight Portrait Sketches + NetEase Art Team

OPPOSITE Necromancer Key Art + Geunjoo Baik, Yongsoon Park

Three pillars were integral in the creation of *Diablo Immortal*'s classes: readability on a small screen, looking good from the game camera, and showcasing a style that fits the *Diablo* universe. But these guidelines were only the beginning.

"We visually retained the class fantasy," says Hunter Schulz. "As well as the themes and shapes that we've seen in the past, a lot of the same elements. Because so many of the classes are returning, we had a really good foundation to work off of. For each class there are themes that you try to tap into, and we tried to draw those out without going too far in reimagining what these classes look like."

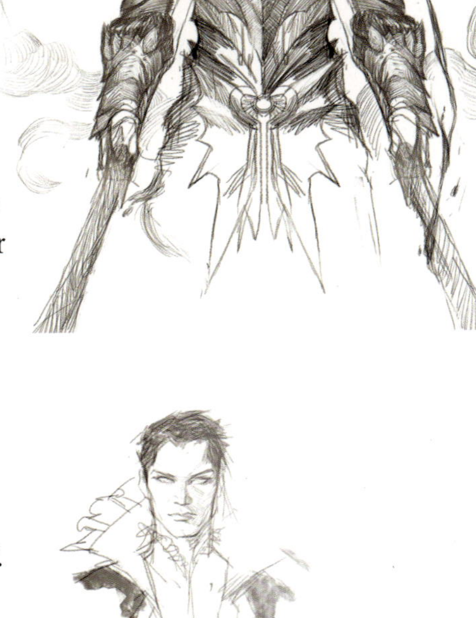

So how do artists maintain class identity? One key element is shape language, which, as the name implies, means using shapes in art to express ideas and themes. An example of this can be found in the contrast between the Necromancer and Monk classes.

"You have death," Schulz explains, "you have skeletal shapes, so you can implement a bone motif or a scythe motif. The scythe, having that beautiful curve with a point, is not something that's just used for the weapon but also for UI elements or borders. You can boil the Necromancer down to sharp shapes, while the Monk is rounder. There's more rhythm and flow to those shapes that go well with the Monk vibe."

Specific armor elements are also used to make classes readily identifiable, such as the Crusader's tabard, shield, and high collar and the Demon Hunter's long scarf. While this is all well and good for established classes, *Diablo Immortal* also included a new addition to the franchise's legendary lineup: the Blood Knight.

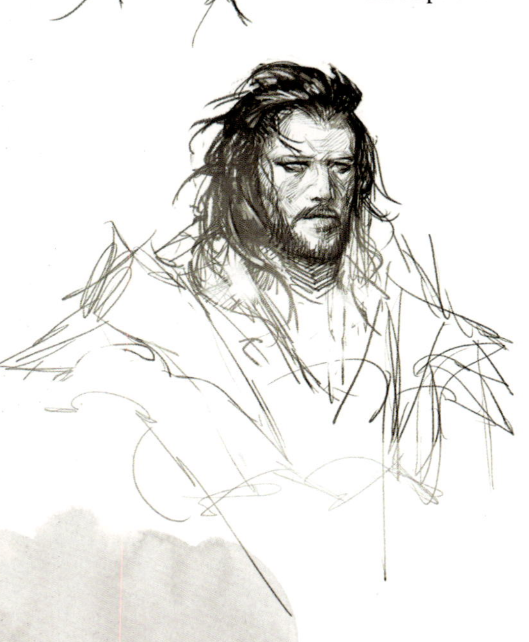

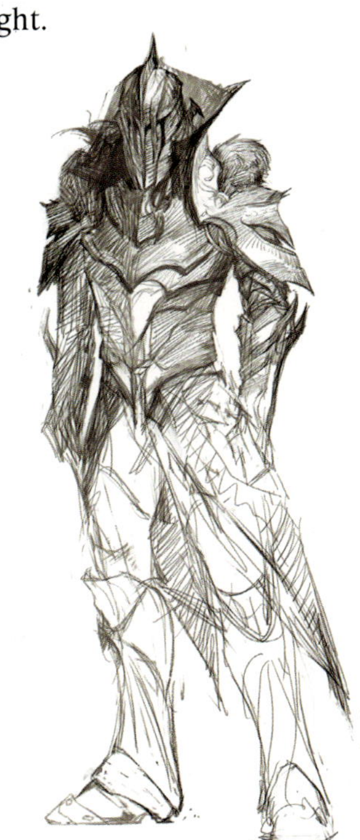

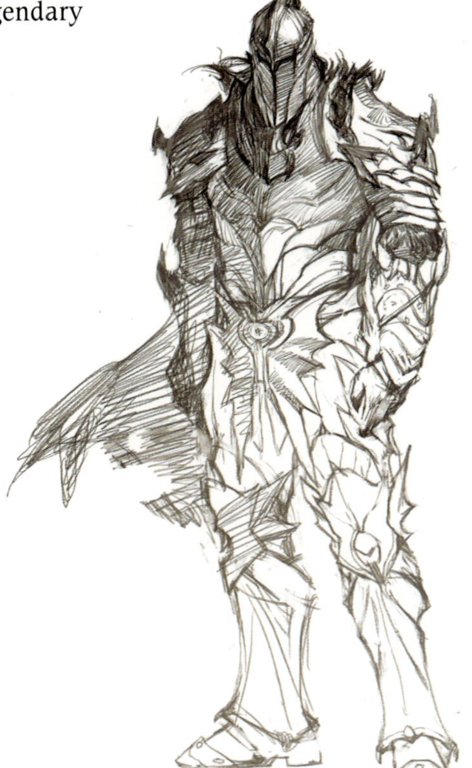

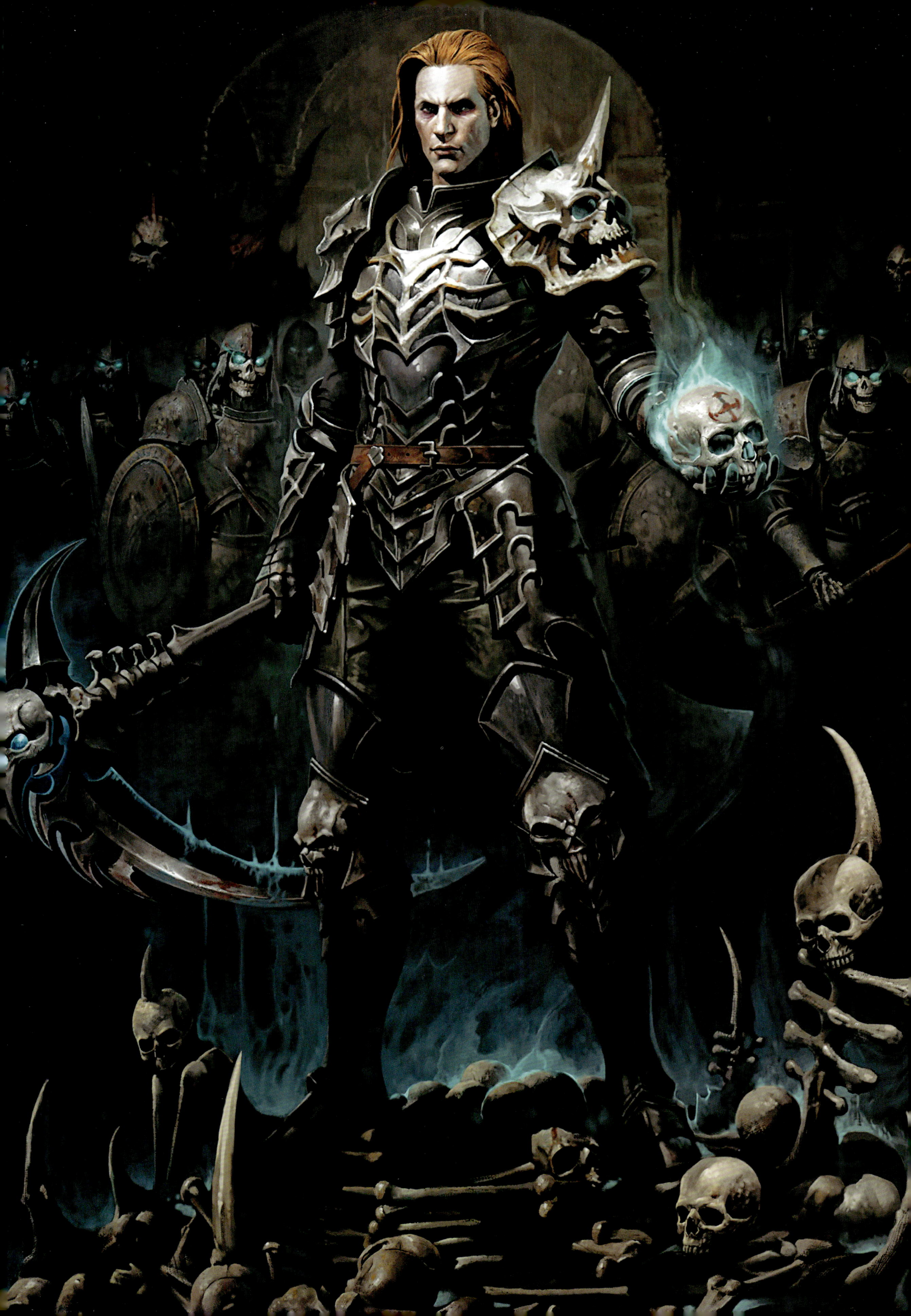

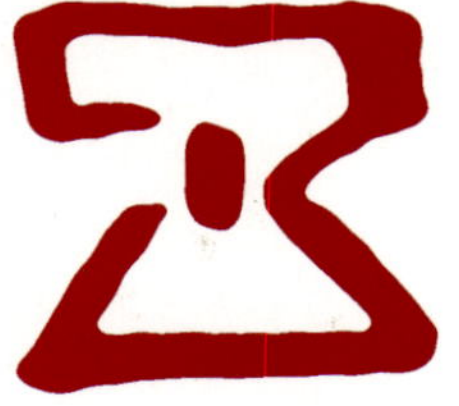

ABOVE Kulle Library Rune + NetEase Art Team

RIGHT Blood Knight Concepts + NetEase Art Team

BELOW Blood Knight Sketch + NetEase Art Team

OPPOSITE Blood Knight Key Art + Sangsoo Jeong

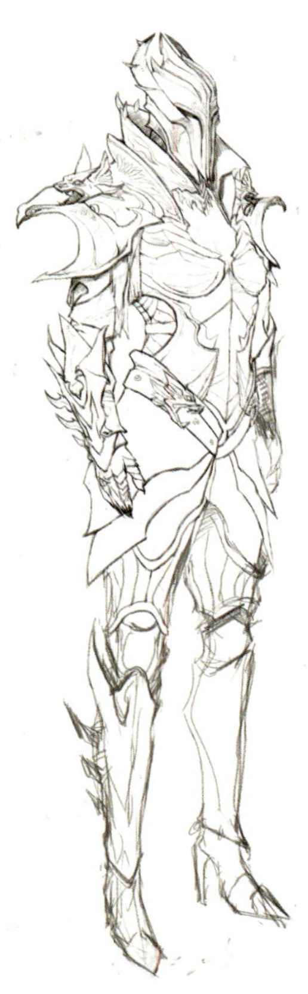

Blood Knights wage a constant struggle against the vampire within. When needed, they can call upon their vampiric abilities to become an unholy abomination. But most of the time they must fight to maintain control of their very humanity. Artists used this conflict as a starting point for the class's design.

"The basic thing we tried to hit," says Schulz, "was to combine the knight aspect—a plated melee character with medieval armor—with the vampire. As we started to combine those elements, we went in a direction that felt like neither. So toward the end of their development, we really leaned into the vampire fantasy. We wanted people to instantly recognize what this character was about."

The resulting design decisions included the use of bat anatomy.

"If you look at the shoulder pads," Schulz notes, "they're sort of these bat wing shapes that flare out with spikes all over the place. Then we have the bat 'thumb' that has the nail on it, a shape that's on the shoulder pads and down at the end of the cape. A lot of the lines are mimicking the skeletal system of a bat wing."

When design enters the final stages for each class, another important step remains, which is to lay out the classes next to each other to see how they interact visually. At this stage, color palette comes to the forefront.

"Even though players will go into the game and get new armor and the color palettes will change," Schulz says, "there is always the poster version for each class—we call them the brand headliners. When we showcase the character in its truest form, the way we really want to portray it, that's what we'll put out there. You'll notice a lot of the cinematics are using similar character designs for each one, which is our brand headliner."

The use of color is more obvious in some classes, like the new Blood Knight.

"When you have a Blood Knight," explains Schulz, "you have a color in the name, so it makes sense to be bold with the brand headliner. Probably 70 percent of the character design is blood red. The Necromancer also stands out, with the greenish-blue to represent the undead they raise, and there's also purple and silver. It's subtle because they're desaturated, but their color palettes are more unified or easier to distinguish than some of the others."

When all is said and done, the result is a line-up of classes that present specific archetypes and have their own individual appeal. For returning classes, they retain the legacy while still feeling unique. And for a premier class like the Blood Knight, they establish a clear theme and a bold new identity.

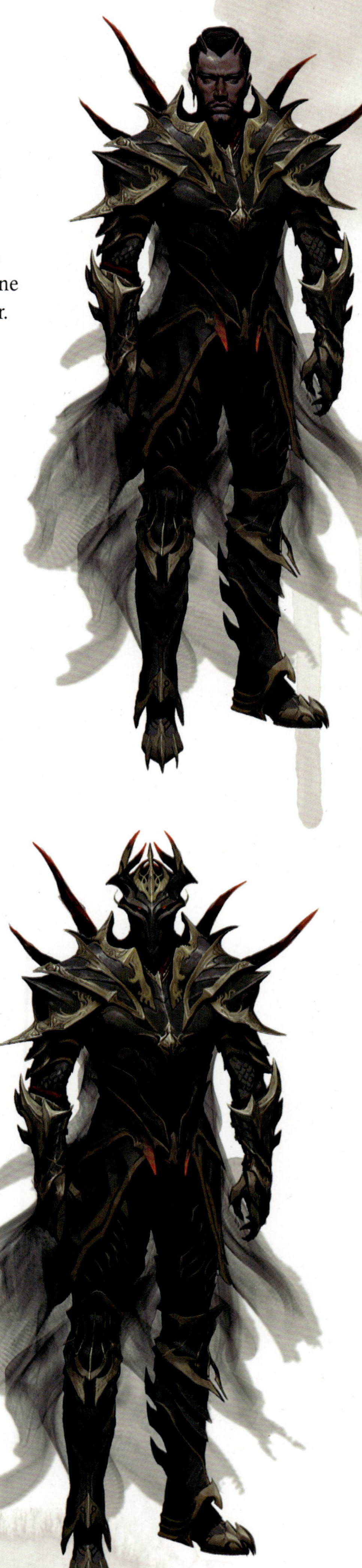

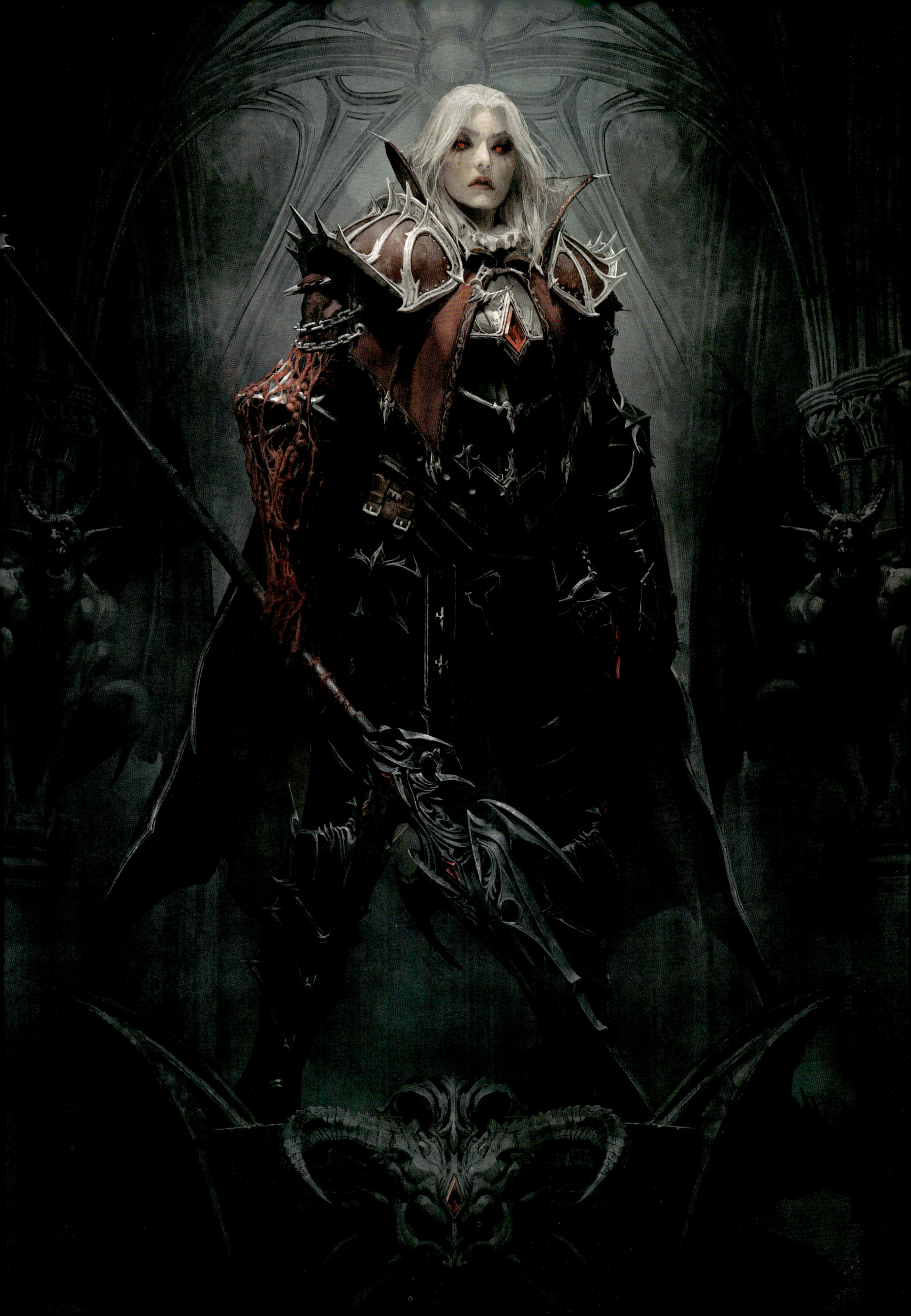

OPPOSITE Crusader Concept • Eunice Ye

BELOW Barbarian Concept • Eunice Ye

"We put a ton of detail into every part of this game, from characters to creatures, environments, cosmetics, and armor sets. With the in-game camera always pointing downward on the characters, we place the majority of the details and interesting shapes on the top half of their body."

—JUSTIN MURRAY, Senior Concept Artist

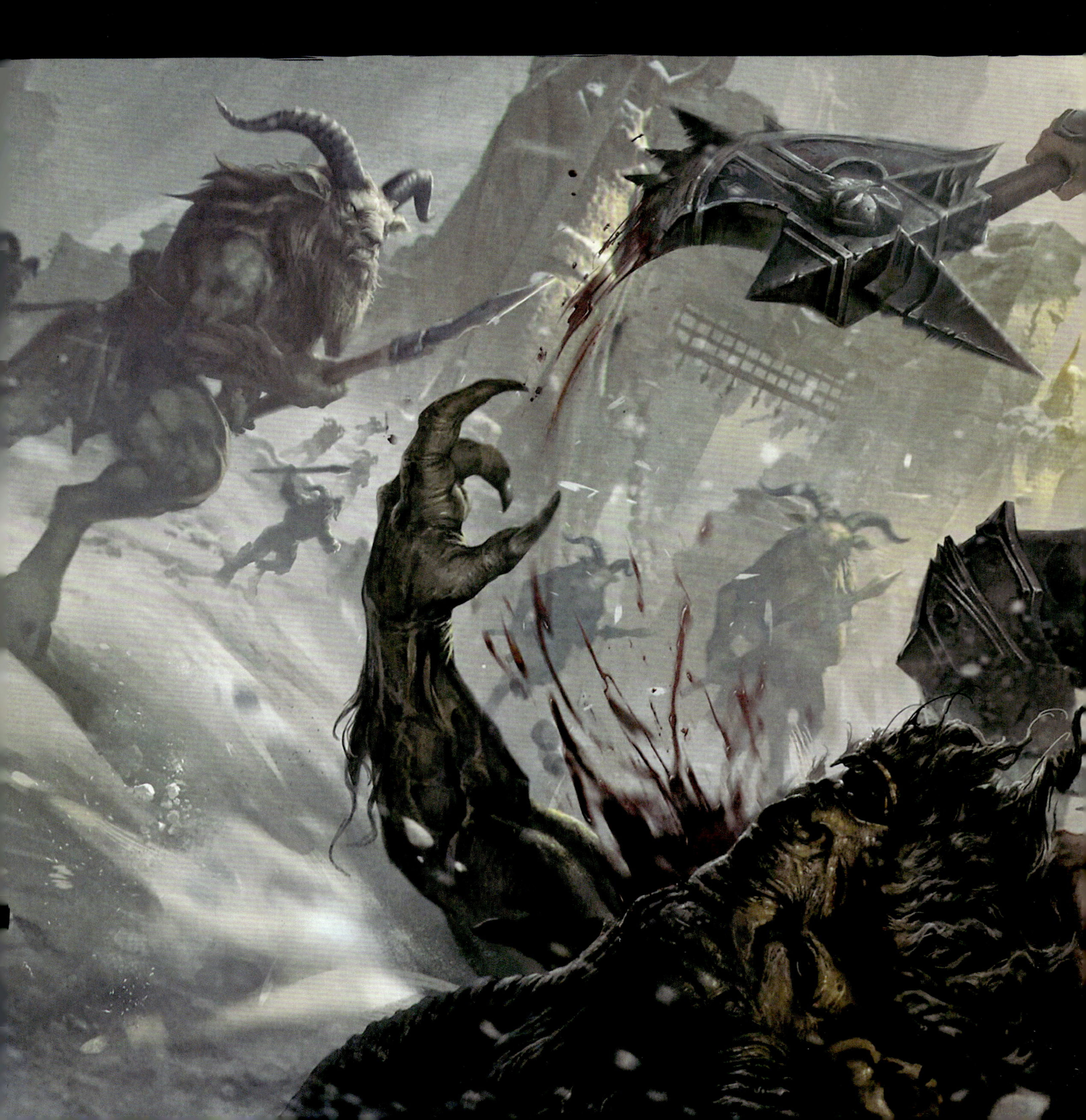

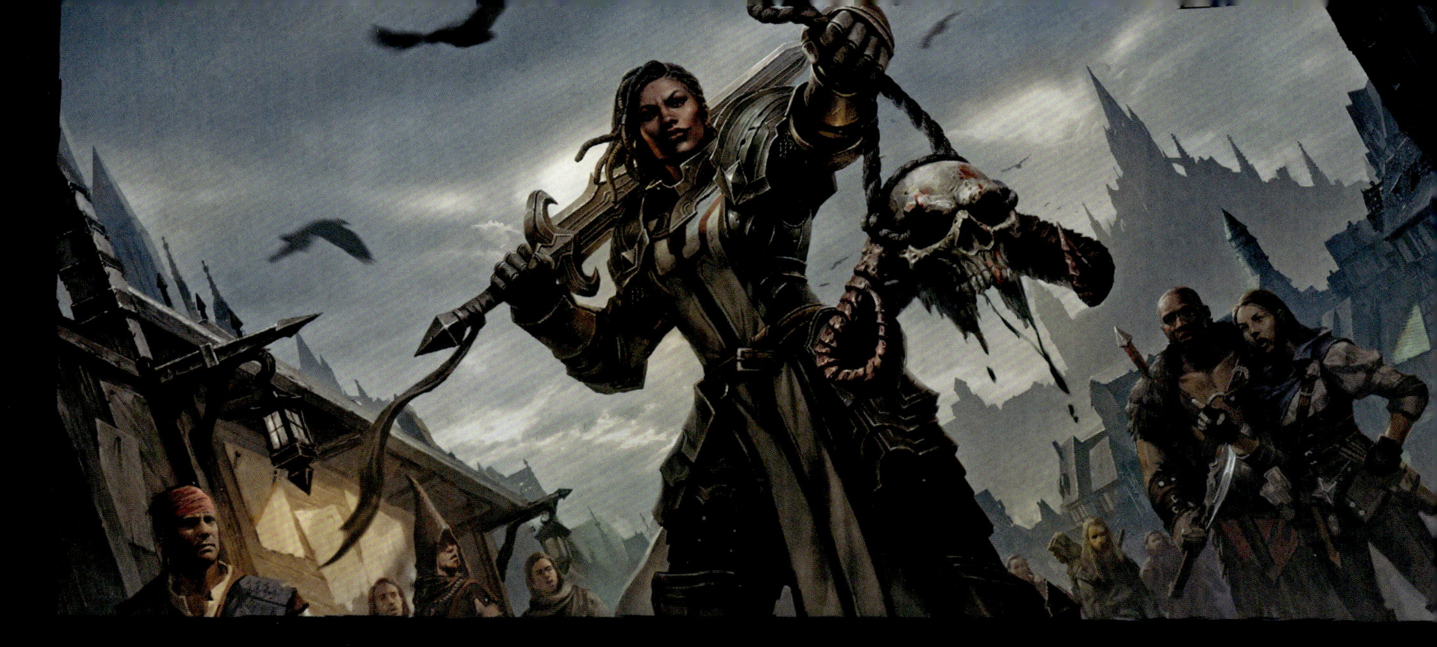

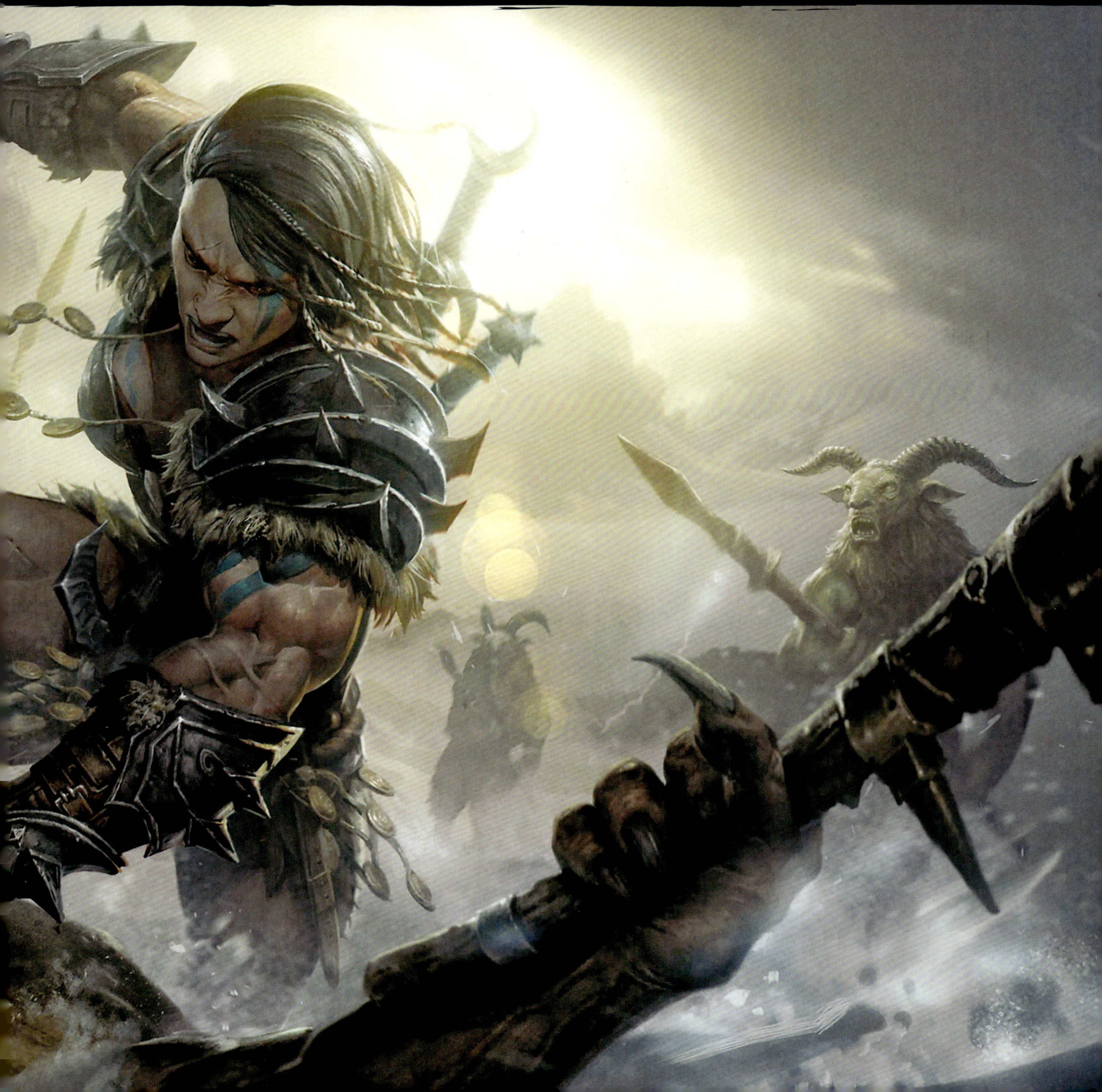

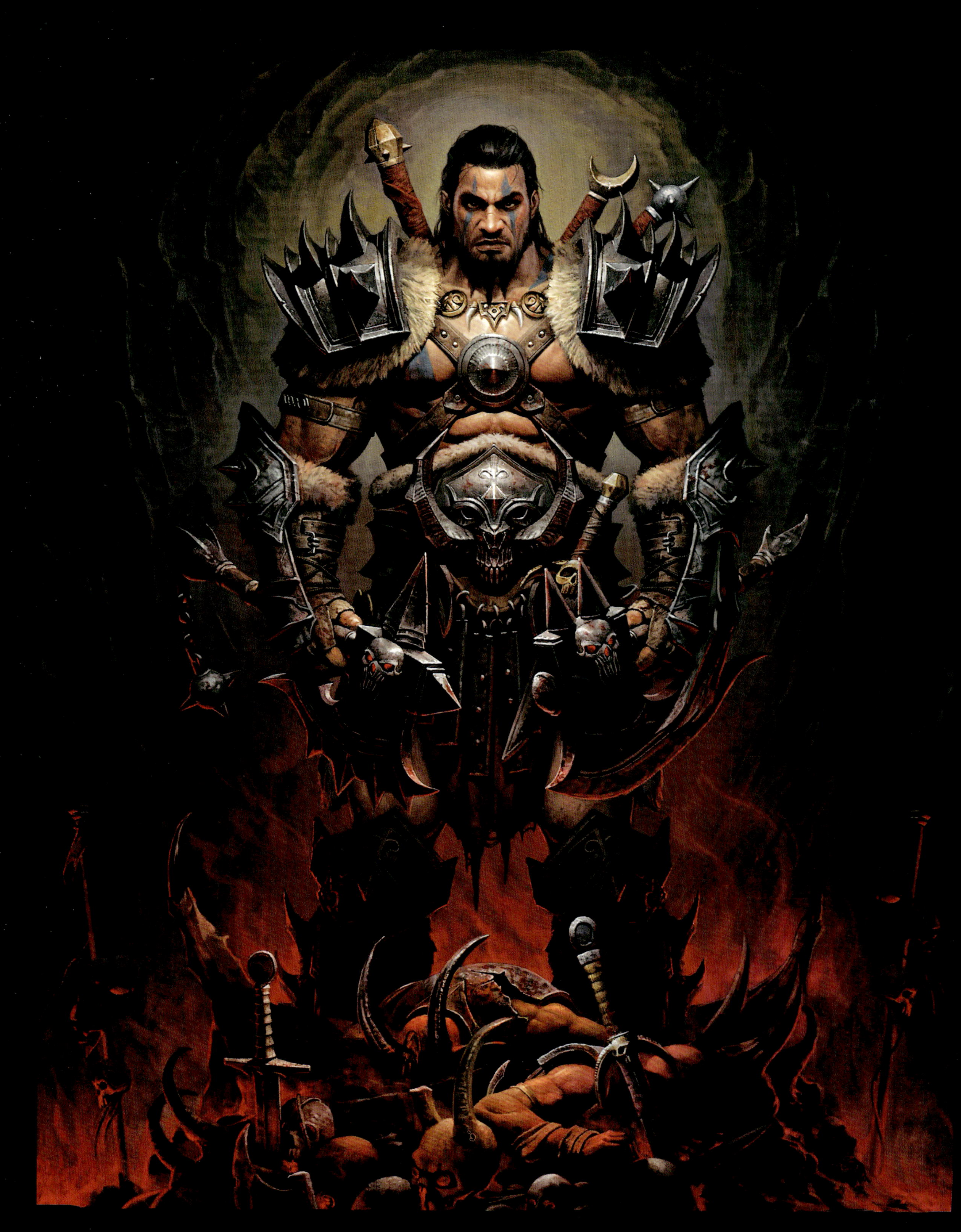

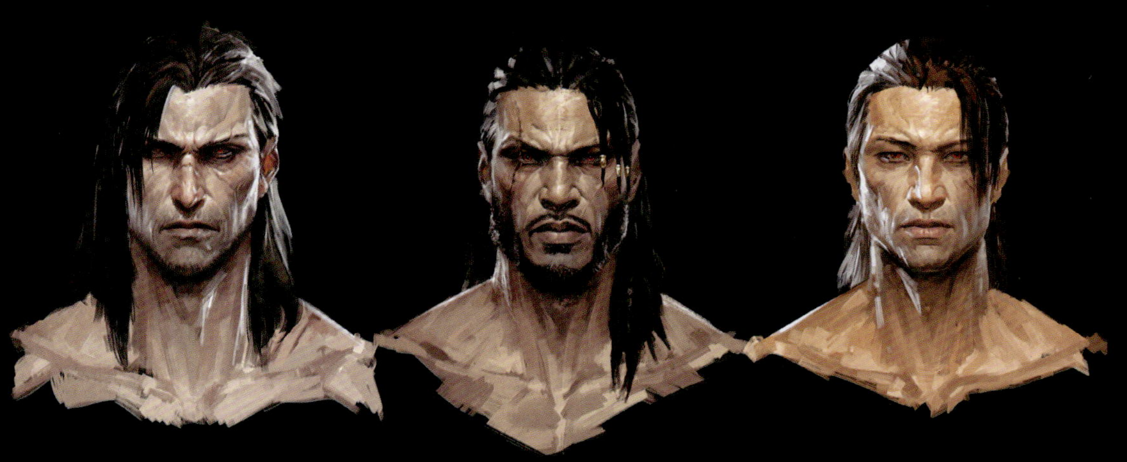

LEFT Blood Knight Customization Concept + NetEase Art Team

MIDDLE Ghosts of Ashwold + NetEase Art Team

BOTTOM, RIGHT Female Crusader Key Art + Geunjoo Baik

BOTTOM, LEFT Male Crusader Key Art + Geunjoo Baik

OPPOSITE Barbarian Key Art + Geunjoo Baik

FOLLOWING SPREAD Blood Knight Concepts + NetEase Art Team

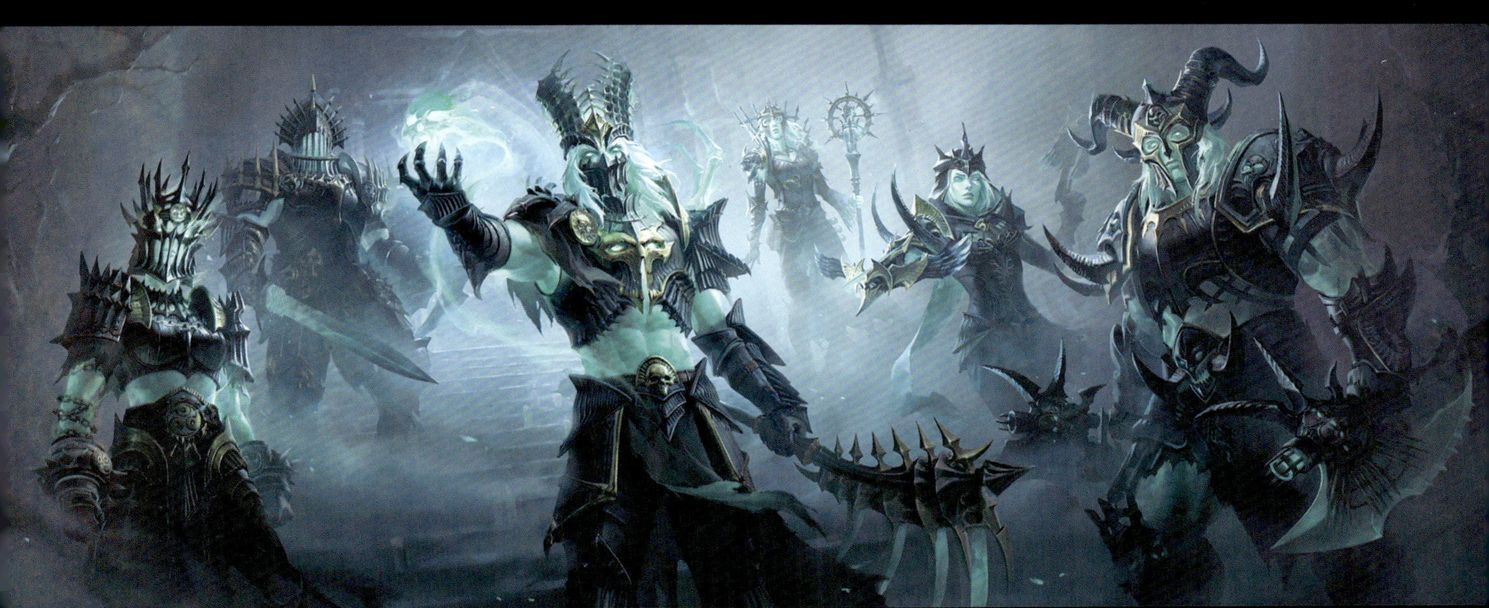

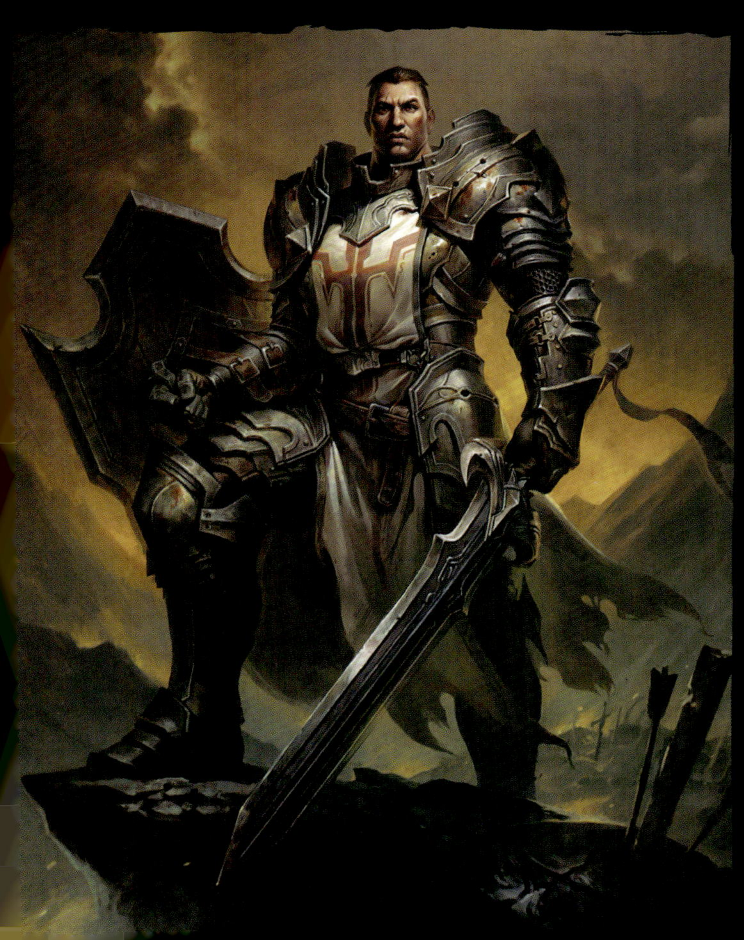

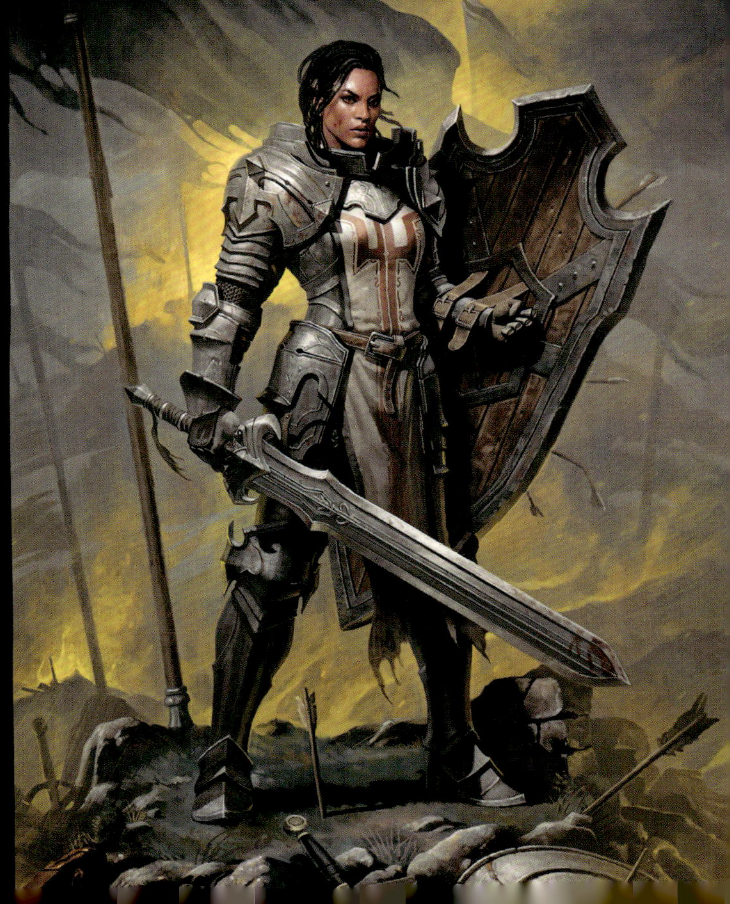

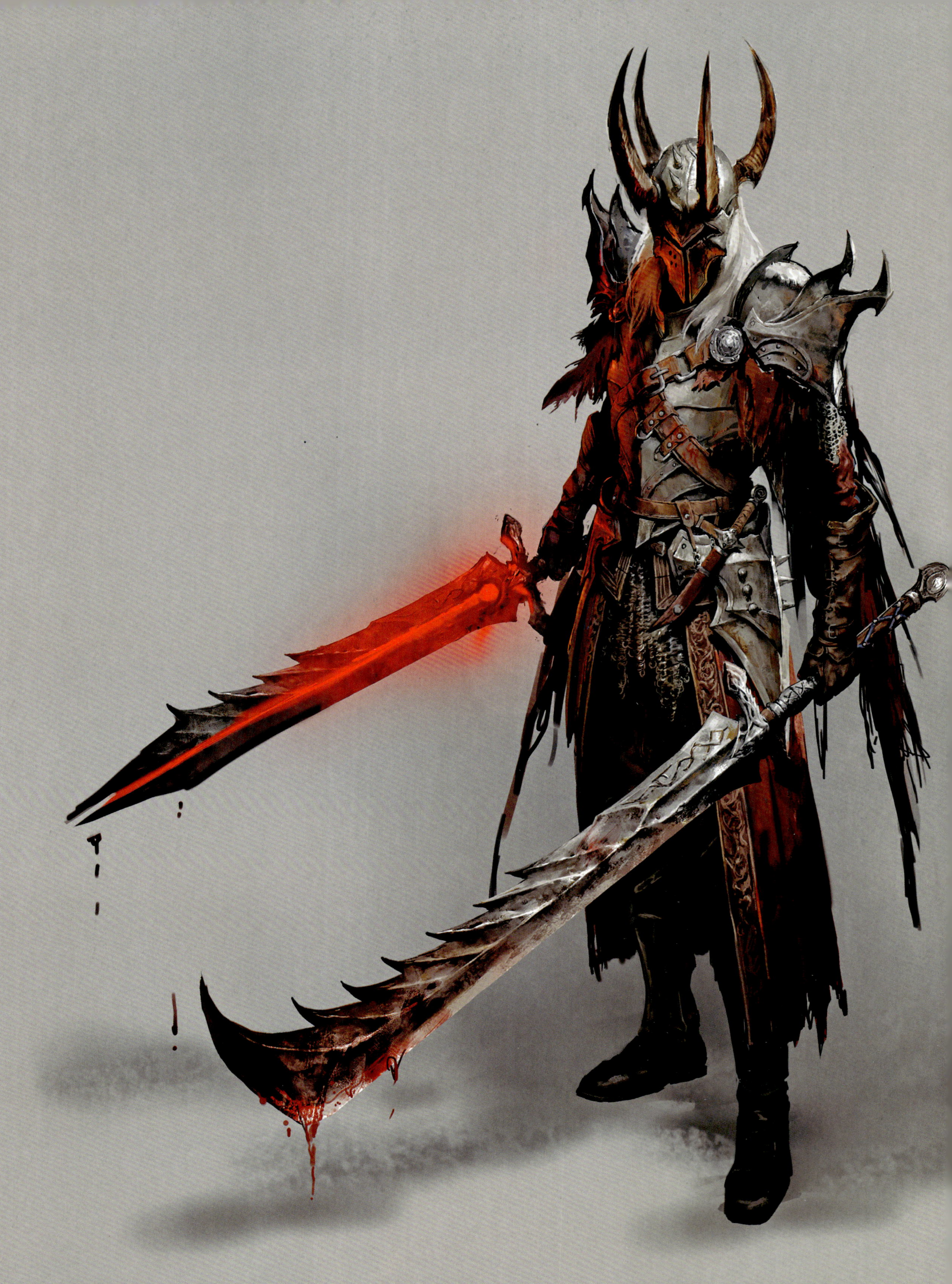

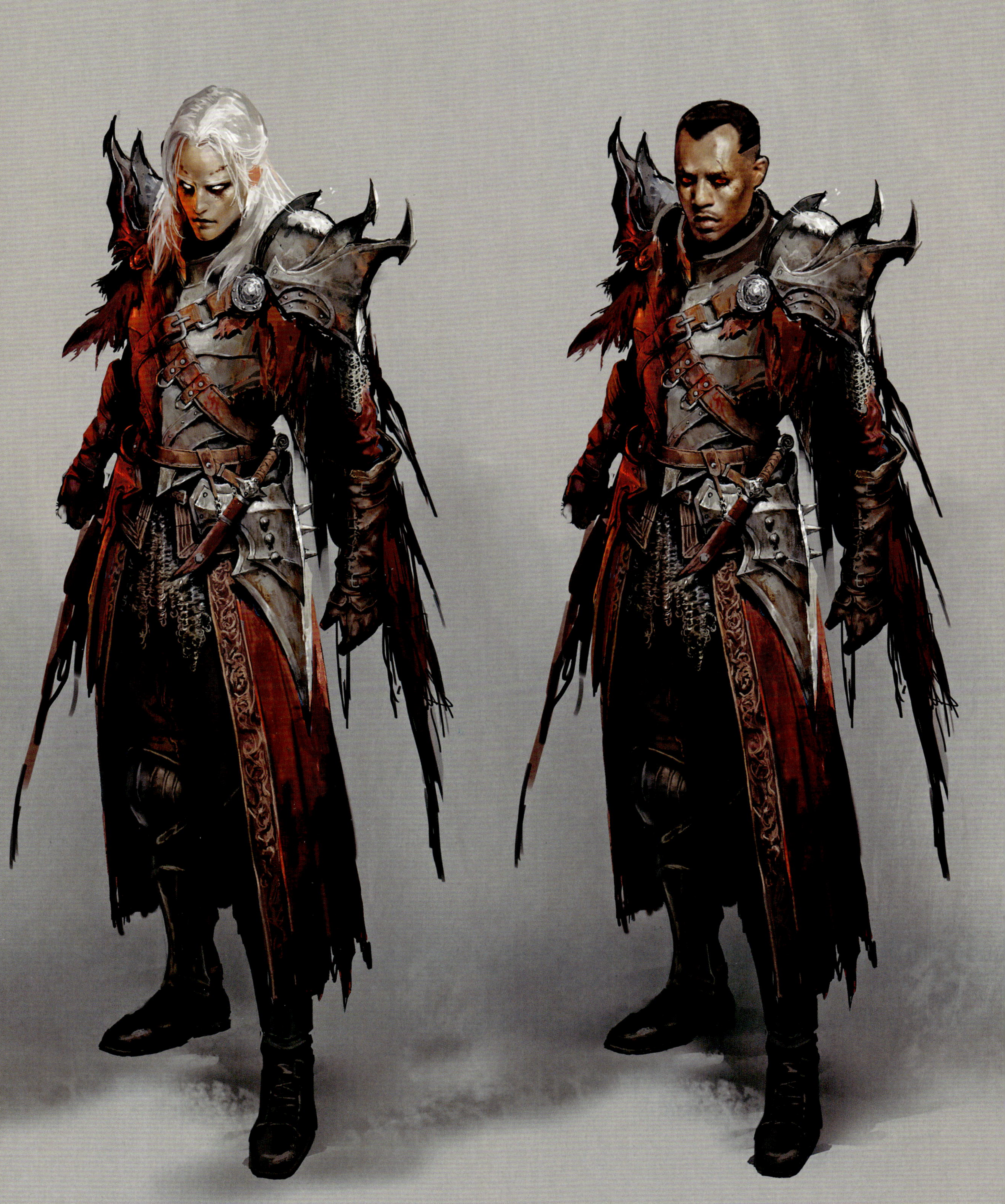

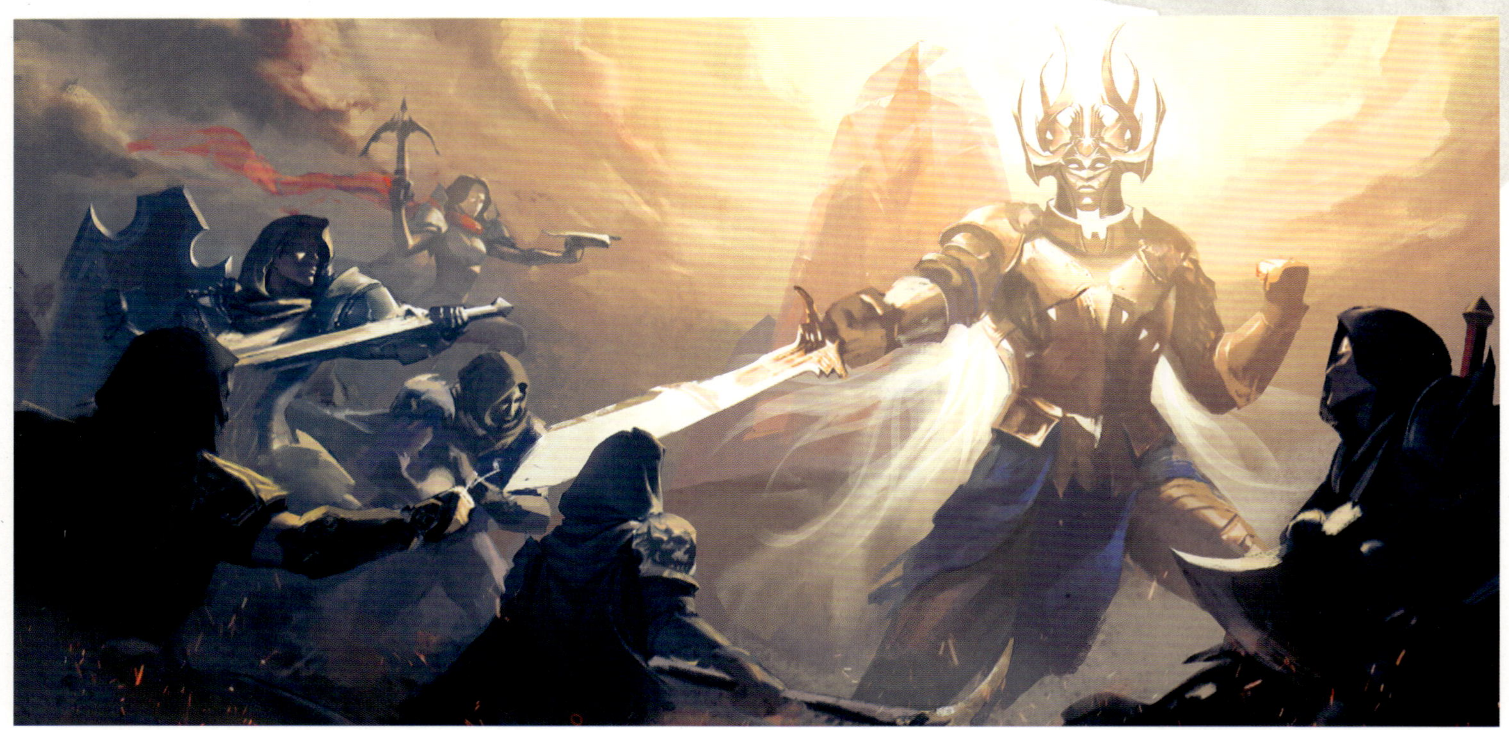

ABOVE Immortal Battle Illustration + NetEase Art Team

BELOW Class Key Art + Geunjoo Baik

OPPOSITE Wizard Key Art + Geunjoo Baik

FOLLOWING SPREAD, LEFT Monk Key Art + Geunjoo Baik

FOLLOWING SPREAD, RIGHT Demon Hunter Key Art + Geunjoo Baik

"You want to make sure that not only is the art clear, visible, and readable but also that everything else is too. You want the players to enjoy the designs, but they also need to understand what they're doing in the world that they're in."

—HUNTER SCHULZ, Art Director

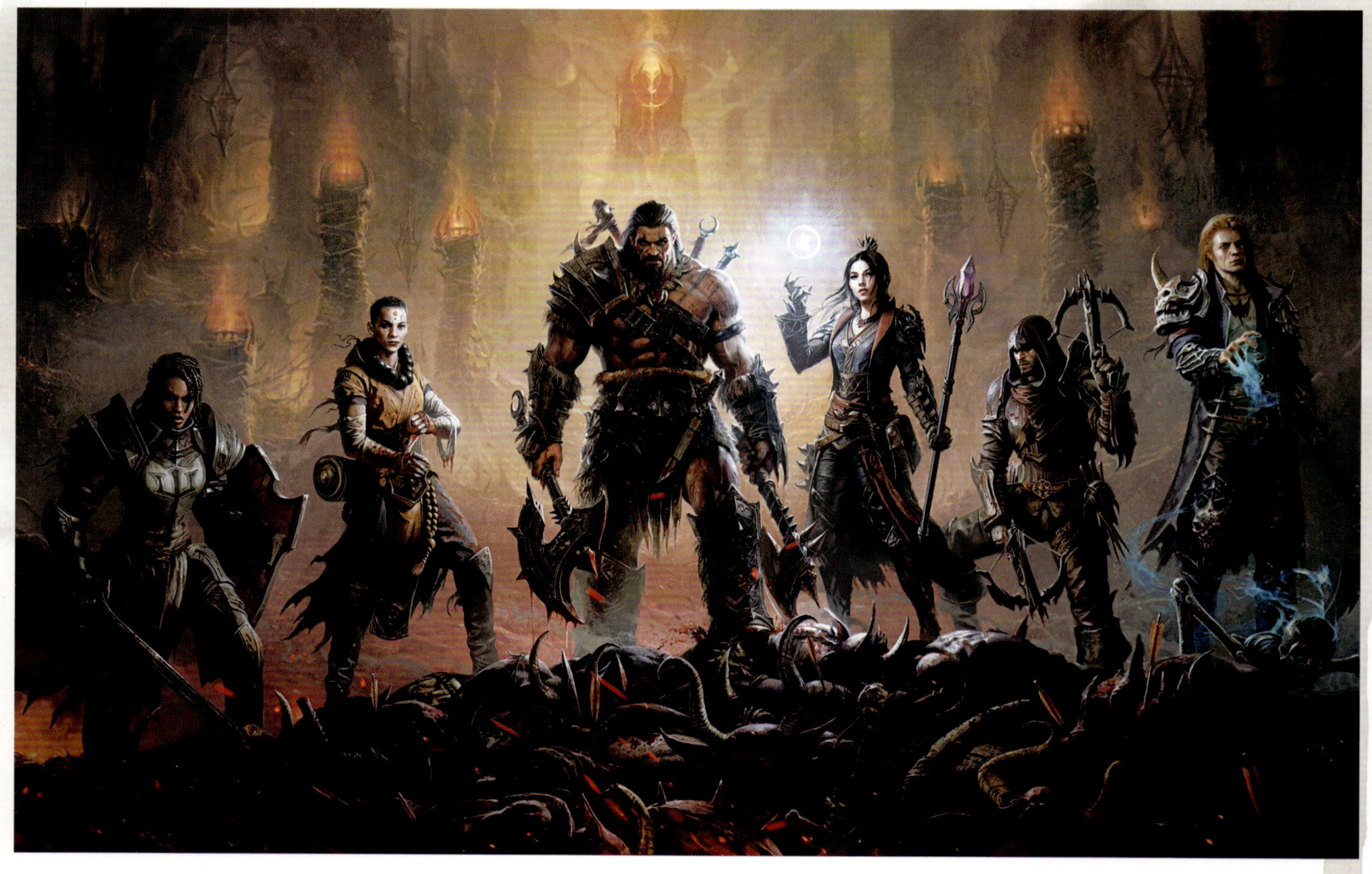

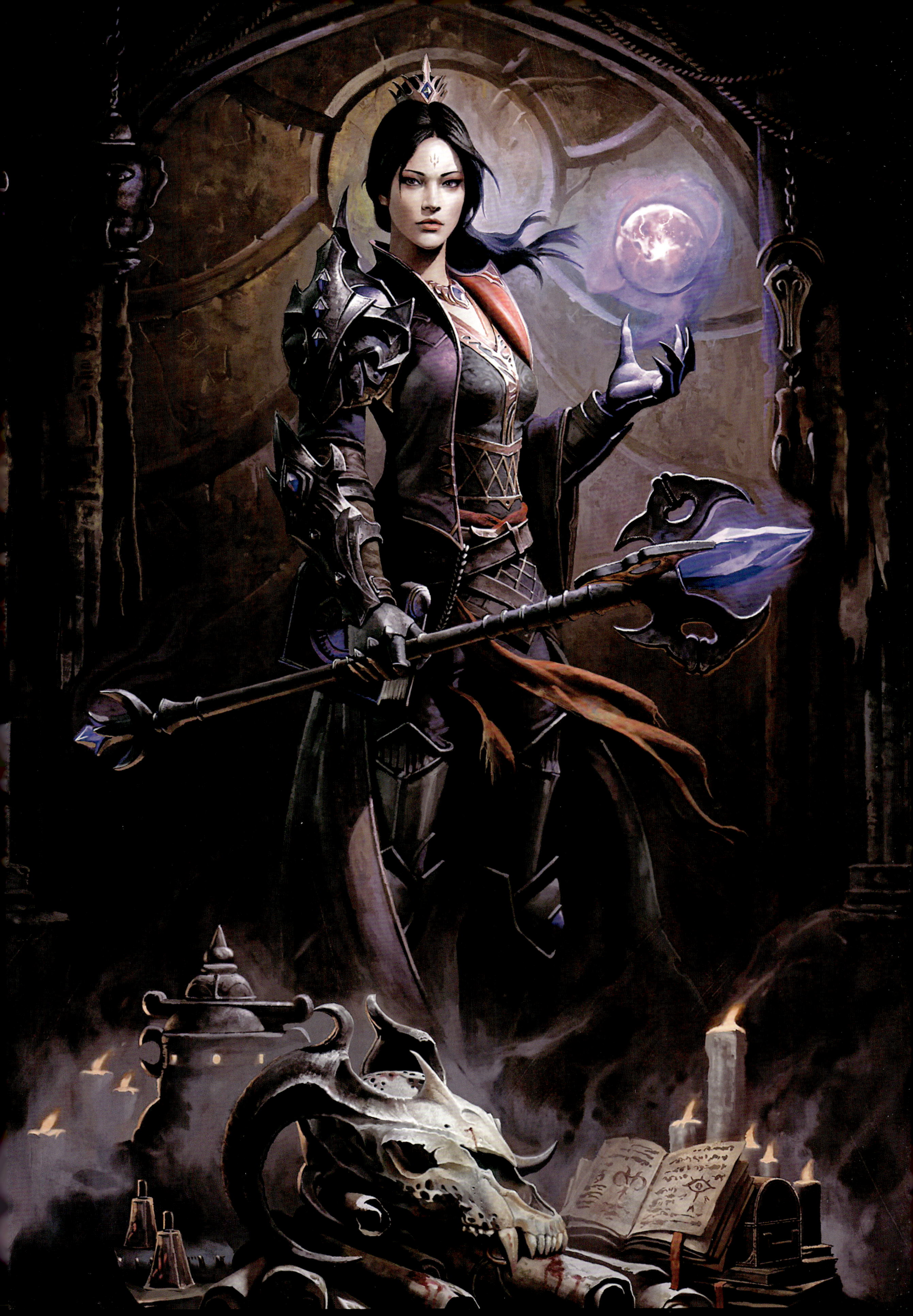

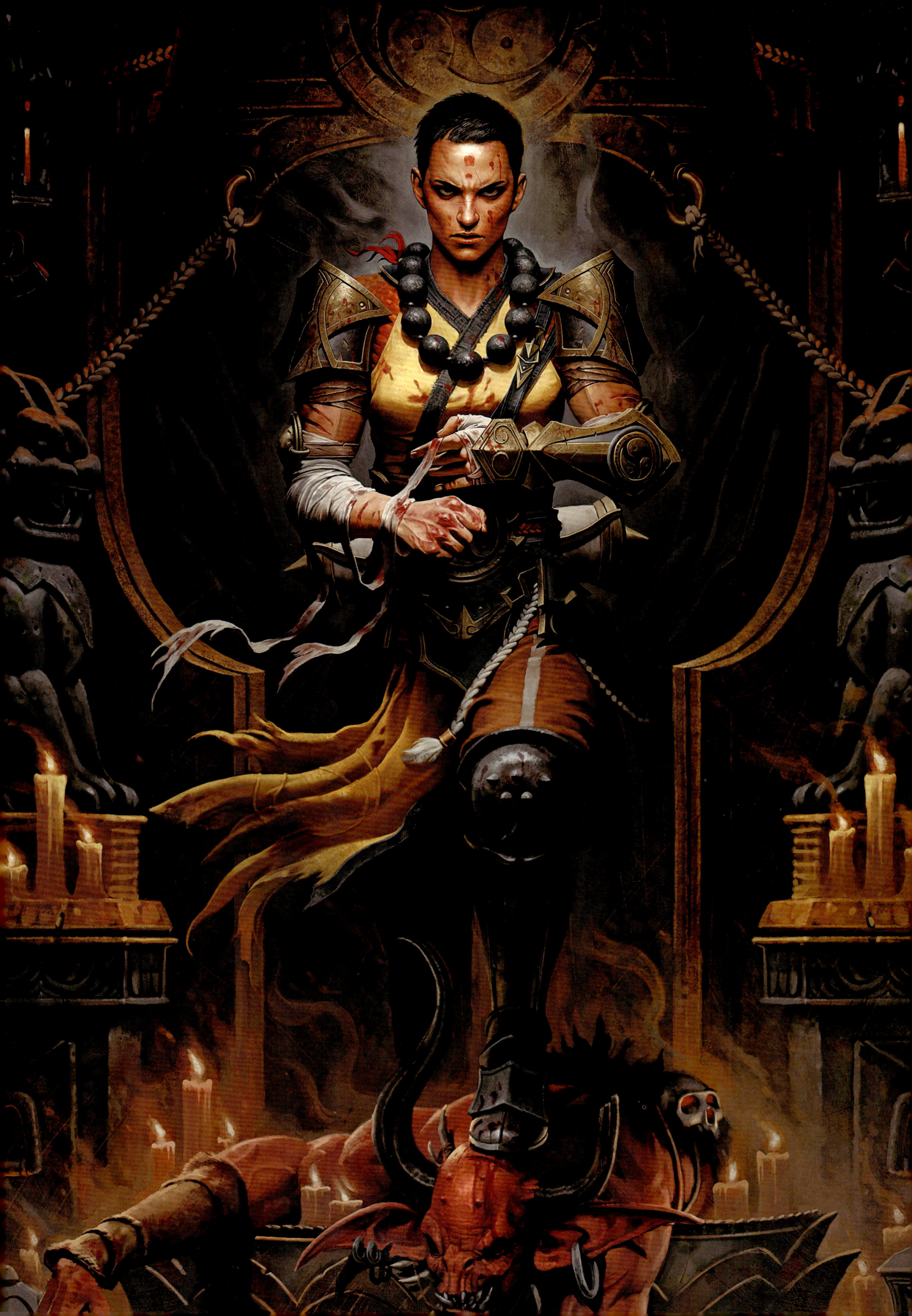

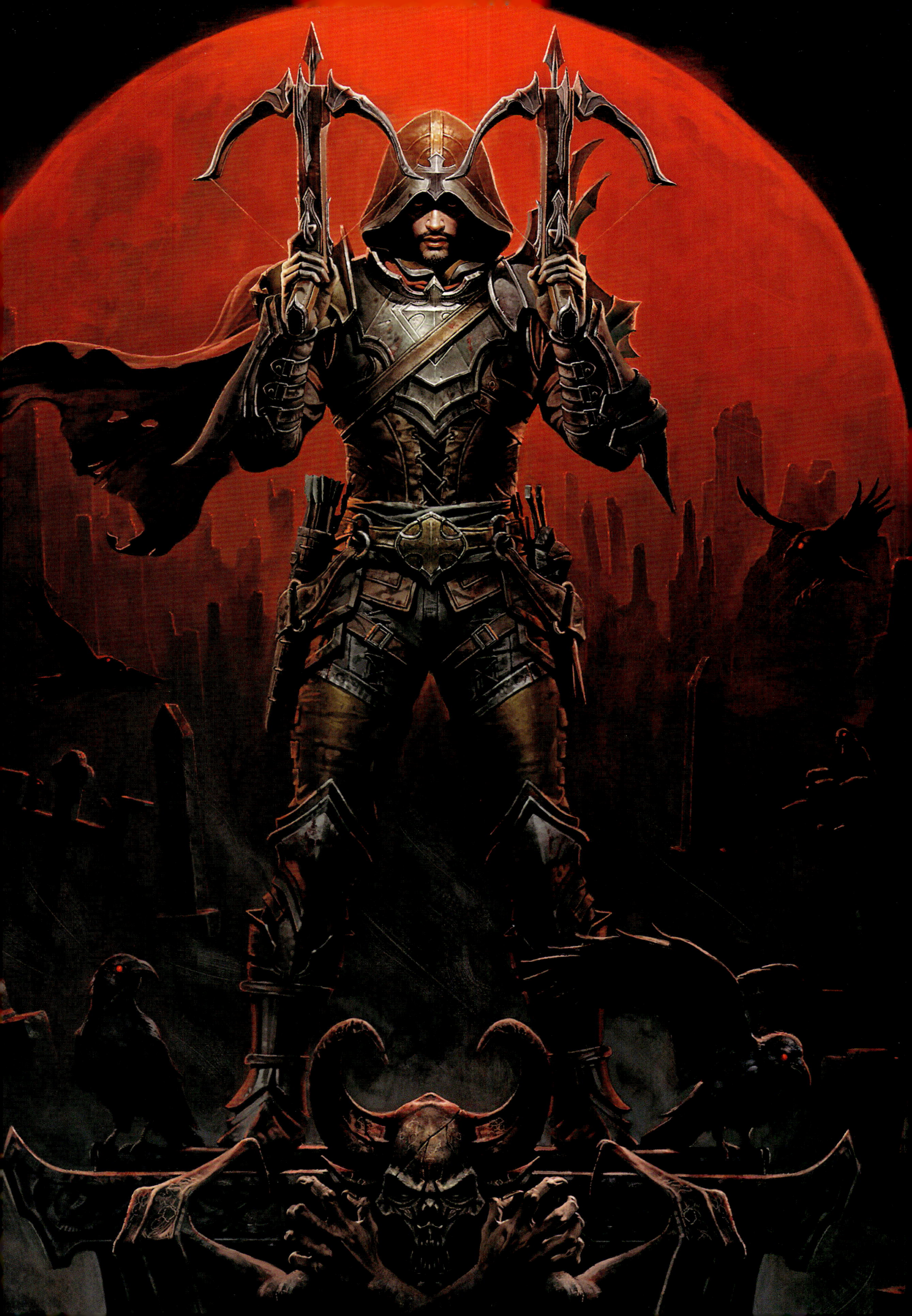

Friends New and Old

ABOVE Kulle Library Rune + NetEase Art Team

RIGHT Skarn Concept + NetEase Art Team

BOTTOM Diablo Key Art + NetEase Art Team

OPPOSITE Shaddox Key Art + NetEase Art Team

While many established characters make appearances in *Diablo Immortal*, there is a host of new characters and monsters as well. And the first stop for all characters—new or old—is the concepting stage.

Concepting is an artistic previsualization process that can be done on paper, in digital paint programs, or in any number of other mediums.

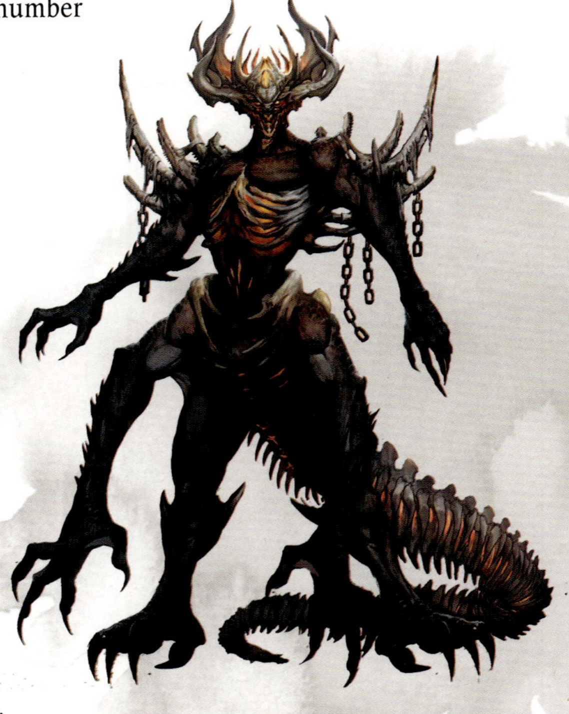

"The concept stage, when it's done right, answers all the questions that need to be answered going into 3D and putting it in the game," says art director Hunter Schulz. "That's something we need to think about, looking at it in a small scale and from an isometric view. A lot of concepts aren't done that way, but when it's done right, you keep in mind what that's going to look like. When it's not done right, you make a cool concept that gets in the game and you may realize something doesn't look right from this angle, in this world."

When designing characters for a mobile game, certain refinements are involved.

"Much of the day-to-day work revolves around sacrificing," says Schulz. "That's the big part of any design, and a big part of clarity. If you have too many cool things happening, they all get subdued, so it's best to get rid of the ones that aren't as important."

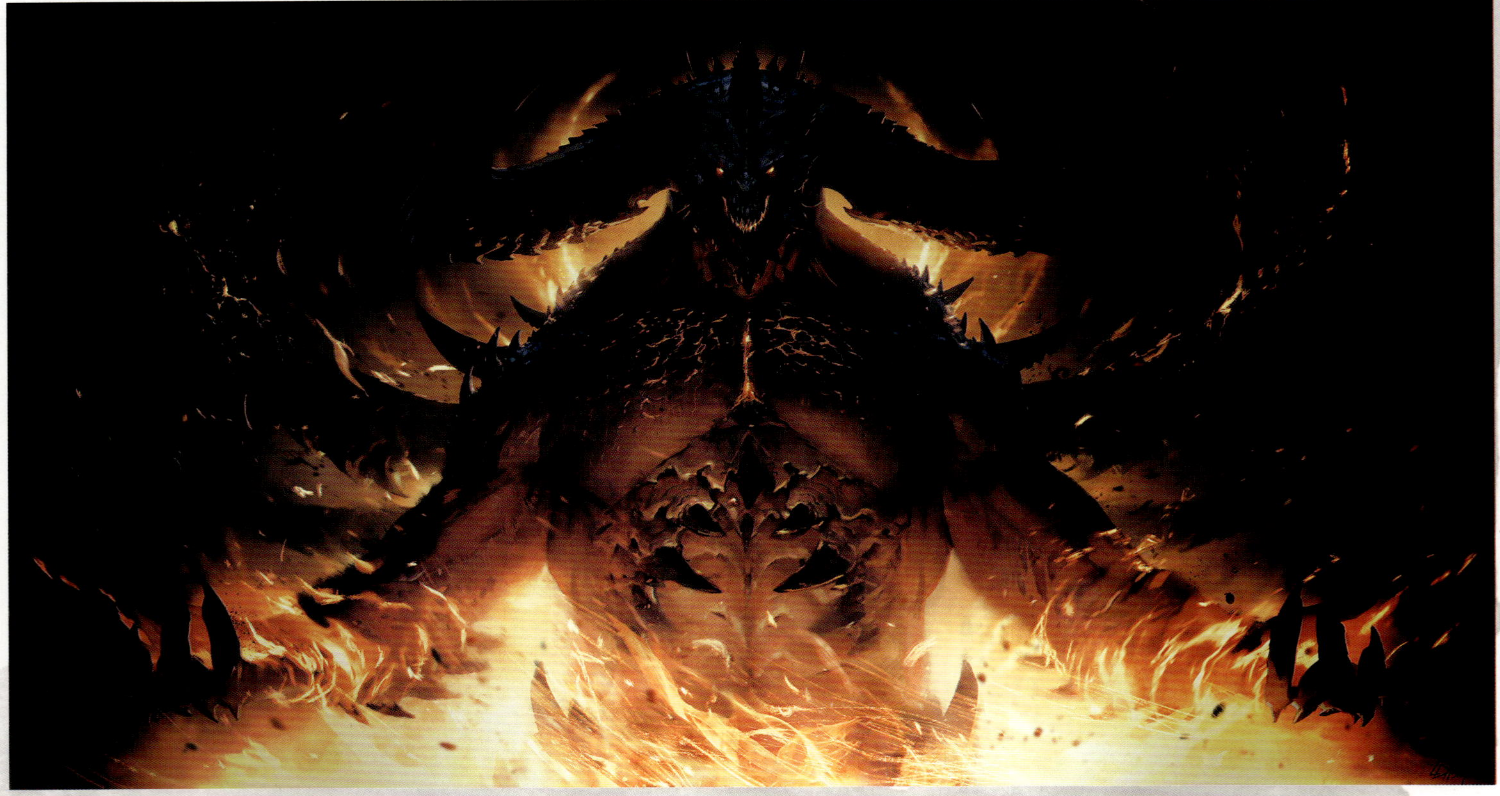

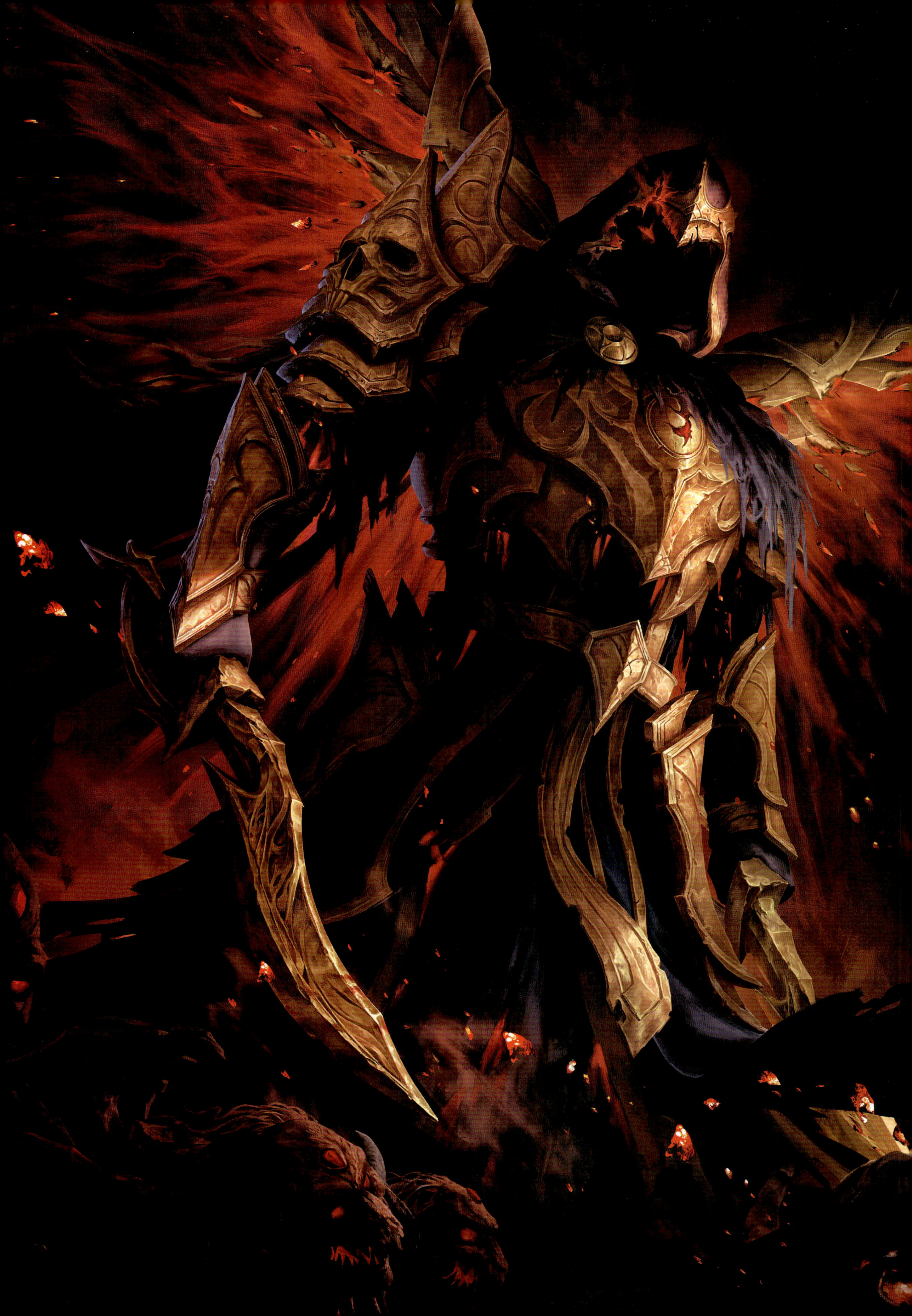

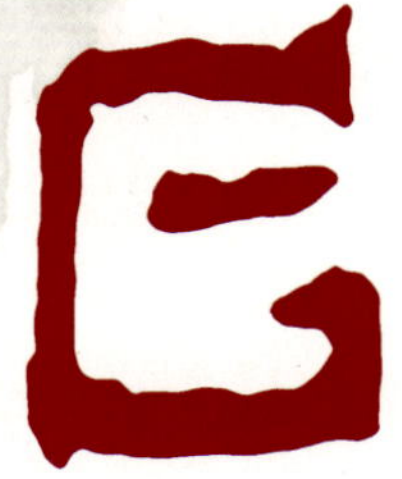

ABOVE Kulle Library Rune + NetEase Art Team

RIGHT Cultist Eskara Concept + NetEase Art Team

BOTTOM Cultist Eskara Key Art + NetEase Art Team

OPPOSITE Lethes Key Art + NetEase Art Team

Silhouette—which is essentially the outline of a character, monster, or even a weapon—is something that is always taken into account.

"A lot of times, there's this urge to do *more*," Schulz remarks. "But you have to make sure the silhouette is strong and readable. They do have a variety of shapes—big, medium, small. But if you don't sacrifice certain elements, then you'll get a pincushion."

Details can be used to enhance any character design. For characters that will be seen at a greater distance, simplicity is key.

"We always harp on the expression 'Look at it from game cam,'" says Richie Marella. "When most artists are making something, they'll go detailed and zoom in. We don't worry about that as long as the details read as big shapes. We create art, look at it on the phone, and ask: 'Is it too busy?'"

Those big shapes play into an overall design philosophy for *Diablo Immortal* that is both simple and effective: "There are endless layers of beautiful detail in this game. We made sure those beautiful layers were extra dark, bloody, badass, and as out of control as Diablo would want," says senior concept artist Justin Murray. "That's what Diablo is—big and badass."

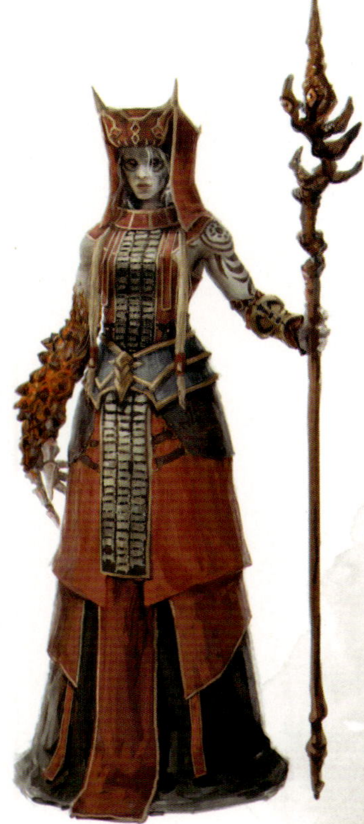

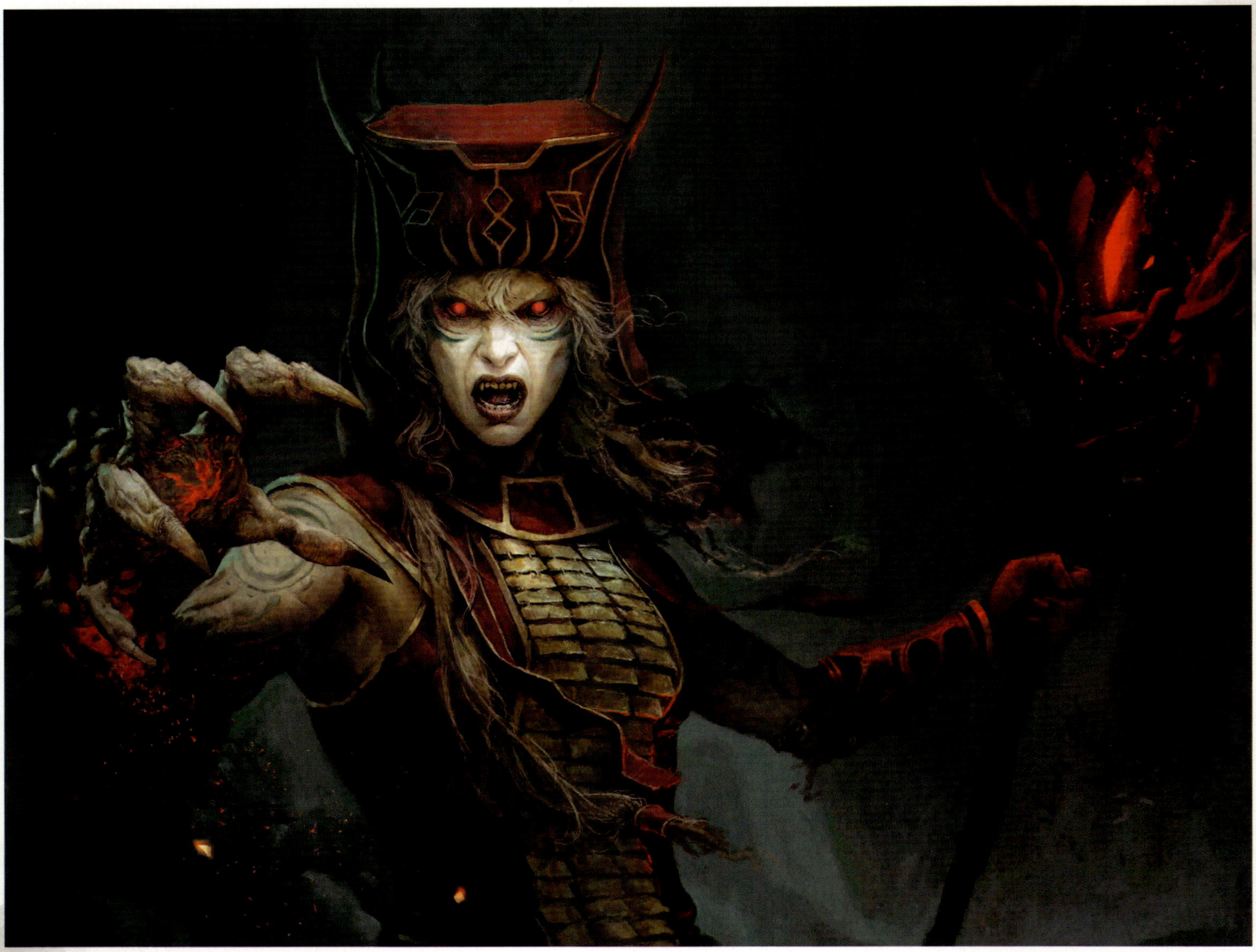

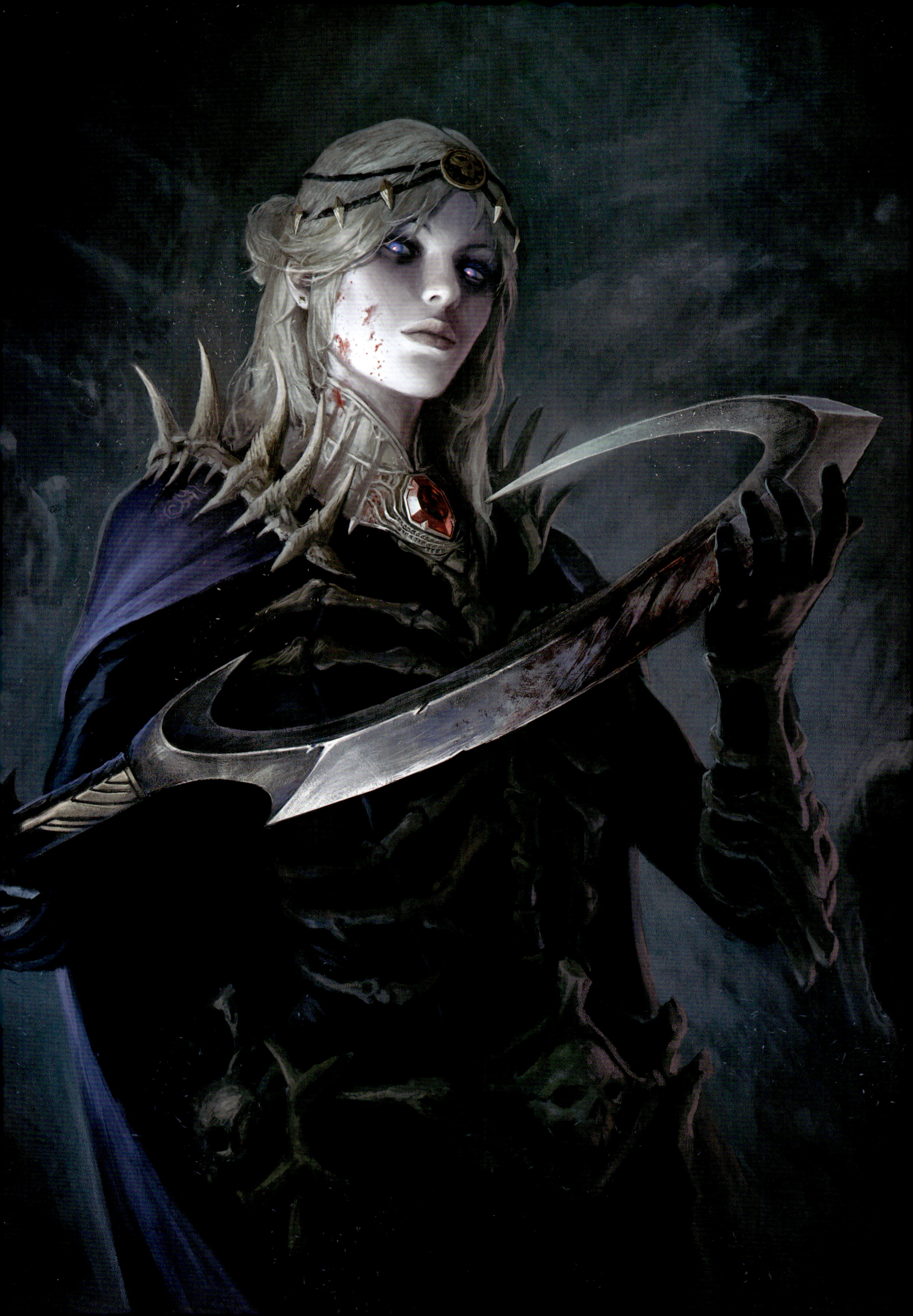

RIGHT Innaloth Portrait • NetEase Art Team

BOTTOM Immortals and Shadows Illustration • NetEase Art Team

OPPOSITE Kion Concept • Xuan Luo

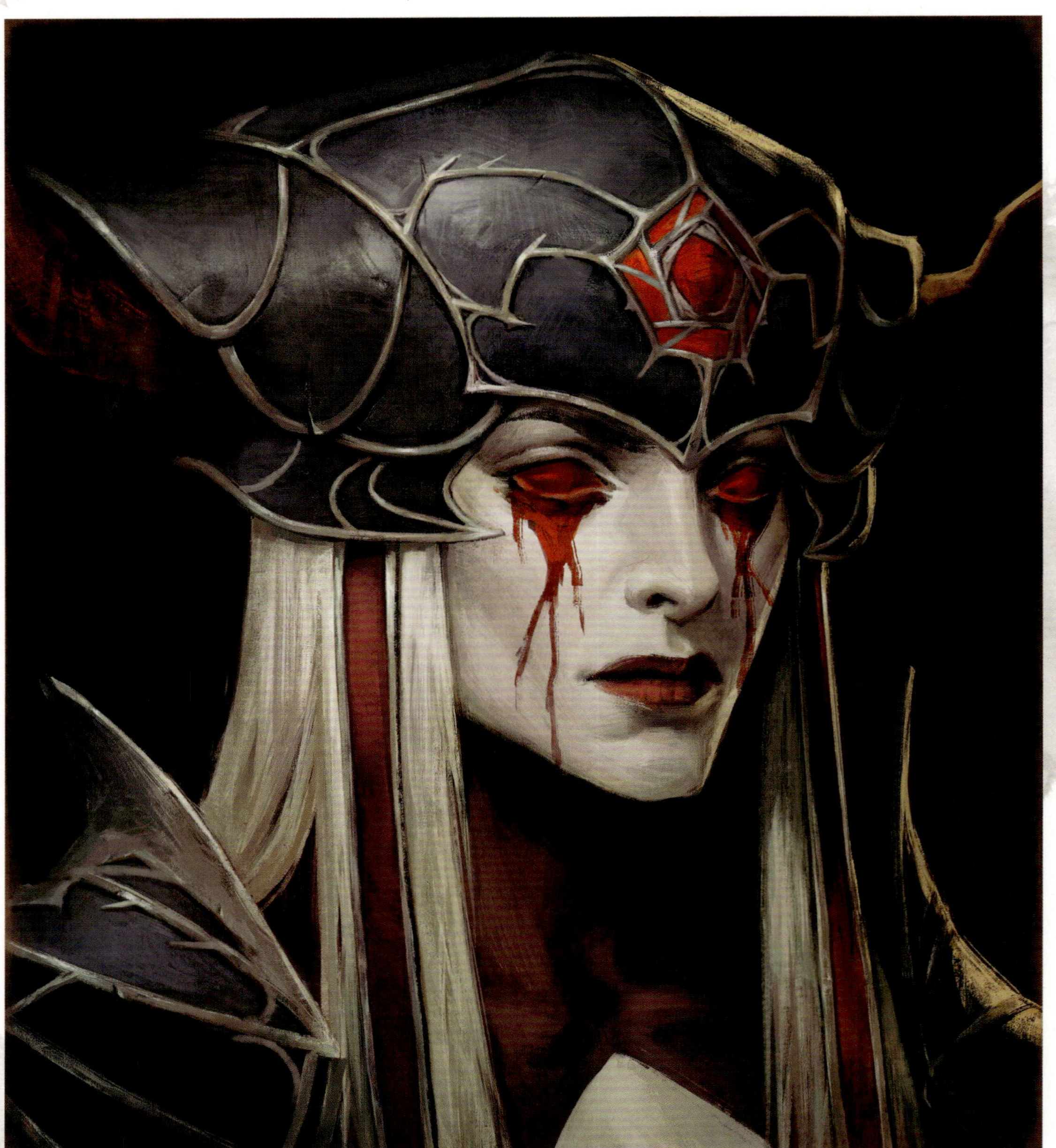

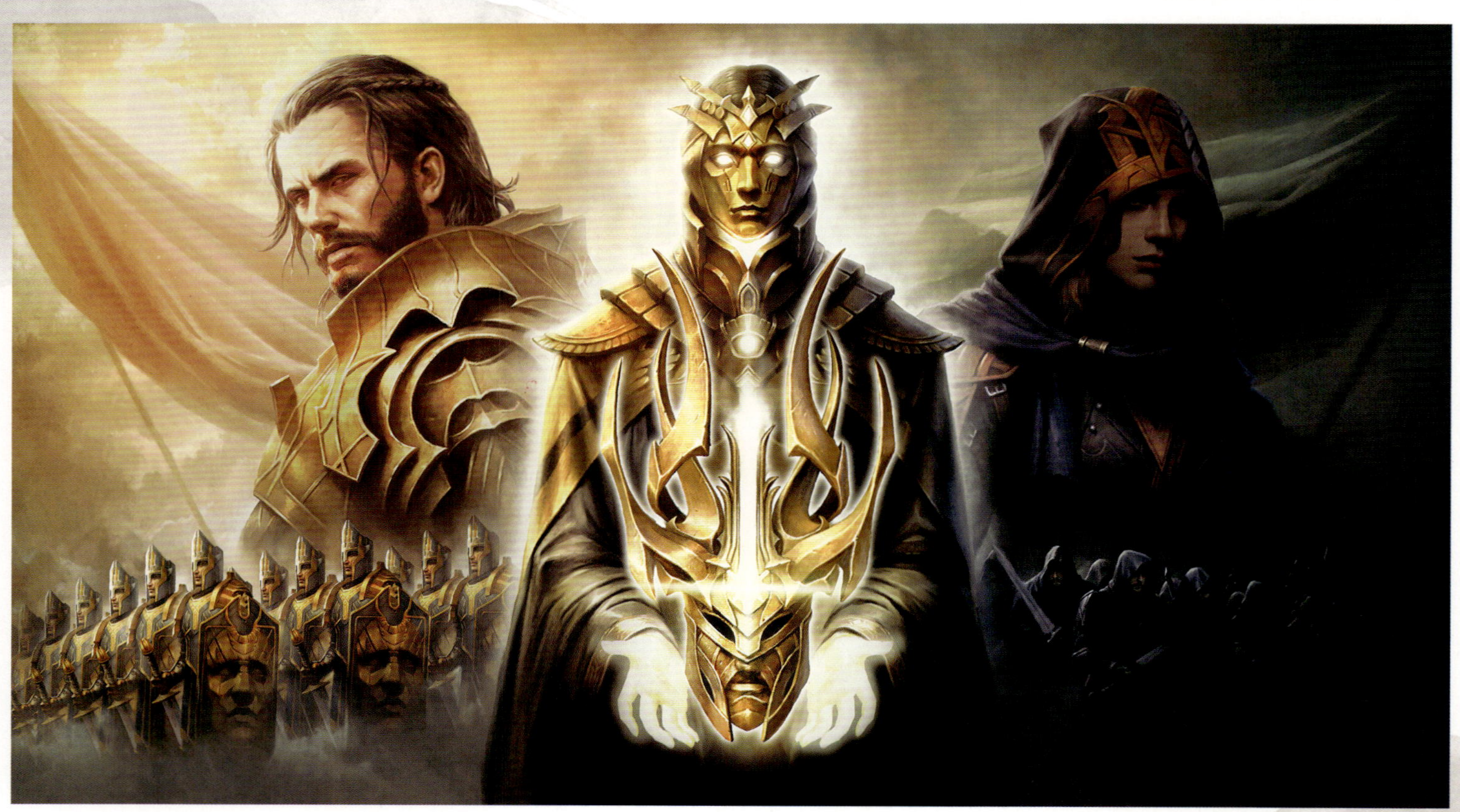

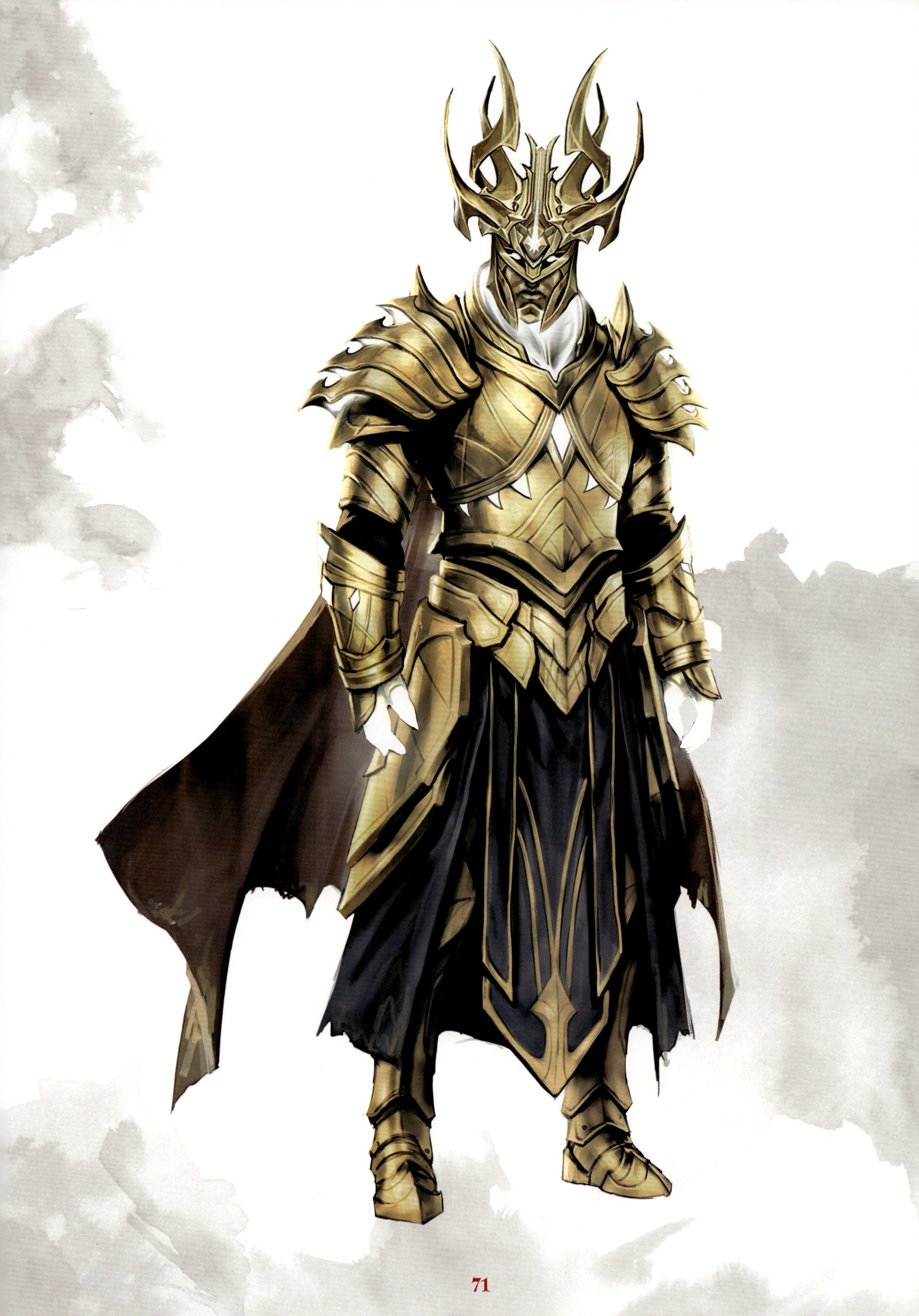

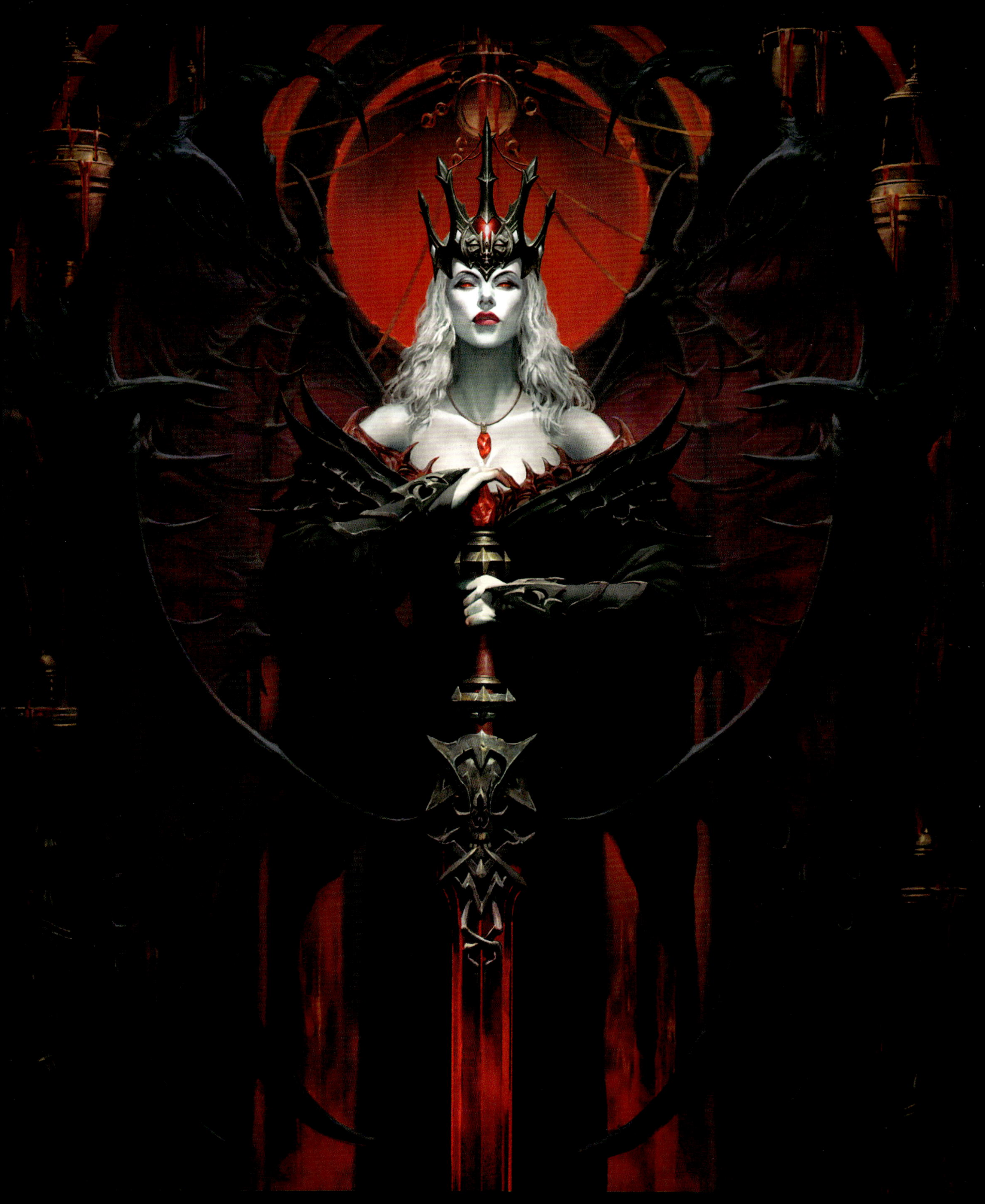

ABOVE The Countess Key Art • Geunjoo Baik, Yongsoon Park

OPPOSITE Baal Key Art • Brom, NetEase Art Team

FOLLOWING SPREAD, LEFT Skarn • Brom, NetEase Art Team

FOLLOWING SPREAD, RIGHT Immortal • Brom, NetEase Art Team

"We have a lot of really impressive effects like hellish fire, ice, and other elements coming off the characters' armor and weapons, which reads well and burns bright. At the same time, it's important that the characters don't get too lost in all the action. The character is the focal point."

—JUSTIN MURRAY, Senior Concept Artist

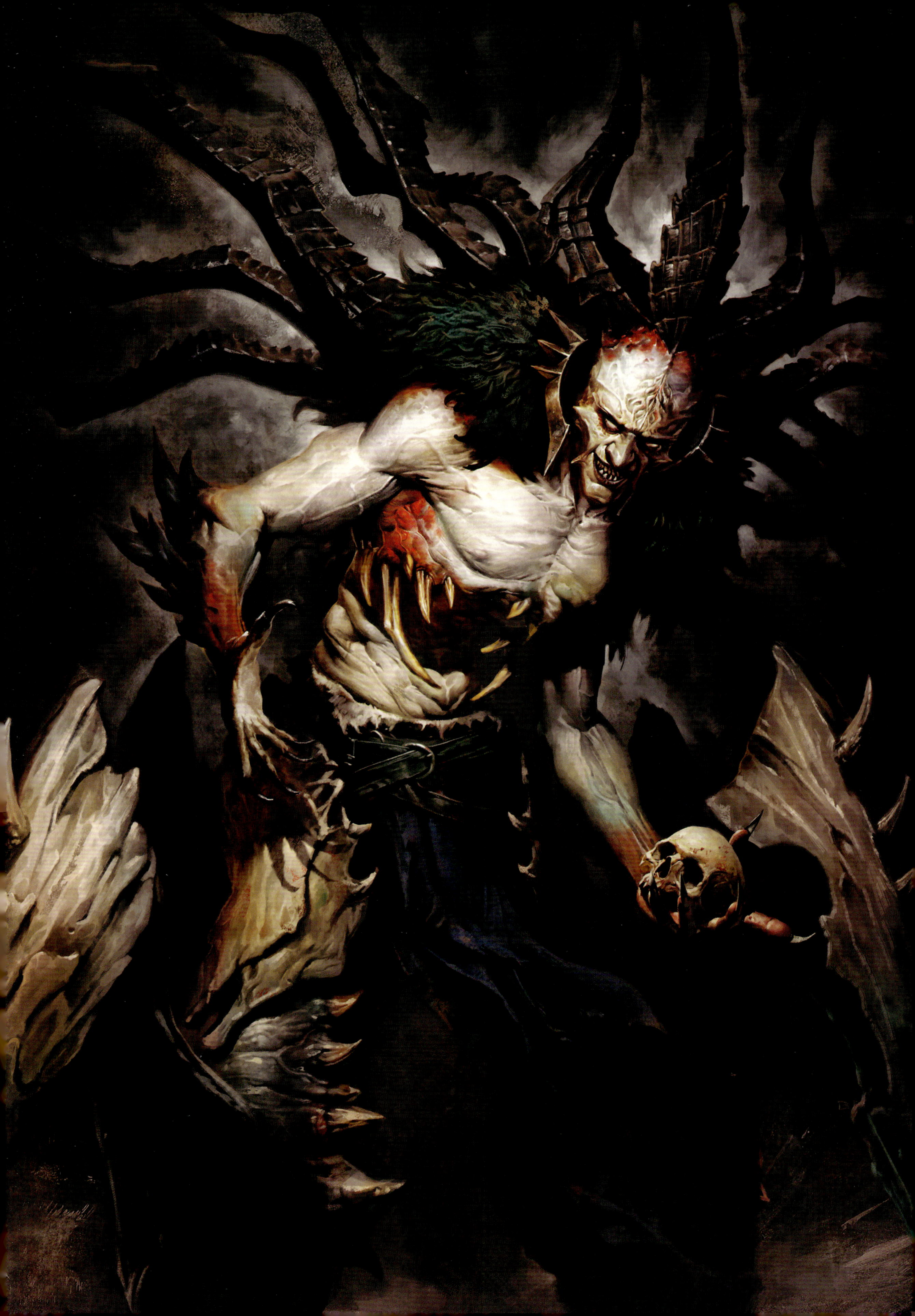

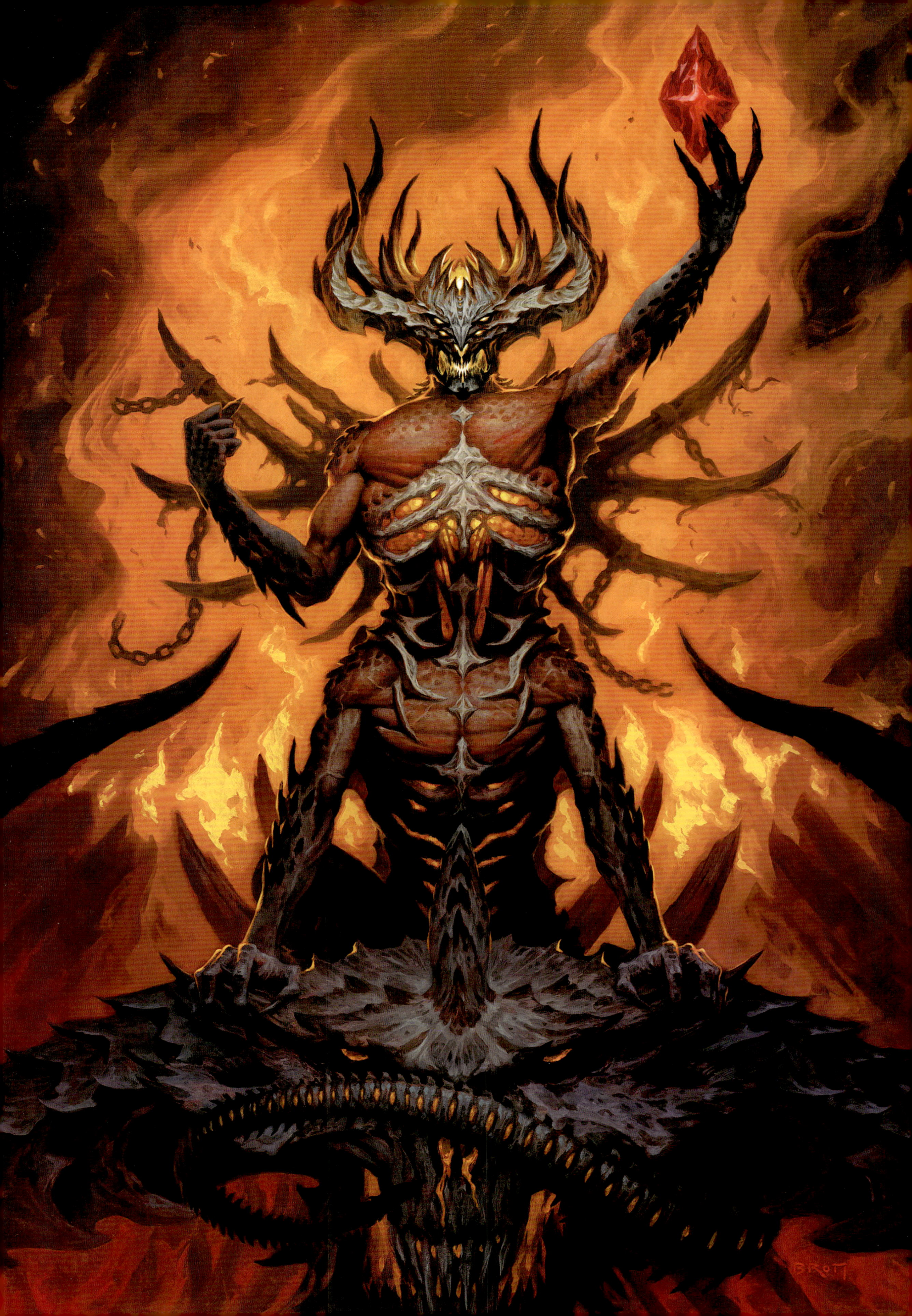
BROM

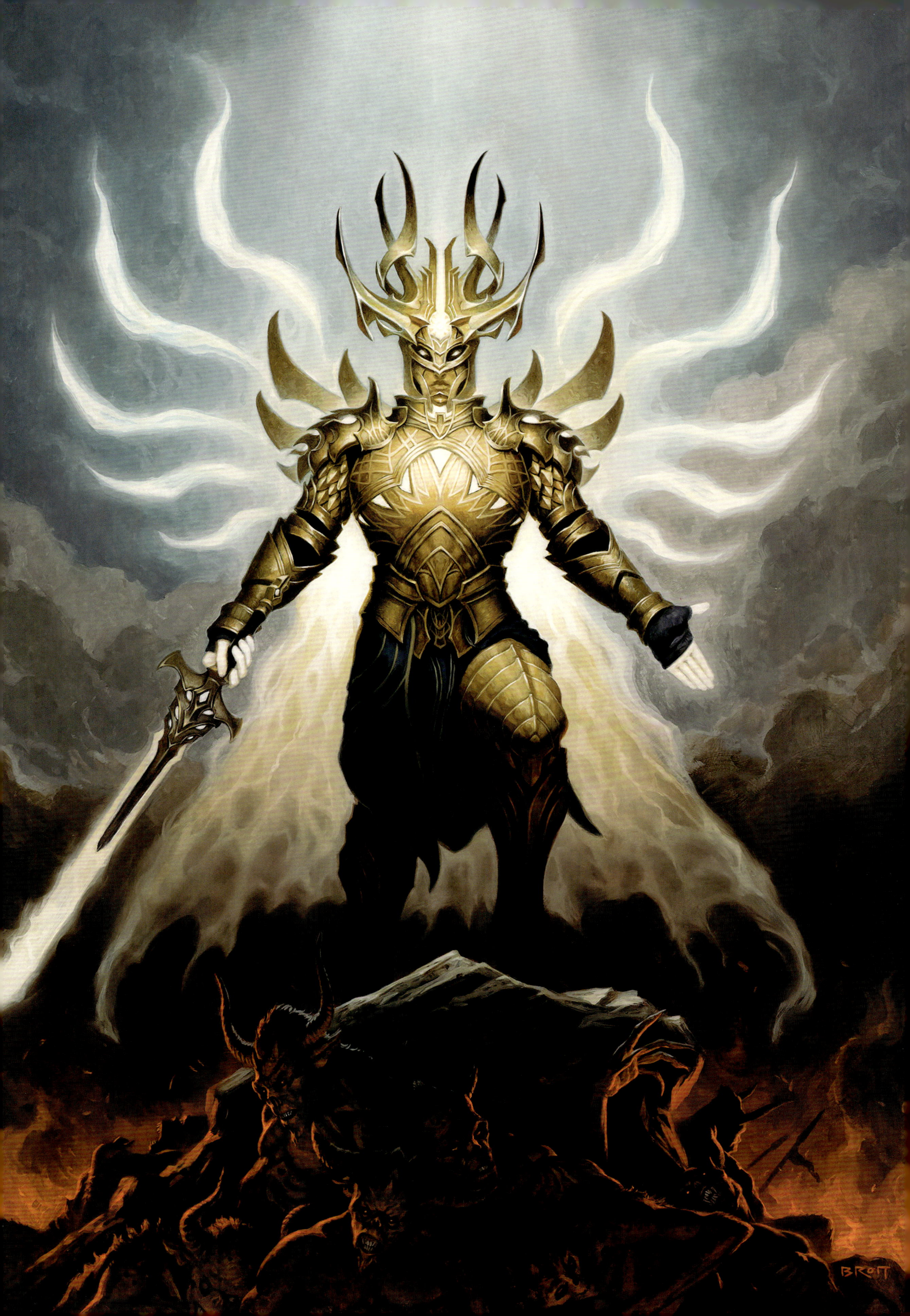
BROM

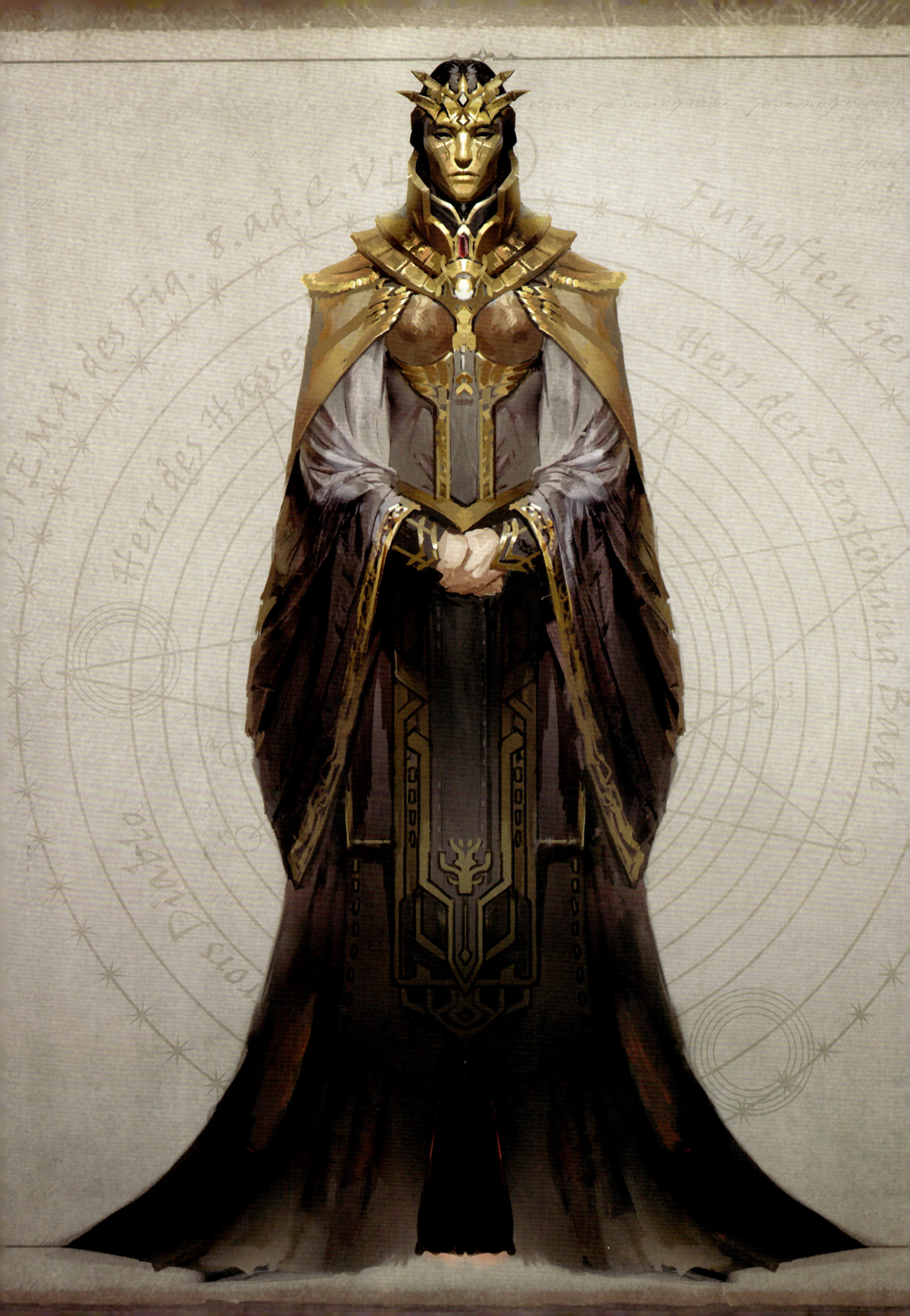
Herr des Hasses
Herr der Zerstörung Baal

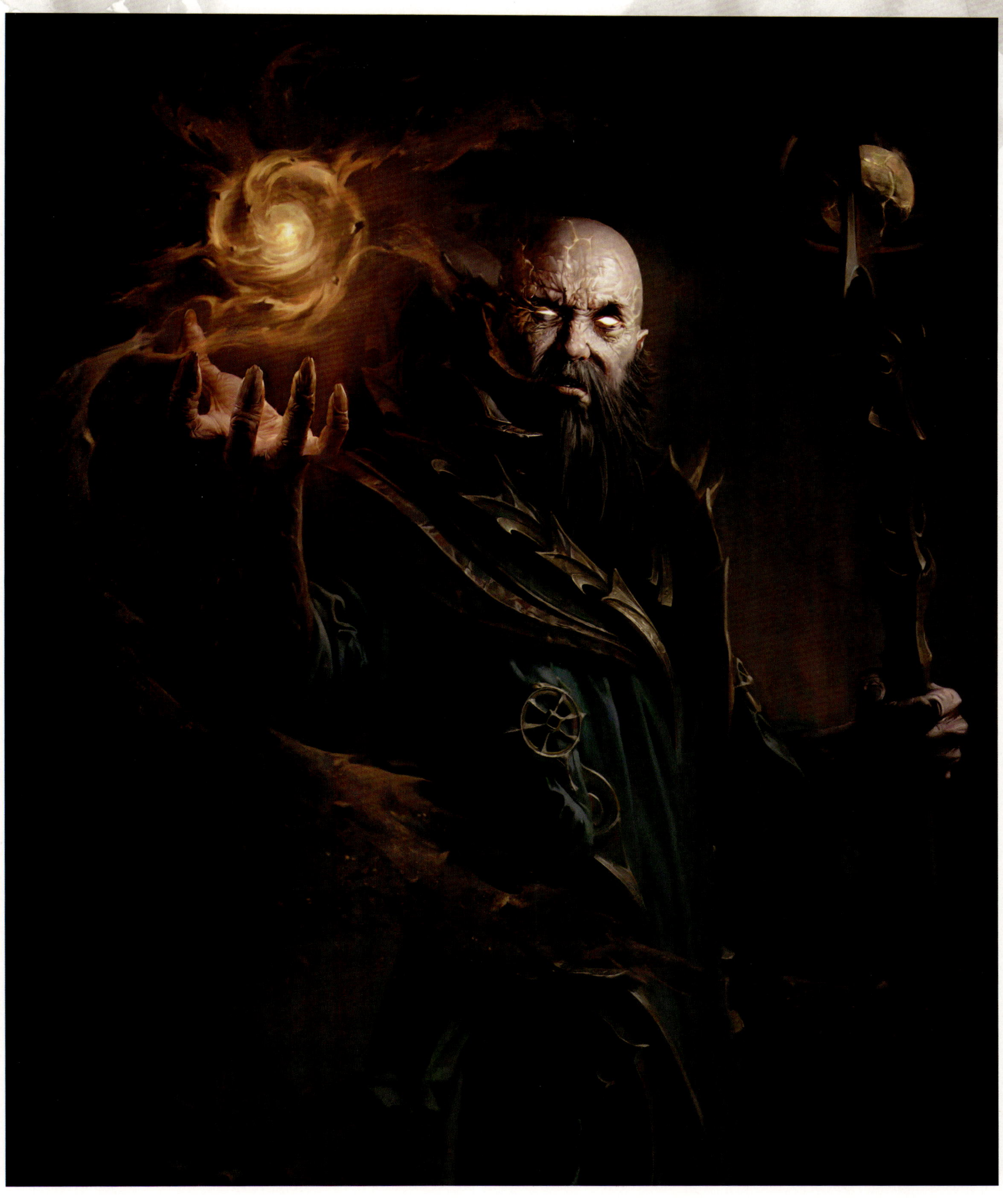

ABOVE The Curator Key Art + Geunjoo Baik

OPPOSITE Daedessa Concept + Zixiang Wei

"We have some style guides that we reference to make sure we have the correct shape language. Style guides are always super important. As for consistency, we're grabbing a lot of the feel from the previous games."

—JUSTIN MURRAY, Senior Concept Artist

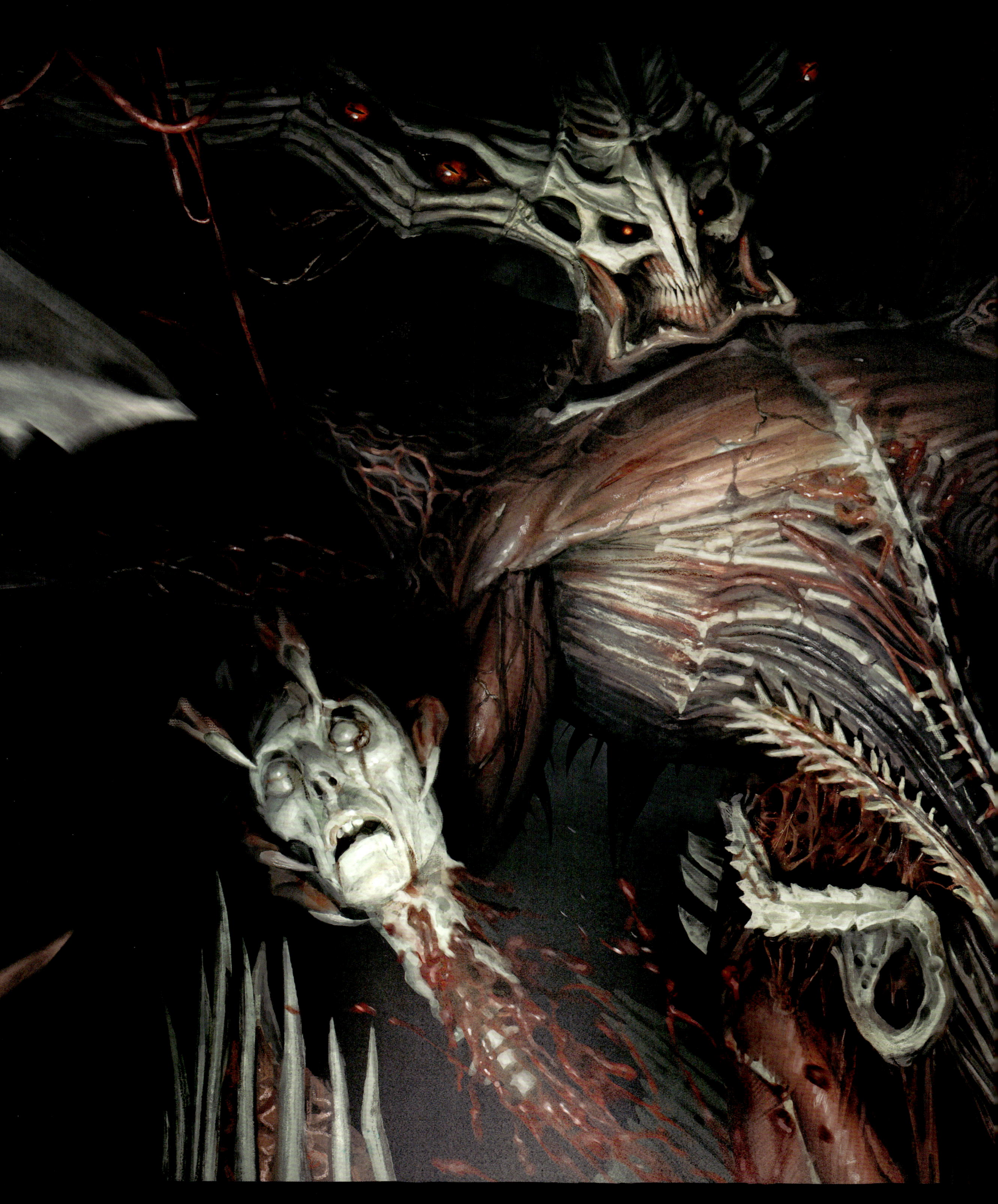

ABOVE Demon Lord Concept • NetEase Art Team

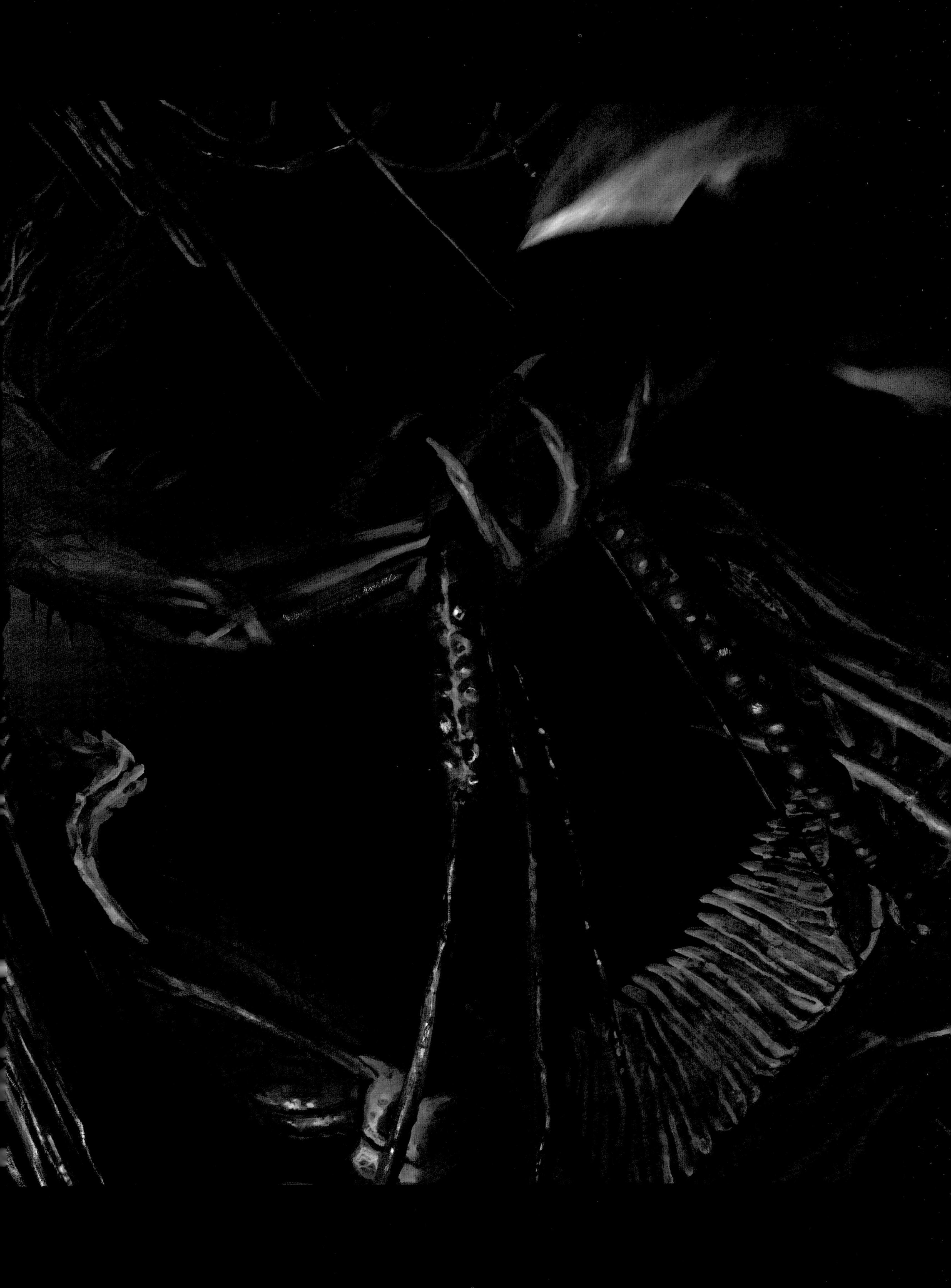

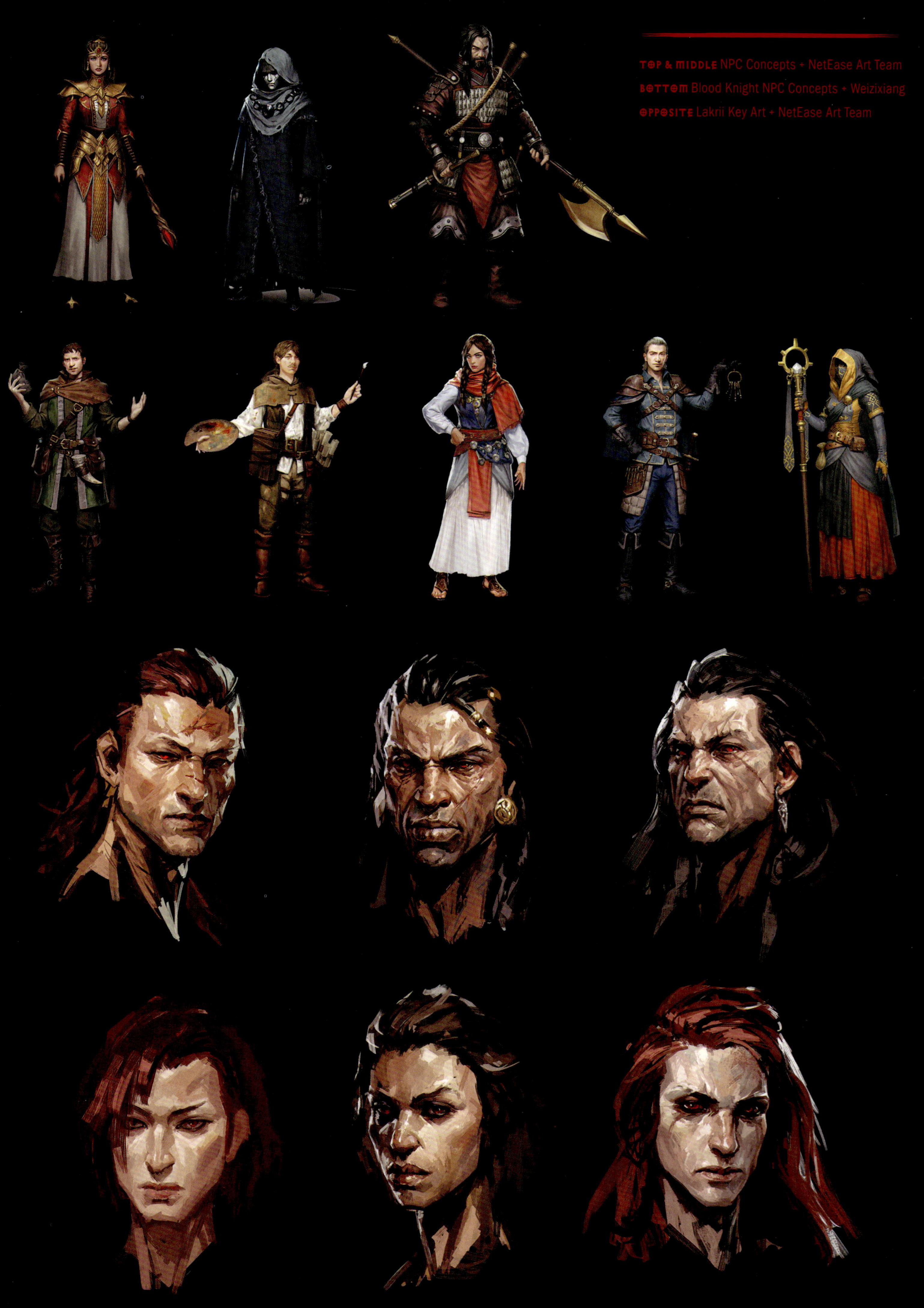

TOP & MIDDLE NPC Concepts • NetEase Art Team
BOTTOM Blood Knight NPC Concepts • Weizixiang
OPPOSITE Lakrii Key Art • NetEase Art Team

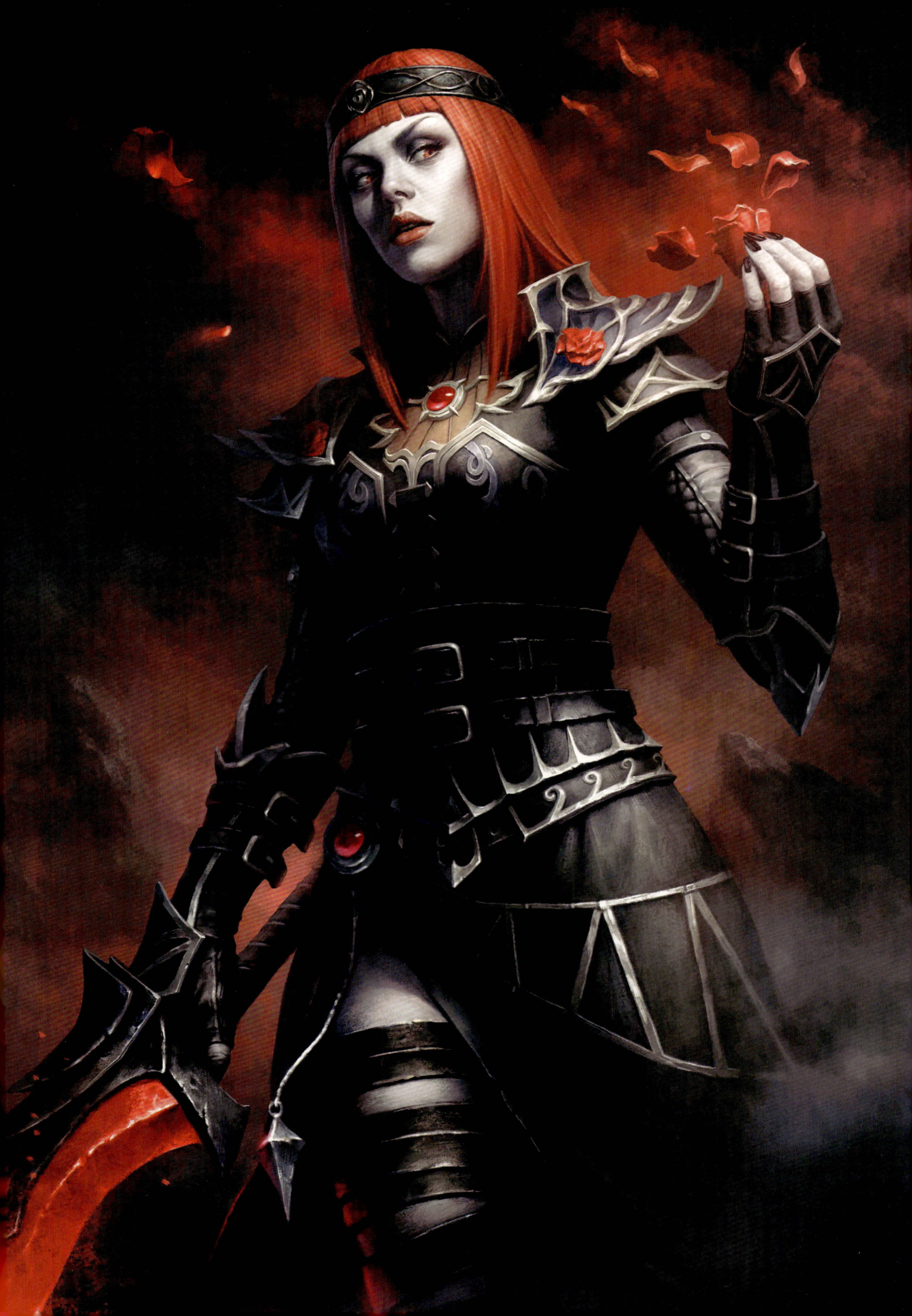

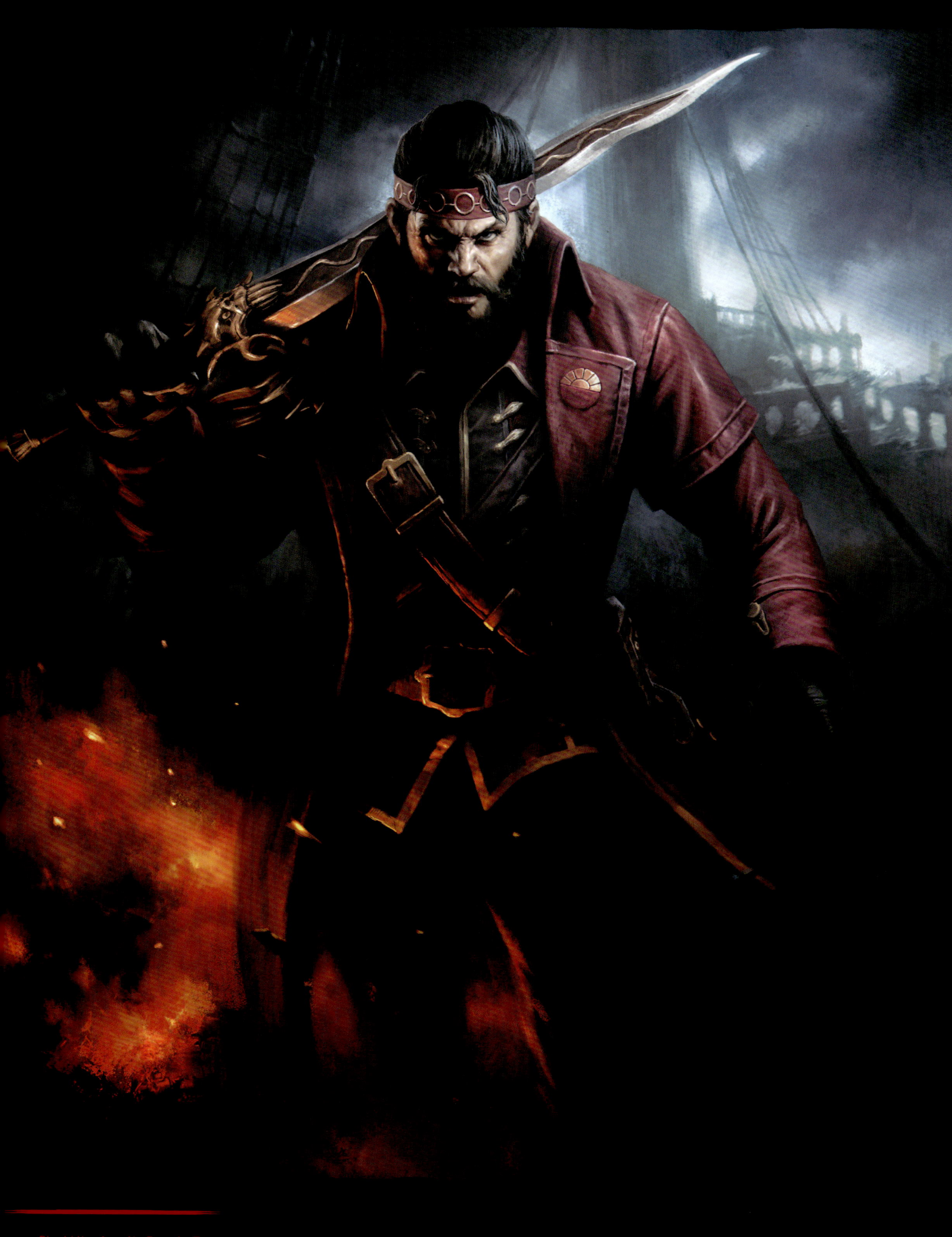

ABOVE Rhodri Key Art • NetEase Art Team
OPPOSITE Manoruk Key Art • Geunjoo Baik

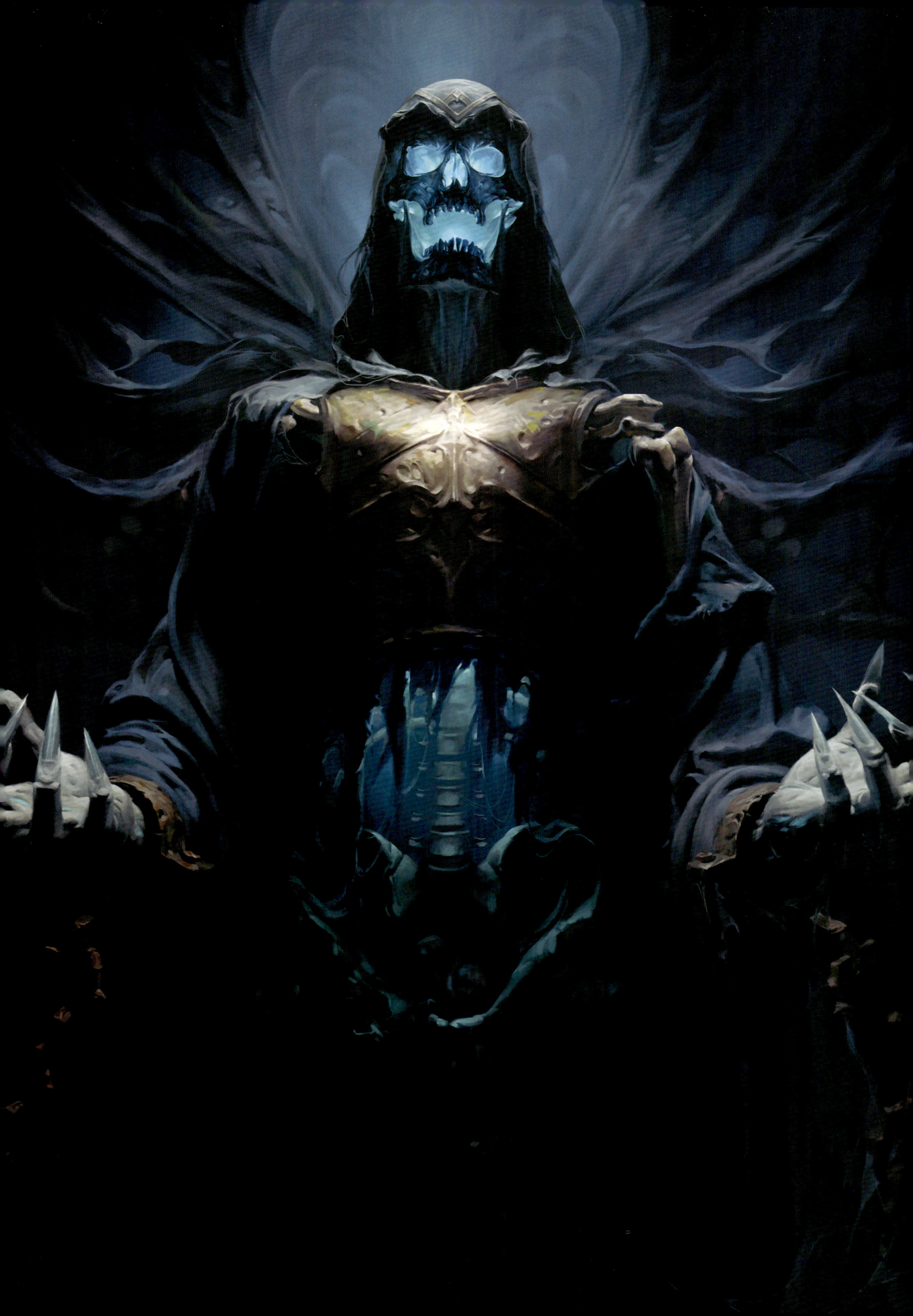

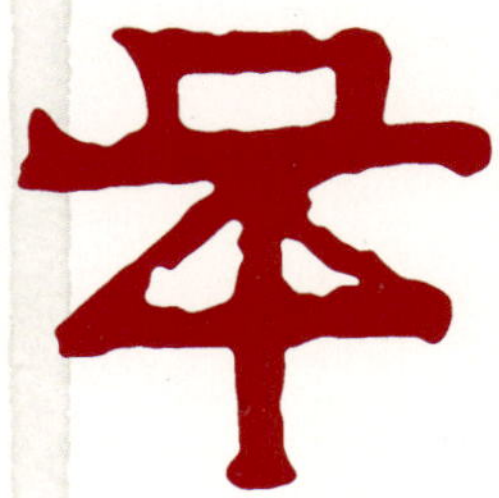

Terrors in the Dark

ABOVE Kulle Library Rune + NetEase Art Team

RIGHT Sand Wasp Color Ideation + NetEase Art Team

BOTTOM Direwolf Concept + NetEase Art Team

BELOW Sand Wasp Concept + NetEase Art Team

OPPOSITE Fallen War Matron Key Art + Geunjoo Baik

Diablo is known for its gruesome, horrific, and extraordinary monsters and demons. When designing creatures for a mobile game, the number one essential is readability. Players must be able to tell at a glance what the monster is and have some indication of what it does.

"You have a brute," says Richie Marella. "They're really big. You have your normal archetypes, like an archer or a fast melee attacker. The difference is one has a visible weapon that does the ranged attack, and one, if it's a caster, has a staff. Those ones you want to separate from the get-go. This way, players know right off the bat that for the brute, they have to keep an eye on him because he charges. Or that the caster summons this thing, and if they don't keep an eye on him, he summons more, or all the things they kill he summons back. Therefore, having iconic looks for each of those important archetypes is critical."

Unique elements are used to make the monster—and the experience of fighting it—unforgettable.

"I try to make it more over-the-top," says Justin Murray. "We design these characters and creatures to work in the environment they live in, but because it's *Diablo*, we push for bigger more aggressive shapes. We've designed an insane amount of creatures with demonic horns, horrific faces with jagged bone structures, gory mutations, and transformations. Horrific things."

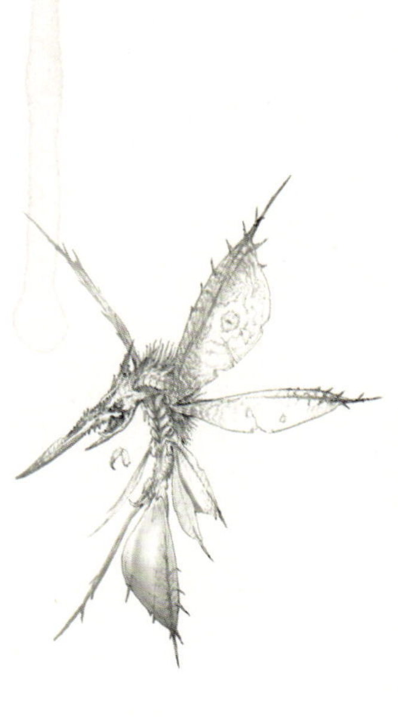

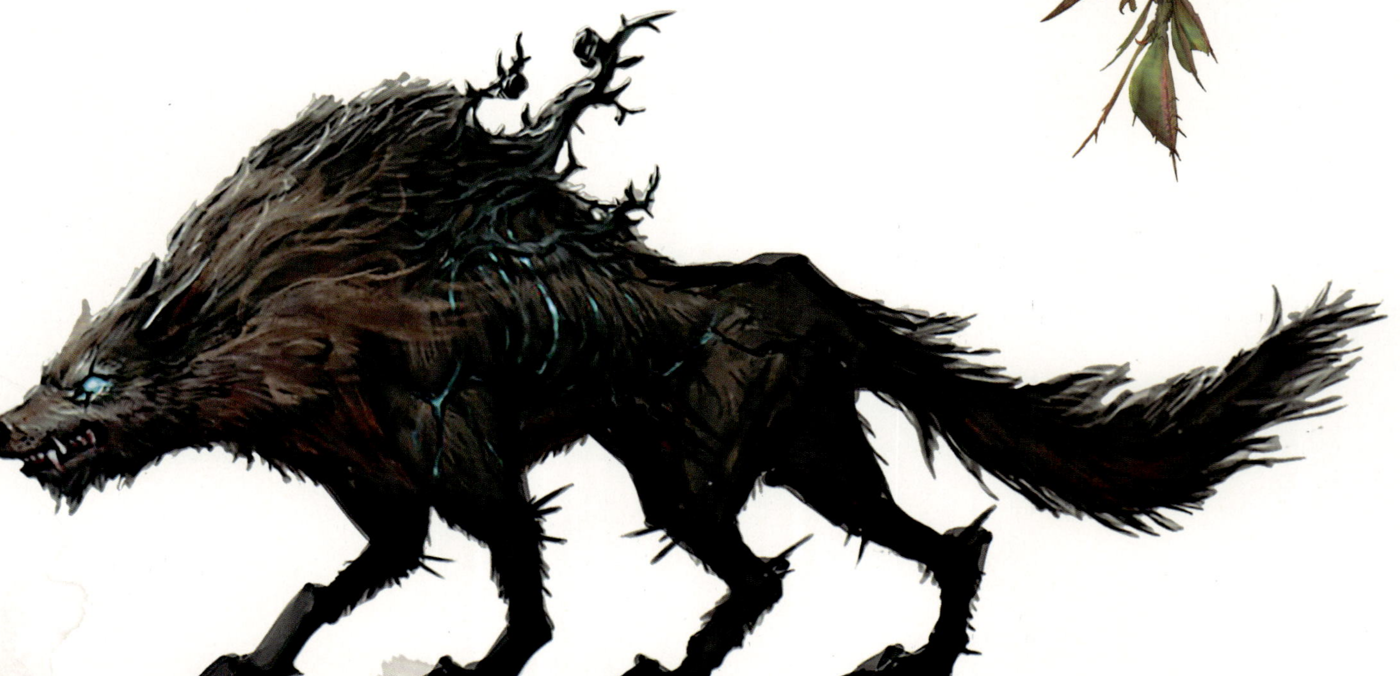

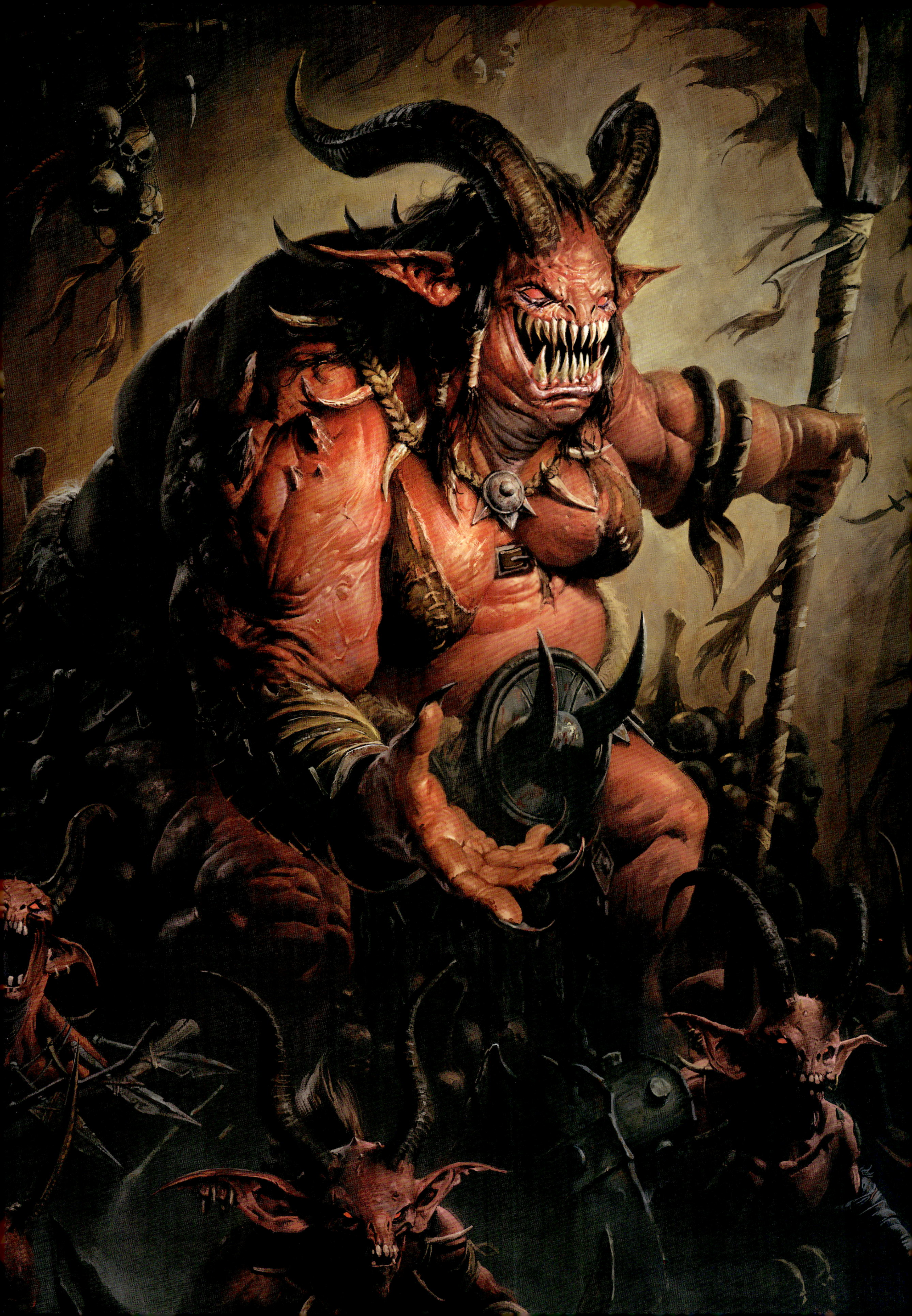

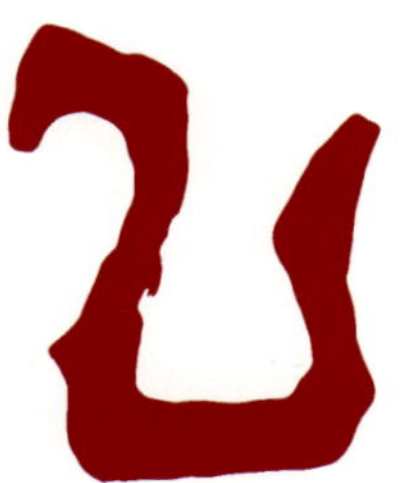

ABOVE Kulle Library Rune + NetEase Art Team

RIGHT Damnation Cultist Concept + NetEase Art Team

BOTTOM Bloodsworn Enemies Concept + NetEase Art Team

OPPOSITE Gishtur and Beledwe Key Art + Geunjoo Baik

Another avenue that artists and designers explore is the element of surprise. A hooded character with glowing eyes may be presented as an ally . . . But in the world of *Diablo*, looks can be deceiving.

"I have a lot of fun coming up with ways a creature can transform into something more brutal," Murray adds. "Makes the gameplay more interesting and has the possibility to alter the environment/boss arena depending on how much destruction is happening."

Transformations such as these are another hallmark of memorable creature design.

"I want the player to wonder what this creature is going to look like next time they fight it," Murray says. "Halfway through the encounter, they'll see that it's getting bigger and harder to kill, but also that it's a lot more fun. Something that goes really well with that is changing the environment, whether the player is wrecking the environment with their battling or maybe the background is part of the monster, like a husk from its skin or part of its body."

But as we've seen before, monsters will always adapt.

"Some of our demons have skinless wings which can no longer be used to fly, the skin rotted away a long time ago," Murray continues. "These things are ancient. The wings take more the shape and function of giant spider legs which it uses to walk on around the twisted landscape of Hell."

Even monsters' deaths have guidelines that are followed.

"When you kill an enemy," says Murray, "the enemy has to die in a very gory way. It's gratifying for the player to defeat the enemy and have blood and guts all over the place as its skeleton falls to the ground."

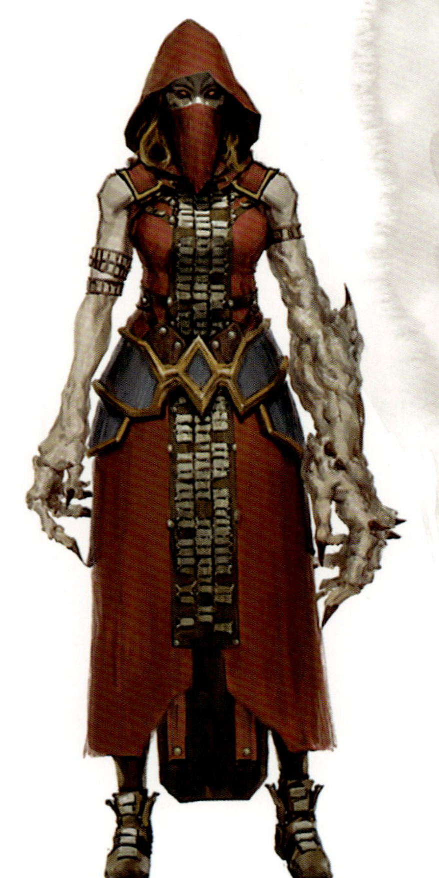

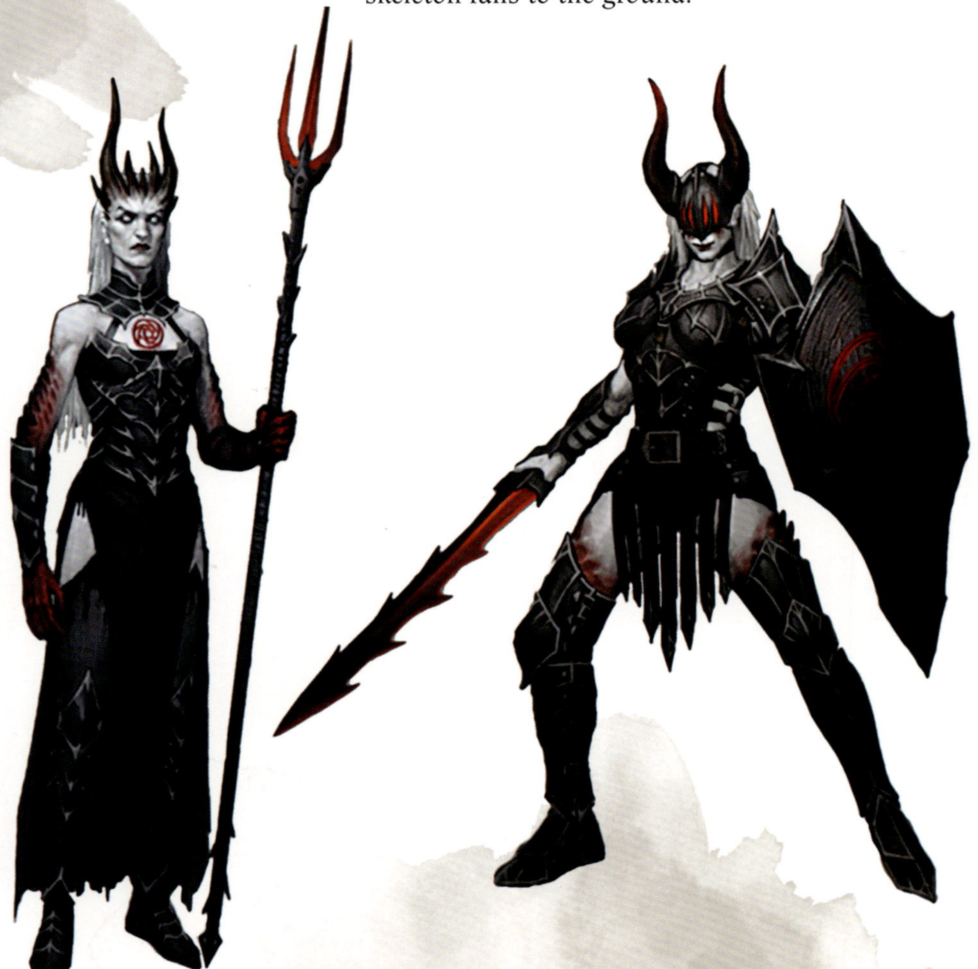

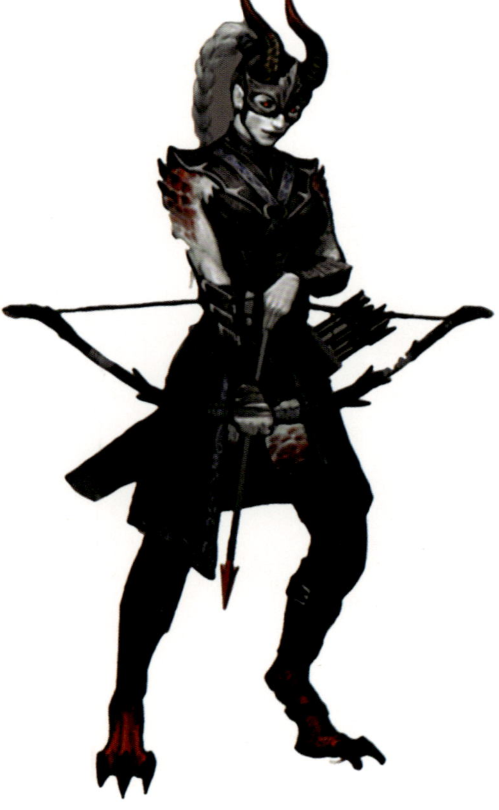

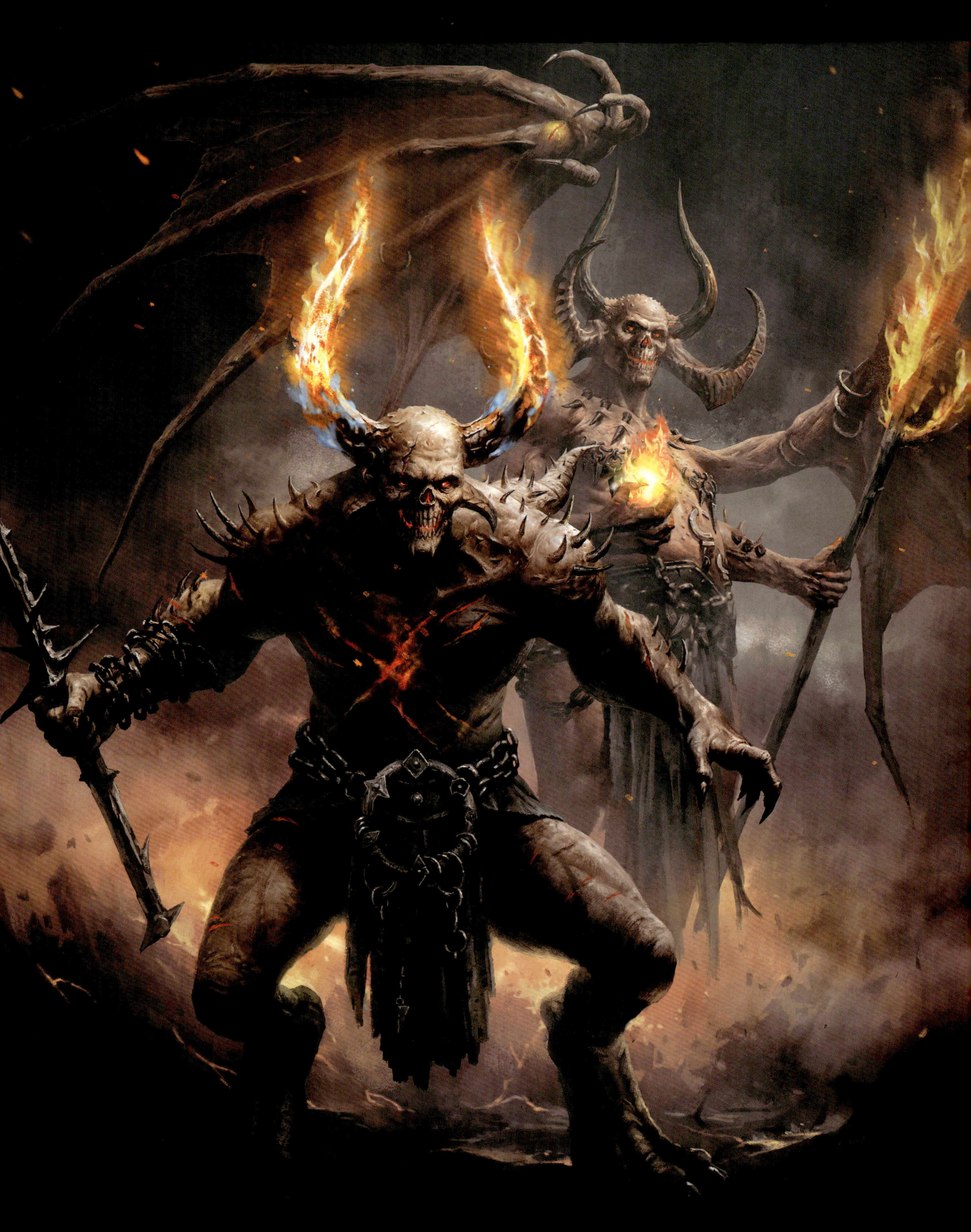

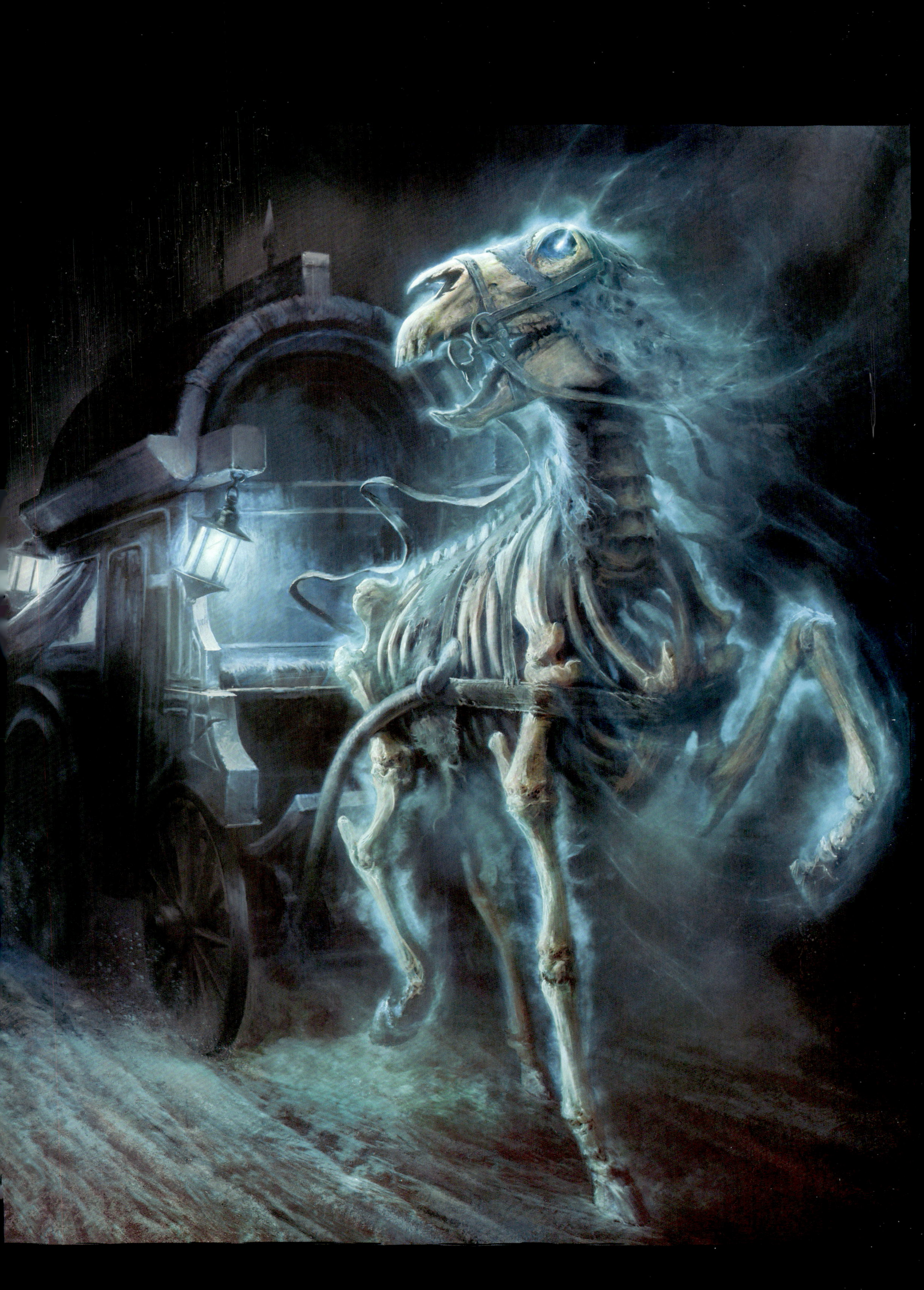

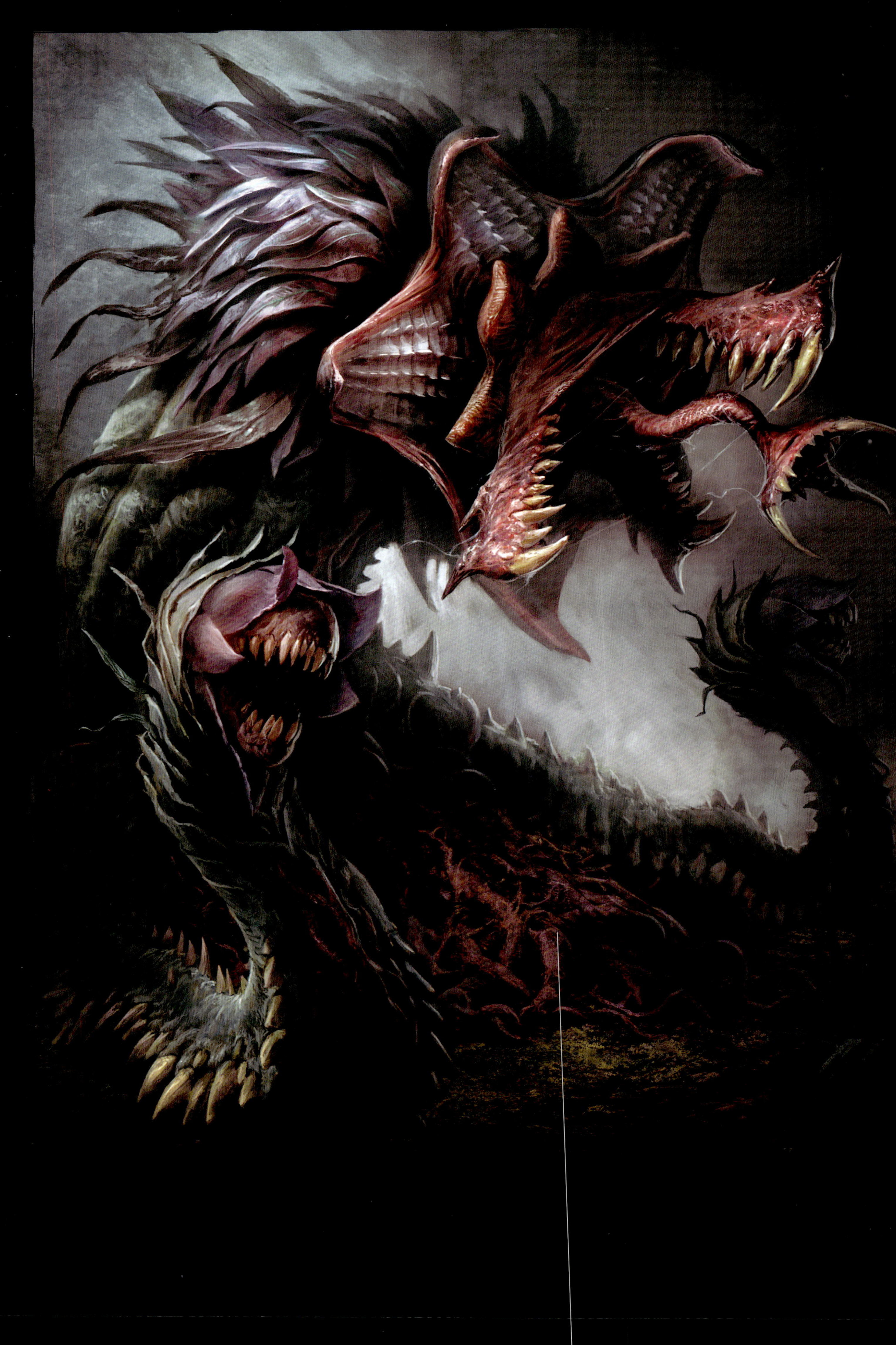

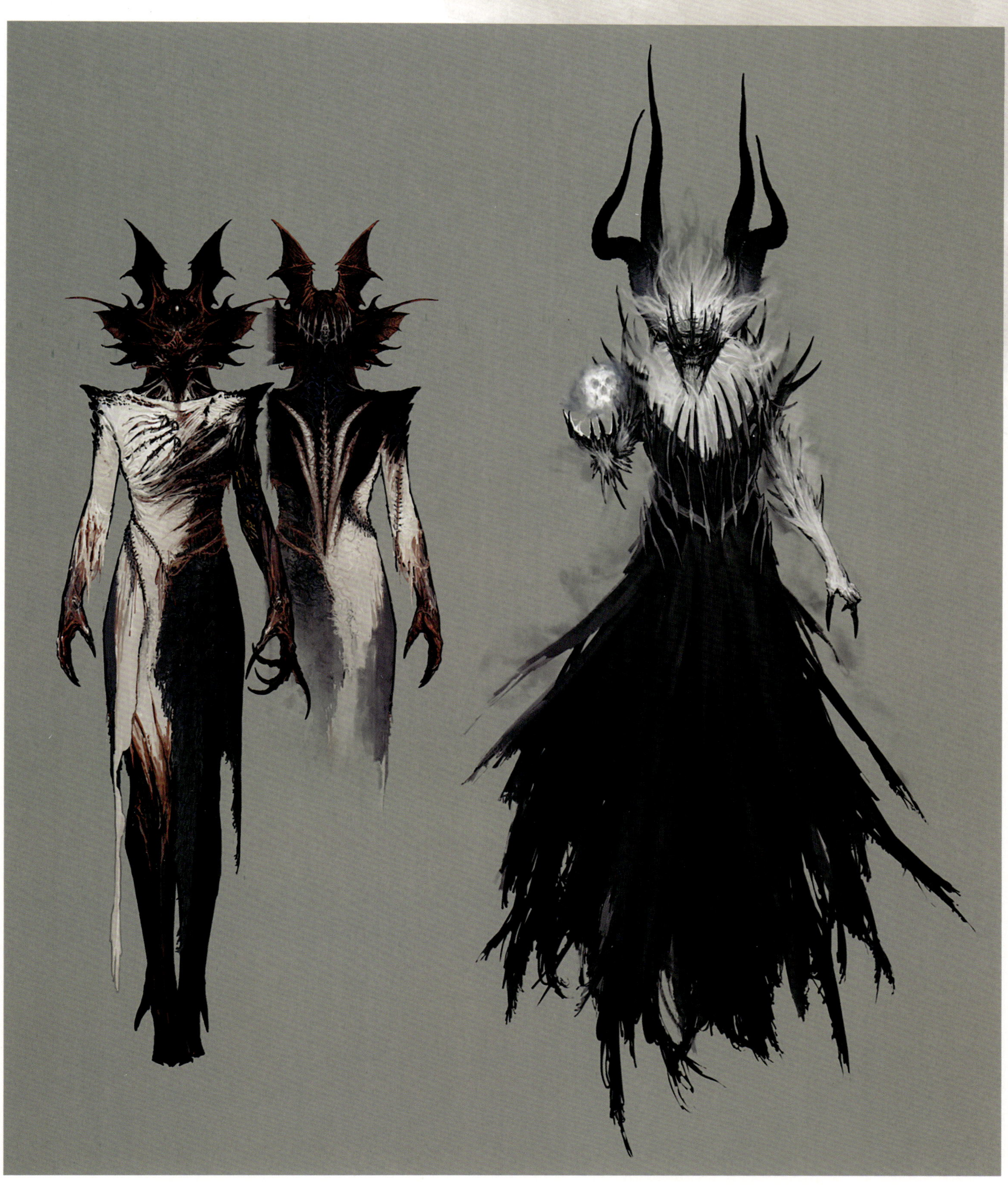

"The biggest challenge is evolving while keeping to the feel of the IP. How many different ways can you design a demon? We're always finding new ways to express that idea. What kind of design is permissible or makes sense for a demon? If we push it too far, does it feel like it's crossing into the realm of science fiction? That's the constant challenge."

—VICTOR LEE, Lead Concept Artist

ABOVE, LEFT Ophinneb the Skin-Veiled Concept + Dean

ABOVE, RIGHT Apothrus, Tamer of the Fallen Concept + Dean

OPPOSITE Haunted Carriage Key Art + Antonio J. Manzanedo

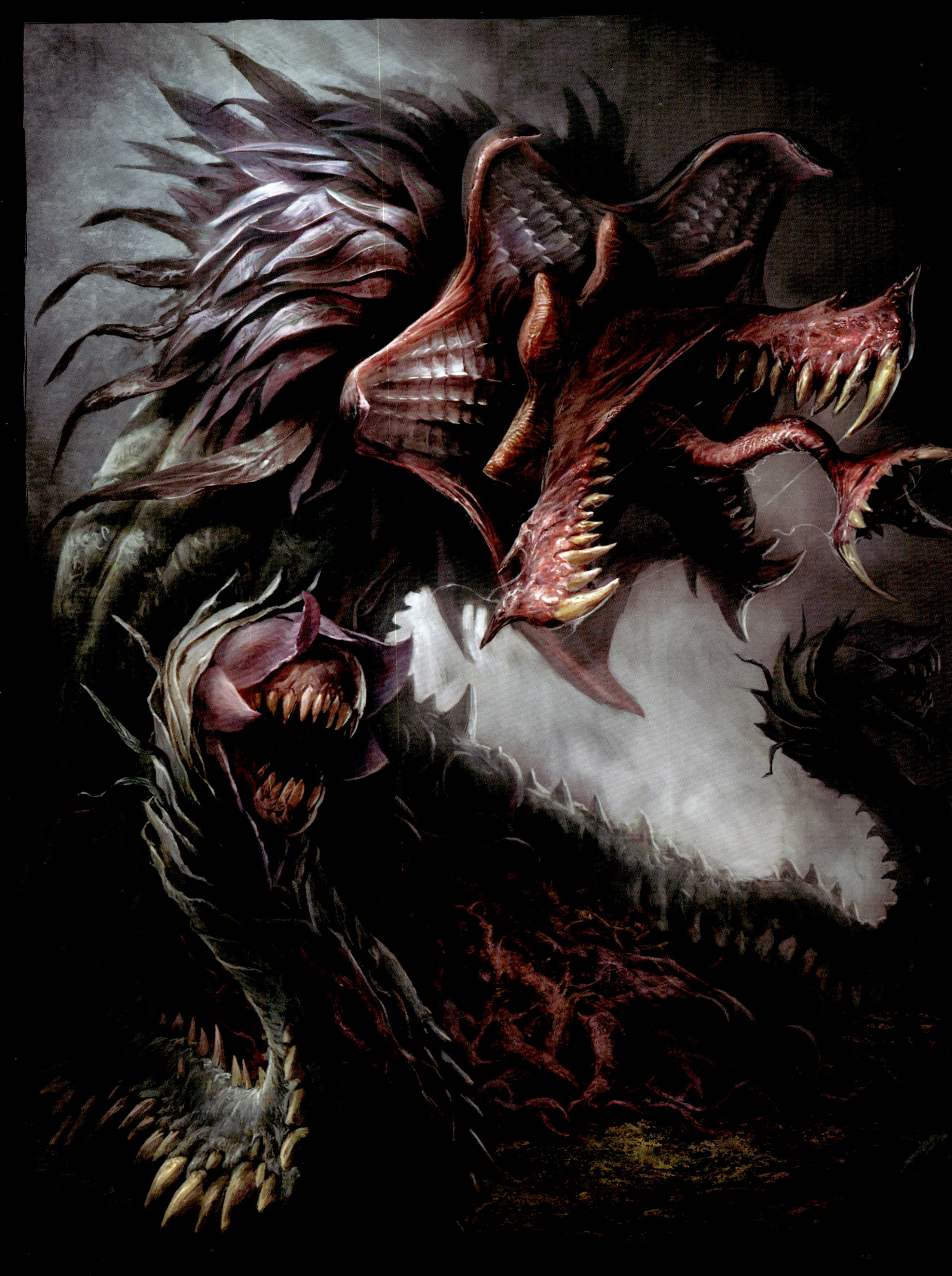

TOP, LEFT Rock Golem Concept + NetEase Art Team

TOP, RIGHT Skull Cleaver Concept + NetEase Art Team

MIDDLE Patchwork Maw Concepts + NetEase Art Team

BOTTOM Boss Lineup Key Art + Xiaofeng Li

OPPOSITE Blood Rose Key Art + Antonio J. Manzanedo

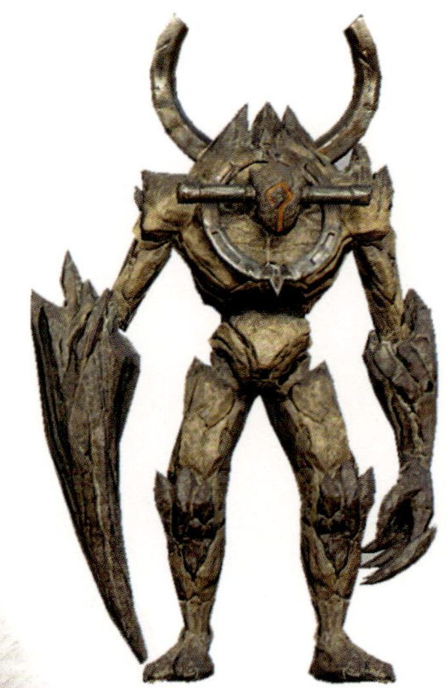

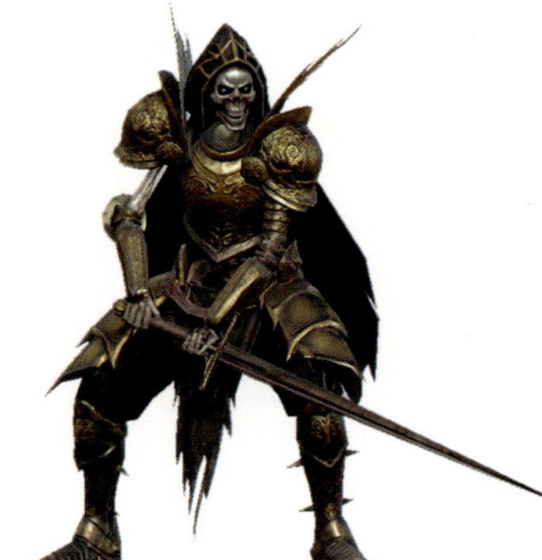

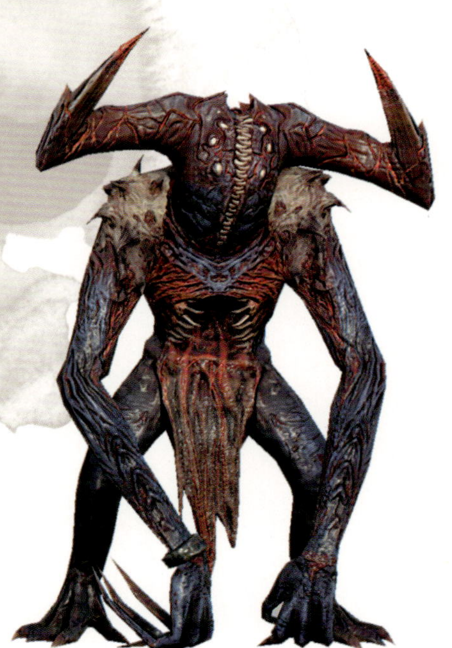

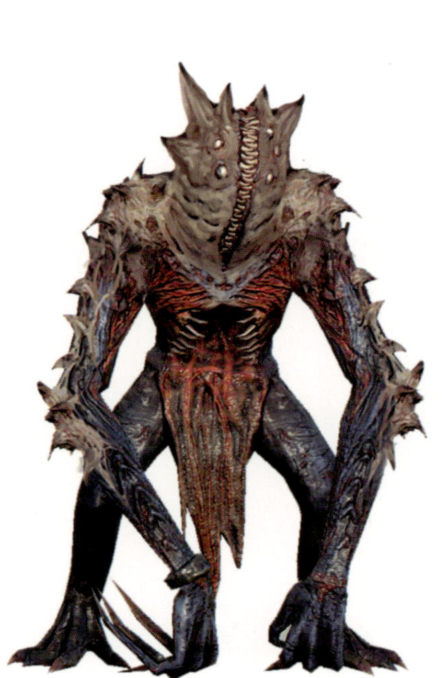

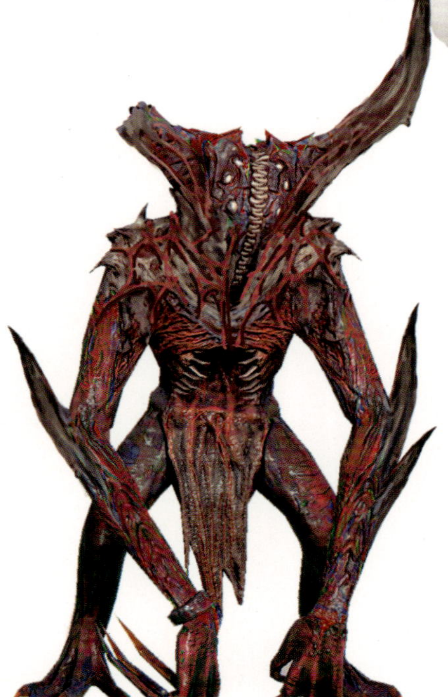

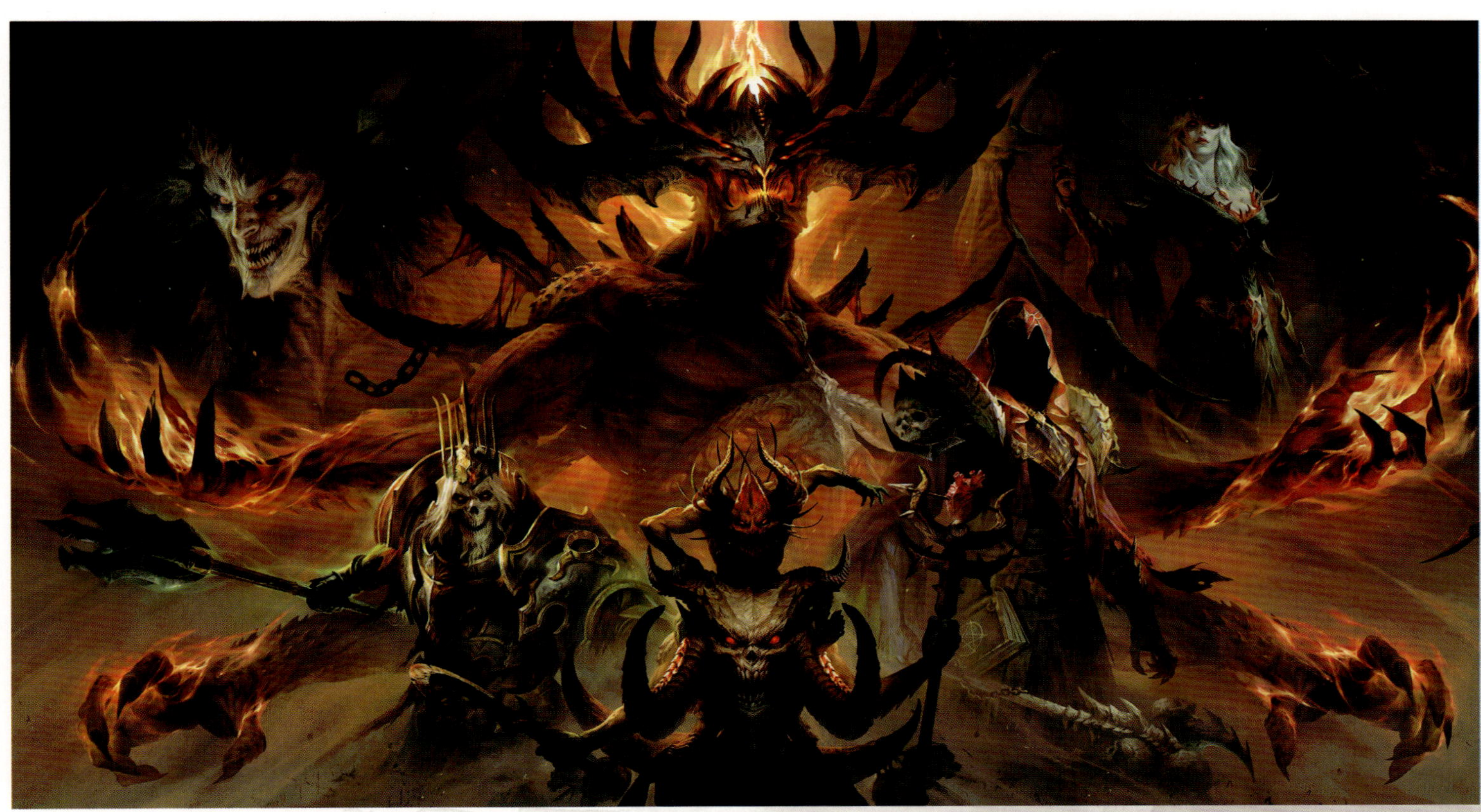

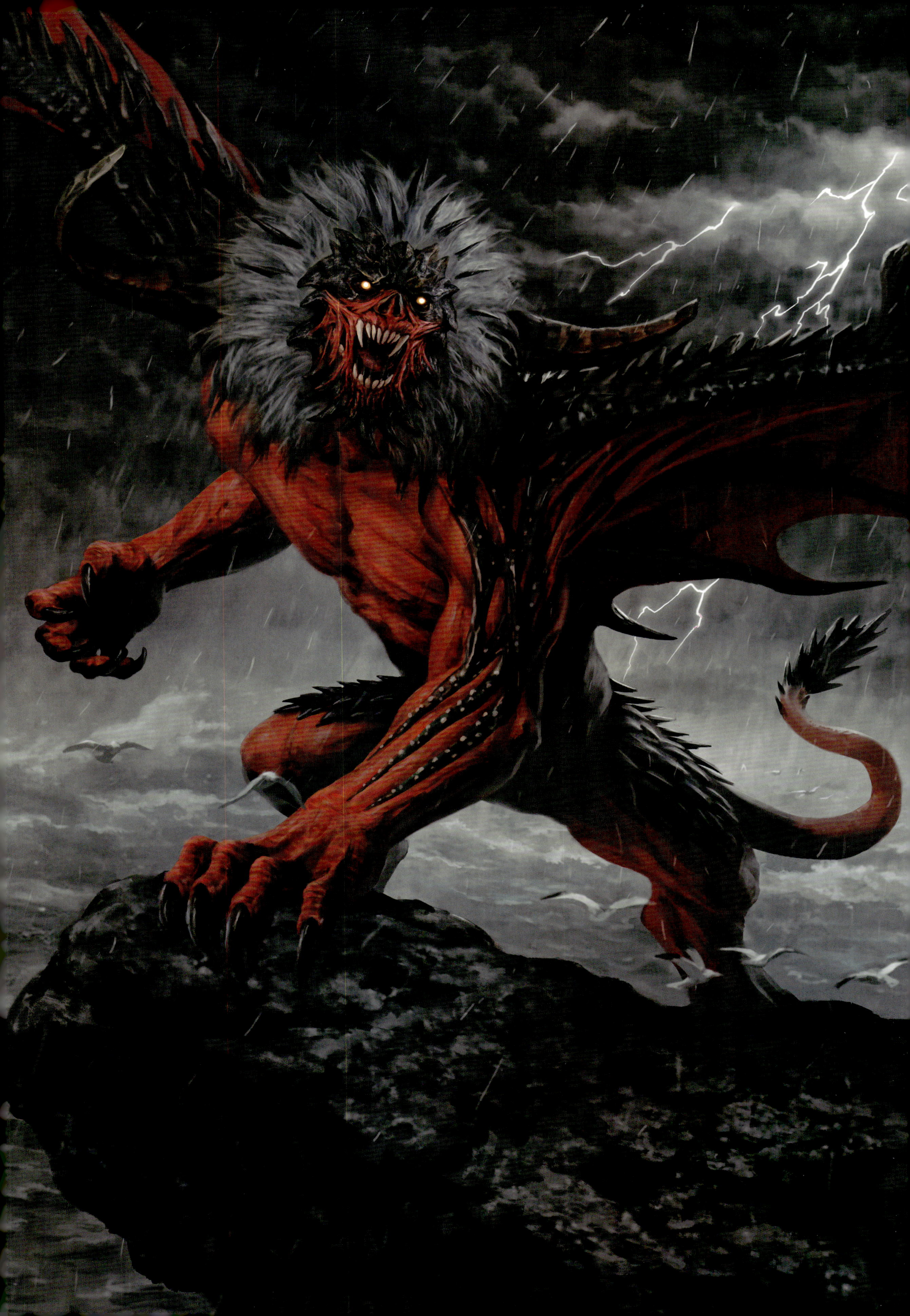

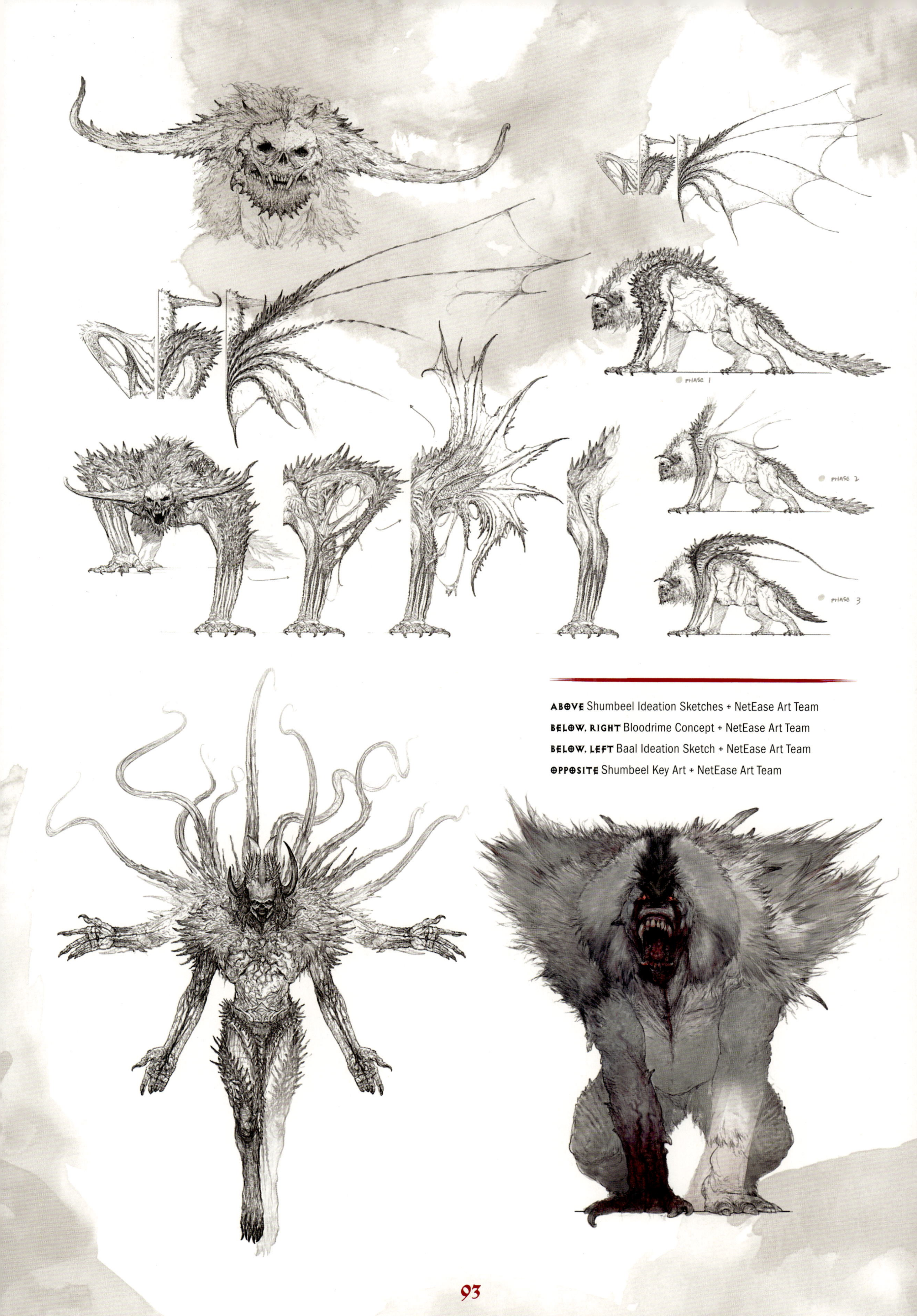

ABOVE Shumbeel Ideation Sketches + NetEase Art Team
BELOW, RIGHT Bloodrime Concept + NetEase Art Team
BELOW, LEFT Baal Ideation Sketch + NetEase Art Team
OPPOSITE Shumbeel Key Art + NetEase Art Team

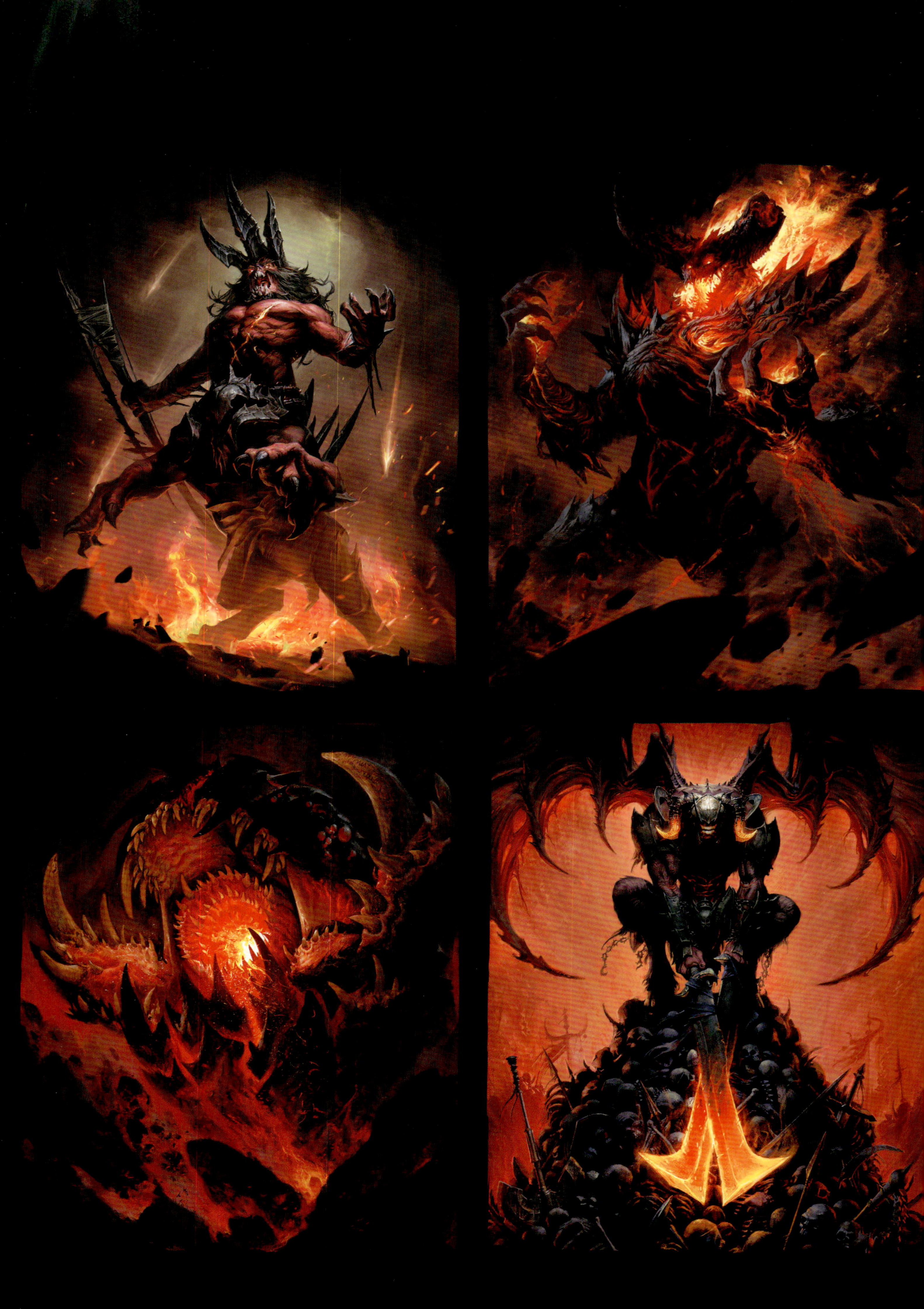

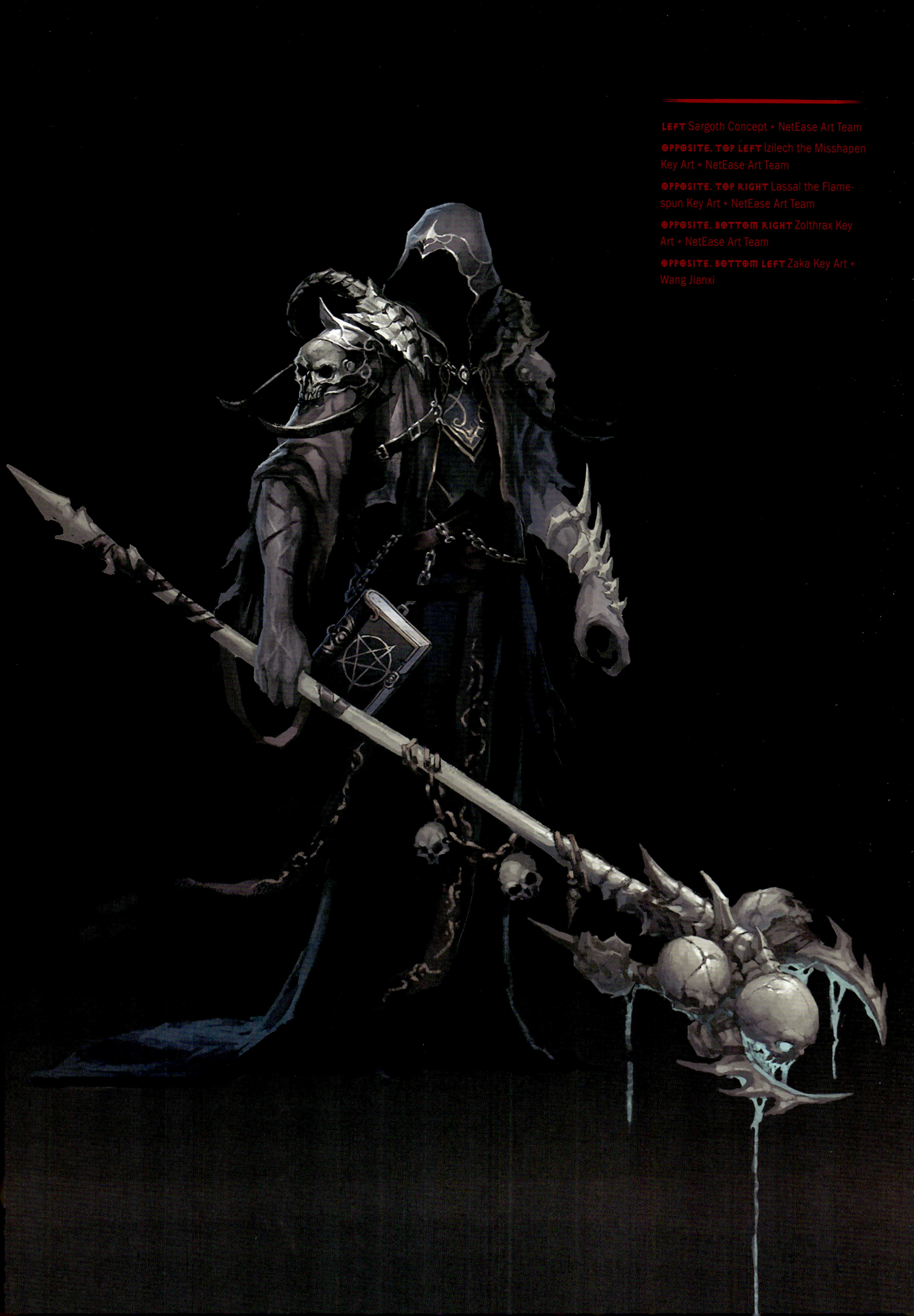

LEFT Sargoth Concept • NetEase Art Team

OPPOSITE, TOP LEFT Izilech the Misshapen Key Art • NetEase Art Team

OPPOSITE, TOP RIGHT Lassal the Flame-spun Key Art • NetEase Art Team

OPPOSITE, BOTTOM RIGHT Zolthrax Key Art • NetEase Art Team

OPPOSITE, BOTTOM LEFT Zaka Key Art • Wang Jianxi

"You can get a hundred characters on the screen. Doing this stuff for so long, it's like we can do anything now, it's fantastic. It's so great to see so many characters on-screen at once with all these wonderful effects going on—and there's no lag. That's what's been really inspiring about this game. It's like we can do whatever we want, and now the tech is better, and it's just great to see—the lighting and effects, the environment, it's all mind-blowing."

—JUSTIN MURRAY, Senior Concept Artist

BELOW Undead Captain Sketch + NetEase Art Team

BOTTOM Dymdrail Concept + NetEase Art Team

LEFT Terror's Tide Monster Concept + NetEase Art Team

OPPOSITE Corphet Key Art + Wang Jianxi

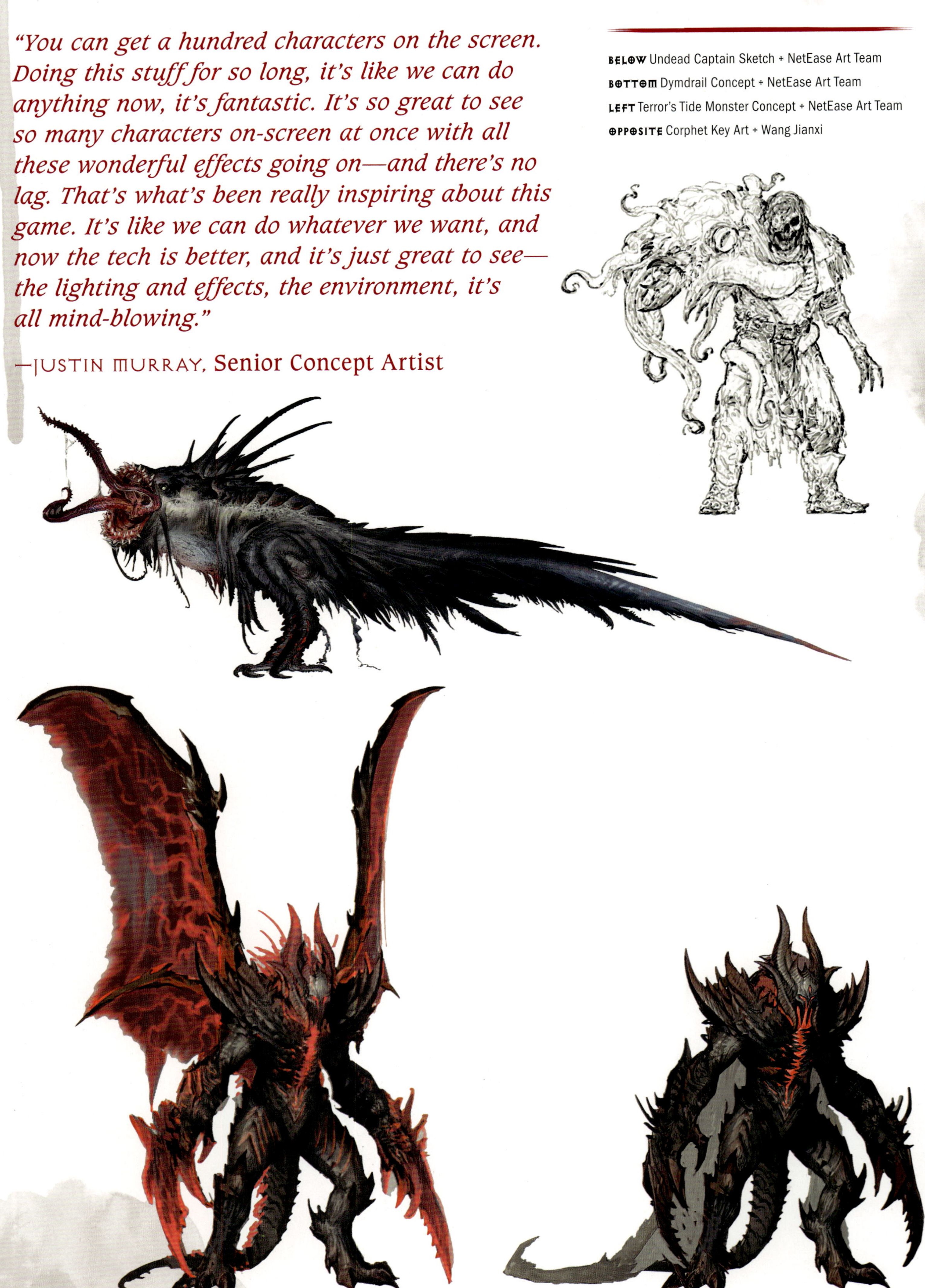

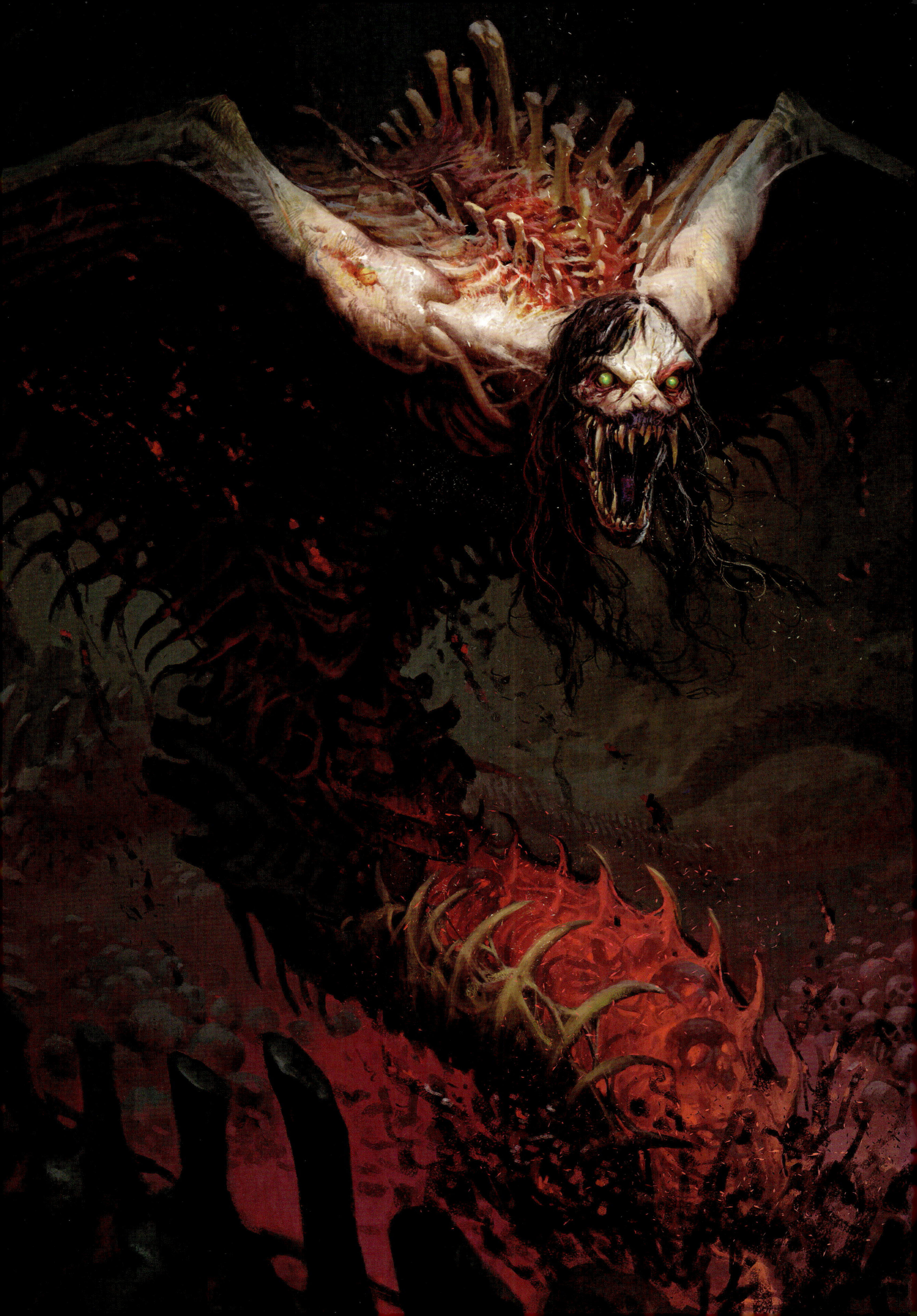

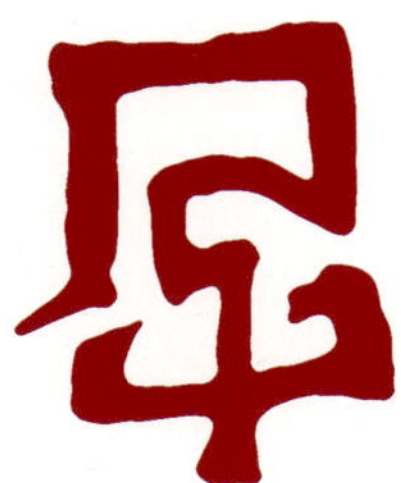

To The Victor Go The Spoils

ABOVE Kulle Library Rune + NetEase Art Team

RIGHT & BOTTOM Barbarian Armor Concept + NetEase Art Team

OPPOSITE Children of Inarius Armor Concept + Pydna

The greatest challenge for *Diablo Immortal* artists is making sure that everything on-screen stands out and is readily identifiable. It is a problem that is compounded by the small size of weapons, items, and pieces of armor.

"The challenge comes down per task," says art director Hunter Schulz, "and the answer isn't always the same. A very thin staff, for instance, would be pixelated and unclear, but overall you want to exaggerate, beef things up, always keep in mind the vantage point of the player and simplify where you can."

When it comes to armor, material selection can have a major impact. Armor can represent any number of substances or components beyond the standard leather or iron.

"We use wood," notes Justin Murray, "where a player can look treelike, which is a lot of fun with the roots. My other favorite is the 'Catacombs in Paris' look—it has that sort of effect where there's repeating patterns of bone and bone parts, like jaw parts with the skull on top."

Detail is used judiciously to create contrast, although at the reduced scale of the *Diablo Immortal* gear, even a small amount of detail can prove to be too much.

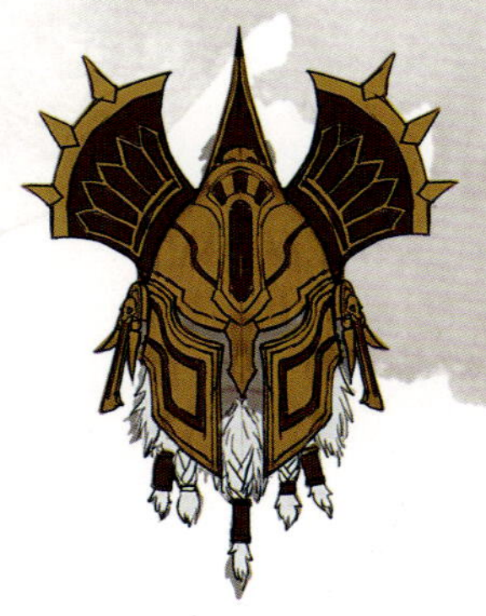

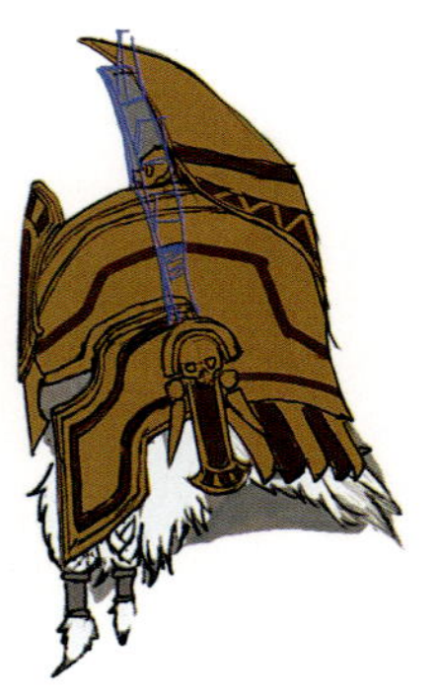

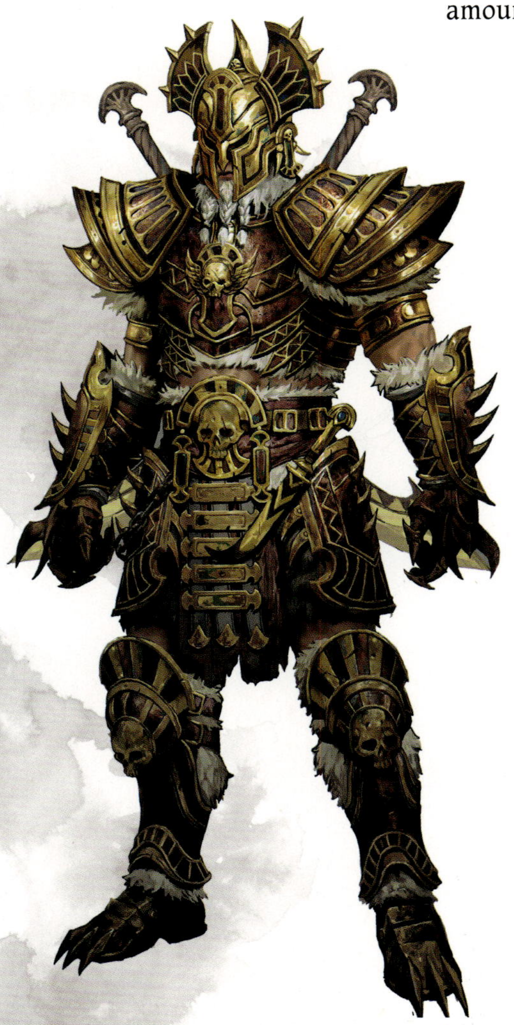

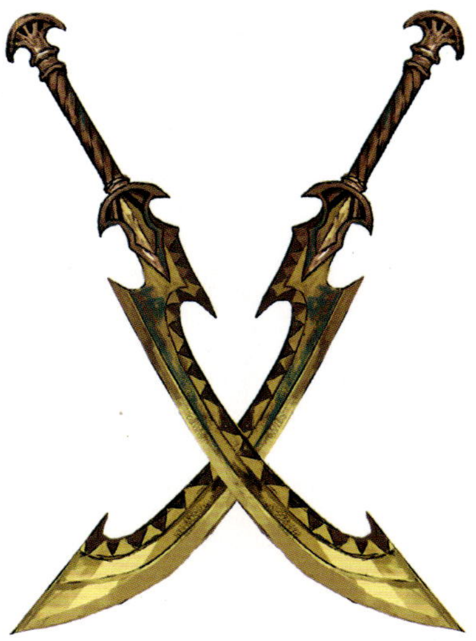

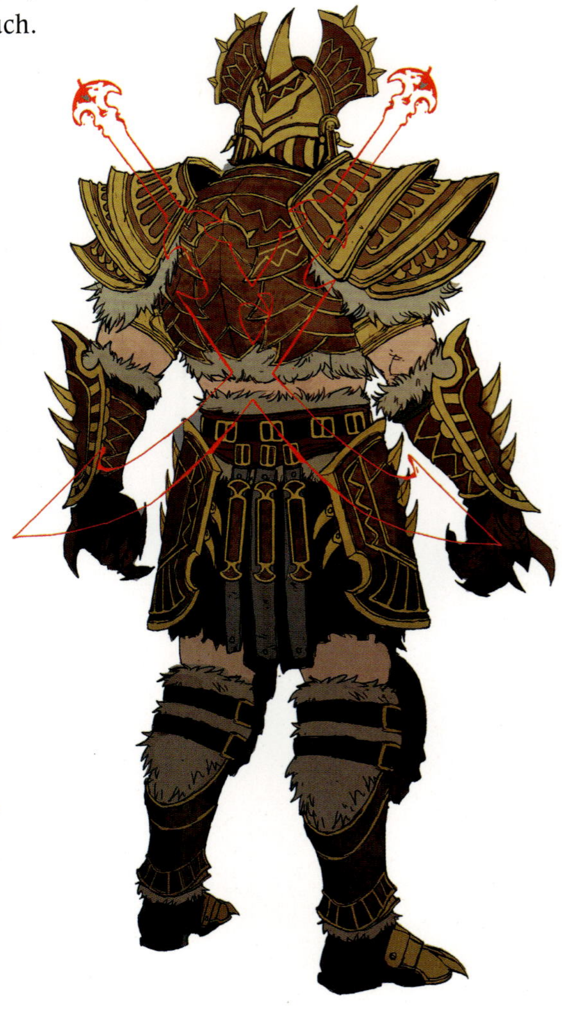

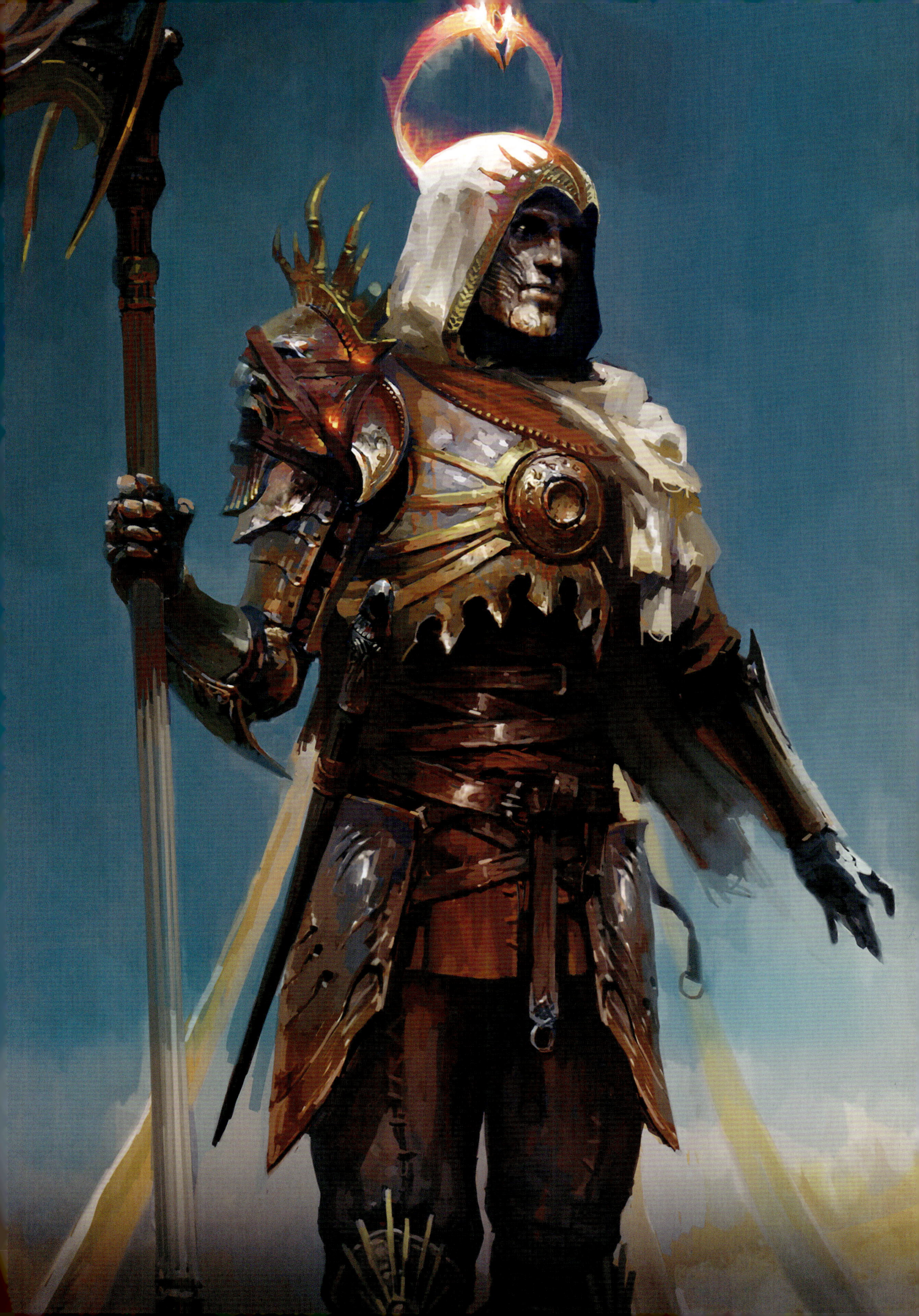

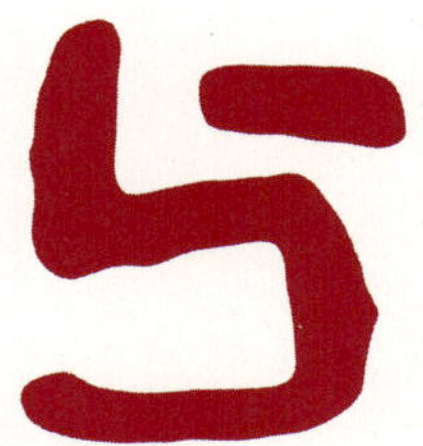

ABOVE Kulle Library Rune • NetEase Art Team

RIGHT Hidden Sun Armor Concept • NetEase Art Team

BOTTOM Lineage of Beasts Armor Set Key Art • NetEase Art Team

OPPOSITE Blood Knight Armor Concept • NetEase Art Team

"Weapons and designs have to read well, and the silhouette has to make sense," Murray continues. "If you're going to have a very busy area with spikes and things, there should be some low detail areas for breathing room."

While some *Diablo* titles, like *Diablo II* and—as we'll see in the following chapter—*Diablo IV*, focused on a grounded realism and functionality for its gear, *Diablo Immortal* loosened those rules to help armor, weapons, and items draw attention.

"*Diablo Immortal* is a bit more relaxed," says Schulz, "allowing for more high fantasy elements. Some of the gear is not very practical—it just looks cool."

Nevertheless, the game follows the same guidelines as all *Diablo* titles when it comes to being mindful of the progression that armor will go through as players level up.

"When I started out," says Murray, "It was very easy to get too detailed on a low level armor set too fast. I thought, 'That's tier one? That looks like tier five!' How do you go up from there? It's going to be so overcrowded. It's going to be shoulder pads on top of shoulder pads."

The key is to start off simple.

"I found that I have to limit myself more than I expect," Murray adds. "When you're doing tier one, it's very basic. It's just like a sheet with a stick and helmet. You don't want anything super amazing on the first one because that's going to go away really fast anyway and you're just going to go on to the next one, and they get bigger and bigger and bigger."

For *Diablo Immortal*, it all boils down to one thing: readability. Using the tools described above, artists ensure that even at the tiniest of sizes, players can quickly determine what any item, weapon, or piece of armor is and also what it does.

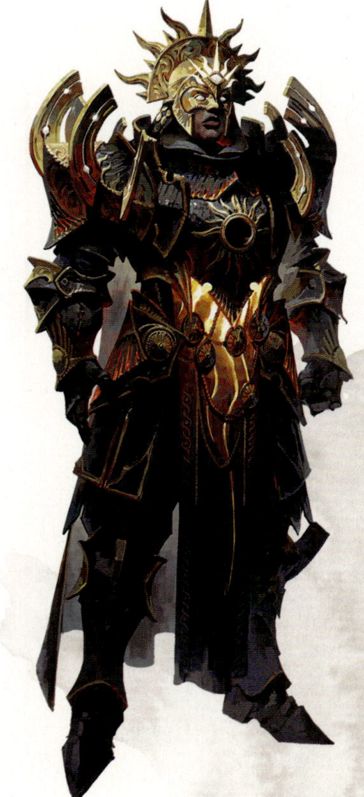

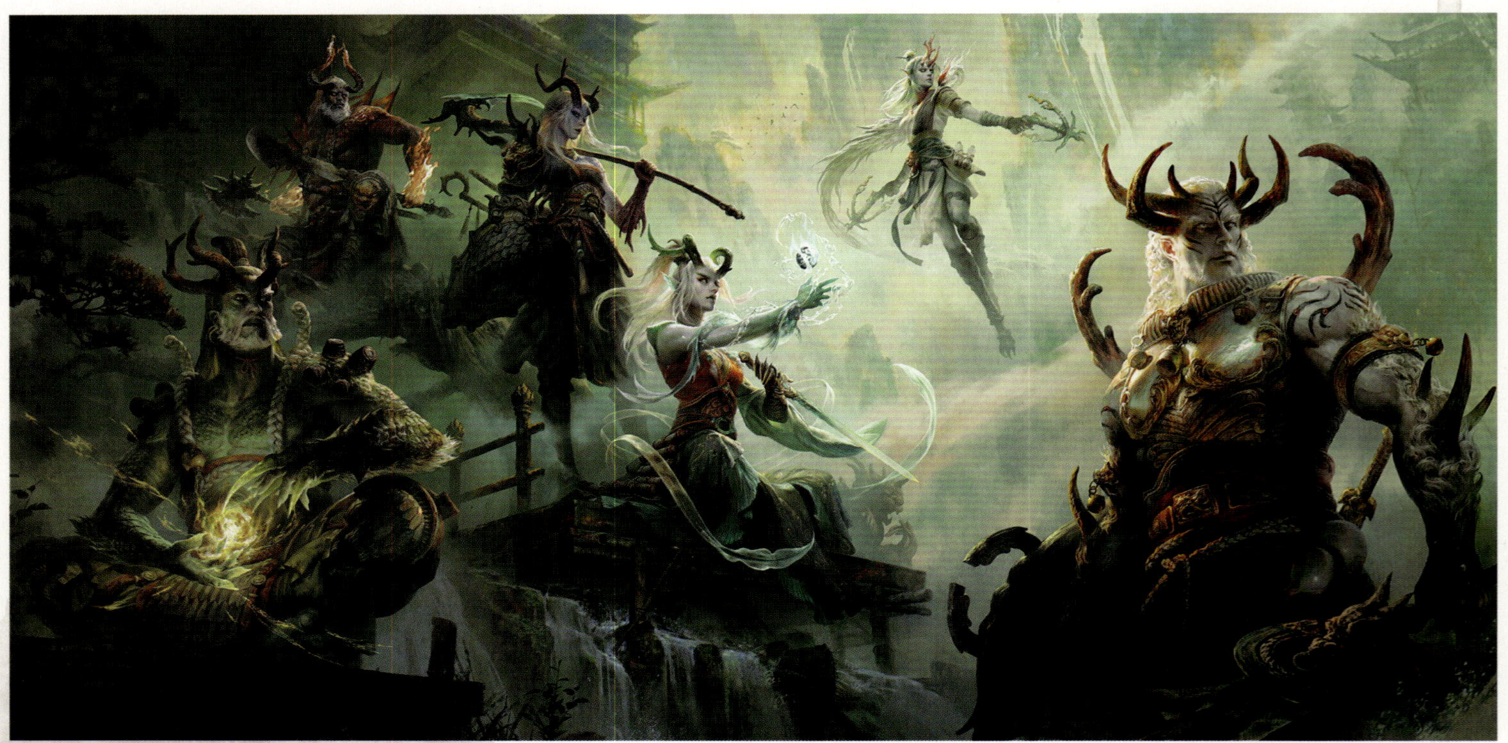

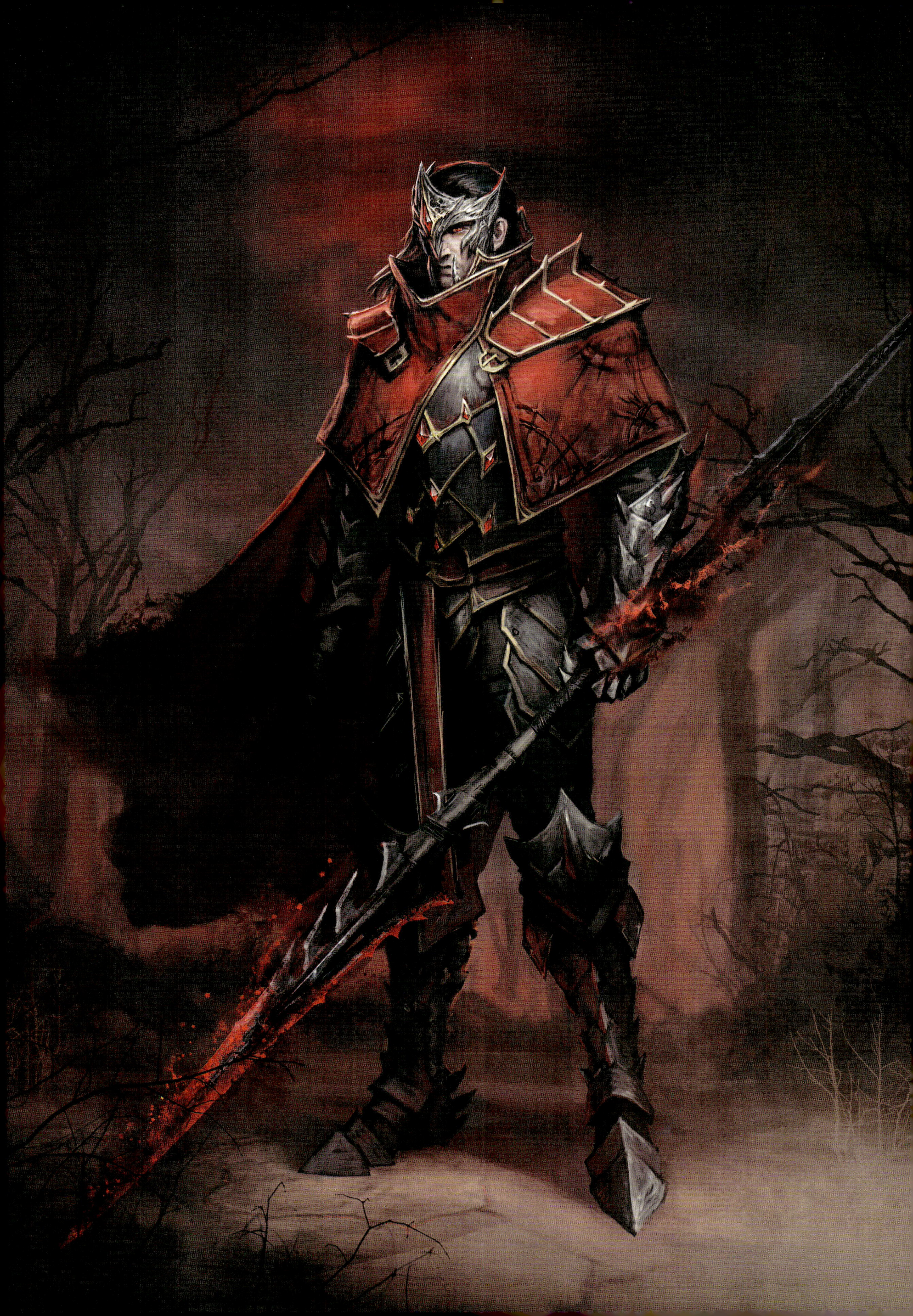

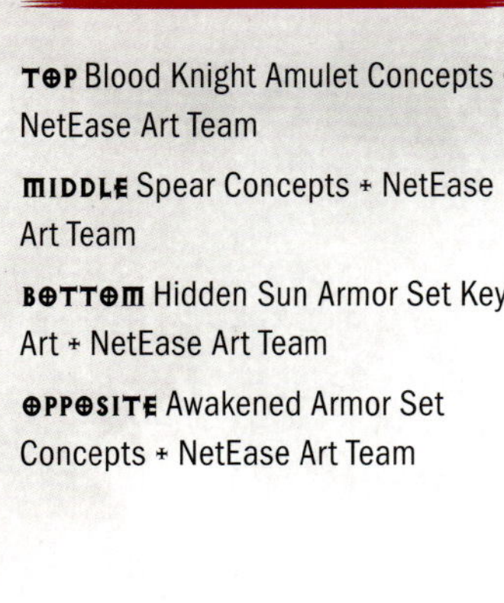

TOP Blood Knight Amulet Concepts • NetEase Art Team

MIDDLE Spear Concepts • NetEase Art Team

BOTTOM Hidden Sun Armor Set Key Art • NetEase Art Team

OPPOSITE Awakened Armor Set Concepts • NetEase Art Team

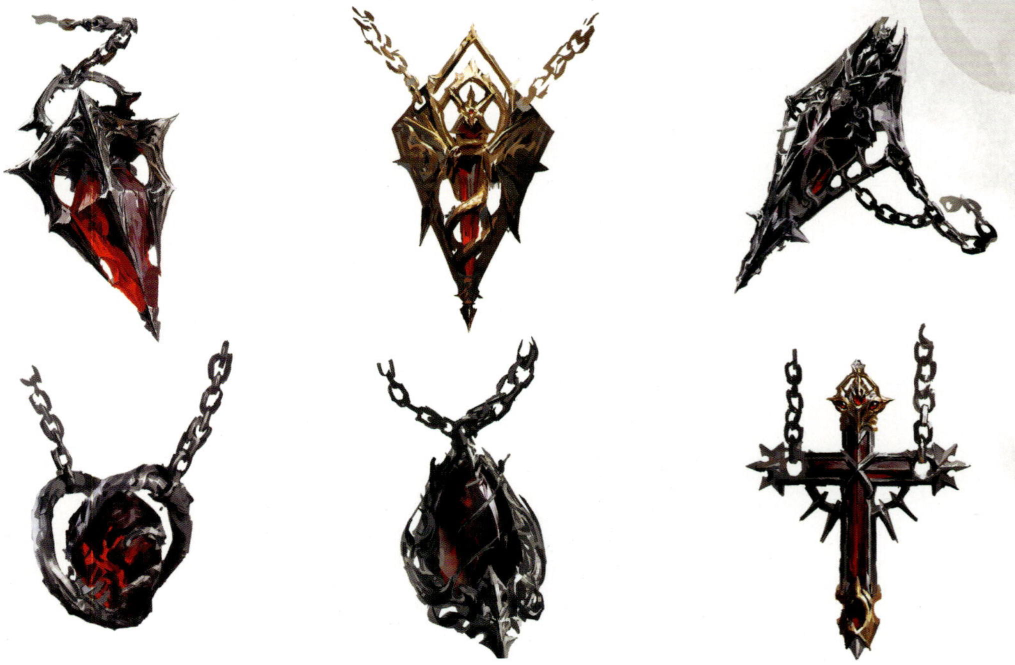

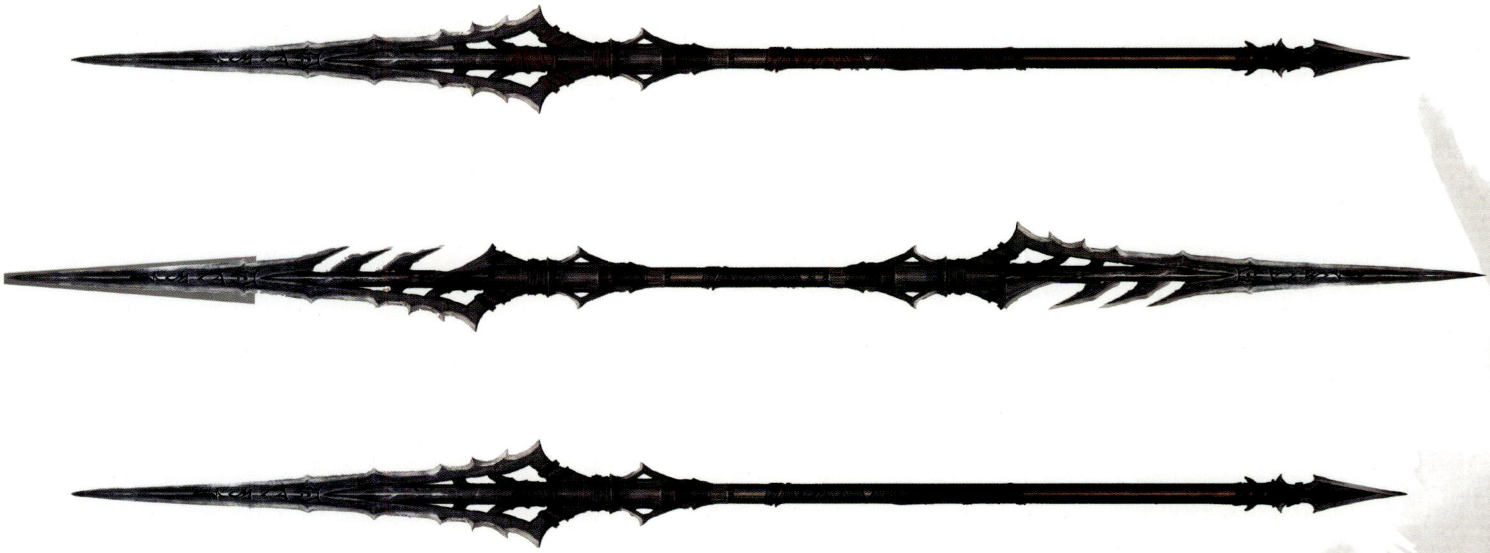

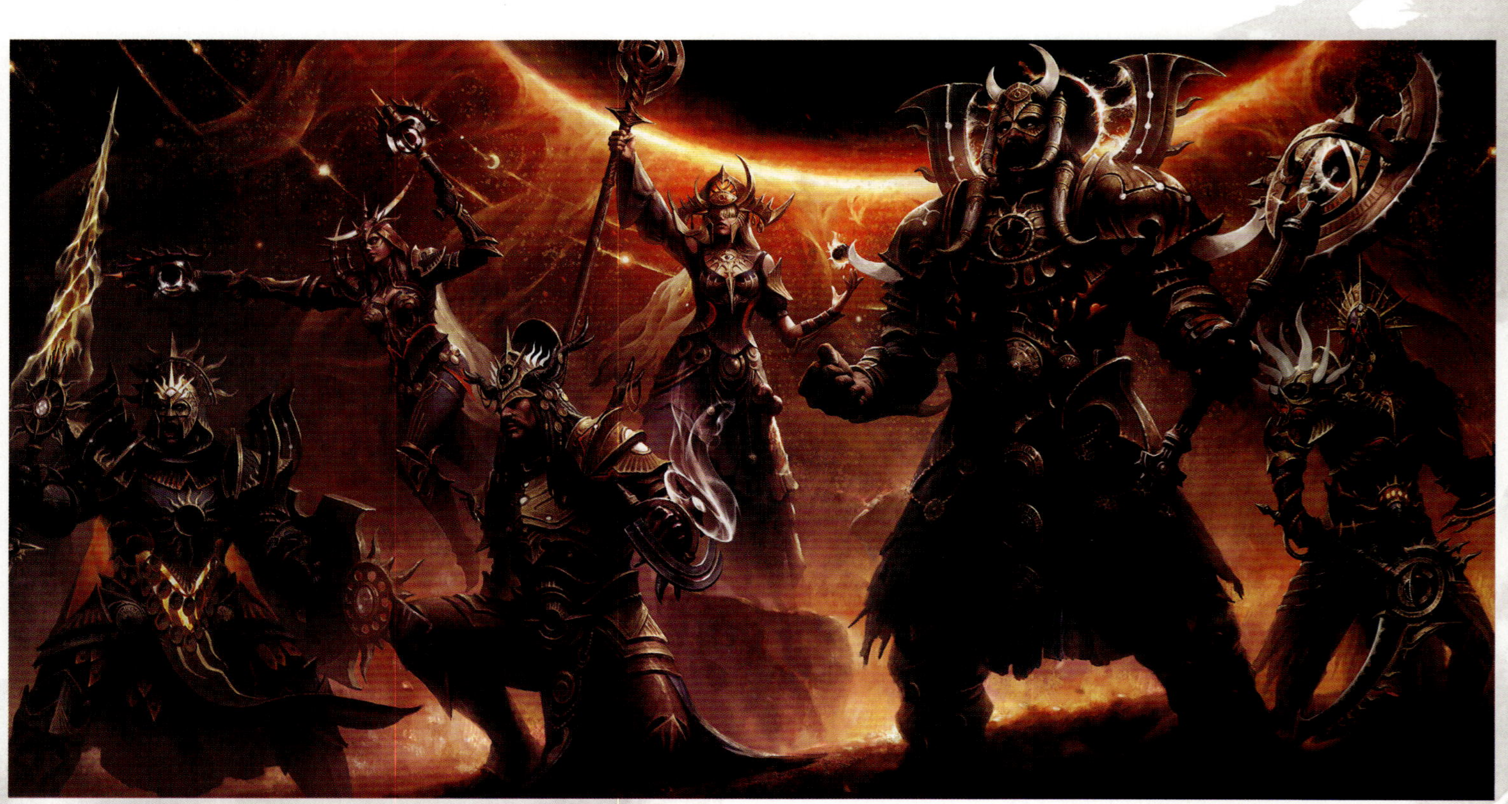

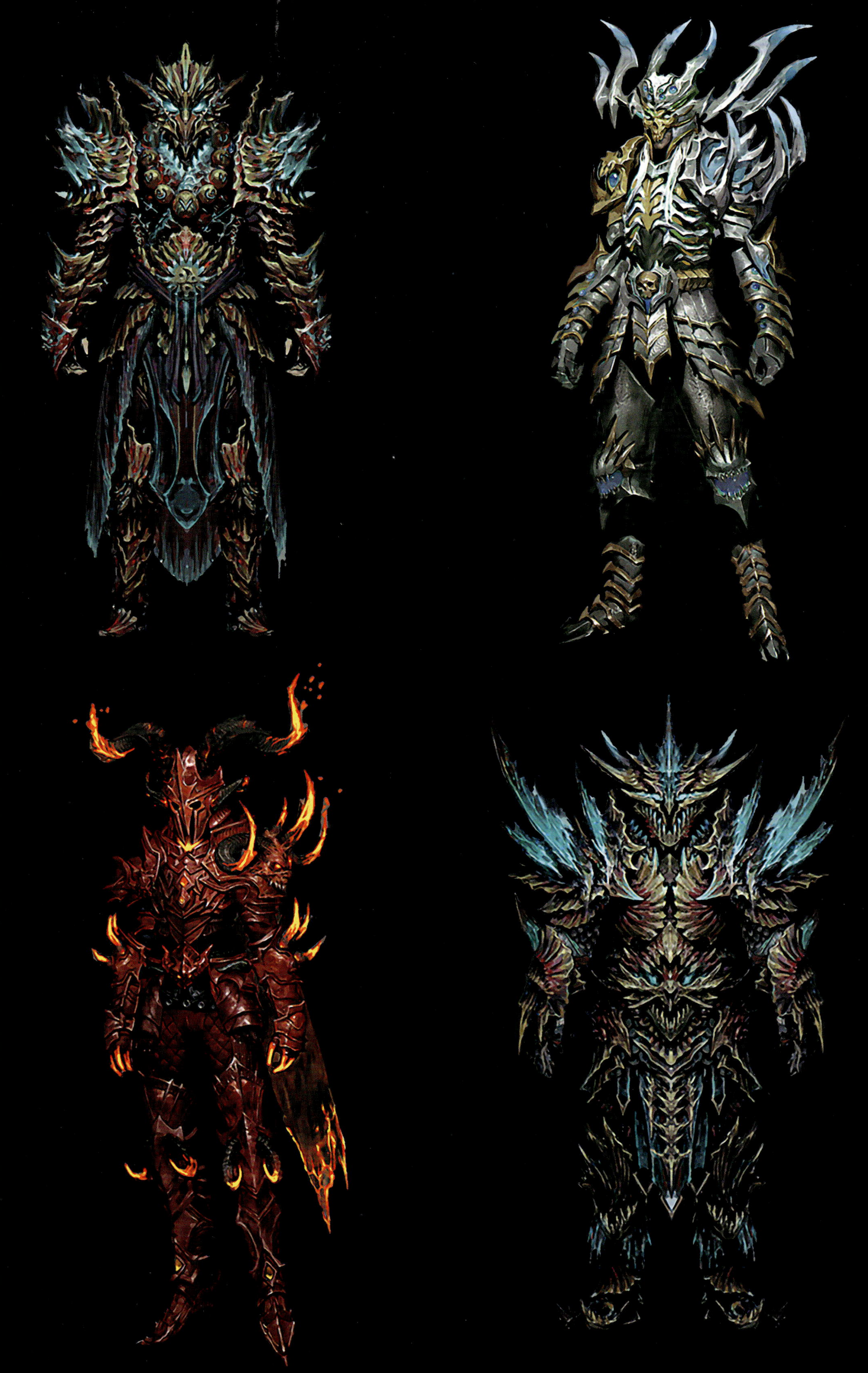

RIGHT Blood Knight Armor Concepts + NetEase Art Team

BOTTOM Barbarian Armor Concepts + NetEase Art Team

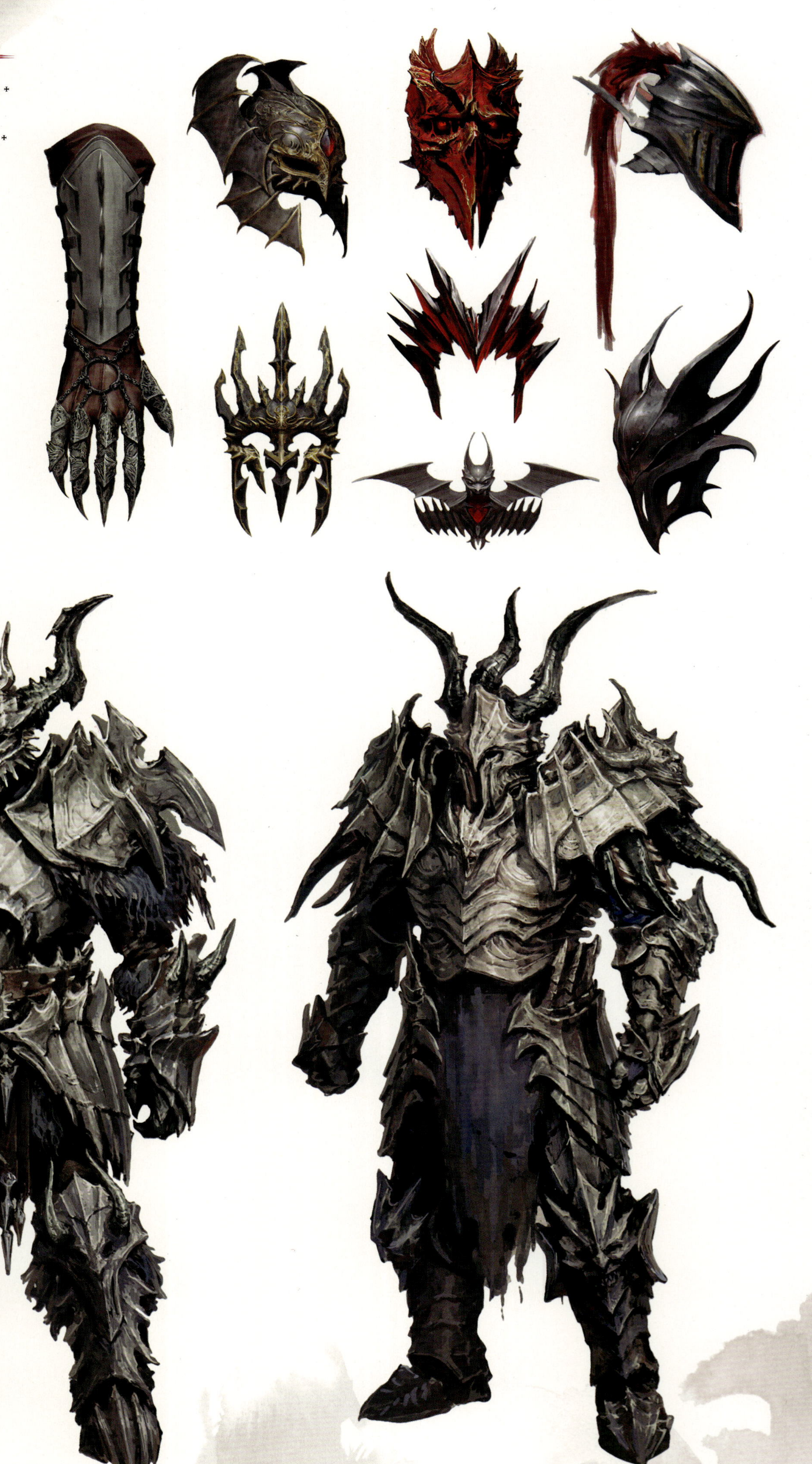

RIGHT & BELOW Blood Knight Armor Concepts • NetEase Art Team

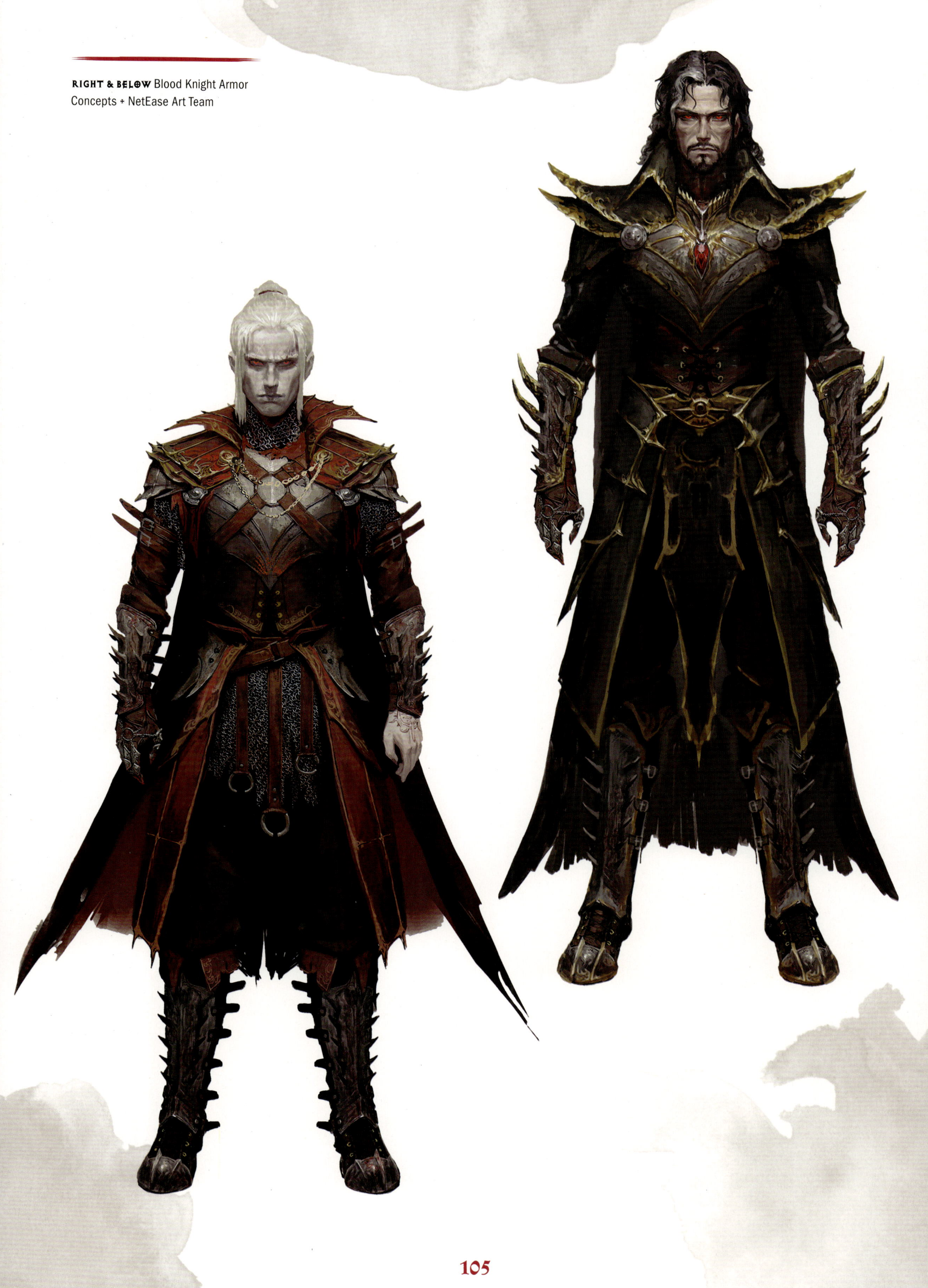

Providing Background

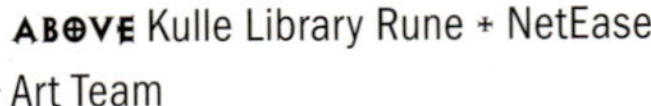

ABOVE Kulle Library Rune + NetEase Art Team

RIGHT Realm of Damnation Concepts + NetEase Art Team

BOTTOM Zone Concept + NetEase Art Team

BELOW Hall of Ascension Concept + Liuweiliang

OPPOSITE Forgotten Tower Illustration + Caozijian

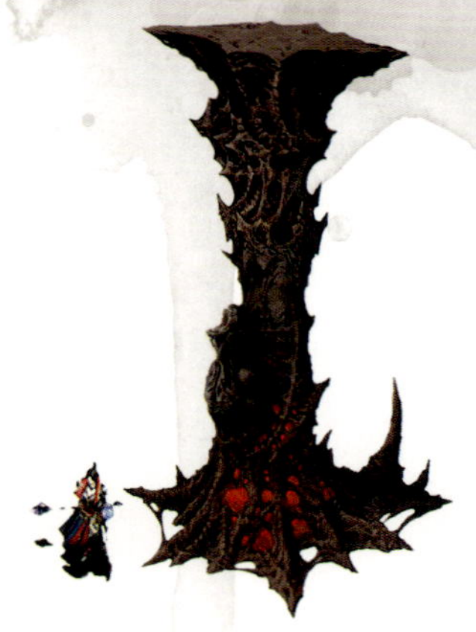

While background colors on *Diablo Immortal* are more enhanced than other installments in the franchise, the environment overall is meant to sit back, or command less attention than the more highly saturated characters, creatures, and especially effects—the elements most important for gameplay.

But there are times when the environment needs to take priority. Often, gameplay will dictate that the character should go in a certain direction or take notice of a particular place of interest. "If there are focal points, you want to make sure they get the most attention in terms of design and color," says art director Hunter Schulz.

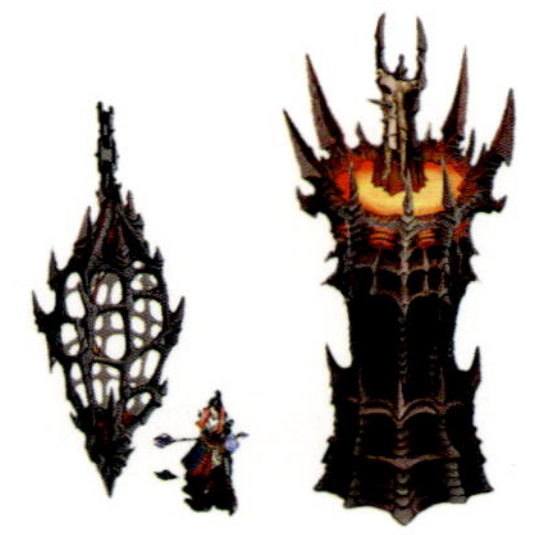

Lighting is one method of directing the player's eye. Schulz uses an in-game wardrobe as an example: "It kind of got lost in the world. You'd just run past it and not even recognize what it was, even though it was interactable. So we ended up putting a spotlight on it, but also giving it a light of its own that it would cast. All of a sudden, it now becomes a place players acknowledge. Even if you're not running to the wardrobe, you take notice of it."

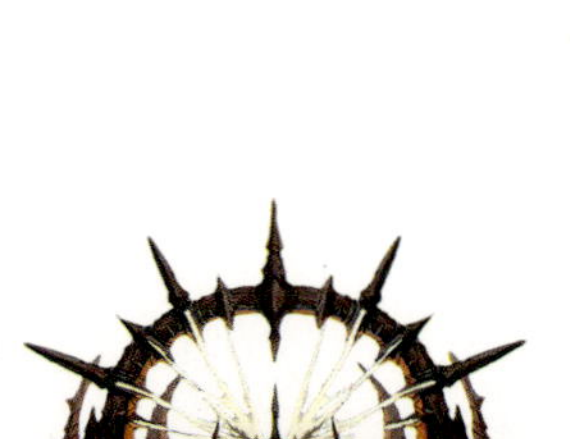

Another point of consideration is distinguishing between zones using color palette, or what is referred to as a "color script."

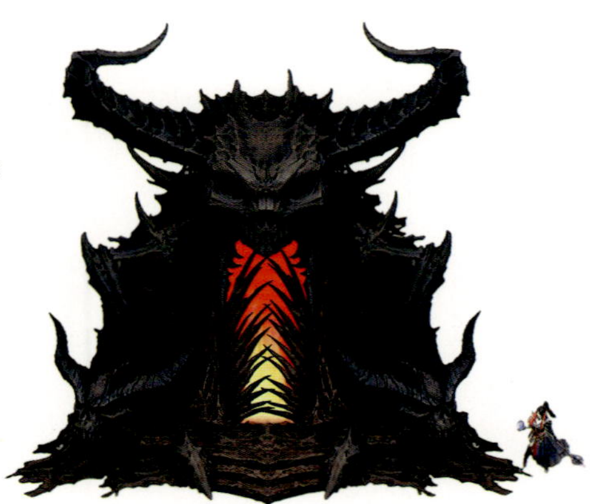

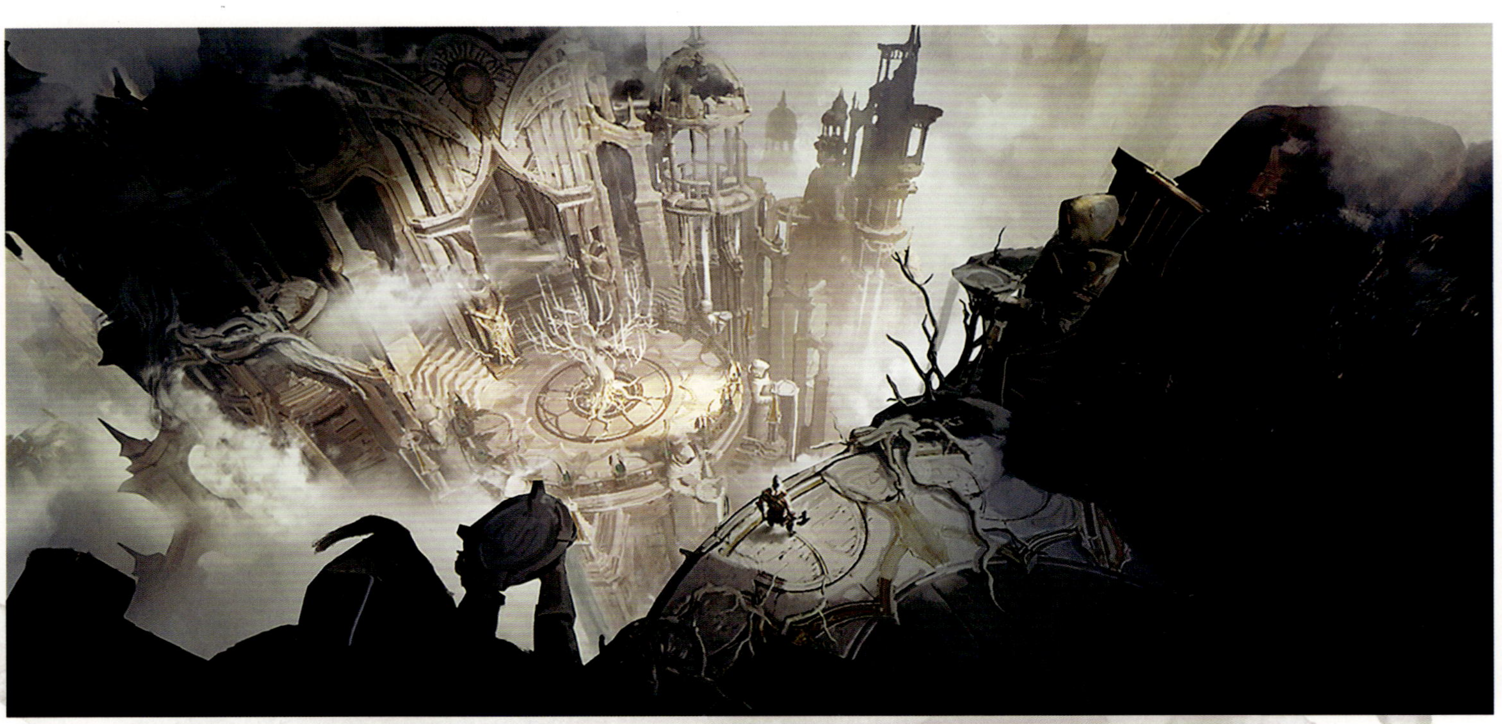

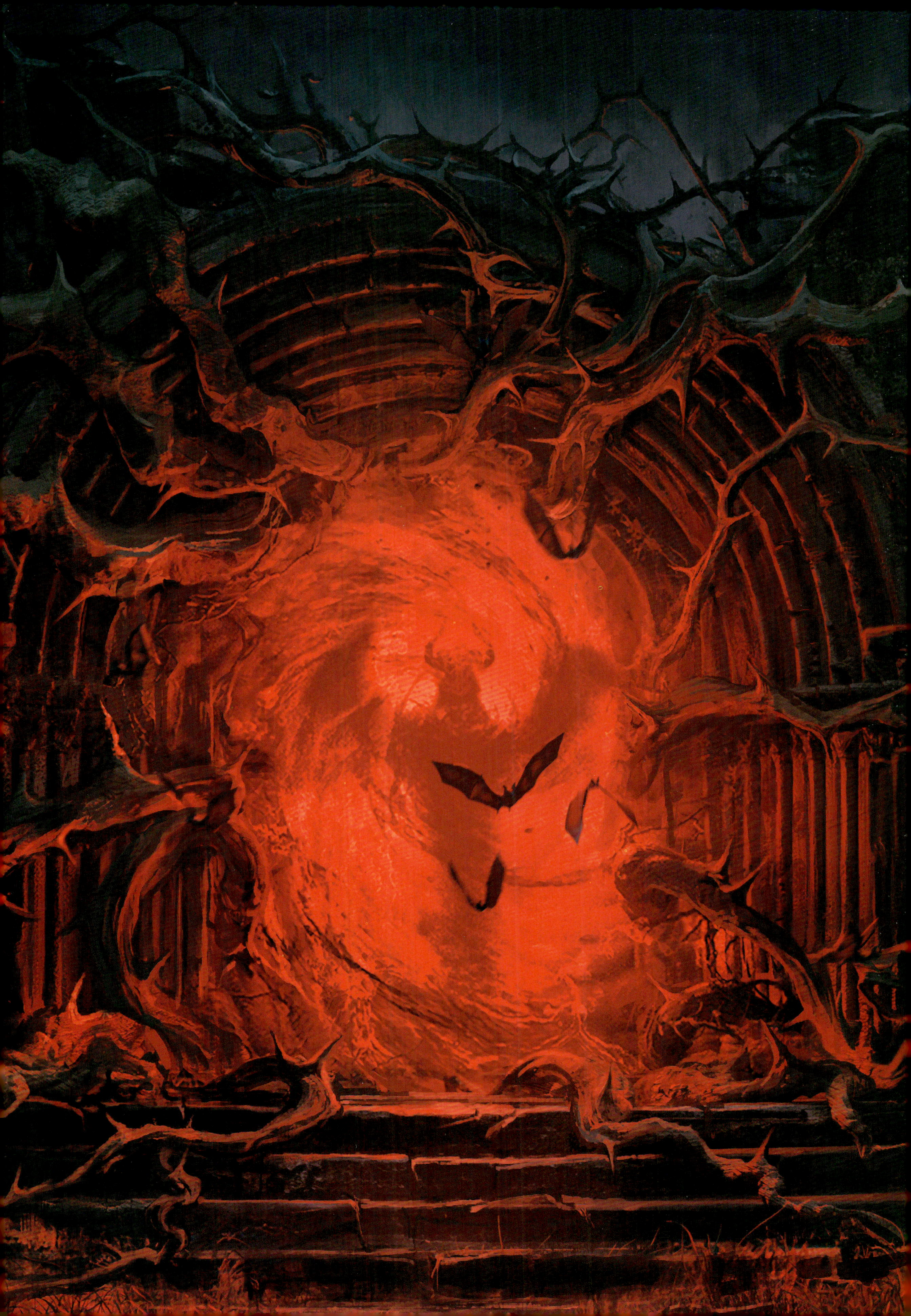

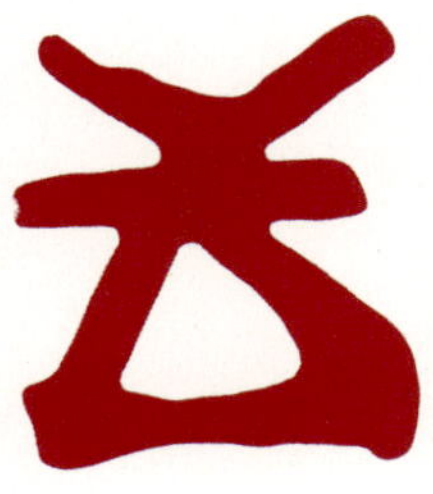

ABOVE Kulle Library Rune • NetEase Art Team

RIGHT, TOP & MIDDLE Shassar Sea Prop Concept • NetEase Art Team

BOTTOM Tree of Inifuss Concept • Rayson

OPPOSITE, TOP Early Westmarch Concept • NetEase Art Team

OPPOSITE, MIDDLE Realm of Damnation Concept • NetEase Art Team

OPPOSITE, BOTTOM Tristram Cathedral Dungeon Illustration • Caozijian

"The big thing for us was making sure each zone had its own palette," says Schulz. "That was always something I was pushing, so that when you ventured into a new zone, you registered it. I think that's important for a few reasons: to remember the zones clearly, to reward the player for advancing through the world in the game, and then just for your eyes to keep you engaged."

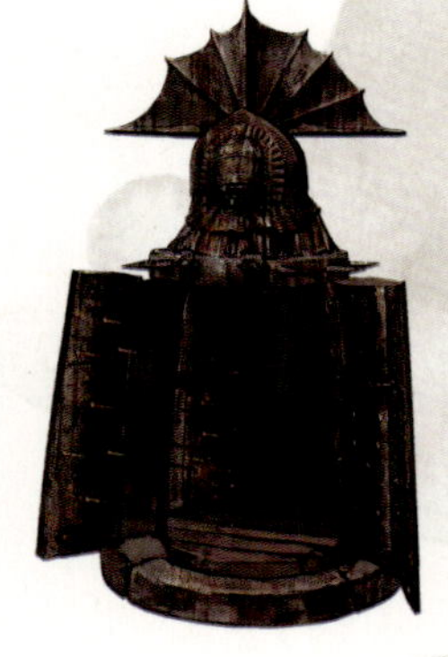

Related to this are the concepts of value and contrast. "Value" refers to the spectrum of a color or hue from light to dark. Differentiating values between characters, monsters, and environment makes for a clearer read.

Associate art director Richie Marella provides an example: "Let's say you have a grassy field. The tall grass would go on the side to create contrast when the shadow at the screen's edge hits it, along with rocks. All of that volume and silhouette is on the outside, and then you have this nice playable space on the inside that has less contrast and is a lot more visible and clean for gameplay."

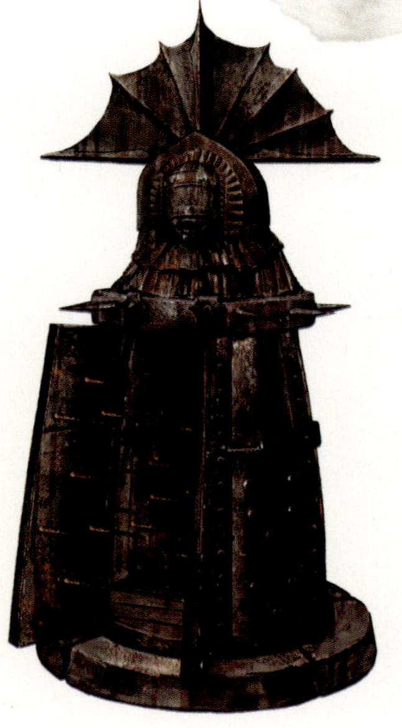

That gameplay space is the most important area of all. The ground texture needs to be relatively clean and simple so that the player can concentrate on gameplay. This is aided by the "hope light" that shines down from above. Rest and detail are also important. "Rest" is the term used for areas of a texture with minimal detail. "When you have a lot of spells going around," Richie continues, "it can get really busy really quickly, so we want to make sure that gameplay space is detailed in the right places."

Diablo Immortal artists used every tool in their toolkit to ensure that environments would sit back in their intended place, only taking center stage when the action of the game called for it.

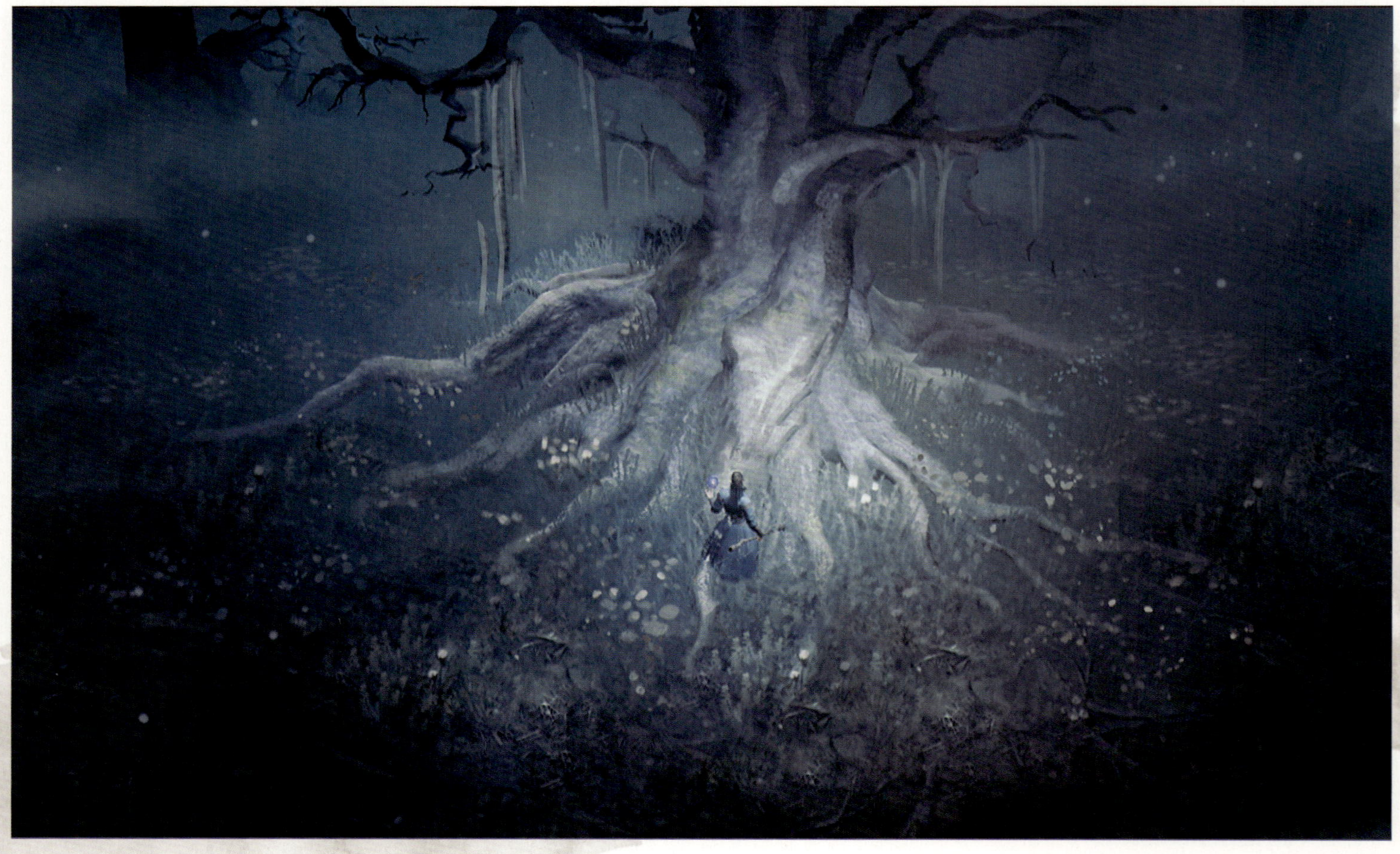

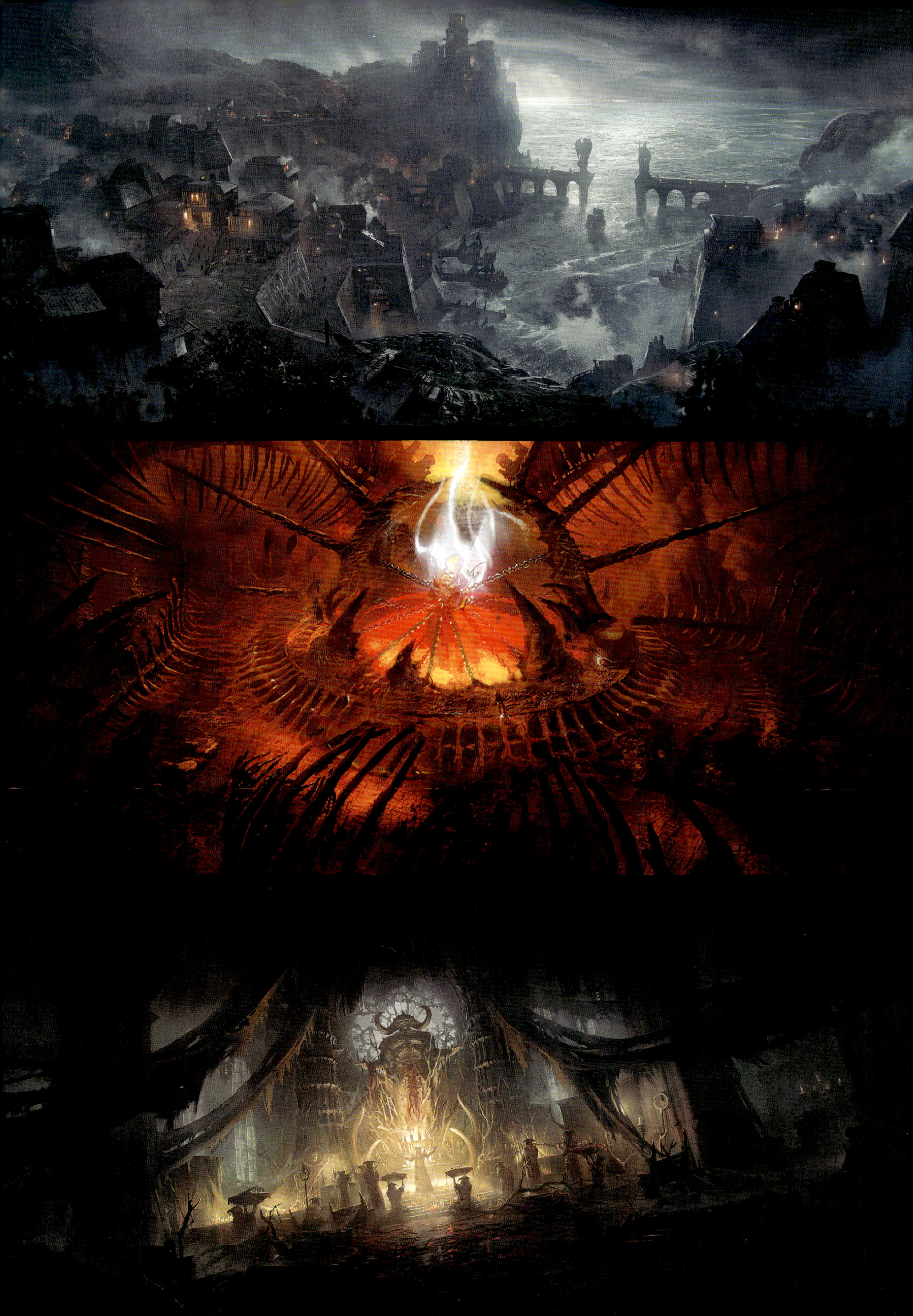

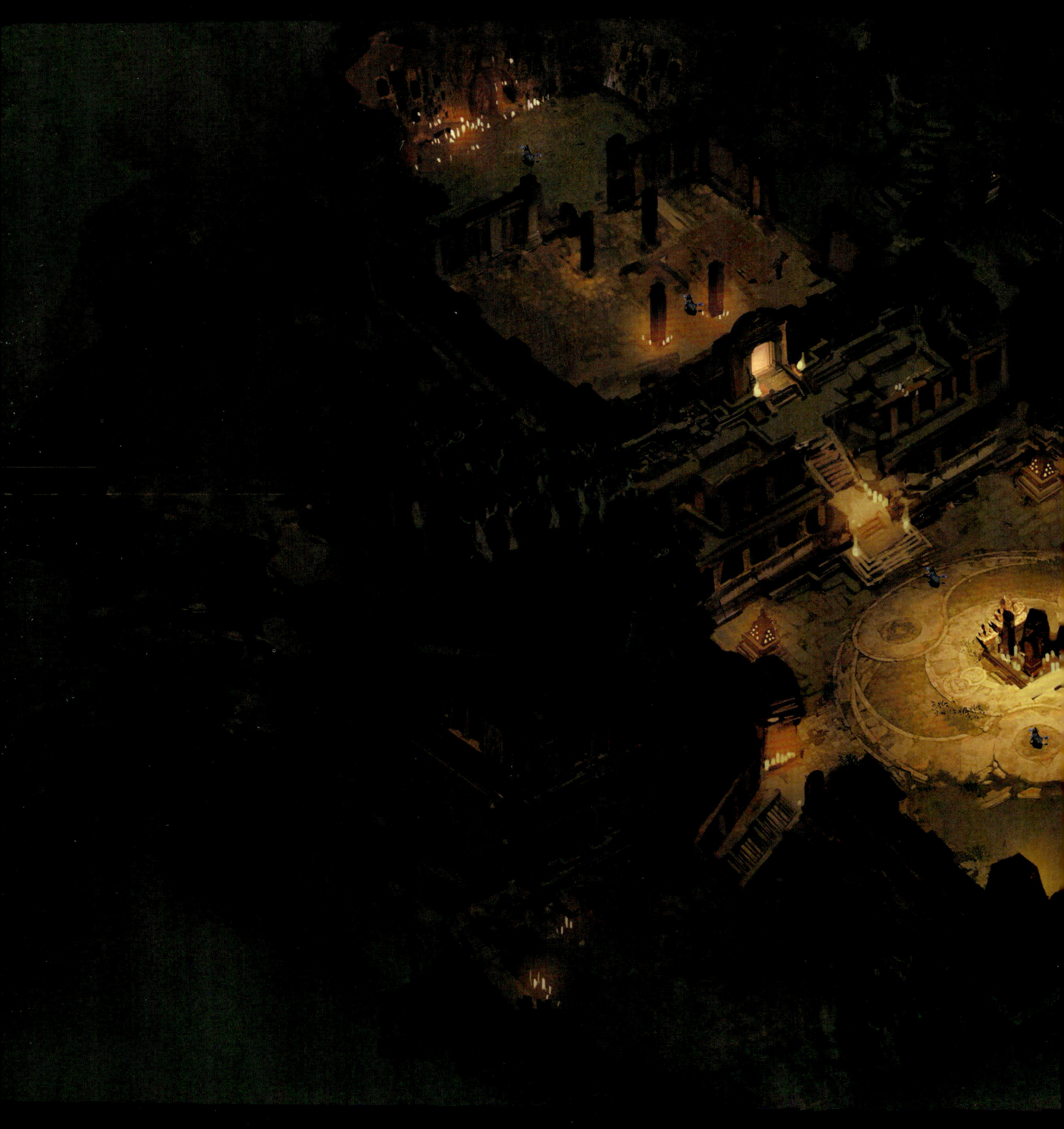

ABOVE Sanctified Earth Monastery Concept • Xiaoquangui

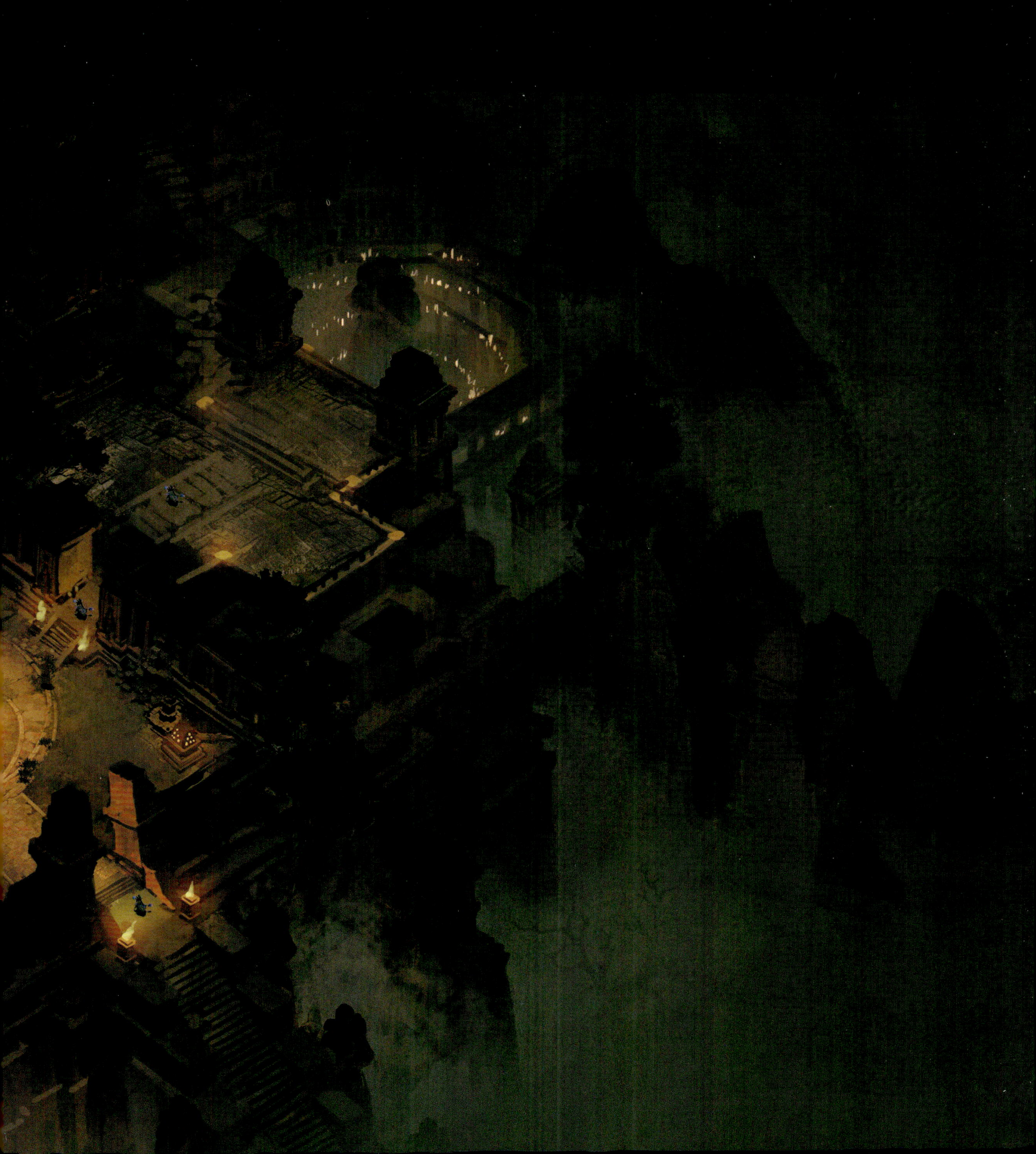

"With lighting, it is exactly what it should be: light the areas where you want the players to go. If there's a point of interest, make sure that is recognizable."

—HUNTER SCHULZ, Art Director

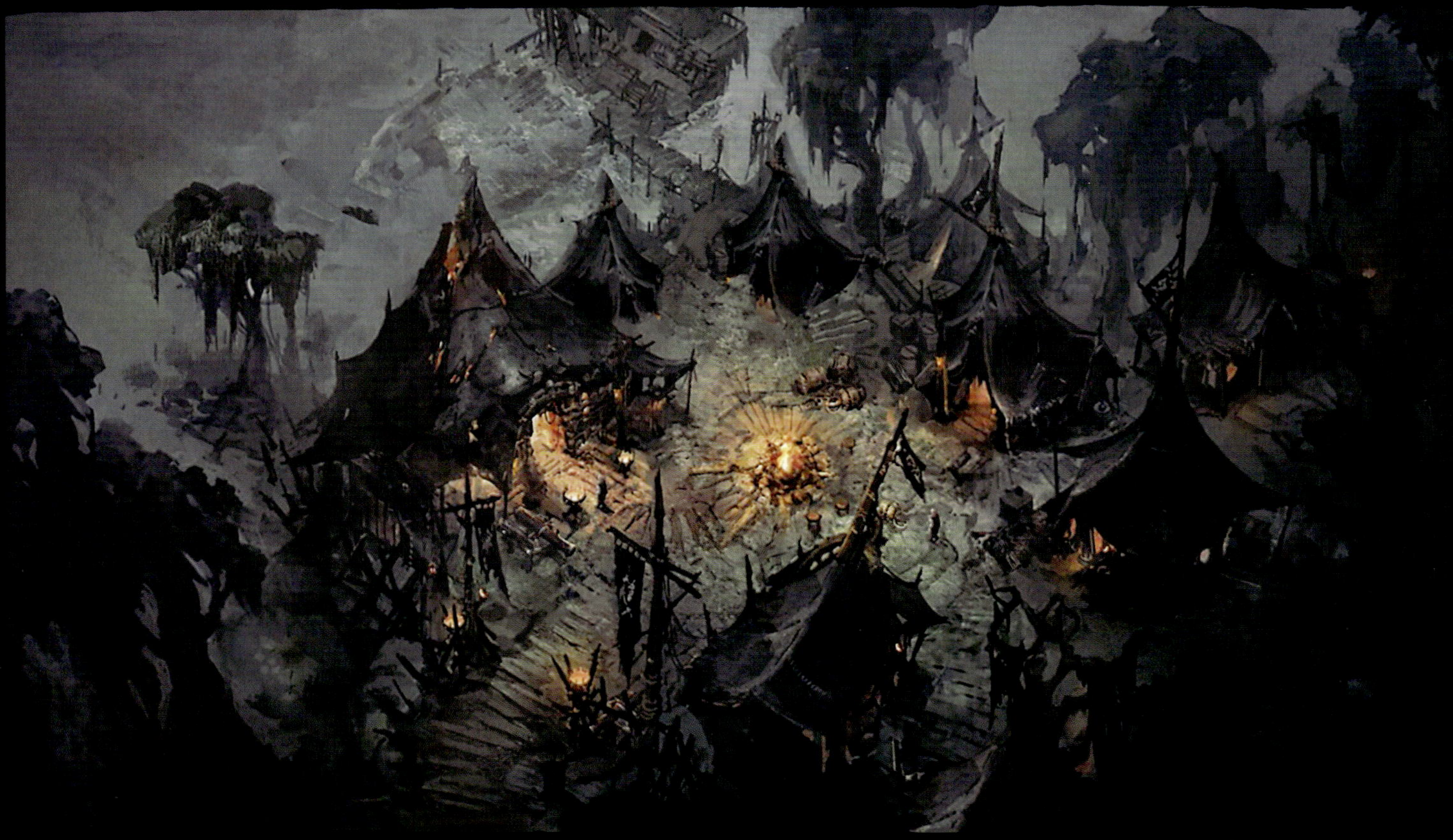

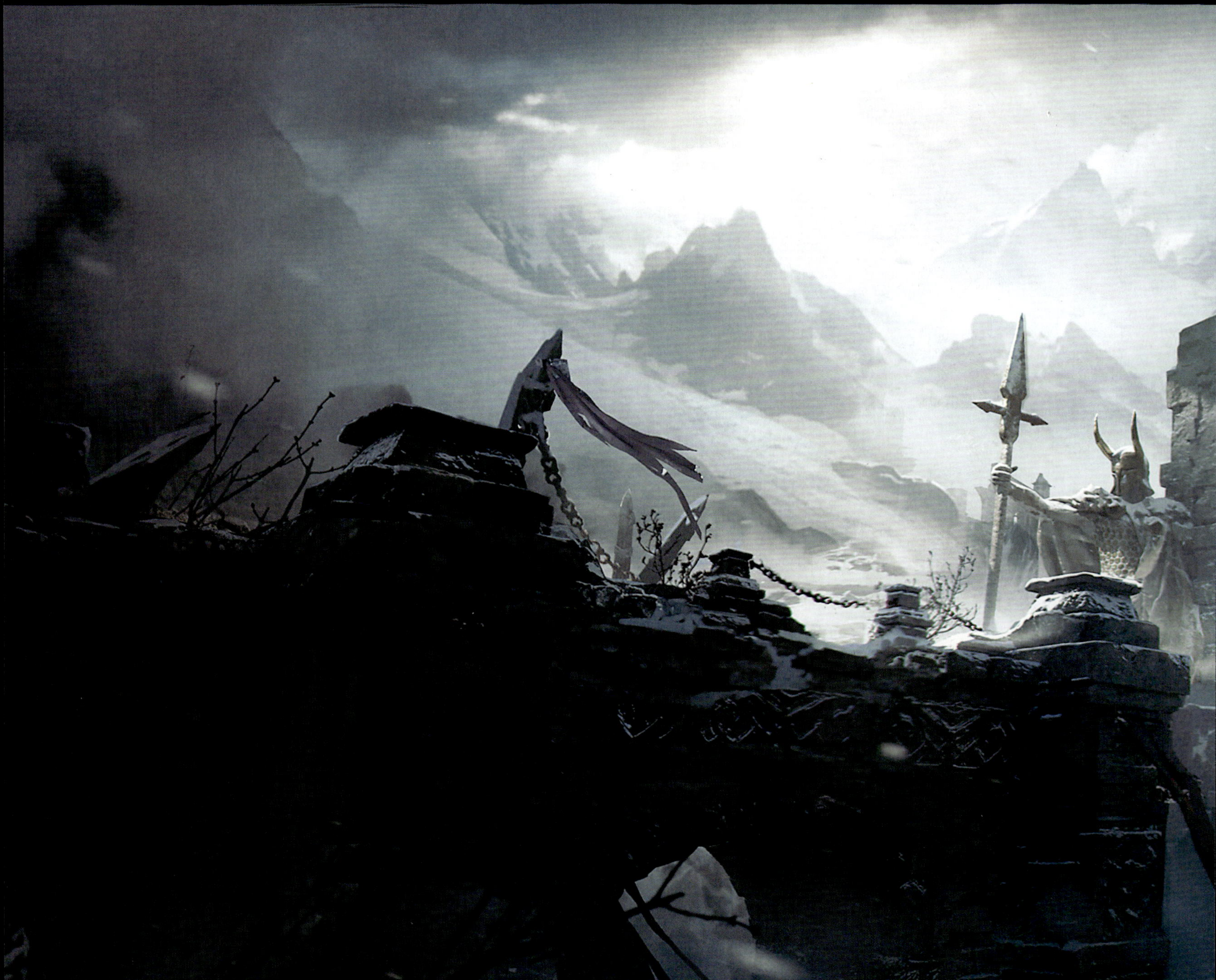

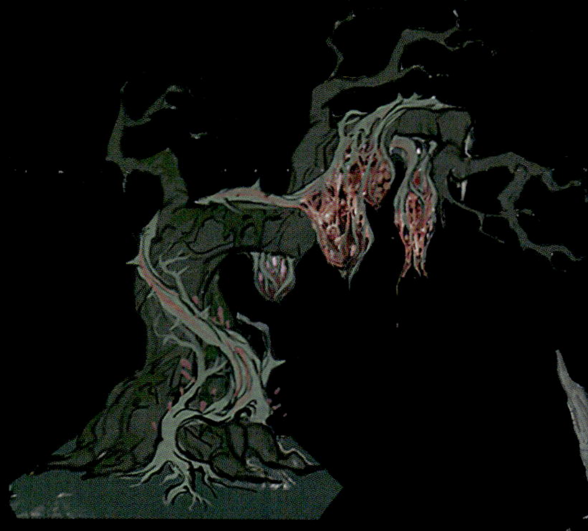

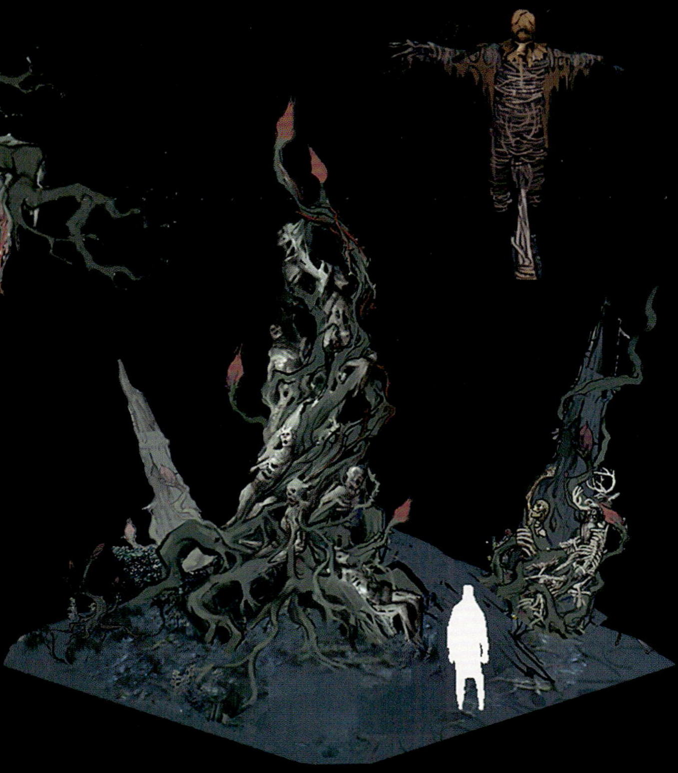

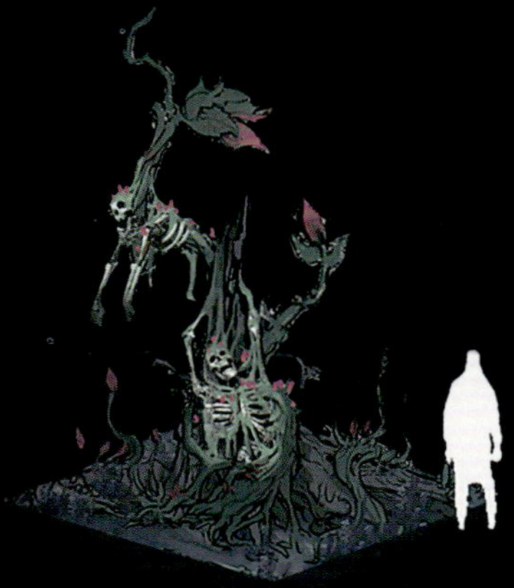

TOP Dark Wood Concepts • NetEase Art Team
BOTTOM Frozen Tundra Key Art • NetEase Art Team
OPPOSITE Bilefen Concept • NetEase Art Team

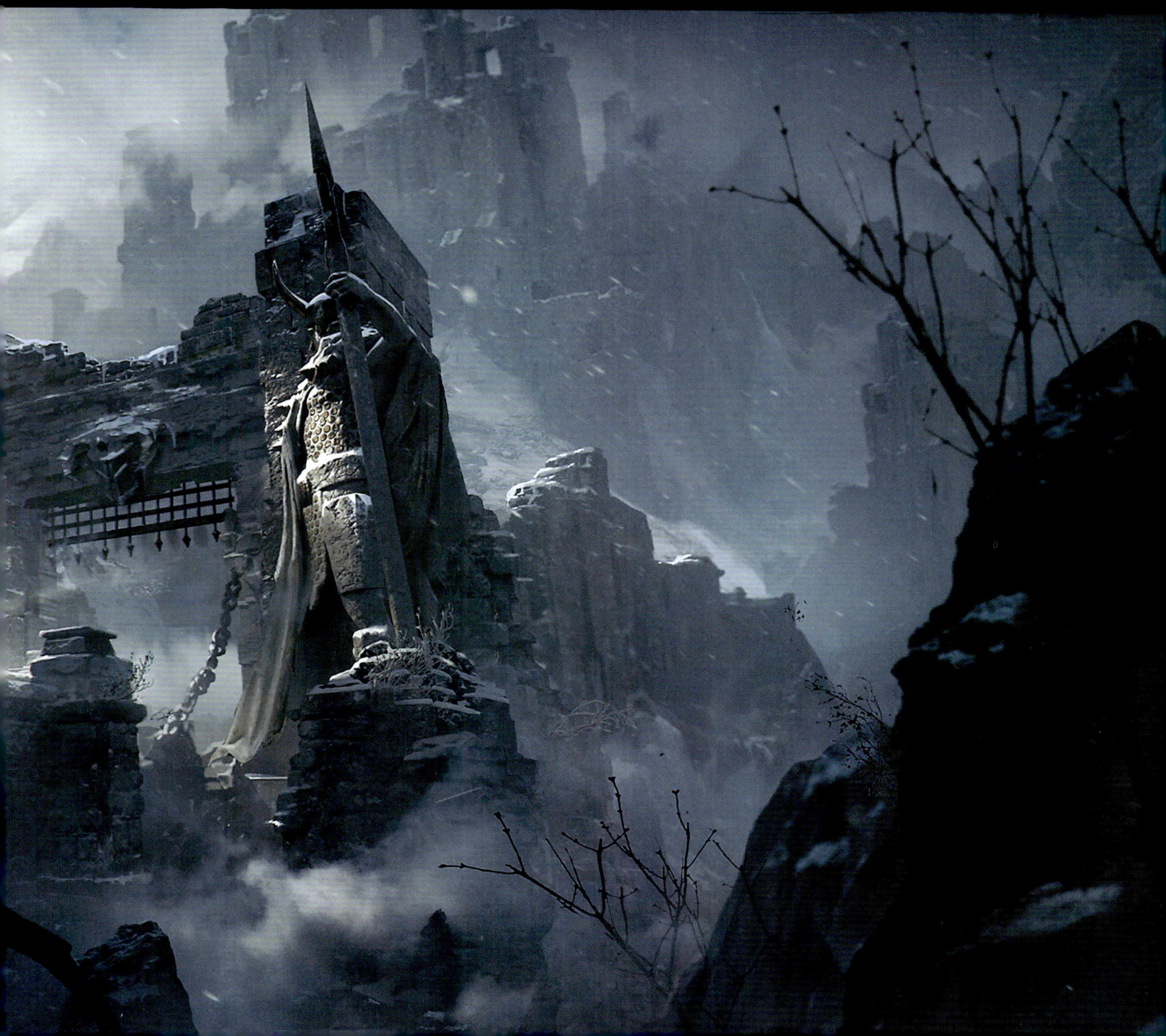

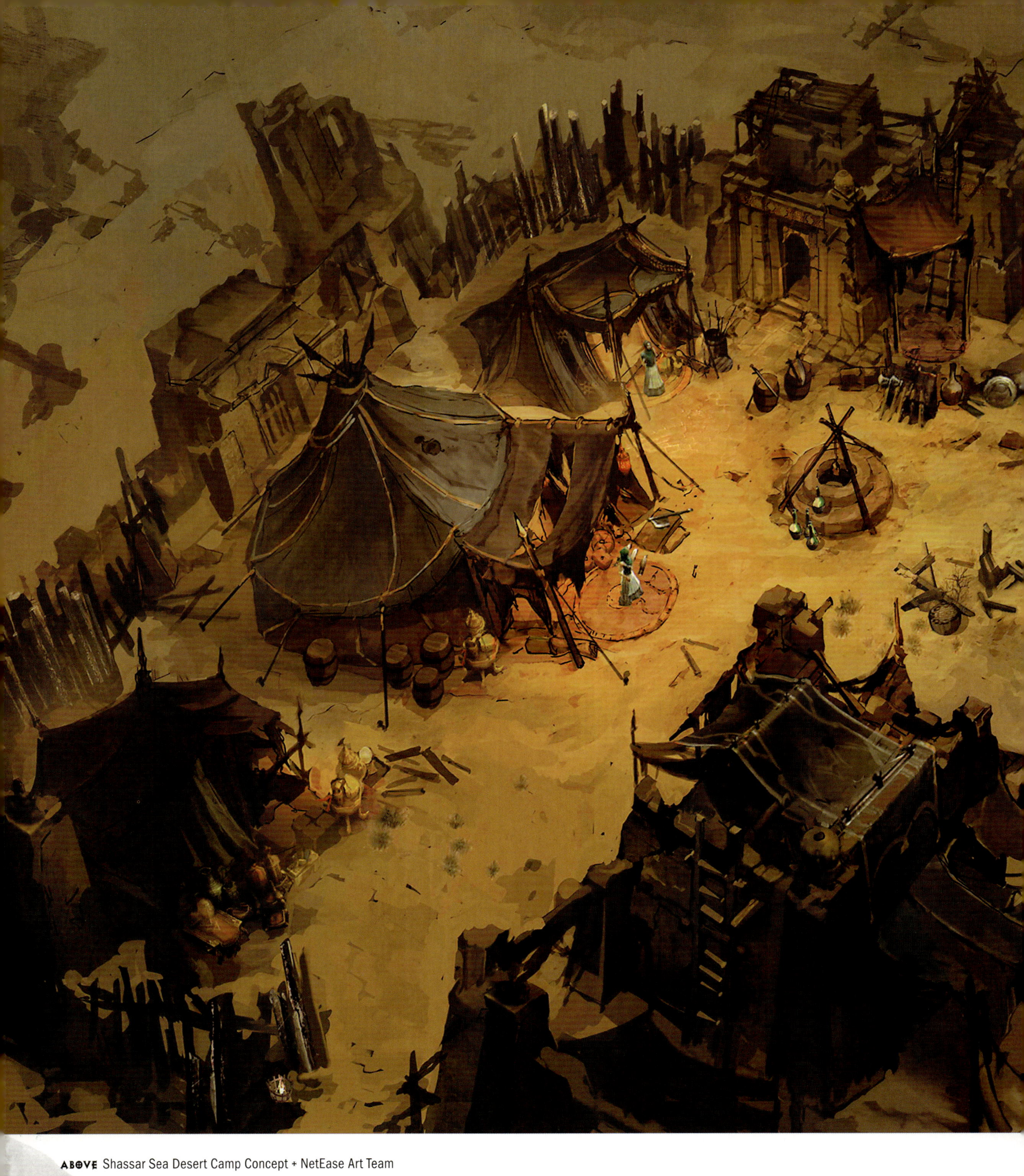

ABOVE Shassar Sea Desert Camp Concept + NetEase Art Team

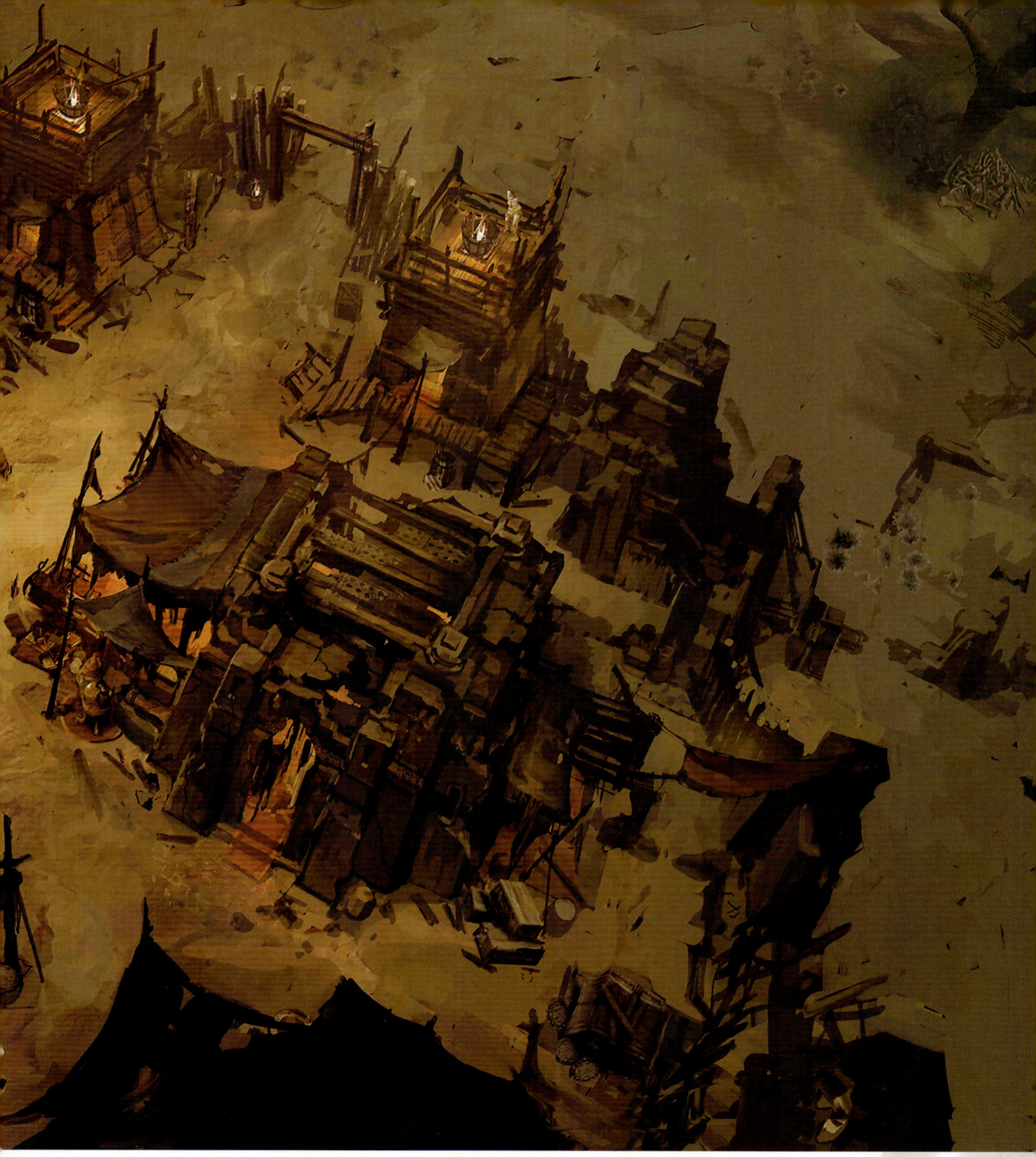

"Characters need to fit in the scene, and the villages have to sit in the landscape so that everything is seamless. Nothing should pop out and draw your attention unintentionally. Even if things look interesting but don't quite fit, it would not be good because that immediately breaks immersion."

—VICTOR LEE, Lead Concept Artist

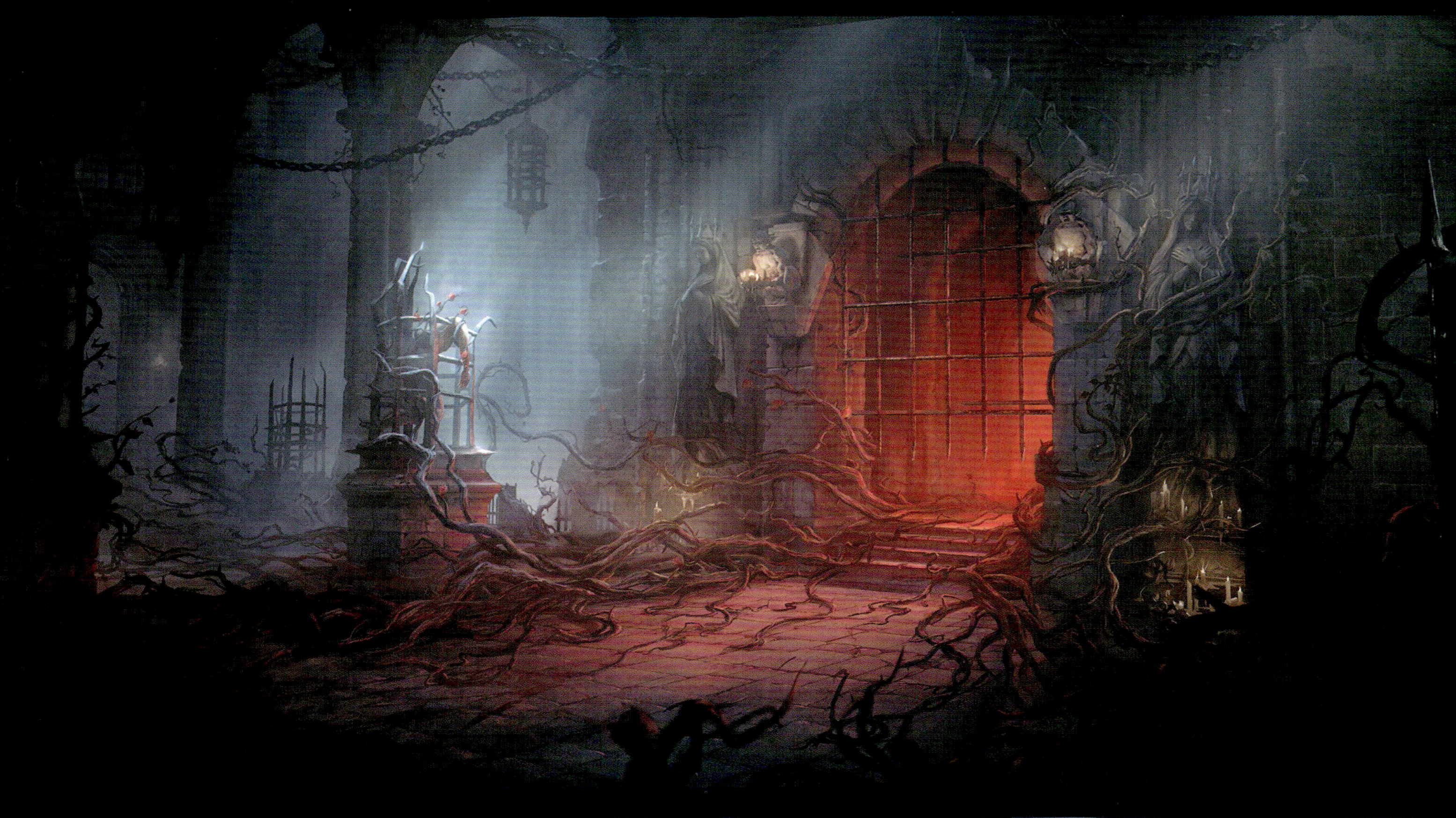

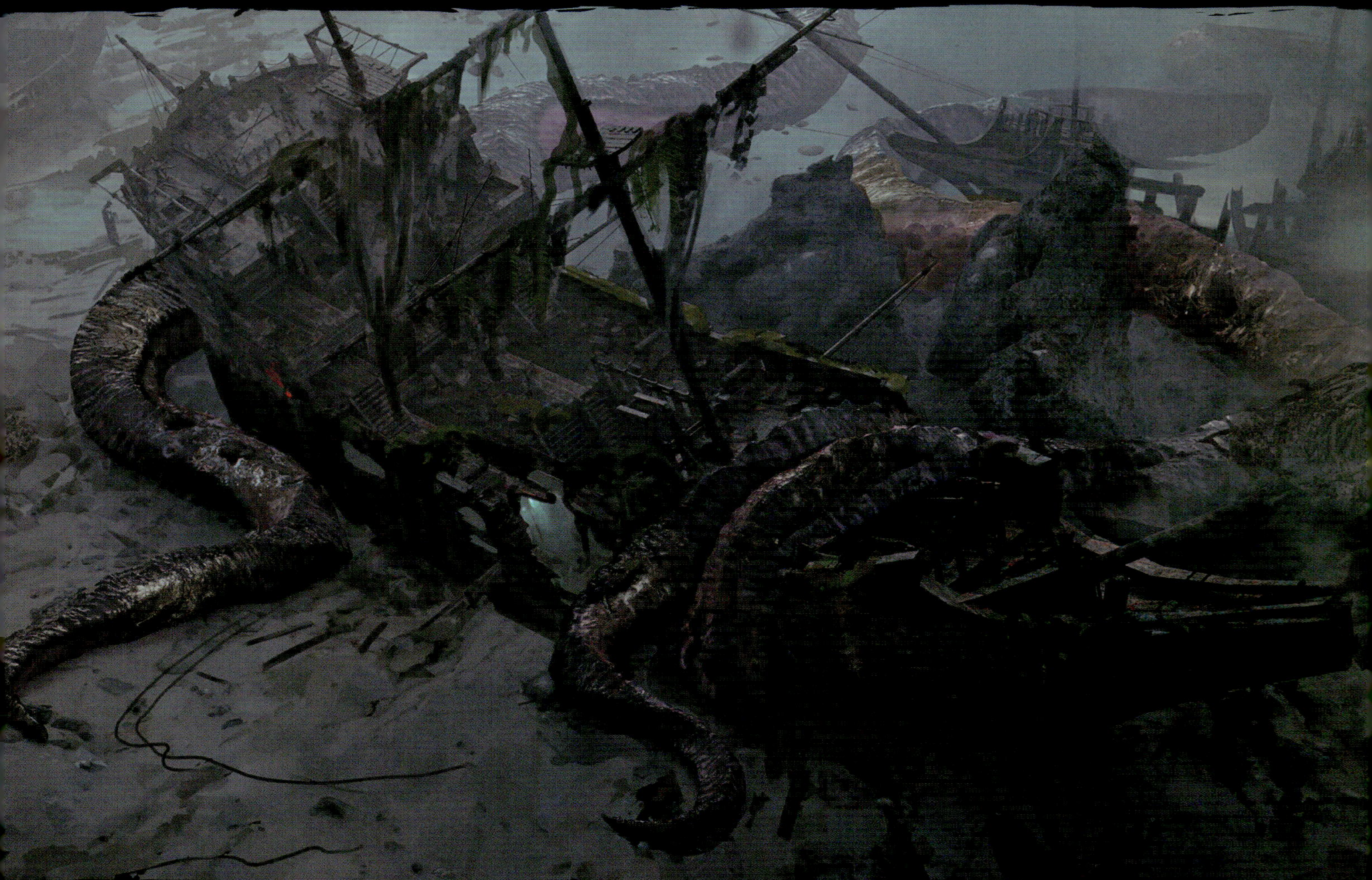

ABOVE, TOP Forgotten Tower Illustration + Shuchuan

ABOVE, BOTTOM Stormpoint Concept + Rayson

RIGHT Highlands Church Wall Concepts + NetEase Art Team

MIDDLE, RIGHT Terror's Tide Concept + NetEase Art Team

MIDDLE, LEFT Destruction's End Concept + NetEase Art Team

BELOW & BOTTOM Forgotten Tower Concepts + NetEase Art Team

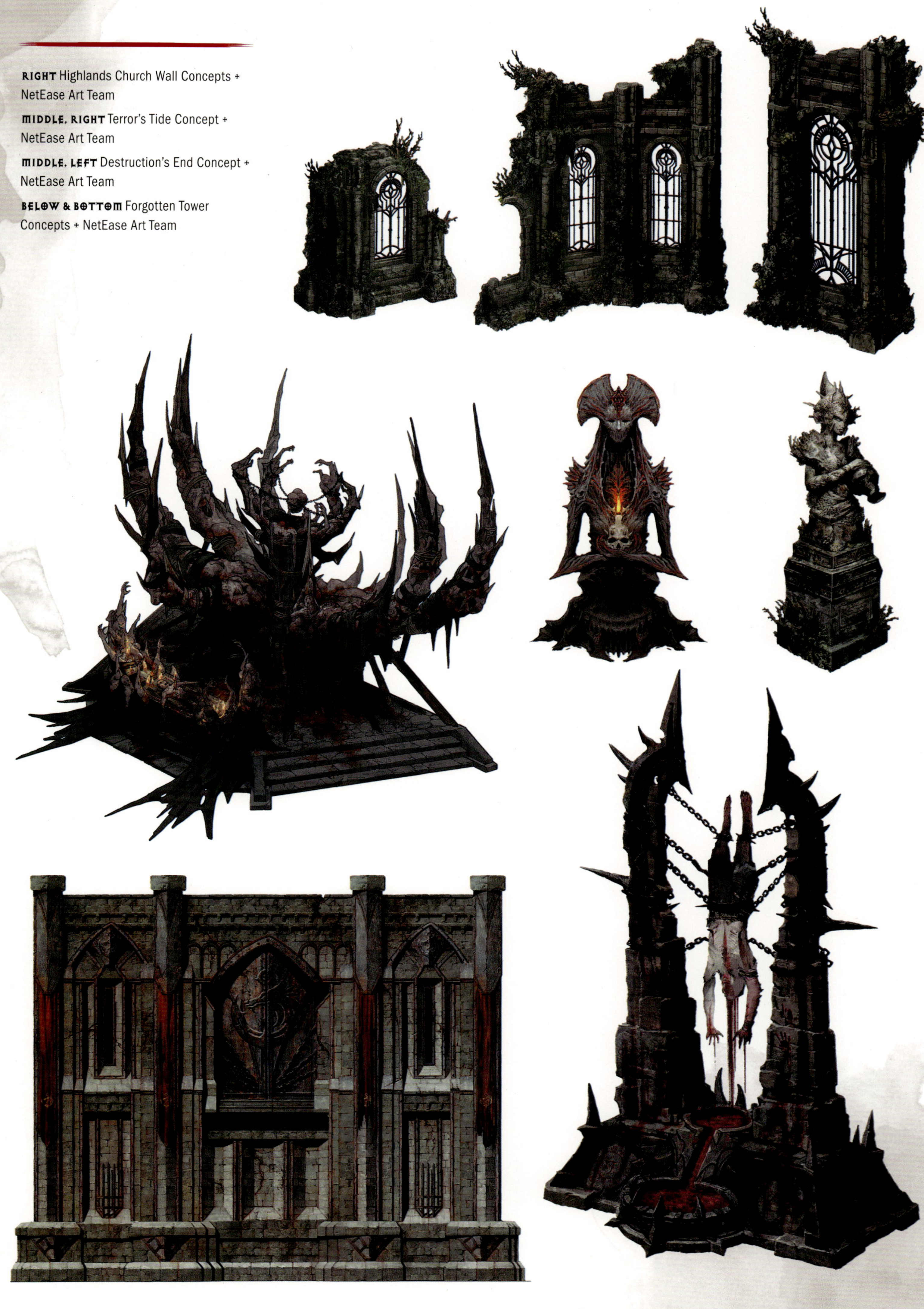

OPPOSITE Stormpoint Concept • NetEase Art Team

BOTTOM Dread Reaver Concept • Liuweiliang

"When we first had our beta, people who looked at it would say, 'Wow, it's almost too dark. The dark is so crushing sometimes.' Then again, you could still see the hesitation because they'd also say, 'I don't know. It's a Diablo *game. I think that's good. I think we want the darkness.'"*

—KEVIN TODISCO, Lead Graphics Engineer

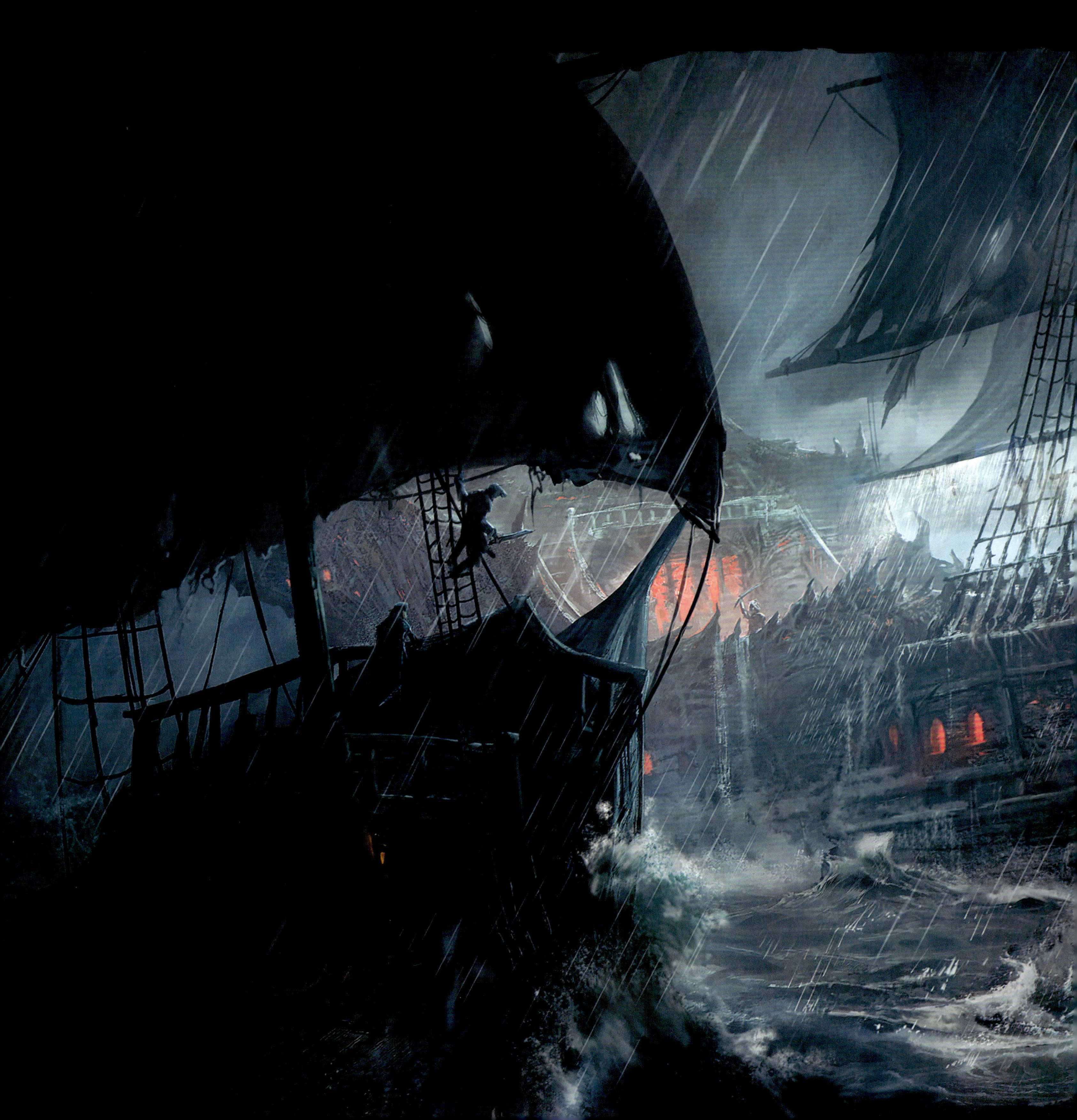

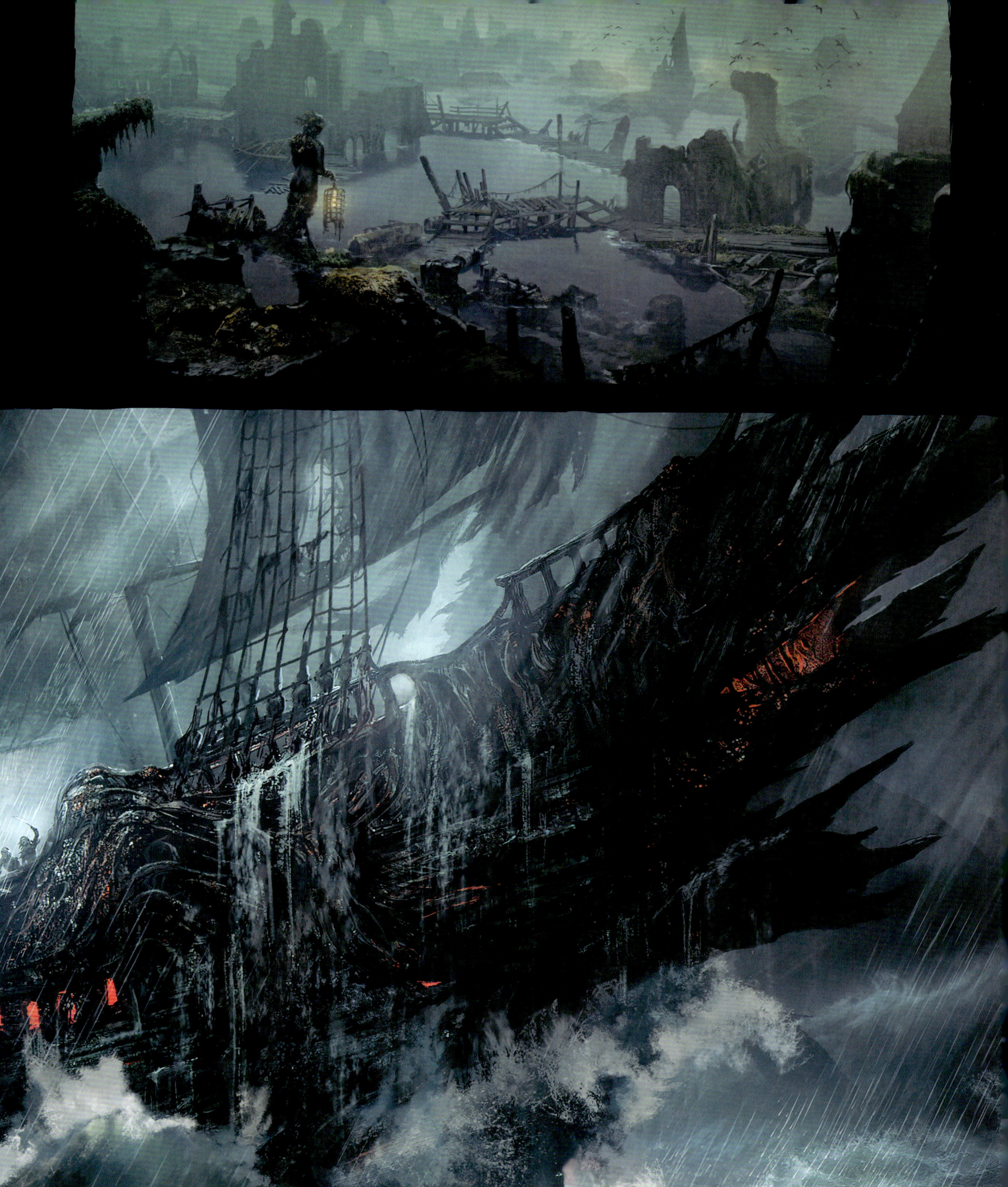

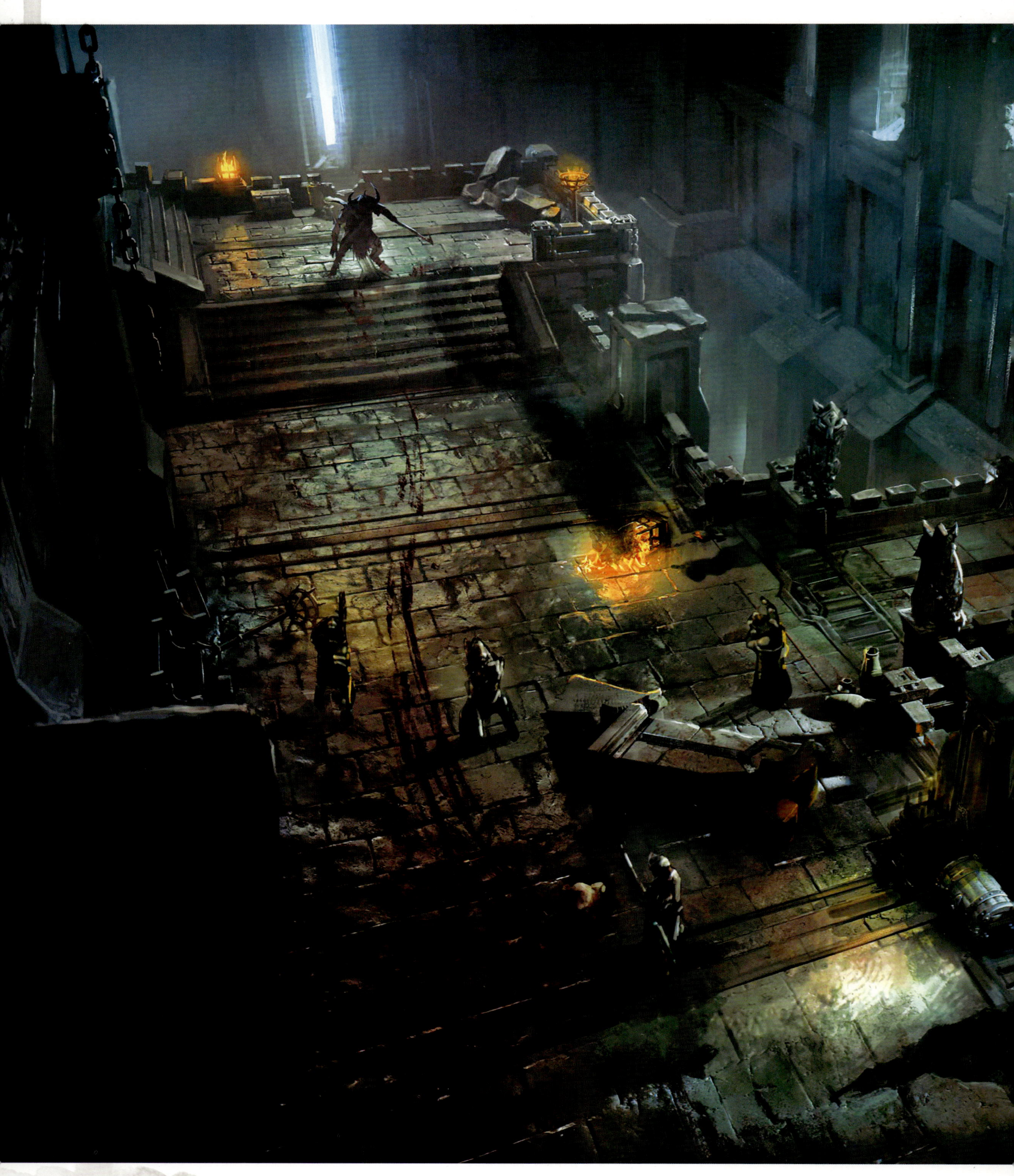

ABOVE Mad King's Breach Concept + NetEase Art Team

FOLLOWING SPREAD Resurrection Chamber Concept + NetEase Art Team

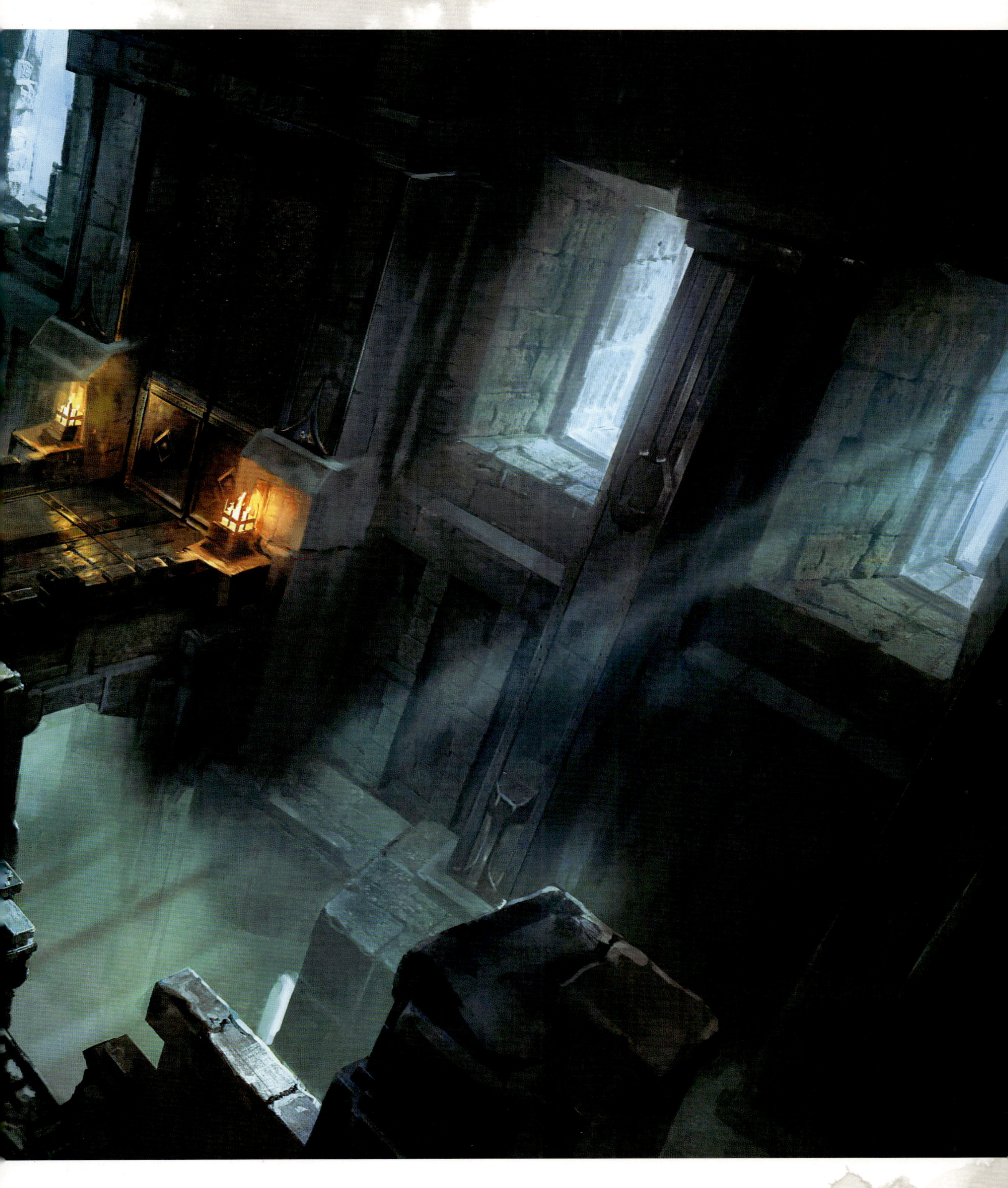

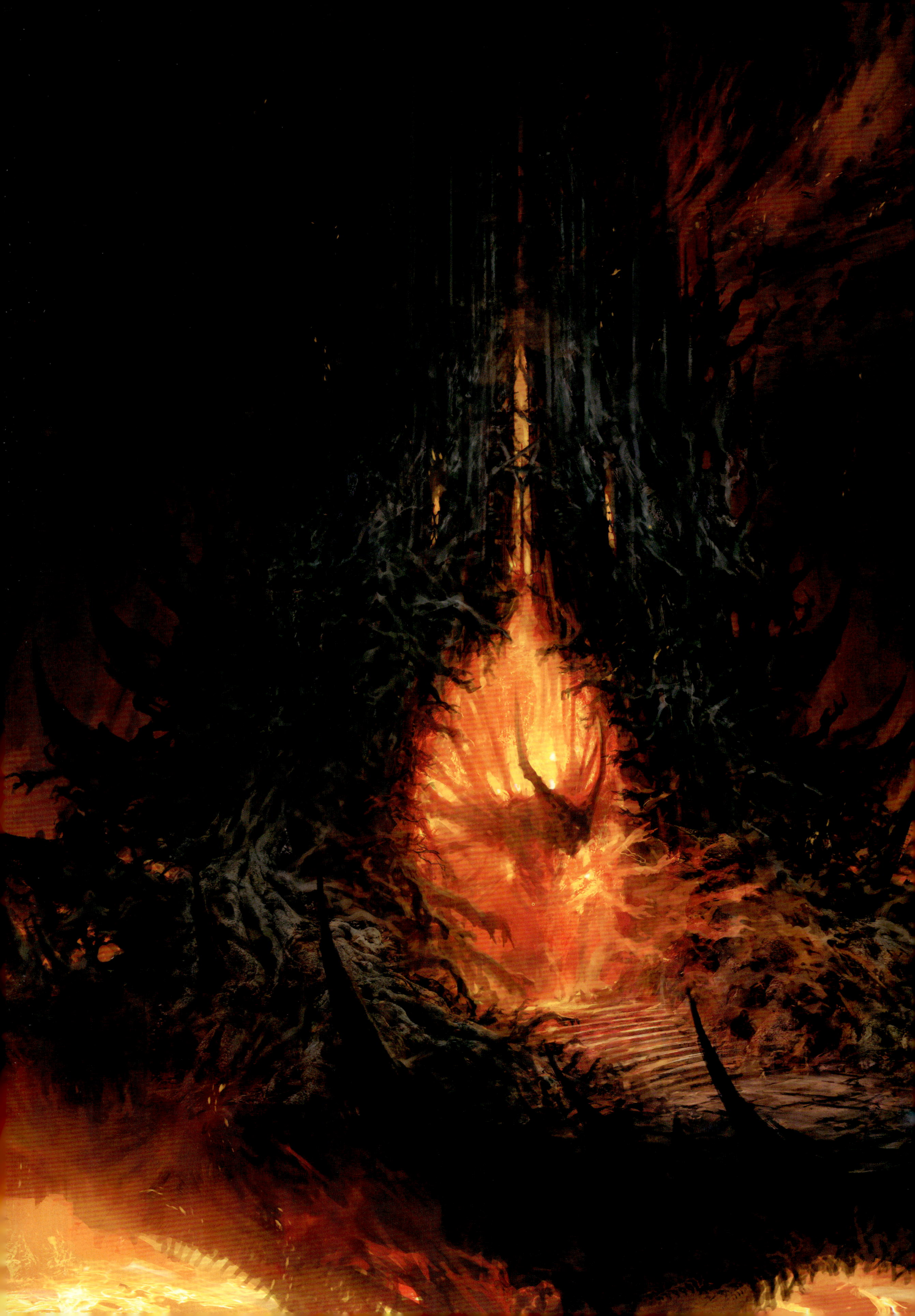

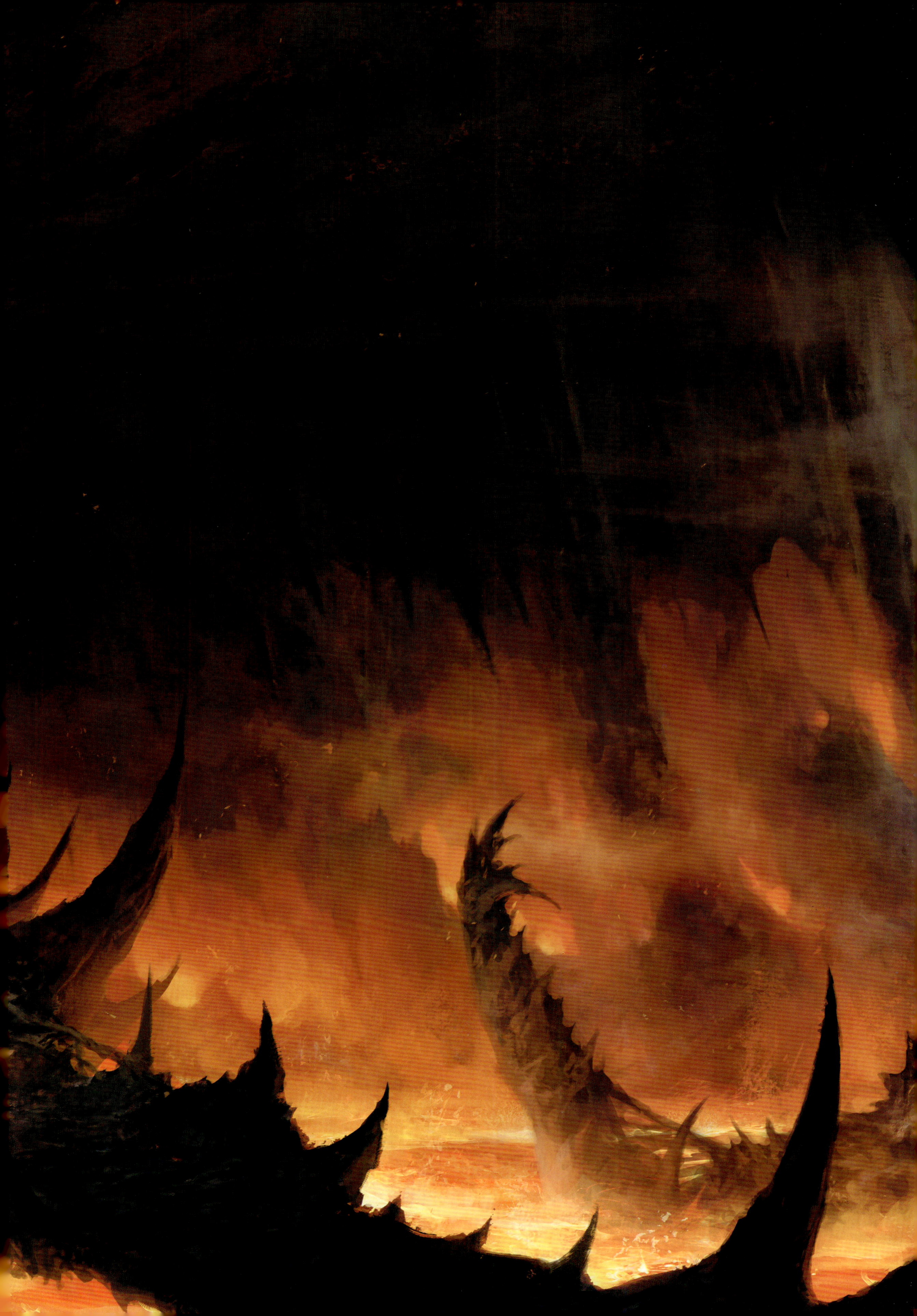

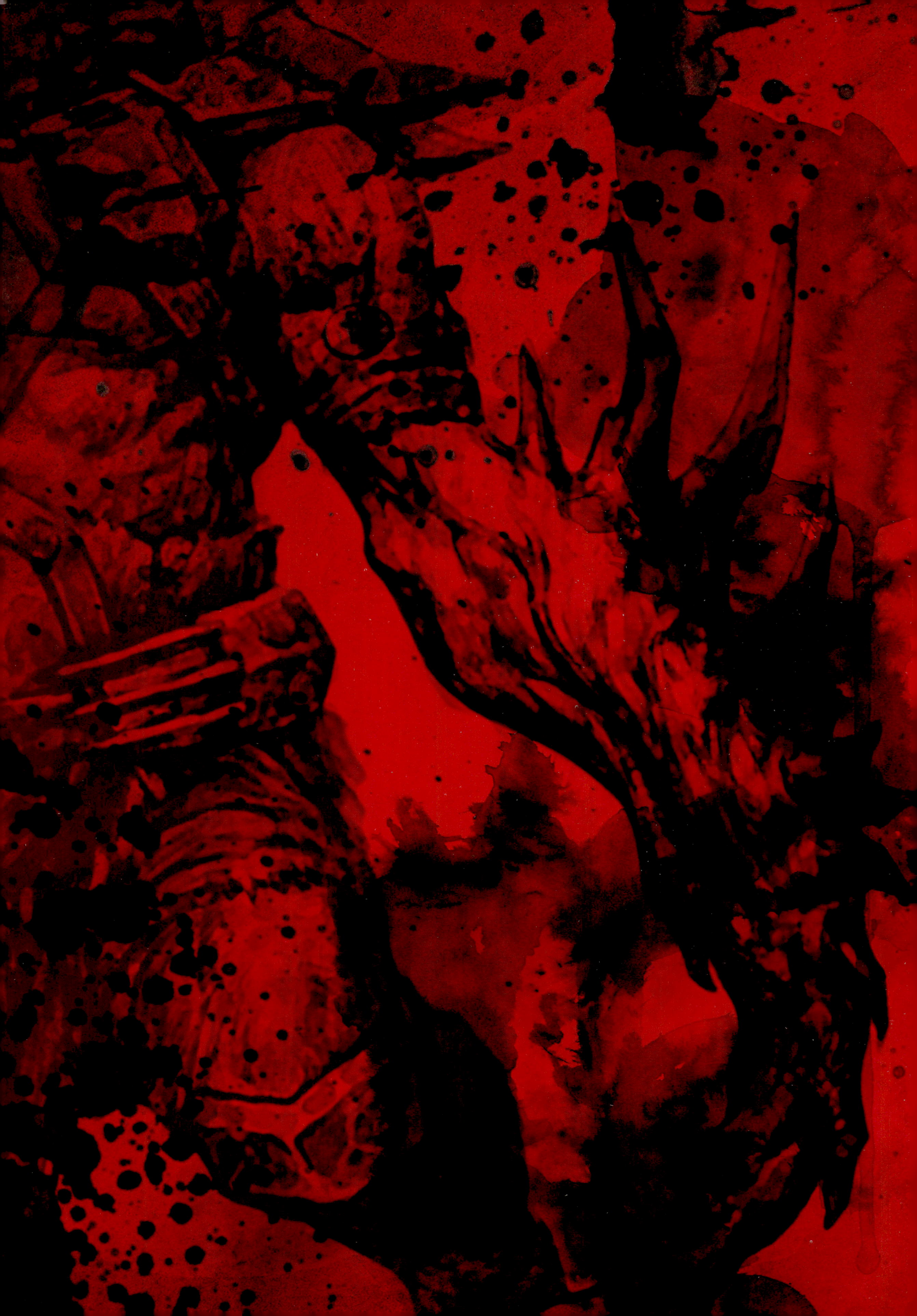

Return to Darkness

Diablo IV introduced a bold aesthetic that broke new artistic ground while maintaining the dark and dismal tones of past entries, a look and feel that was only discovered after a long journey of exploration.

"Early on, there was a question of style," says *Diablo* art director John Mueller. "How stylized was *Diablo IV* going to be? You think of *World of Warcraft* and *Overwatch* as having very distinct, colorful styles . . . and then there's *Diablo*. To me, the right move was to make something that felt wholly unique but also embraced what makes *Diablo* beloved to our fans. That made us look at *Diablo II* because it has a more grounded aesthetic, and I sometimes said that our goal was to thread the needle between *Diablo II* and *Diablo III* . . . but with the technology of today."

The *Diablo IV* team wanted an aesthetic that was more graphic and classical than *Diablo III*. But the balance between *Diablo II* and *III* was a delicate one to achieve.

As development continued, certain guidelines began to emerge to help keep the style grounded and separate from your standard high fantasy. The decision was made to stay away from a lot of colorful crystals and magical objects that floated at random. Spots where the game *did* engage with higher fantasy were focused and intentional. "Everything is more grounded," explains lead concept artist Victor Lee. "Like the materials in the armor. Everything has to be readable—whether it's understanding that something is leather or metal—and doesn't include fantastical materials. There are no plastic-looking things. Everything had to look like it could have been made in that environment in that time period with the appropriate craftspeople, like a blacksmith or a leatherworker."

Another pillar that *Diablo IV* was built on was known as the "old masters pillar," based around a painting style called the Hudson River School, which focuses on the beauty of nature.

"There's a lot of a 'tonal wash' appearance," says character lead Cory Turner. "A liberal use of fog and depth. Making sure things stand out and don't fall too much in shadow or get too washed out. Making sure the colors aren't too underbaked. It's like you're doing a painting, then you're doing a glaze, ensuring that the integrity of the individual assets and colors still show through."

All of these choices were measured against the most important question of all: Does it look and feel like *Diablo*? Hitting that mark was a process that evolved over time and oftentimes involved revisiting old art.

The end result is a new kind of Sanctuary, one forged by dedicated artisans equipped with bleeding-edge tools and new techniques: a classical, old masters' painting come to life.

In the Company of Heroes

ABOVE Barbarian Lettering + Fernando Pinilla

RIGHT Early Witch Concept + Victor Lee

BOTTOM, RIGHT Early Witch Concept + Victor Lee

BOTTOM, LEFT Early Witch Concept + Victor Lee

BELOW Early Witch Concept + Victor Lee

OPPOSITE Early Witch Concept + Victor Lee

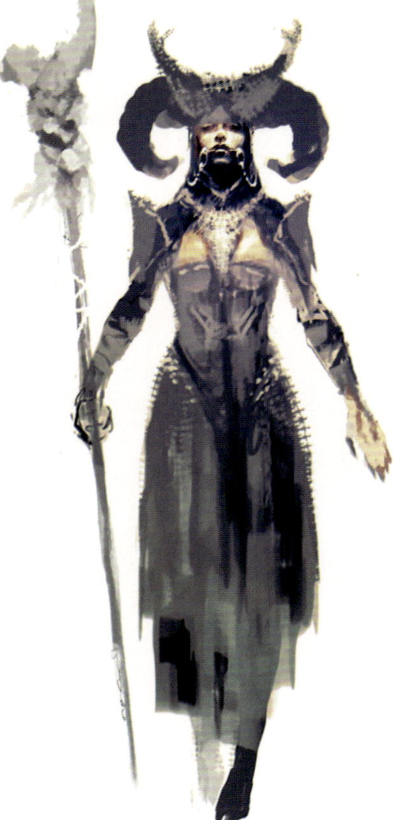

Although the franchise had been firmly established when the creators of *Diablo IV* set to work, the development of classes began with a period of exploration.

"The Sorceress was called the Witch class," says principal concept artist Rob Sevilla. "The Rogue was called the Assassin. So for some of the classes, we were bouncing around trying to figure out what to settle on."

It was necessary for all of these classes to adhere to the overall vision for *Diablo IV*—a return to darkness.

"If you look at the tonal spectrum," Sevilla continues, "you have the Sorcerer and the Barbarian on the lighter end in terms of how dark the class should feel, versus the Necromancer, who is completely on the other side of that."

Nearer to the middle of the spectrum, the Assassin class began as a kind of brutal mercenary for hire before evolving into its final form as the Rogue, a character that is equally as deadly, yet fights with a code of honor.

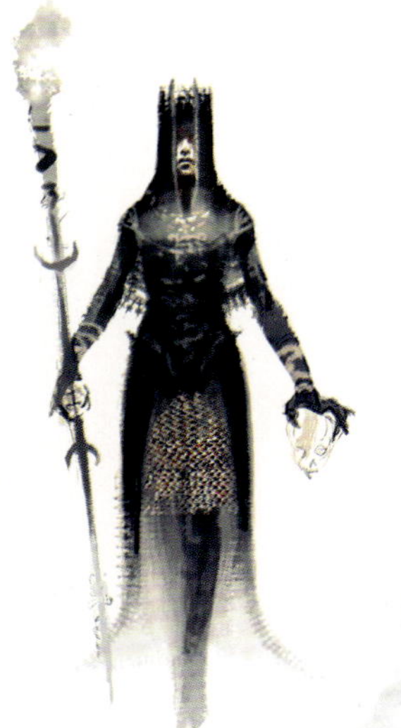

In addition to hitting the right tone, class designs needed to feel grounded, gothic, and of course . . . dark. But what exactly does that mean when it comes to design choices?

Sevilla explains: "What dark meant to me, was that it can't have anything that felt like it would overly fantasize a certain design. With the Necromancer, for example, I designed a skull with a gibbet around the skull. That felt more grounded than having a skull that was floating with magic."

Another important early consideration was diversity, including both ethnicity and gender.

"We wanted this customization to let people do what they want to do," says associate art director Arnaud Kotelnikoff. "In different parts of the world, people picture a class like the Barbarian differently. We want people to express themselves. We have to be true to the class but still give freedom."

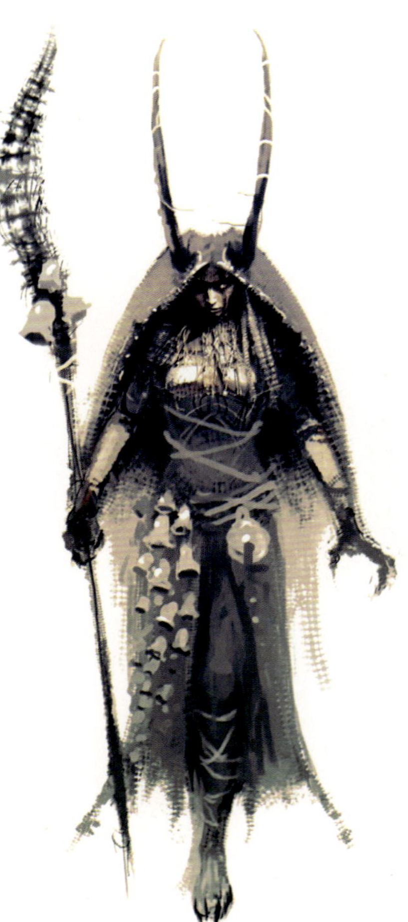

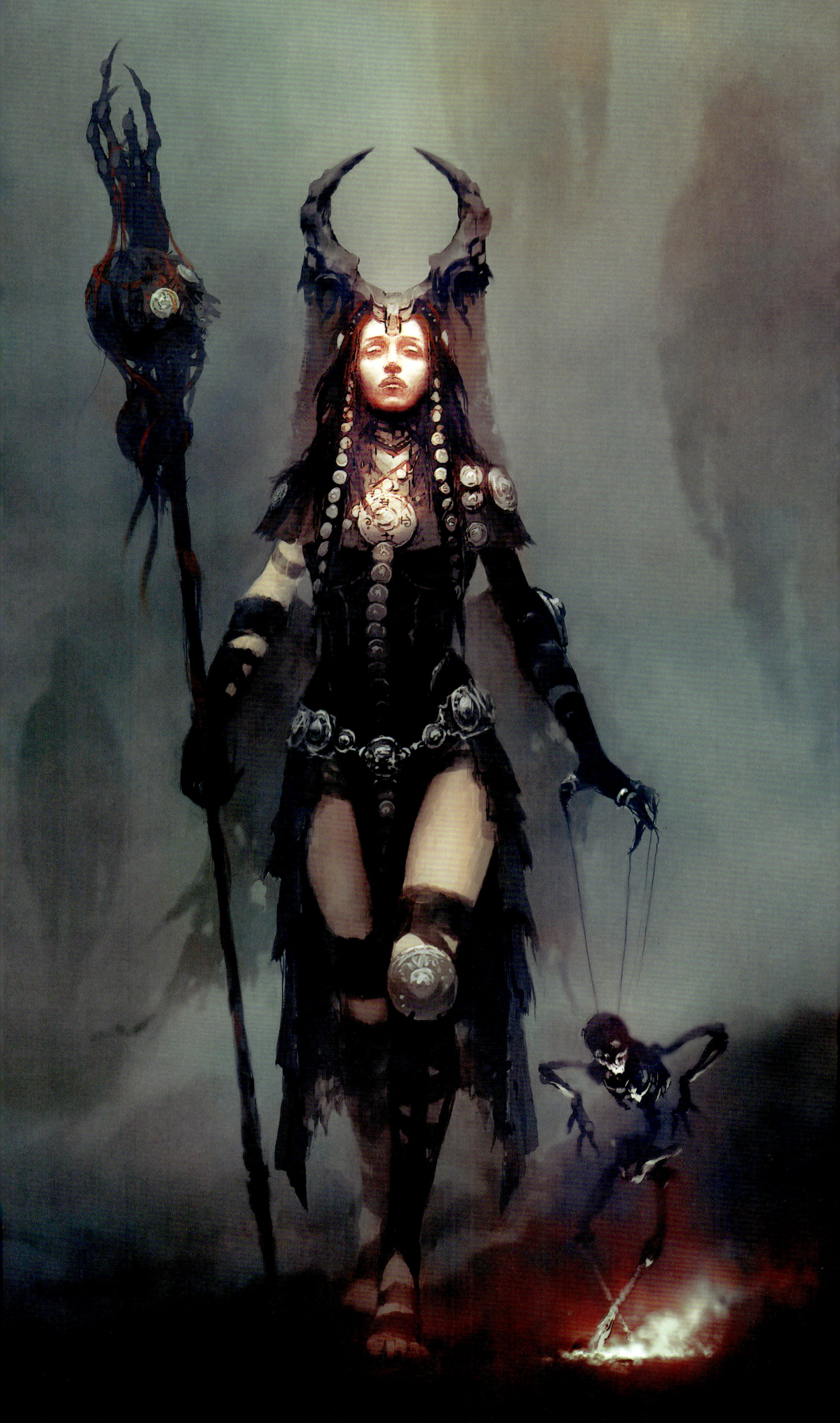

ABOVE Barbarian Lettering + Fernando Pinilla

RIGHT, TOP Necromancer Concept + Victor Lee

RIGHT, BOTTOM Rogue Ritual Tattoo Concept + Hyun Lee

BELOW Druid Tattoo Concept + Ted Beargeon

OPPOSITE Rogue Concept + Igor Sidorenko

FOLLOWING SPREAD Class Key Art + Igor Sidorenko

Once the classes were created, the time came to pose and animate them. The demeanor of each archetype factored heavily into their animation.

"I try to think about 'What is the space they take up, and how would they do that?'" says animation director Nick Chilano. "The Barbarian is at a higher level; they punch first and ask questions later, so we think of stances. Heavy shoulders, the arms hang, broad shoulders. They look like a square in front of you. They are going to face whatever is in front of them head-on."

The more tactical Rogue was depicted in a sideways stance to allow for ease of movement, their eyes and head constantly moving, always assessing their environment. A class like the Druid was seen as big and extremely physical but also thoughtful, knowing when to use their strength. Sorceresses were animated with a flow that was meant to represent the confidence that comes with mastering their discipline and commanding the elements.

"If you think about the Druid, the Druid is our biggest and most physical class, yet they're thoughtful and mindful enough to know what they're going to do," Chilano explains. "They know when to use their strength. They're in tune with nature and the elements around them. They're in tune with the world, and they've grounded themselves in that. We have them barrel-chested and upright, not as heavy and ready to fight, but they do feel imposing. We slightly turn them and we have them looking down at people as if to say, 'If you do something wrong, I'll correct it.'"

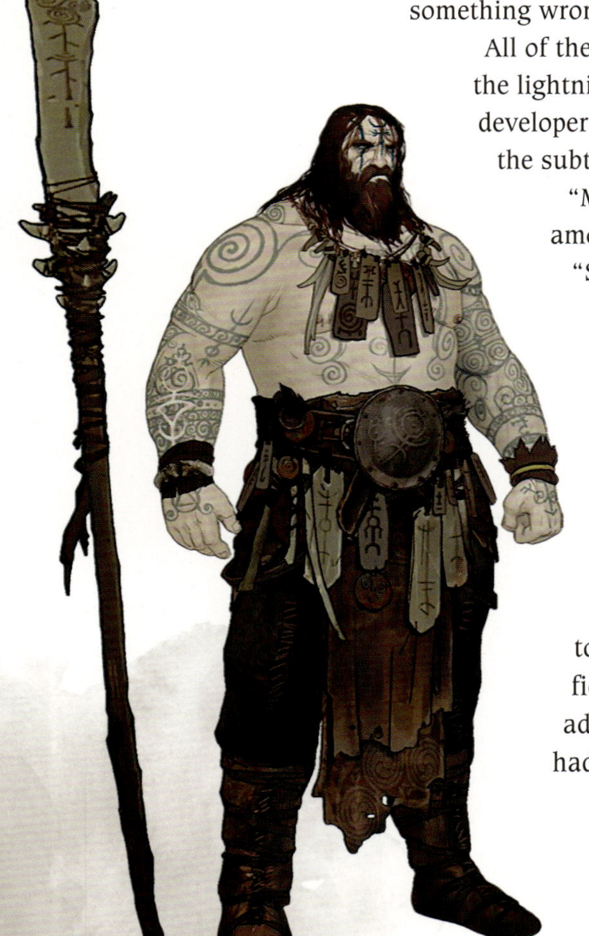

All of these nuances were not easy to convey in the lightning-fast gameplay of an action RPG. But developers found other means of communicating the subtleties to players.

"Marketing is going to do a certain amount of that lifting," Chilano continues. "So will the front-end screen at the campfire and the wardrobe pose, the character select screen, the paper doll, and the cinematics."

A great deal of hard work went into making the *Diablo IV* classes as amazing as they are. For Chilano, it was time well spent. "I think improving the character creation experience, bringing the art to where it needed to be, upping that fidelity level, and creating an open world, adding all of these things that *Diablo* never had, those were the right places to focus."

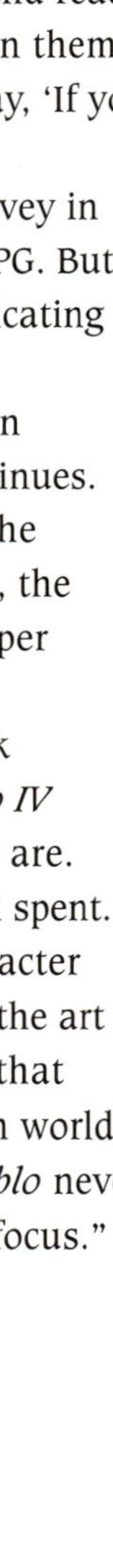

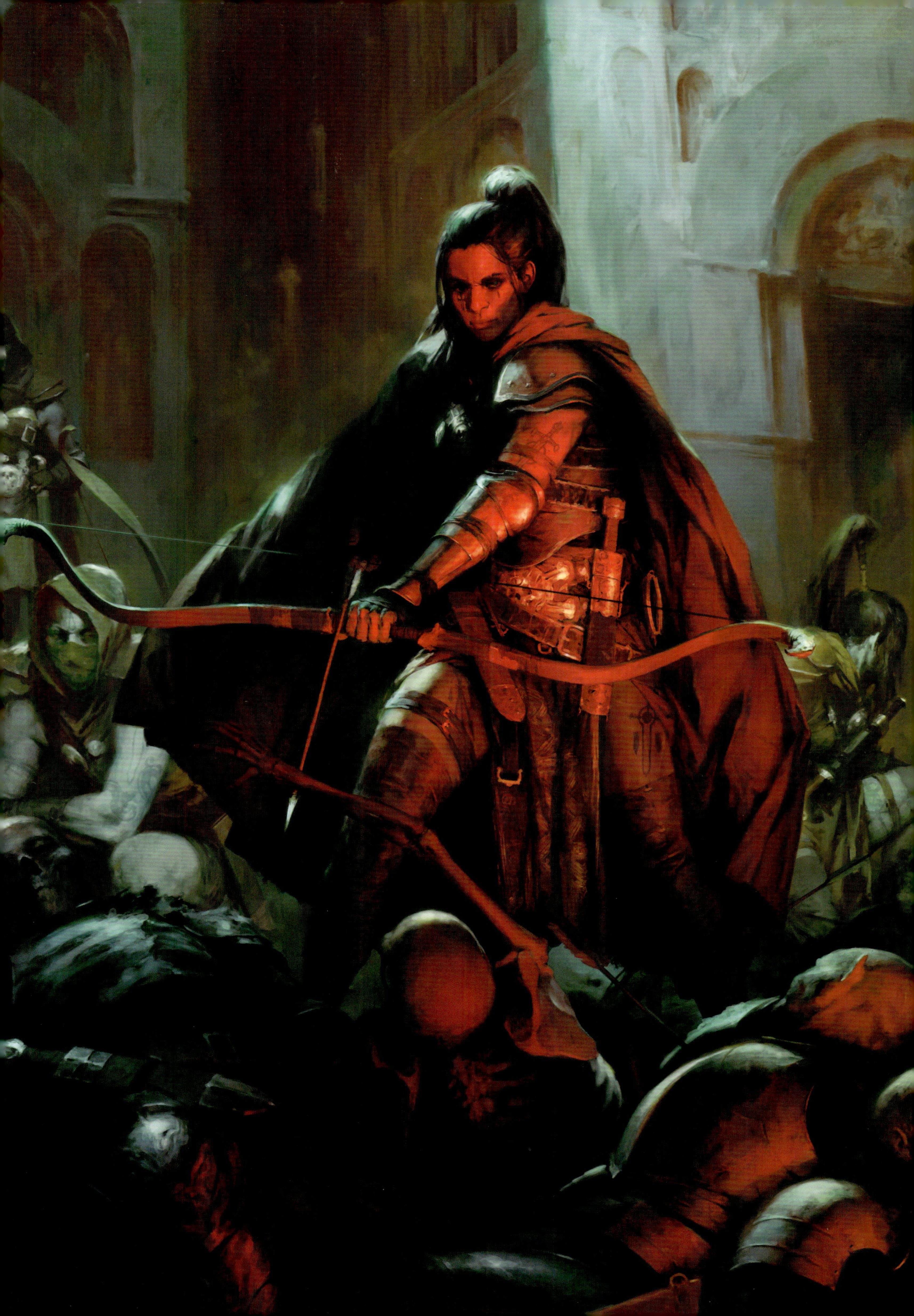

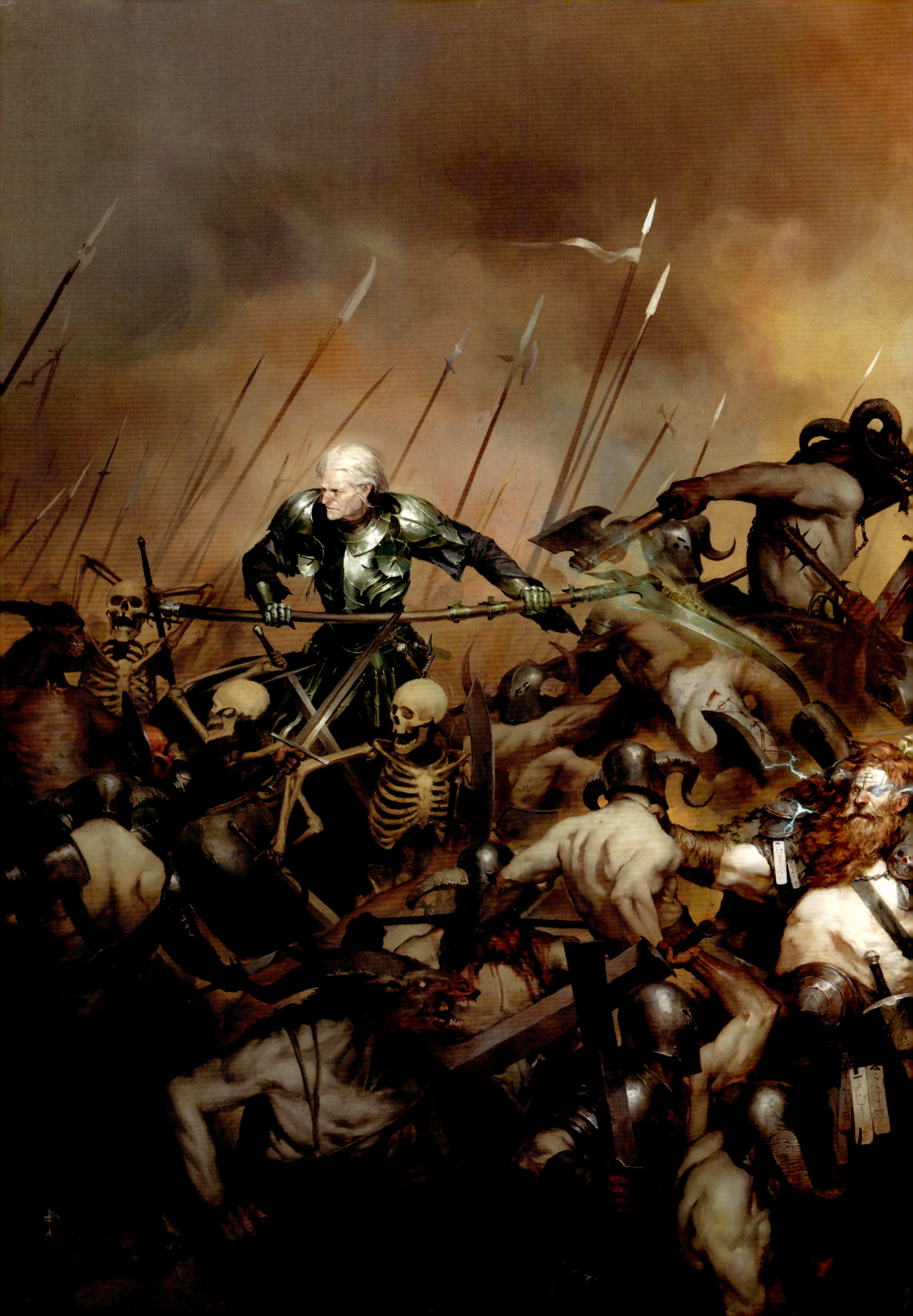

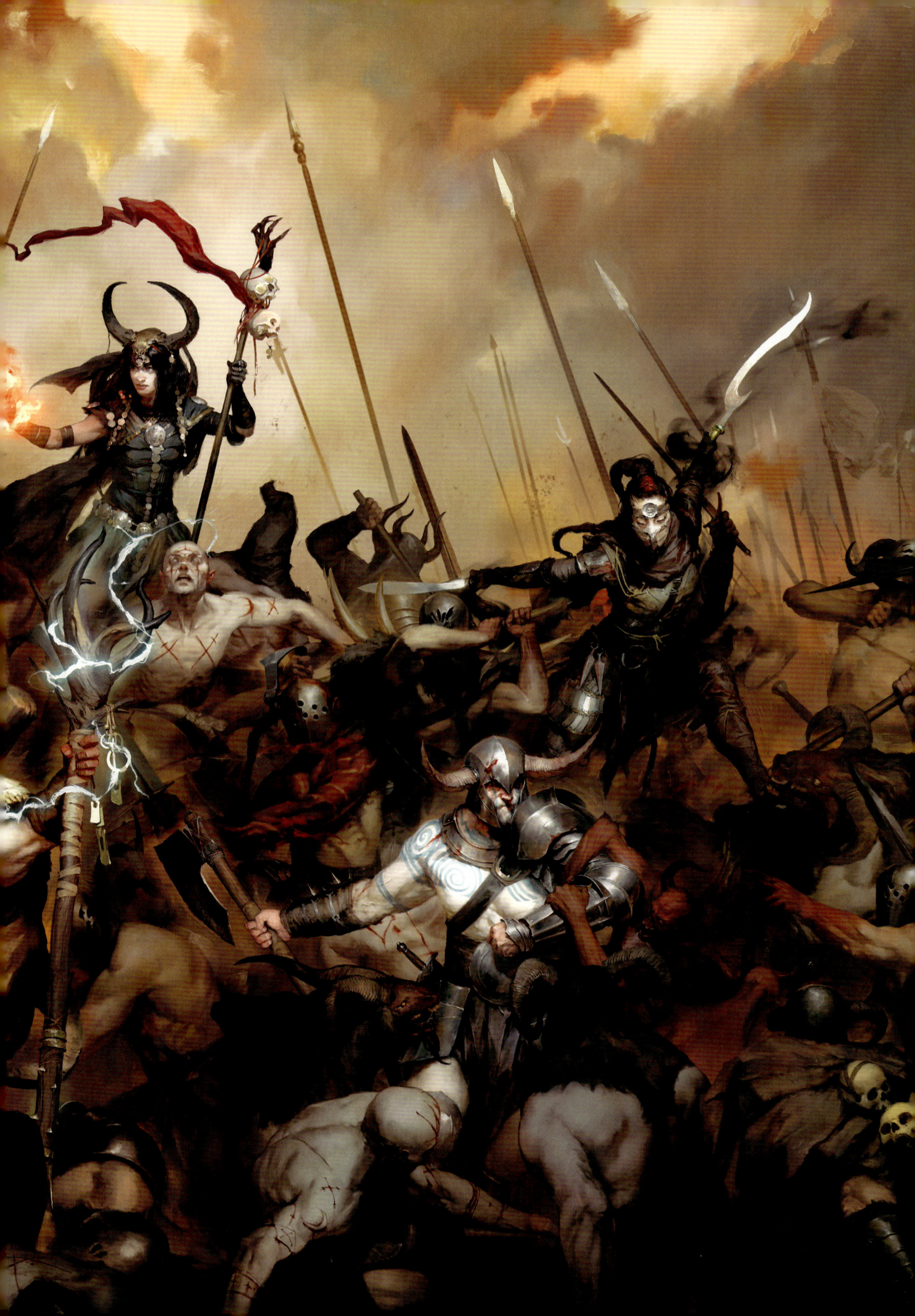

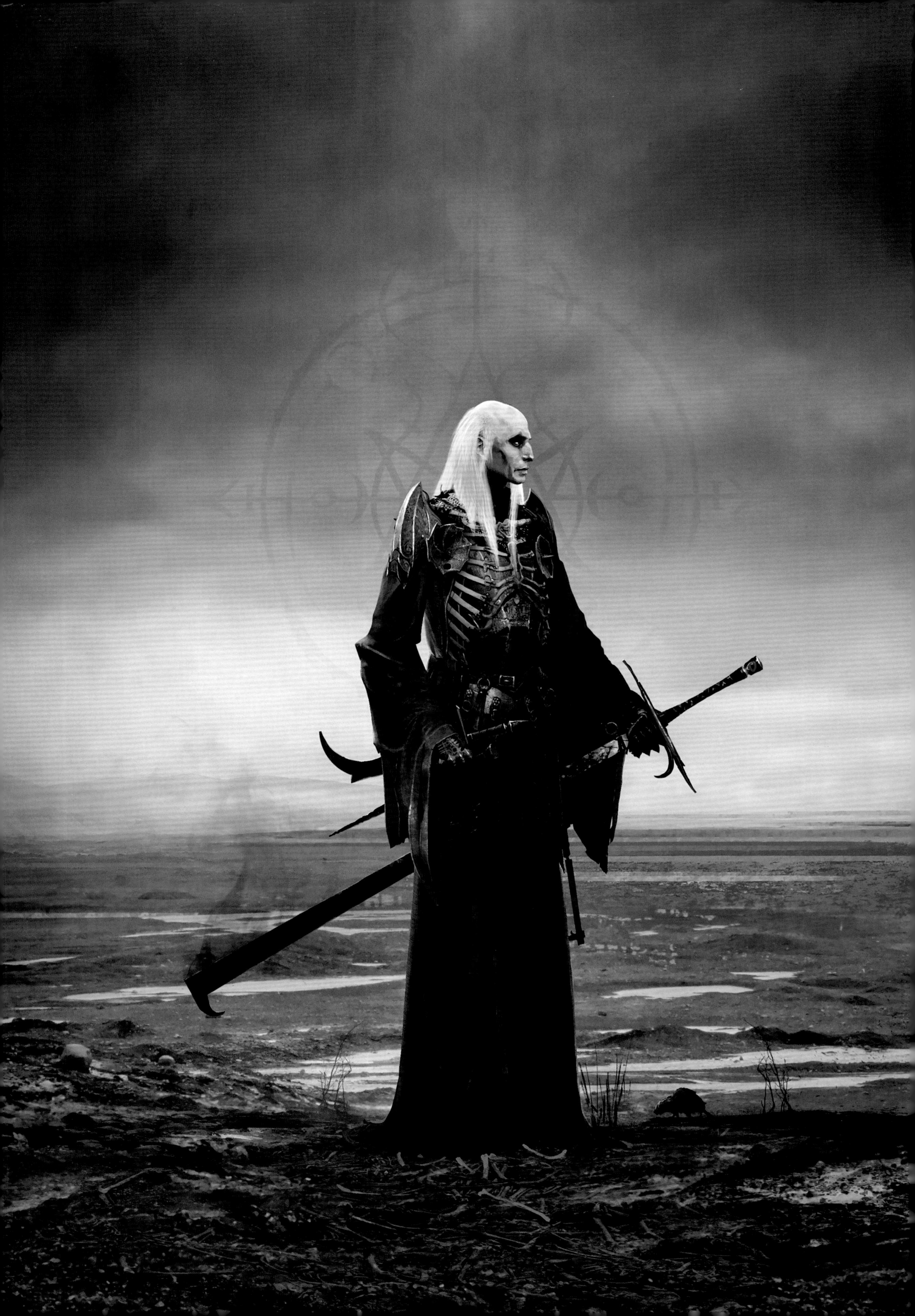

"All of our classes need to be as inclusive as possible, meaning gender, ethnicity, any type of inclusion. That's what we work on very solidly, and we will continue to double down on that as we create each class."

—ARNAUD KOTELNIKOFF, Associate Art Director

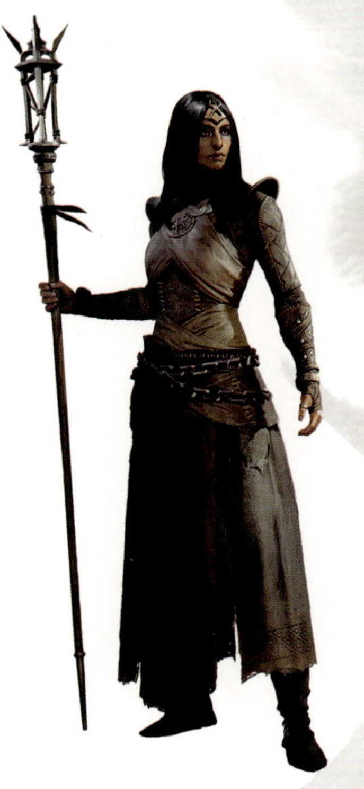

RIGHT Sorcerer Concept + Igor Sidorenko

BOTTOM Sorcerer Key Art + Igor Sidorenko

OPPOSITE Early Necromancer Concept + Ted Beargeon

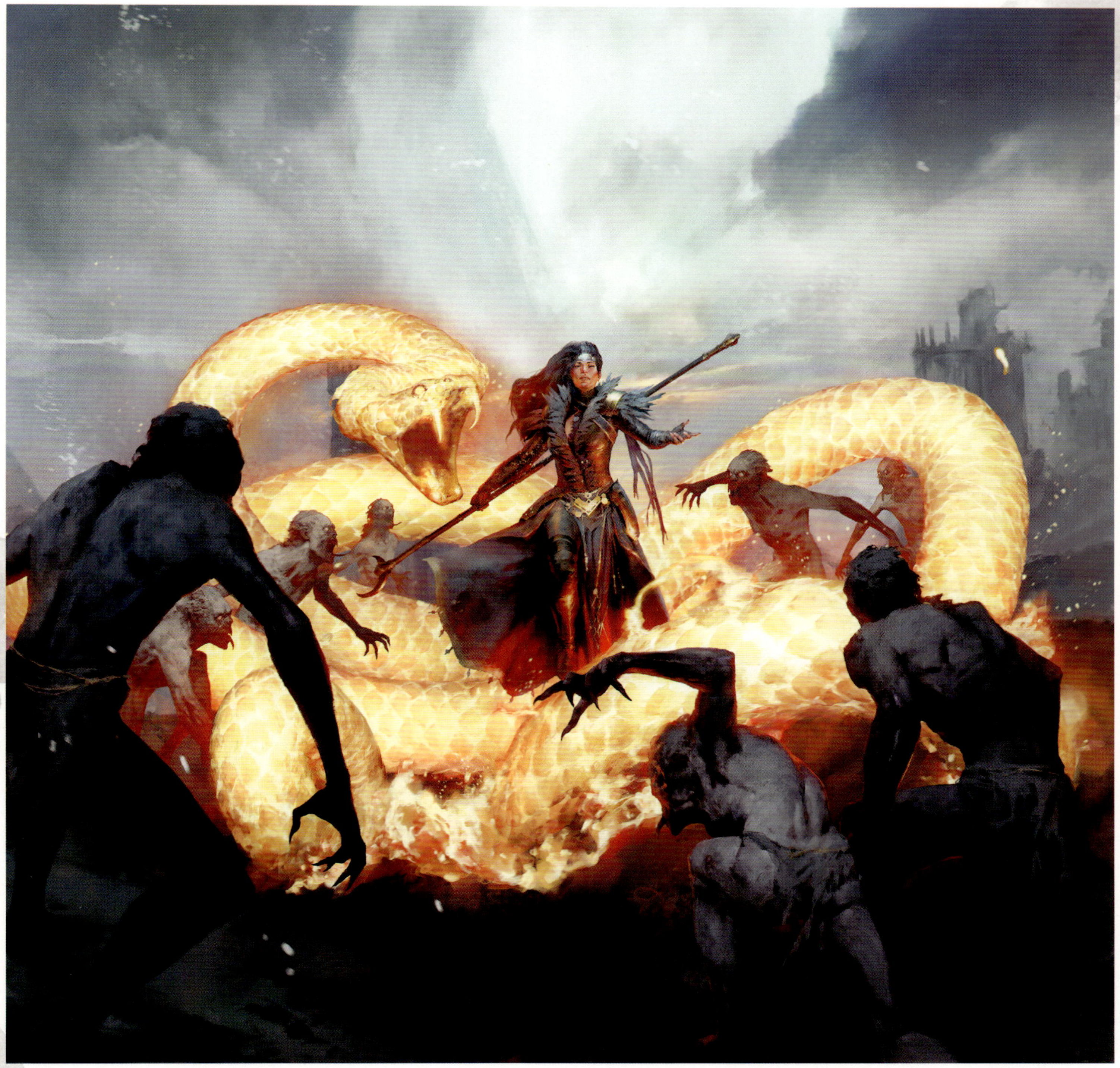

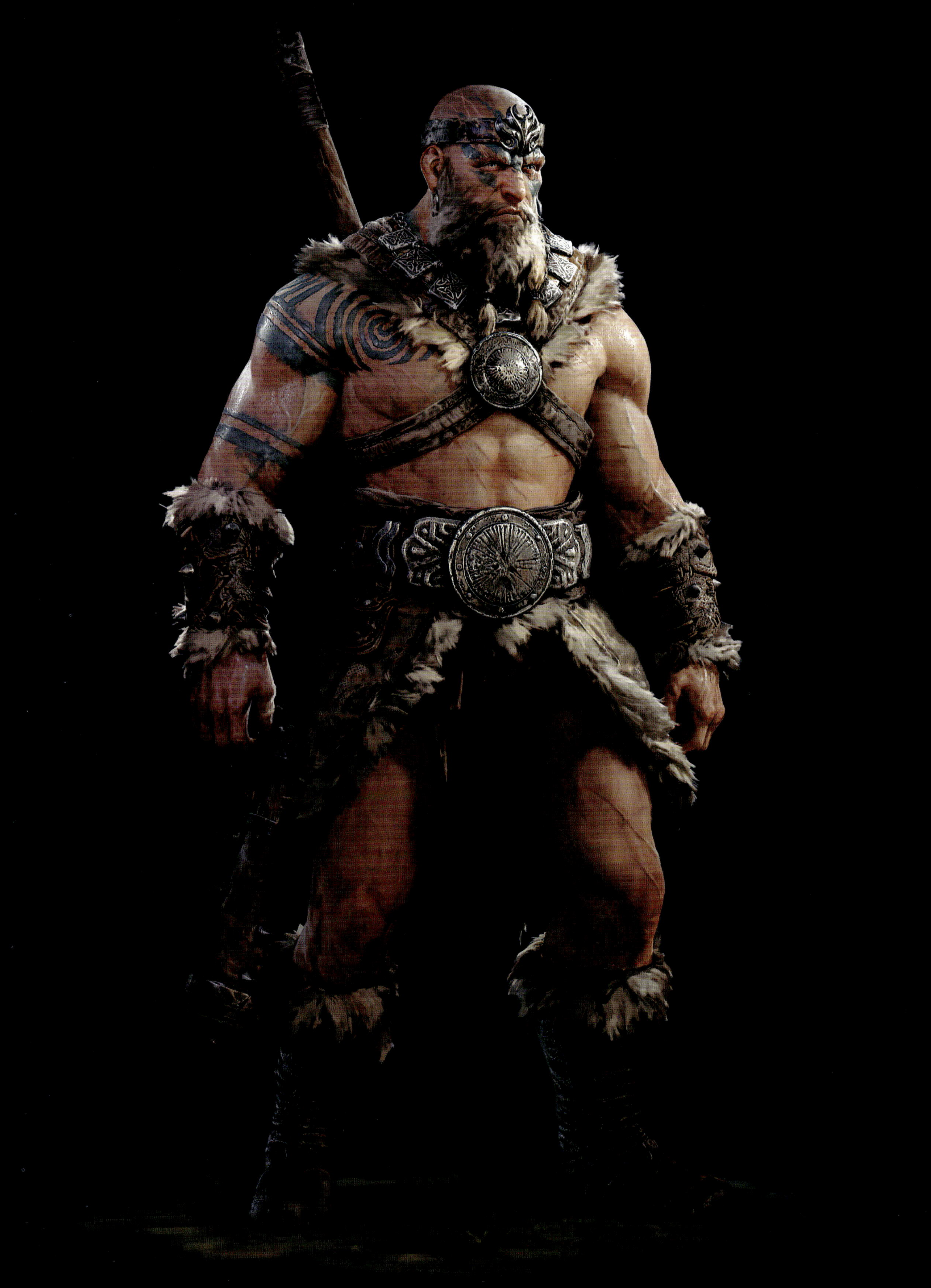

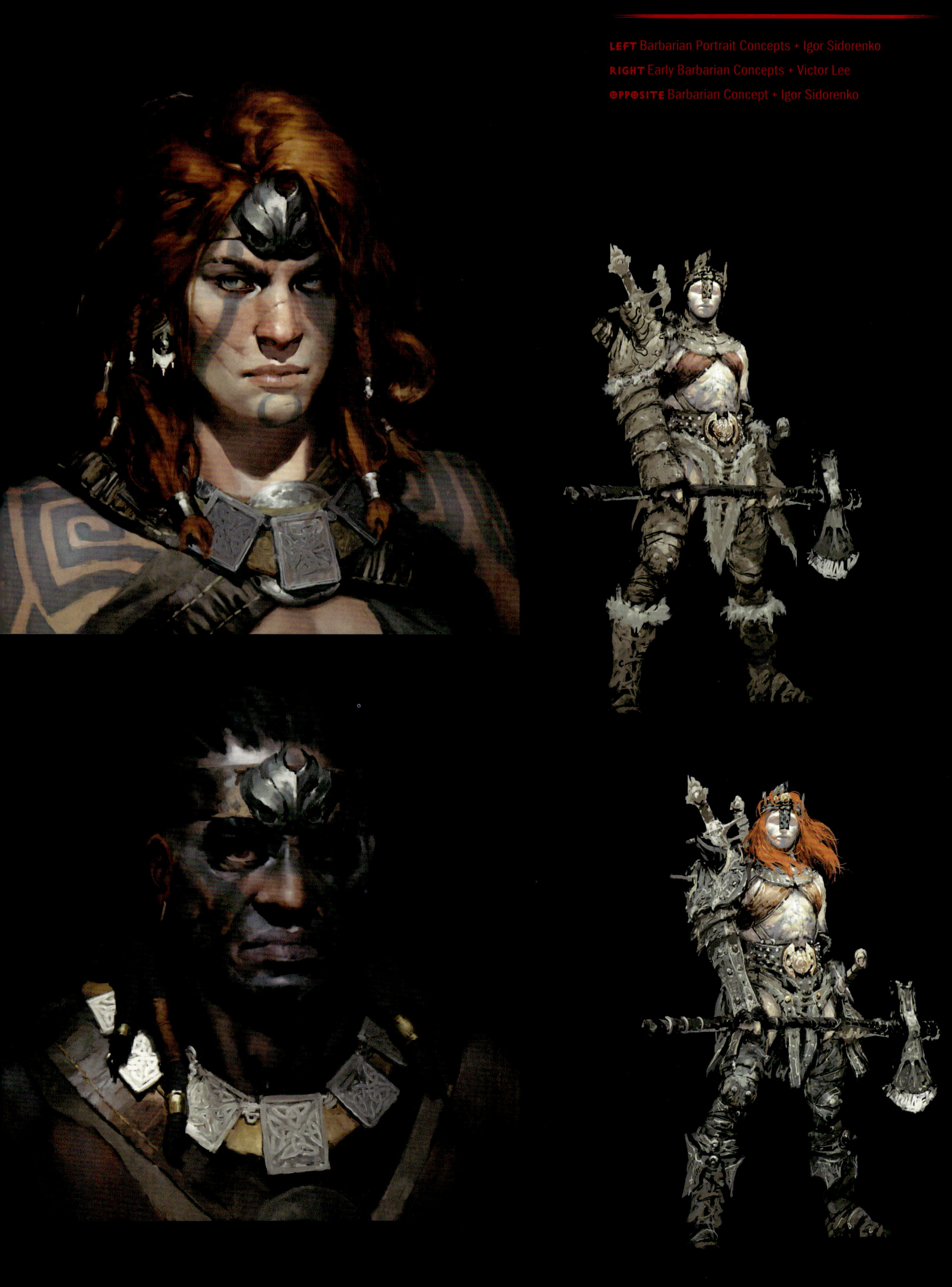

LEFT Barbarian Portrait Concepts • Igor Sidorenko

RIGHT Early Barbarian Concepts • Victor Lee

OPPOSITE Barbarian Concept • Igor Sidorenko

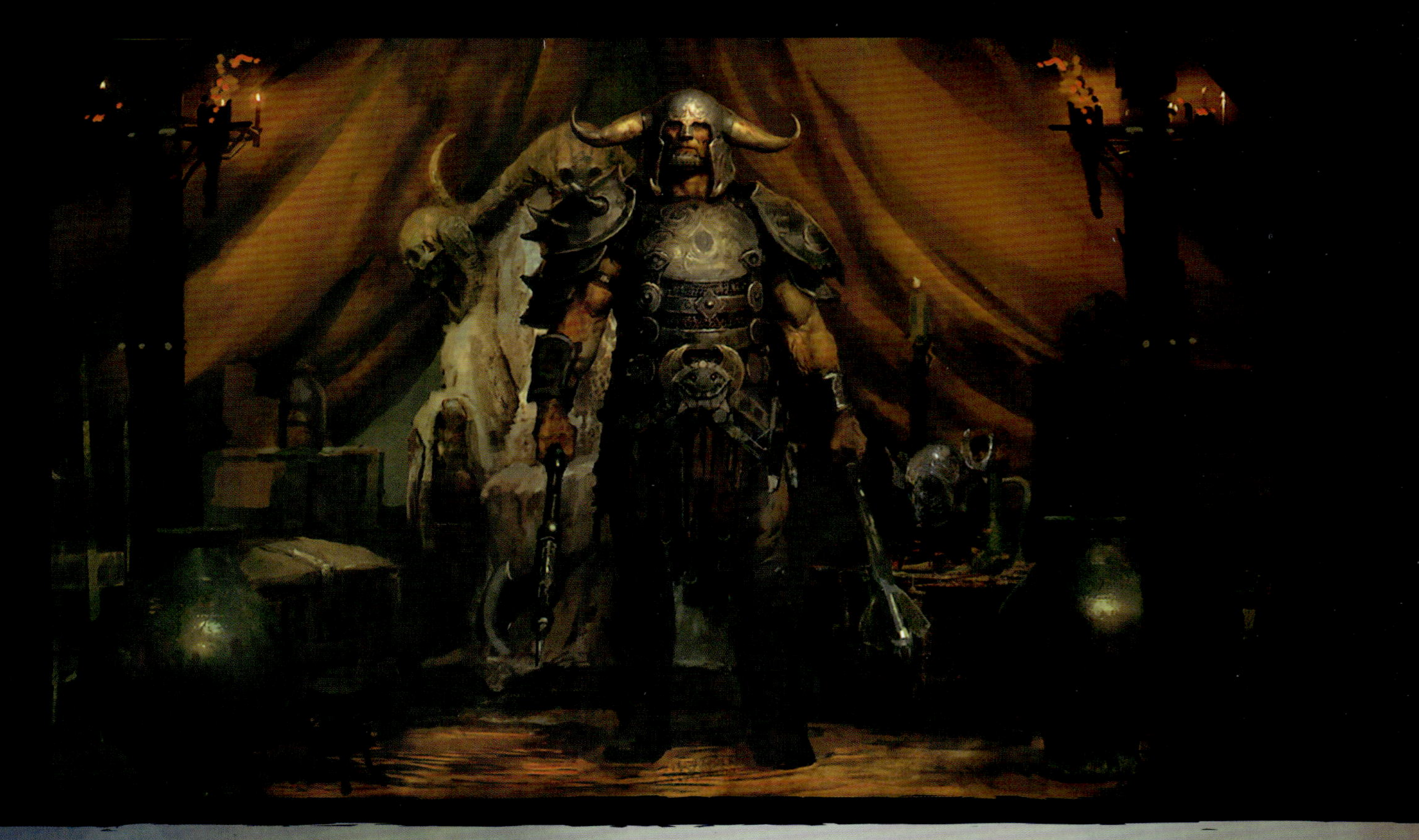

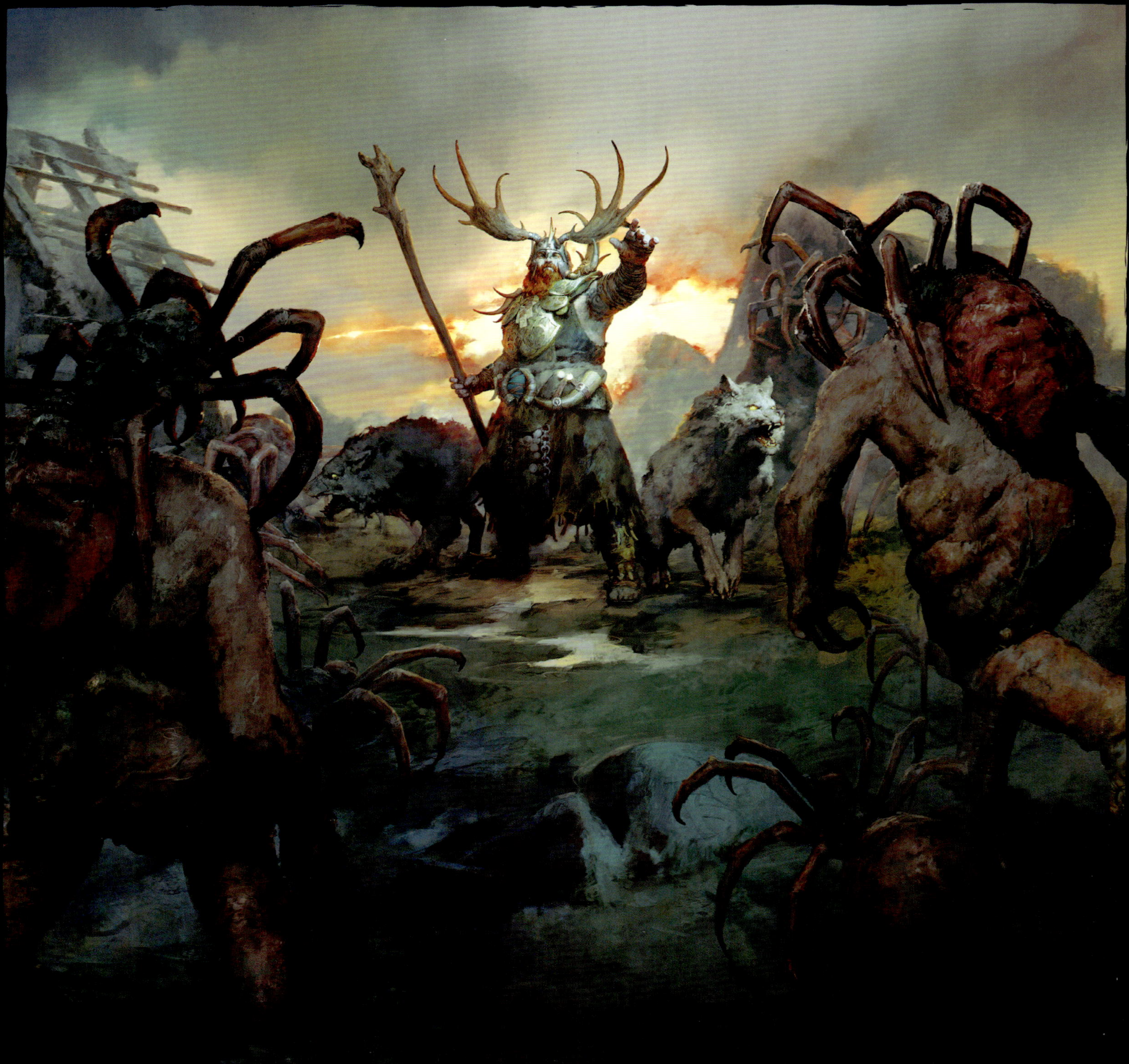

THIS PAGE Early Druid Concepts + Cedric Peyravernay
OPPOSITE, TOP Barbarian Tent Concept + Justin Sweet
OPPOSITE, BOTTOM Druid Key Art + Igor Sidorenko

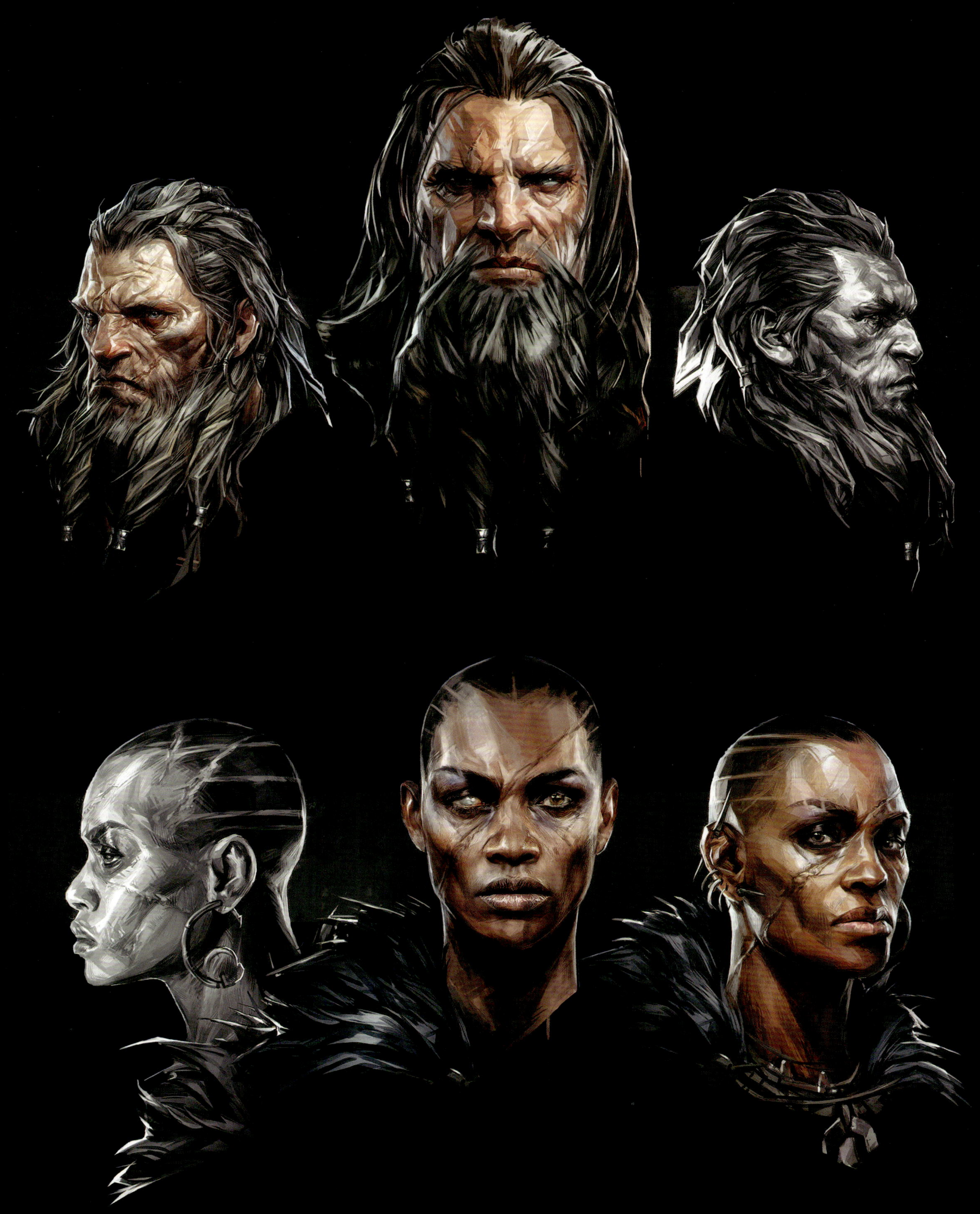

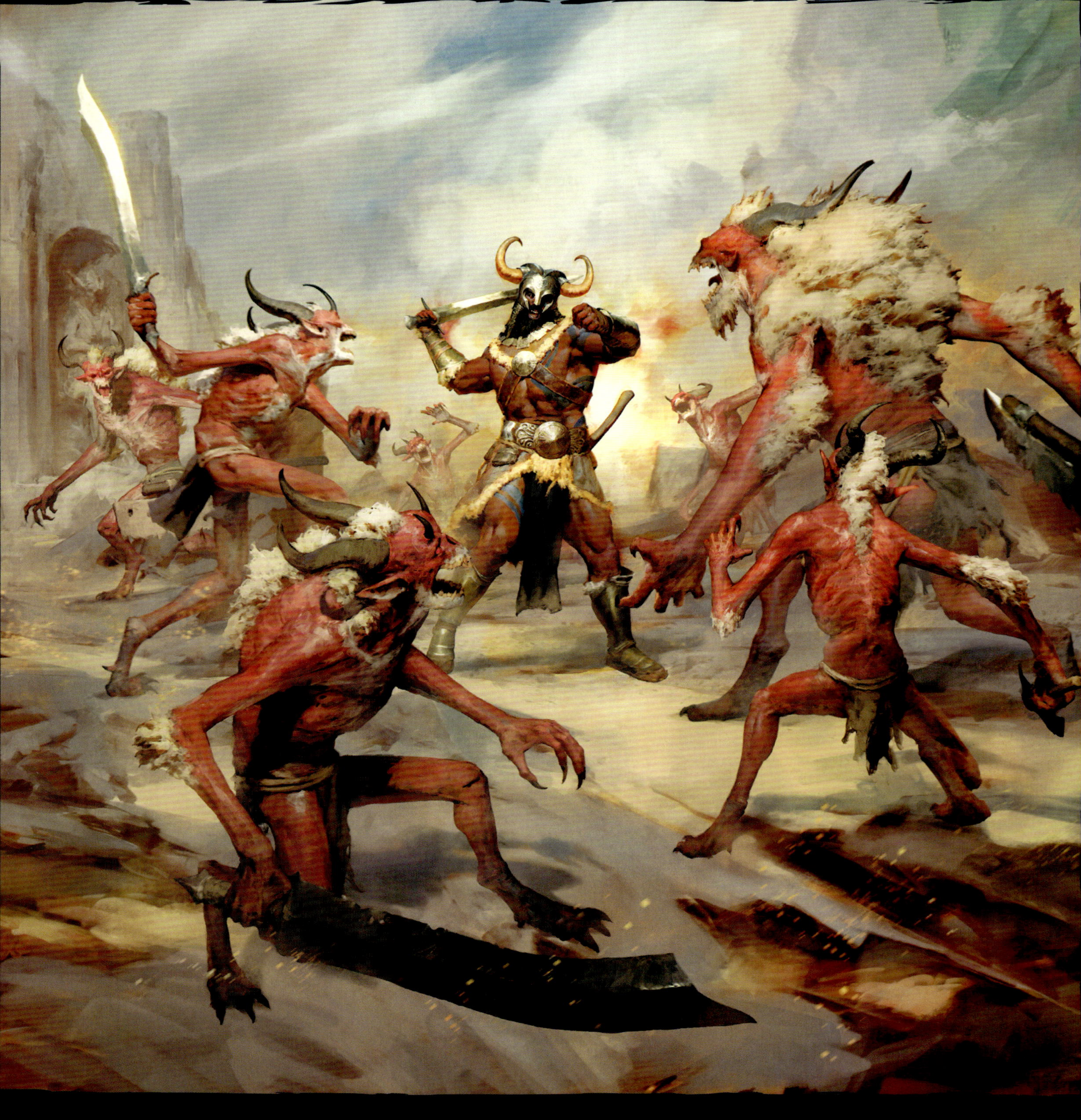

ABOVE Barbarian Key Art • Igor Sidorenko

"The fidelity of what is possible today is so much higher than Diablo III. *We pushed the detail to new highs in* Diablo IV."

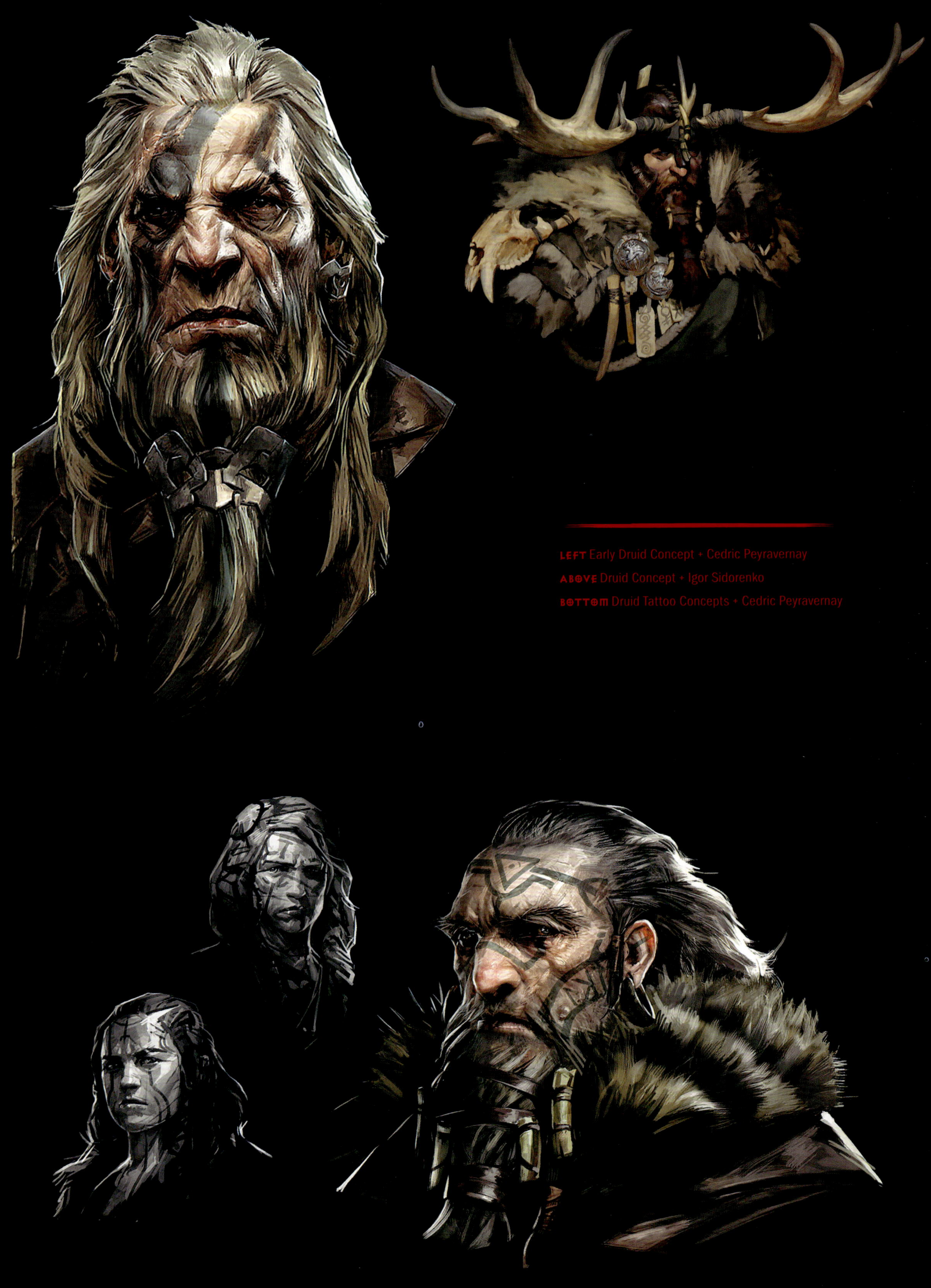

LEFT Early Druid Concept • Cedric Peyravernay

ABOVE Druid Concept • Igor Sidorenko

BOTTOM Druid Tattoo Concepts • Cedric Peyravernay

TOP, LEFT Druid Dire Werebear Concept + Victor Lee

TOP, RIGHT Druid Concept + Mike Franchina

BOTTOM Druid Illustration + Mike Franchina

OPPOSITE Early Druid Concept + Mike Franchina

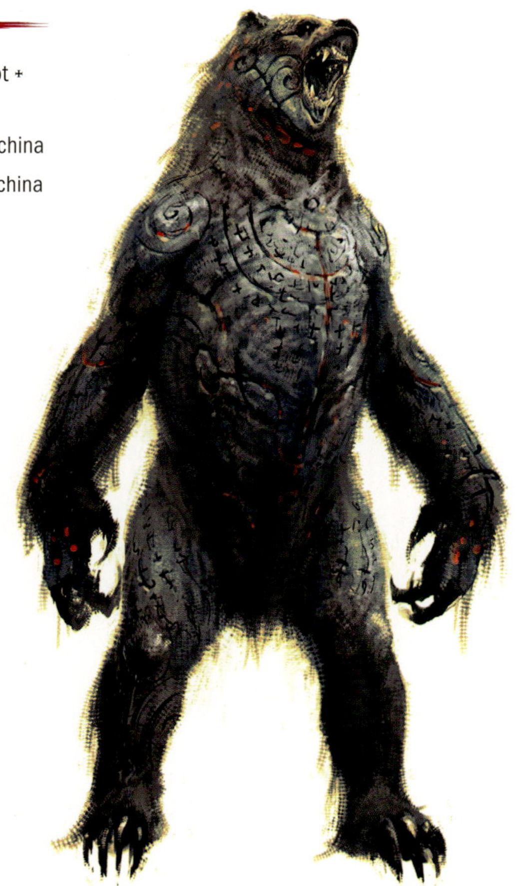

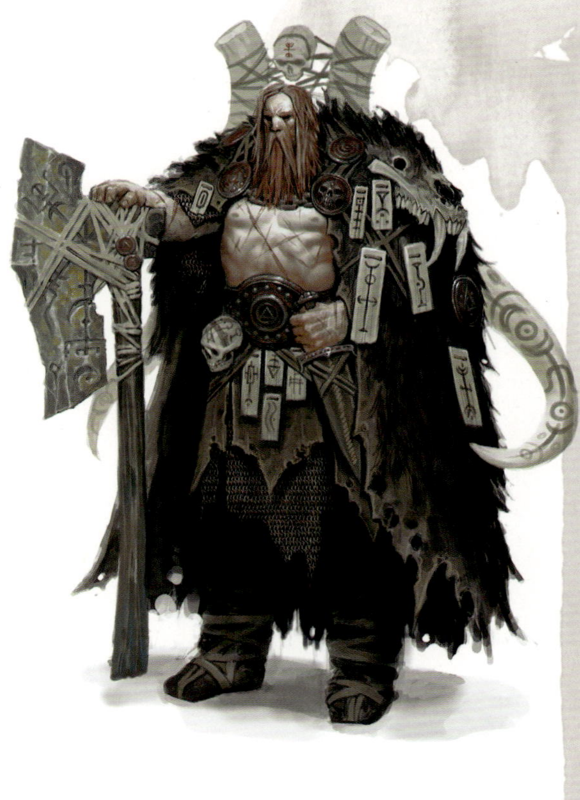

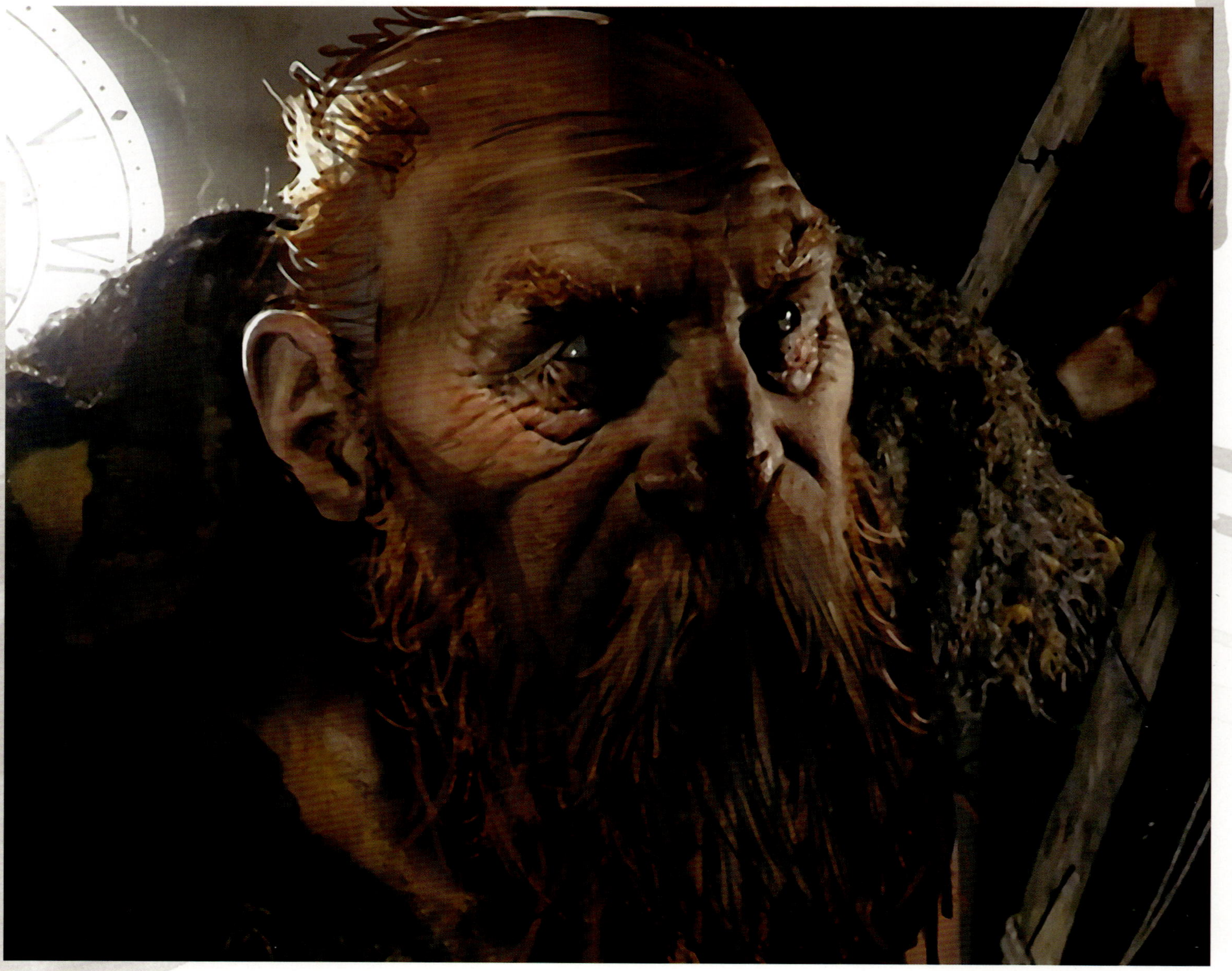

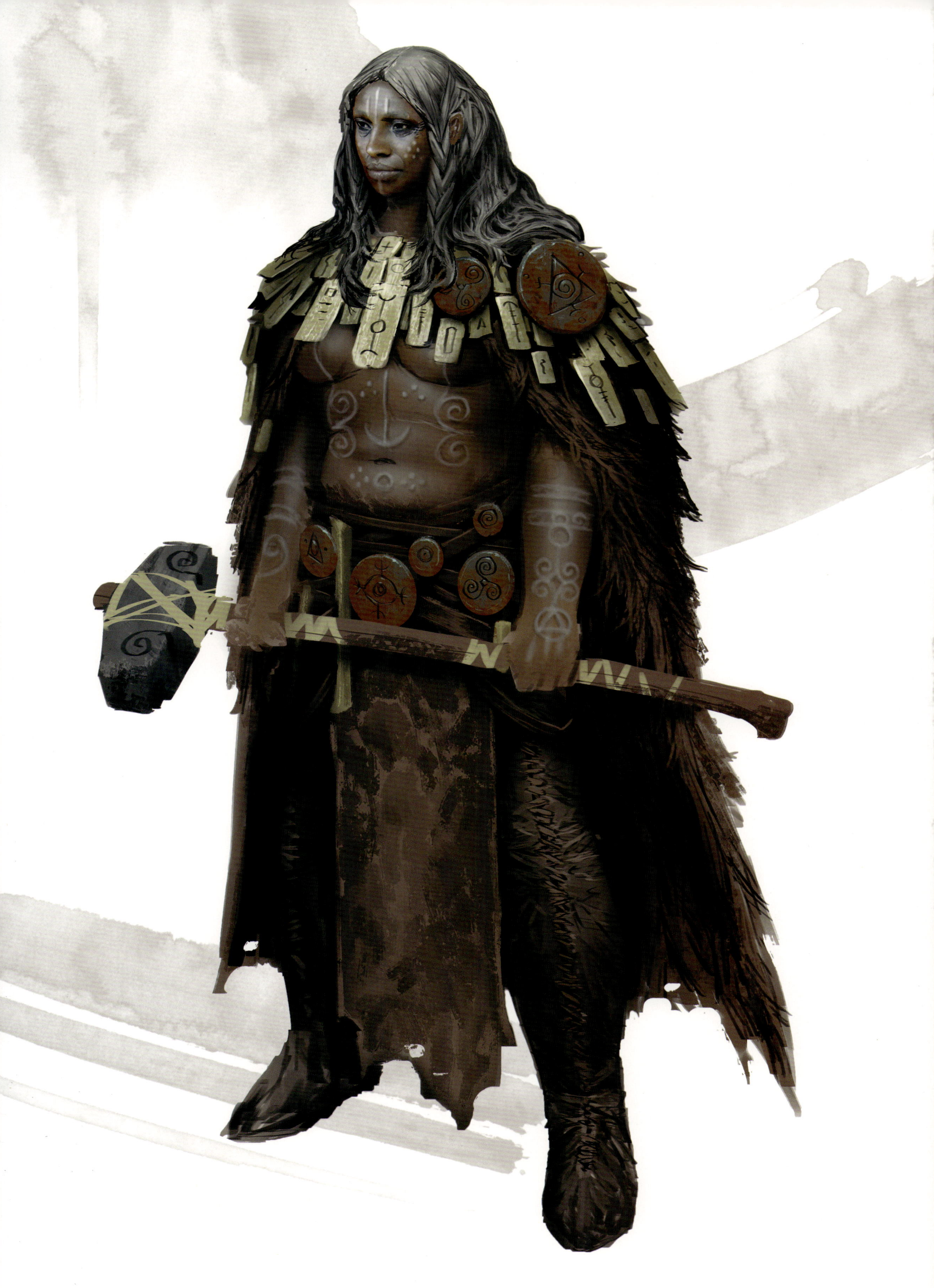

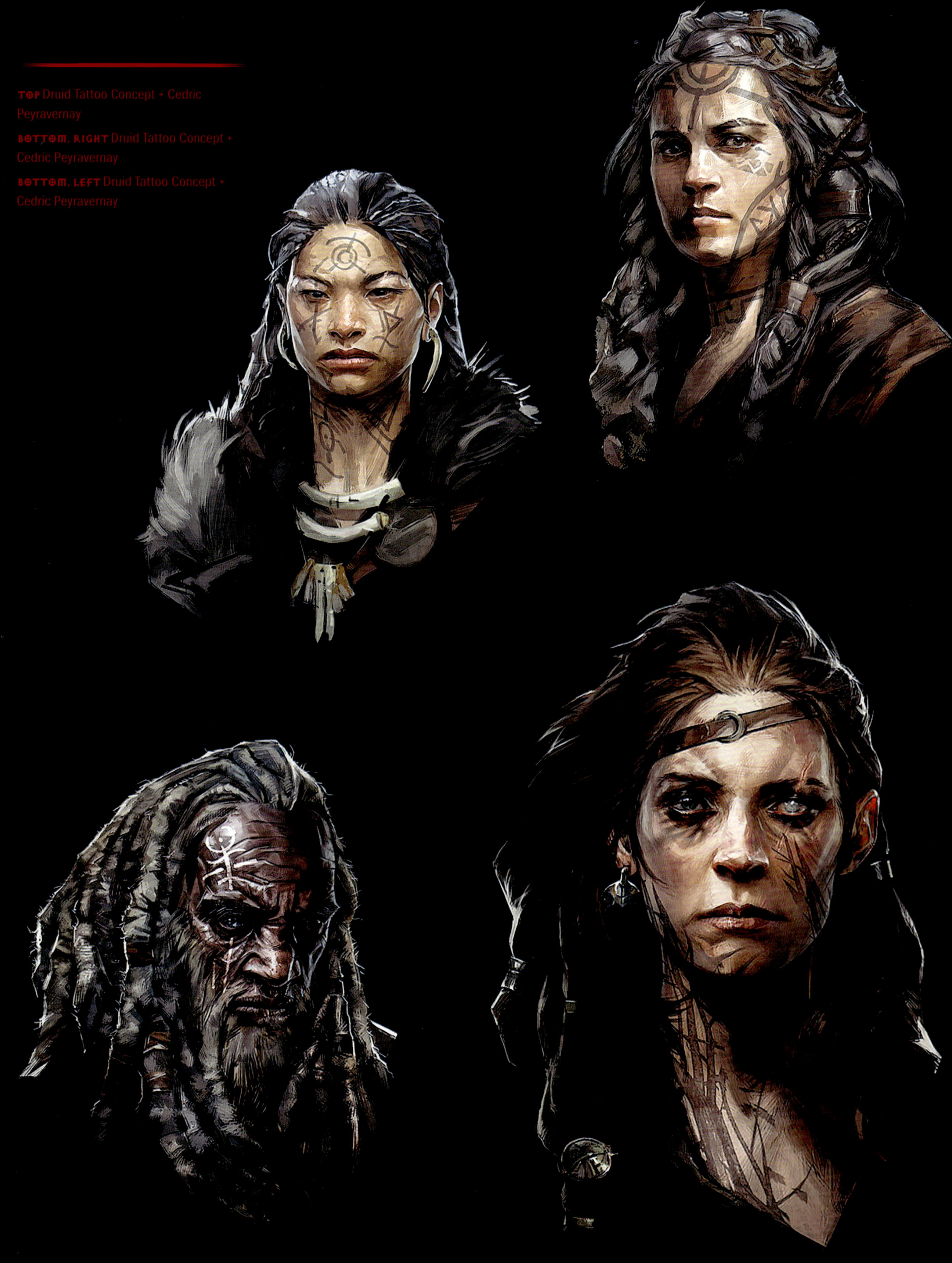

TOP Druid Tattoo Concept • Cedric Peyravernay

BOTTOM, RIGHT Druid Tattoo Concept • Cedric Peyravernay

BOTTOM, LEFT Druid Tattoo Concept • Cedric Peyravernay

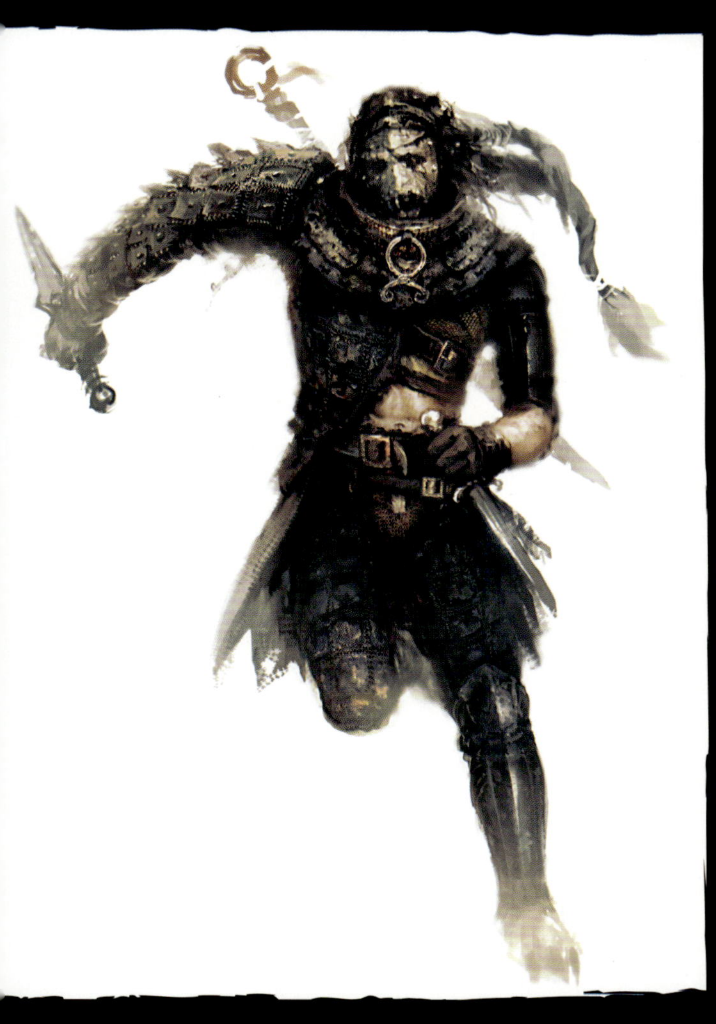

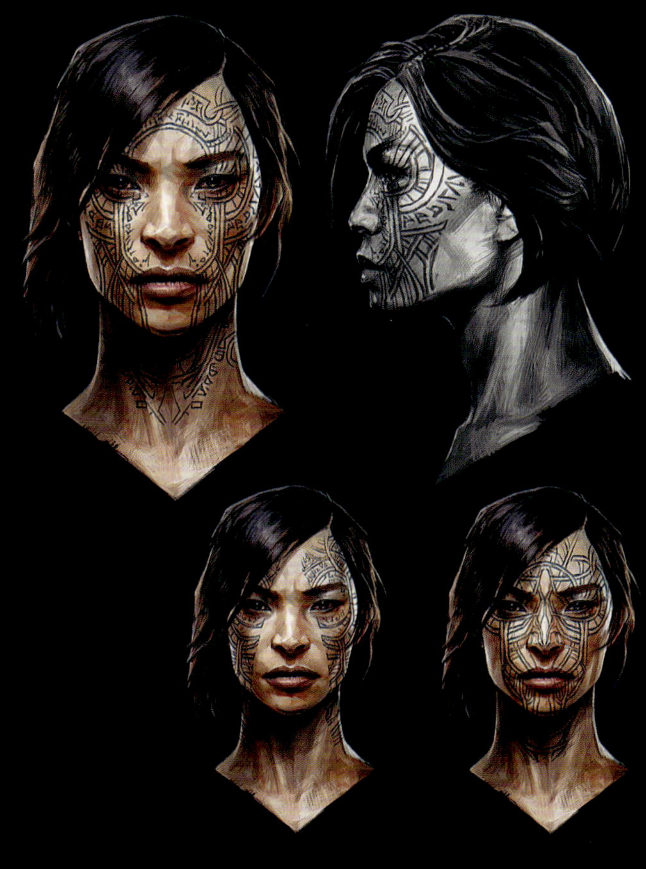

LEFT Early Assassin Concept • Victor Lee

ABOVE Early Tattoo Concept • Cedric Peyravernay

BOTTOM Early Assassin Concept • Victor Lee

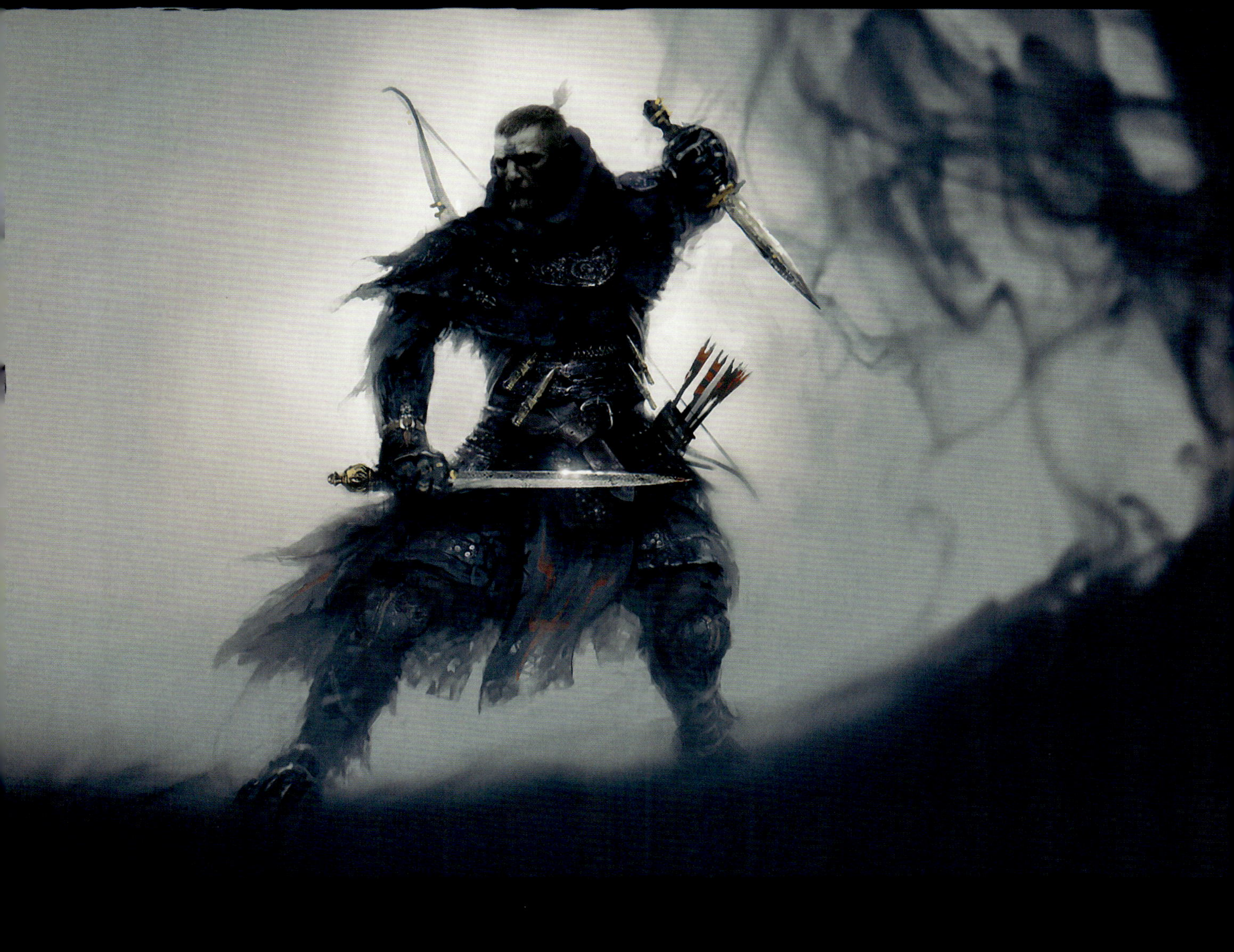

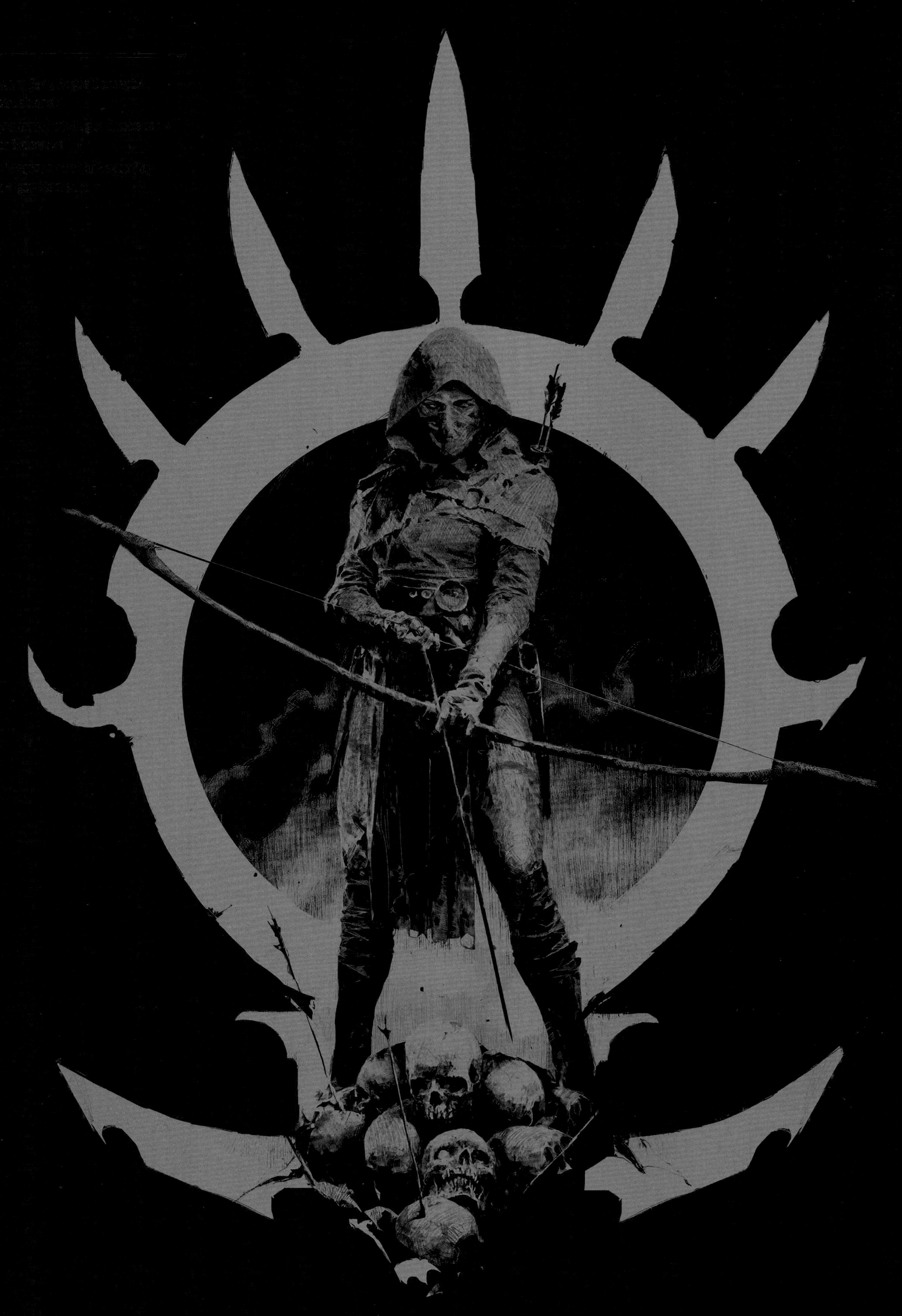

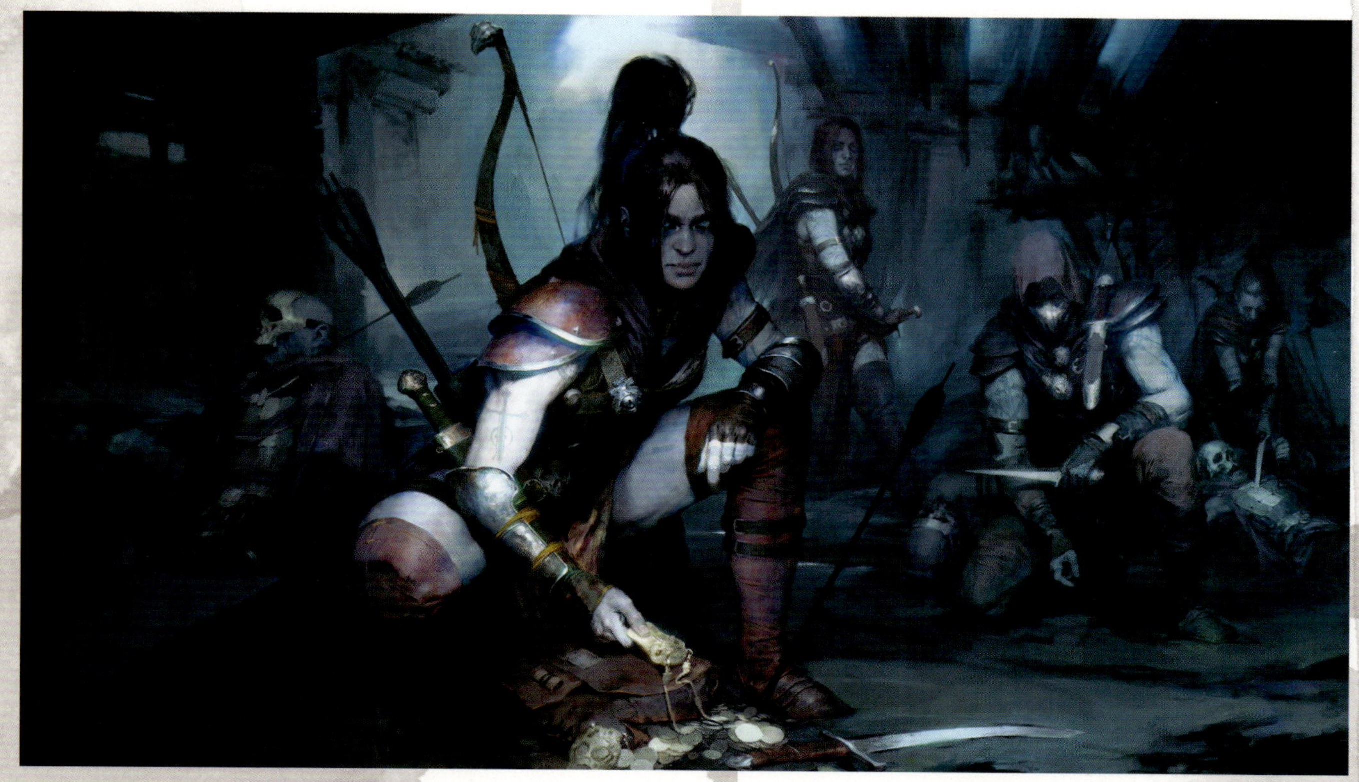

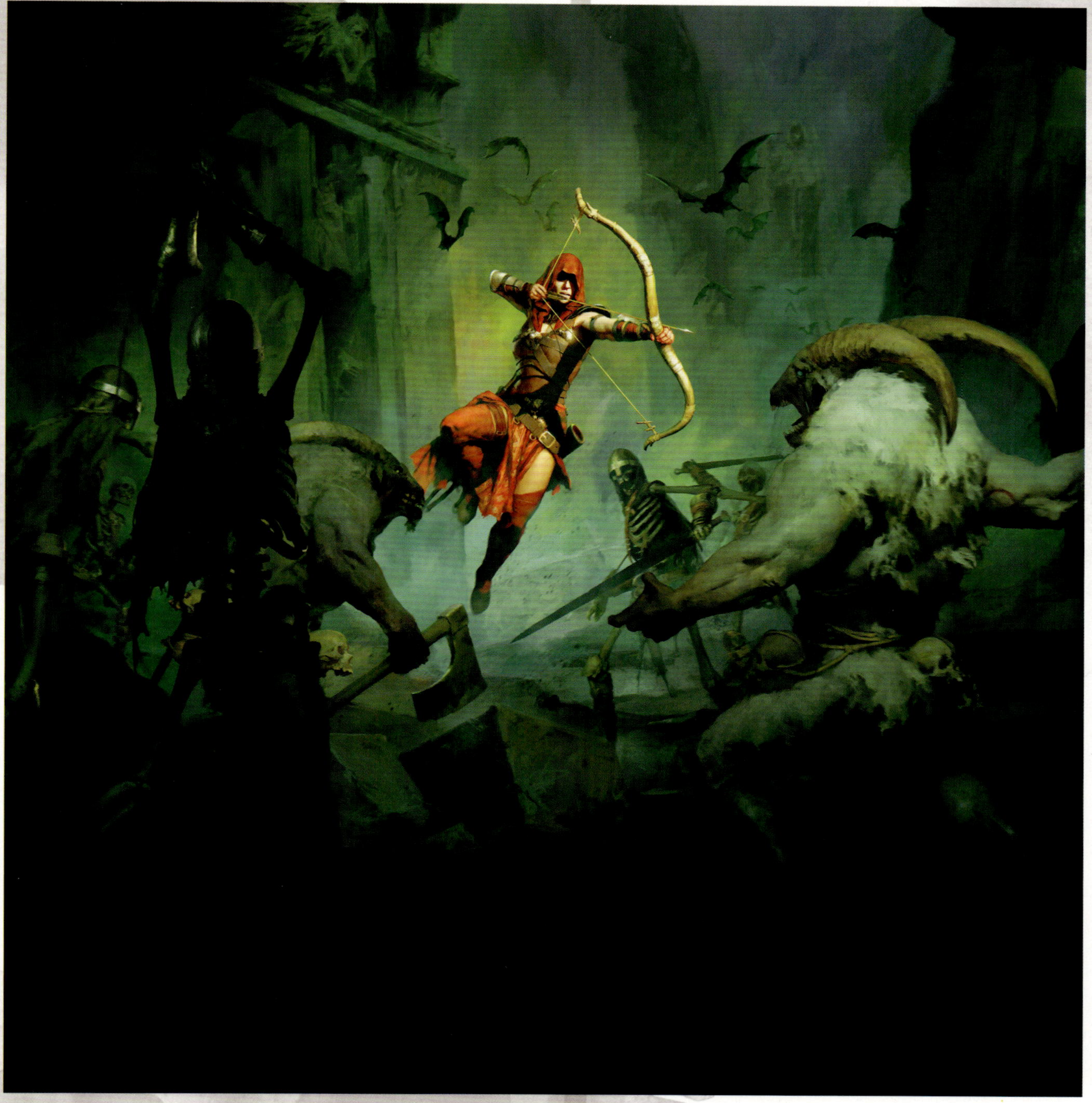

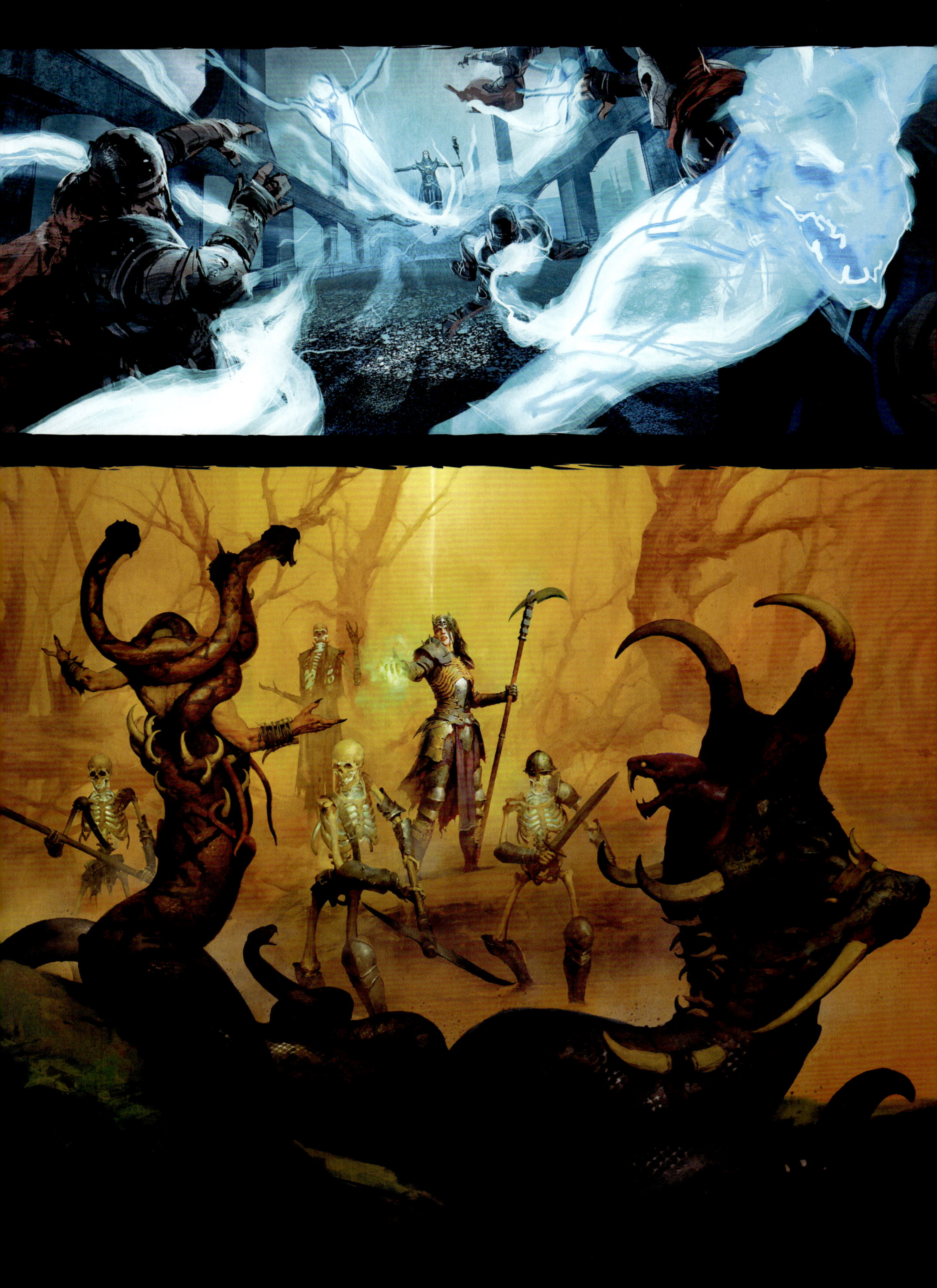

"The Necromancer, he's reanimating the dead, dealing with dark magic. They get a little gaunt over the years, they wither a little bit, there's some wear and tear on them. If you think about lines, angles, the Necromancer always has breaks in their lines. So if they're standing with their arms down, we turn the wrist a little bit, we bring the neck down and shoulders. We break them a little bit so their posture isn't clean because they're controlling something that doesn't want to be controlled."

—NICK CHILANO, Animation Director

THIS PAGE Necromancer Illustrations + Piotr Jablonski

OPPOSITE, TOP Undead Illustration + Dan Milligan

OPPOSITE, BOTTOM Necromancer Key Art + Igor Sidorenko

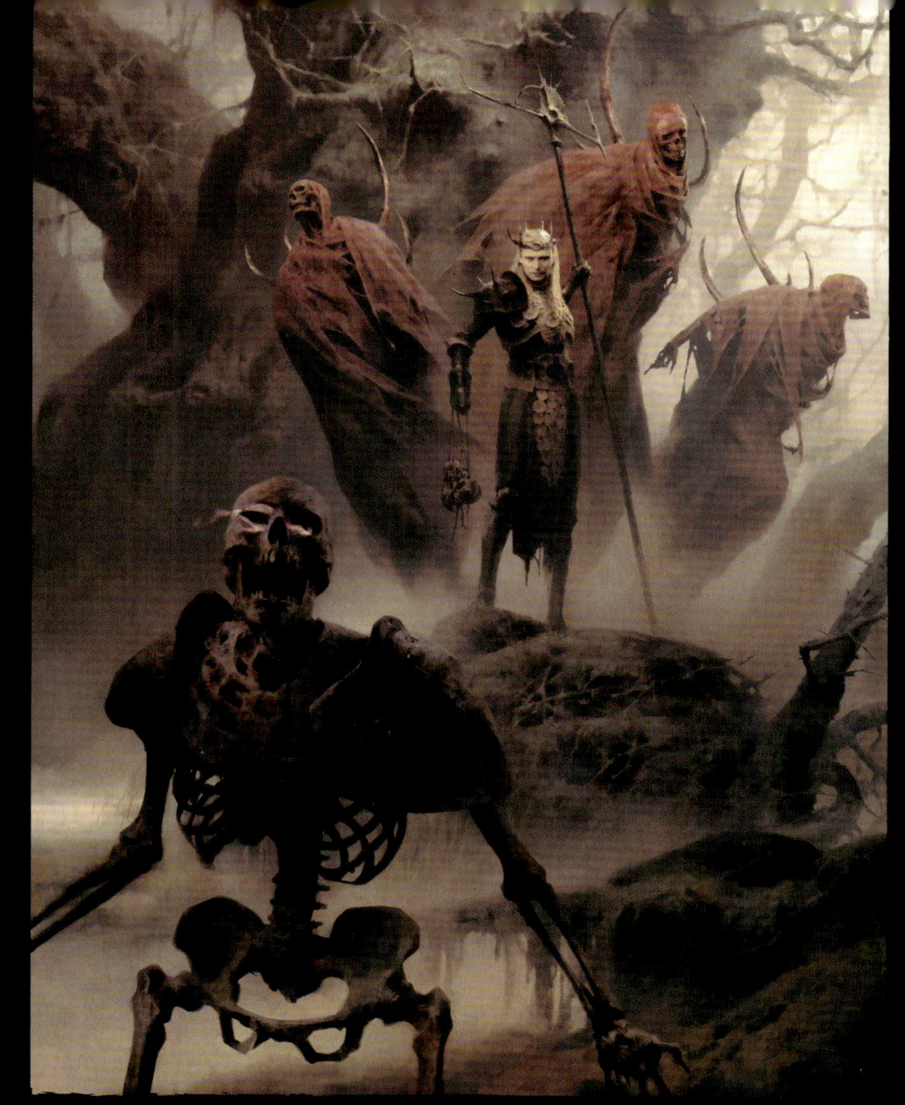

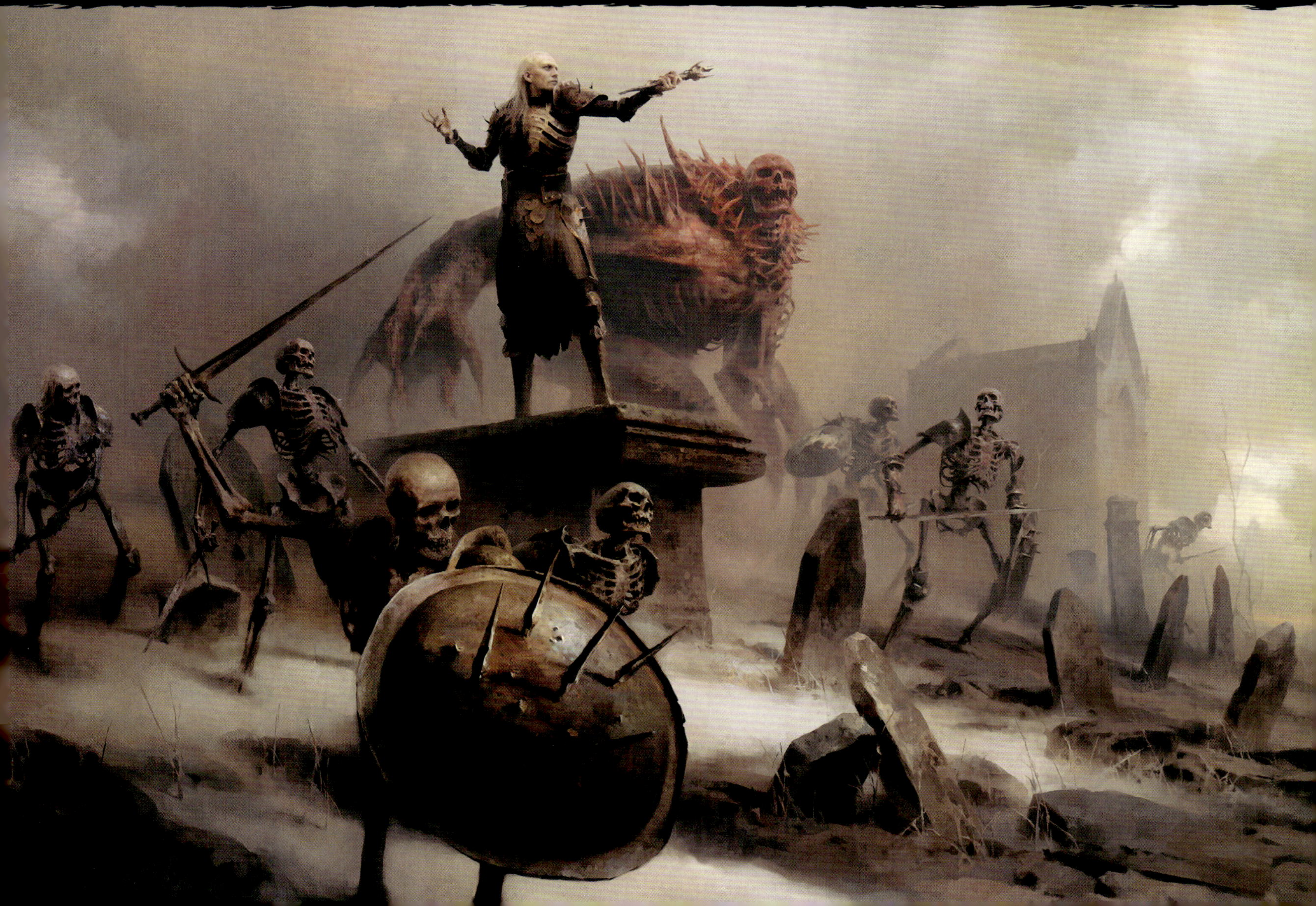

Brave, Bold, and Brutal

ABOVE Dry Steppes Lettering + Fernando Pinilla

RIGHT, TOP Cultist NPC Concept + Mike Franchina

RIGHT, MIDDLE Exorcist Concept + Mike Franchina

BOTTOM, RIGHT Exorcist Concept + Mike Franchina

BOTTOM, LEFT Healer Concept + Mike Franchina

BELOW Healer Concept + Mike Franchina

OPPOSITE Inarius Concept + Igor Sidorenko

Diablo IV features an all-new cast of exciting and unforgettable characters: Neyrelle, a young adventurer with a thirst for knowledge; Reverend Mother Prava, a zealot and second-in-command of the Cathedral of Light; Elias, the mysterious right-hand man of the new big bad—and even a few familiar faces like Lorath Nahr, first met in *Reaper of Souls*, and Lyndon, the Scoundrel of *Diablo III* fame. Before any of these actors can take the stage, however, they must go through a developmental journey.

"It mostly comes from the story team," says character lead Cory Turner. "Sometimes we'll receive a fully fleshed-out concept, from the written word down to the concept art. Sometimes it's looser, when we must figure out exactly what something needs. And sometimes it's literally a sketch or a drawing rather than fully painted concept art, and we help define what it is."

Depending on the amount of information provided at the outset, various questions are posed: Will the character fulfill a certain fantasy? Can they be built efficiently and to budget? What is their role?

"Then it comes down to character design and balance," says Hunter Schulz, concept art lead for *Diablo IV*. When the character is far enough along, it will be reviewed by the animation and 3D and modeling team. Next comes the 3D modeling phase, where details are added.

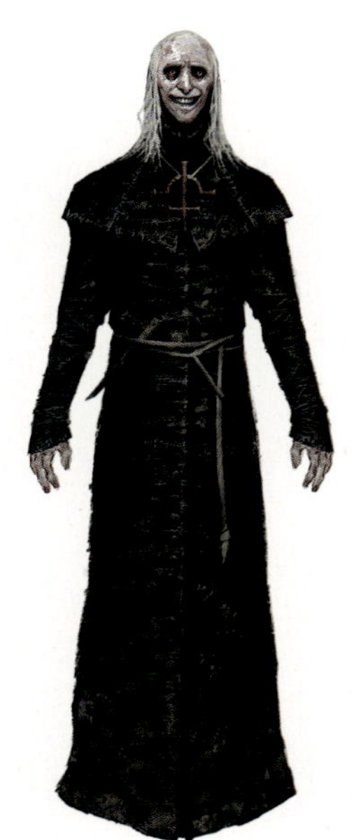

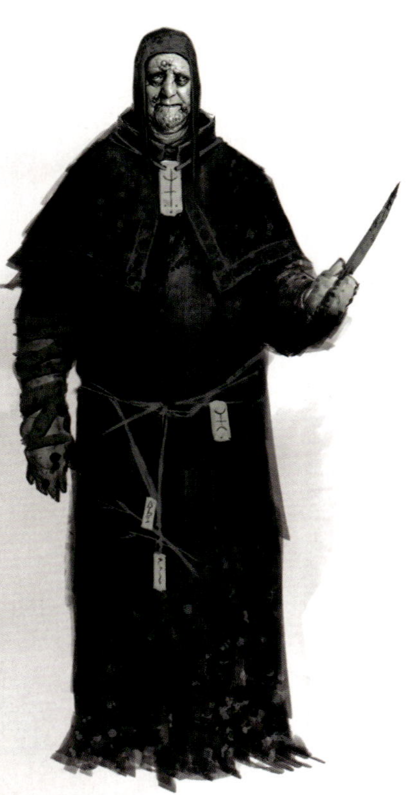

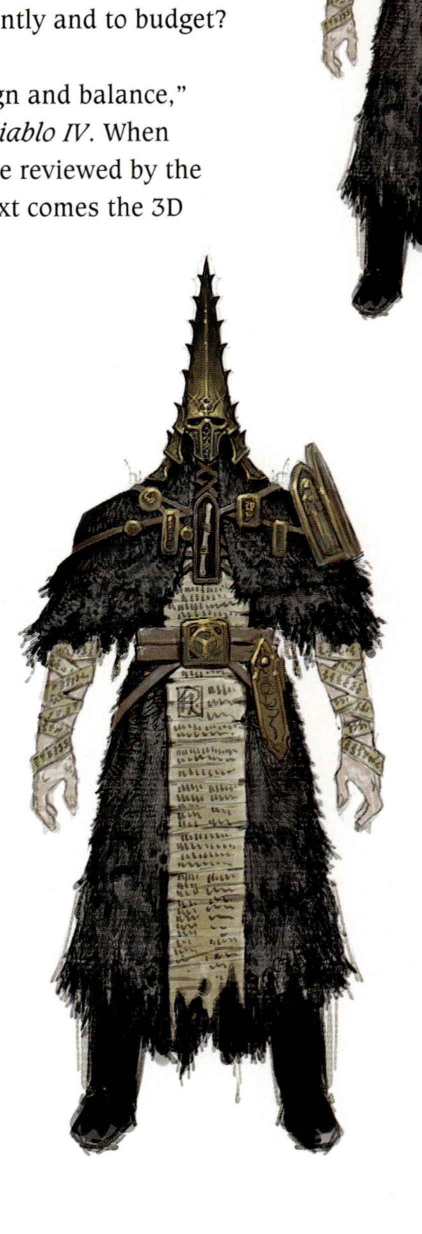

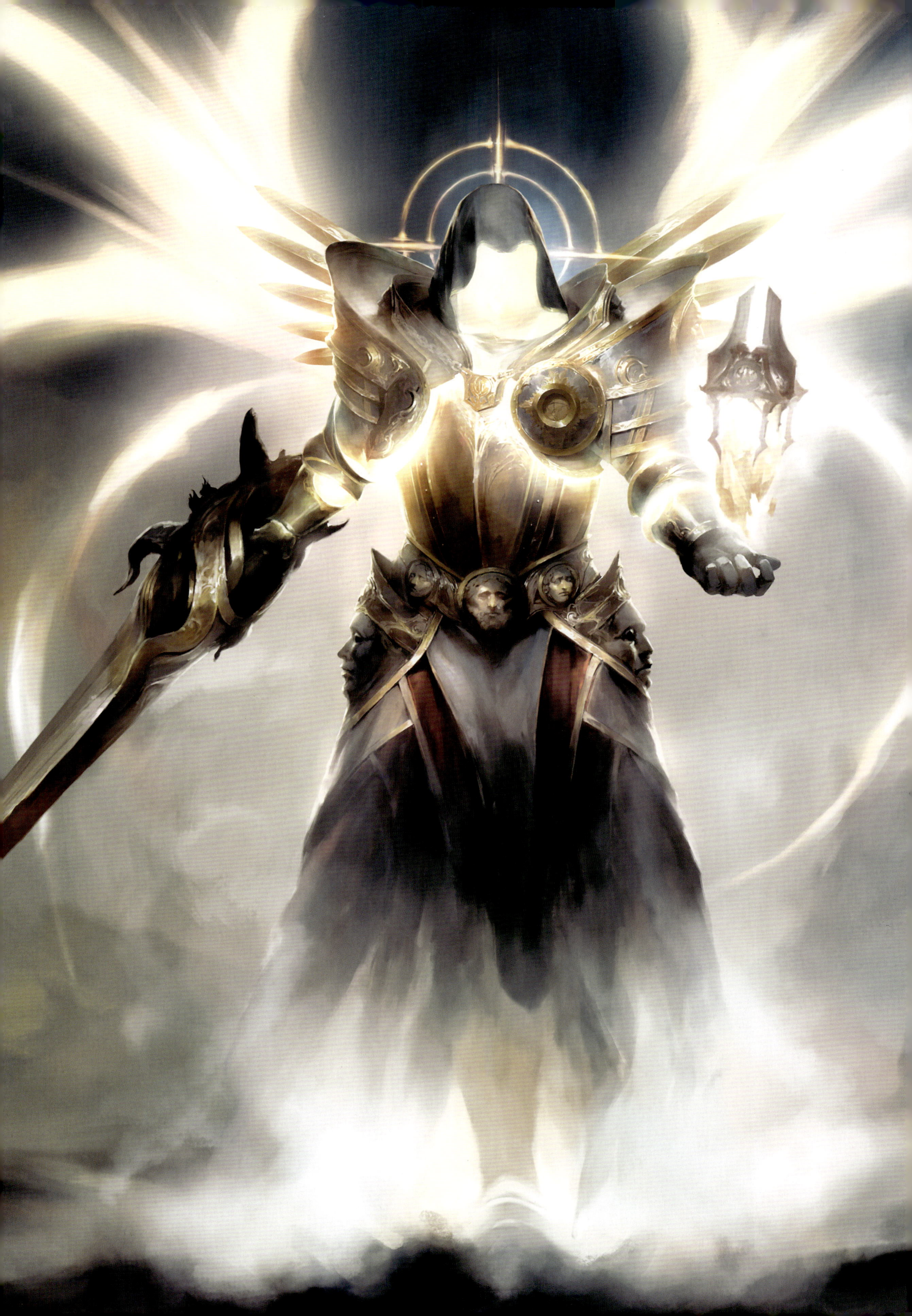

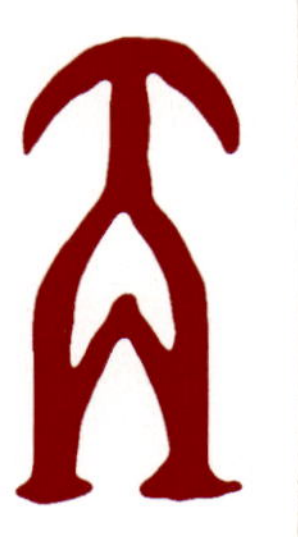

ABOVE Fractured Peaks Lettering + Fernando Pinilla

RIGHT & BOTTOM Butcher Concepts + Gray Rogers

BELOW, TOP Butcher Hook Concept + Gray Rogers

BELOW, BOTTOM Butcher Cleaver Concept + Gray Rogers

OPPOSITE Lilith Throne Illustration + Igor Sidorenko

"The important thing is the lens we're looking through," John Mueller notes. "The *Diablo III* lens was much more heroic, where *Diablo II* was very grounded aesthetically. Our character art in *Diablo IV* has grown so much in its complexity. There are so many layers. It really felt like character art was the perfect thing to go all-in on. You can really get close and they hold up remarkably well as far as the level of detail, it really adds so much to the sense of immersion for the class fantasy."

With all of *Diablo IV*'s customization, even players get to become characters . . . and those characters have a more active role to play in the story than ever before. In fact, the level of character quality in *Diablo IV* is so good, they nearly rival the models created for the cinematics.

"We're getting close," says Mueller. "We try to treat our characters the way Blizzard Animation treats theirs. We've invested a huge amount of effort into research and development and technology, striving to bring these characters to a level of fidelity that feels like it's at the cutting edge of game development."

The goal is for players to create characters who feel like real people inhabiting a real world.

"In previous games, the Barbarian looked a certain way," says Nick Chilano. "So players were kind of stuck with the gray-haired Barbarian. Now I think we've pushed past that . . . If you look at the story, a lot of it is delivered through Lorath, Neyrelle, Donan, and these other characters, and you're there with them. I think we're in a good spot to say, 'This is what Lorath would do, but you as a character are in a situation where maybe you can start to do things the way you want.' You want to imprint yourself in the character, and I think we've turned a corner where we're starting to get into that space with *Diablo IV*."

Of course, the star of the show this time around is Lilith, a character just as beautiful as she is deadly.

"There's a lot of nastiness in the game, so when there is beauty, it's in stark contrast to that," says Hunter. "With Lilith, there's a lot of beauty in that design. Some people don't understand how you can be drawn to dark art or dark stuff in general. It's very primal. It's a part of our nature. You can do horror with something that's grotesque and makes your skin crawl, or you can do it with something that is almost alluring. And there's terror in that as well. Aesthetically, I think a good design should be beautiful. Doesn't mean it can't scare the hell out of you."

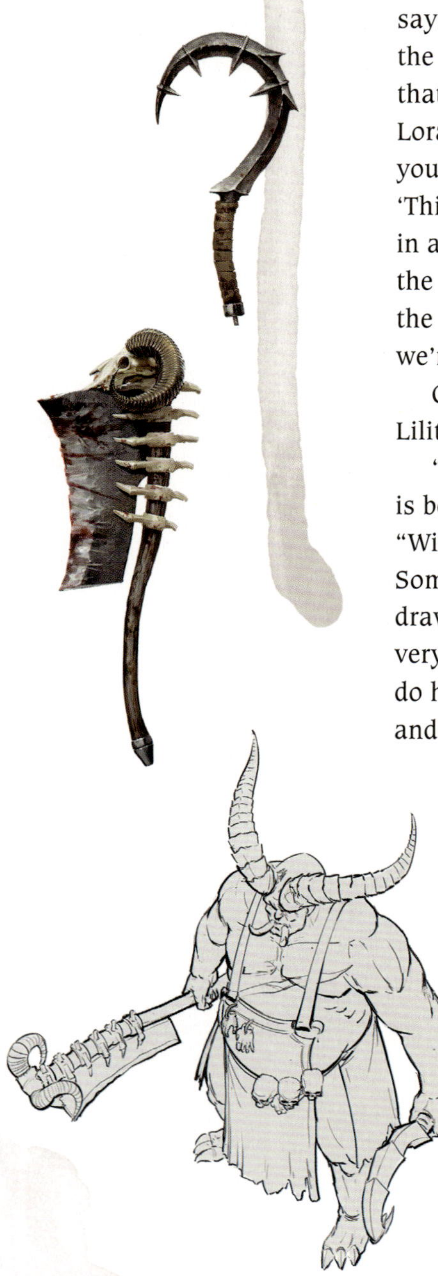

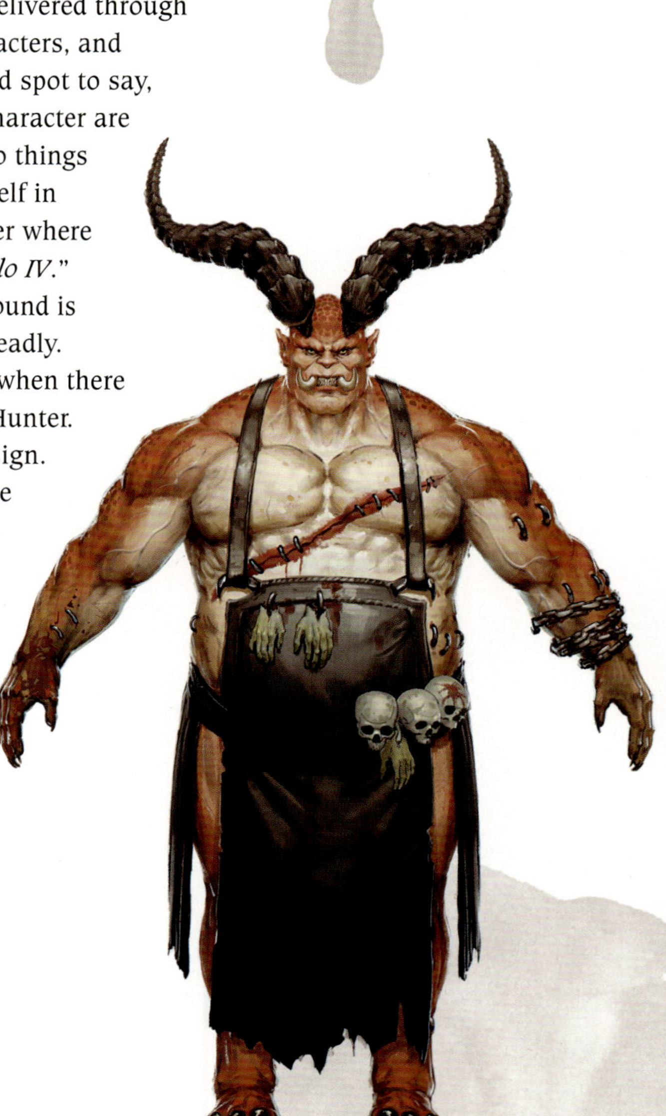

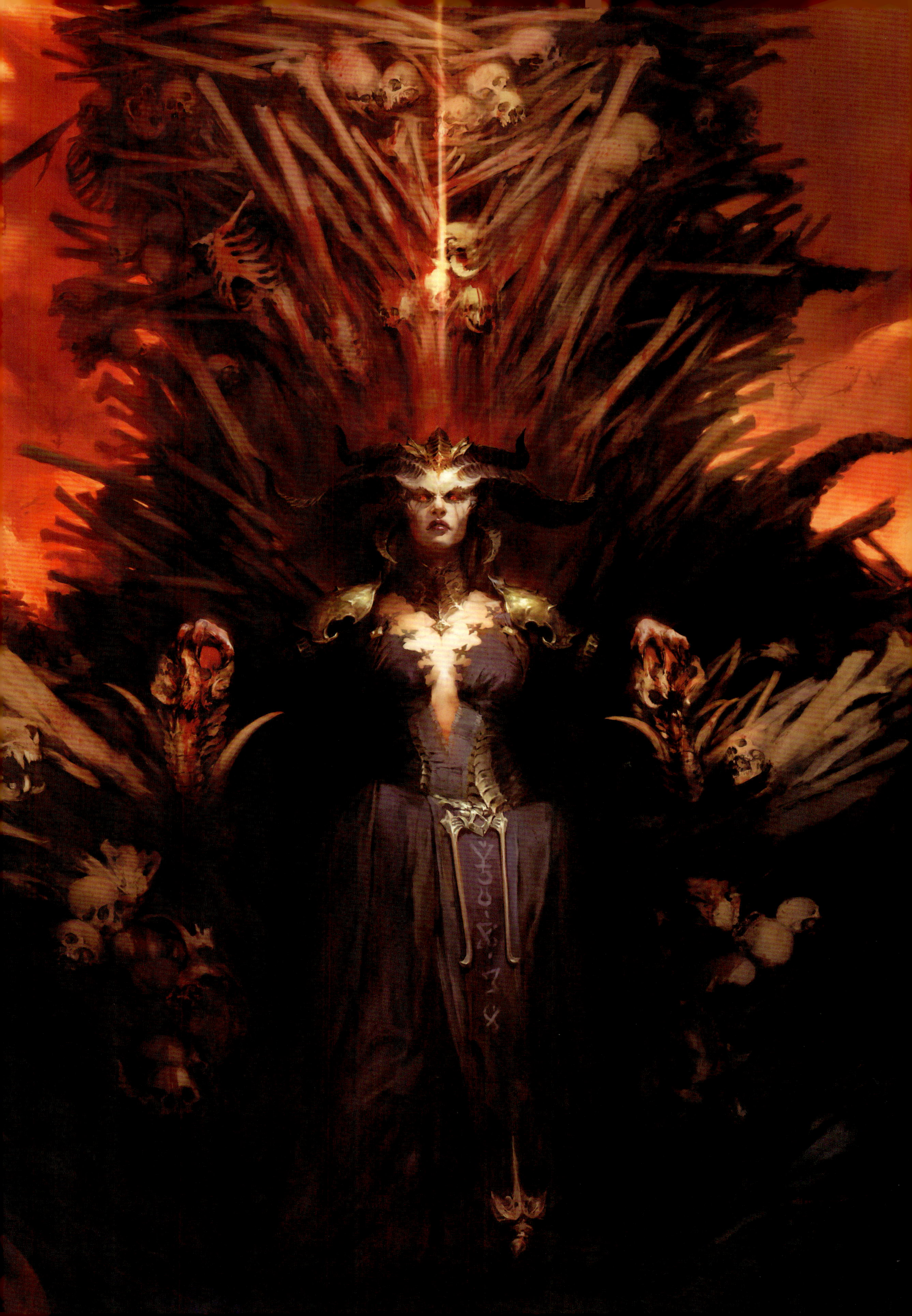

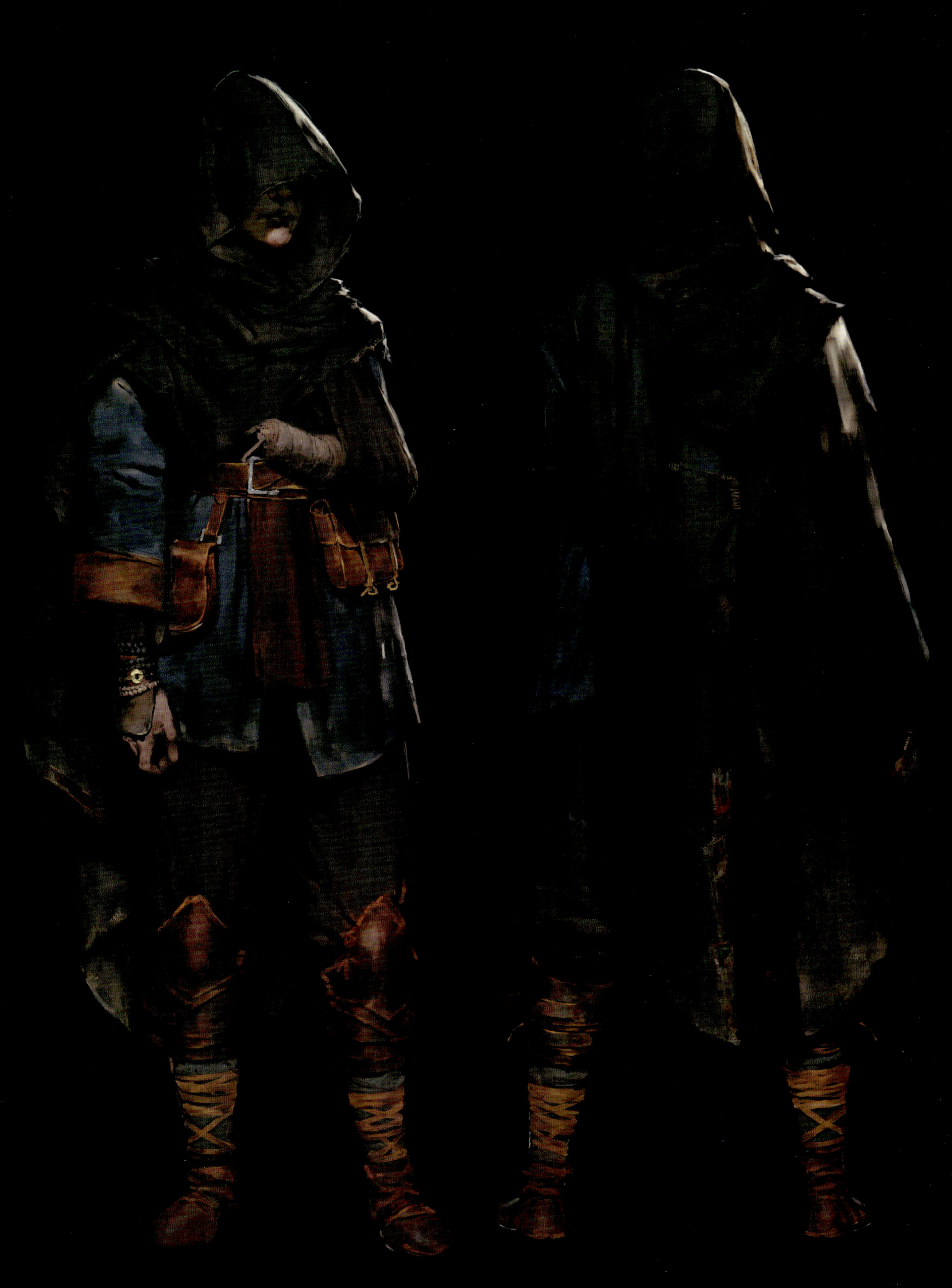

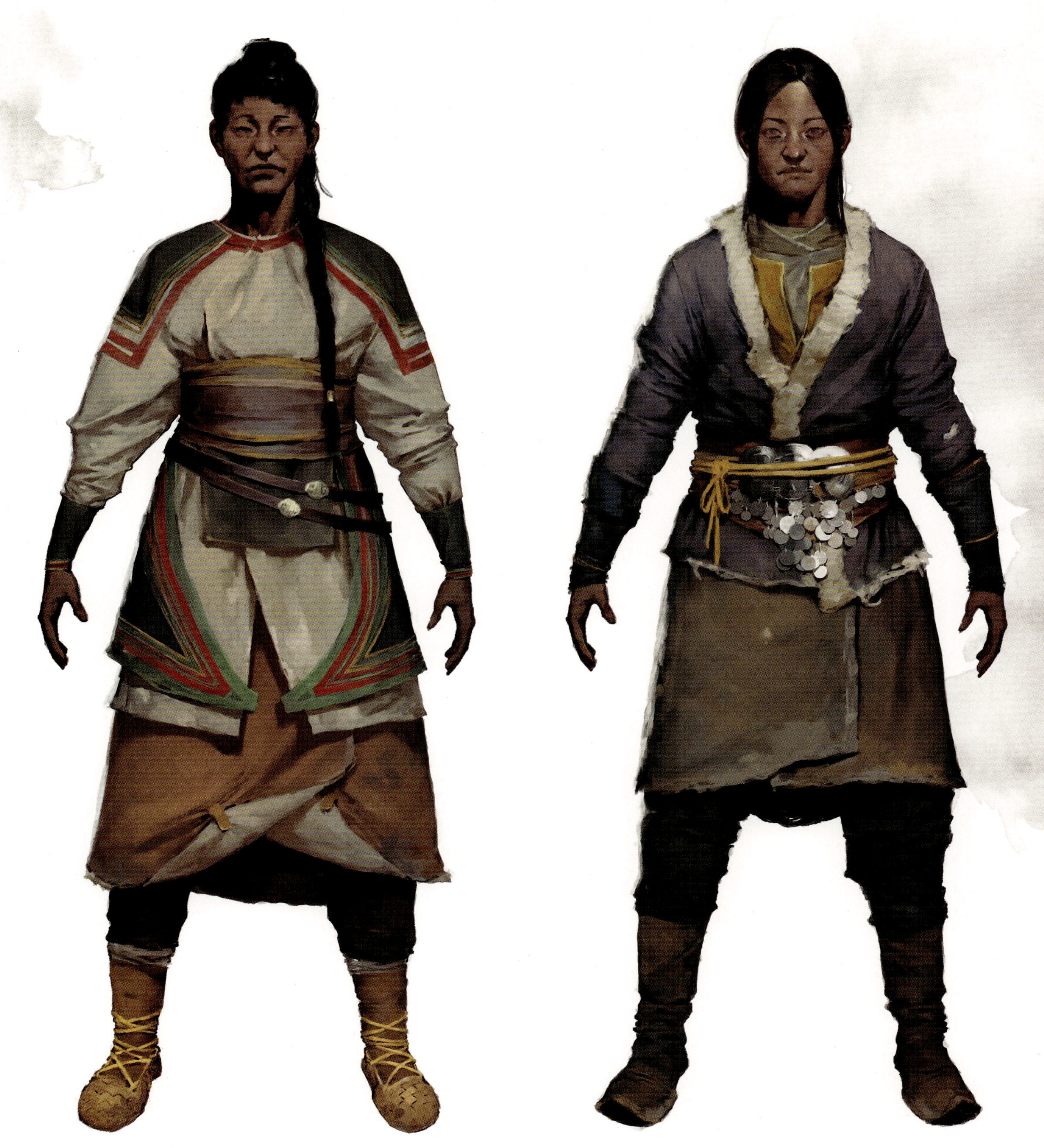

"A lot of times, we latch on to things that are popular, like a certain hairstyle or skin marking like a tattoo, and it appears in the game and then it's no longer popular and the game is just locked into that time period. So that's always on my mind: how to keep things timeless. It's not easy because everybody wants to use things—design elements and visuals—that are popular currently. We just have to be aware of it."

—VICTOR LEE, Lead Concept Artist

ABOVE Dry Steppes Villager Concept • Igor Sidorenko

OPPOSITE Neyrelle Concept • Igor Sidorenko

RIGHT Early Lyndon Concept + Hyun Lee

BOTTOM Early Donan Concept + Victor Lee

OPPOSITE Dry Steppes Villager Concept + Igor Sidorenko

FOLLOWING SPREAD, LEFT Early Lilith Concept + Victor Lee

FOLLOWING SPREAD, RIGHT Herald of Hatred + Victor Lee

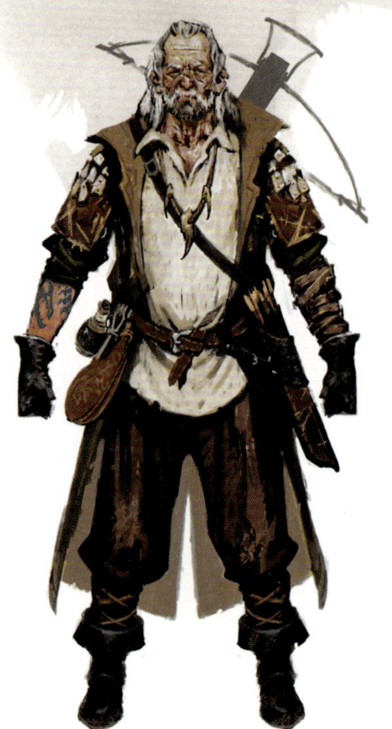

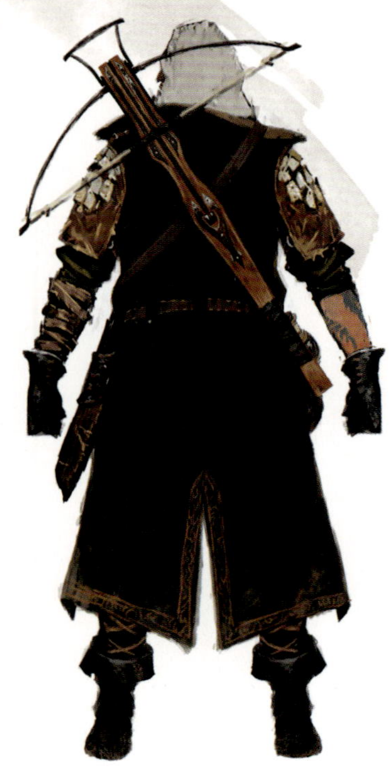

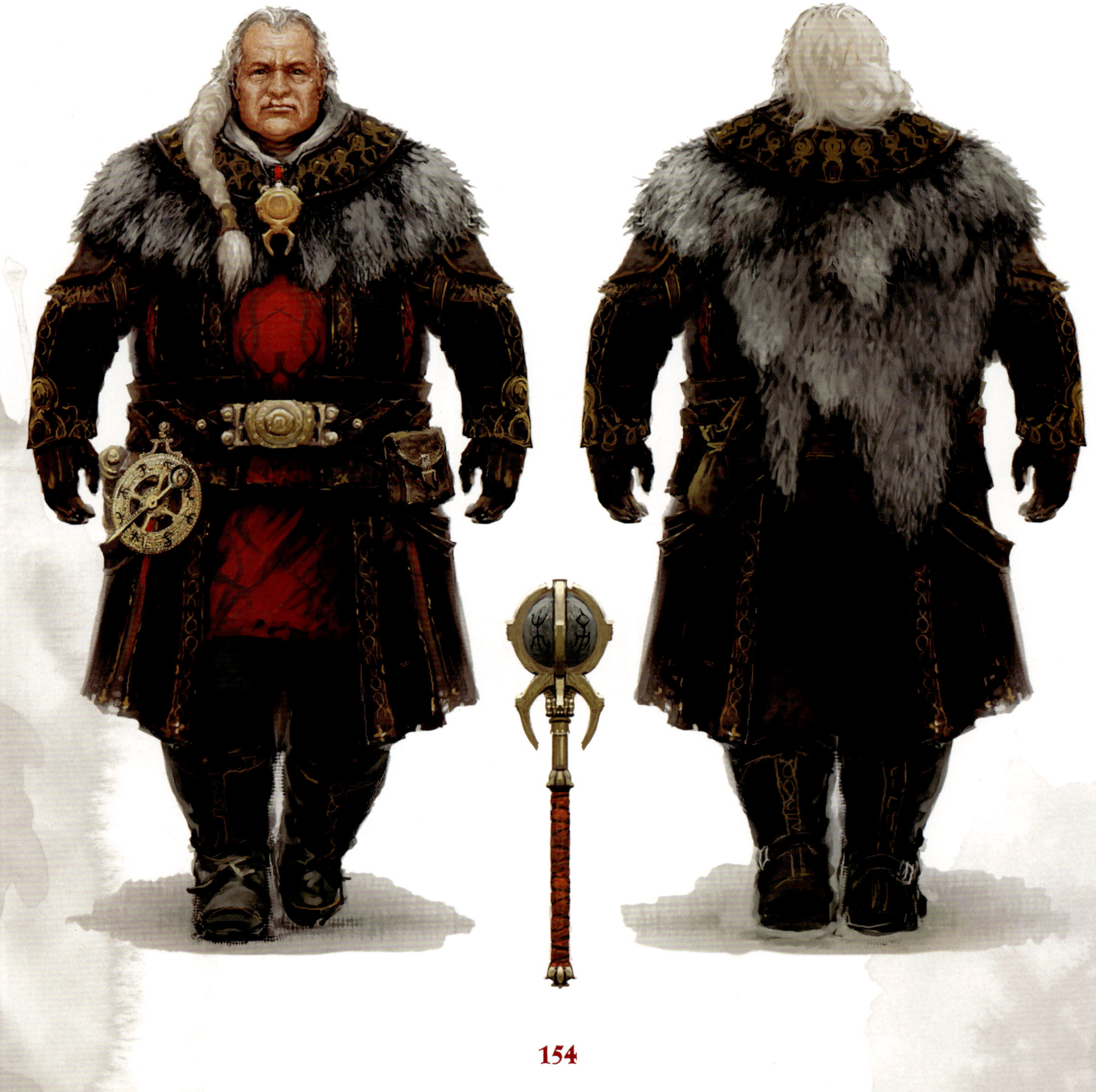

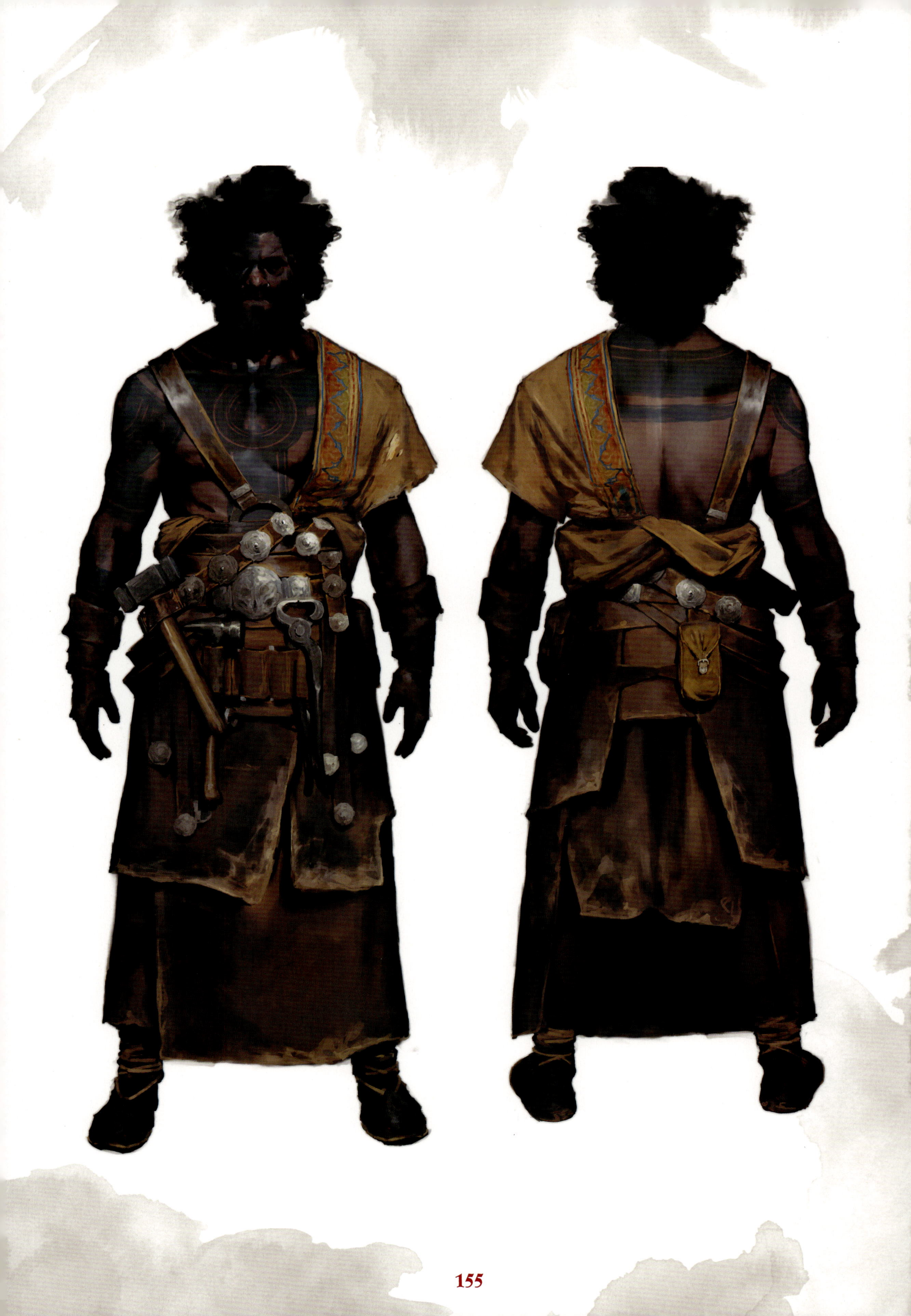

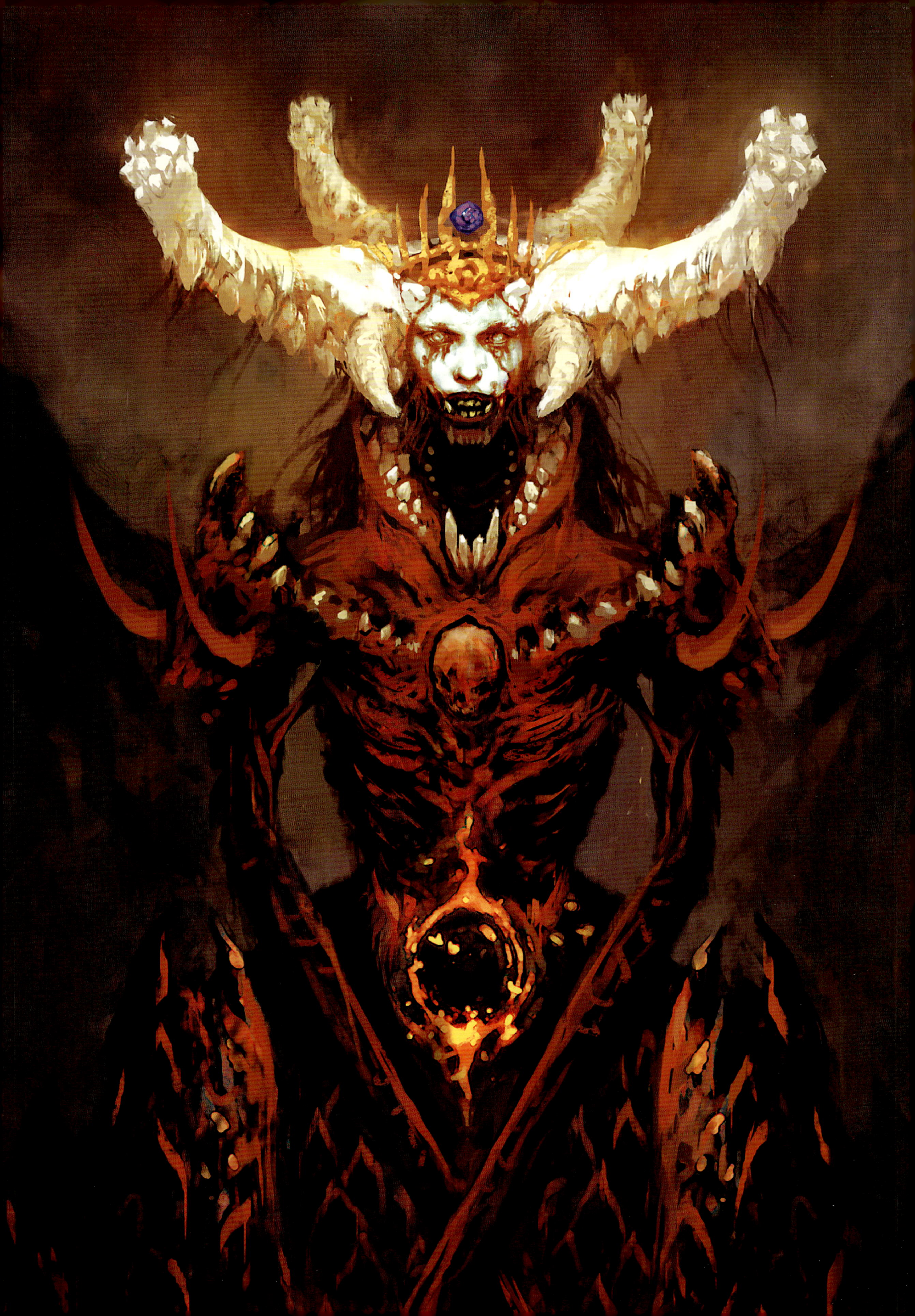

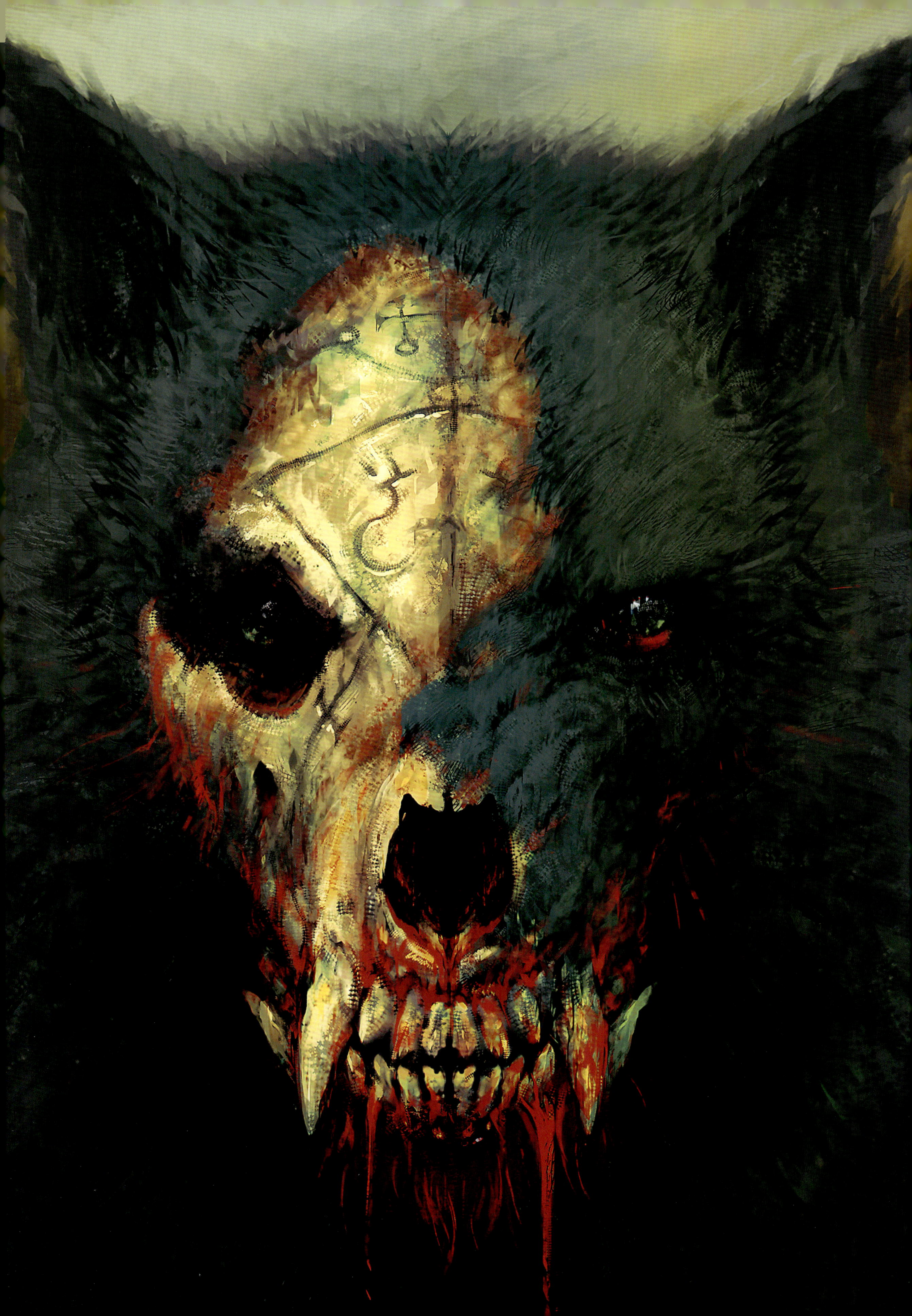

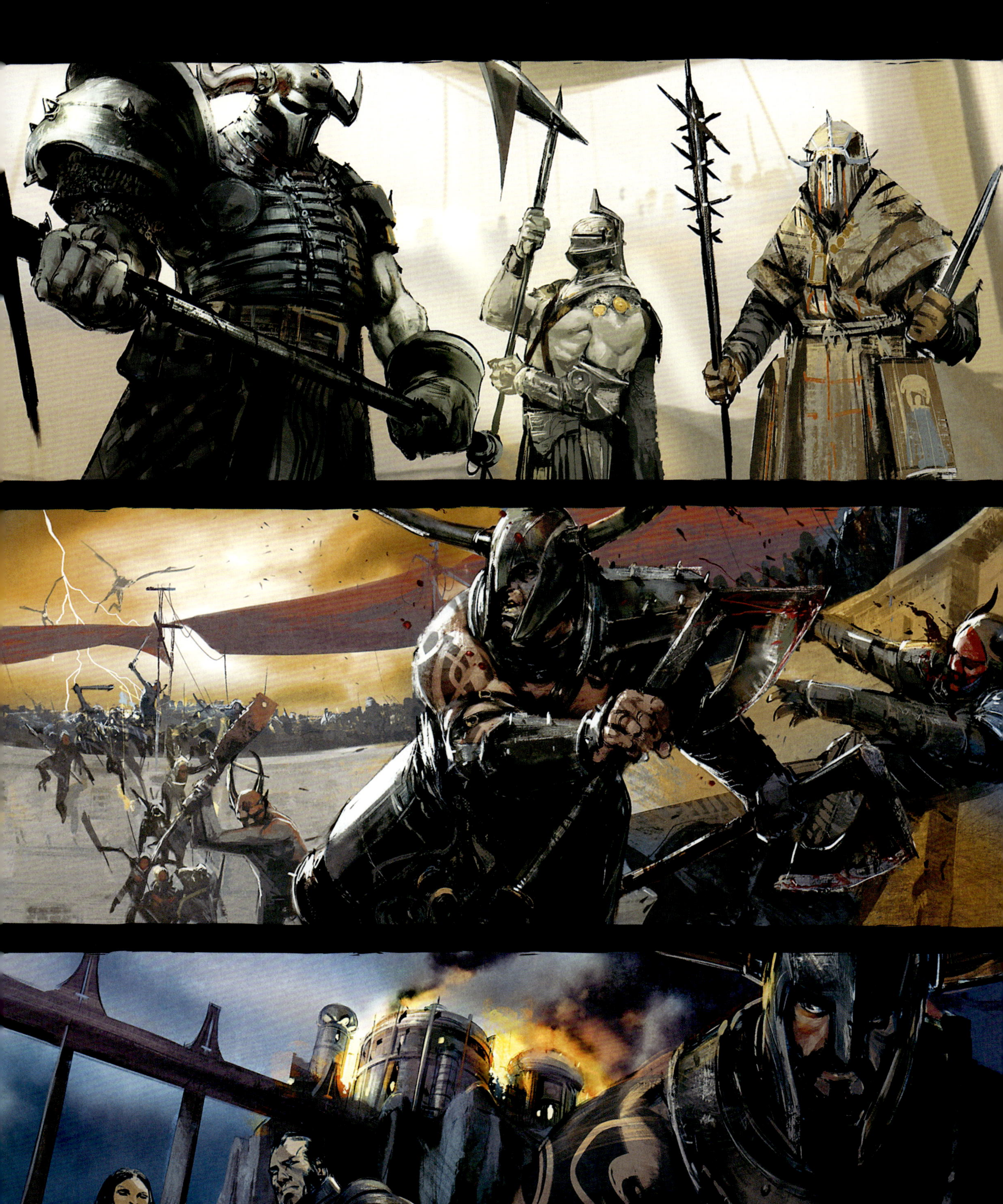

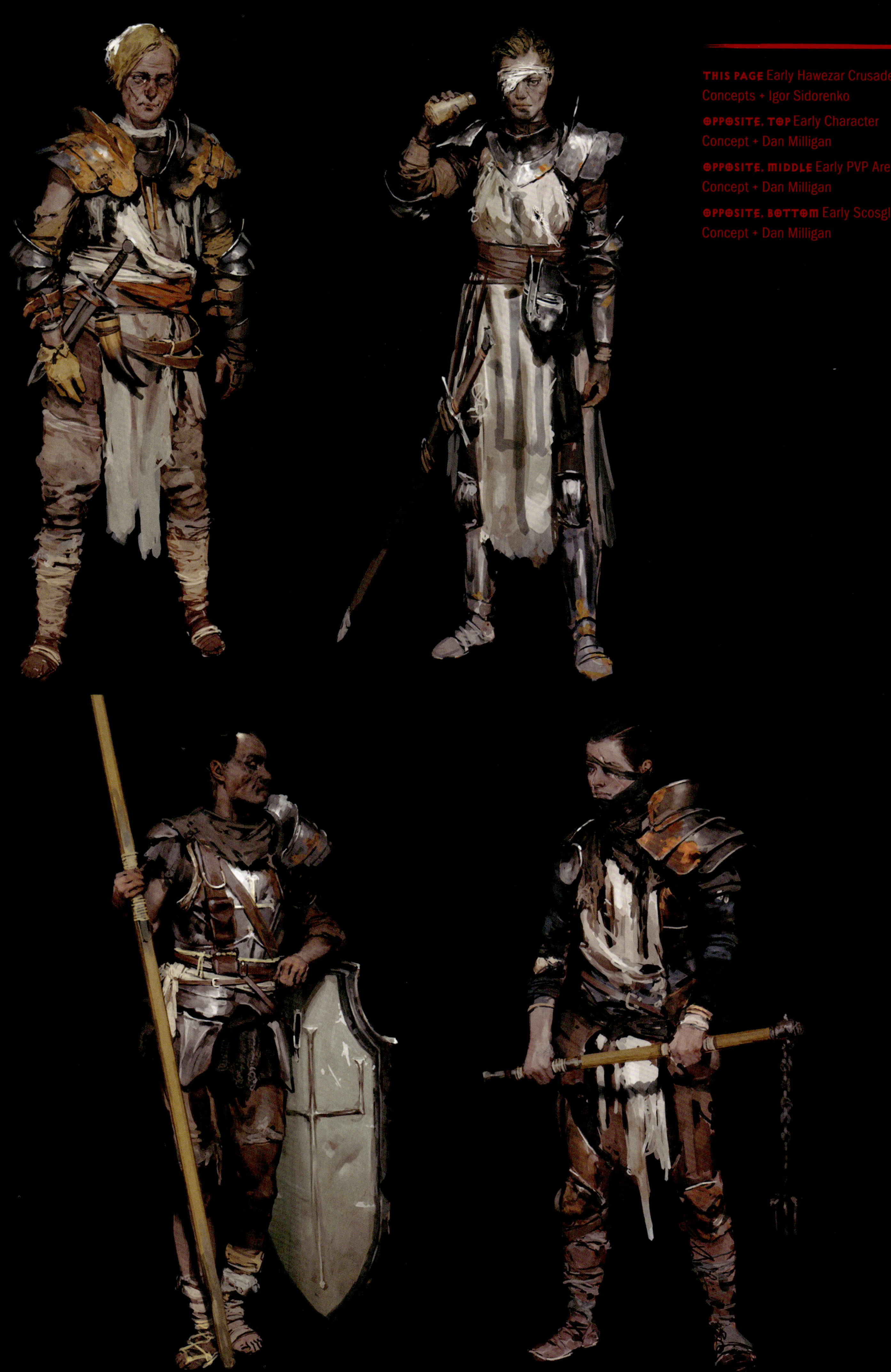

THIS PAGE Early Hawezar Crusader Concepts + Igor Sidorenko

OPPOSITE, TOP Early Character Concept + Dan Milligan

OPPOSITE, MIDDLE Early PVP Arena Concept + Dan Milligan

OPPOSITE, BOTTOM Early Scosglen Concept + Dan Milligan

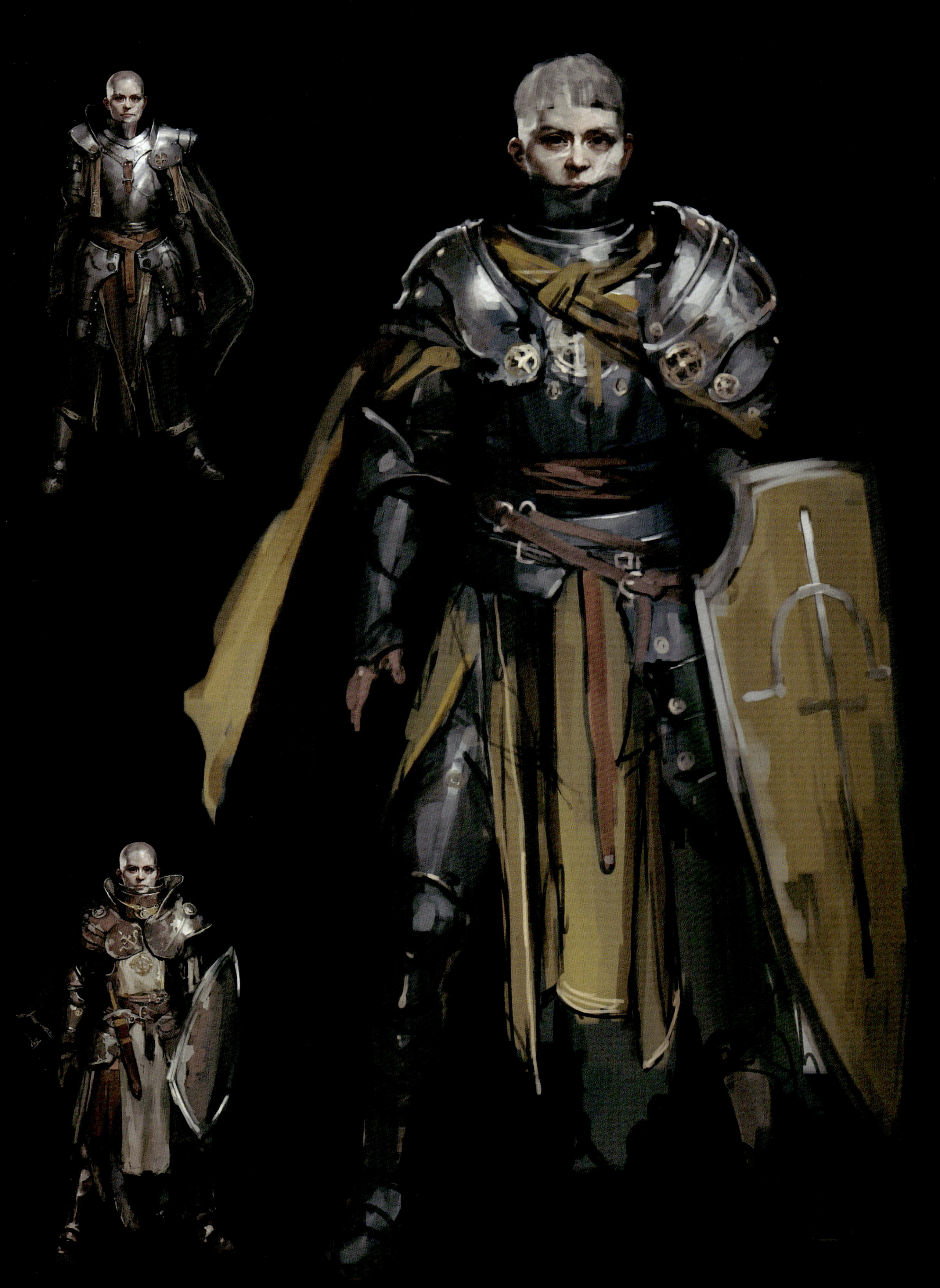

RIGHT Early Enemy Concept + Mike Franchina
BOTTOM Lilith Concept + Igor Sidorenko
OPPOSITE Early Fractured Peaks Knight Concepts + gor Sidorenko

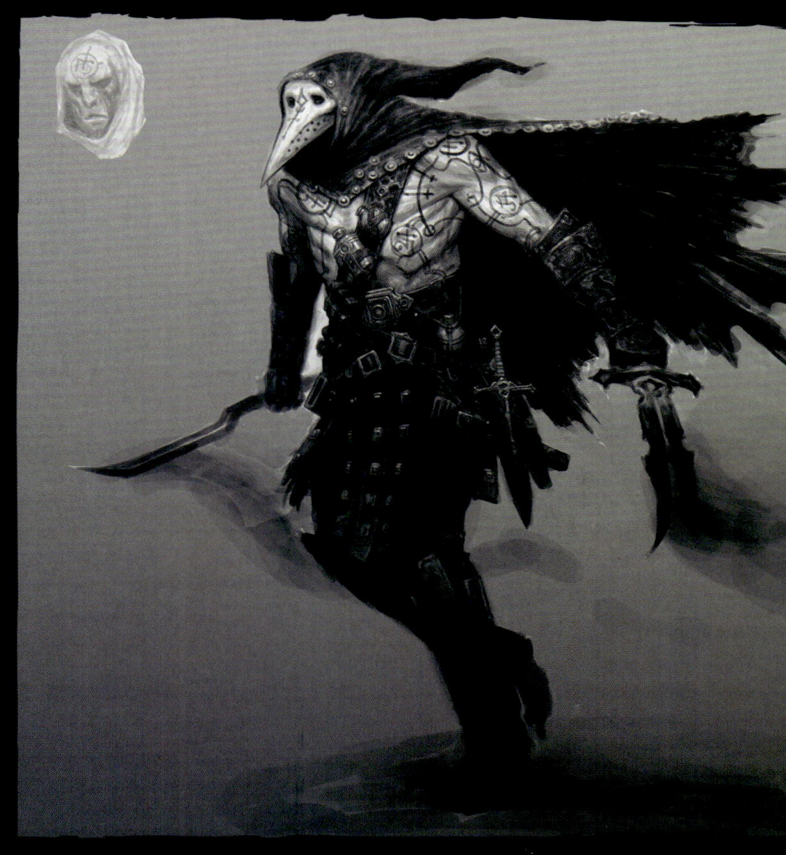

'The characters don't feel like hey're in a comic book; they eel like real characters in a real vorld, and the armor and the details all feel very real."

—JOHN MUELLER, Art Director

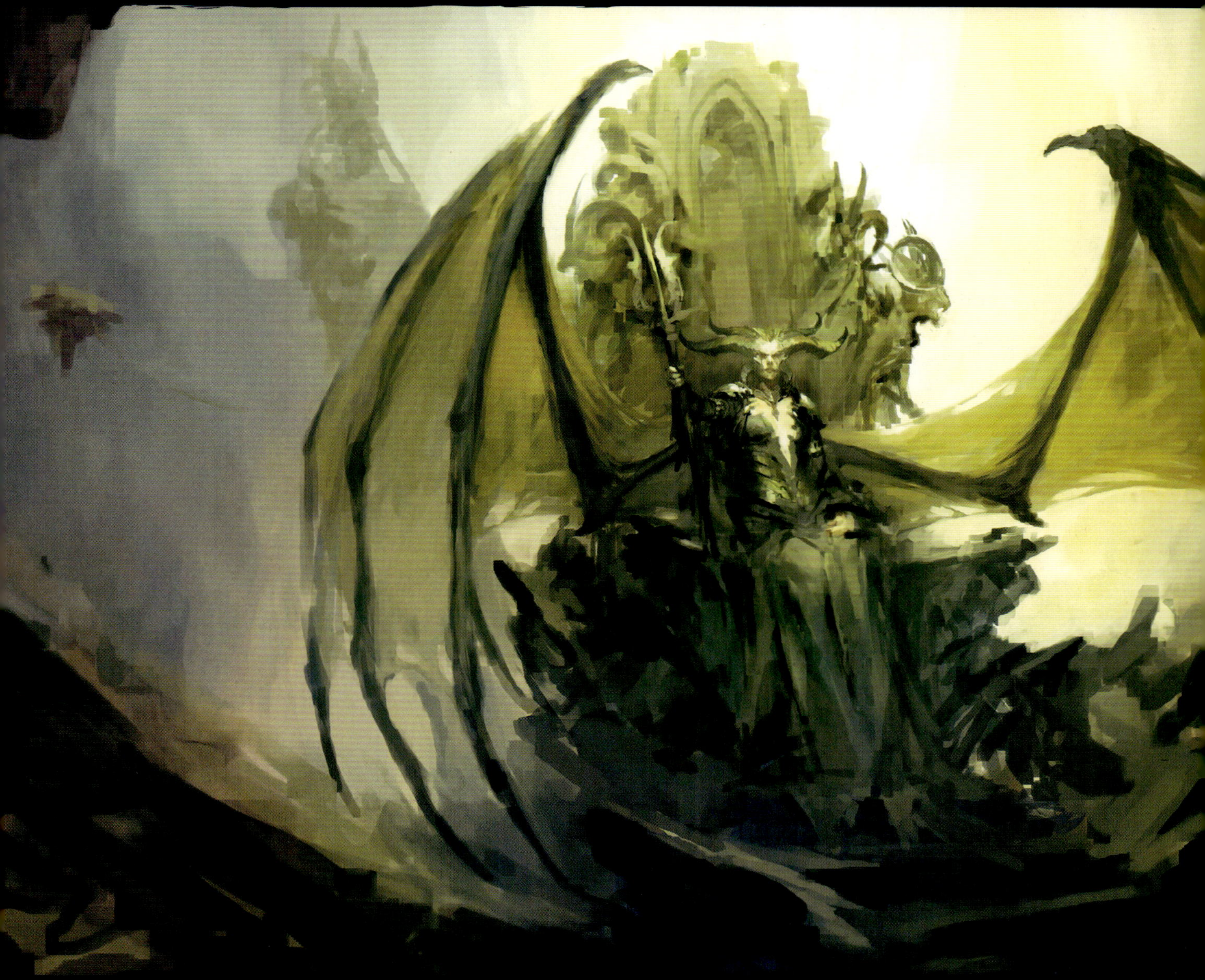

TOP, LEFT Hawezar Infected Concept + Igor Sidorenko

TOP, RIGHT Tejal Concept + Igor Sidorenko

BELOW & BOTTOM Hawezar Infected Concepts + Igor Sidorenko

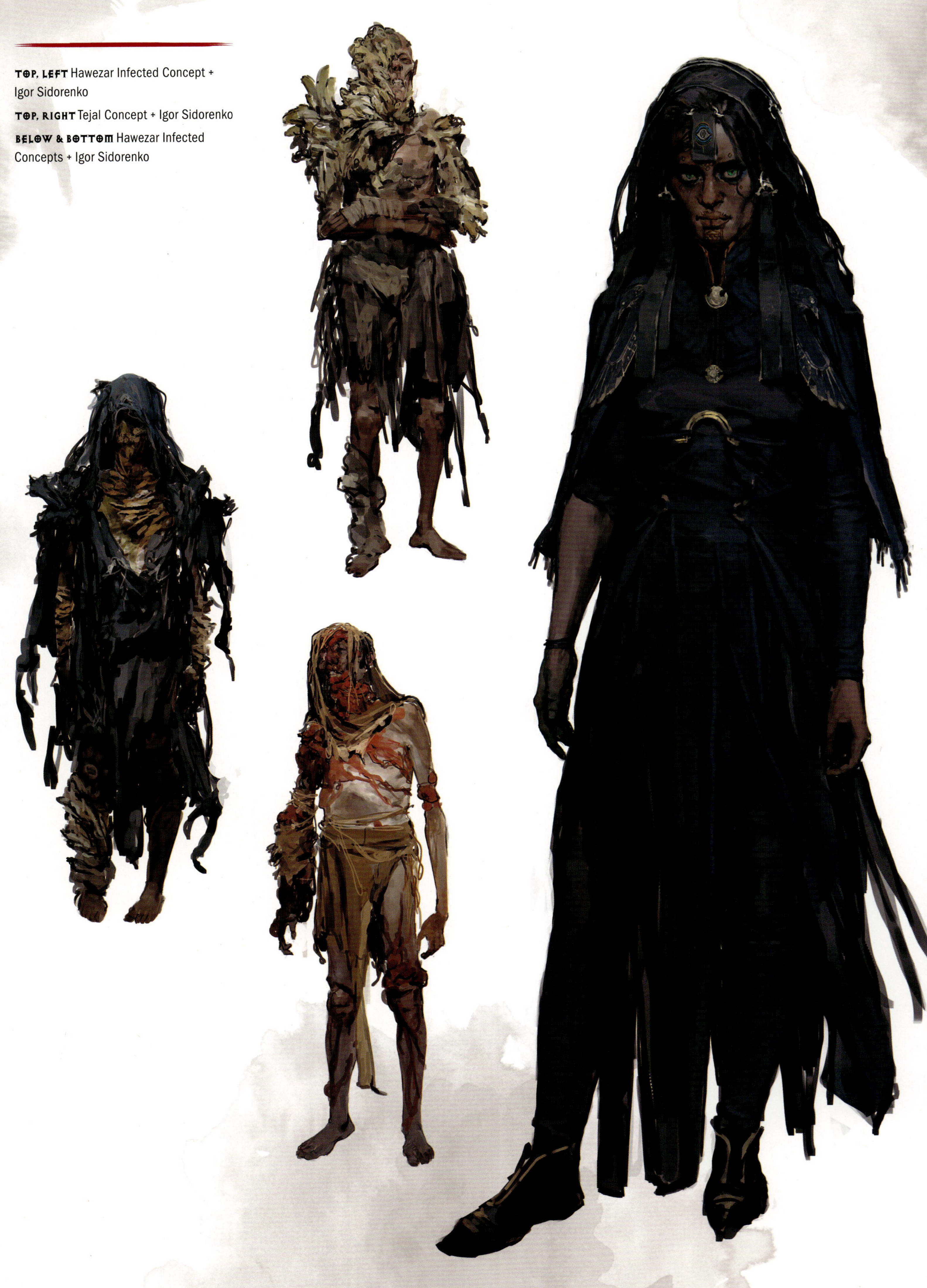

LEFT Neyrelle Concept + Igor Sidorenko

RIGHT Alchemist Concept + Igor Sidorenko

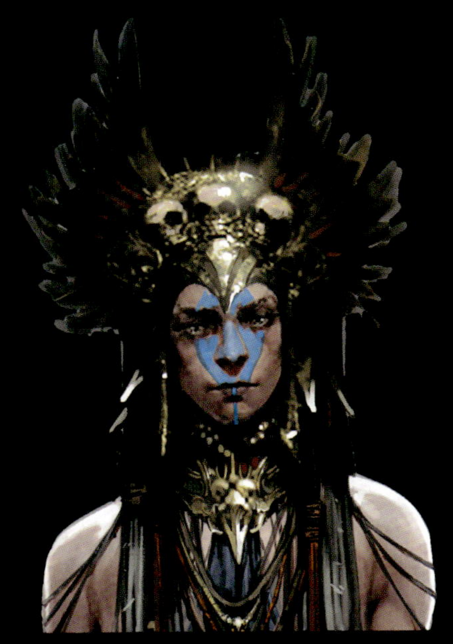
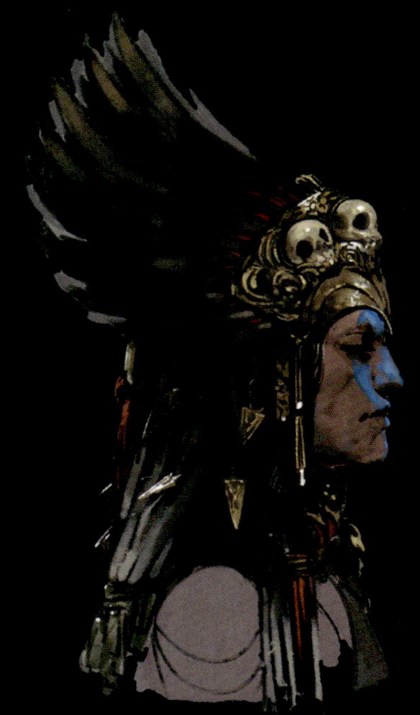
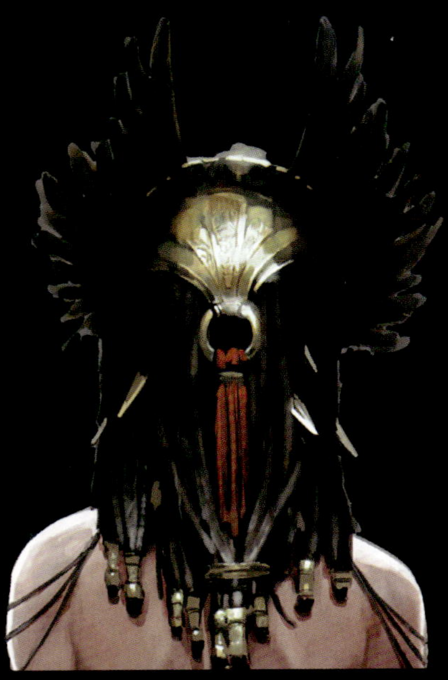

ABOVE Early Taissa Headdress Concepts + Peet Cooper

RIGHT Early Taissa Concept + Konstantin Vavilov

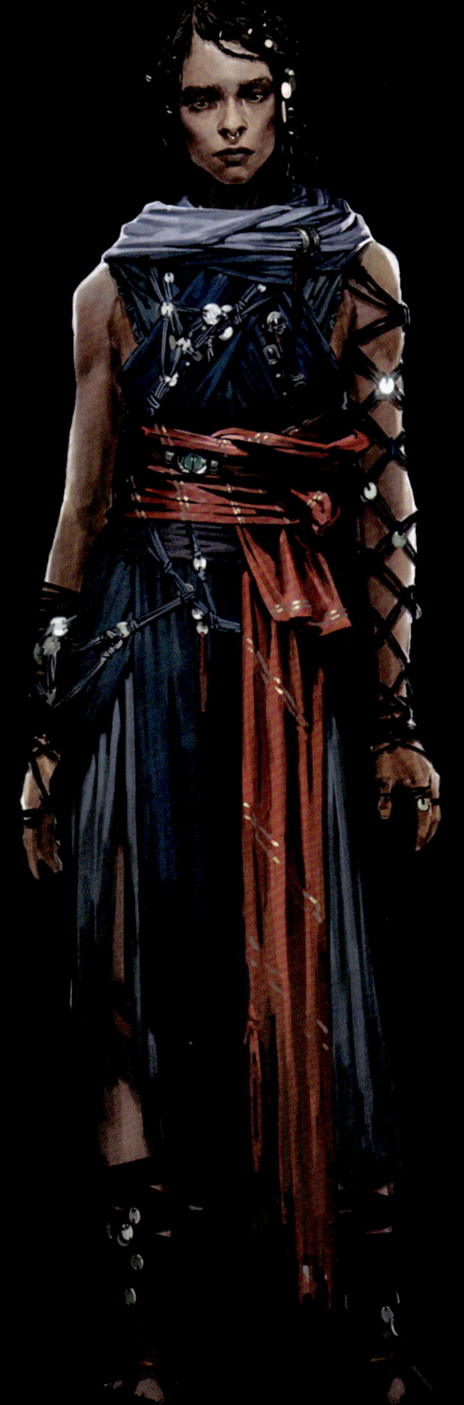
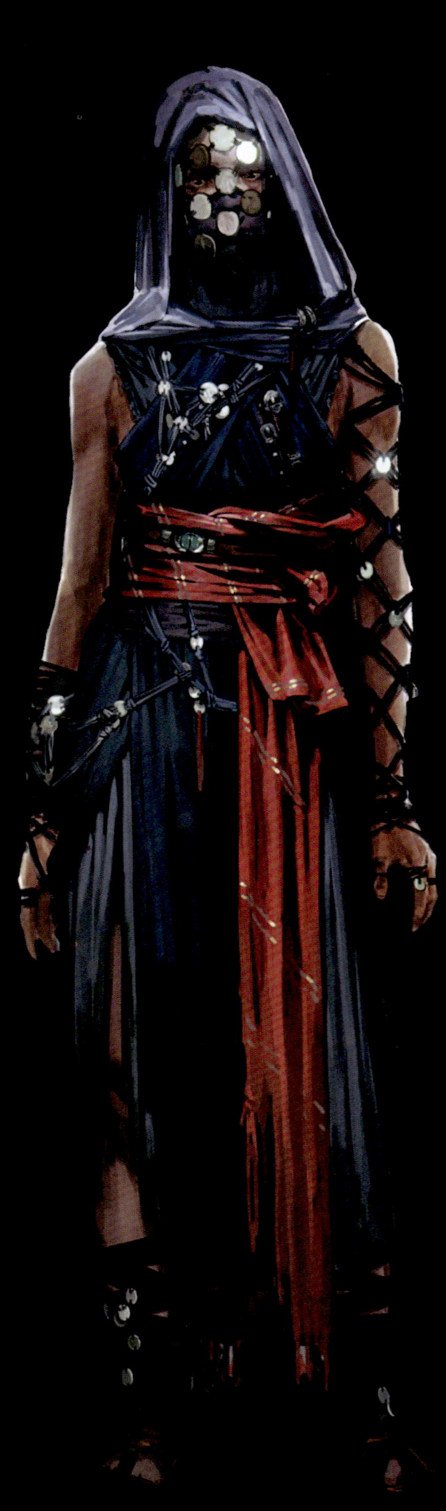

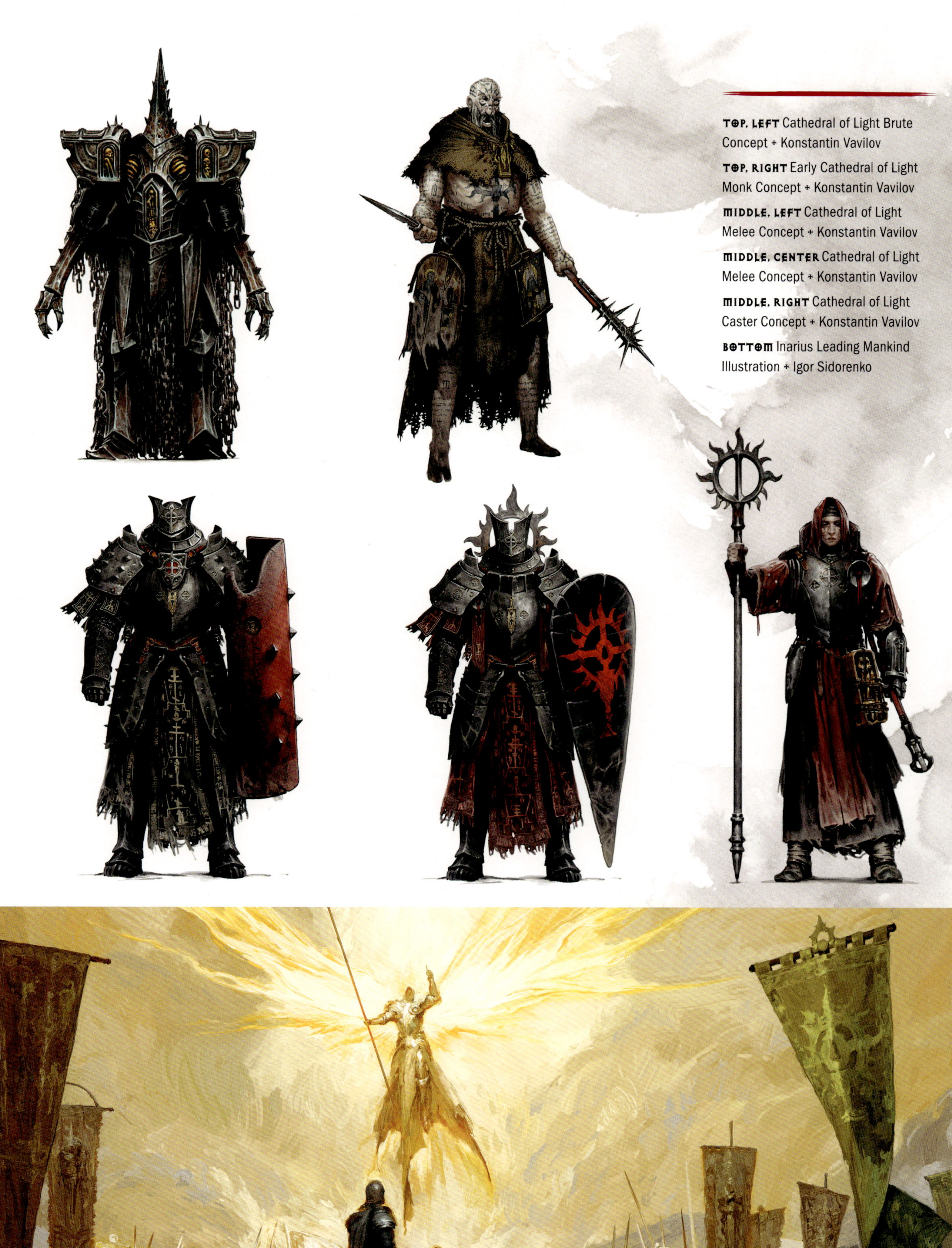

TOP, LEFT Cathedral of Light Brute Concept + Konstantin Vavilov

TOP, RIGHT Early Cathedral of Light Monk Concept + Konstantin Vavilov

MIDDLE, LEFT Cathedral of Light Melee Concept + Konstantin Vavilov

MIDDLE, CENTER Cathedral of Light Melee Concept + Konstantin Vavilov

MIDDLE, RIGHT Cathedral of Light Caster Concept + Konstantin Vavilov

BOTTOM Inarius Leading Mankind Illustration + Igor Sidorenko

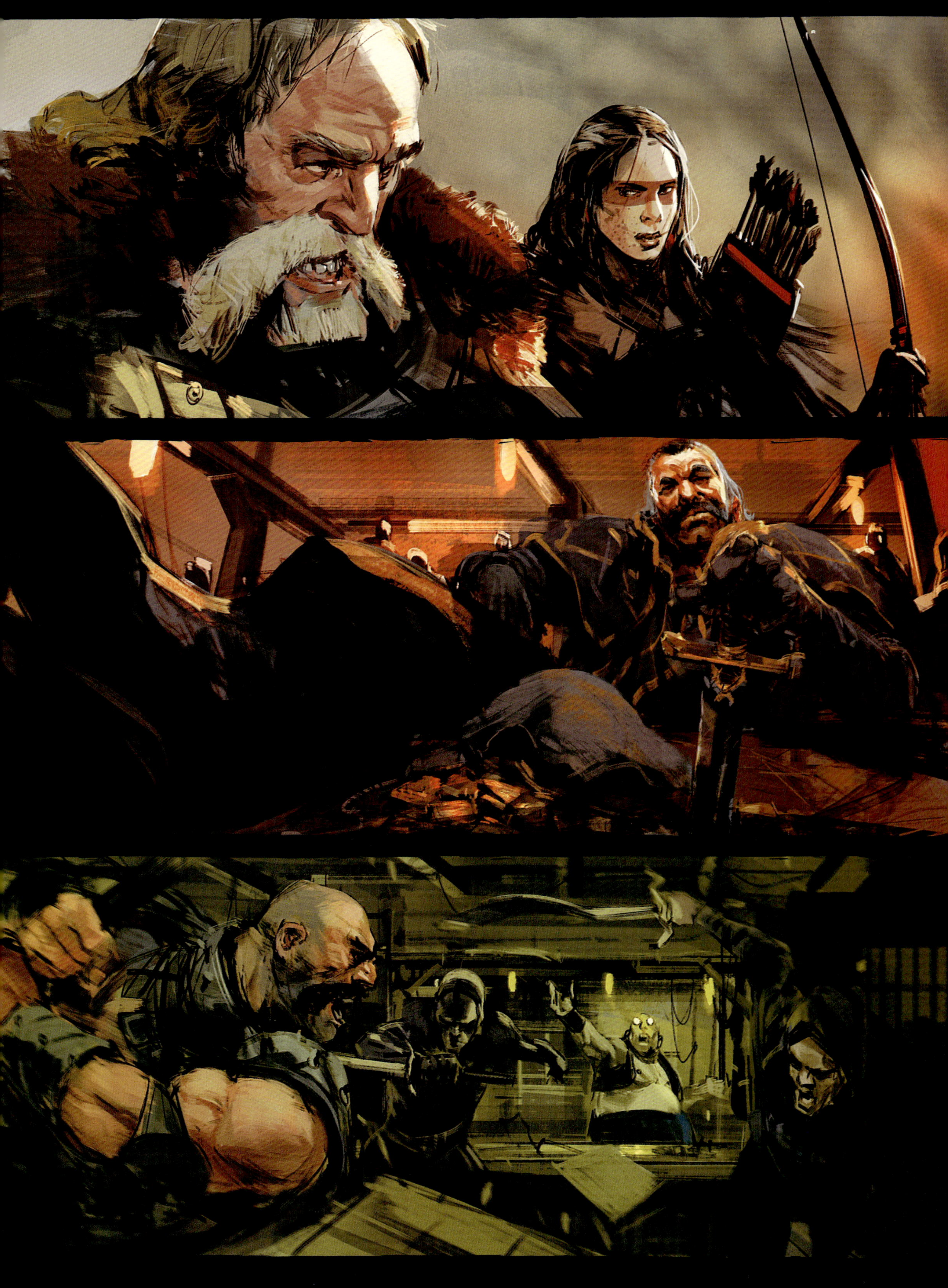

"In Diablo IV, *the detail level on the armor sets just blows my mind with how much we can do in the variants. A lot of our character artists and character leads are masters of pushing the variety and the aesthetics of the design and making sure each face has a nice aesthetic where they look like individual characters."*

—RICHIE MARELLA, Associate Art Director

BELOW Yorin Concept + Victor Lee

OPPOSITE, TOP Early Scosglen Concept + Dan Milligan

OPPOSITE, MIDDLE Lyndon Concept + Dan Milligan

OPPOSITE, BOTTOM Early Tavern Brawl Concept + Dan Milligan

FOLLOWING SPREAD Inarius Heals Prava Illustration + Igor Sidorenko

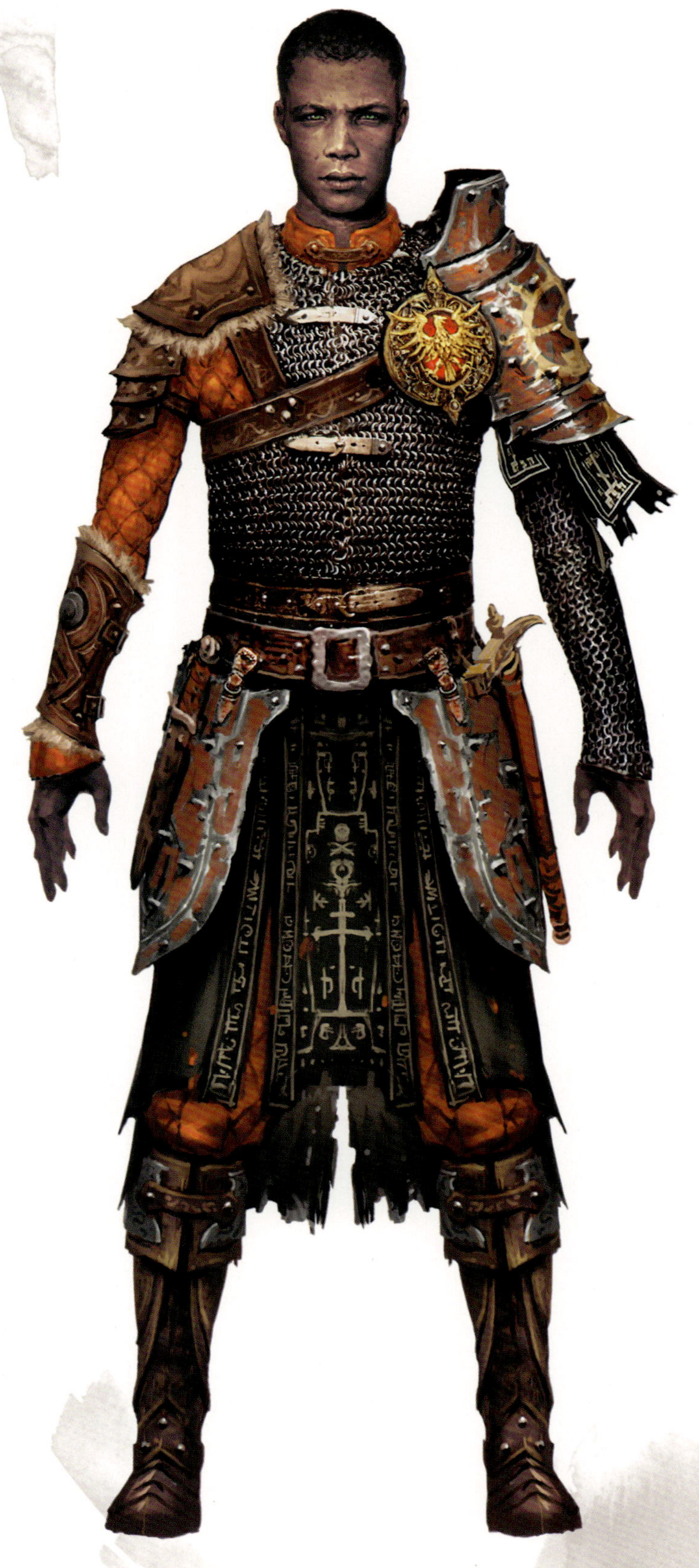

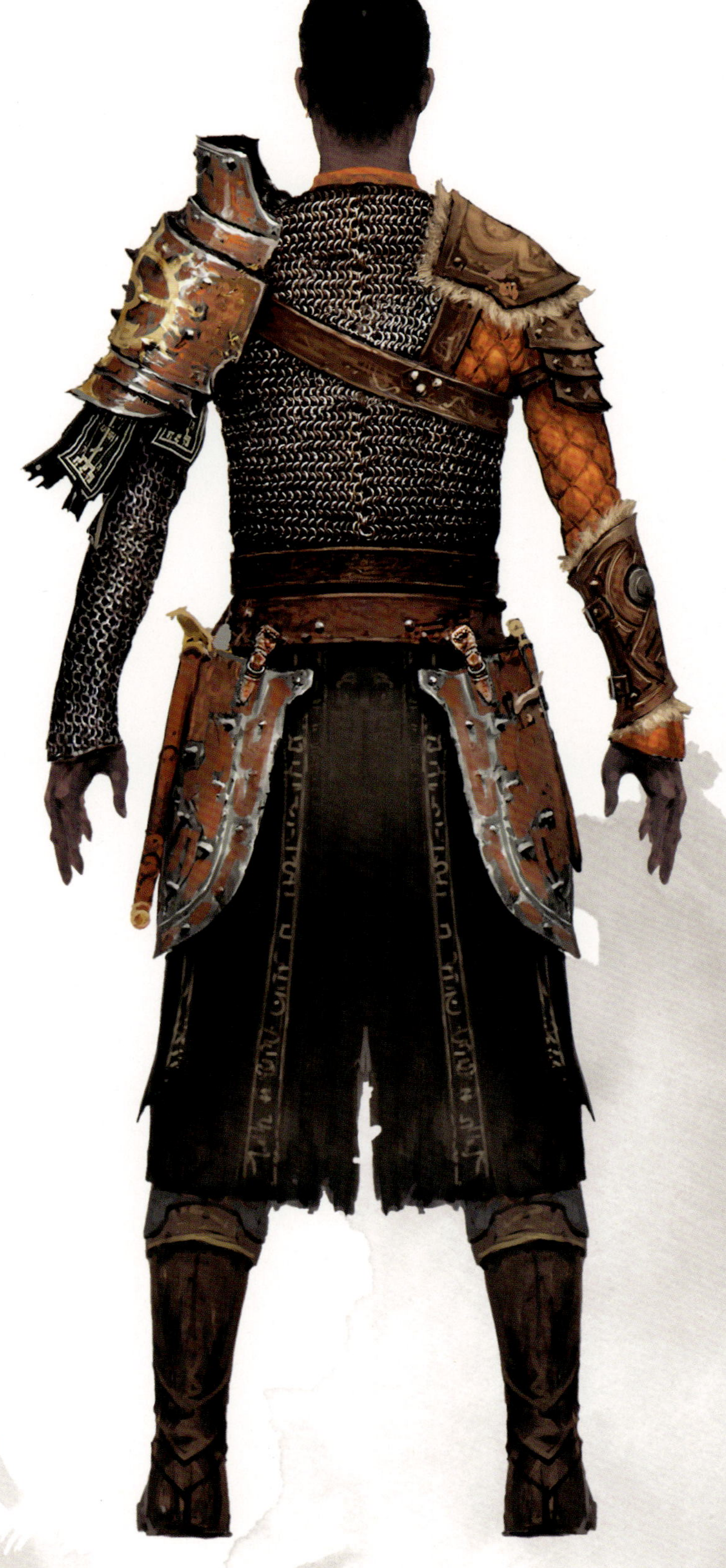

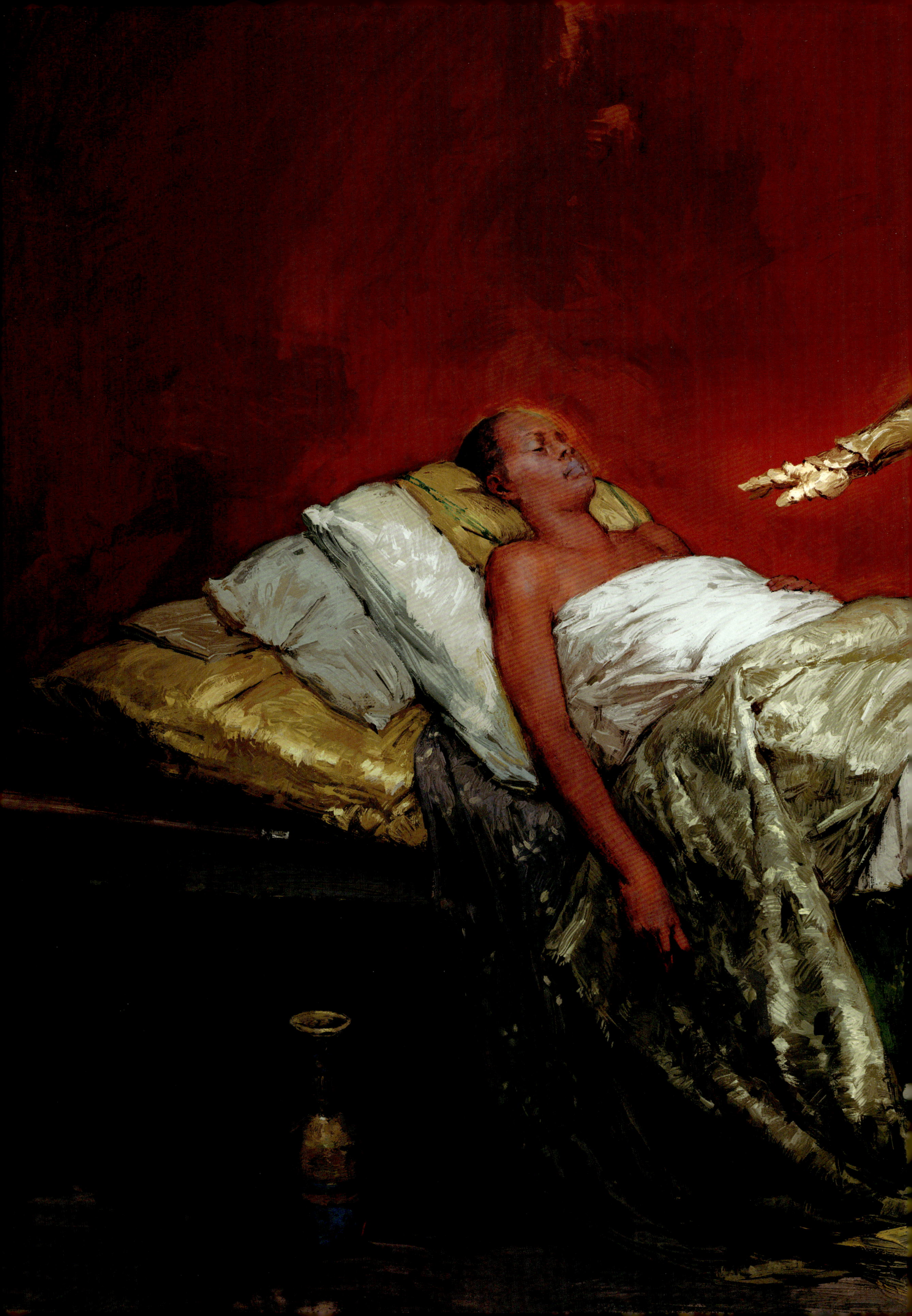

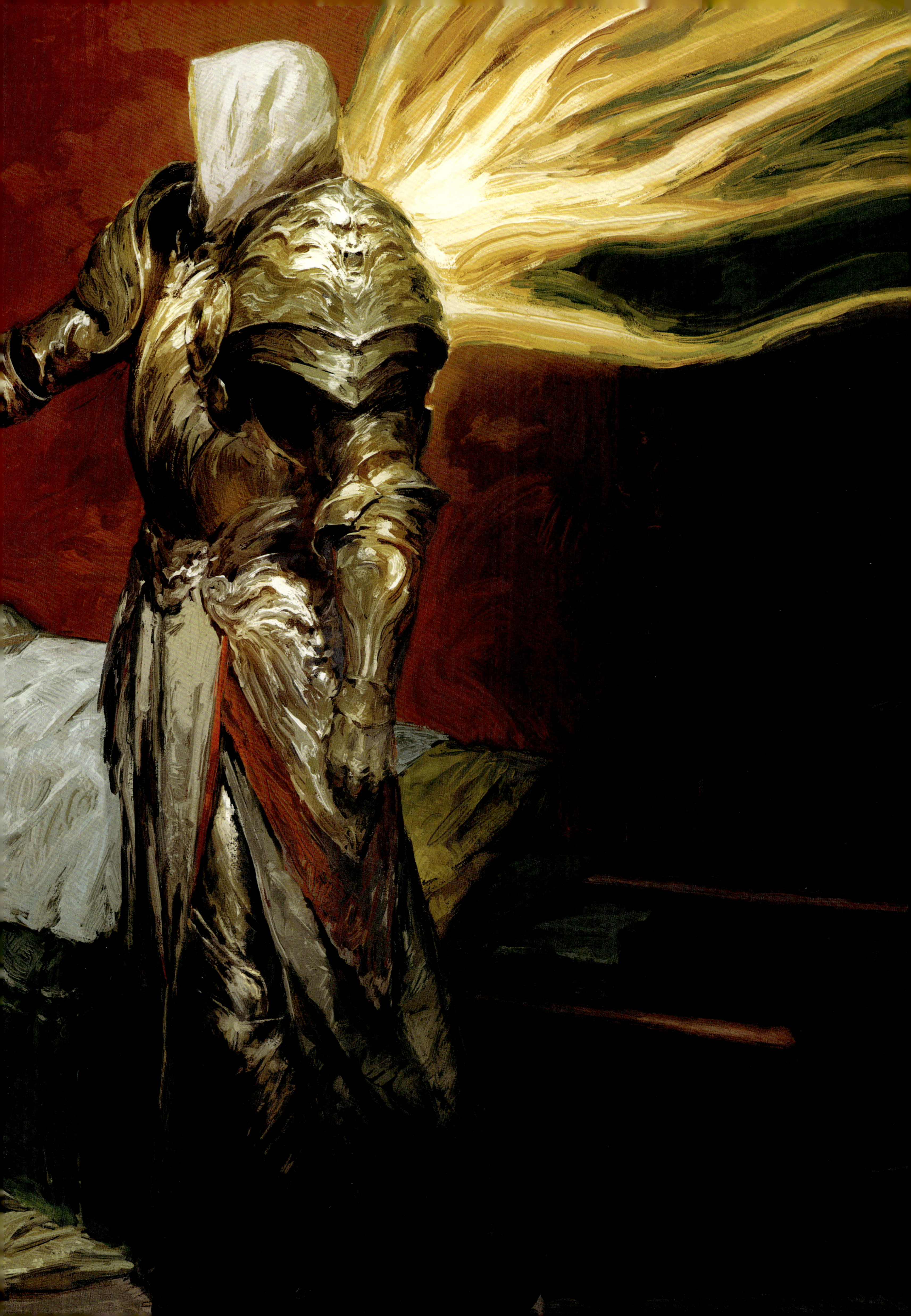

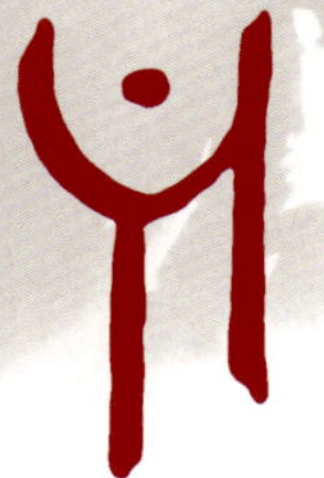

Dark Imaginings

ABOVE Druid Lettering + Fernando Pinilla

RIGHT & BOTTOM Early Monster Concepts + Gray Rogers

OPPOSITE Lilith Reborn Concept + Victor Lee

D*iablo IV*'s demons and monsters are more terrifying than anything that has come before. As with characters, the creation process for the creatures began with an idea. For a long-running franchise like *Diablo*, one might assume that coming up with new monster types would be challenging. "It's the opposite," says concept art lead Hunter Schulz. "I wish I had more time to get them all out. Even with a fast sketch, there could be a lot of other ideas you want to put out there. Ideas get more difficult when you start to narrow in on something and focus on smaller details and visual problem-solving."

A great deal of consideration goes into the creation of new monsters and monster types. One key component that developers look for is visual variety. Related to this concept is the importance of a clear silhouette, which essentially means the outline of the monster. Can you tell at a glance that it's a magic caster rather than a brute? The answer could mean life or death for the player.

Readability, function, and theme are paramount. "We have to almost immediately understand what the creature's about," says lead concept artist Victor Lee. "The story that it's telling. It can't be vague. And to keep things interesting, a lot of times we'll add a little twist to a traditional idea just to evolve it and keep it fresh."

Another way *Diablo IV* encourages fresh ideas is through something called "ideation weeks," periods of time once a month where artists can pitch their own ideas, rather than working on assigned tasks.

"We play a build of the game," says Rob Sevilla, "and ask ourselves, 'What is it missing?' or 'I have this idea that's been floating around in my head, and I finally have a chance to pitch it.' Ideation weeks were super important because a lot of what ended up in the game came from them."

One concept from ideation that made it into the game was the Tree of Whispers, a wish-granting tree with a sinister twist. Another was the world boss Avarice, the Gold Cursed, an enormous death-dealing Treasure Goblin.

Other new monster types introduce entirely new mythologies to the franchise.

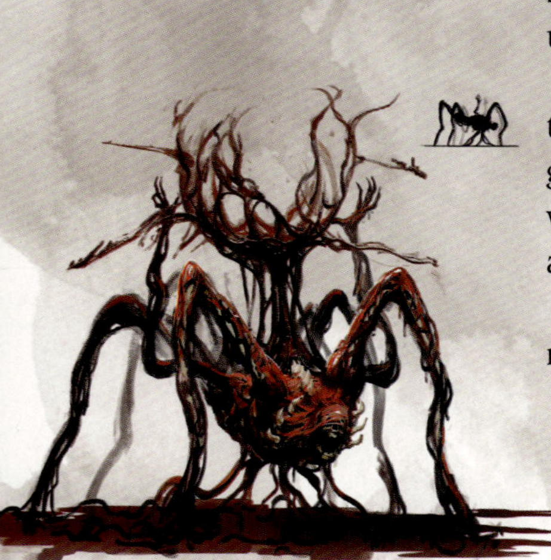

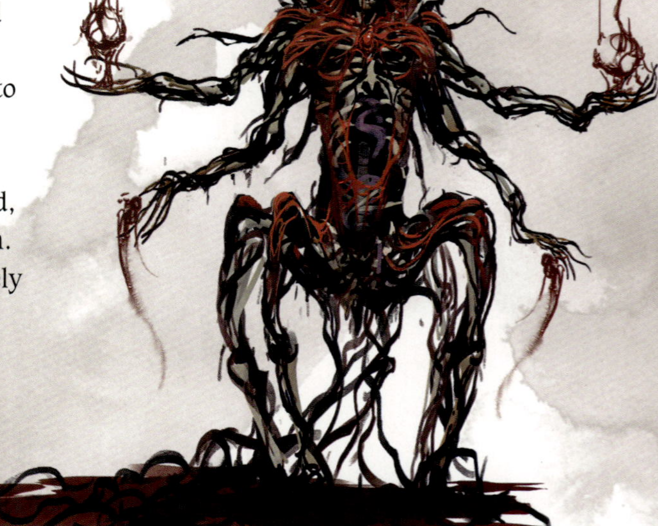

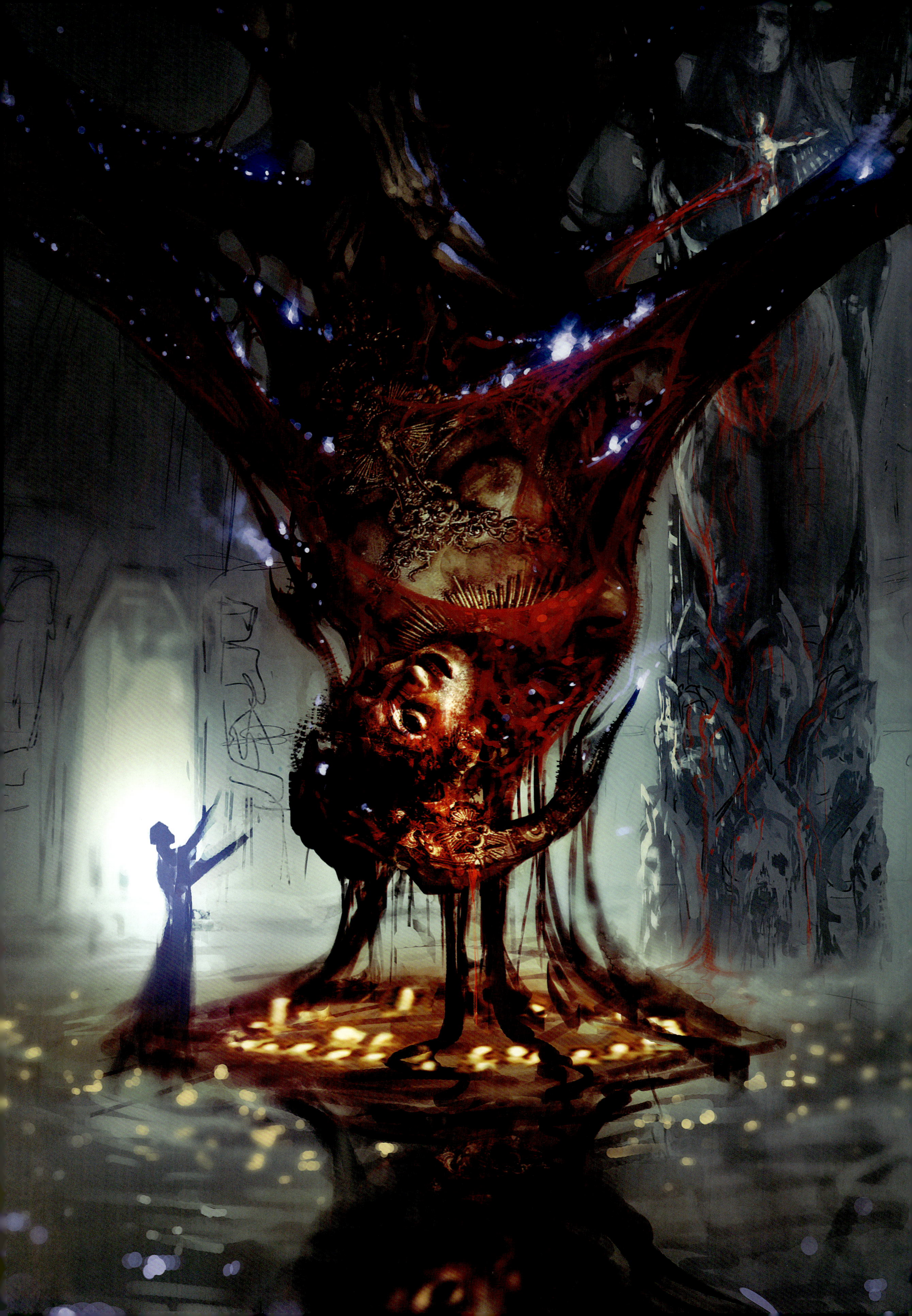

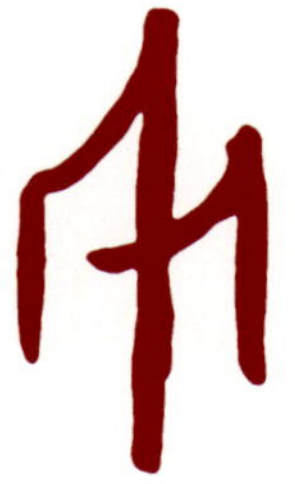

ABOVE Druid Lettering + Fernando Pinilla

RIGHT & BELOW Nangari Markings Concepts + Hyun Lee

BOTTOM Nangari Concepts + Hyun Lee

OPPOSITE Fallen Illustration + Igor Sidorenko

"We asked ourselves what kind of demons live in the ocean," says John Mueller. "We came up with a drowned monster family, this cursed faction of lost sailors, a mythos of what happens to people when they go to sea and they're never heard from again. It's not high fantasy. It's not heroic fantasy. It really leans into *dark* fantasy."

While new ideas are always welcome, old concepts are not discarded. "We have this huge collection of concept art," says Lee, "some of which we could not use at the time, but we constantly ask ourselves, 'What about that one we did four years ago?' We'll bring it out and wonder, 'Can we use it here? Could we tweak it to make it work?' We'll work on evolving that design to take it to the next level and see what happens. Nothing goes to waste."

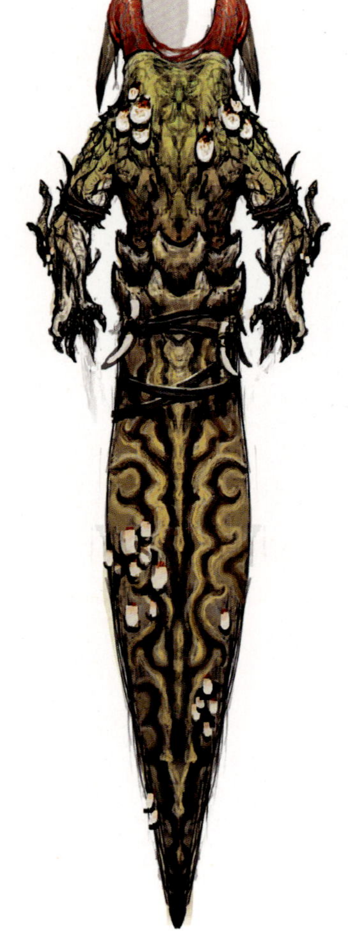

With *Diablo IV*'s advanced technology, creators are able to explore options with monsters that either didn't exist previously or were far more limited in their capabilities and scope.

"In earlier games, you could not have a creature with too many limbs because it would be too expensive," says Lee. "Now we can push more into that area. For a boss creature, we have more room to put things like tentacles, which means a lot of joints. Even with shaders and the textures, the textures are higher resolution images so we can see more detail on the surfacing."

Even with these increased capabilities, limitations do still exist. In *Diablo*, monsters are categorized into types or classes. "We have brutes," says Lee. "They're the tough, big creatures. Then we have the swarmers. Many of those will appear on-screen at once. If a creature appears in numbers of ones and twos on-screen, it can be more complex. If you see twenty on-screen at once, then you have to keep them relatively simple."

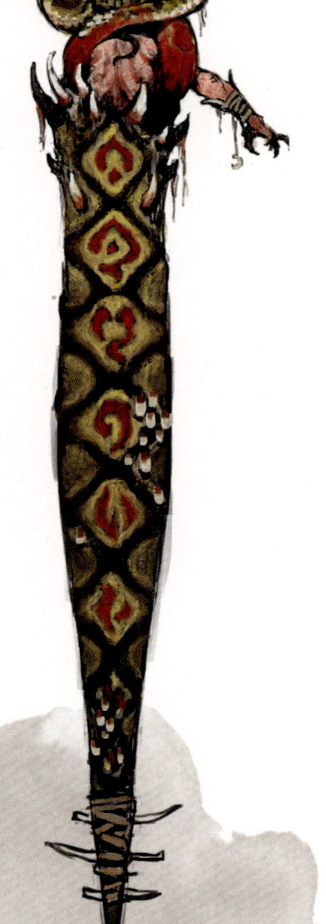

Another important element that artists have to keep in mind is *Diablo*'s isometric camera angle. Artists will sometimes mock up monsters in 3D just to see how they look from that particular view.

"I sometimes do sketches from that angle," says Schulz. "Everybody should have that in mind, because if you have a bulky guy with a big stomach and short legs, he's probably going to look like he's floating."

Diablo IV proves that the franchise's classic monsters are just as terrifying as they've ever been, and that creators continue to breathe life into the most horrific, nightmare-inducing creatures imaginable.

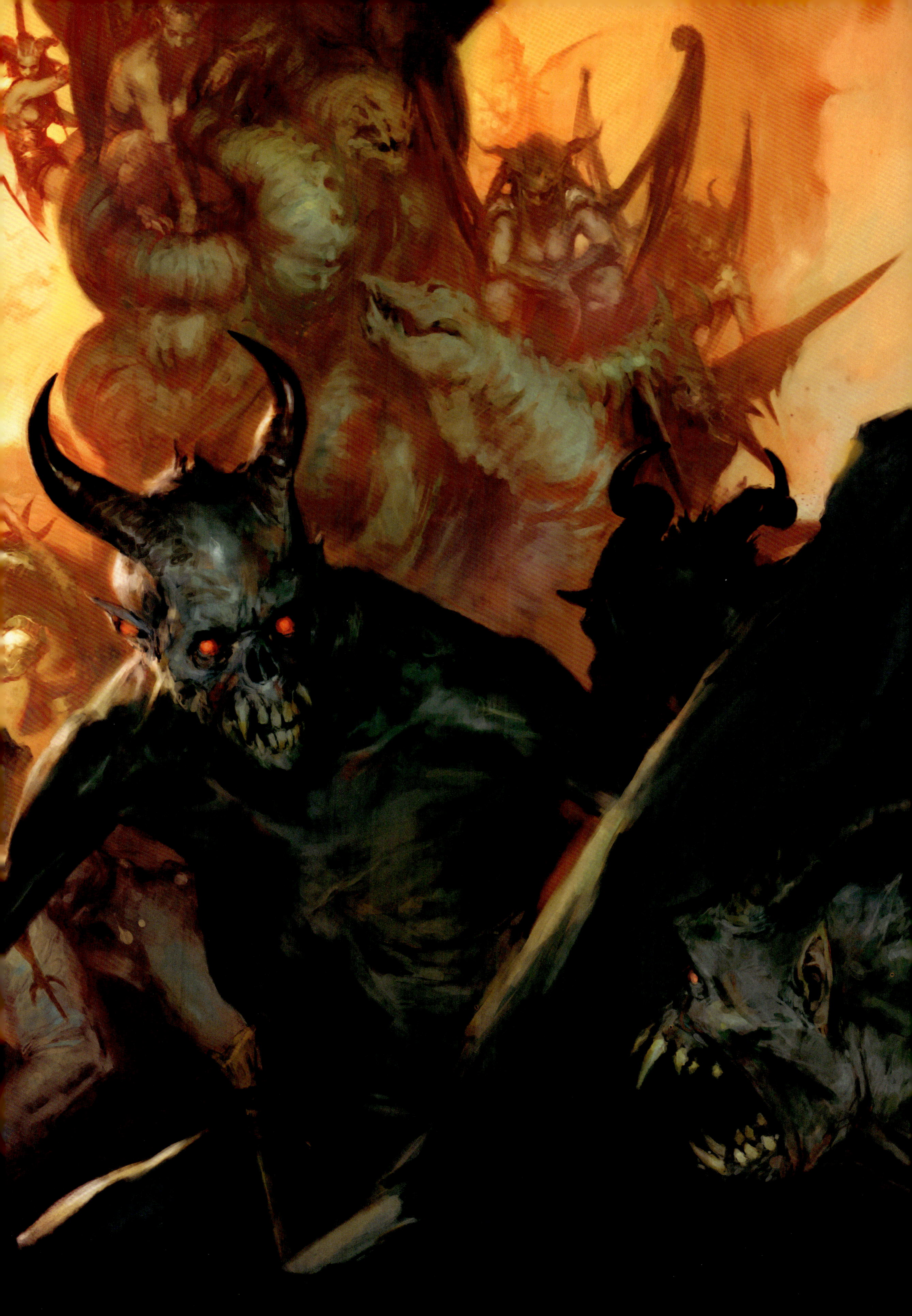

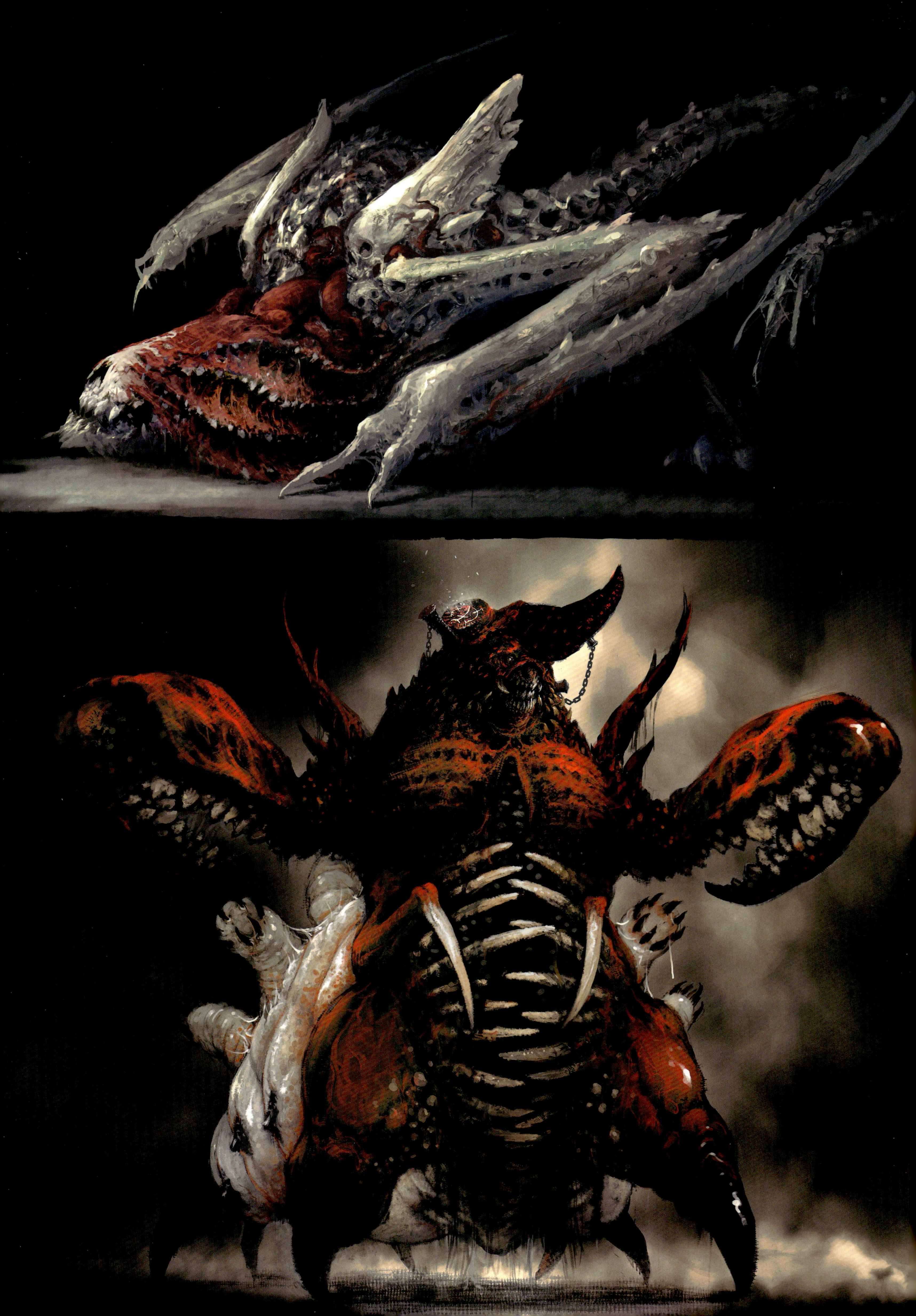

"A dark world can sometimes be portrayed in a narrow sense—maybe just throw some mud on a skeleton with an axe and send it out there—but you can only do that so much before it becomes redundant. We always try to push new and interesting ideas forward, try to find some depth behind a design, give it a purpose and sense of belonging to a large and rich world."

—HUNTER SCHULZ, Concept Art Lead

BELOW Early Bat Monster Concept + Guy Davis

OPPOSITE, TOP Ashava the Pestilent Concept + Victor Lee

OPPOSITE, BOTTOM Early Duriel Concept + Victor Lee

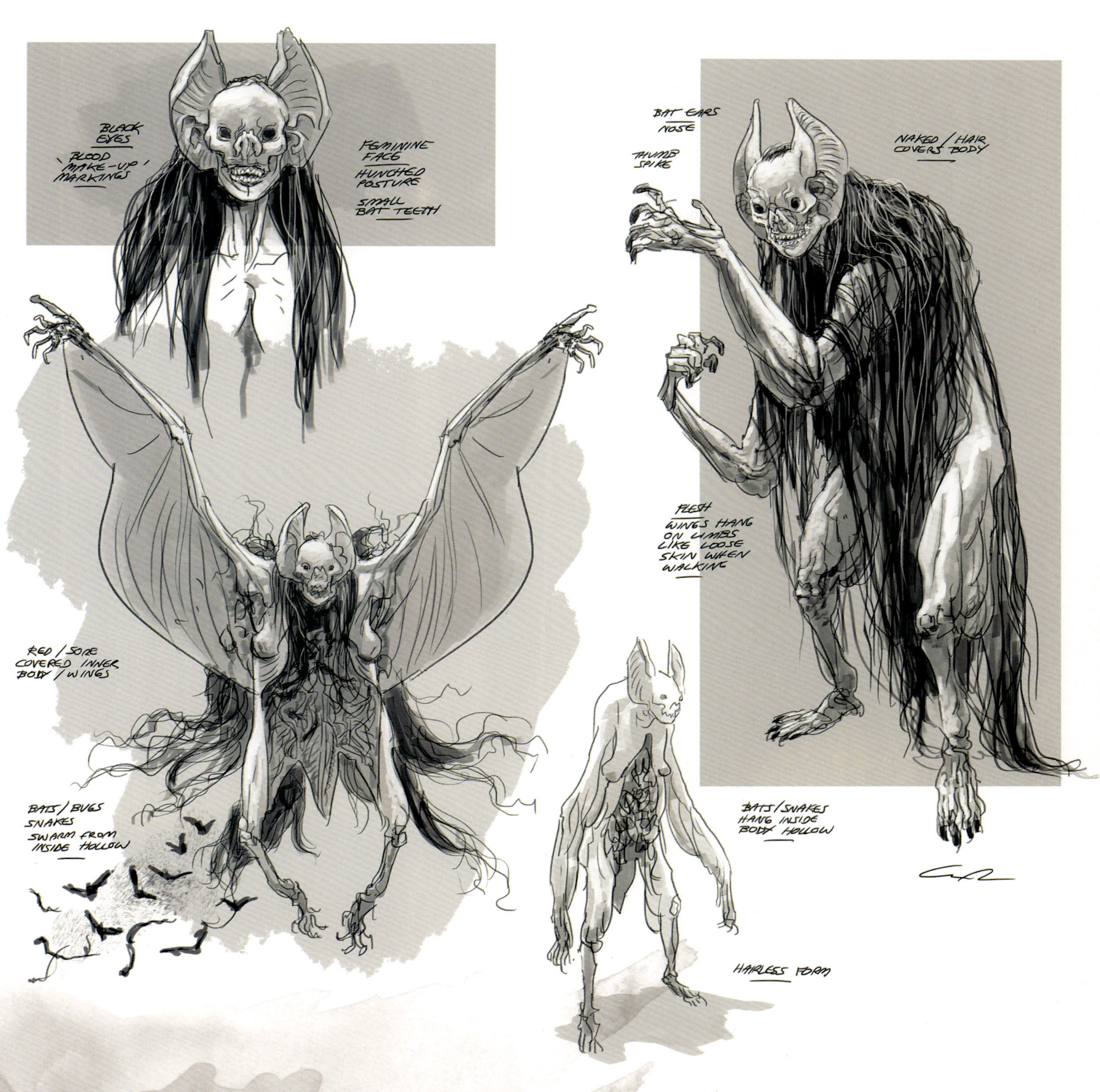

RIGHT Skittering Abomination
Concept + Victor Lee

BOTTOM Astaroth With Mount
Concept + Rob Sevilla

BELOW Amalgam of Rage
Concepts + Richie Marella

OPPOSITE Werewolf Abomination
Concept + Victor Lee

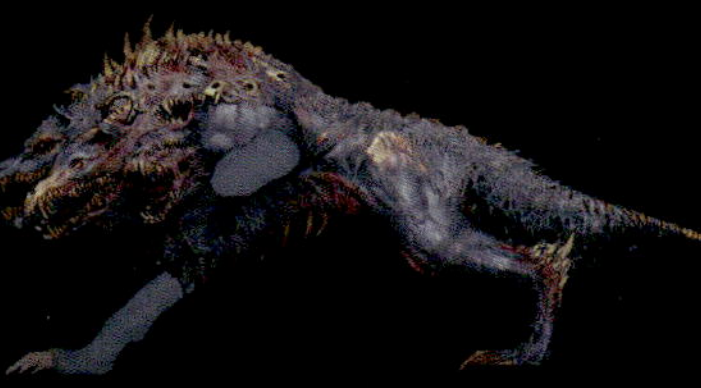

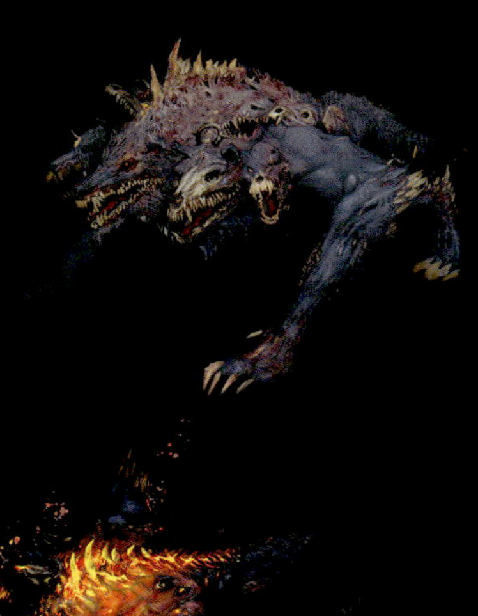

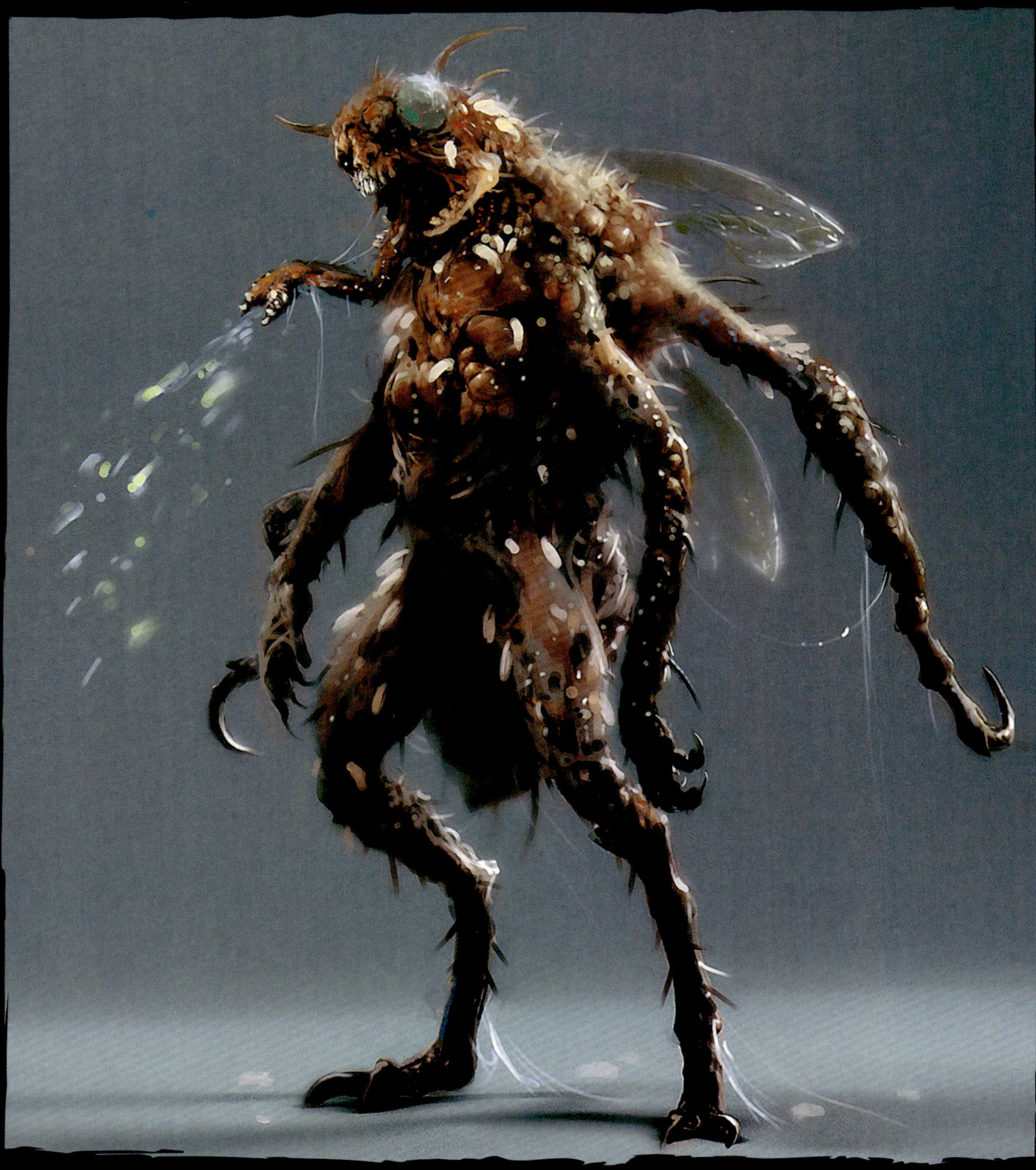

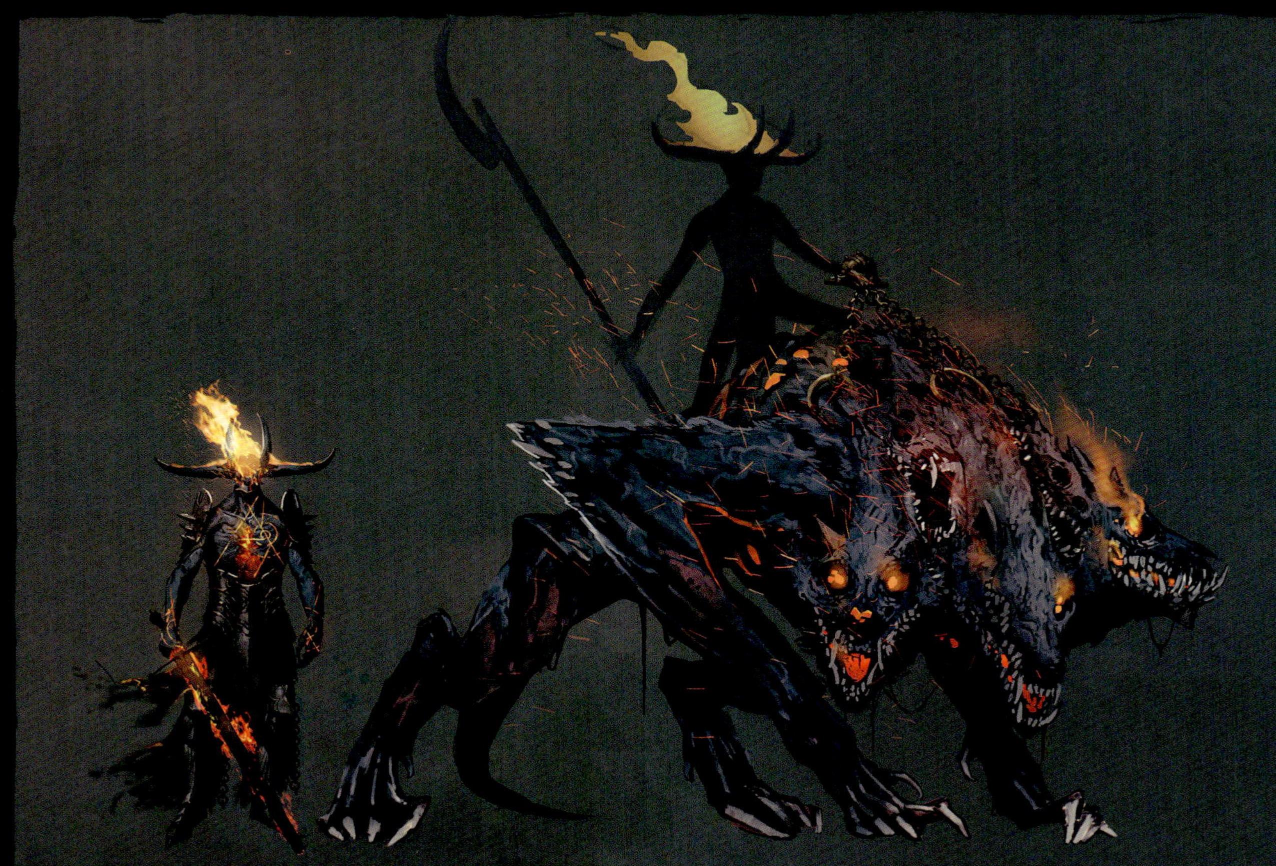

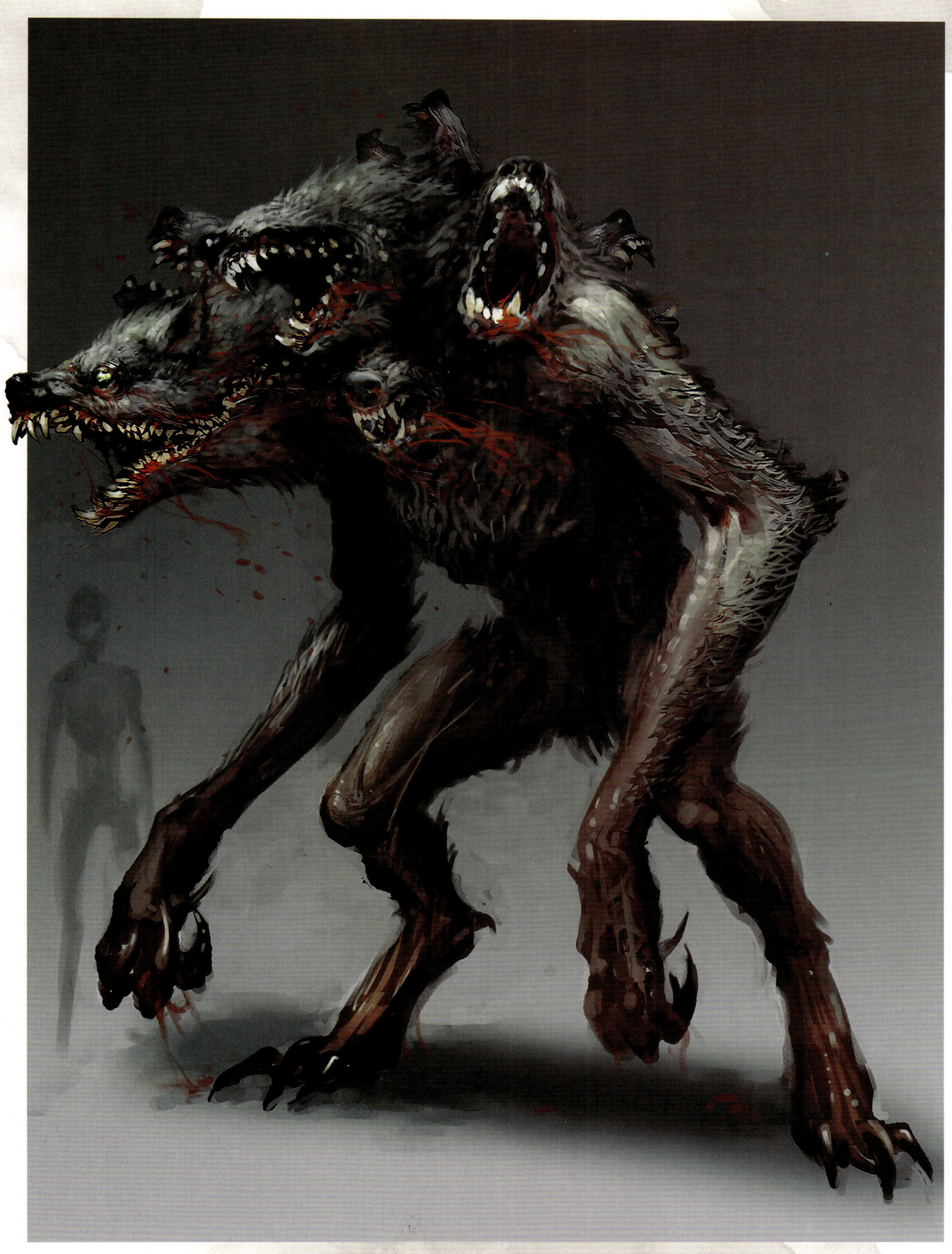

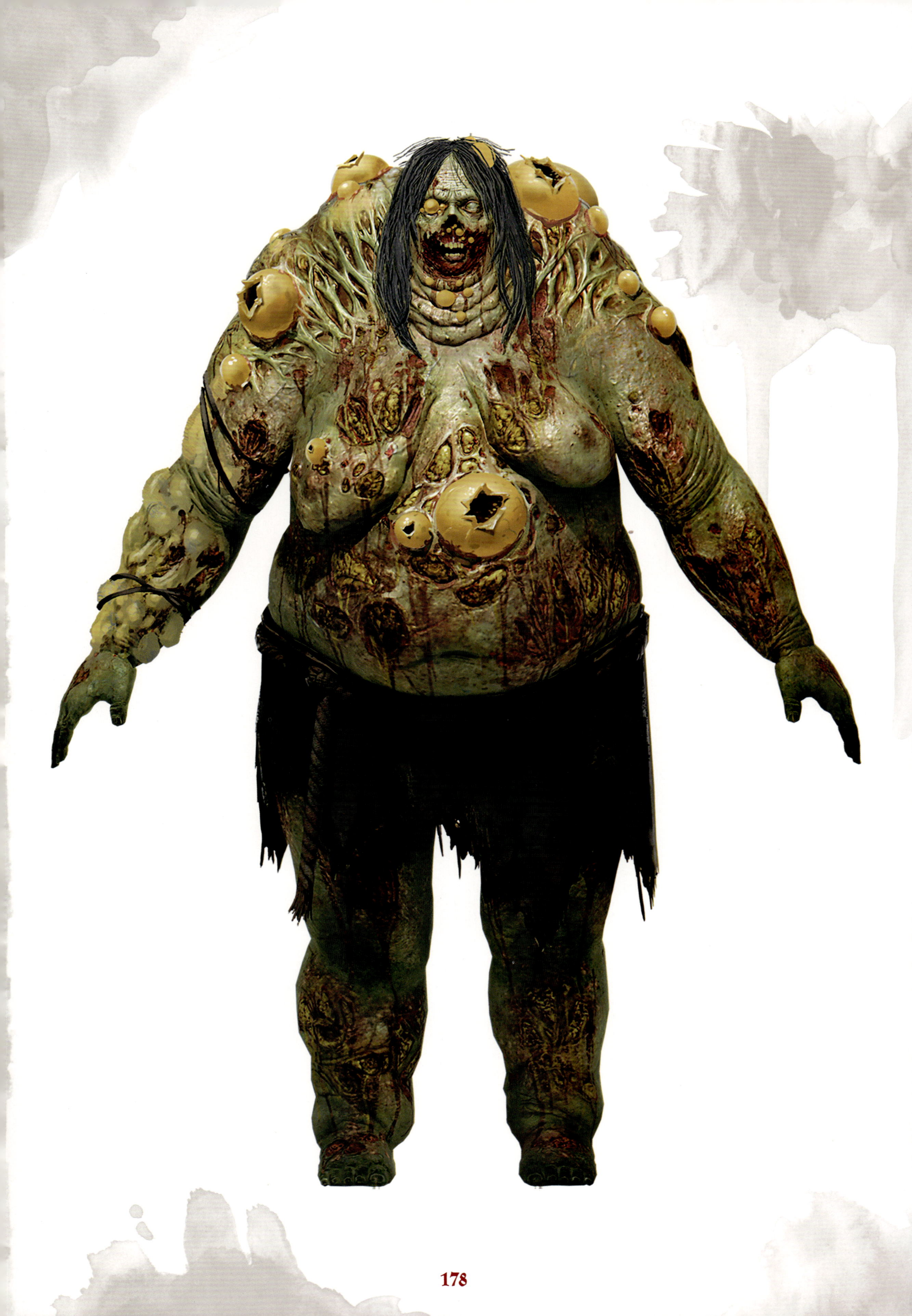

RIGHT Avarice, the Gold Cursed Concept + Gray Rogers

BOTTOM Plague Maggot Concept + Mike Franchina

BELOW Spider Concept + Mike Franchina

OPPOSITE Zombie Brute Concept + Gray Rogers

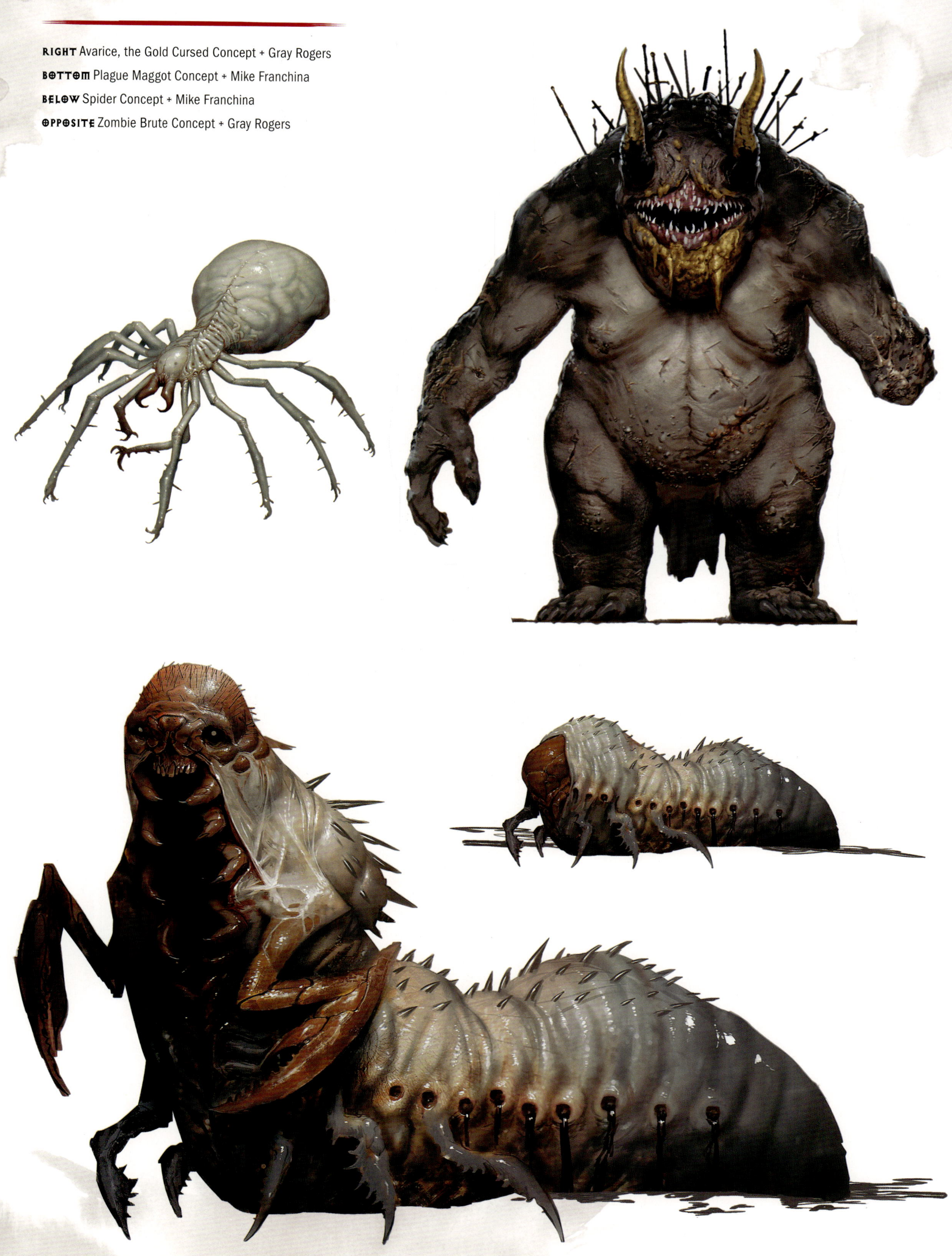

RIGHT & BELOW Undead Sketches + Guy Davis

BOTTOM Early Monster Concept + Guy Davis

OPPOSITE, TOP Early Wood Wraith Concept + Guy Davis

OPPOSITE, BOTTOM Early Treasure Goblin Concept + Guy Davis

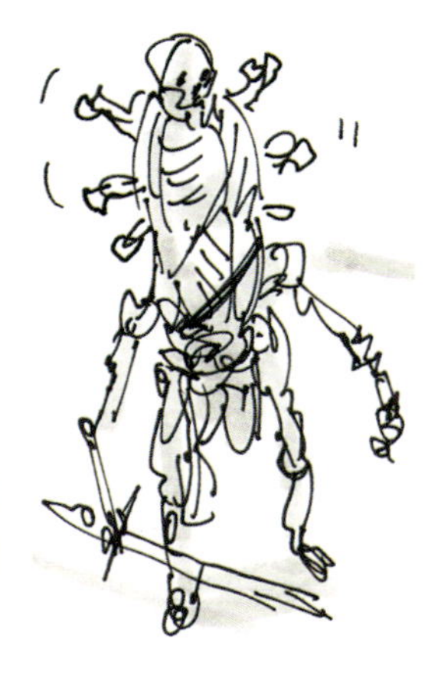

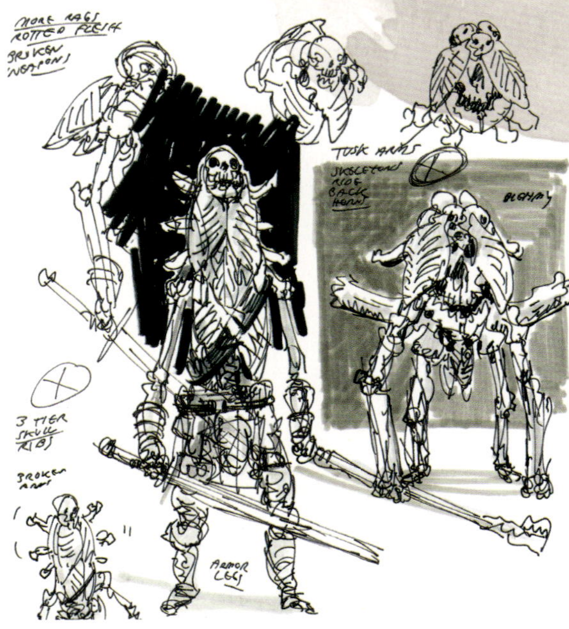

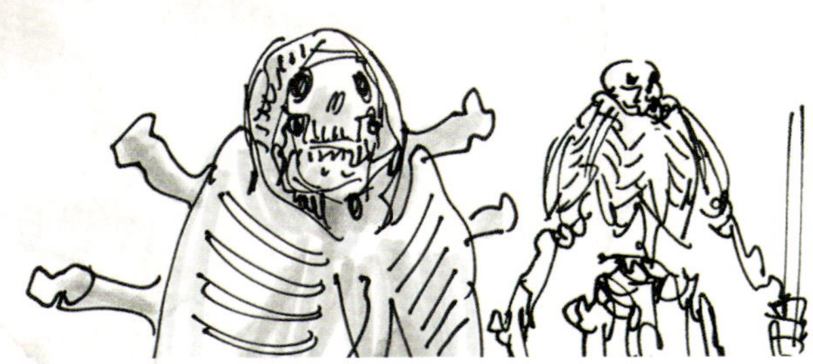

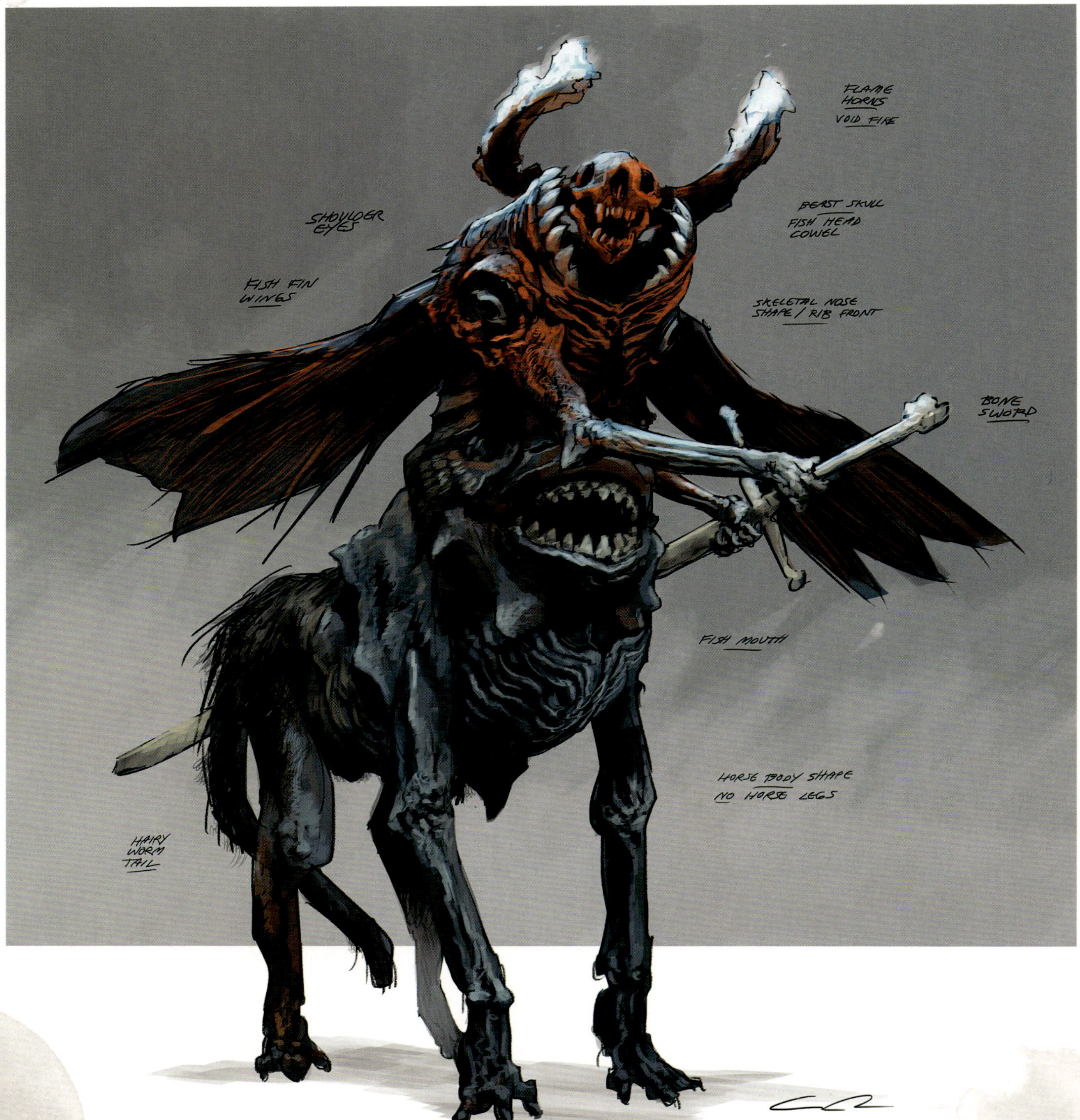

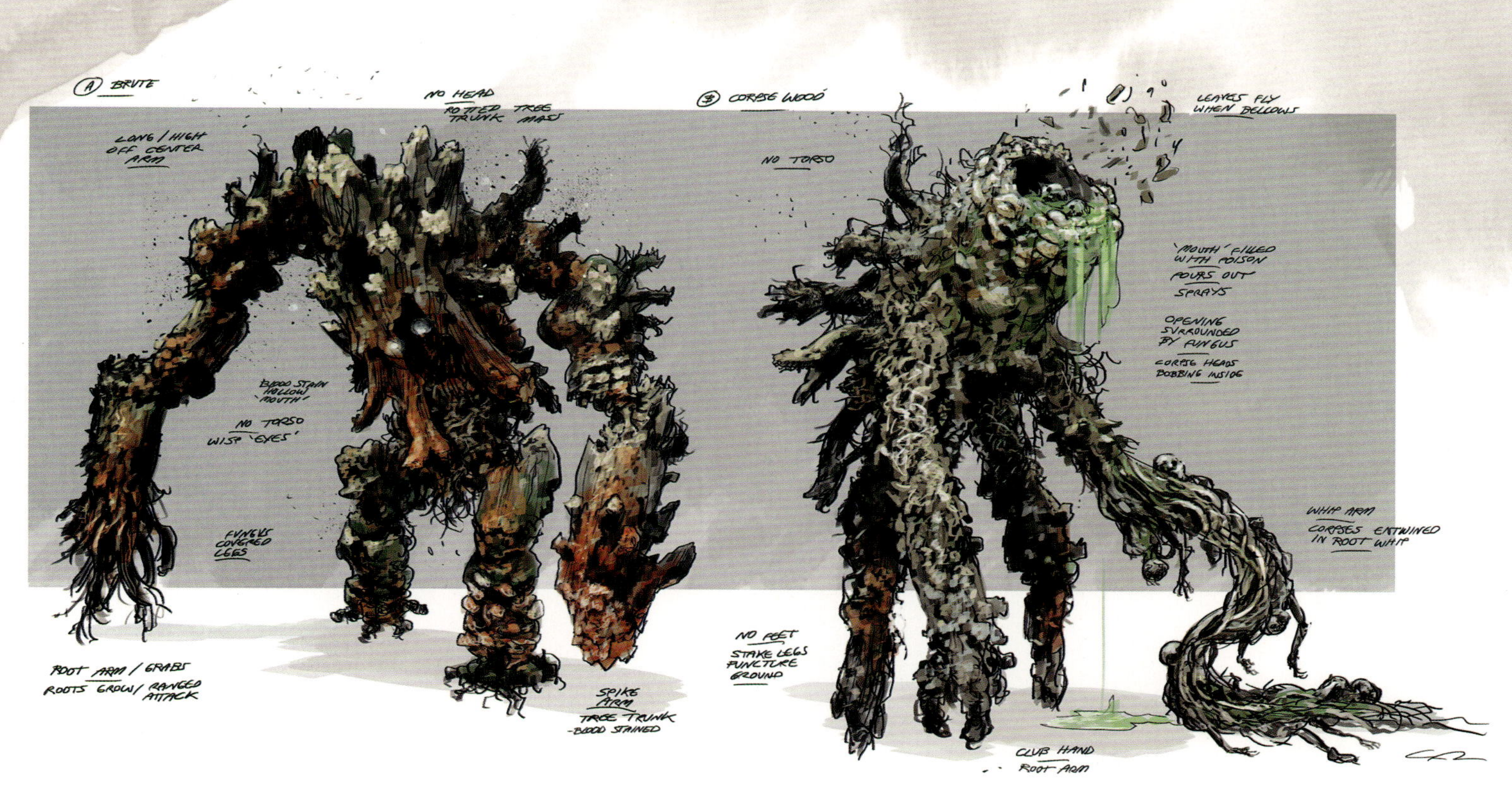

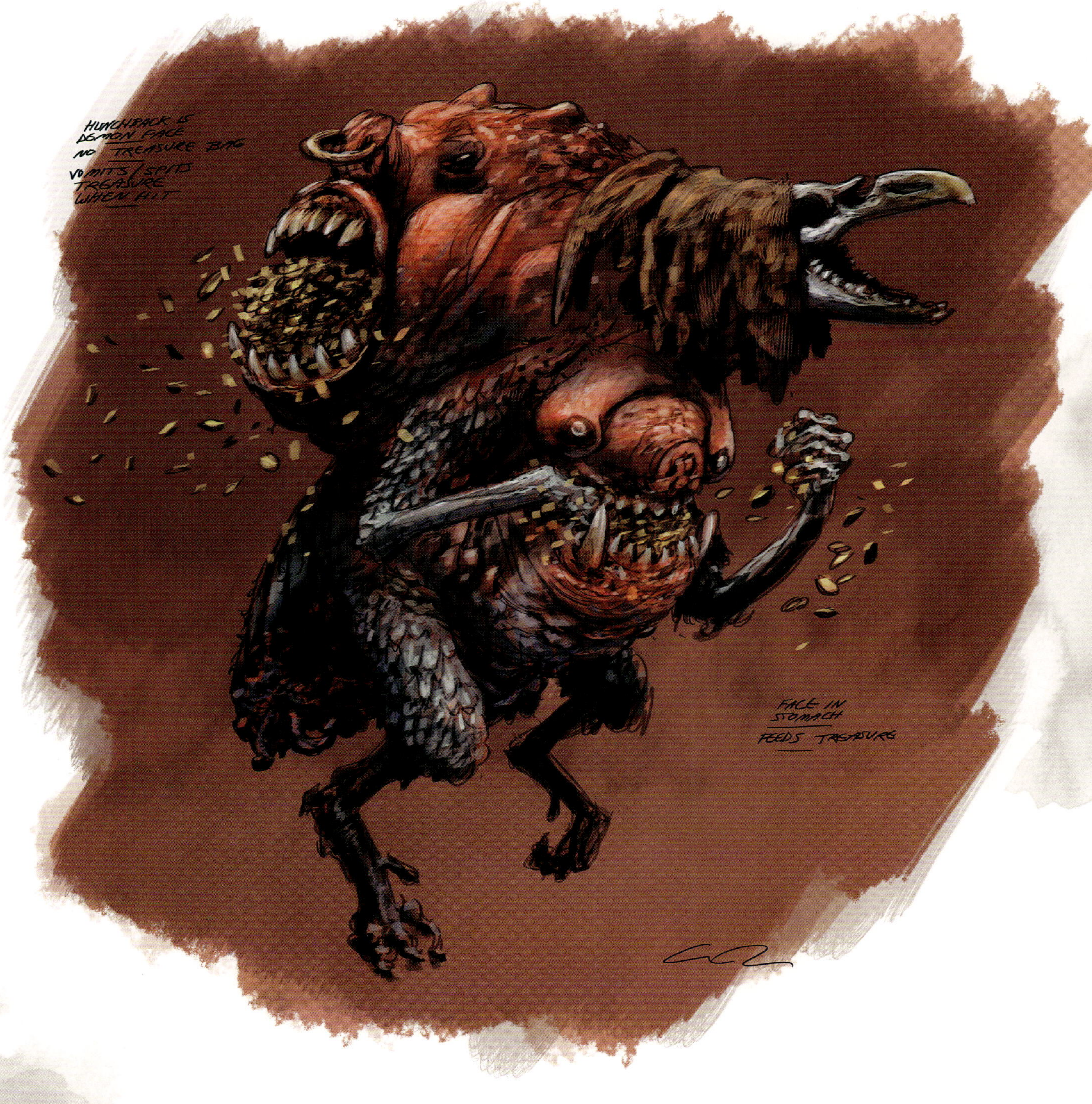

HUNCHBACK IS DEMON FACE
NO TREASURE BAG
VOMITS / SPITS TREASURE WHEN HIT

FACE IN STOMACH
FEEDS TREASURE

BELOW Ashava Concept + Victor Lee

RIGHT Early Monster Concept + Mike Franchina

BOTTOM Early Monster Concept + Rob Sevilla

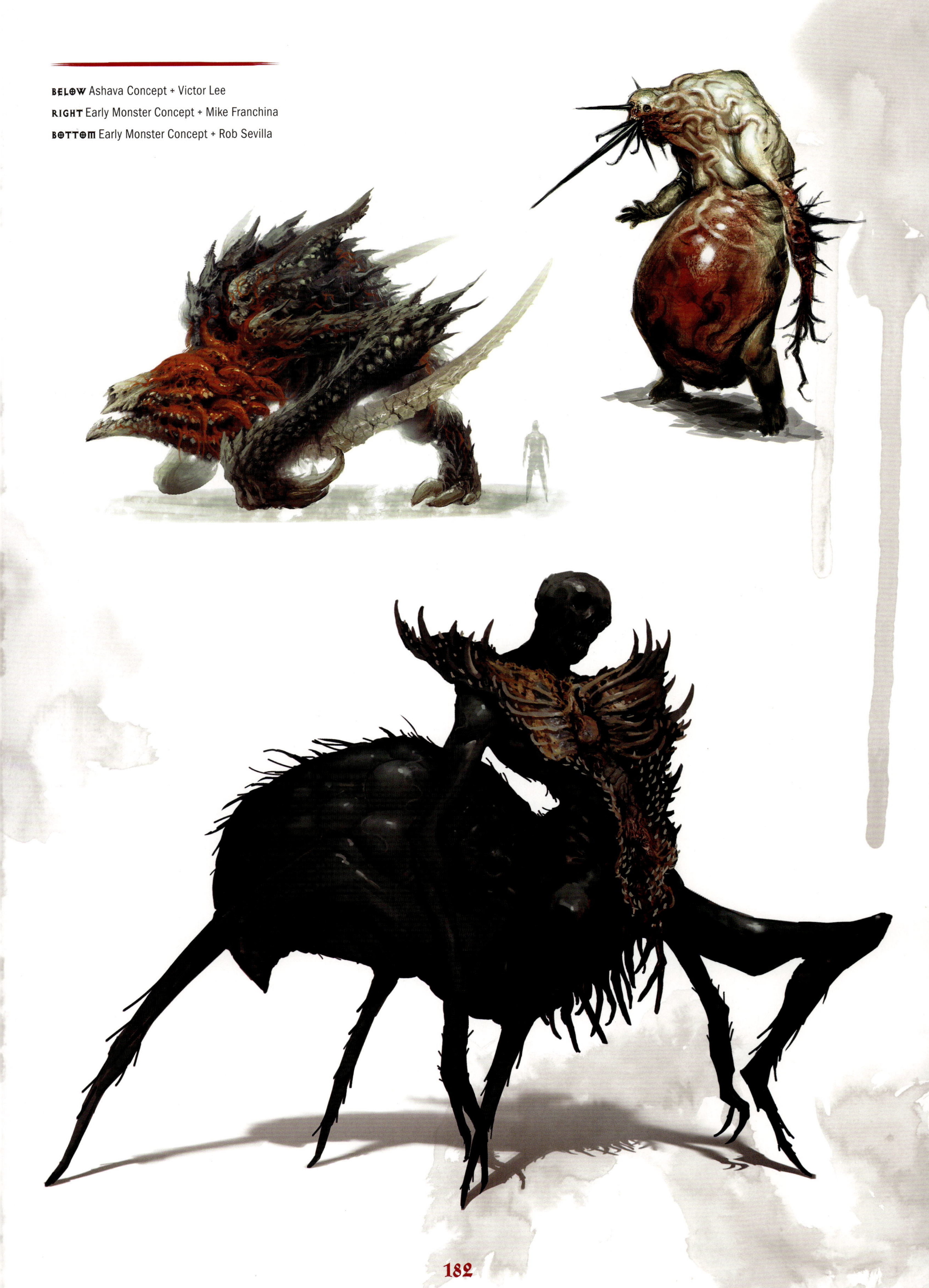

TOP Duriel Concept + Victor Lee

BELOW Mephisto Regeneration Concept + Victor Lee

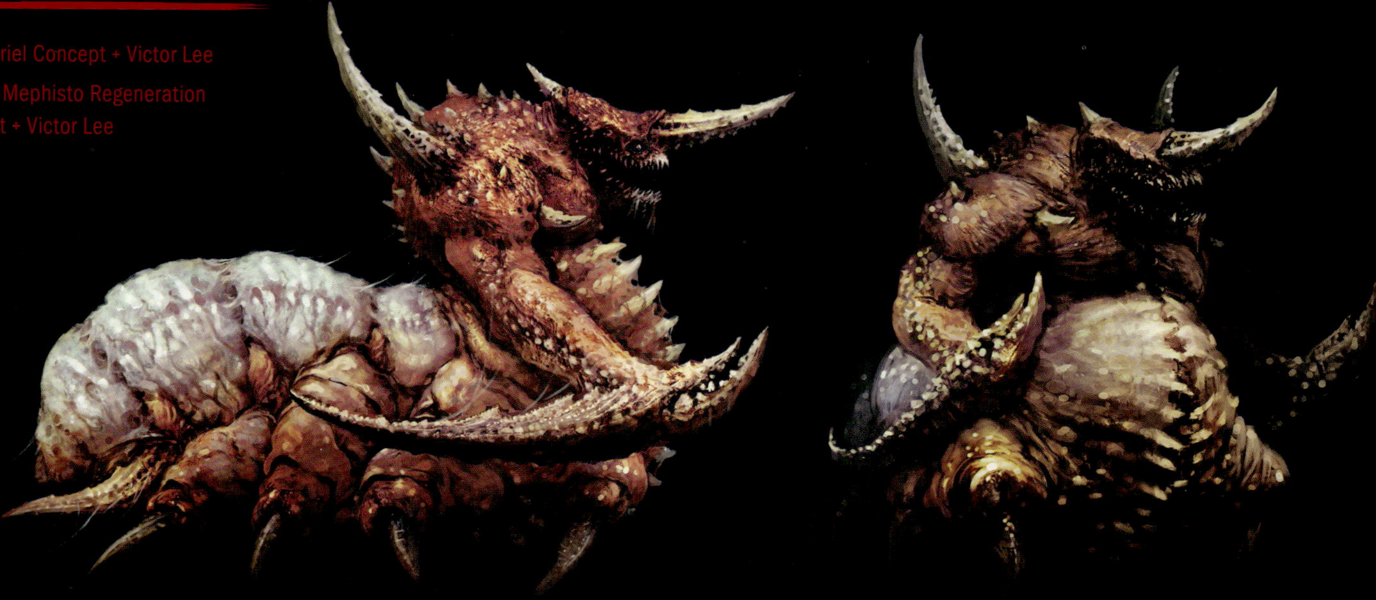

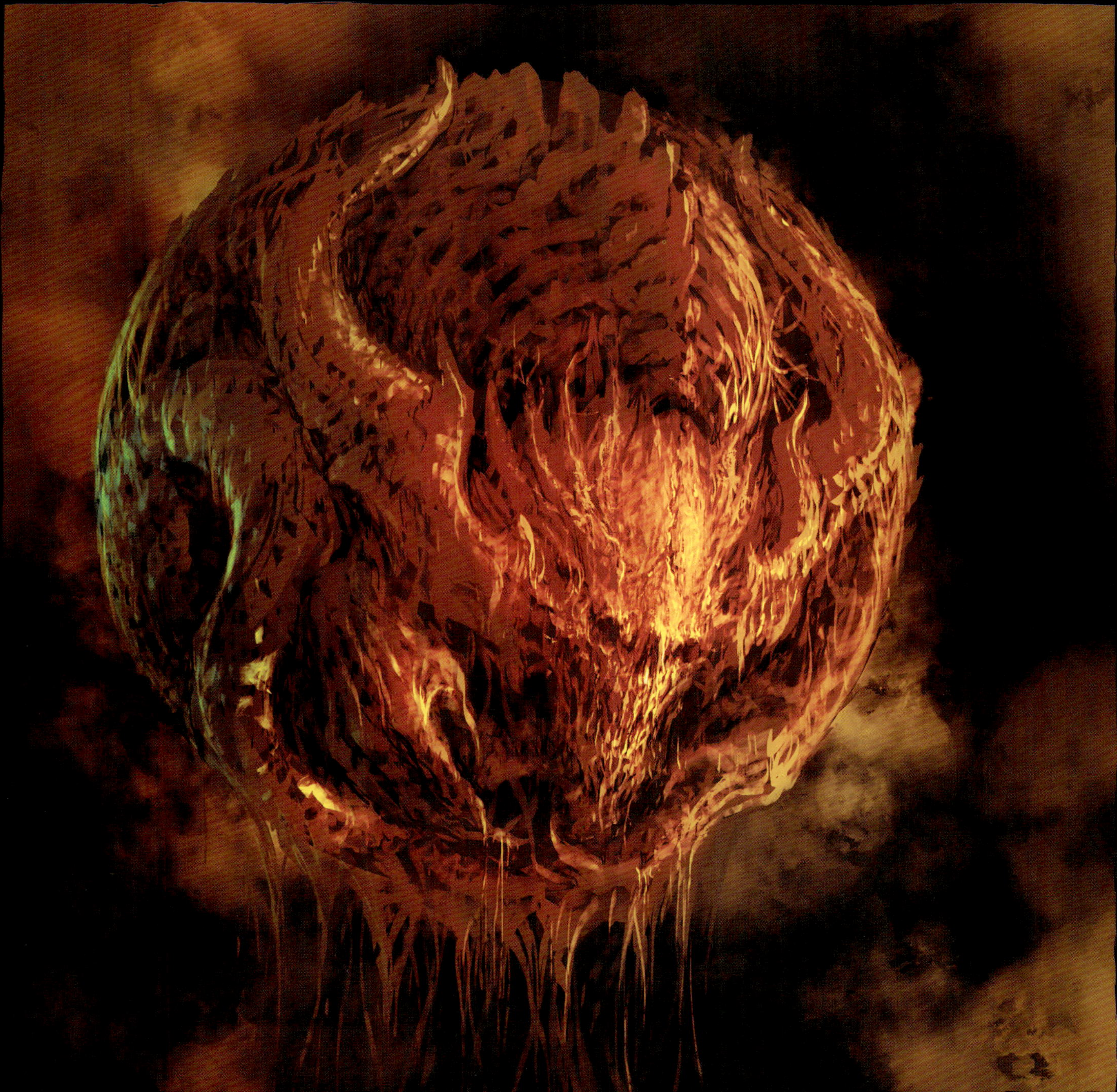

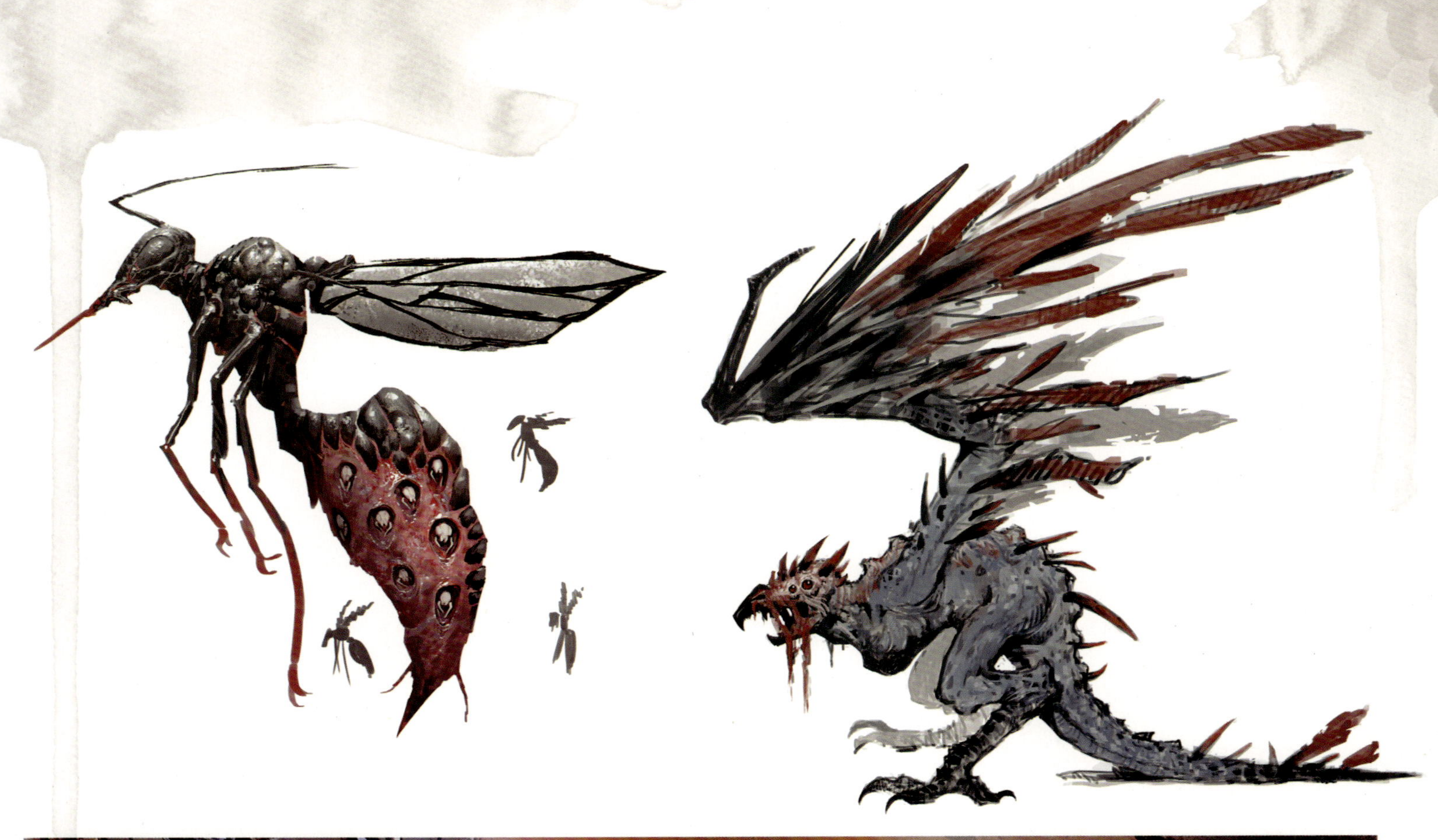

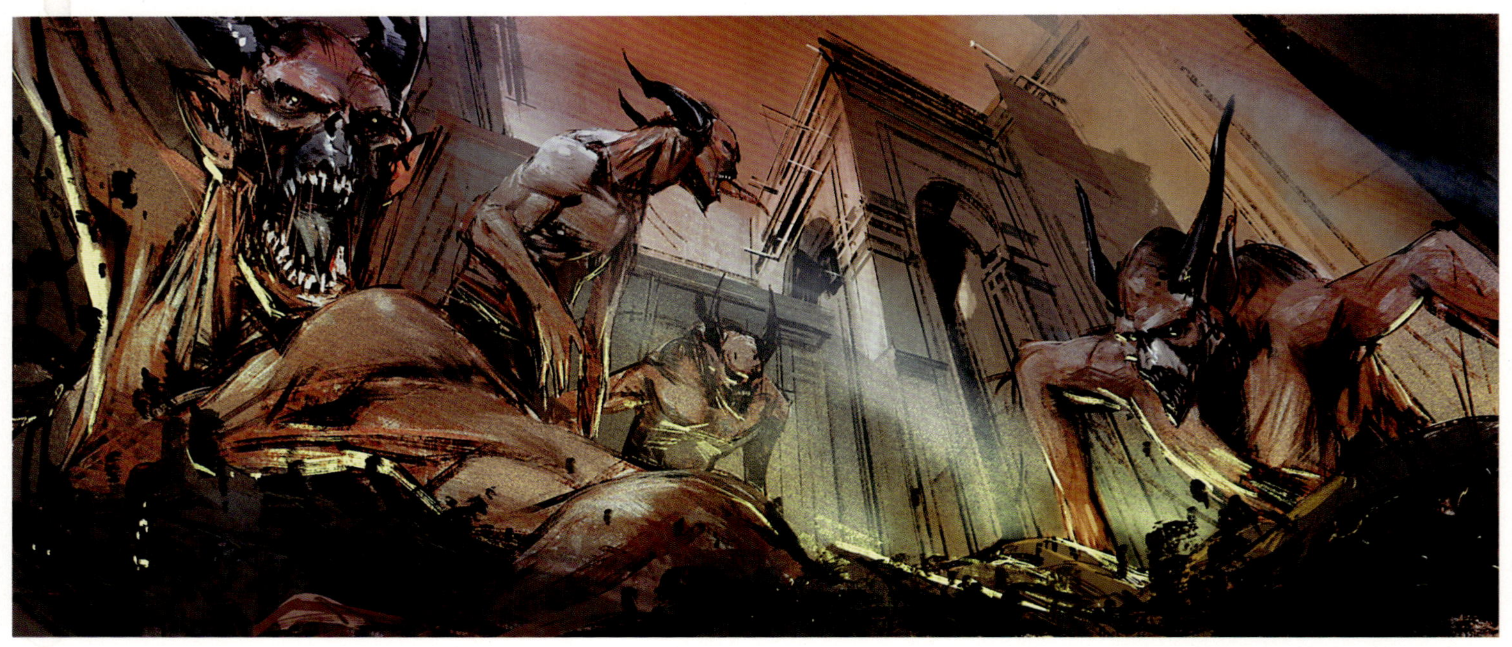

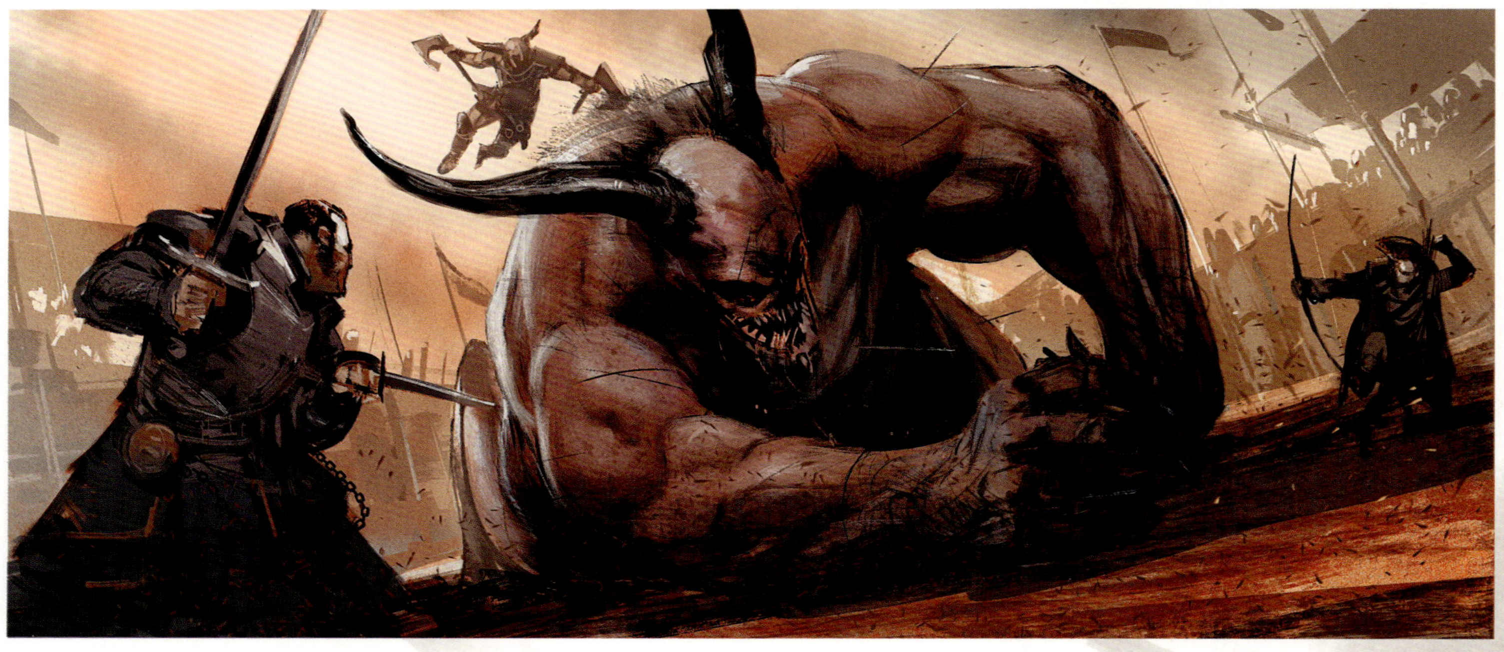

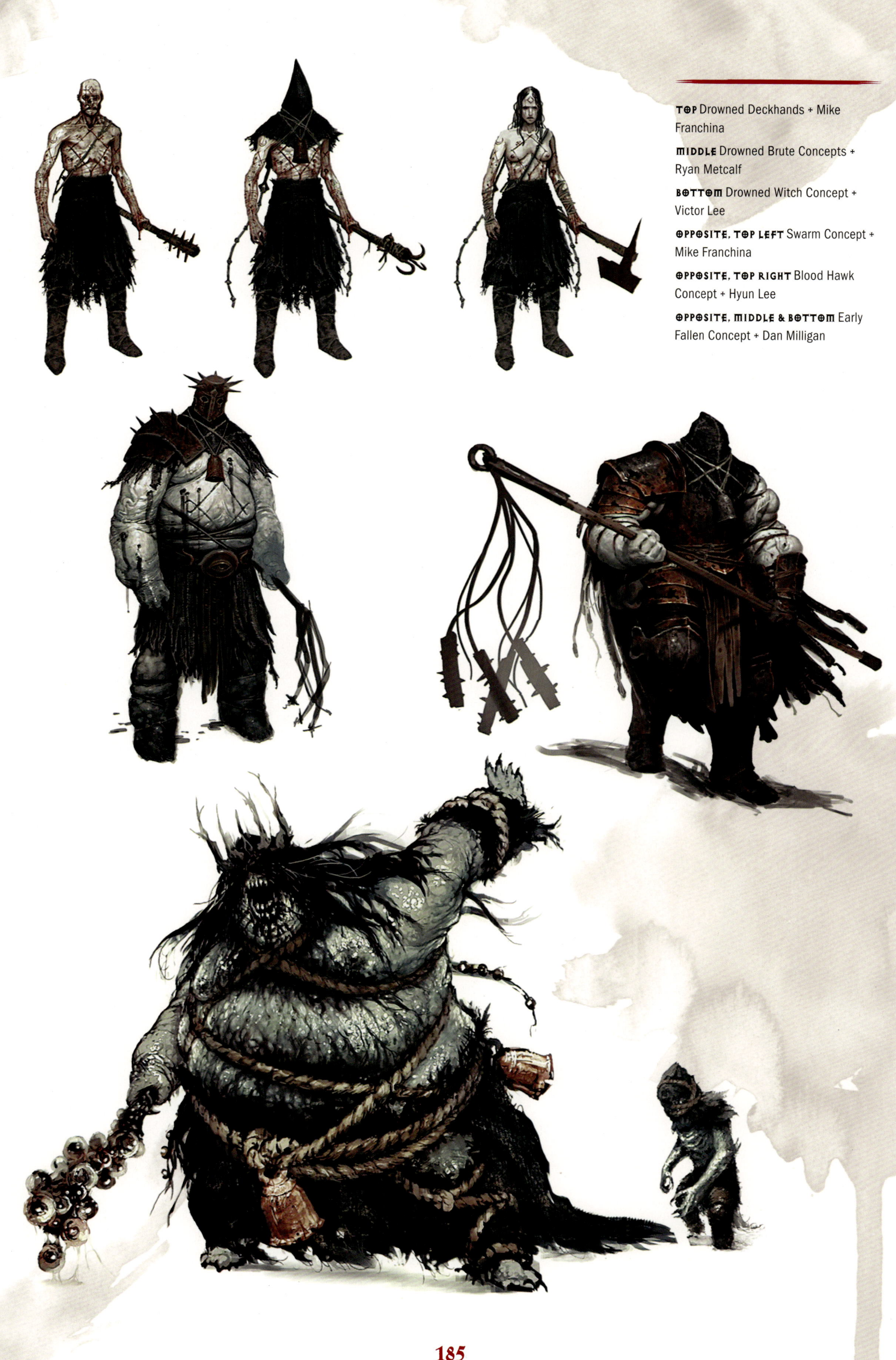

TOP Drowned Deckhands + Mike Franchina

MIDDLE Drowned Brute Concepts + Ryan Metcalf

BOTTOM Drowned Witch Concept + Victor Lee

OPPOSITE, TOP LEFT Swarm Concept + Mike Franchina

OPPOSITE, TOP RIGHT Blood Hawk Concept + Hyun Lee

OPPOSITE, MIDDLE & BOTTOM Early Fallen Concept + Dan Milligan

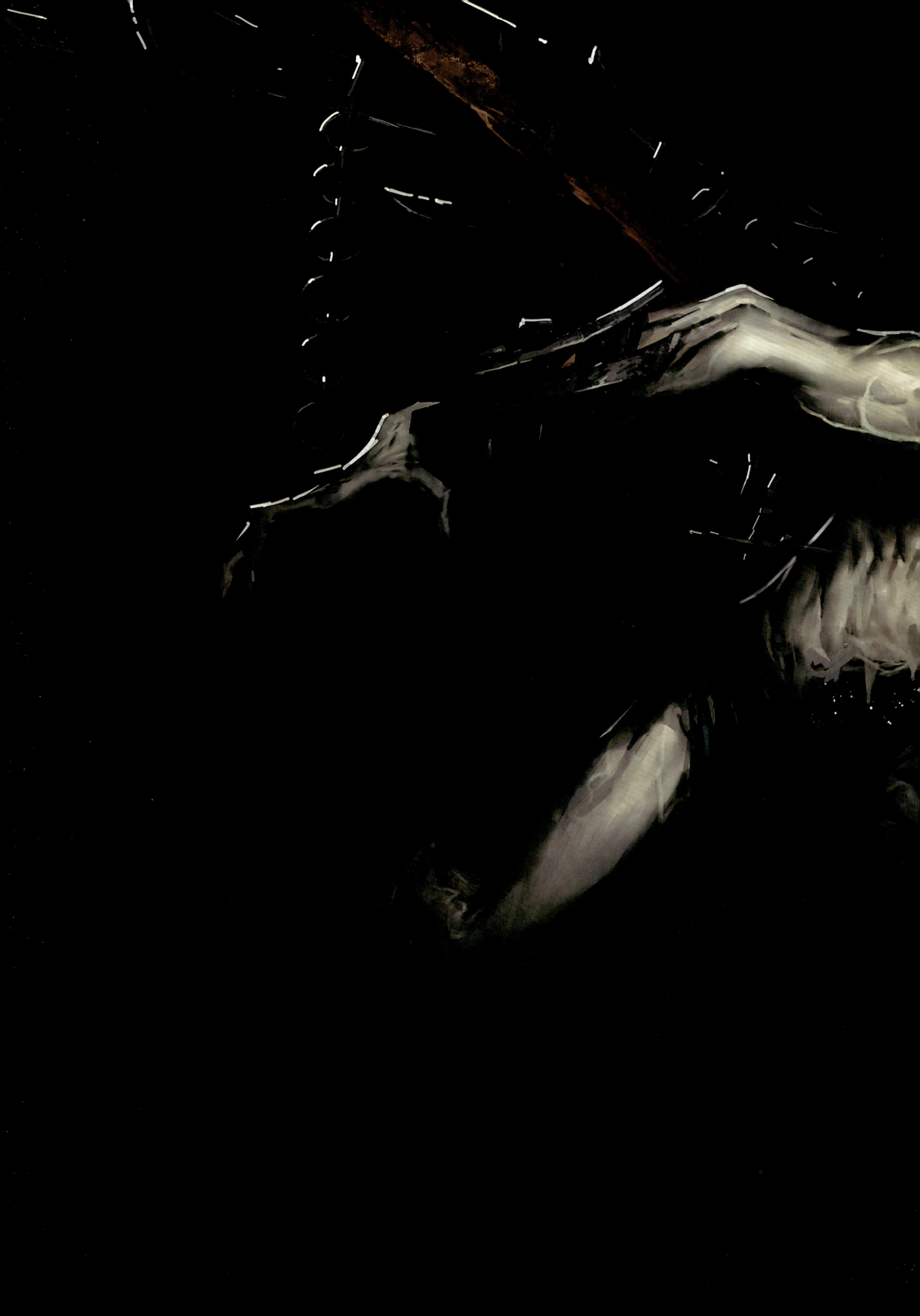

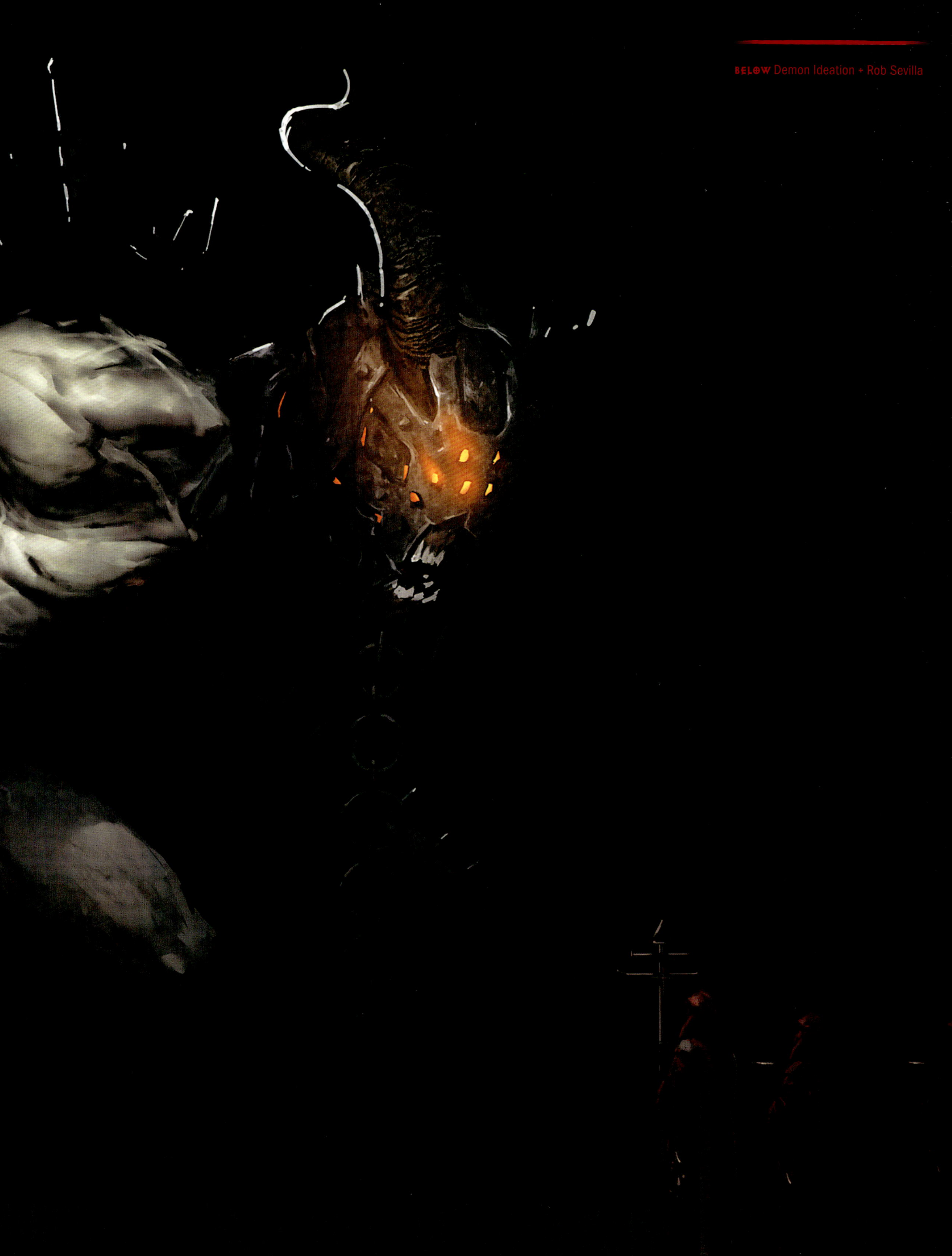

BELOW Demon Ideation • Rob Sevilla

And Hell Rides With Them

ABOVE Barbarian Lettering + Fernando Pinilla

RIGHT Trophy Concepts + Rob Sevilla

BOTTOM Spectral Charger Set Concept + Rob Sevilla

BELOW Trophy Concept + Rob Sevilla

OPPOSITE Temptation Set Concept + BOSi

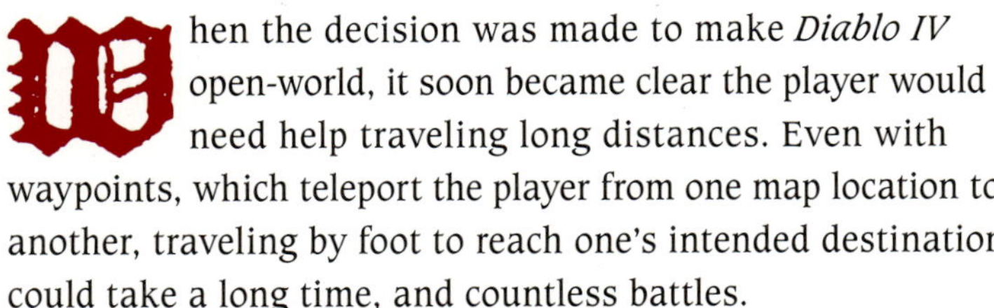

When the decision was made to make *Diablo IV* open-world, it soon became clear the player would need help traveling long distances. Even with waypoints, which teleport the player from one map location to another, traveling by foot to reach one's intended destination could take a long time, and countless battles.

"The space is huge," says Nick Chilano. "So mounts just seemed like a totally natural transportation device that thematically fit into the game and made complete sense."

The goal quickly became to not just make horses, but horses that feel like they belong in the *Diablo* universe.

"You start to see all the possibilities," Chilano explains. "You can have horses with markings on them, cultist runes, plus all the armor you can put on them. It essentially starts to become an extension of your character."

As a part of that extension, barding for horses is designed to synchronize so the player and mount can wear the same style of armor. While exciting, this direction did present challenges.

"There were limitations," says Rob Sevilla, "like how far does the armor go versus the saddle? How far can we design the saddle? Does it go all the way to the tail? Does it include the neck of the horse, or is that part of the barding?"

Mount trophies—awards obtained by players for killing certain enemies—also factor into the equations.

"If we put them toward the front of the horse," says Sevilla, "does it get in the way when the horse is running? We figured out that the hip area is the best place to put the mount trophy because it's out of the way of the player and out of the way of the animation."

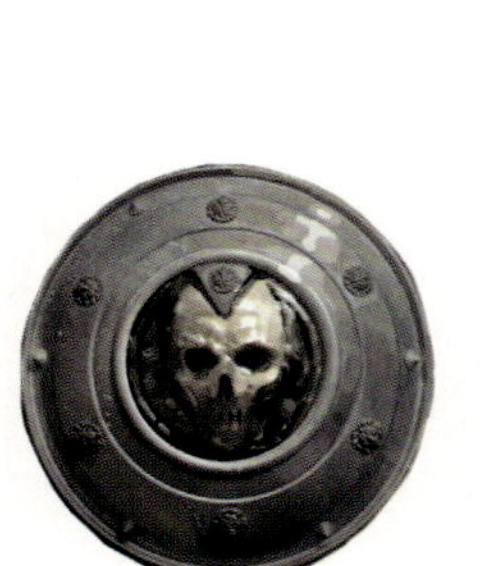

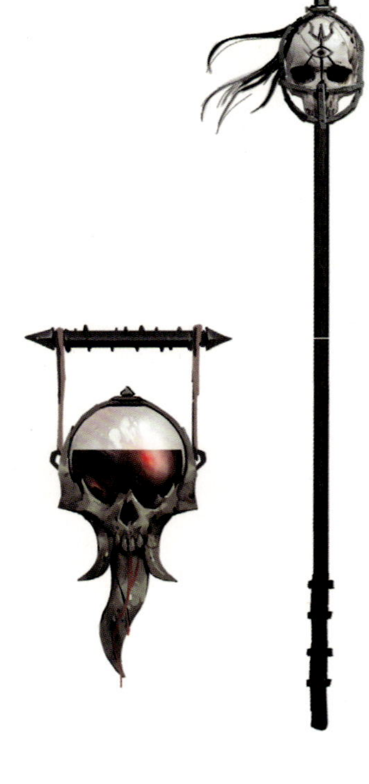

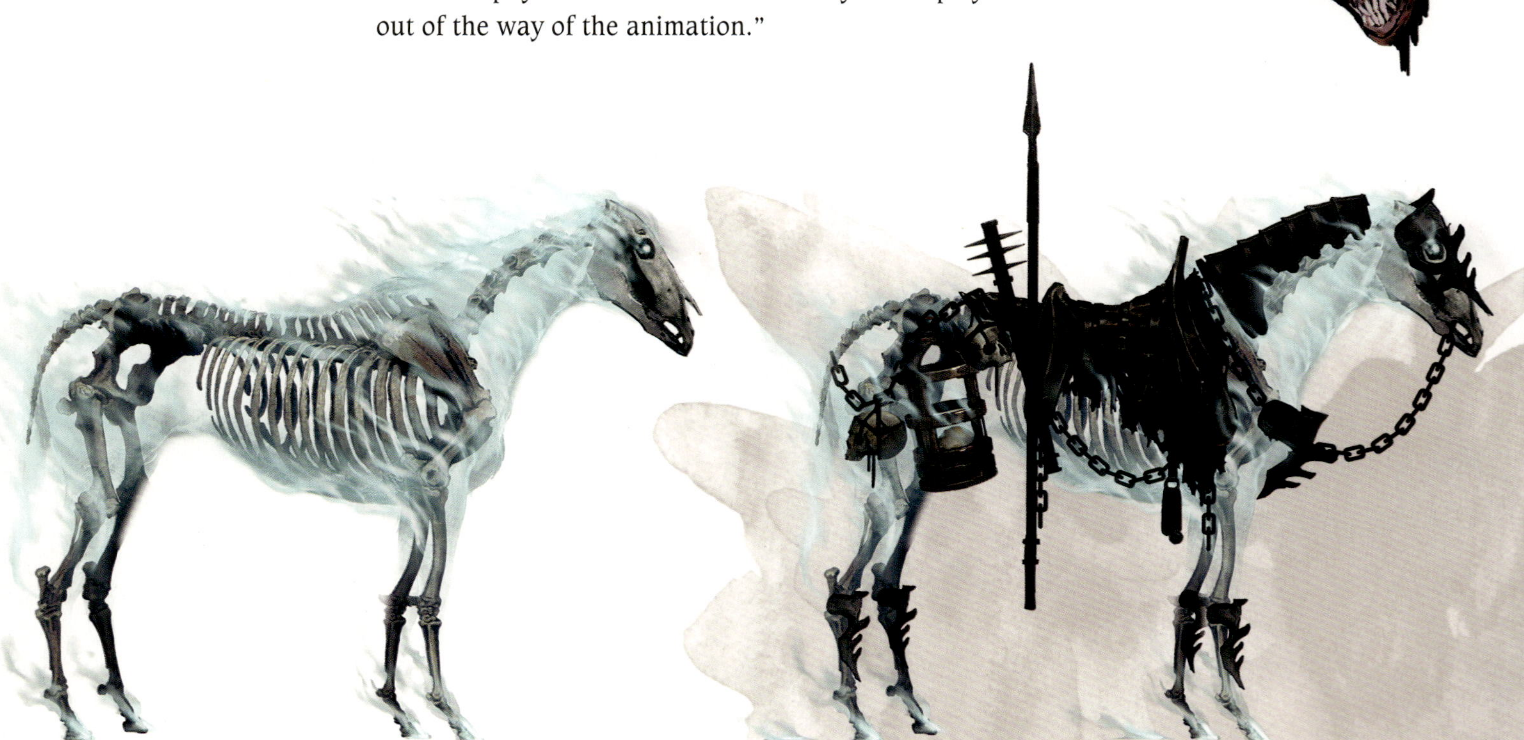

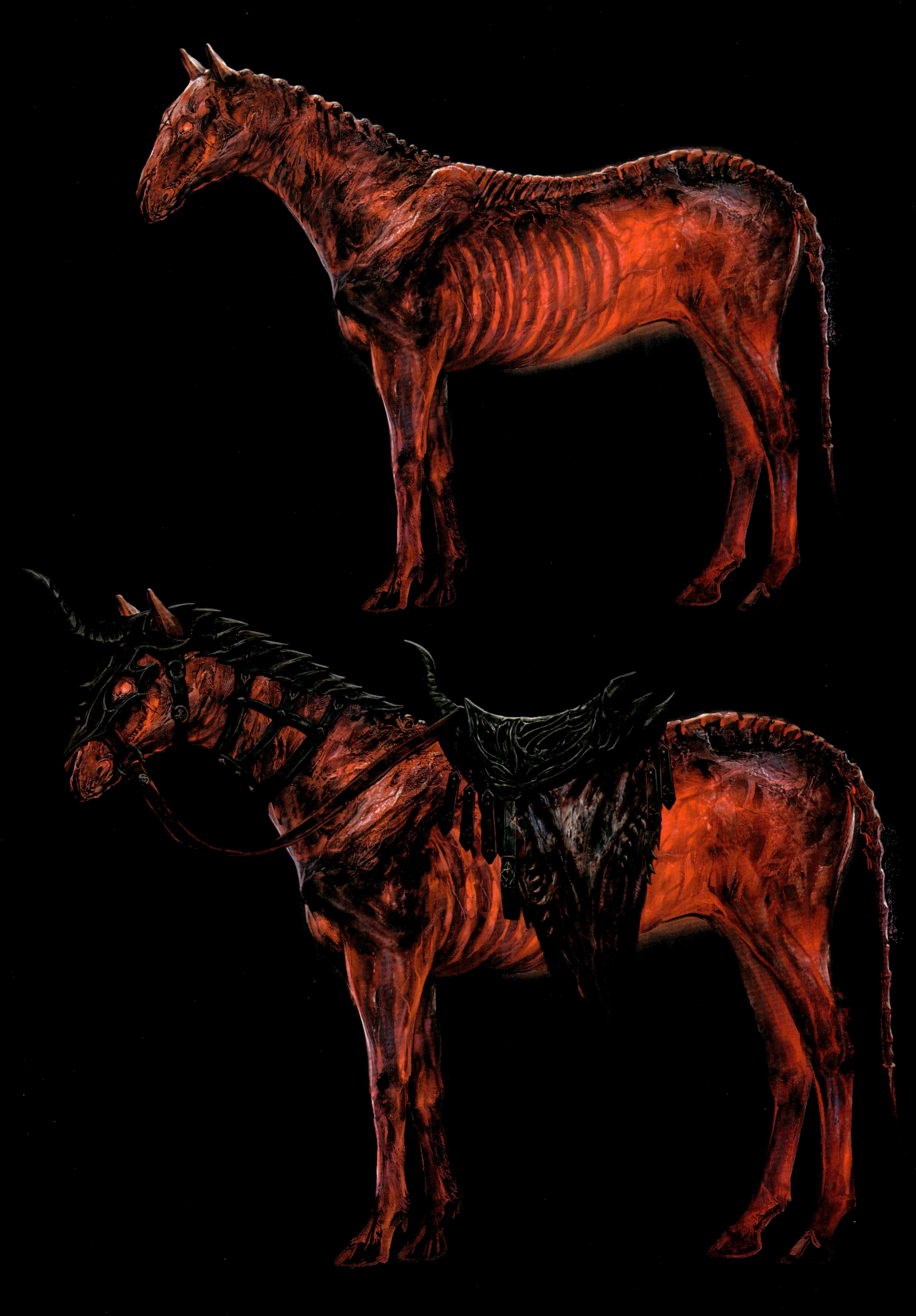

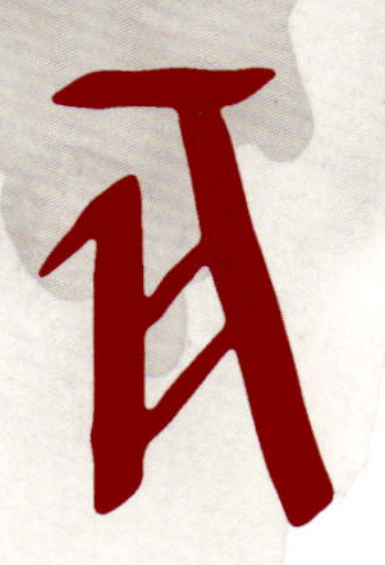

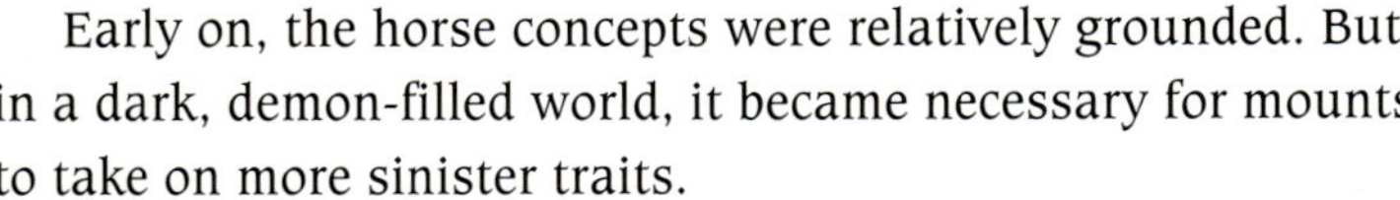

Early on, the horse concepts were relatively grounded. But in a dark, demon-filled world, it became necessary for mounts to take on more sinister traits.

As Sevilla notes, "Toward the end, we realized that we had to go from a horse to a death horse and all the different hellish versions of what that could be. Like a horse themed after a Fallen, with Fallen type horns, and others themed after creature families like the Drowned, so we had a horse that felt like it had been rotting in the ocean, with flesh coming off."

Yet no matter how fantastical designs may become, the pillar that the team works around is that mounts still need to look like a horse. And one action that is naturally associated with a horse is mounting and dismounting. In the beginning, the animations of getting on and off the horse were deemed too slow.

"We have to keep the *Diablo* player in mind," says Chilano. "So you need to hop on and hop off. Then we realized that doing an attack while getting off the mount is really fun. You can ride into a group, hit a button, and your Rogue jumps up and shoots arrows down and lands and rolls. These are really cool moments where you can say, 'Who's the character or the class, and what can they do getting off this mount that supports what is really the heart and soul of *Diablo*?' which is combat to get loot. It's always fun being a Druid and jumping off the mount and turning into a bear."

The addition of mounts required the team to take into account another element introduced in *Diablo IV*—traversals. Traversals allow players to jump gaps and climb cliffs, ropes, and more, exploiting verticality in a way that had previously been impossible. But what did this mean for mounts?

Chilano and the team had a few ideas. "When you jump across a chasm, a horse jumping totally makes sense. Then we have cases like a one-way traversal, which is sliding down a slope. We had to figure out a way to make the horse go down the slope at the same speed as a player so you're not being punished for using the horse."

With all the work that has gone into mounts thus far, one natural question might be, where will they go from here? One thing is certain: the future is full of possibilities.

ABOVE Barbarian Lettering + Fernando Pinilla

RIGHT Flower Armor Concept + Mengtian Mei

BOTTOM & BELOW Celestial Armor Concepts + BOSi

OPPOSITE, TOP Flower Armor Concept + Mengtian Mei

OPPOSITE, BOTTOM Celestial Armor Concept + BOSi

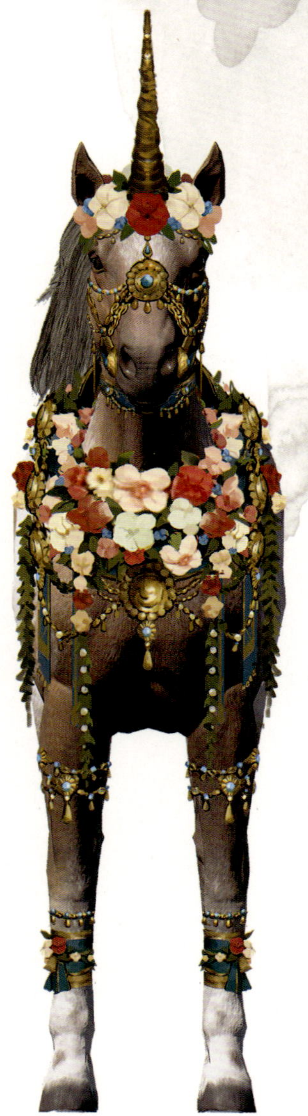

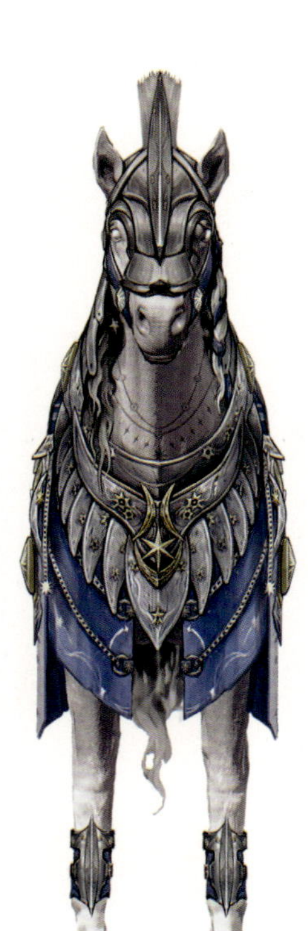

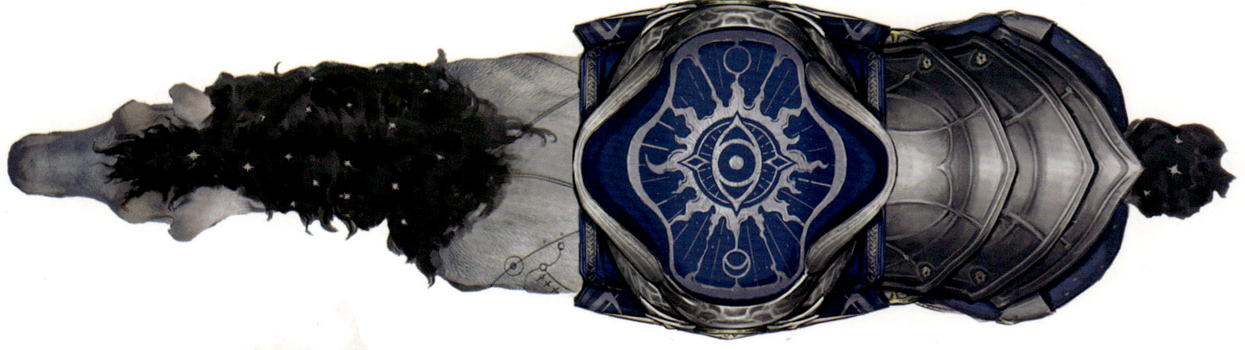

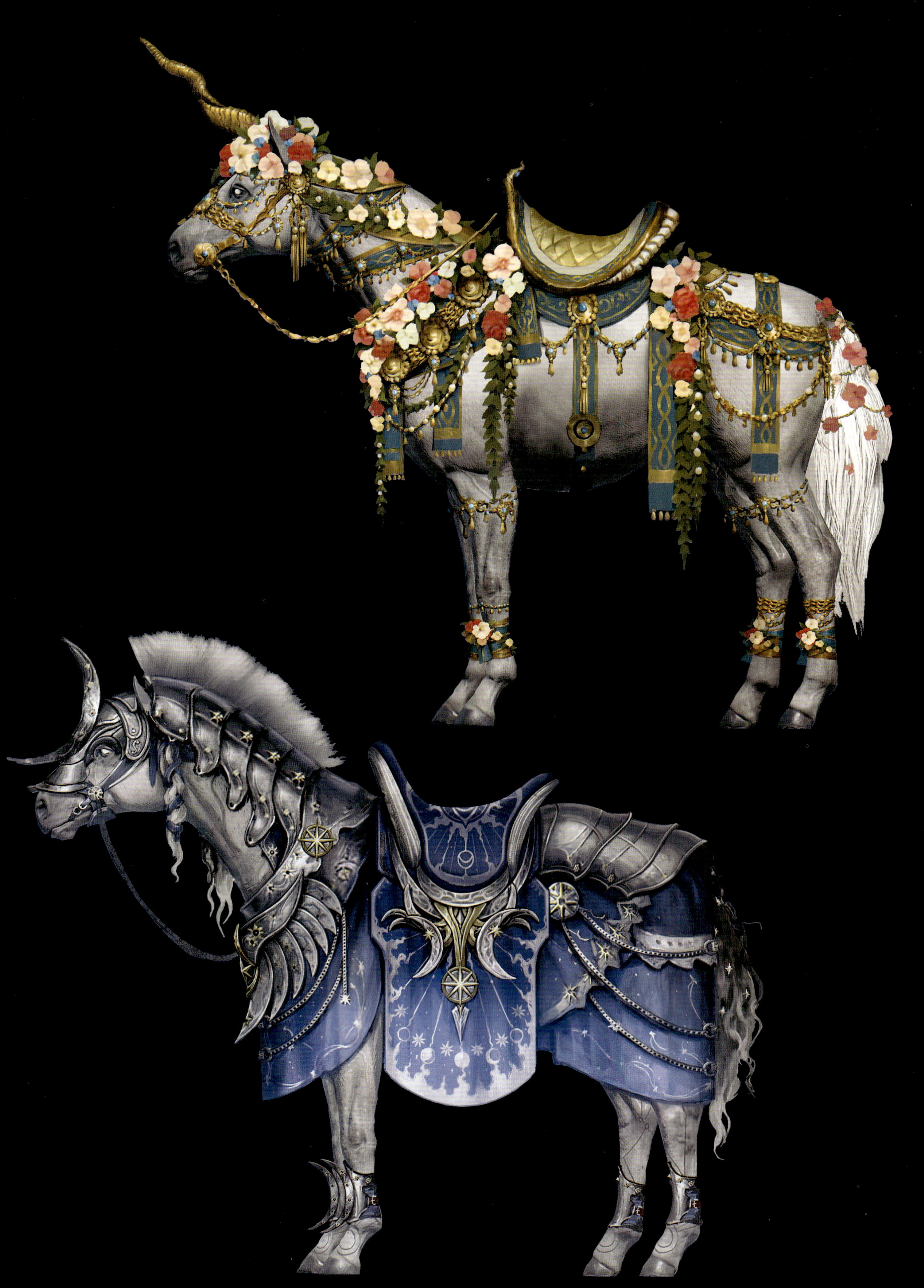

RIGHT Demon Armor Concept • Sora Kim

BOTTOM Inarius Armor Concept • Rob Sevilla

OPPOSITE, TOP LEFT Rogue Concept • Sora Kim

OPPOSITE, TOP RIGHT Gold Plate Armor Concept • Sora Kim

OPPOSITE, MIDDLE RIGHT Avarice Armor Concept • Mac Smith

OPPOSITE, BOTTOM RIGHT Bathed in Blood Armor Concept • Max Yenin

OPPOSITE, BOTTOM LEFT Penitent Armor Concept • BOSi

OPPOSITE, MIDDLE LEFT Necromancer Armor Concept • Sora Kim

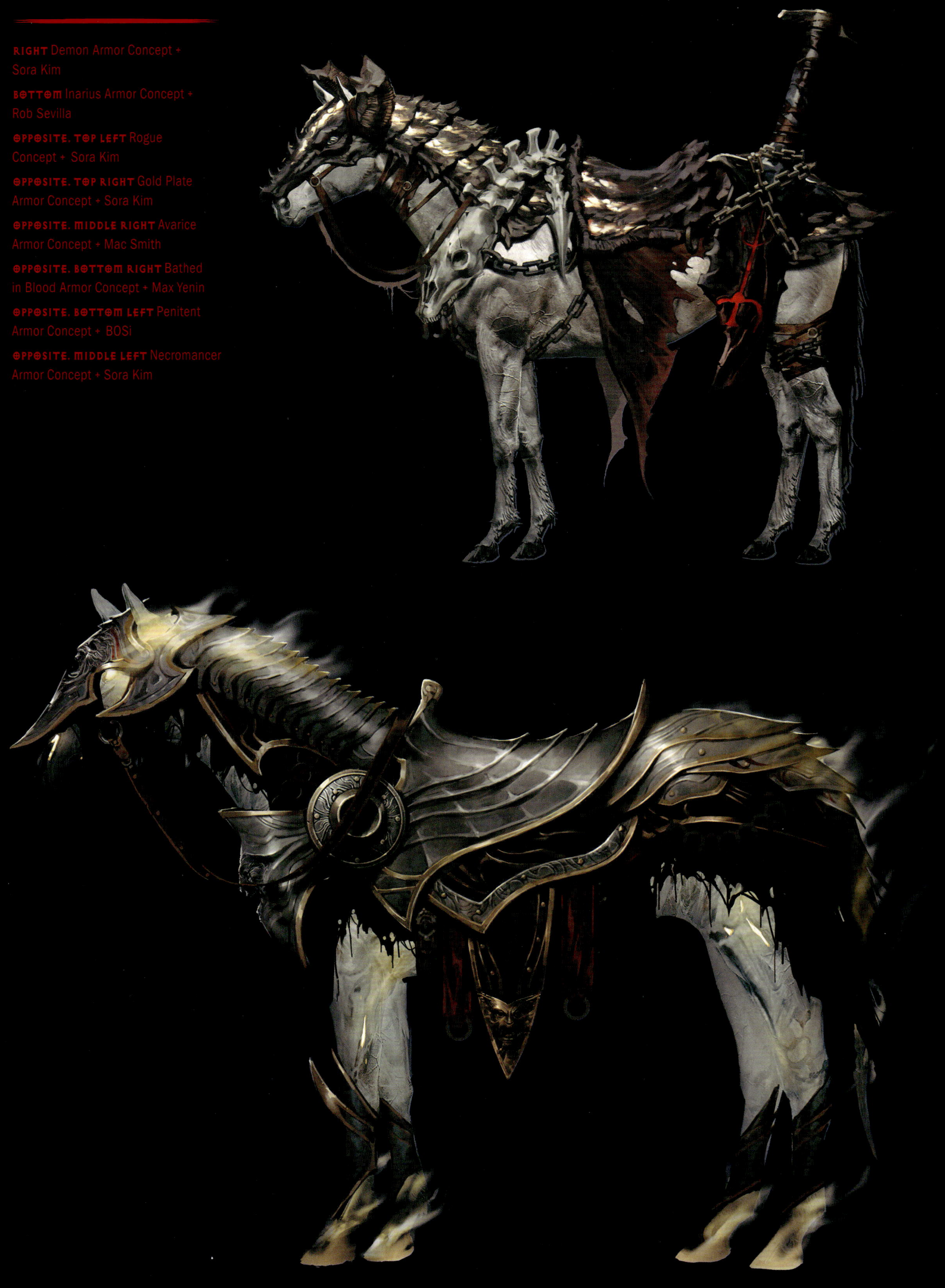

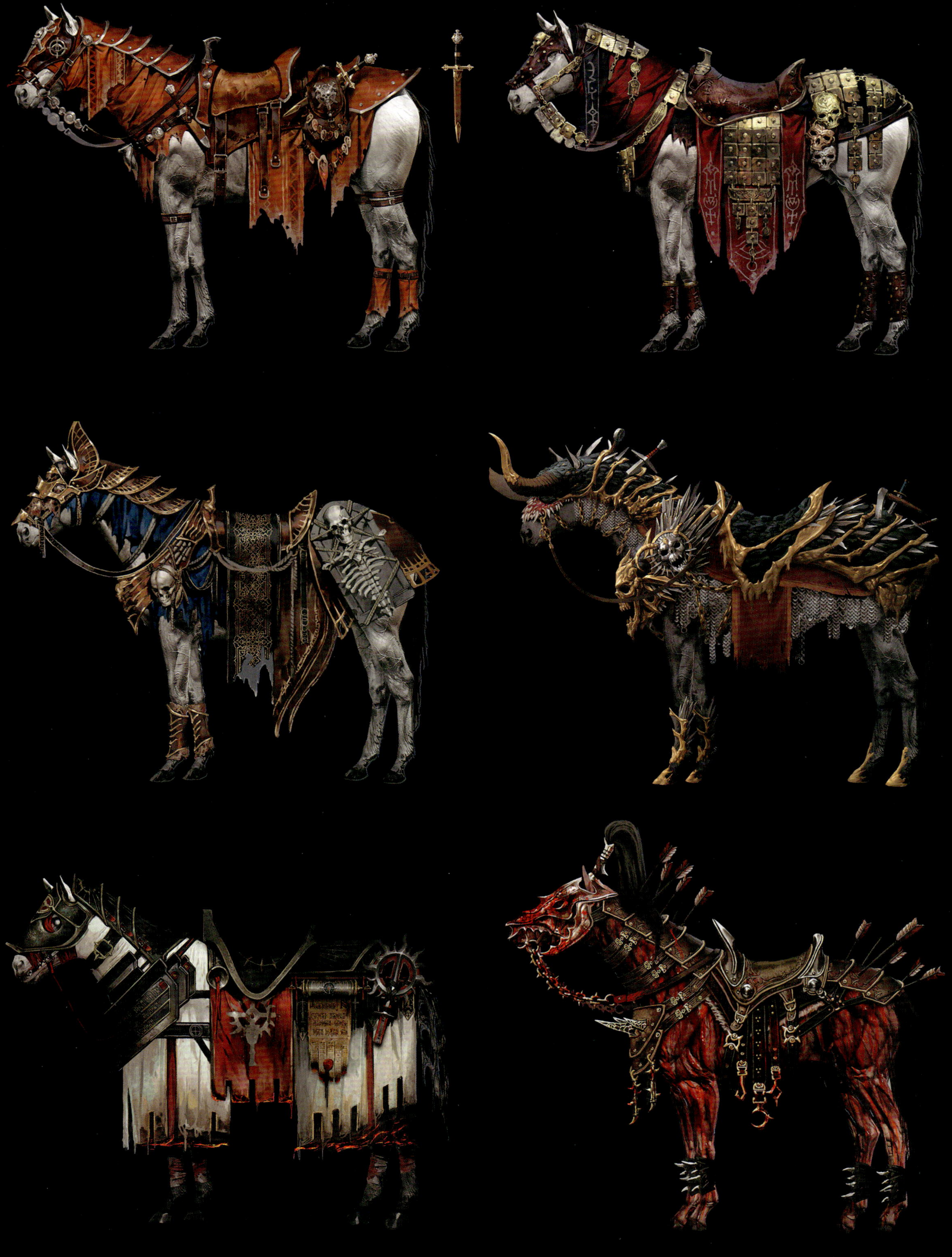

RIGHT Drowned Armor Concept + Gabriel Santos

BELOW Fallen Hunter Armor Concept + Rob Sevilla

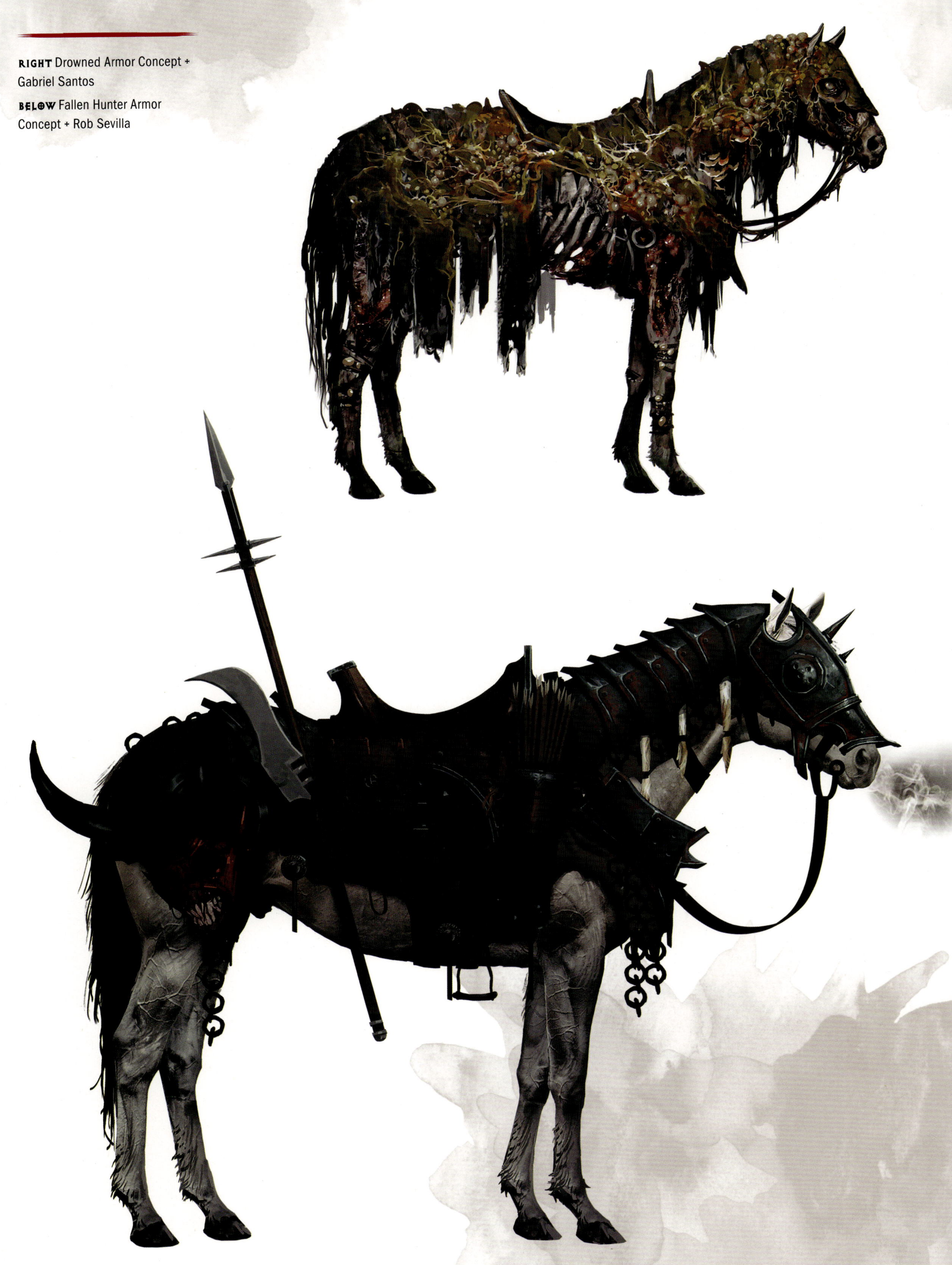

THIS PAGE Ice Armor Concept + Thanh Tuan

"So the challenge was really finding that sweet spot of how is it tuned, how does it feel, how do we animate it so that it makes sense to just hop on and off or to just have the mount appear. We obviously want to find that spot where we're making it walk and trot and run and it feels nice and smooth and it feels good, but we also can't make that aggravate the player. So we're always trying to find that balance."

—NICK CHILANO, Animation Director

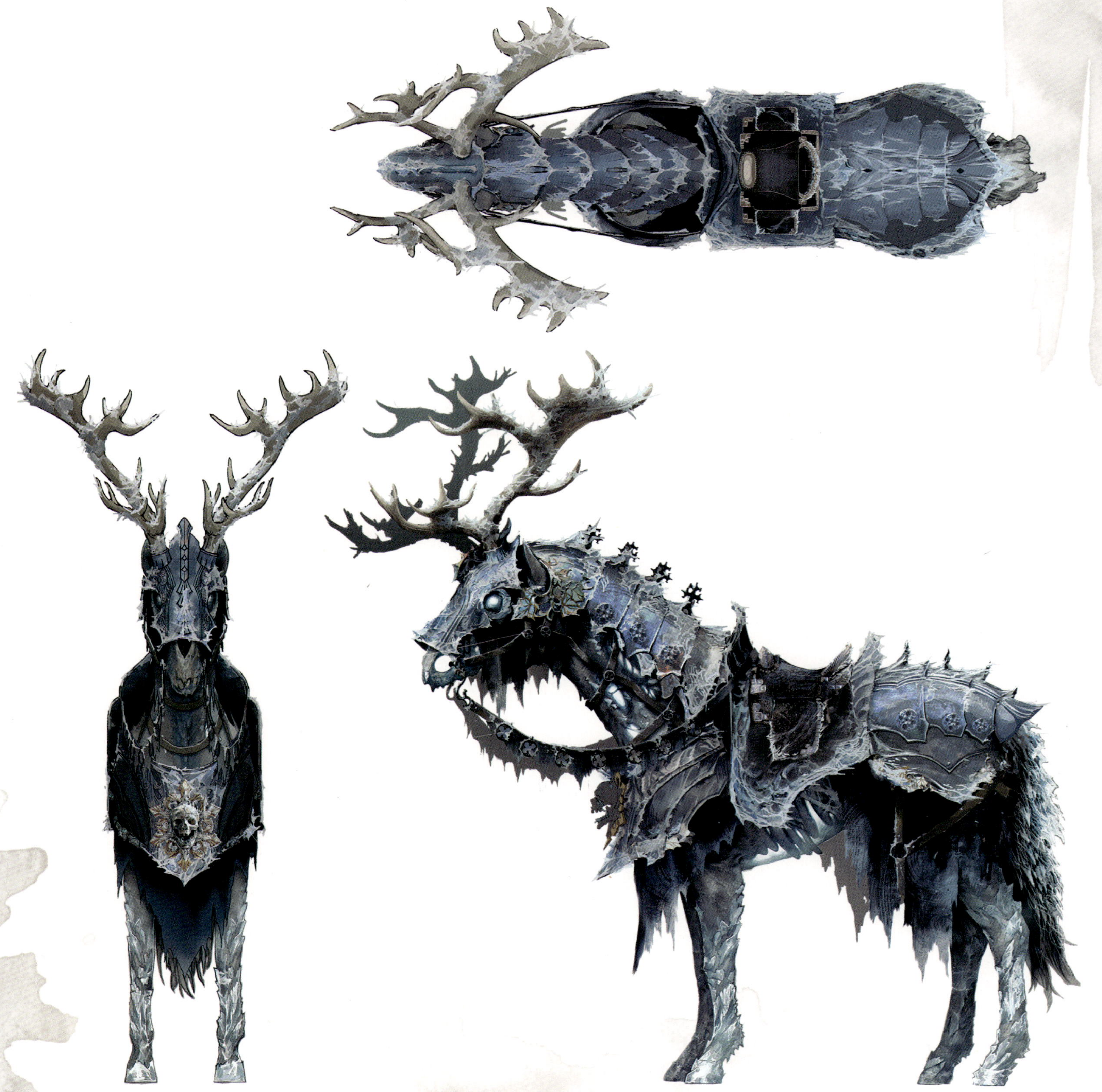

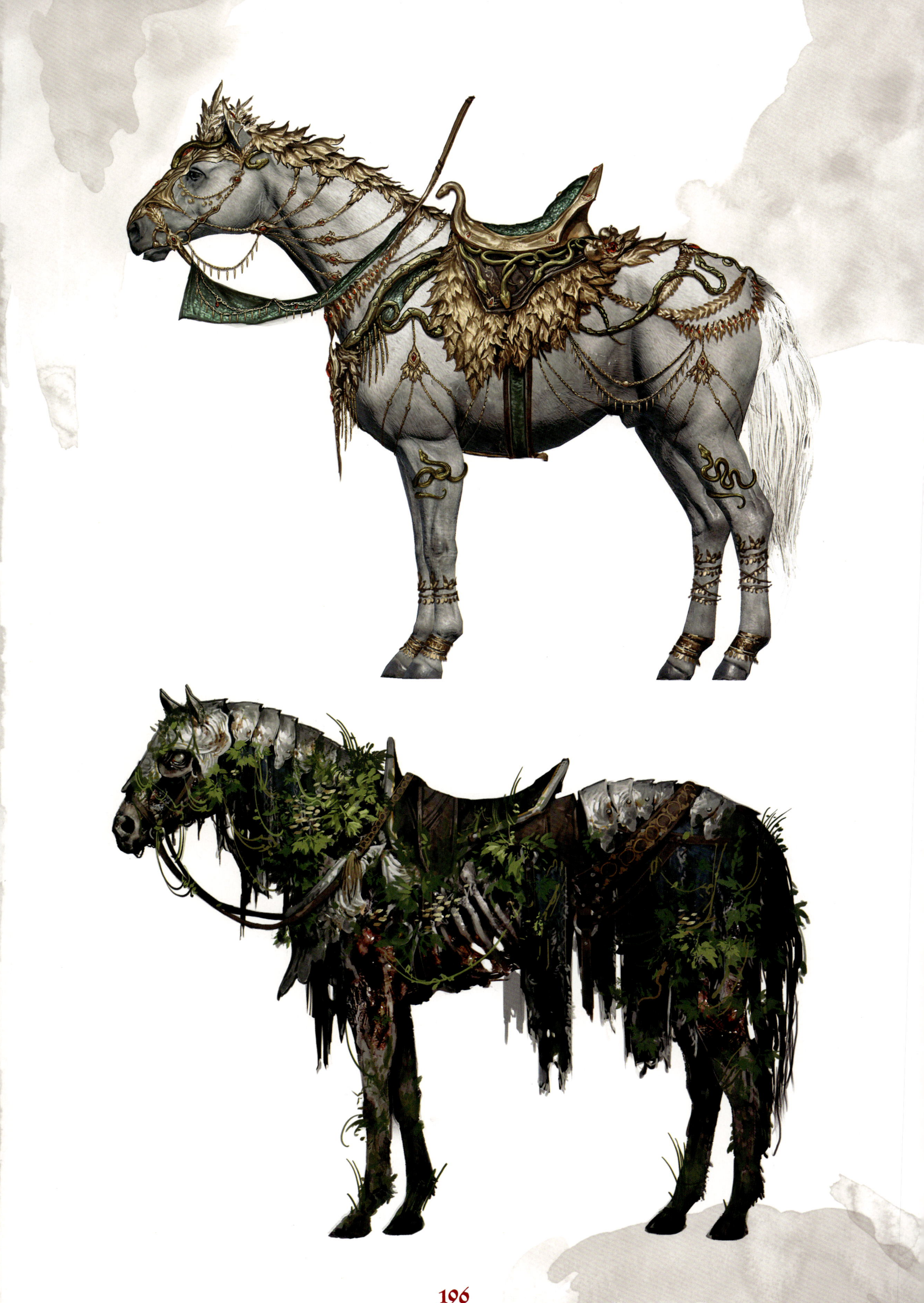

RIGHT, TOP Hellfire Mount Concept + Rob Sevilla

RIGHT, MIDDLE Flayed Mount Concept + Rob Sevilla

RIGHT, BOTTOM Fallen Mount Concept + Rob Sevilla

BOTTOM Vain Monarch Parade Mount Armor Concept + Maxim Zaytsev

OPPOSITE, TOP Envious Lust Mount Armor Concept + Jiamin Lin

OPPOSITE, BOTTOM Fleshrot Overgrowth Mount Concept + Gabriel Santos

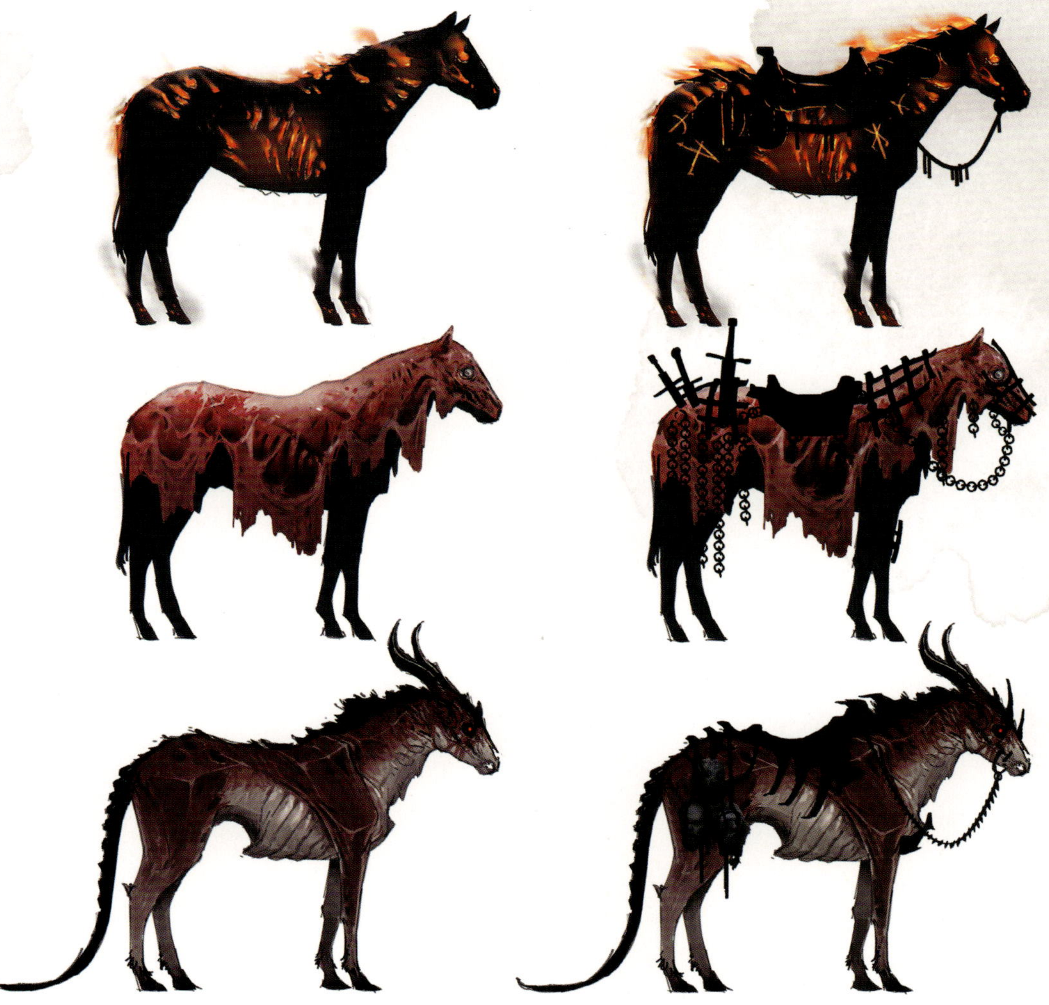

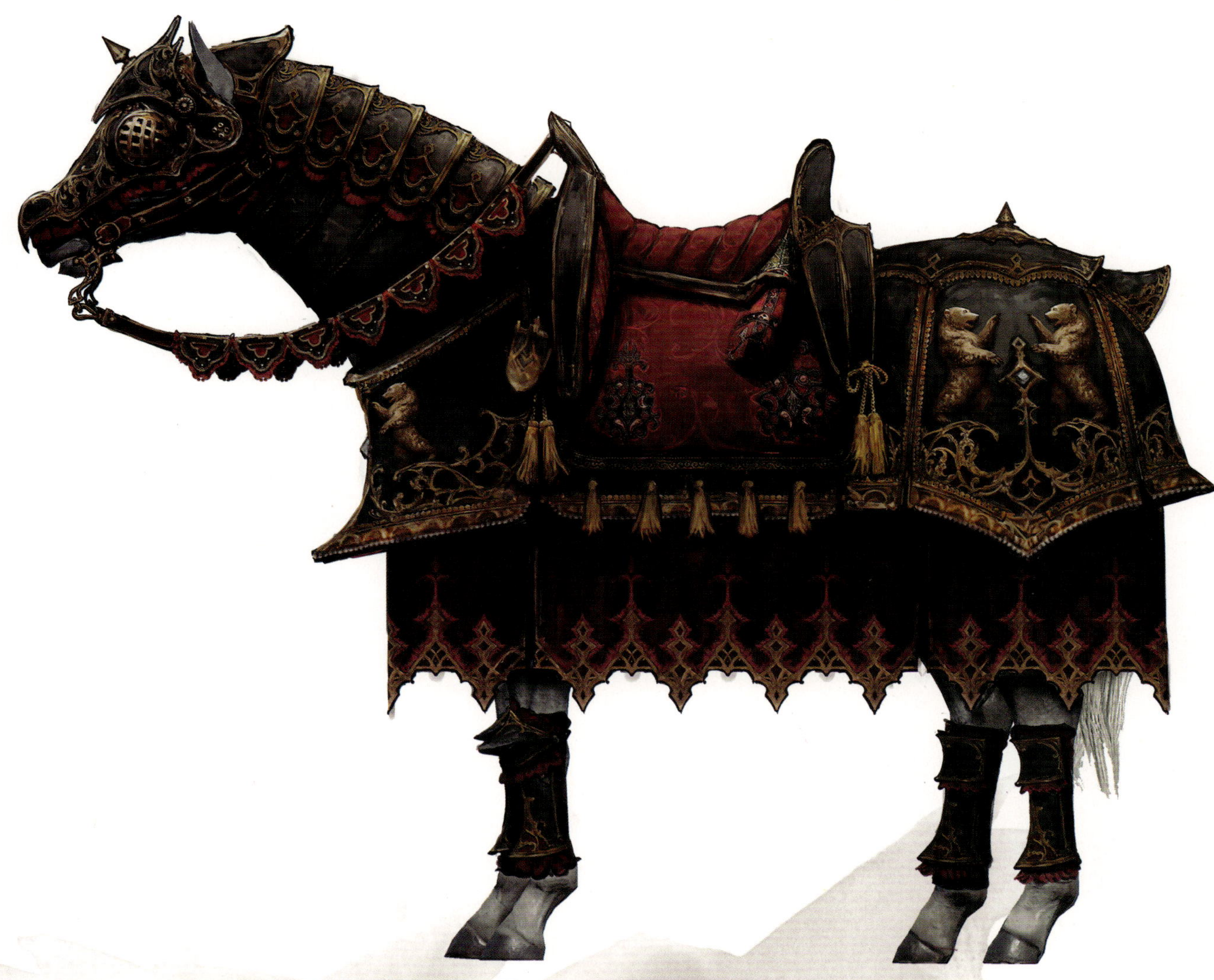

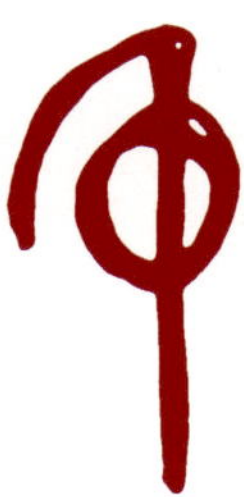

A Weapon For Every Occasion

ABOVE Druid Lettering + Fernando Pinilla

RIGHT Two-Handed Axe Concept + Mike Franchina

BOTTOM, RIGHT Polearm Concept + Mike Franchina

BOTTOM, MIDDLE Scythe Concepts + Mike Franchina

BELOW Polearm Concept + Mike Franchina

OPPOSITE Lilith Deluxe Armor Concepts + Min Fu

Diablo IV allows players to get more up close and personal with their armor, weapons, and items than ever before. The game's physically based rendering provides for gear that is textural, believable, and made up of components that mimic easily identifiable real-world materials.

Every class has its own suit of armor and weapons. So when artists start out, many times they focus on the class's theme. In the case of Necromancer armor, the theme is death.

"*Diablo IV* appreciates bold ideas," says Hunter Schulz. "If you had leather straps and shoulder pads with a skull on it and a spike, you can make that look cool through a really good design. But what if you ask questions such as: How did the Necromancer make this gear? What materials did they use? How did they put it together? *Why* did they put it together? That's when it gets really interesting."

Artists keep the interchangeable nature of the armor in mind as well, knowing that players may collect an entire set or only ever wear certain pieces. "We build things in a set," explains Cory Turner, "but armor's not presented to the player that way. It's presented in isolation so that a player might only ever see the boots. They might never get a drop or think to combine two sets together. So for us, making sure that everything will come together in a way that looks pleasing and not broken is a huge undertaking."

Adding to the complexity is the topic of cosmetics, such as dyes that players can use to change the color of armor and weapons.

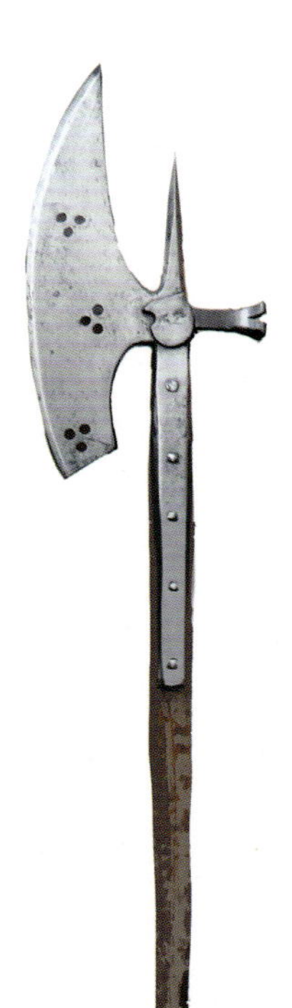

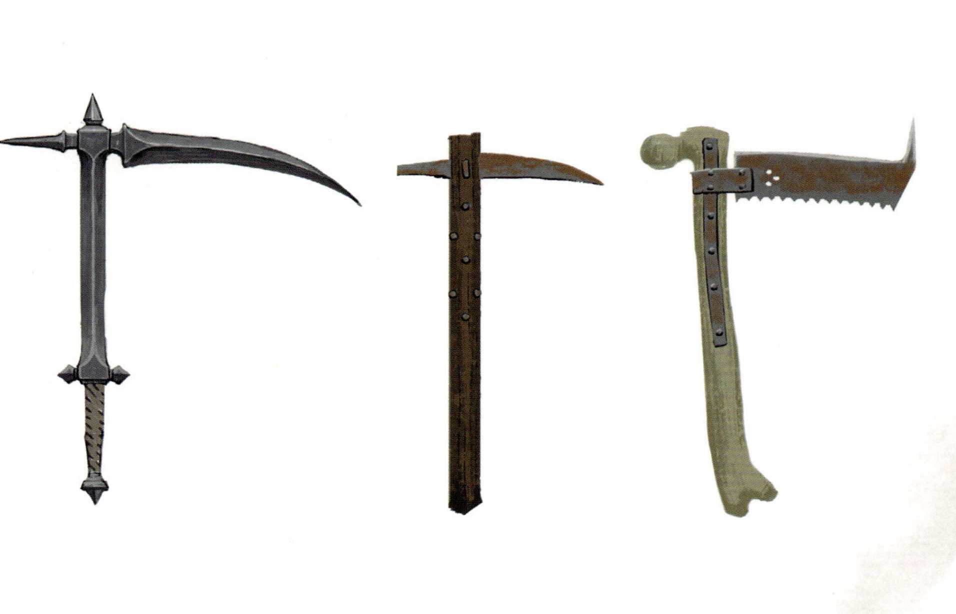

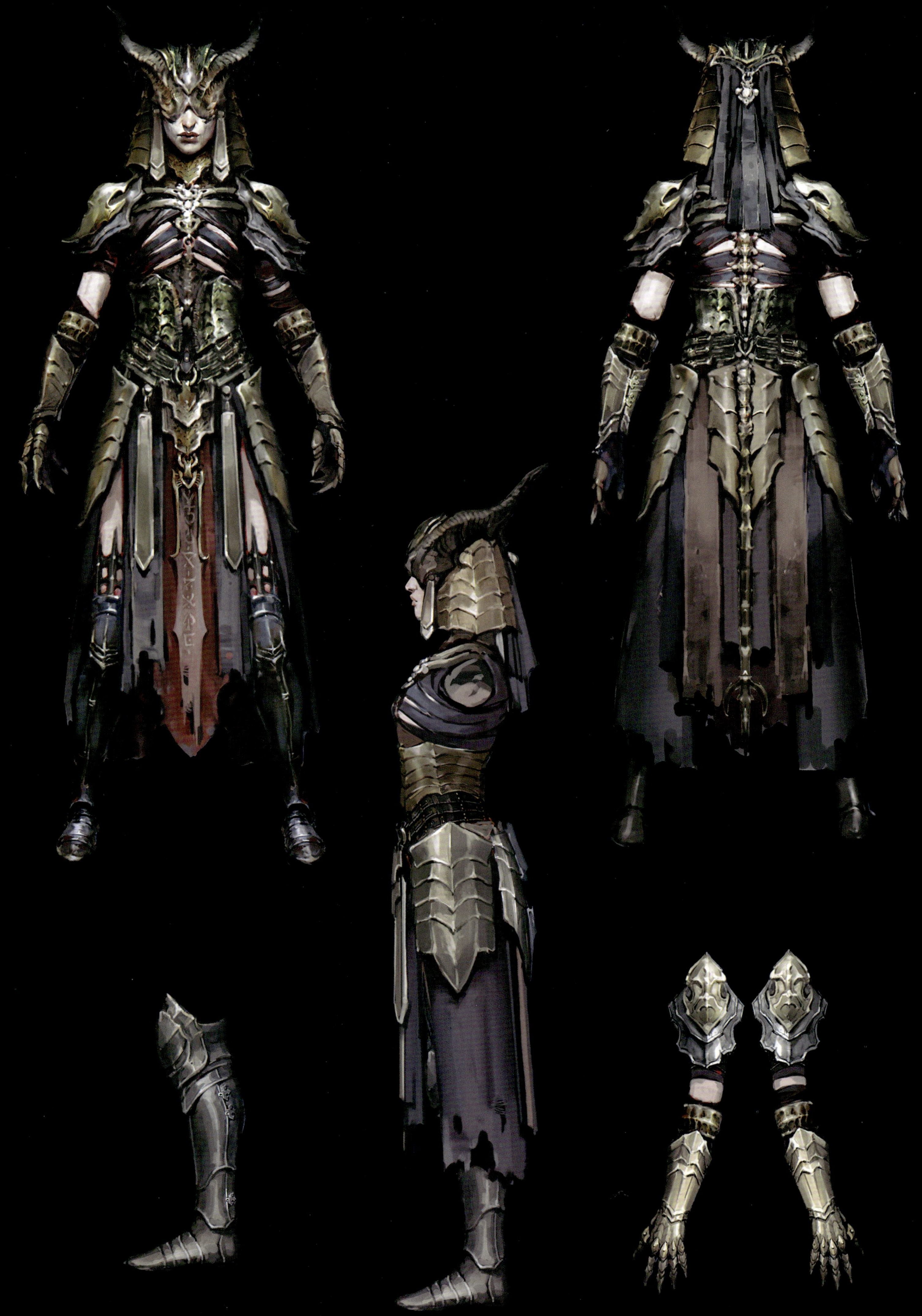

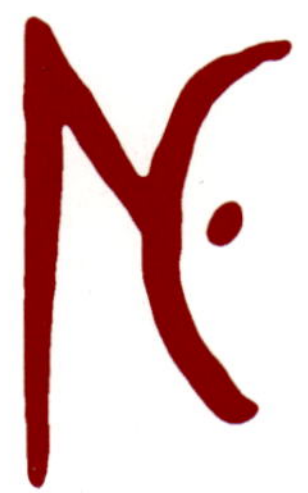

ABOVE Druid Lettering + Fernando Pinilla

RIGHT Host of Chaos Mace Concept + Bjorn Hurri

BOTTOM Host of Chaos Dagger Concept + Bjorn Hurri

BELOW Focus Concept + Jin Xiaodi

OPPOSITE Staff Concepts + Victor Lee, Jin Xiaodi, BOSi

"The player is going to want a satisfying experience when they apply color to a piece," says Turner. "We don't want them to think, 'I applied the green dye to my boots, yet there is no green on my boots. Something must be wrong.' We want them to make themselves look however they want, which is a big change for *Diablo*. There was color application in *Diablo III*, but armor was mostly skintight with a few flourishes. In *Diablo IV*, everything is very rounded out and three-dimensional. Plus, there's much more complex interactions between materials and geometry."

Given the near-limitless range of *Diablo* gear, artists apply this golden rule in the early design stages: keep it simple.

"The eternal challenge is always how not to escalate," says Victor Lee. "As you progress from simple armor to stronger armor, it has to get more complex, better looking, with better materials, cooler shapes, and cooler silhouettes. How we tend to achieve that is to tack things onto it. That is a dangerous practice because you start to get more and more layered and cluttered. What we try to do is leave room for visual progression so in the end you don't have this monstrous thing."

The same rule applies to weapons, Lee notes. "The beginning weapon should look very simple, something that a villager would find or make. It shouldn't be too exotic."

On top of it all, special attention is given to how armor pieces come together.

"You have to be vigilant about minding the borders," says Turner. "The seams of a helmet. A hood and the chest. An arm and a sleeve. A belt and the torso. You have to make sure they all play with each other and that they never look like they're crashing or conflicting. There can't be any gaps between them either."

All these aspects add to the functionality and believability of *Diablo IV* gear, which in turn supports the overall style of the game.

"The armor and the world," says Schulz. "Everything looks like it should work. It's meant to mirror a medieval universe. It should feel tangible, like something that is very much grounded in the real world."

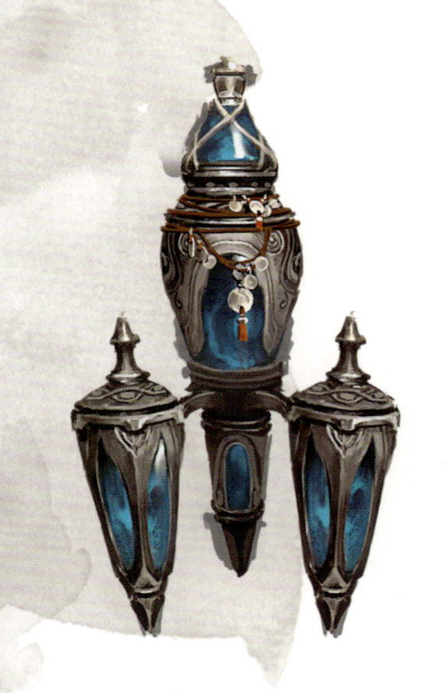

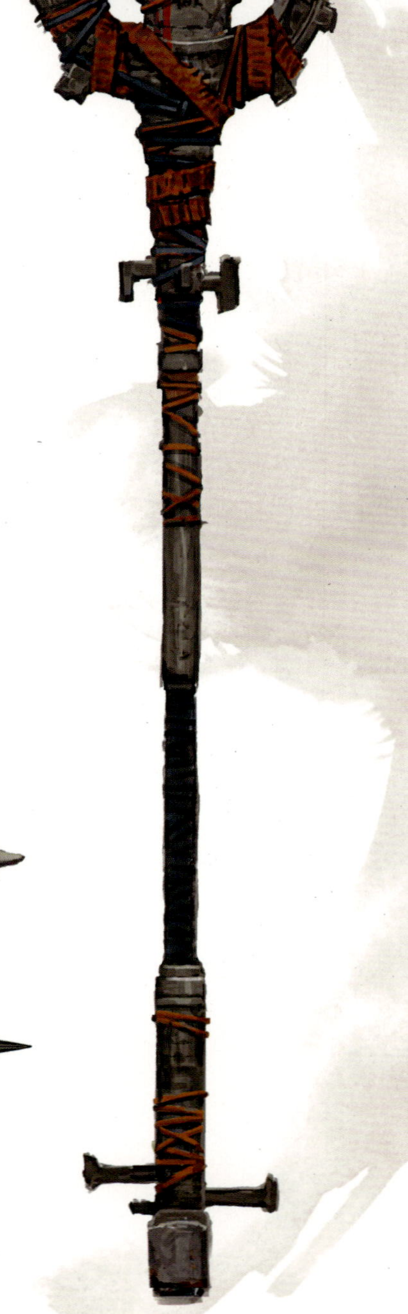

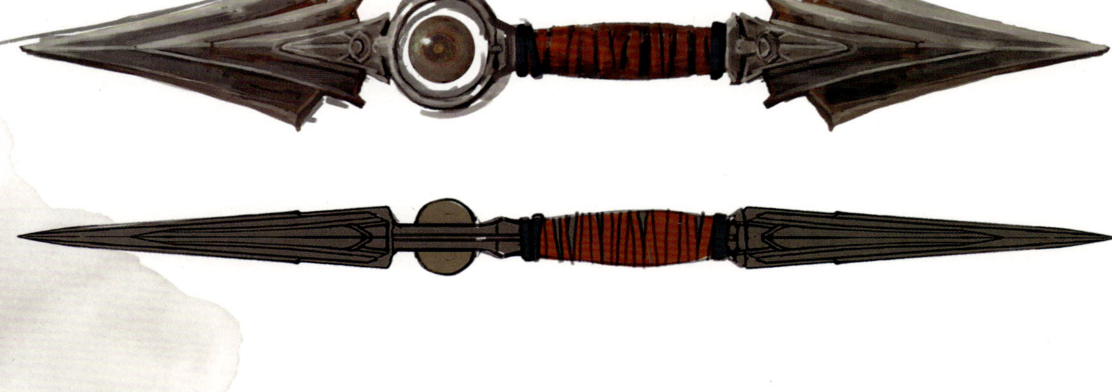

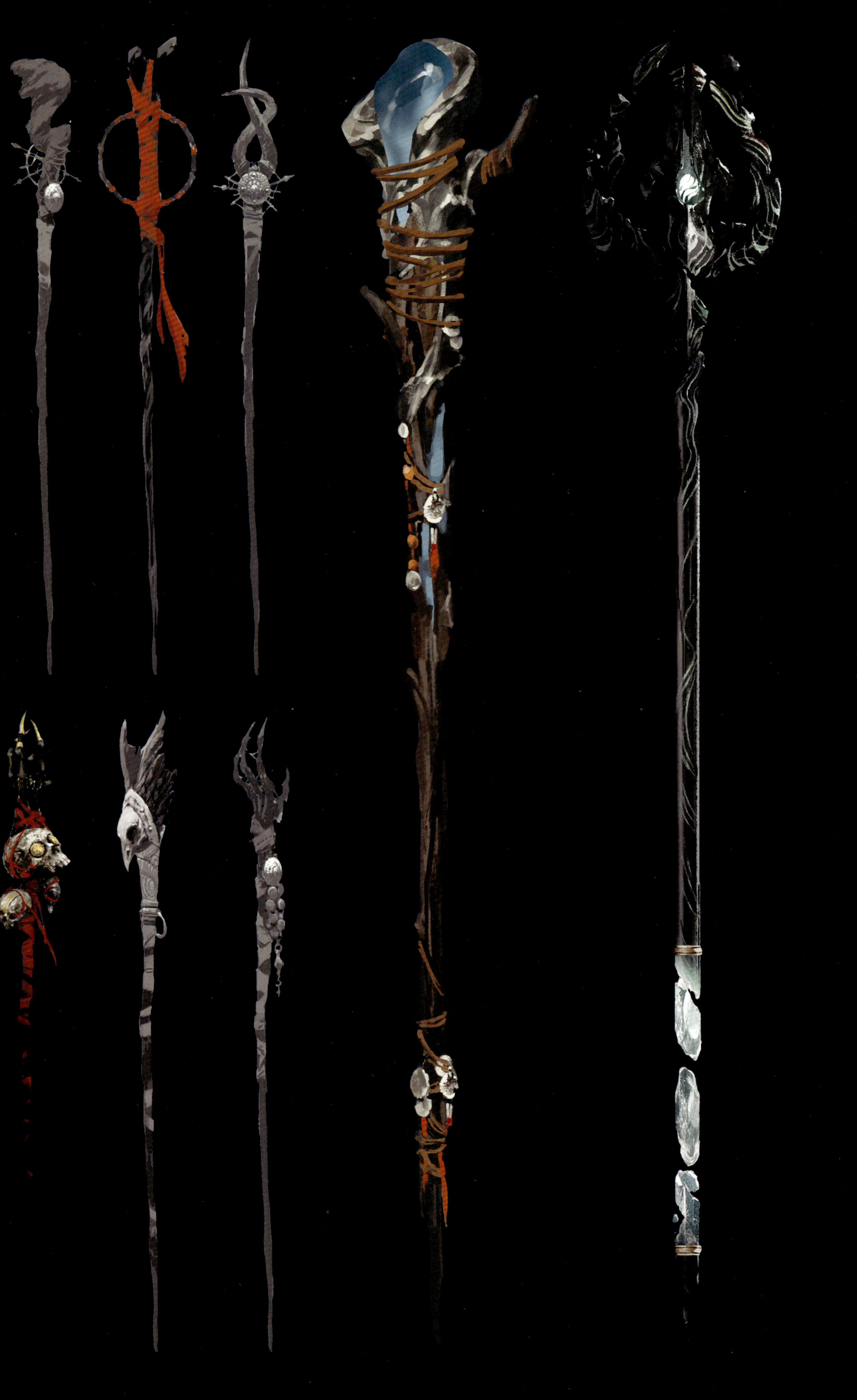

RIGHT Wand Concepts + Mike Franchina

BOTTOM, RIGHT Legendary Polearm Concept + T-Rex Lab

BOTTOM, MIDDLE Legendary Two-Handed Mace Concept + T-Rex Lab

BOTTOM, LEFT Legendary Scythe Concept + T-Rex Lab

BELOW Axe Concepts + Mike Franchina

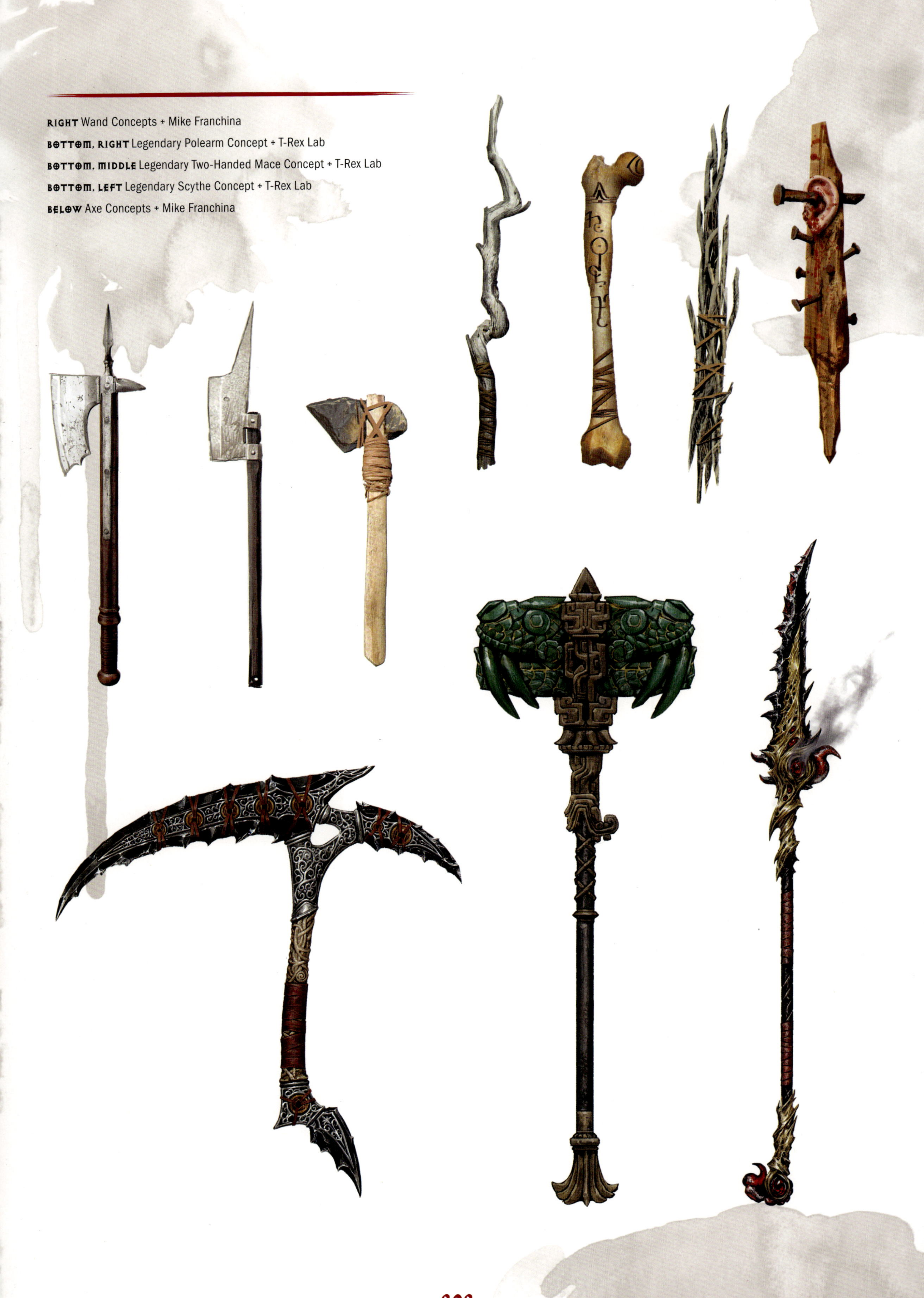

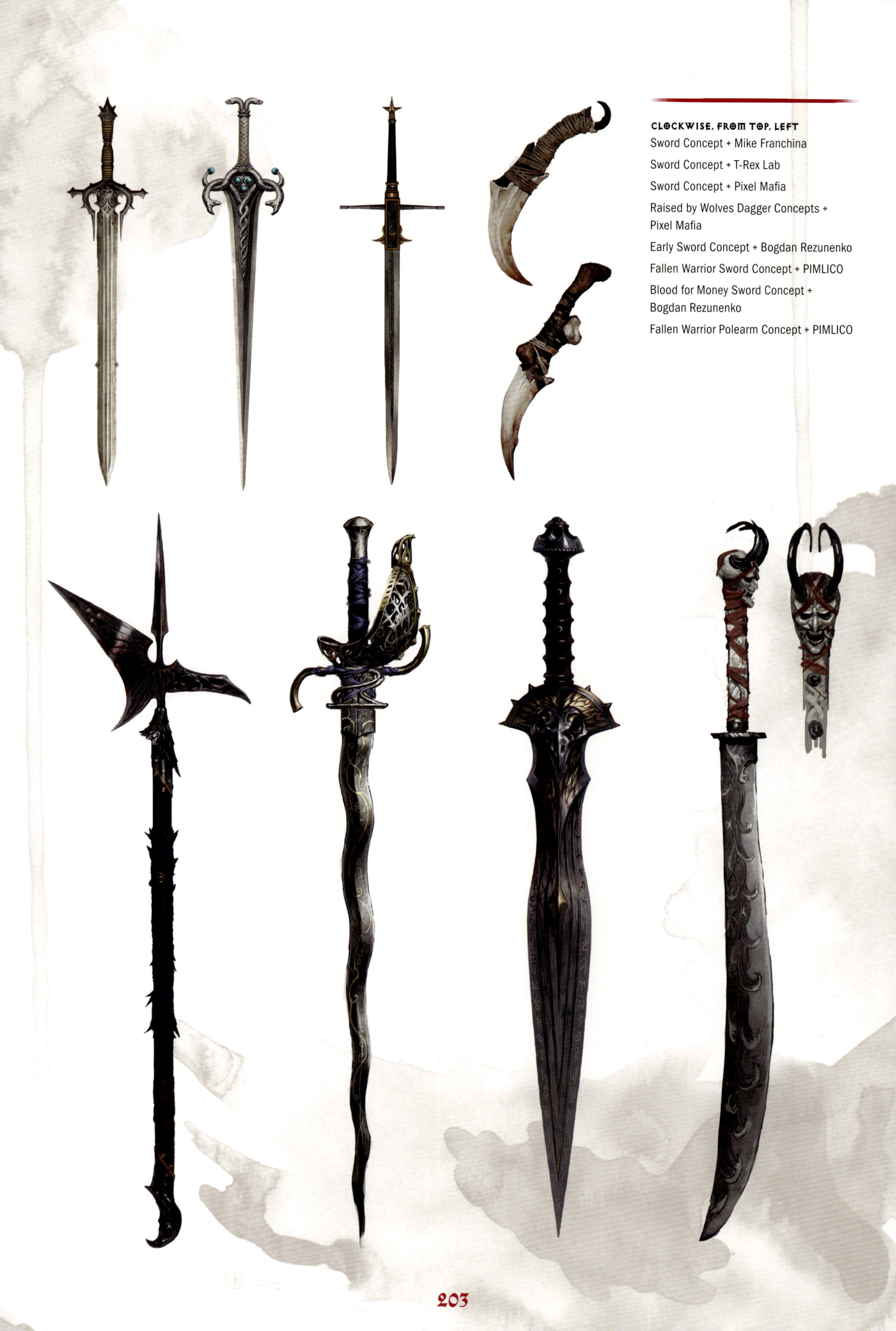

CLOCKWISE, FROM TOP, LEFT

Sword Concept + Mike Franchina

Sword Concept + T-Rex Lab

Sword Concept + Pixel Mafia

Raised by Wolves Dagger Concepts + Pixel Mafia

Early Sword Concept + Bogdan Rezunenko

Fallen Warrior Sword Concept + PIMLICO

Blood for Money Sword Concept + Bogdan Rezunenko

Fallen Warrior Polearm Concept + PIMLICO

"From the beginning, we wanted the armor to have a good base that's realistic and down-to-earth. We wanted to have a nice variety of materials in order to really take into account that realistic visual variety when you're able to inspect your character in a wardrobe. In Diablo III, *we never went that far into material variety because we did not use PBR."*

—RICHIE MARELLA,
Associate Art Director

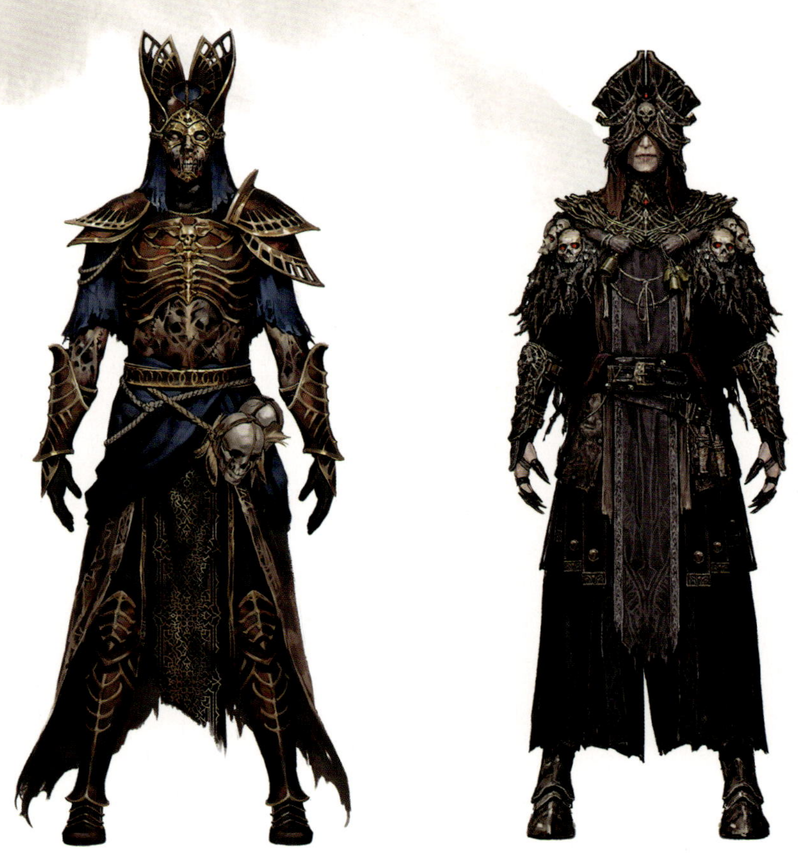

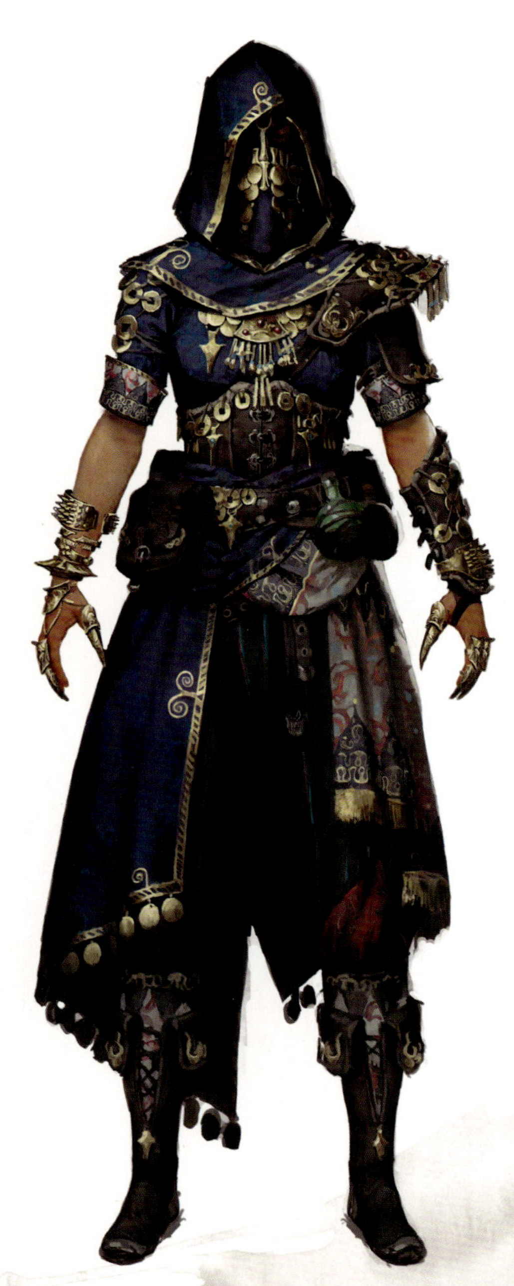

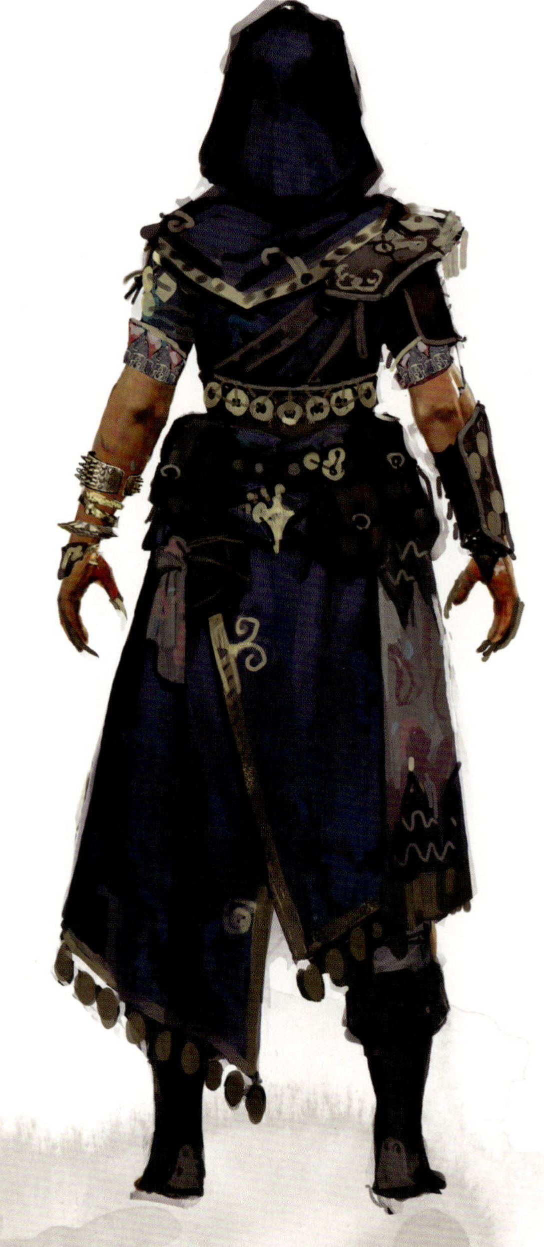

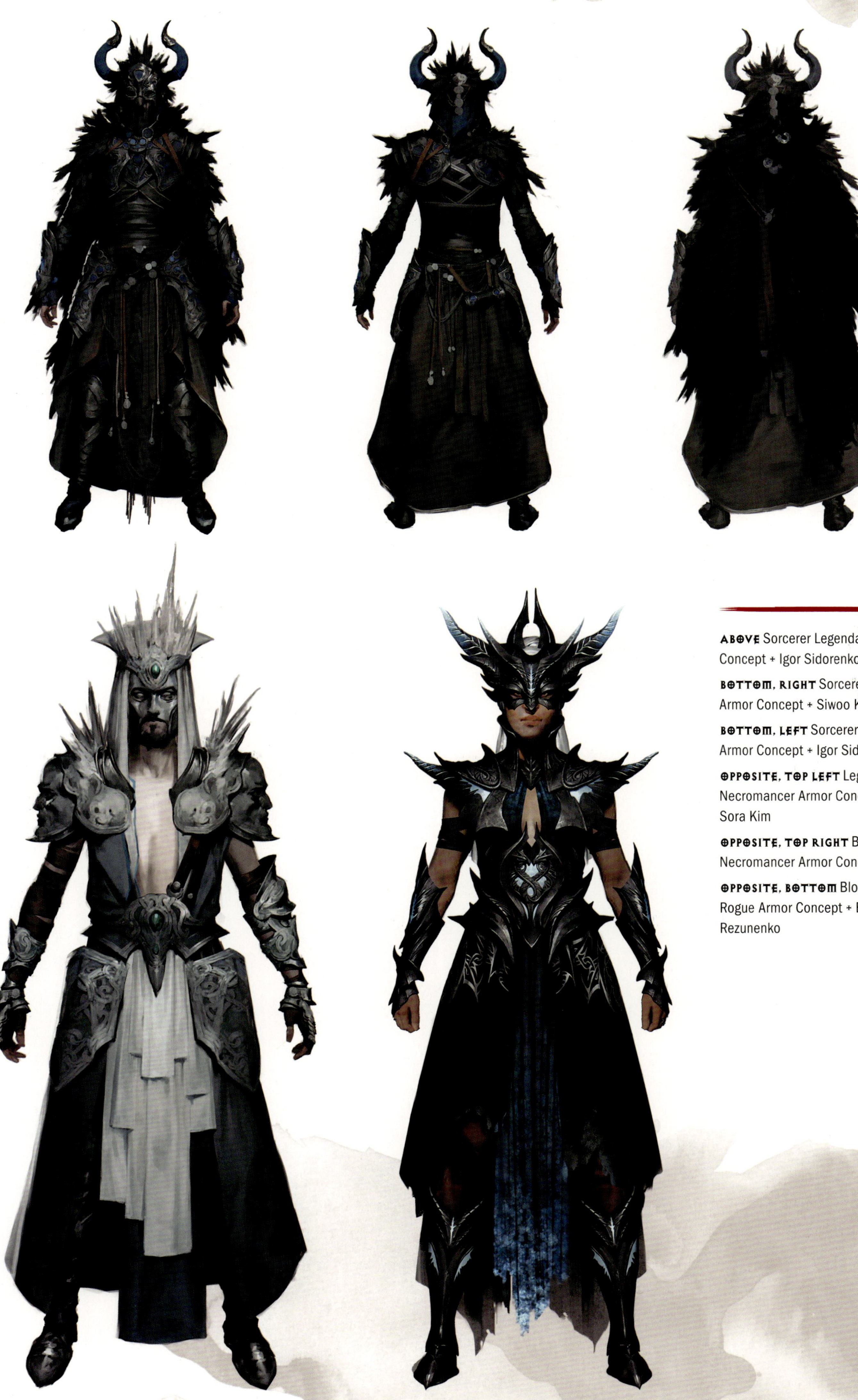

Above Sorcerer Legendary Armor Concept + Igor Sidorenko

Bottom, Right Sorcerer Legendary Armor Concept + Siwoo Kim

Bottom, Left Sorcerer Legendary Armor Concept + Igor Sidorenko

Opposite, Top Left Legendary Necromancer Armor Concept + Sora Kim

Opposite, Top Right Belladonna Necromancer Armor Concept + Asher

Opposite, Bottom Blood for Money Rogue Armor Concept + Bogdan Rezunenko

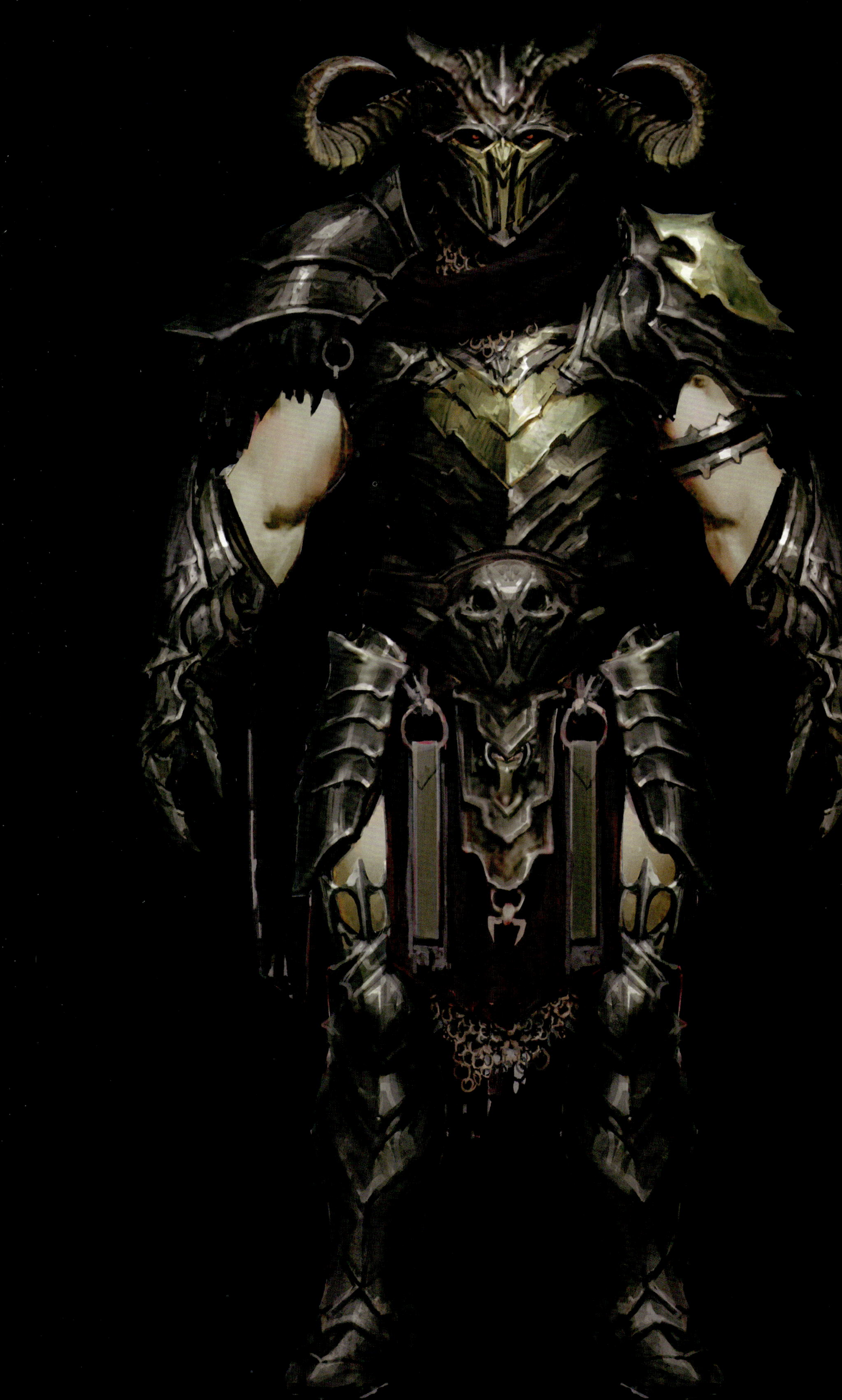

THIS PAGE Warlord Barbarian Armor Concepts + Igor Sidorenko

OPPOSITE Lilith Barbarian Armor Concept + Bjorn Hurri

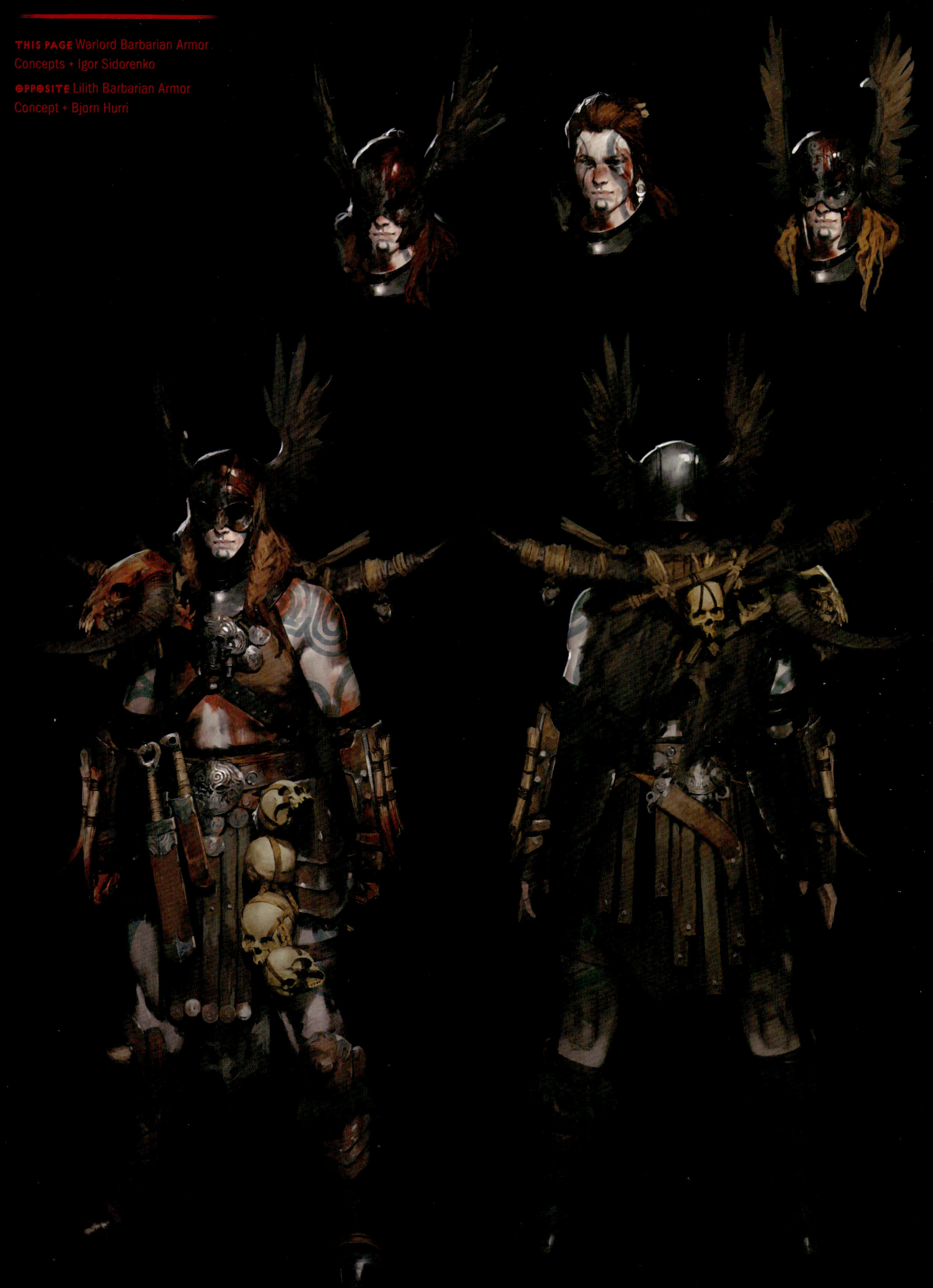

TOP, LEFT Druid Armor Concept + Igor Sidorenko

TOP, RIGHT Druid PvP Armor Concept + Igor Sidorenko

BOTTOM, RIGHT Legendary Druid Armor Concept + Rob Sevilla

BOTTOM, LEFT Oaken Keeper Druid Concept + Pavel Shut

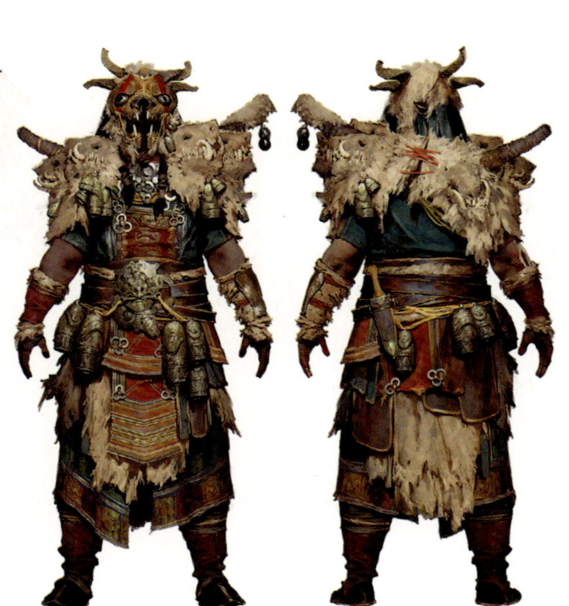

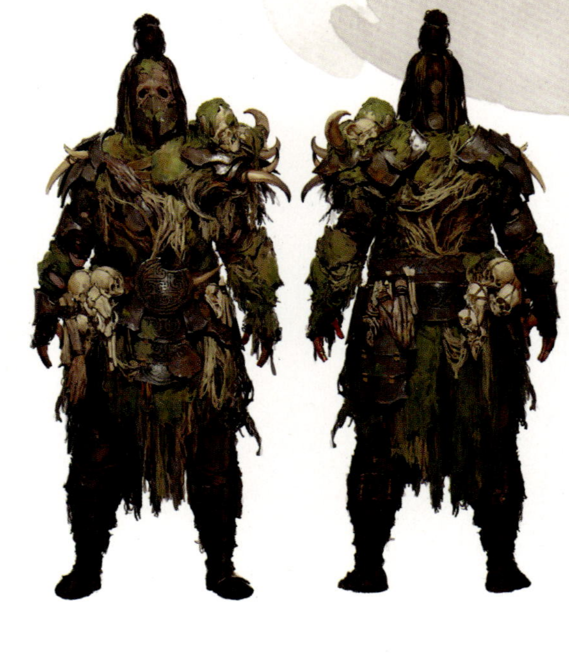

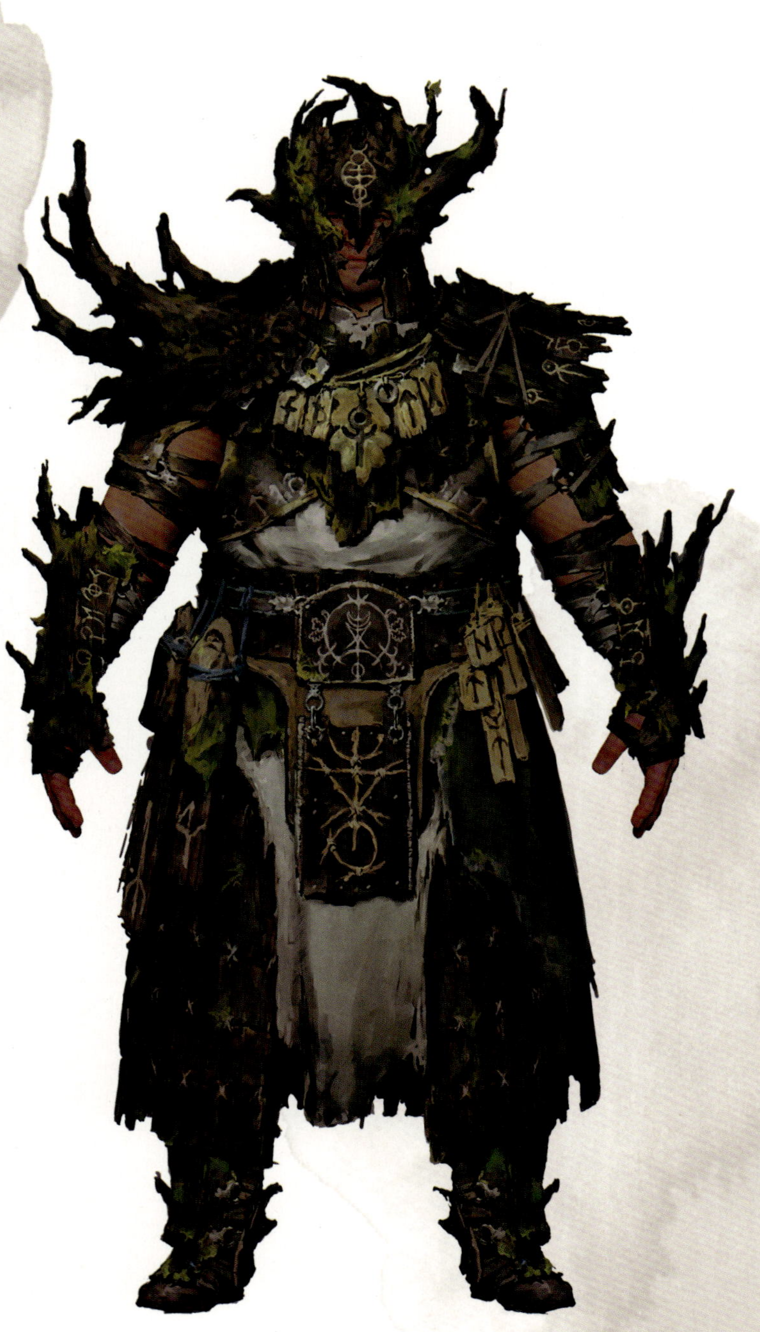

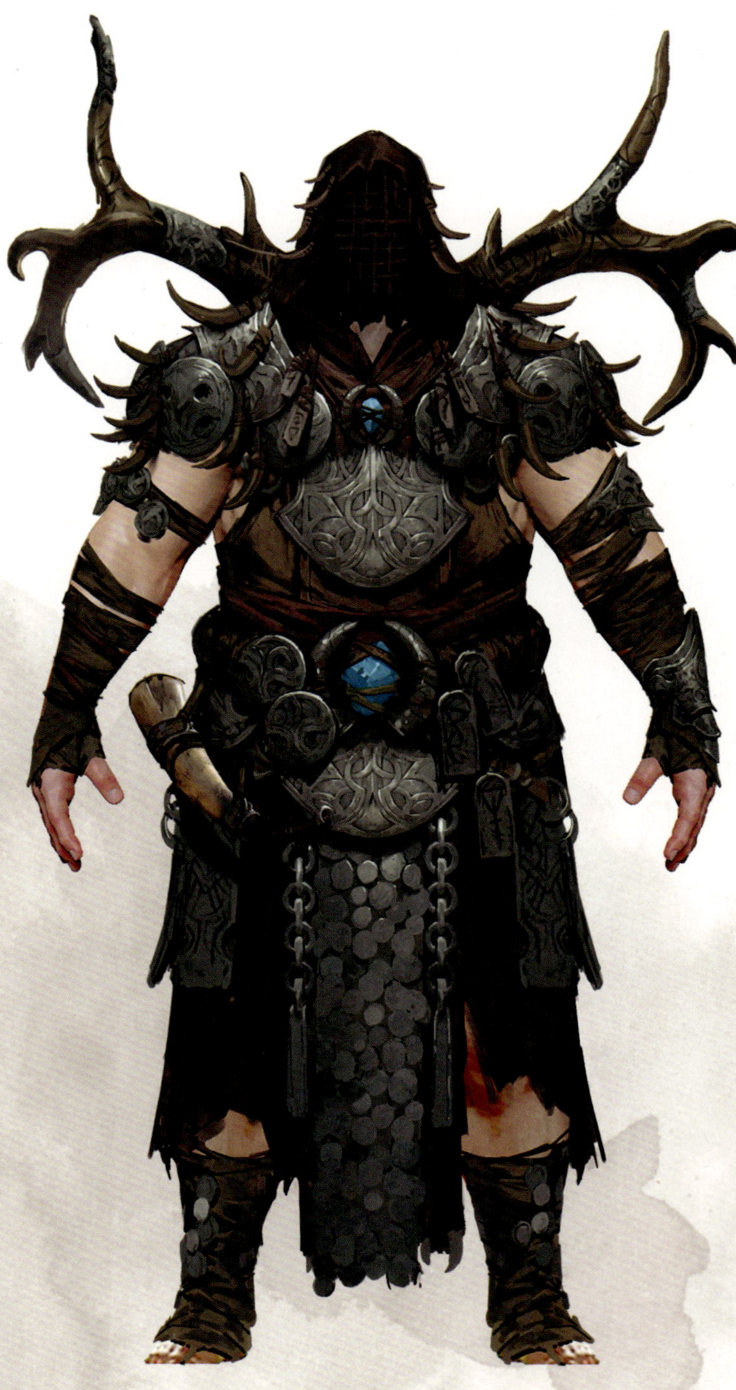

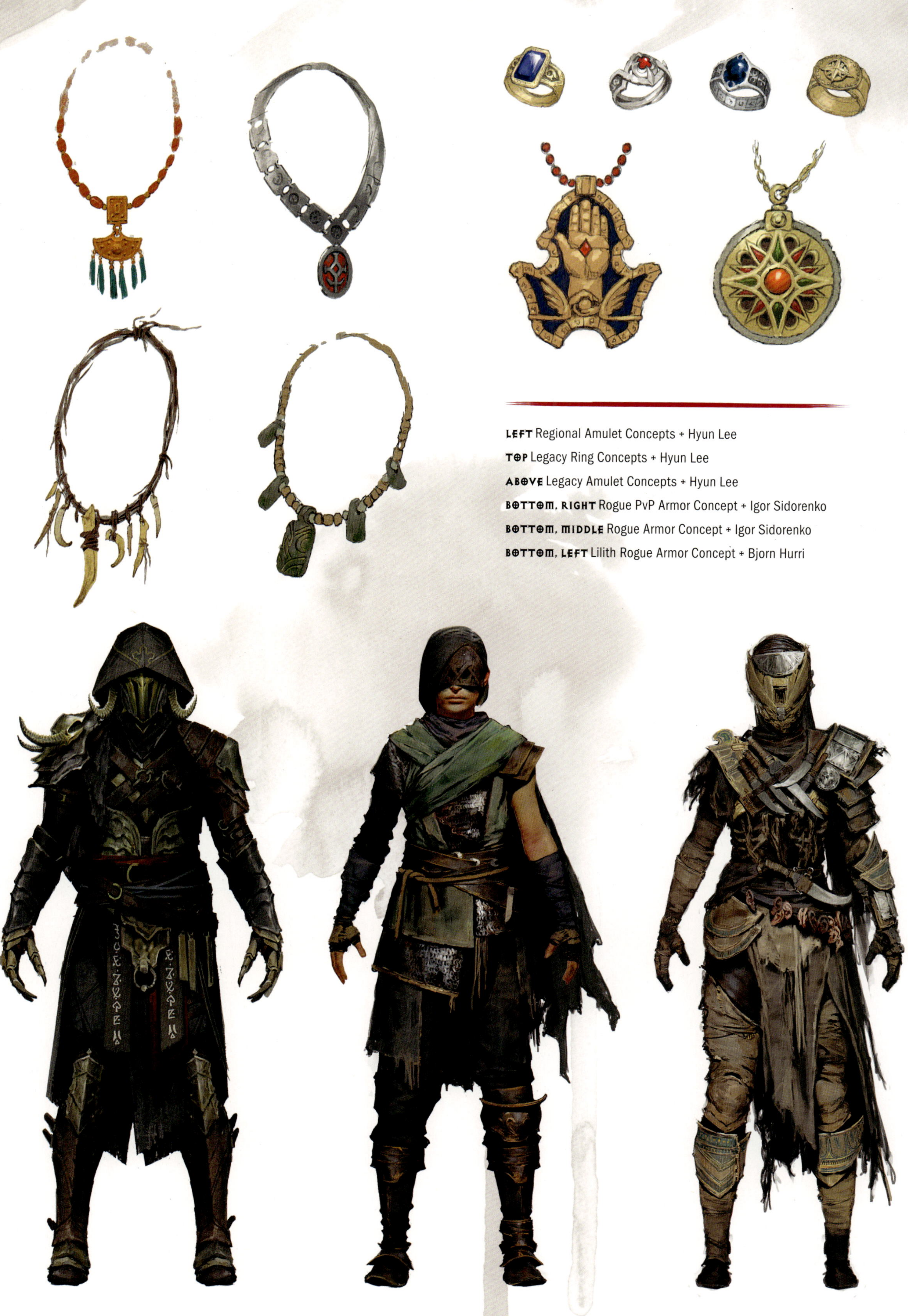

LEFT Regional Amulet Concepts + Hyun Lee
TOP Legacy Ring Concepts + Hyun Lee
ABOVE Legacy Amulet Concepts + Hyun Lee
BOTTOM, RIGHT Rogue PvP Armor Concept + Igor Sidorenko
BOTTOM, MIDDLE Rogue Armor Concept + Igor Sidorenko
BOTTOM, LEFT Lilith Rogue Armor Concept + Bjorn Hurri

The Whole Wide World

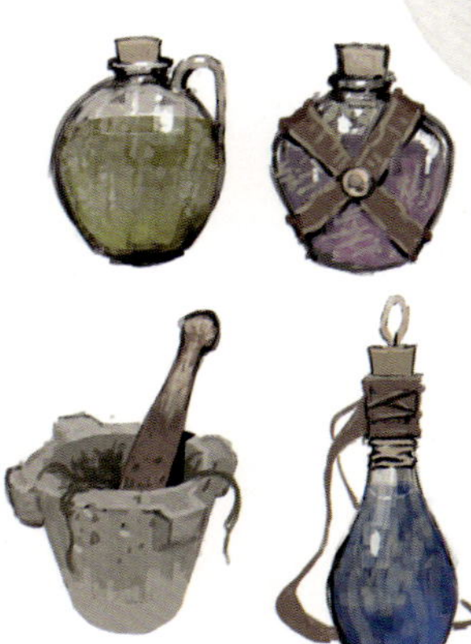

ABOVE Fractured Peaks Lettering + Fernando Pinilla

RIGHT, TOP Potions Concepts + Hyun Lee

RIGHT, MIDDLE Alchemist Storage Concept + Hyun Lee

BOTTOM, RIGHT Alchemist Press Concept + Hyun Lee

BOTTOM, LEFT Alchemist Distiller Concept + Hyun Lee

OPPOSITE Inarius Creates Sanctuary Illustration + Igor Sidorenko

Many of the environments in *Diablo IV* were built around the concept of *a world in decline*, a world that was once majestic and beautiful, ground down not only by the Eternal Conflict between angels and demons . . . but by humanity's own destructive impulses as well.

"Nothing in this world is new," says *Diablo* art director John Mueller. "Nothing was built yesterday. It was all built thousands of years ago. There are a lot of patinas and age. We wanted to get across a very neutral, dark palette. If you think about horror movies, they're often shot in this bleak cinematography style—and that's what we were going for here."

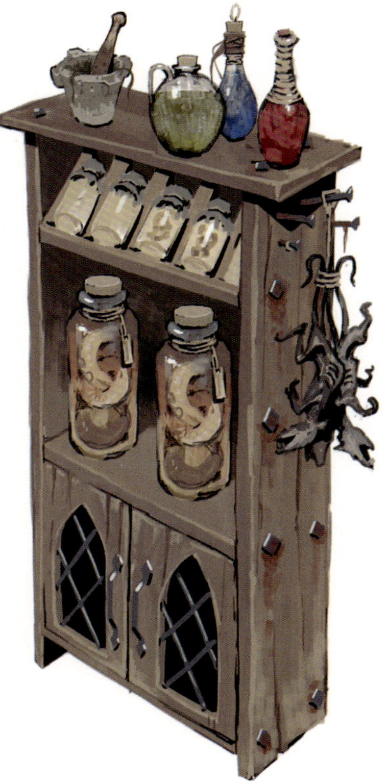

However, even a dismal, dark world such as *Diablo* needs a few bright spots.

"If *everything* is dreary looking, then the pacing will be off," says Victor Lee. "After a while, the player will just be numb to it. So after a long stretch of muted colors, austere visuals, and negative art, we try to have something—an area or a zone—that's more colorful and more upbeat. We try to have things that are more normal to give viewers a bit of a recharge so that the next time they enter a dark zone, they will get that feeling of blood-chilling terror."

In *Diablo IV*, even Hell itself defies expectations. In place of lava, the team created what they refer to as "soul soup," composed of the spirits of the damned. This departure allowed for the use of strong color accents. This reimagining of Hell included careful consideration of the materials used in any structures where Hell is mentioned, such as a church.

"It should feel like a cathedral, but there's no brick and mortar," Mueller explains. "Nothing is built from stone. It has to be built from souls and pain and suffering and bodies and viscera. You could make church-like shapes, but there's no mortar. Nobody's casting bricks in Hell."

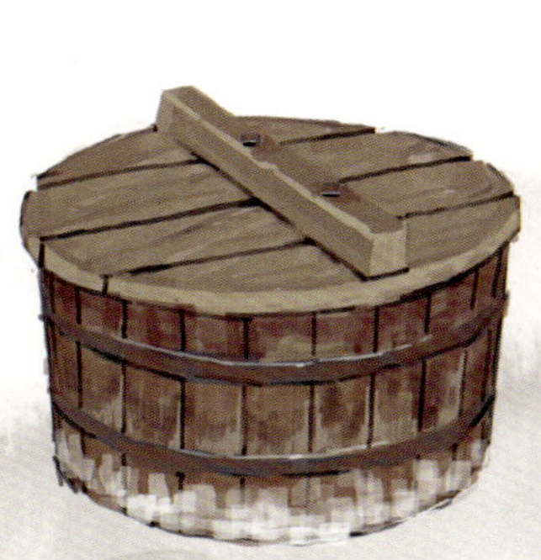

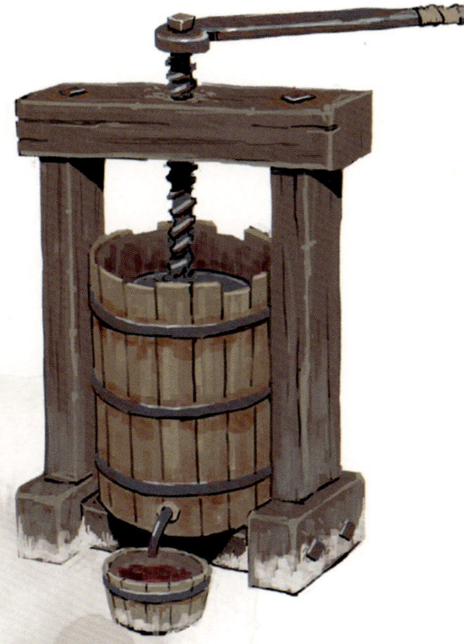

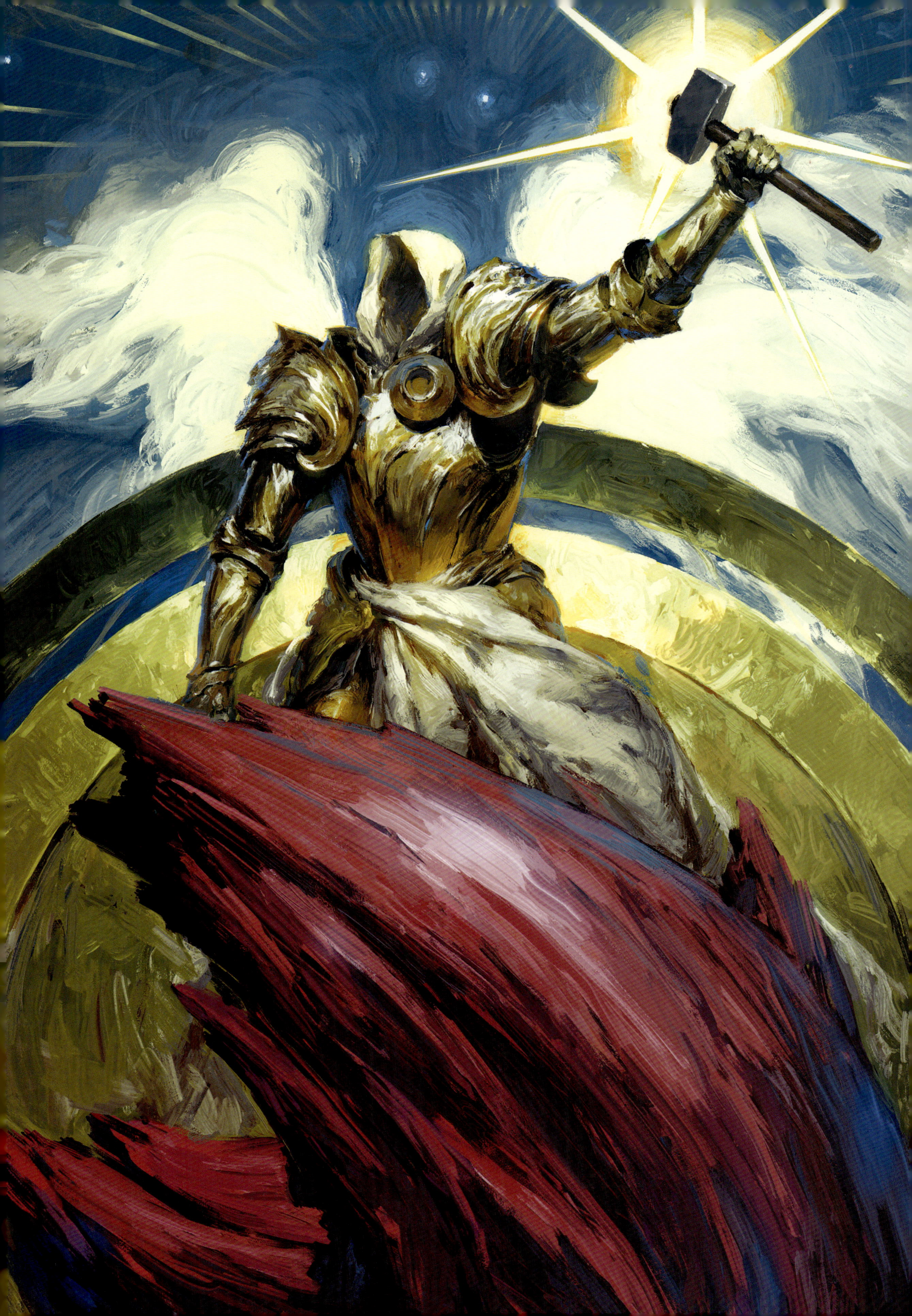

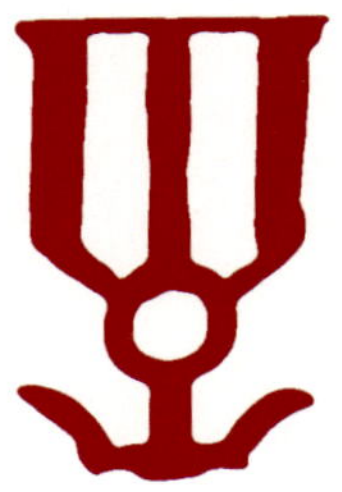

ABOVE Fractured Peaks Lettering + Fernando Pinilla

RIGHT & BELOW Hell Dungeon Decoratives + Galina Lobyshova

OPPOSITE Dry Steppes Canyon Illustration + Victor Lee

Perhaps the greatest aspect of *Diablo IV*'s environment is the introduction of open-world play. One goal in this new, wide-open Sanctuary was not to create pocket locations that would make the world feel strange and disconnected.

"It's not just isolated," says associate art director Richie Marella. "It's all connected. So the planning was very different as to how things flow. In *Diablo III*, we always had regions that players ported to, but it never felt like a connected, real world. Now those places are real and permanent, and there's storytelling of how each of these regions connect and how the populations interact with each other."

One challenge in creating a cohesive Sanctuary came with the game's isometric camera angle.

"When you think of an open world, you just naturally think of a grand horizon," says lead exterior artist Jeffrey Lee. "But when the camera is staring at the ground, how can you make the world feel large? How can we convey to a player that a certain location is a desirable place to be? How can we help shape the experience in a way that feels like an invisible hand pushing the player?"

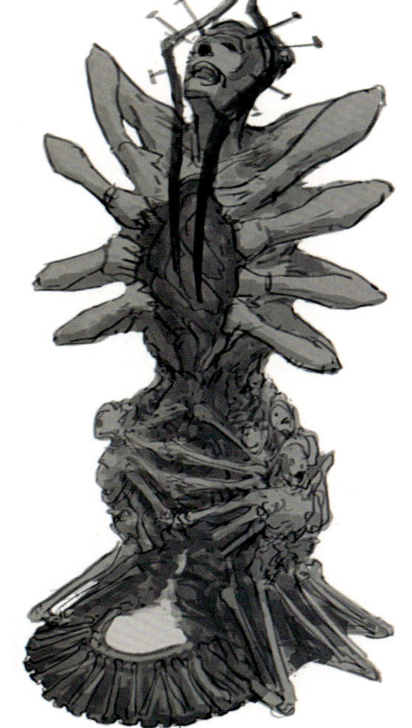

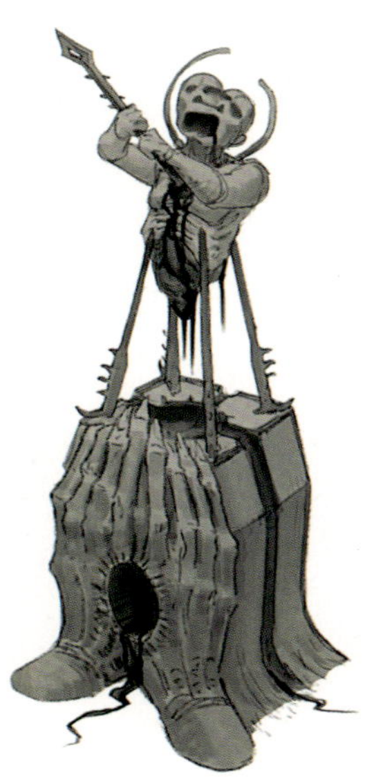

This guiding of the player through the world is accomplished through various means, such as architectural practices like lighting and positive or negative space. Sometimes it's artistic principles such as composition, in order to lead the eye—and the player—in a desired direction. Cinematic techniques are used as well, such as passing the character from a claustrophobic area to a wide-open space for a big reveal. And sometimes the geography of the environment will literally point the way.

"In Stinging Winds, we have these really sharp, jagged rocks that look like arrows," Lee says. "We can use these pointy directional rocks in a way to make the player naturally want to go in a direction . . . even if it's subliminal."

With all the hard work the team has put into environments, and with all the firsts and surprises awaiting the player, Mueller sums it up best: "I believe we've created a fun world, ripe for exploration."

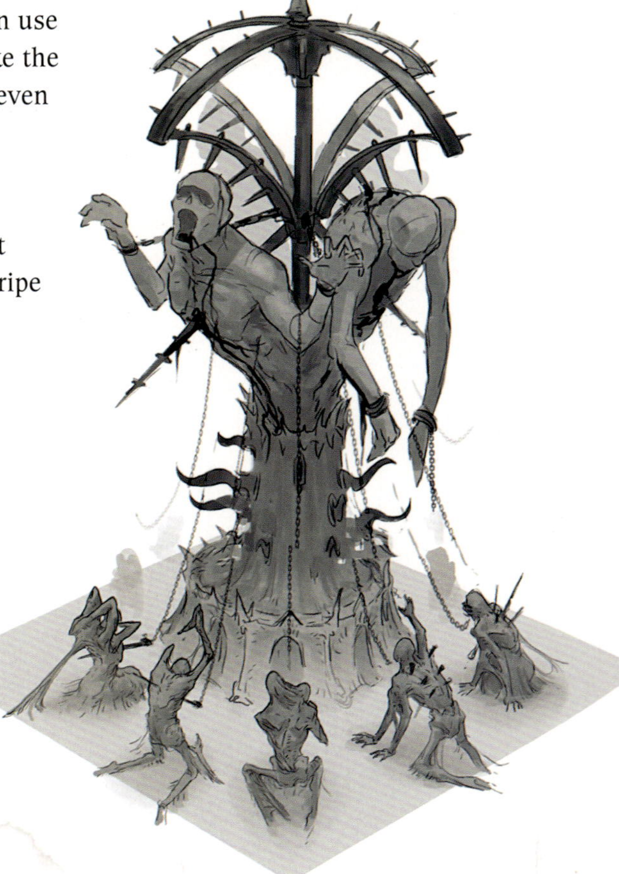

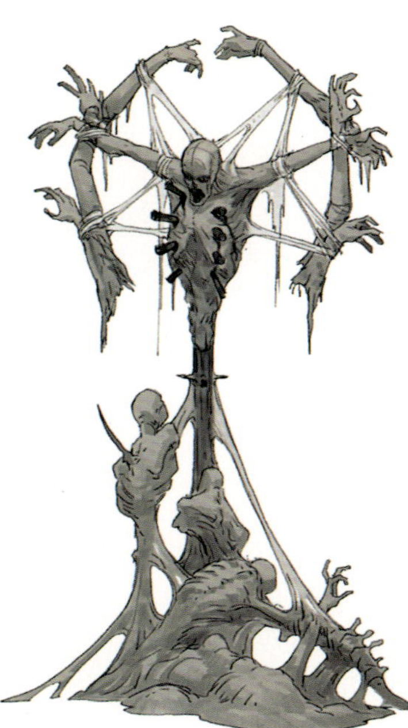

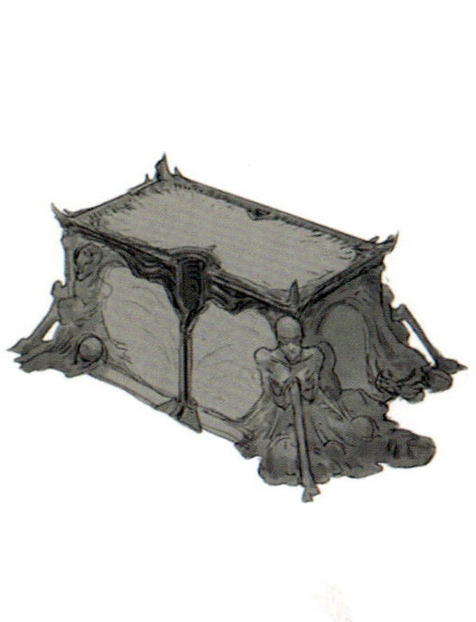

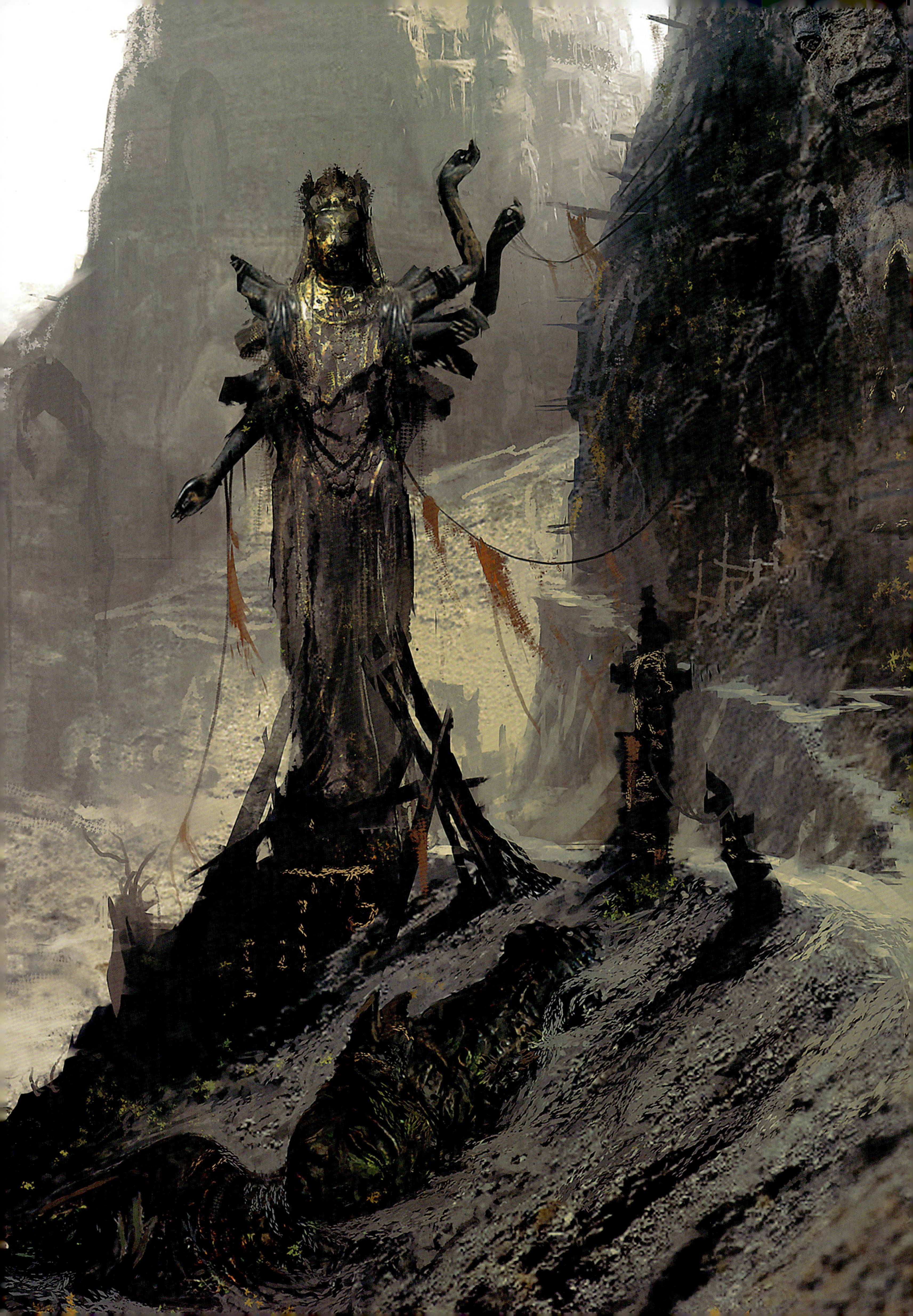

TOP Khazra Cave Concept • Mike Franchina

BOTTOM Nafain Tree Concept • Galina Lobyshova

OPPOSITE, TOP LEFT Gates of Hell Concept • Hyun Lee

OPPOSITE, TOP MIDDLE Hell Banner Concepts • Konstantin Vavilov

OPPOSITE, TOP RIGHT Hell Decor Concept • Konstantin Vavilov

OPPOSITE, MIDDLE RIGHT Hell Banner Concept • Konstantin Vavilov

OPPOSITE, BOTTOM Blood Obelisk Magic Concept • Jin Kim

OPPOSITE, MIDDLE LEFT Blood Obelisk Concepts • Jin Kim

"Art gets noisy in pursuit of realism. But if everything is detailed, then nothing is. Diablo IV *has this intentional use of noise where the environment is meant to be the background. It is not meant to draw your eye . . . until it is."*

—JEFFREY LEE, Lead Exterior Artist

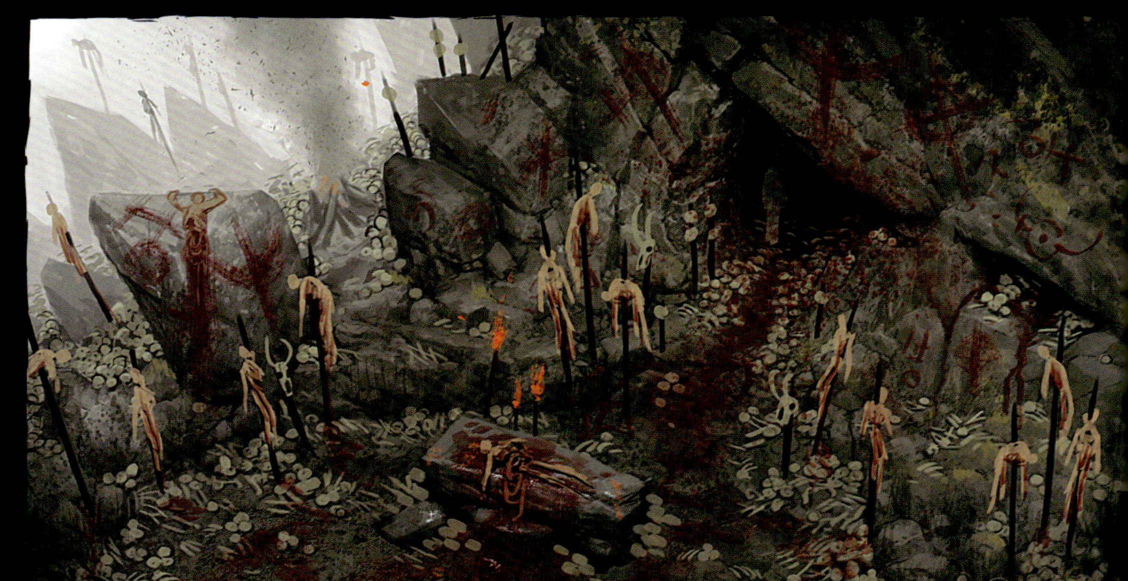

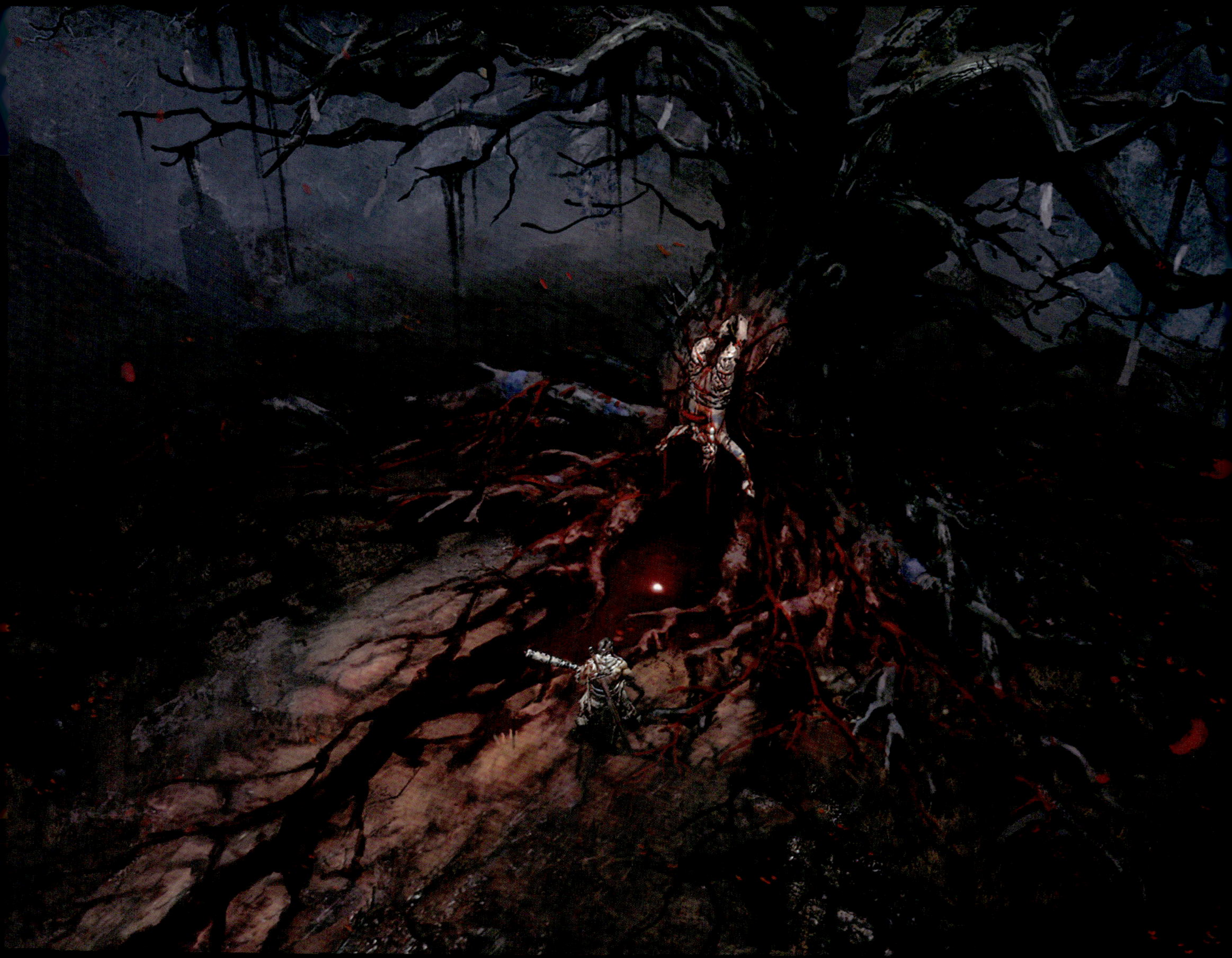

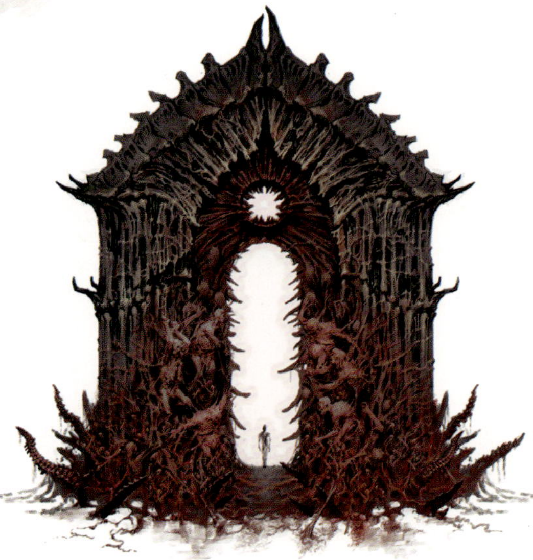

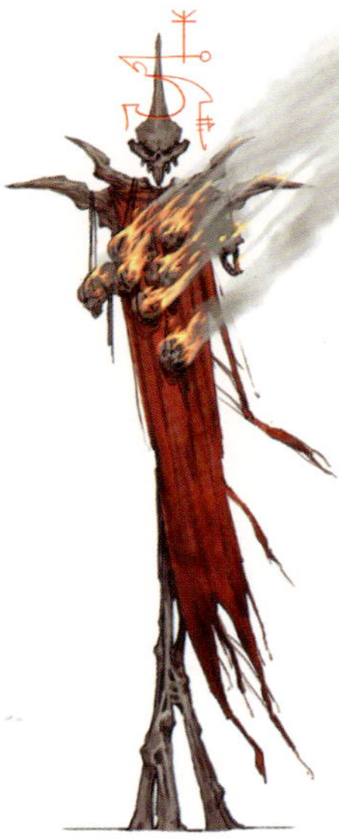

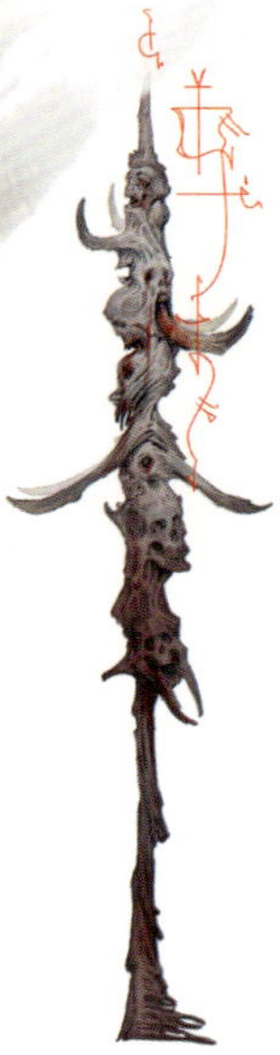

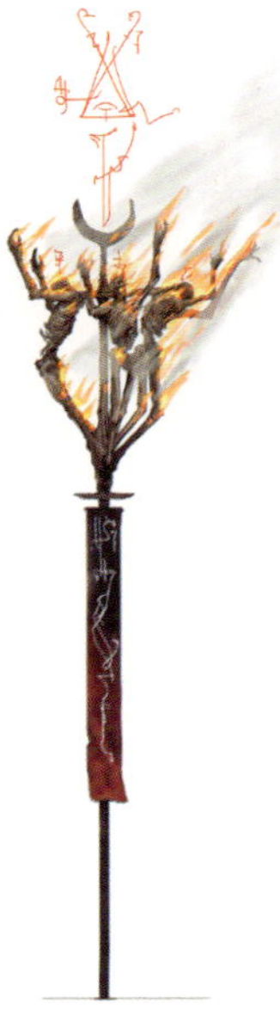

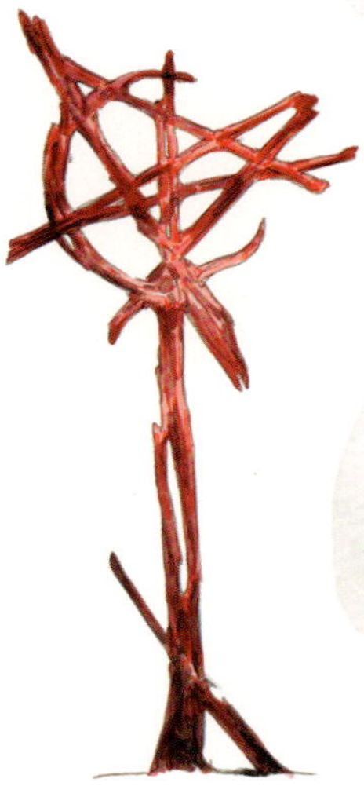

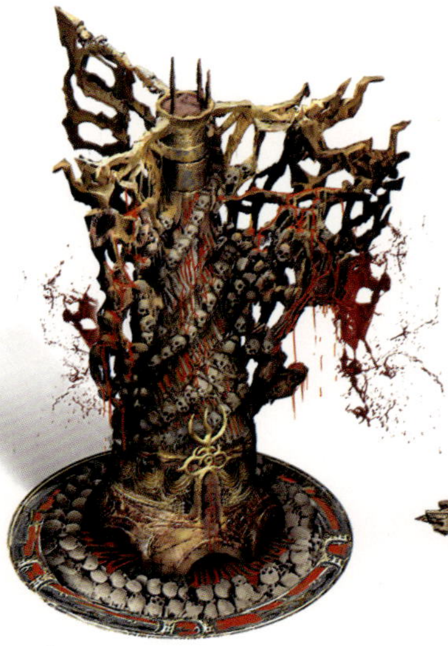

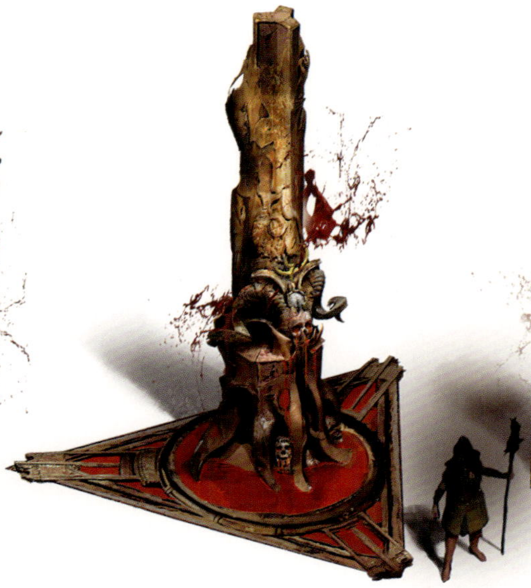

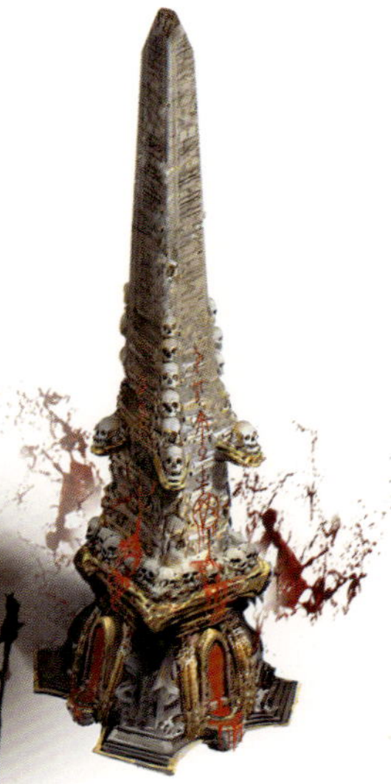

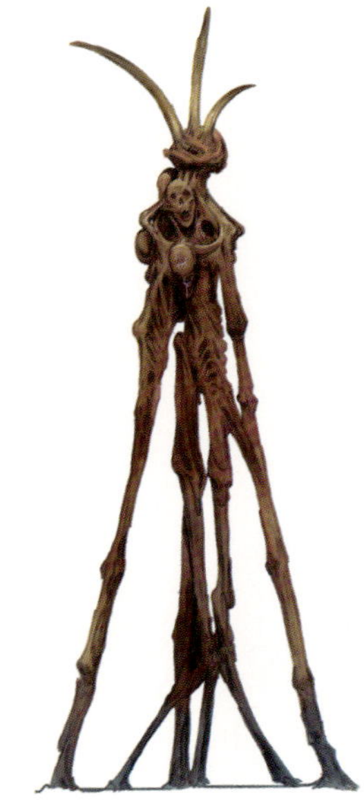

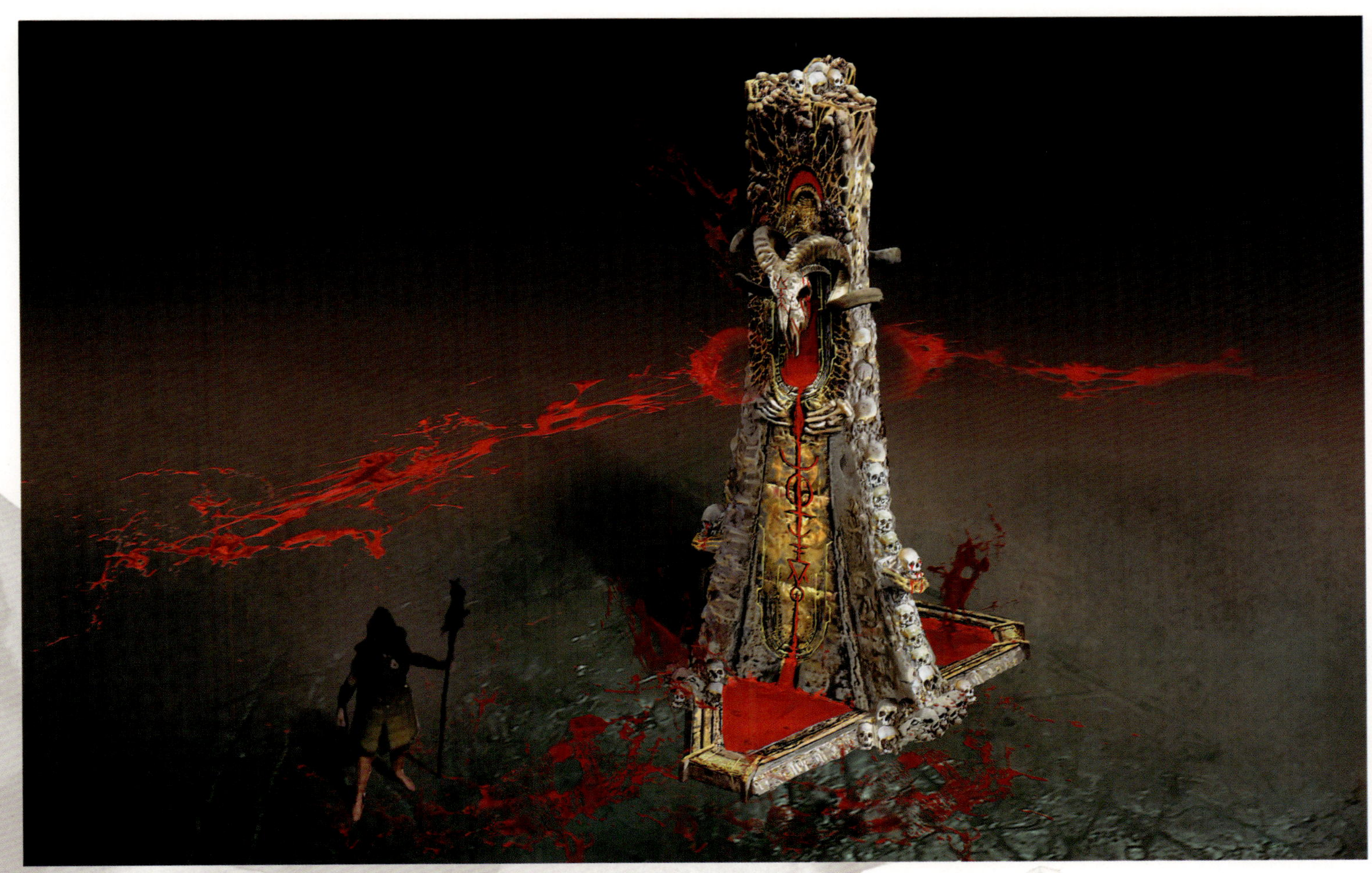

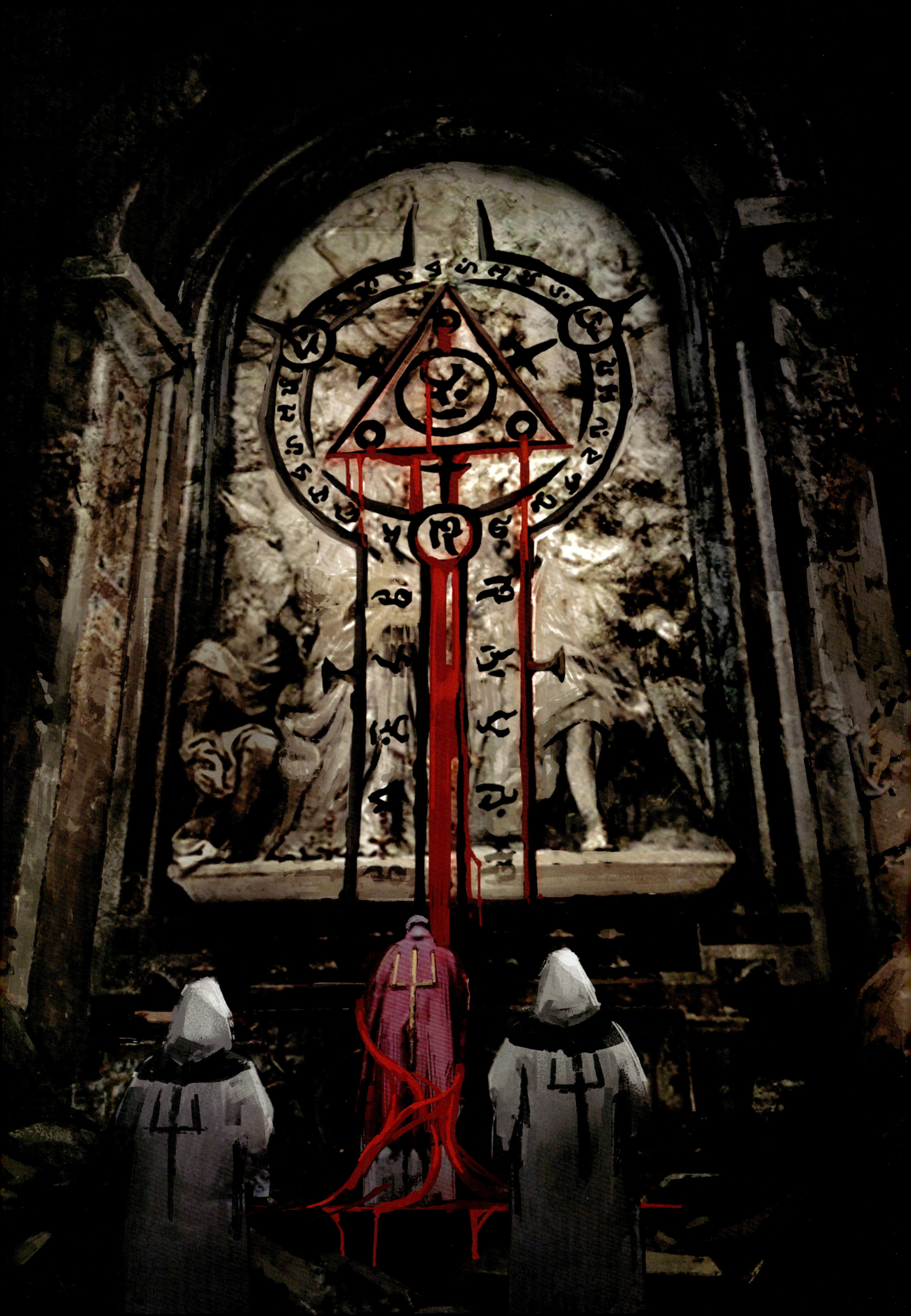

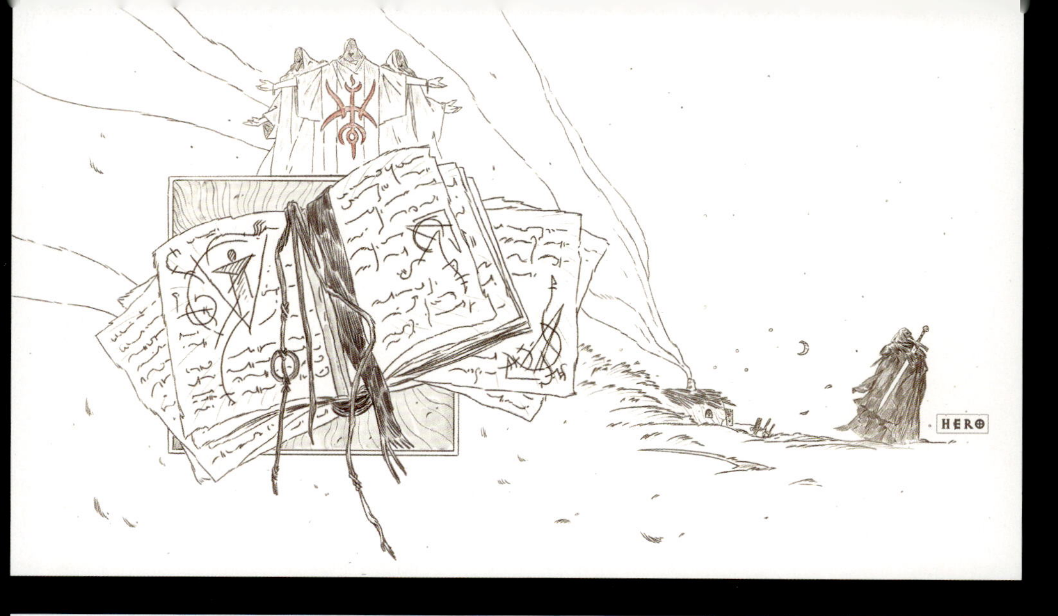

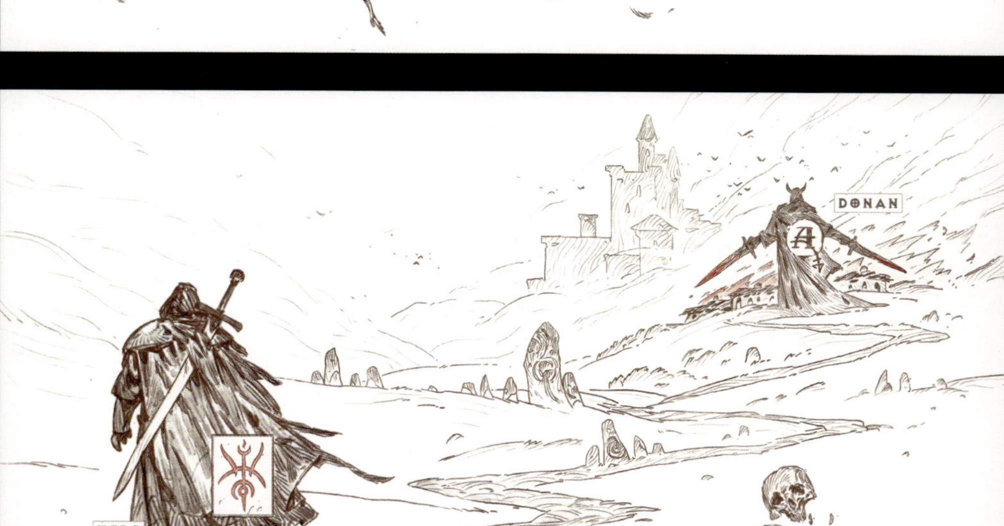

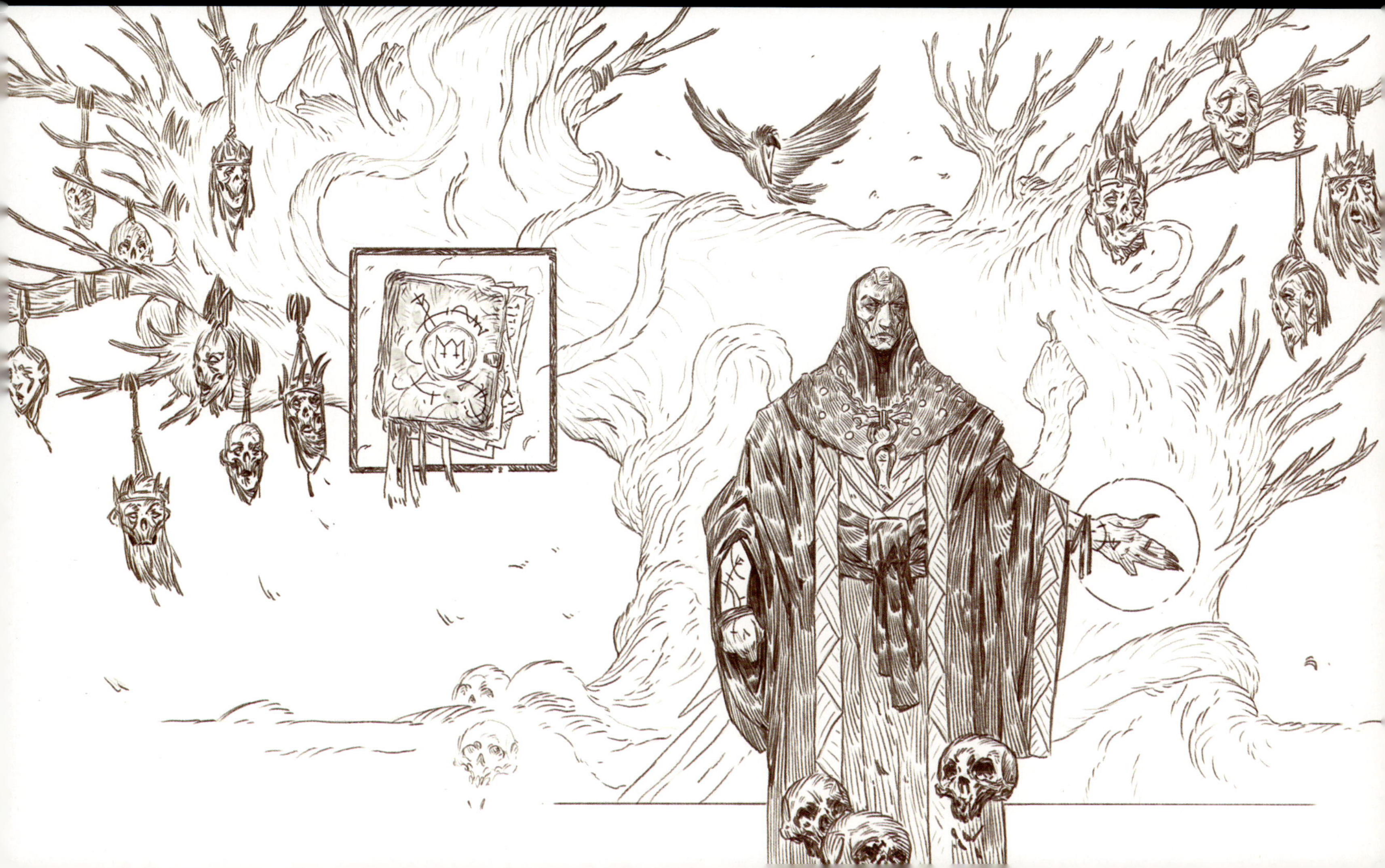

TOP Early Fractured Peaks Concept • Konstantin Vavilov

MIDDLE Early Scosglen Concept • Konstantin Vavilov

BOTTOM Early Tree of Whispers Concept • Konstantin Vavilov

OPPOSITE Early Jirindai Concept • Rob Sevilla

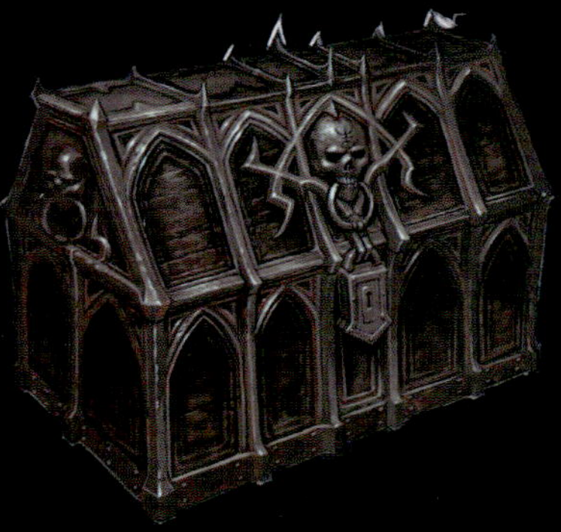

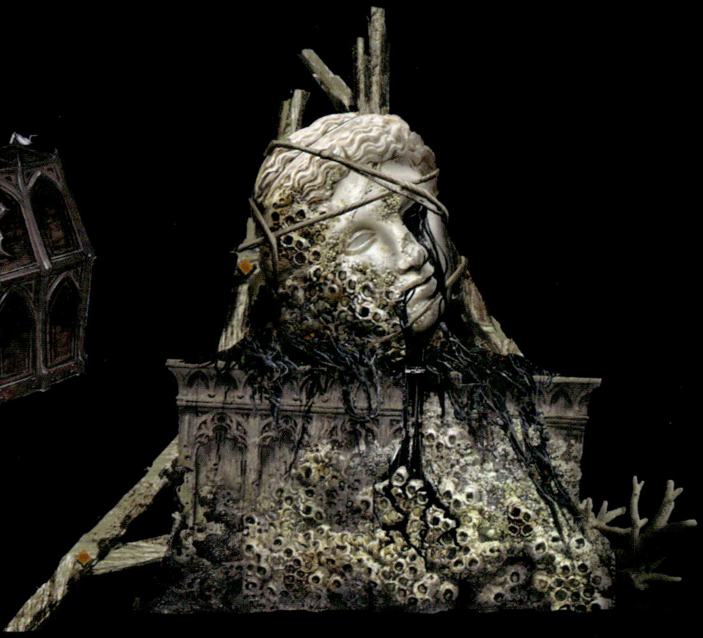

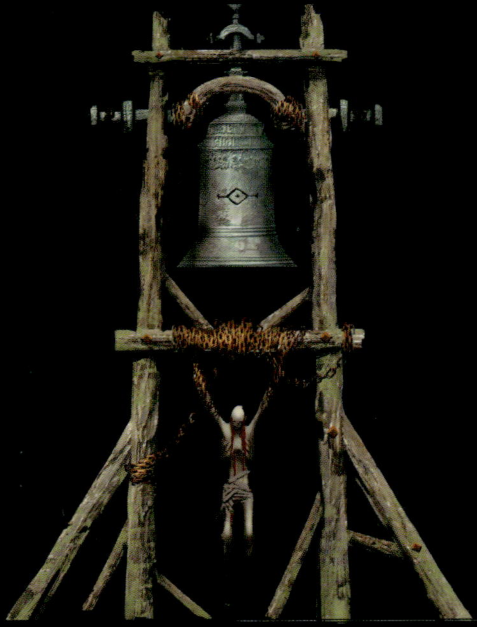

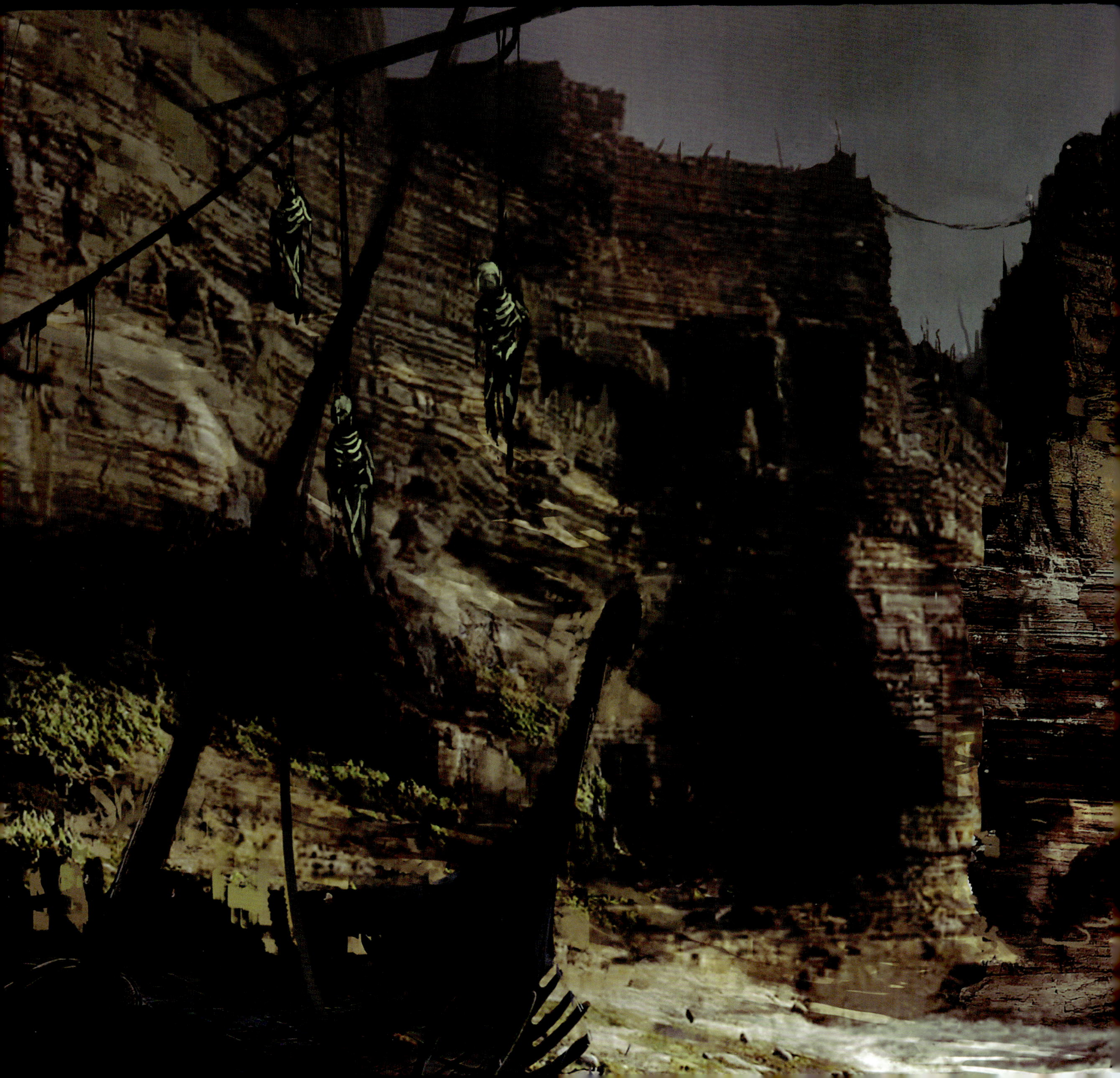

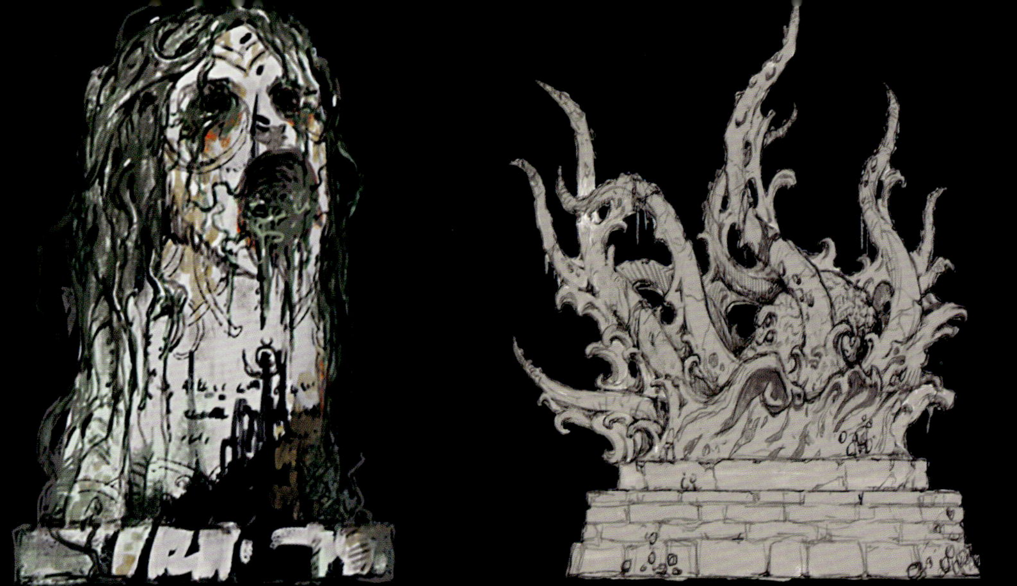

TOP, LEFT Wight Stone Concept + Hyun Lee

TOP, RIGHT Sea Creature Statue Concept + Hyun Lee

BOTTOM Scosglen Coast Concept + Victor Lee

OPPOSITE, LEFT Chest Concept + Mike Franchina

OPPOSITE, MIDDLE Drowned Altar Concept + Mike Franchina

OPPOSITE, RIGHT Drowned Belltower Concept + Mike Franchina

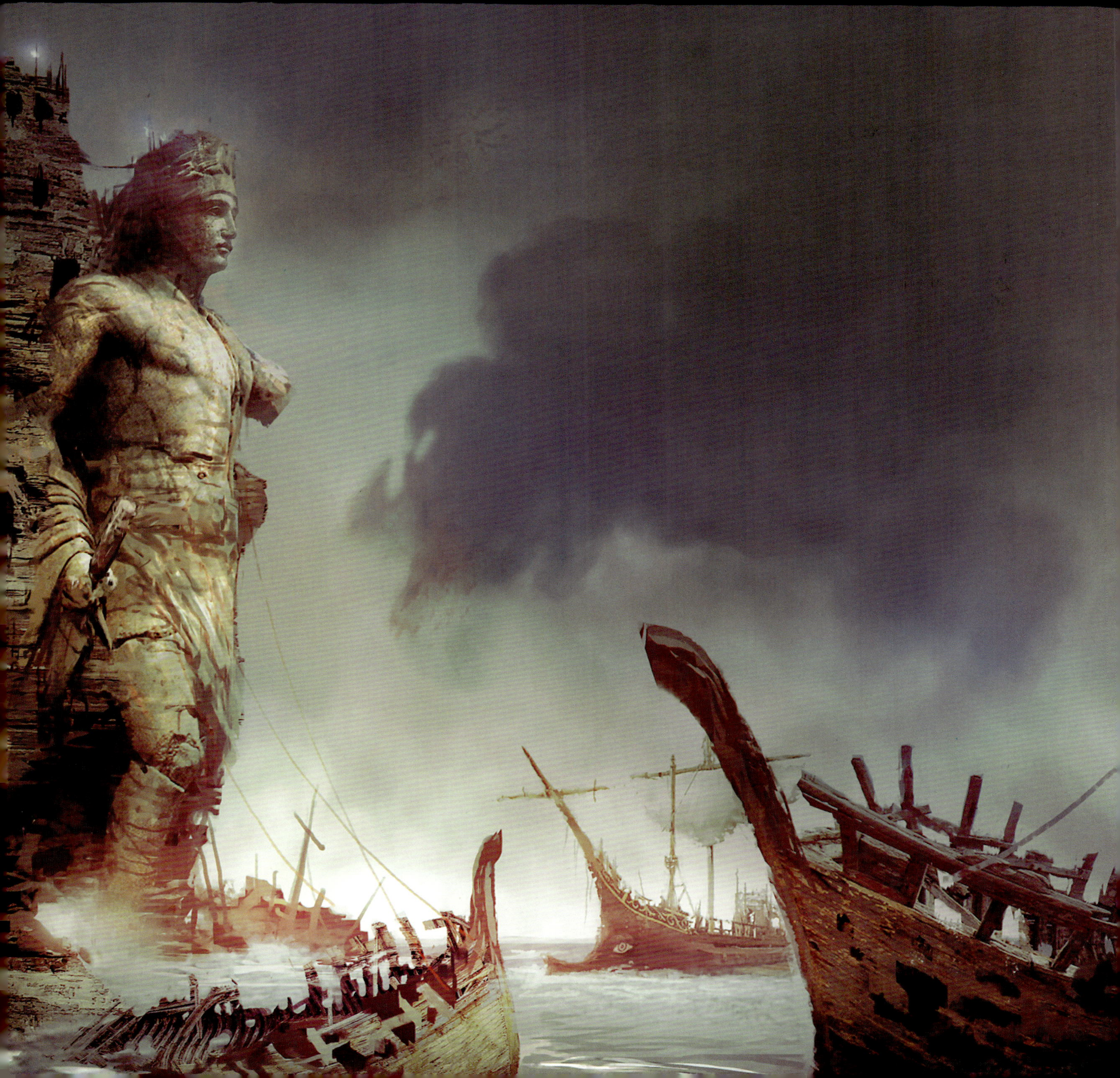

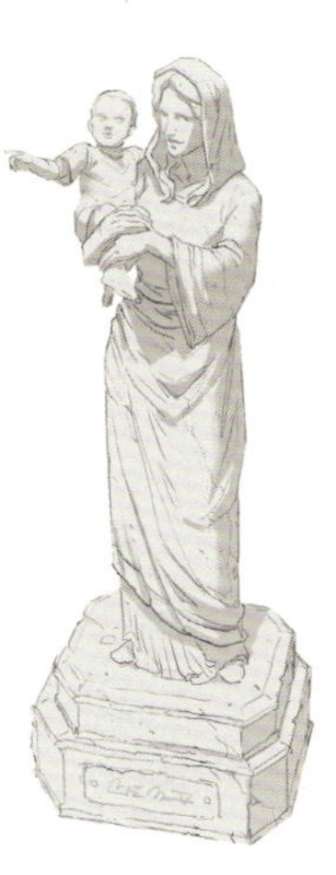

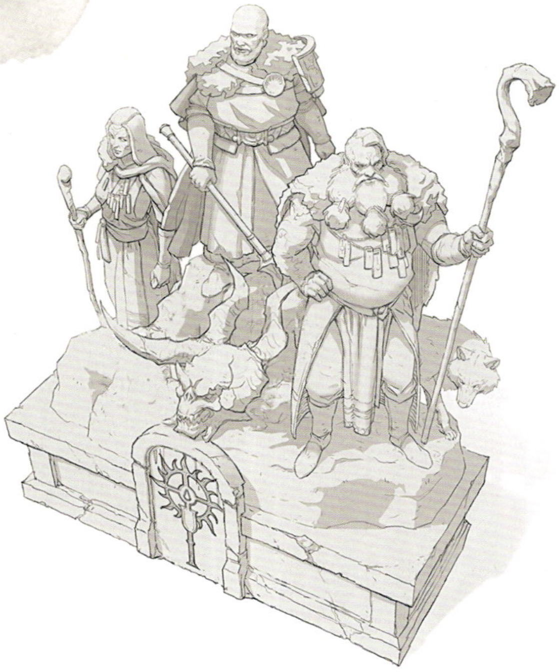

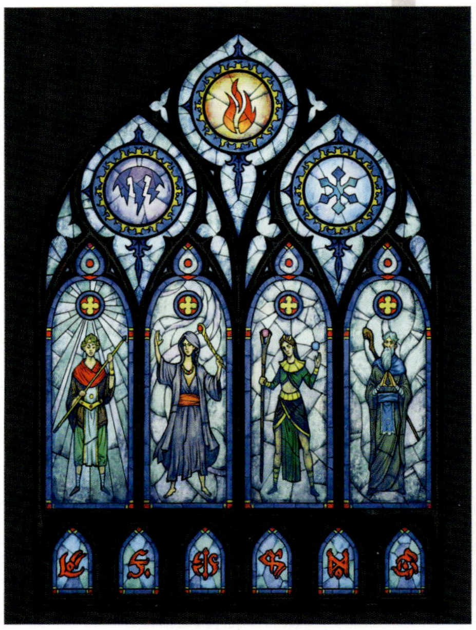

ABOVE Braega Statue Concept + Galina Lobyshova

TOP, MIDDLE Scosglen Heroes Monument Concept + Galina Lobyshova

TOP, RIGHT Sorcerery Stained Glass Concept + Hyun Lee

MIDDLE Church Dungeon Concept + Galina Lobyshova

BOTTOM Cathedral of Light Interior Concept + Jin Kim

BELOW Cathedral of Light Prop Ideation + Konstantin Vavilov

OPPOSITE Alabaster Monastery Concept + Rob Sevilla

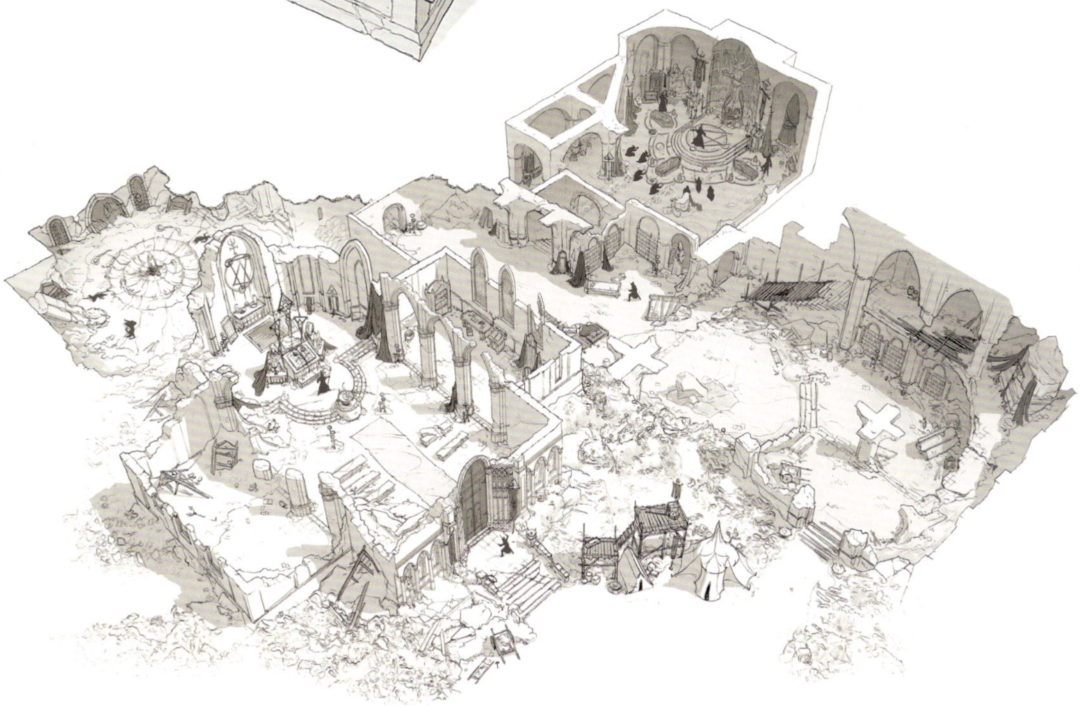

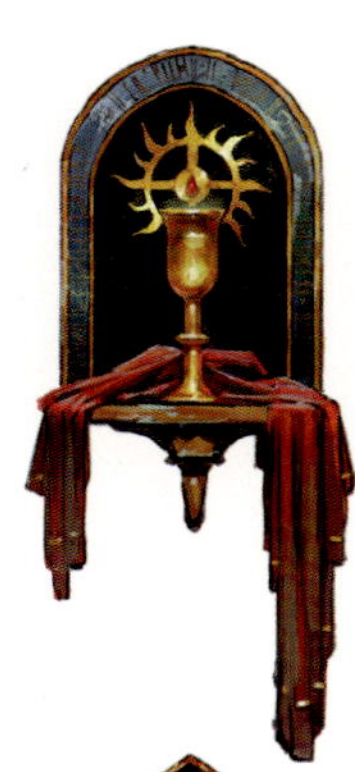

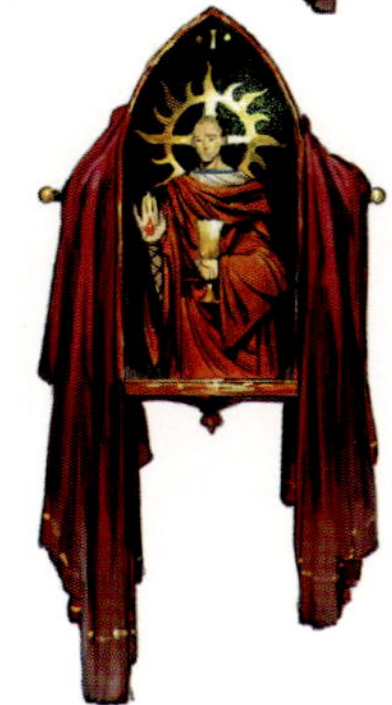

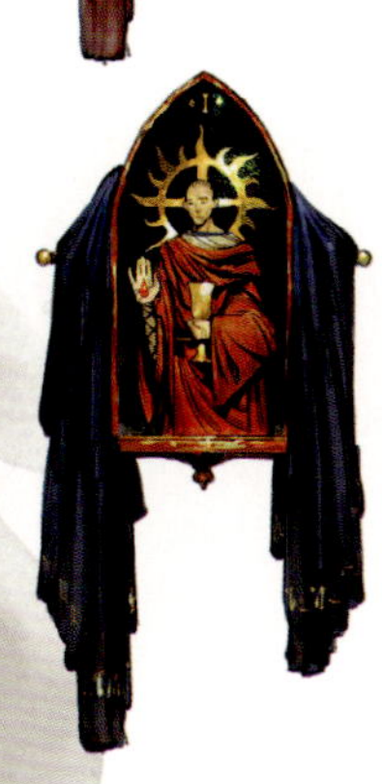

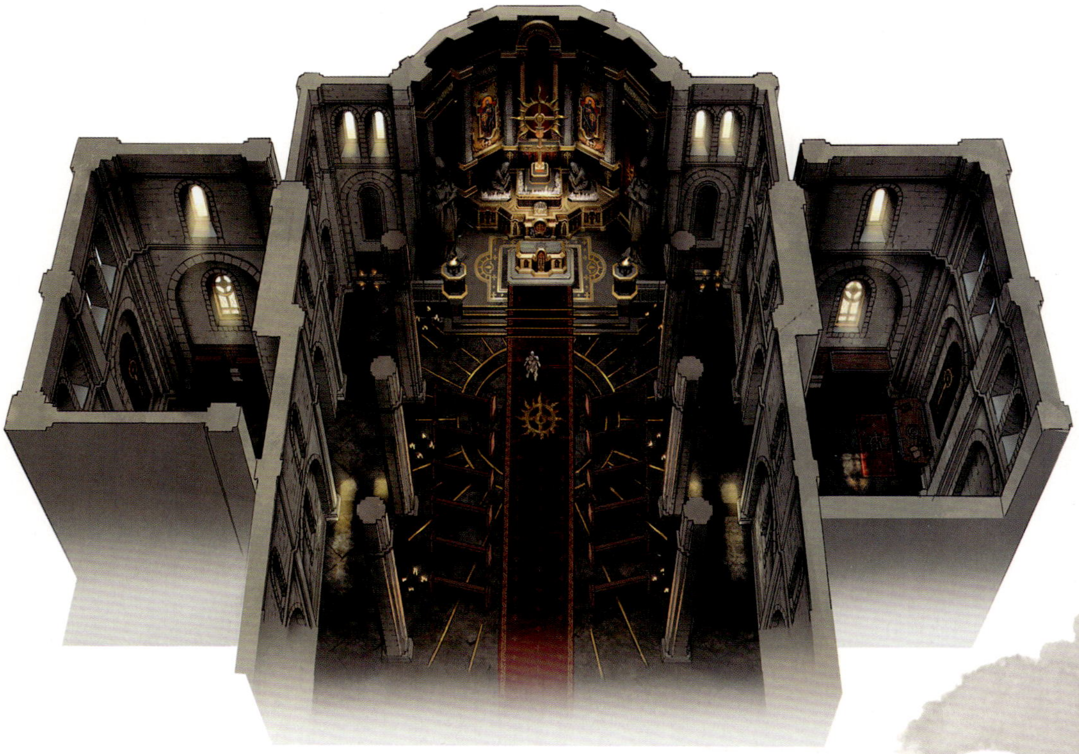

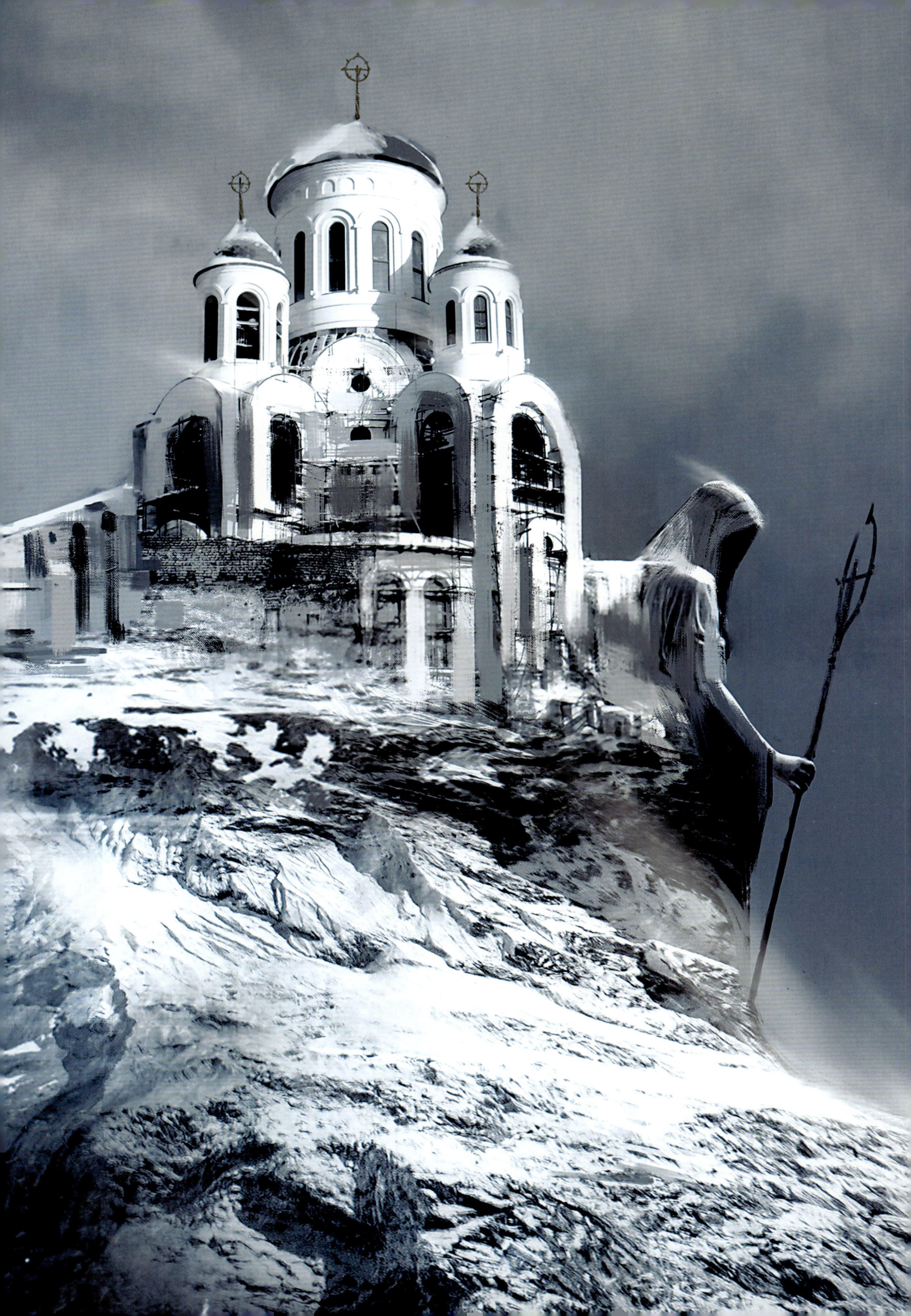

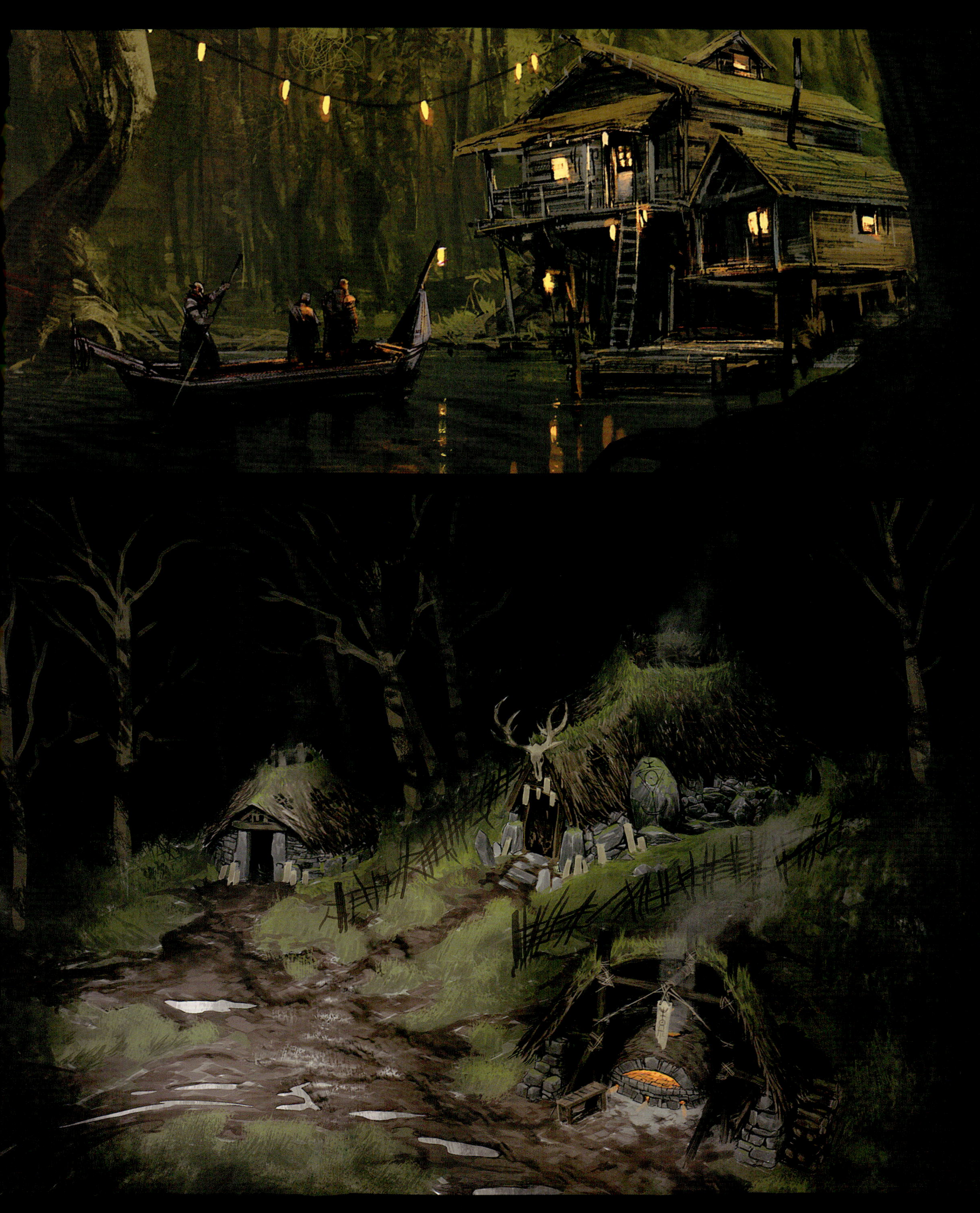

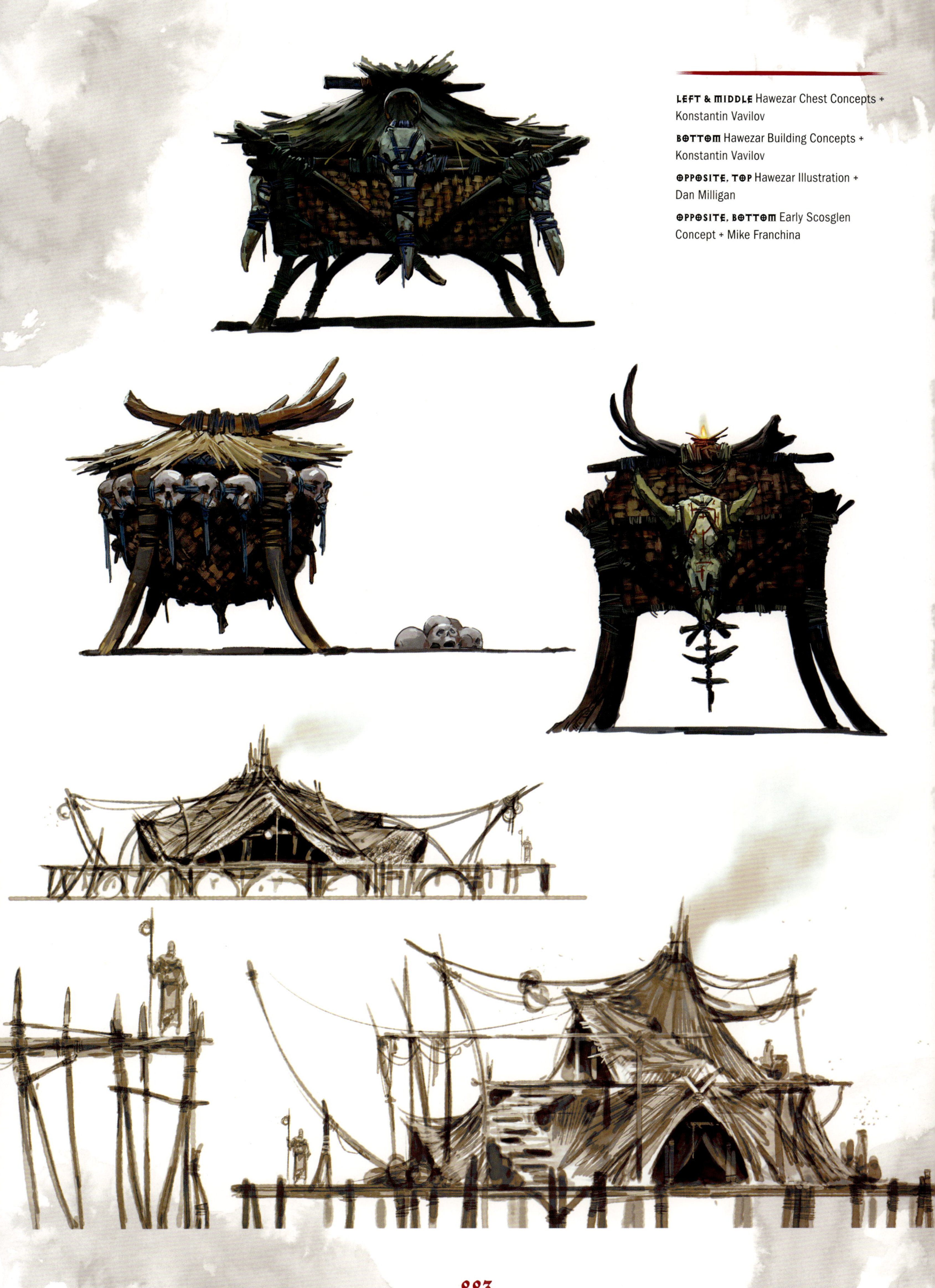

LEFT & MIDDLE Hawezar Chest Concepts + Konstantin Vavilov

BOTTOM Hawezar Building Concepts + Konstantin Vavilov

OPPOSITE, TOP Hawezar Illustration + Dan Milligan

OPPOSITE, BOTTOM Early Scosglen Concept + Mike Franchina

"We know that in Diablo the screen could get absolutely bananas with all the things going on, so we wanted to keep the ground and the environments pretty neutral as far as not a lot of highly saturated colors, not overly detailed. We have this idea of areas of rest, which is that we want the play space to be clean for the player so they can see what's happening on screen."

—JOHN MUELLER, Art Director

OPPOSITE Fractured Peaks Environment Concept + Victor Lee

BOTTOM Orbei Monastery Concept + Victor Lee

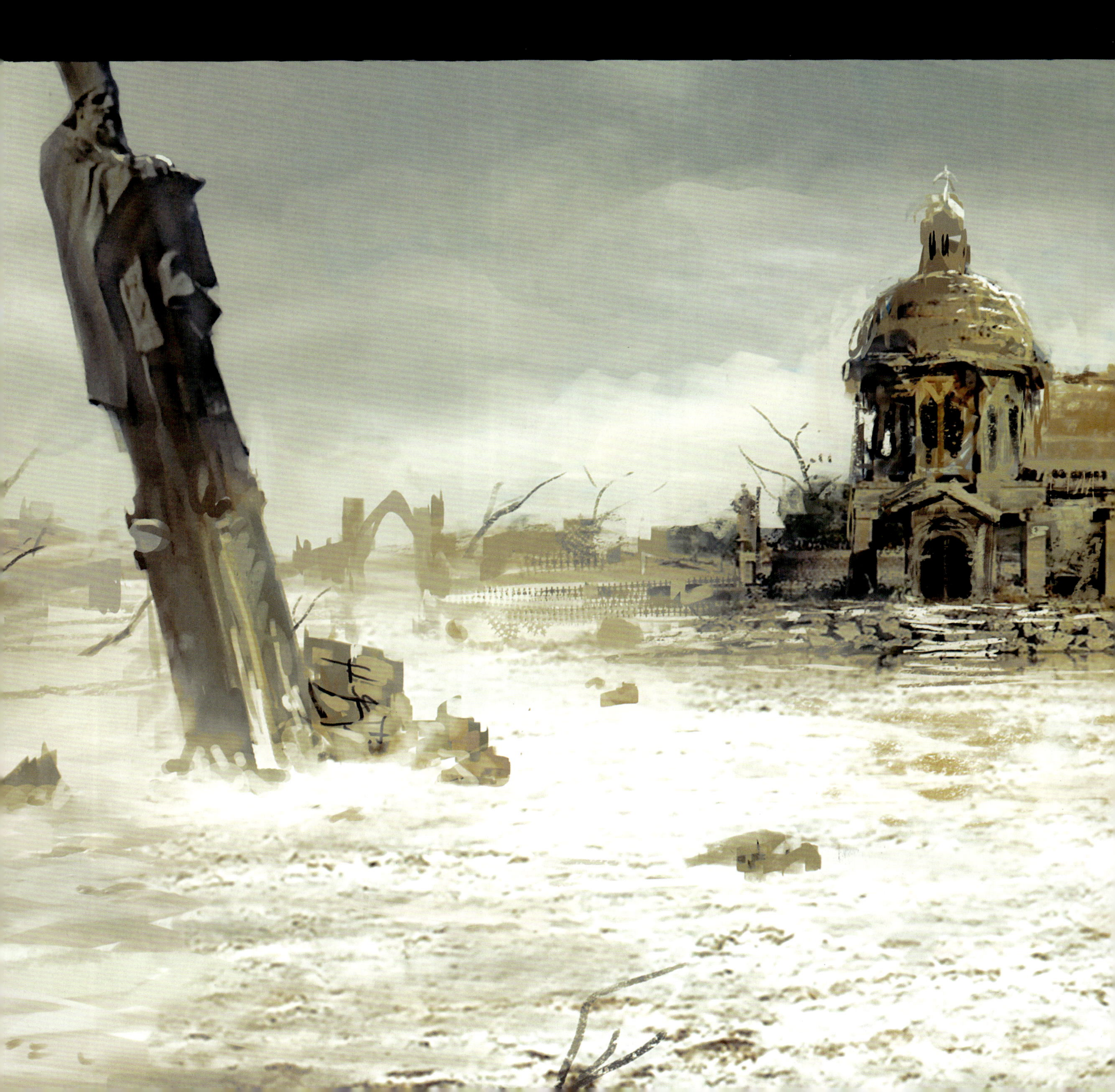

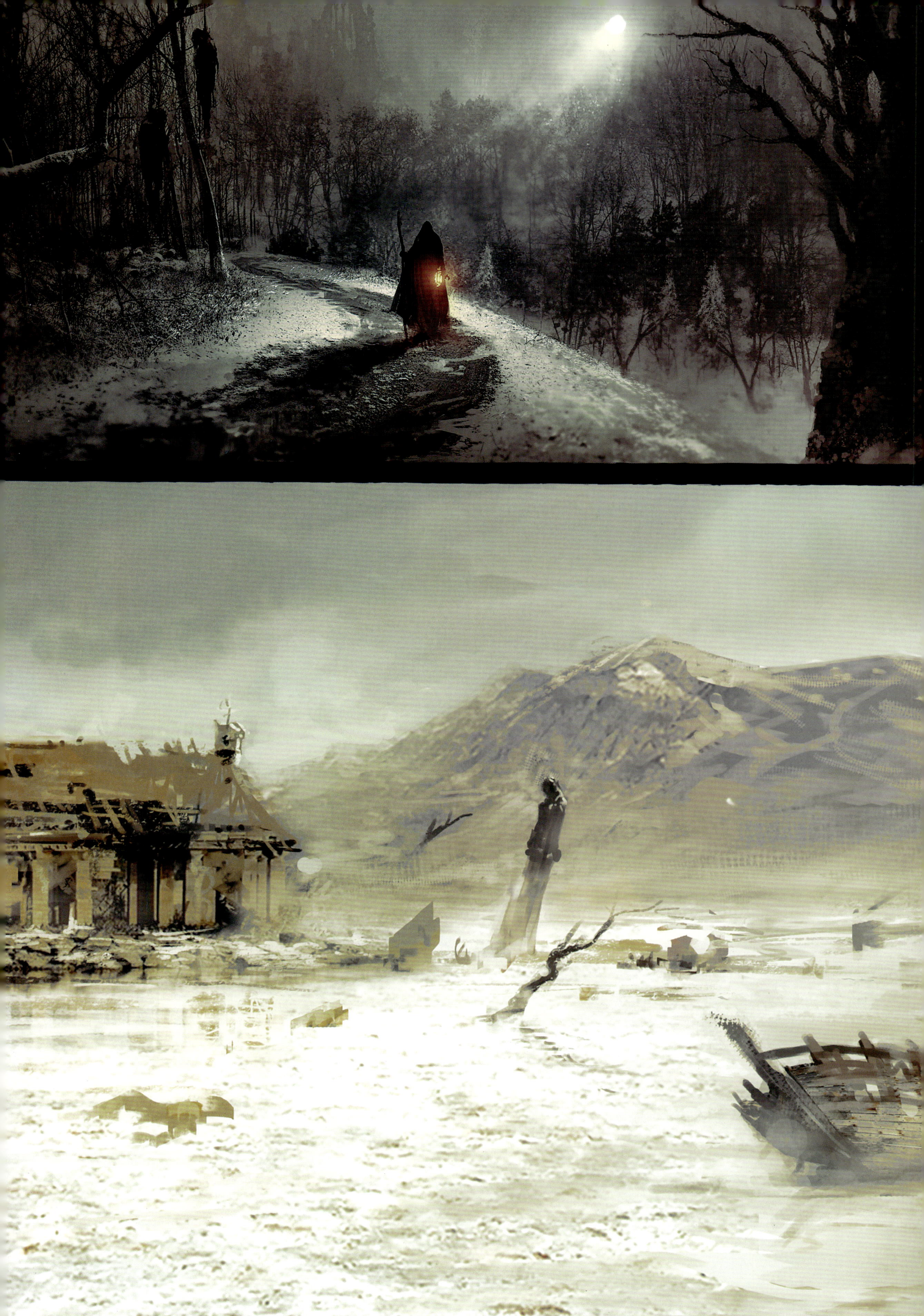

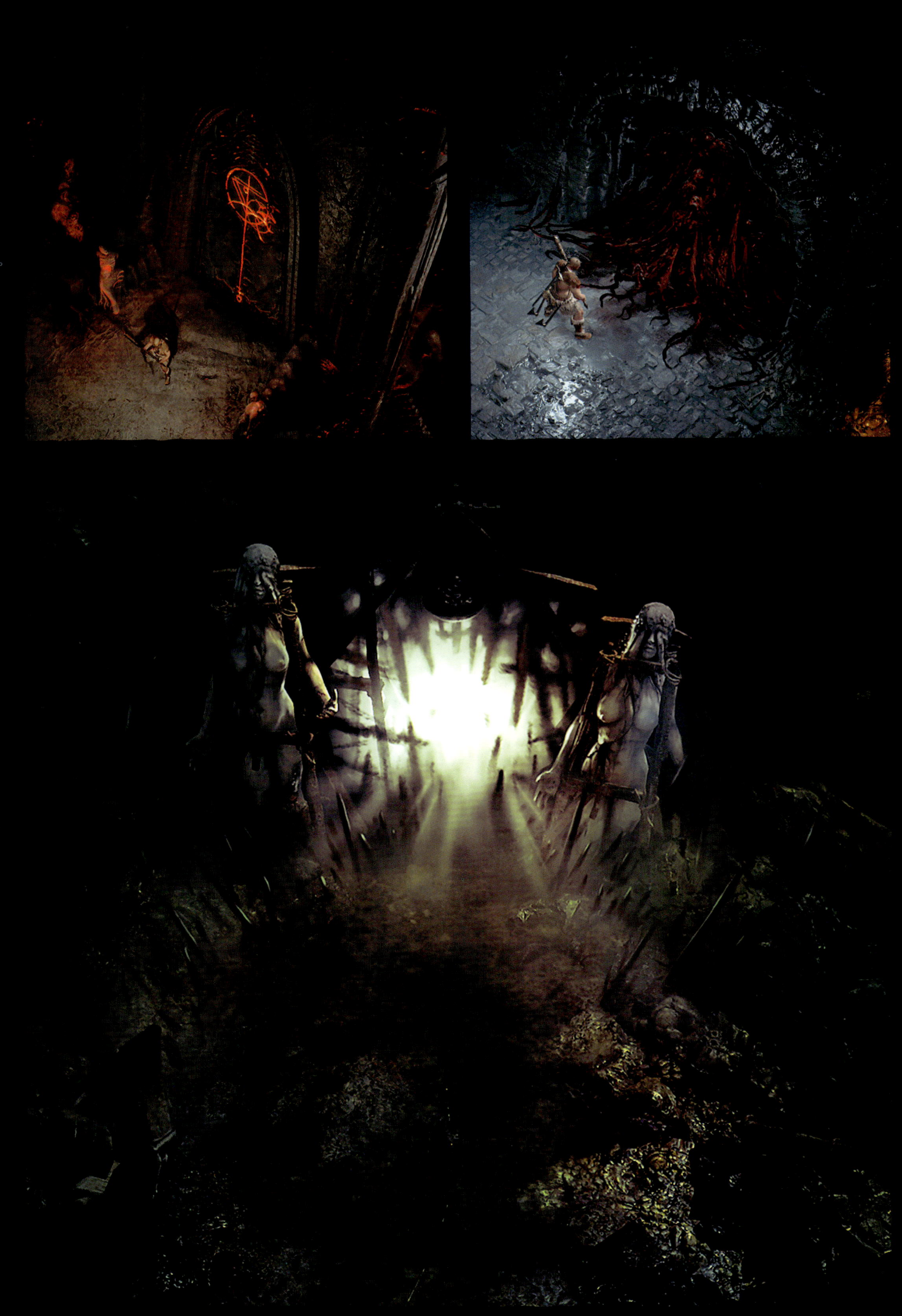

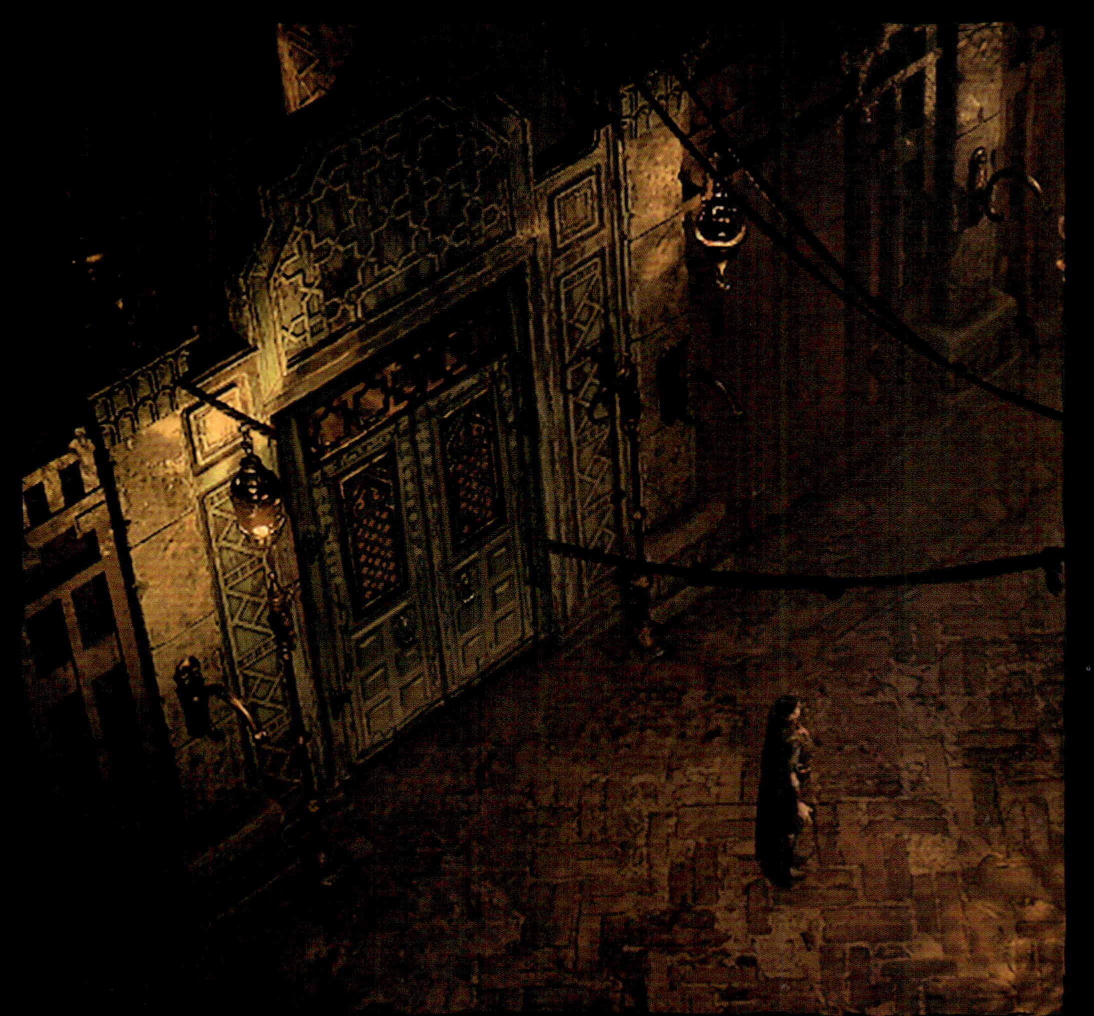

TOP Caldeum Door Concept + Galina Lobyshova

BOTTOM Drowned Dungeon Entrance Concept + Rob Sevilla

OPPOSITE, TOP LEFT Hellfort Blocker Concept + Galina Lobyshova

OPPOSITE, TOP RIGHT Vampire Blocker Concept + Galina Lobyshova

OPPOSITE, BOTTOM Hell Fort Concept + Victor Lee

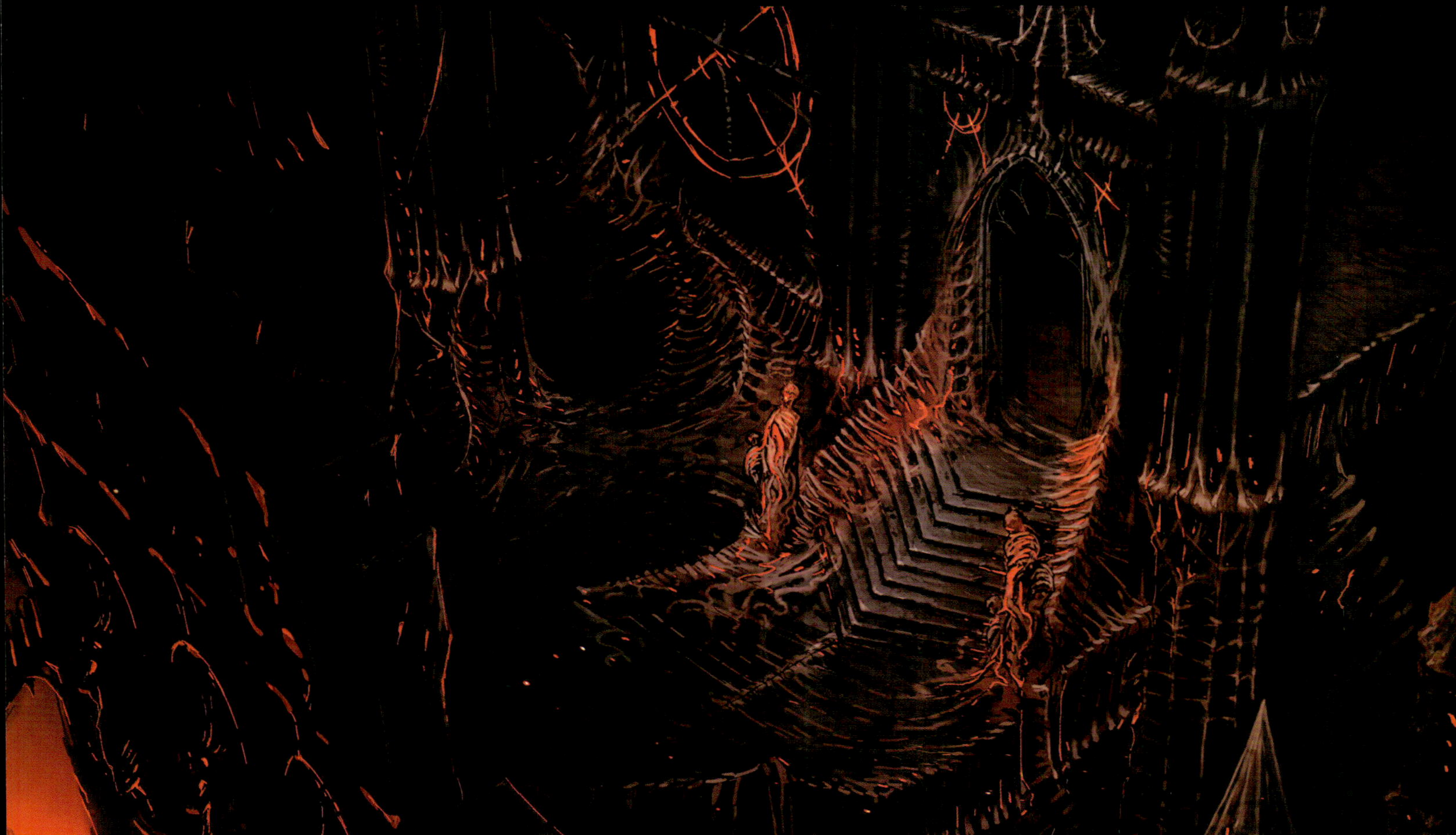

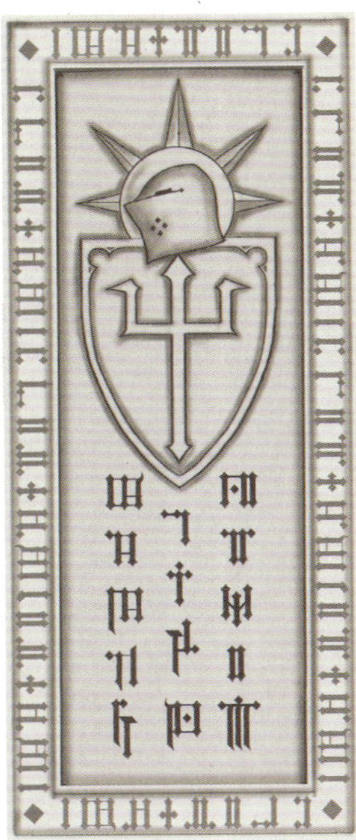

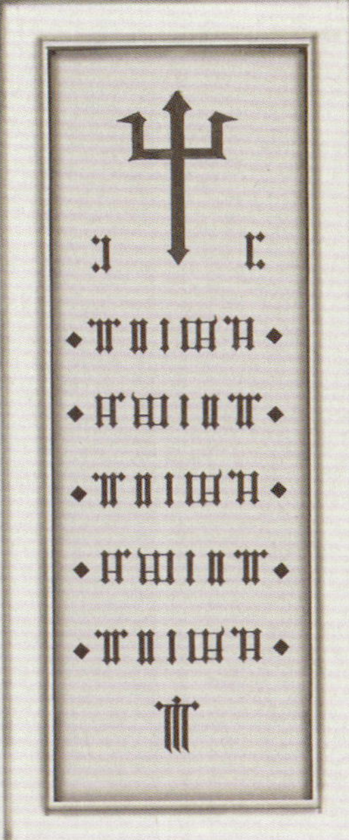

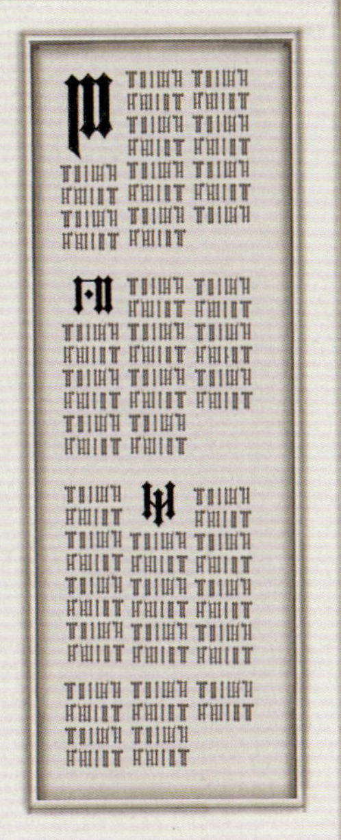

RIGHT Zakarum Prop Concepts + Mike Franchina

RIGHT, MIDDLE Lantern Prop Concept + Mike Franchina

RIGHT, BOTTOM Torture Cage Concept + Mike Franchina

BELOW Dungeon Torture Decor Concept + Mike Franchina

OPPOSITE, TOP & BOTTOM Early Zakarum Dungeon Illustrations + Mike Franchina

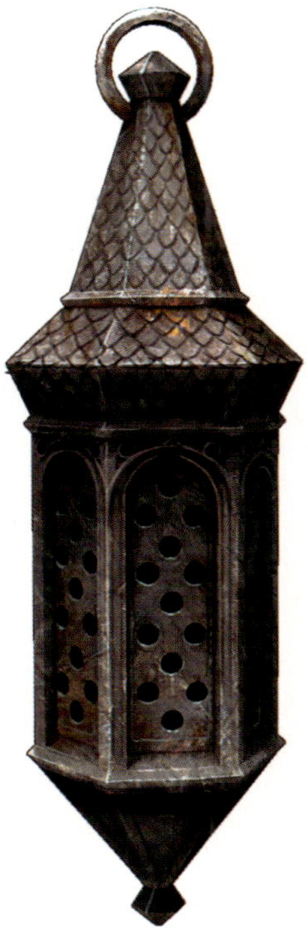

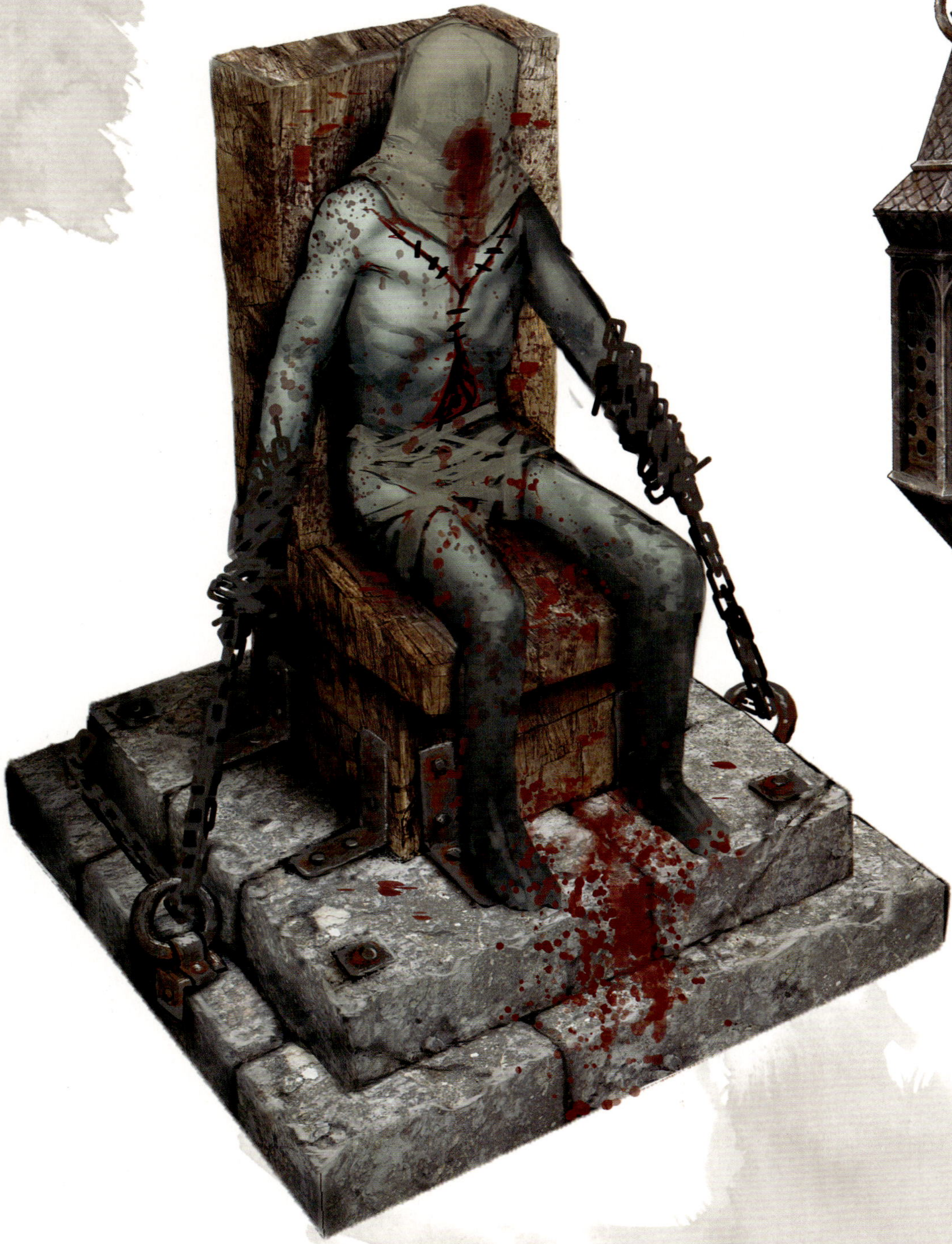

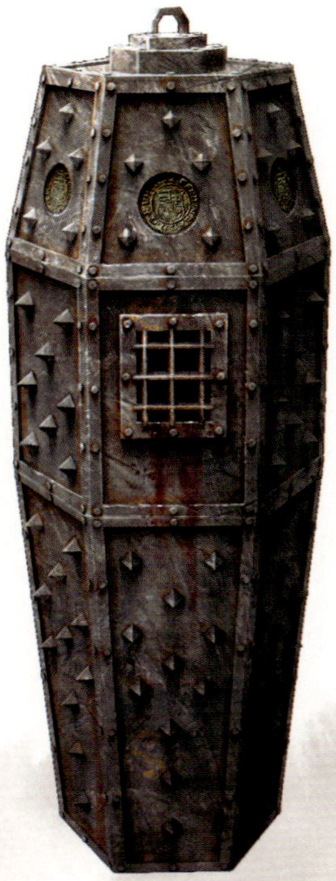

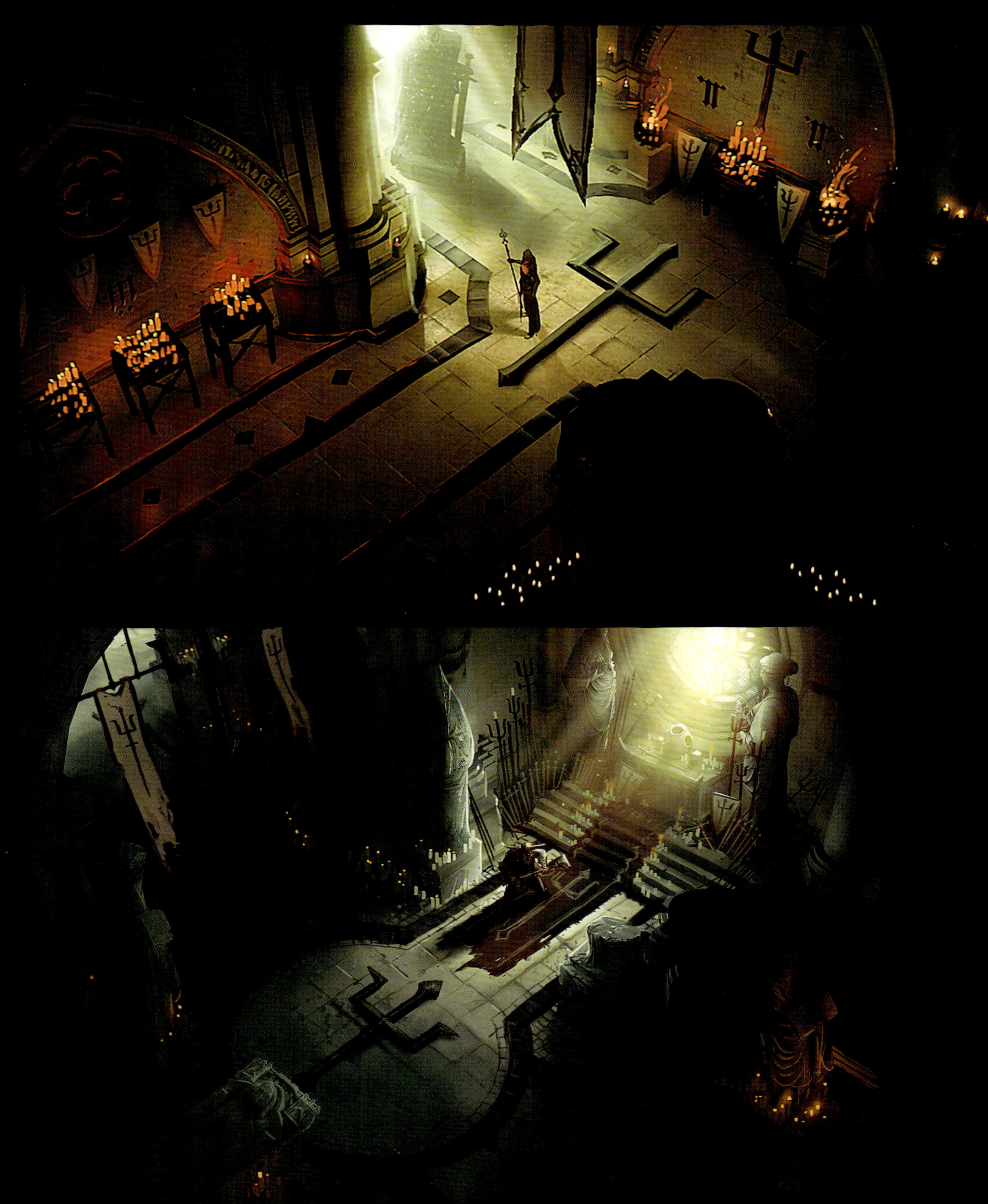

"With the open world, we needed to create interesting locations. Not only interesting, but also fun. You need to have a theme, and then you need to execute on it and make it evident while you're having fun. So we work with the designers to find the soul, the hook of this one place, and we try to make it permeate throughout the experience."

—JEFFREY LEE, Lead Exterior Artist

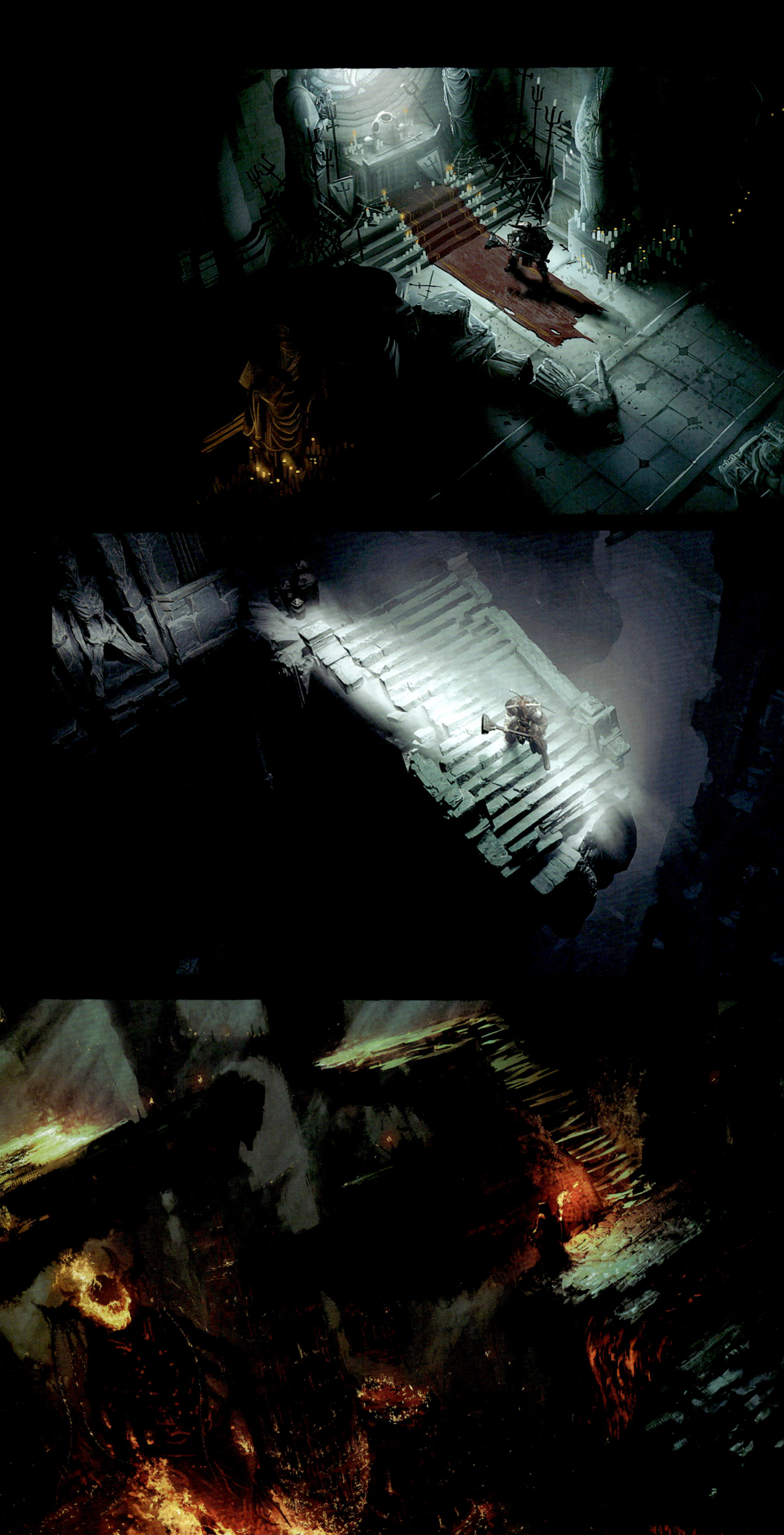

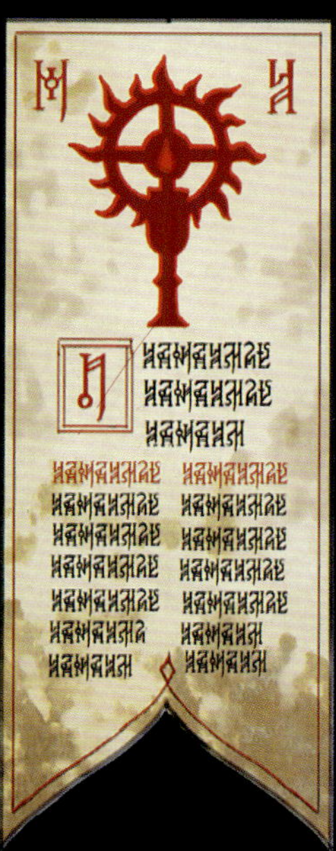

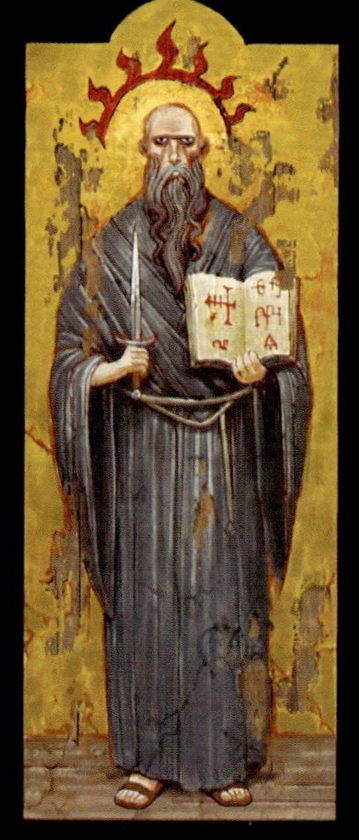

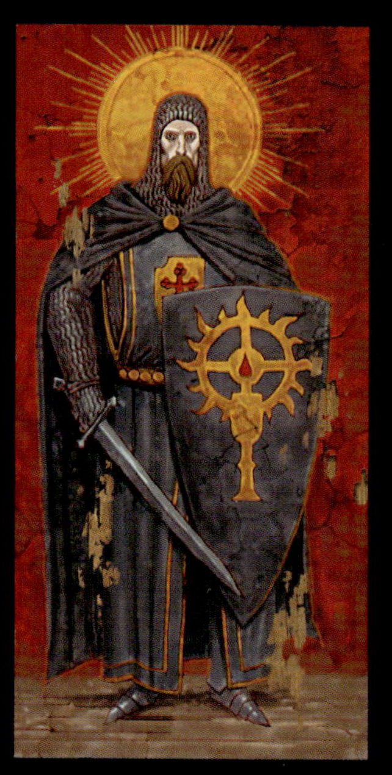

LEFT Cathedral of Light Tapestries • Mike Franchina

BOTTOM, RIGHT Cathedral of Light Murals • Mike Franchina

BOTTOM, LEFT Early Zakarum Stained Glass • Mike Franchina

OPPOSITE, TOP Zakarum Dungeon Illustration • Mike Franchina

OPPOSITE, MIDDLE Ancients Dungeon Illustration • Victor Lee

OPPOSITE, BOTTOM Early Dungeon Concept • Victor Lee

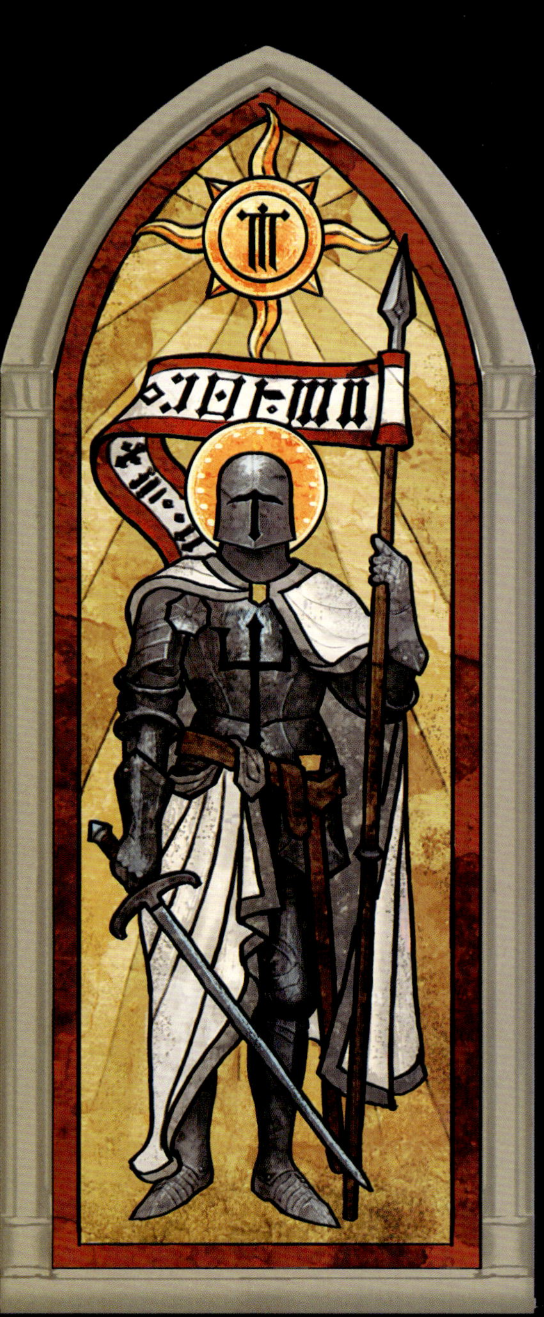

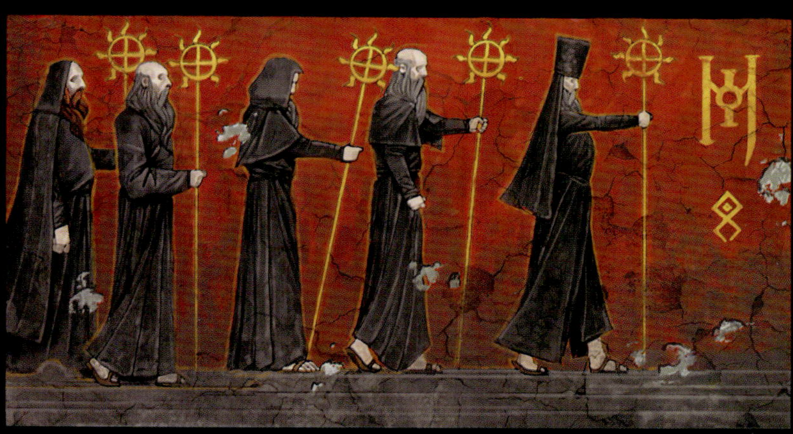

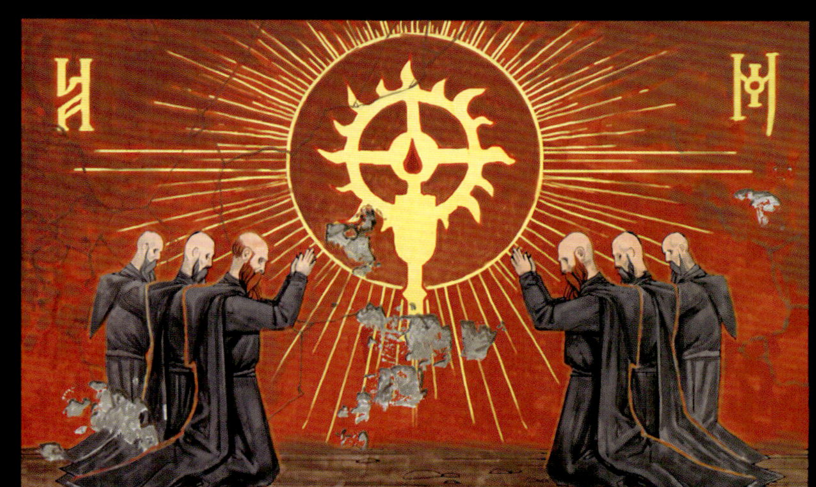

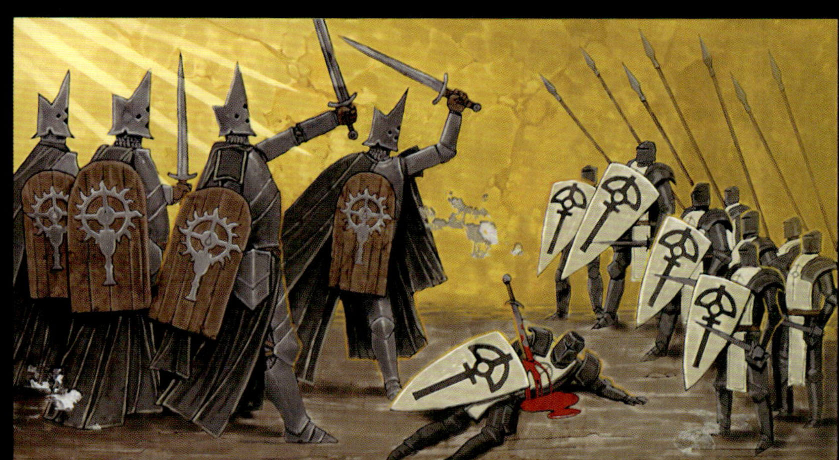

RIGHT Early Zakarum Crusader Relief Concept + Mike Franchina

MIDDLE Great Serpent Mural + Konstantin Vavilov

BOTTOM Sarcophagus Prop Concept + Victor Lee

OPPOSITE Mephisto Stained Glass Concept + Konstantin Vavilov

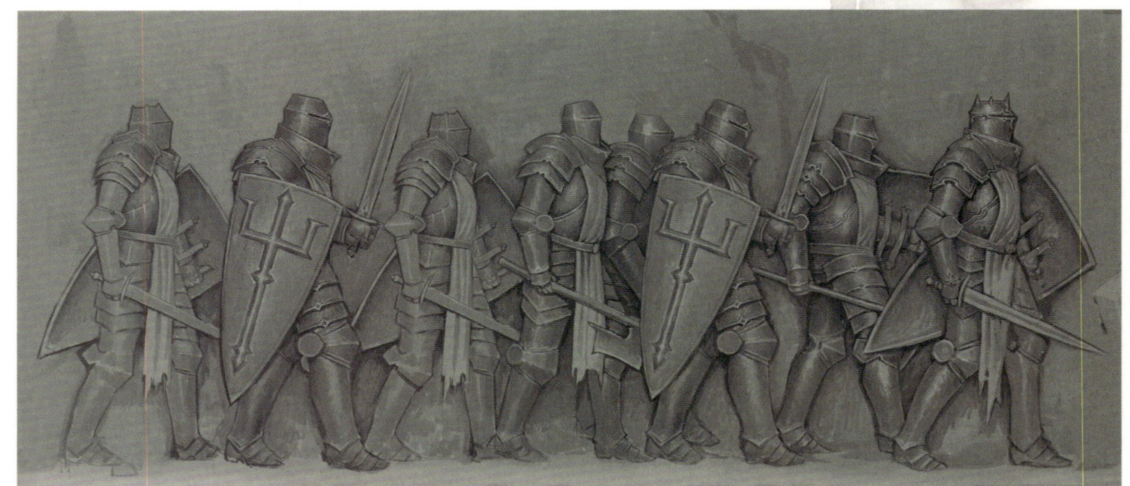

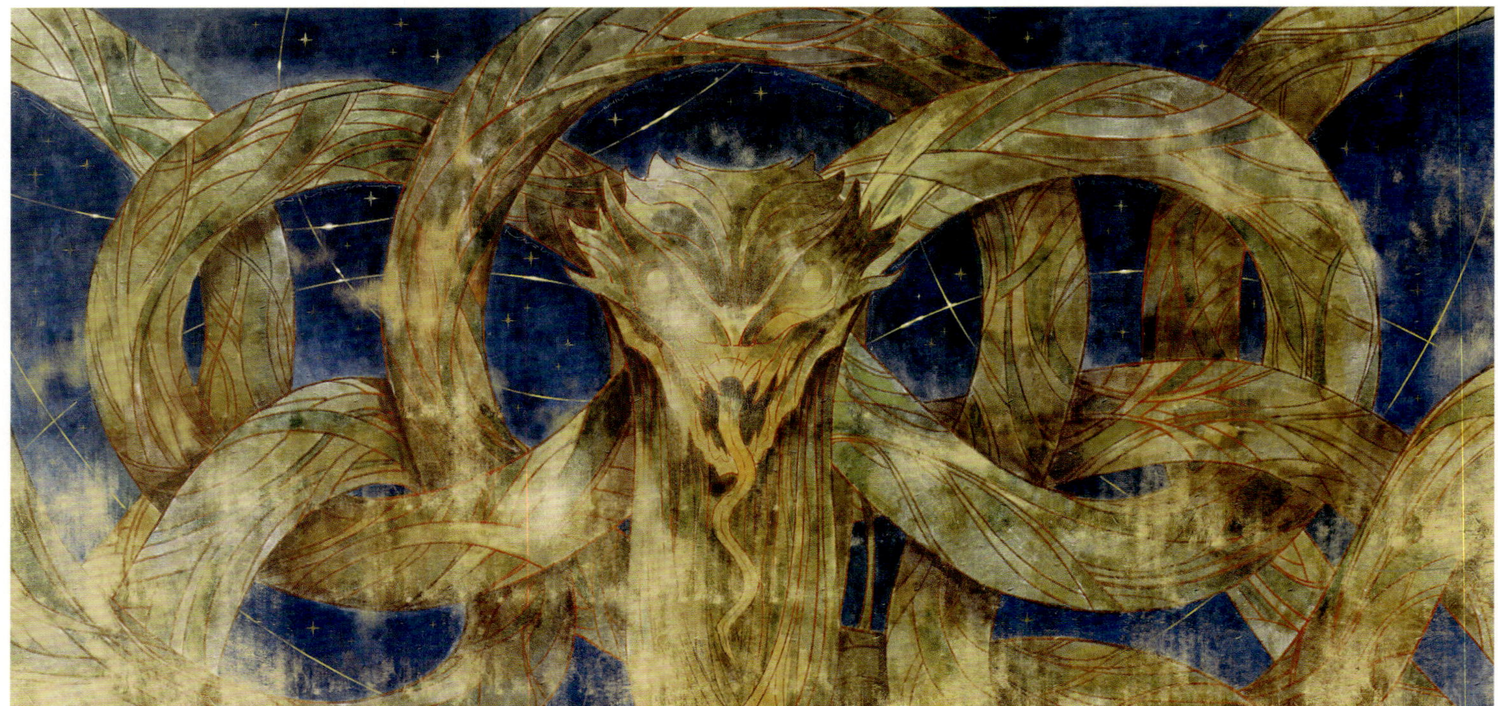

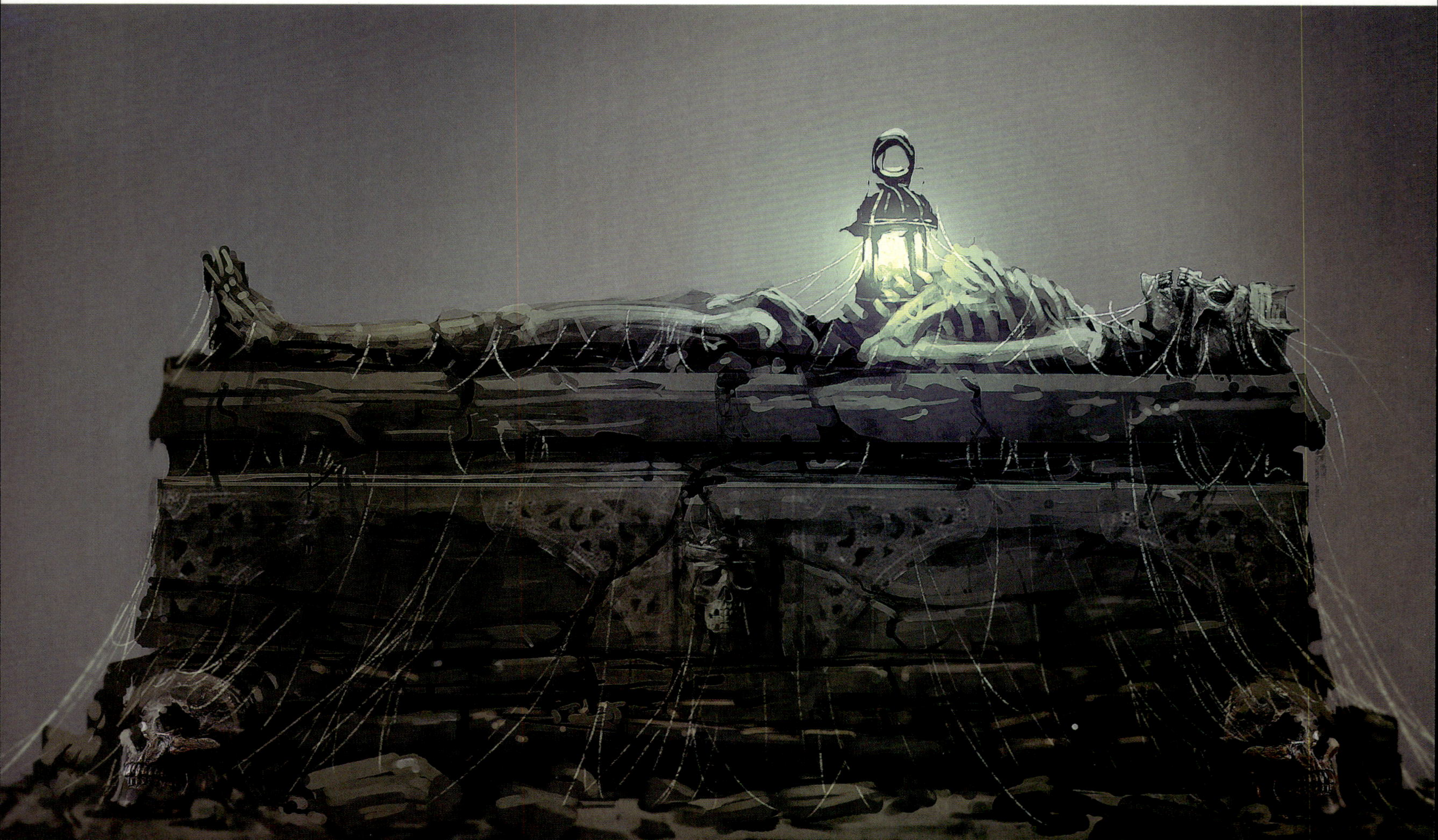

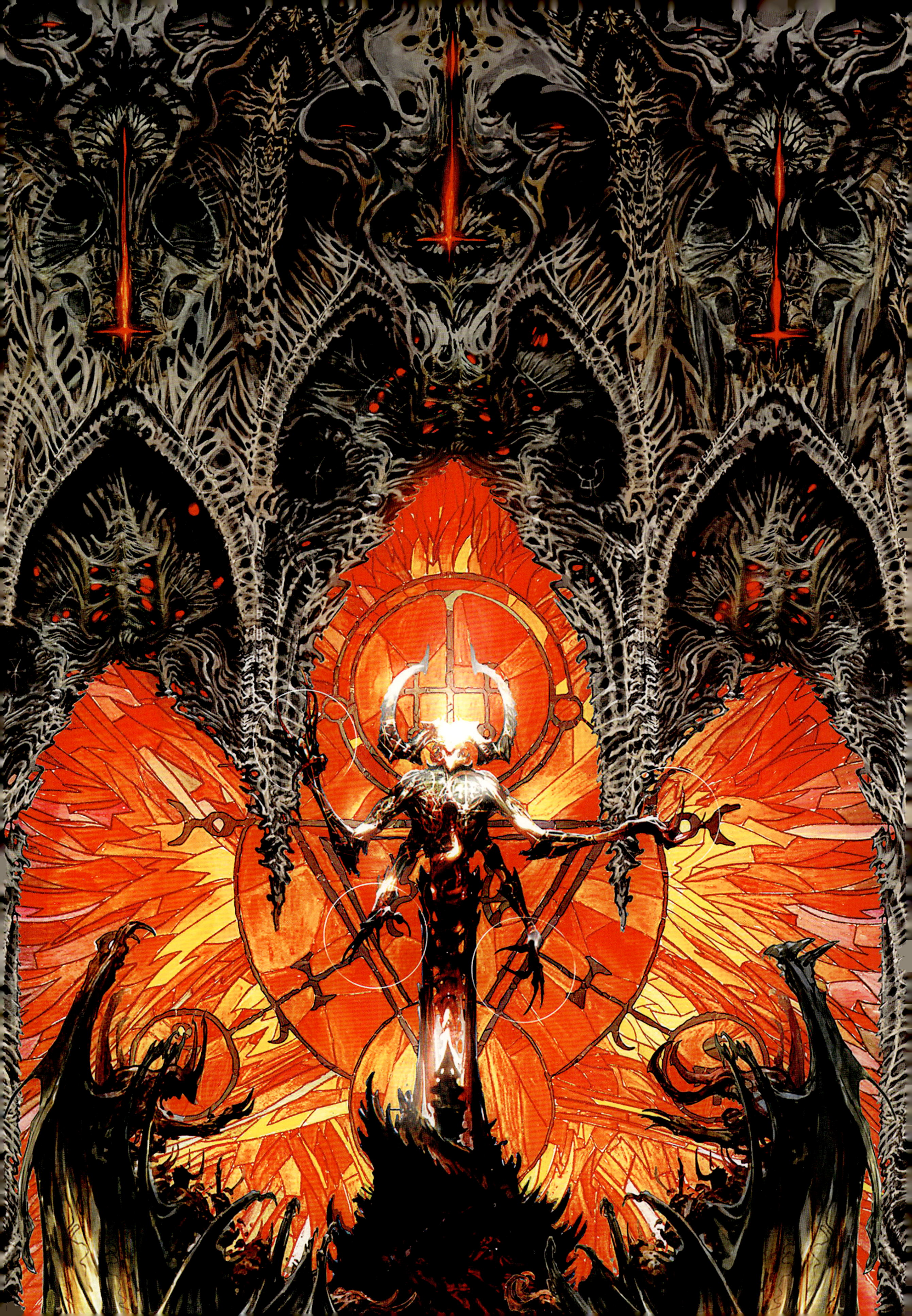

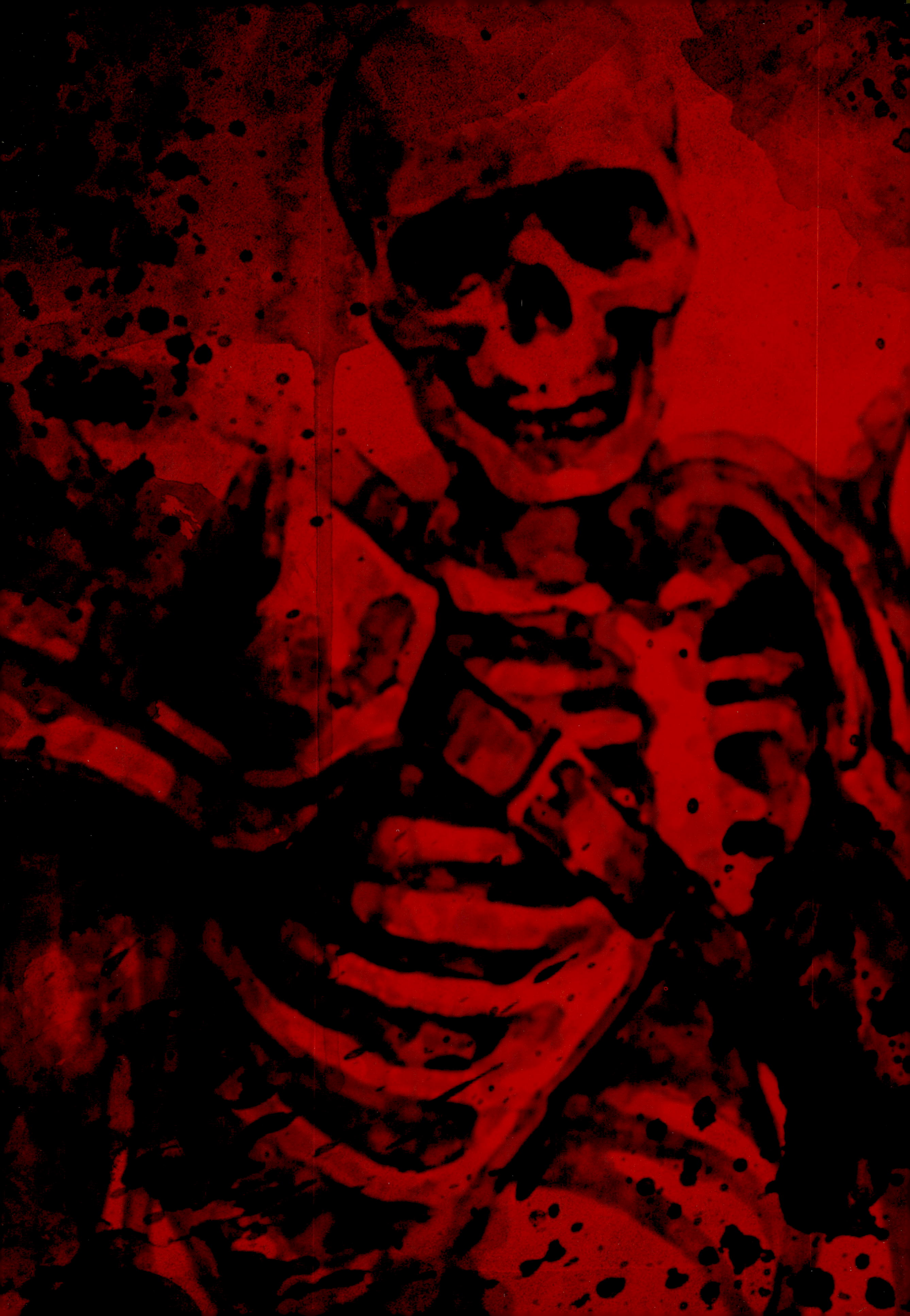

The Heart of Darkness

Diablo IV opened up the world of Sanctuary, quite literally, and underwent a style evolution even as developers faced obstacles in development and in the real world.

"We navigated a million hurdles as a team," says art director John Mueller, "and that's the thing I'm most proud of. Given the complexity of new pipelines, new technology, and challenges outside the game—like the pandemic and remote work—I'm most proud of the team and how we got through it. Not only did we get through it—we thrived. After finishing the game, our team is in such a good place, and we're set up to make a ton of beautiful content post-ship."

Such a welcome statement inevitably sparks the question: What shape will this new content take?

Enter the new *Diablo* expansion, *Vessel of Hatred*.

Here, players will be joined by exciting new characters as they explore Sanctuary's eastern jungles, as well as an entirely new region that will feature more monsters than any other in the game.

"There's a lot of variety and a lot of new content," says Mueller. "We basically get to put a ton of effort into one region of the world and really breathe life into it."

Leading players on this journey will be Neyrelle, a character who accompanied the player in *Diablo IV*, became an adept of the Horadrim only to leave it behind . . . and was last seen leaving on a boat at the end of the game with one very unique and dangerous item: "She has the Soulstone of Mephisto with her," Mueller explains. "She has left Lorath behind. She's on a personal journey, wrestling with her own demons—both metaphorically and literally—with Mephisto trying to corrupt her mind."

Mueller promises that *Vessel of Hatred* will take players to the source of all evil, and good, as Neyrelle explores what developers are calling "the Heart of Darkness."

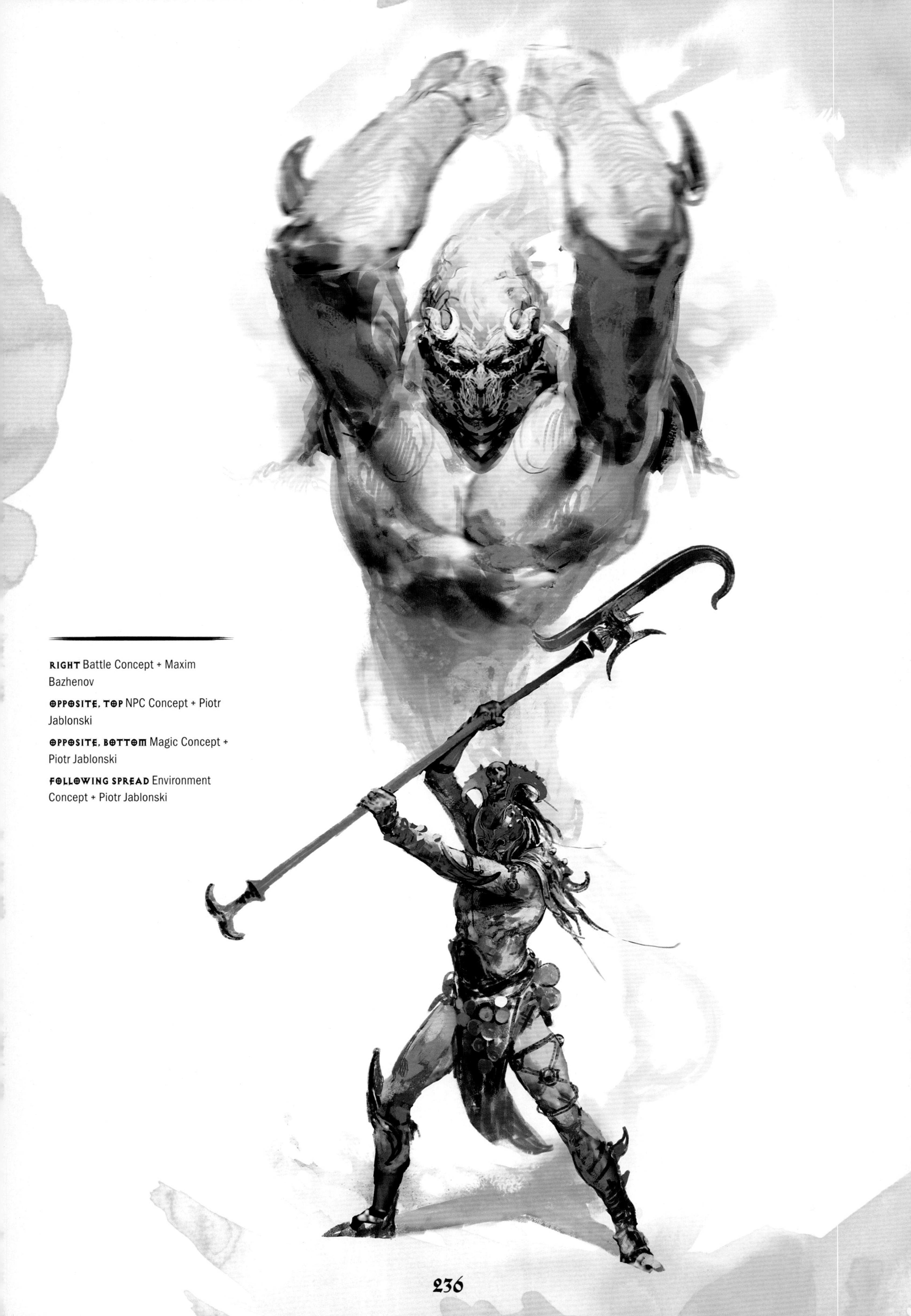

RIGHT Battle Concept + Maxim Bazhenov

OPPOSITE, TOP NPC Concept + Piotr Jablonski

OPPOSITE, BOTTOM Magic Concept + Piotr Jablonski

FOLLOWING SPREAD Environment Concept + Piotr Jablonski

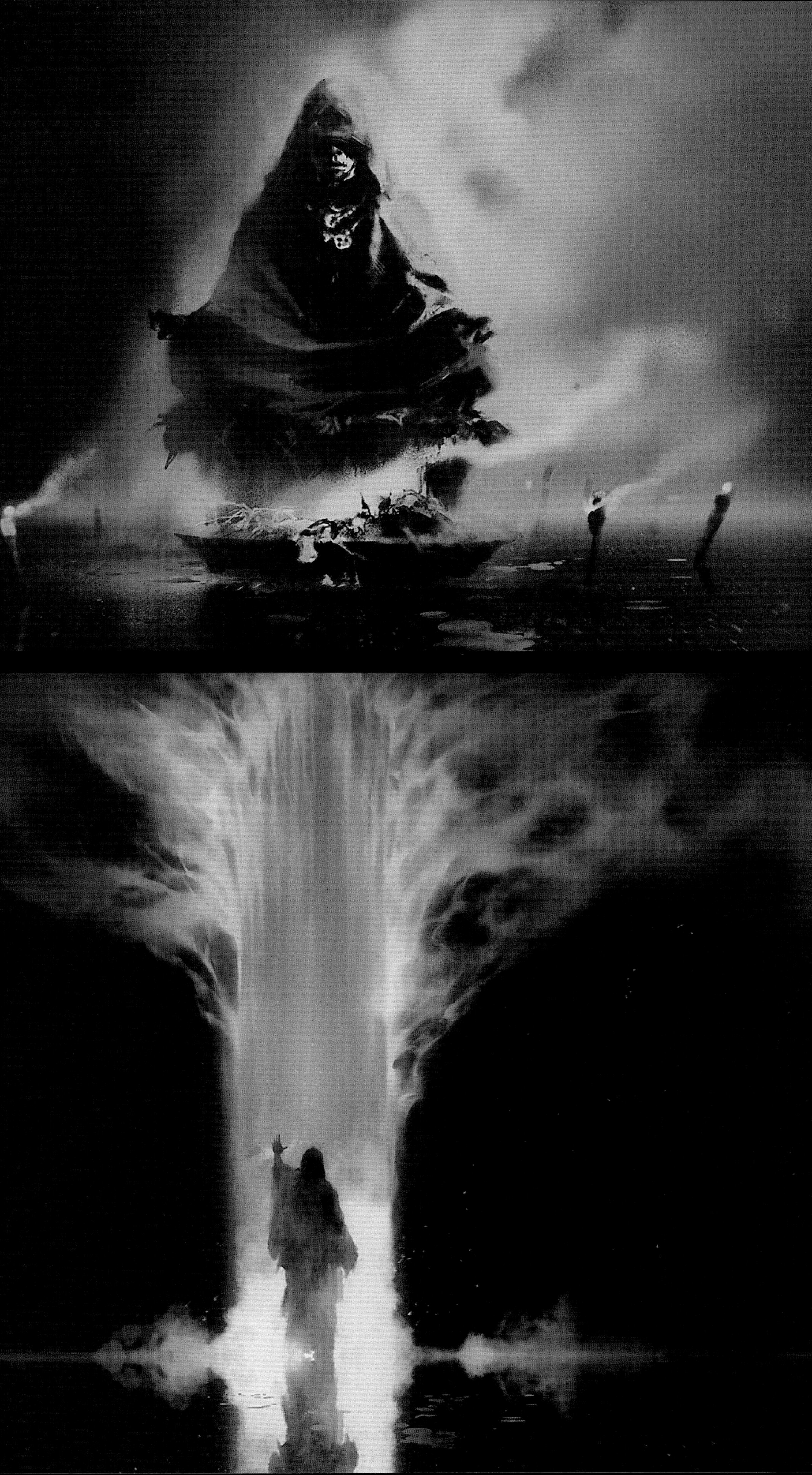

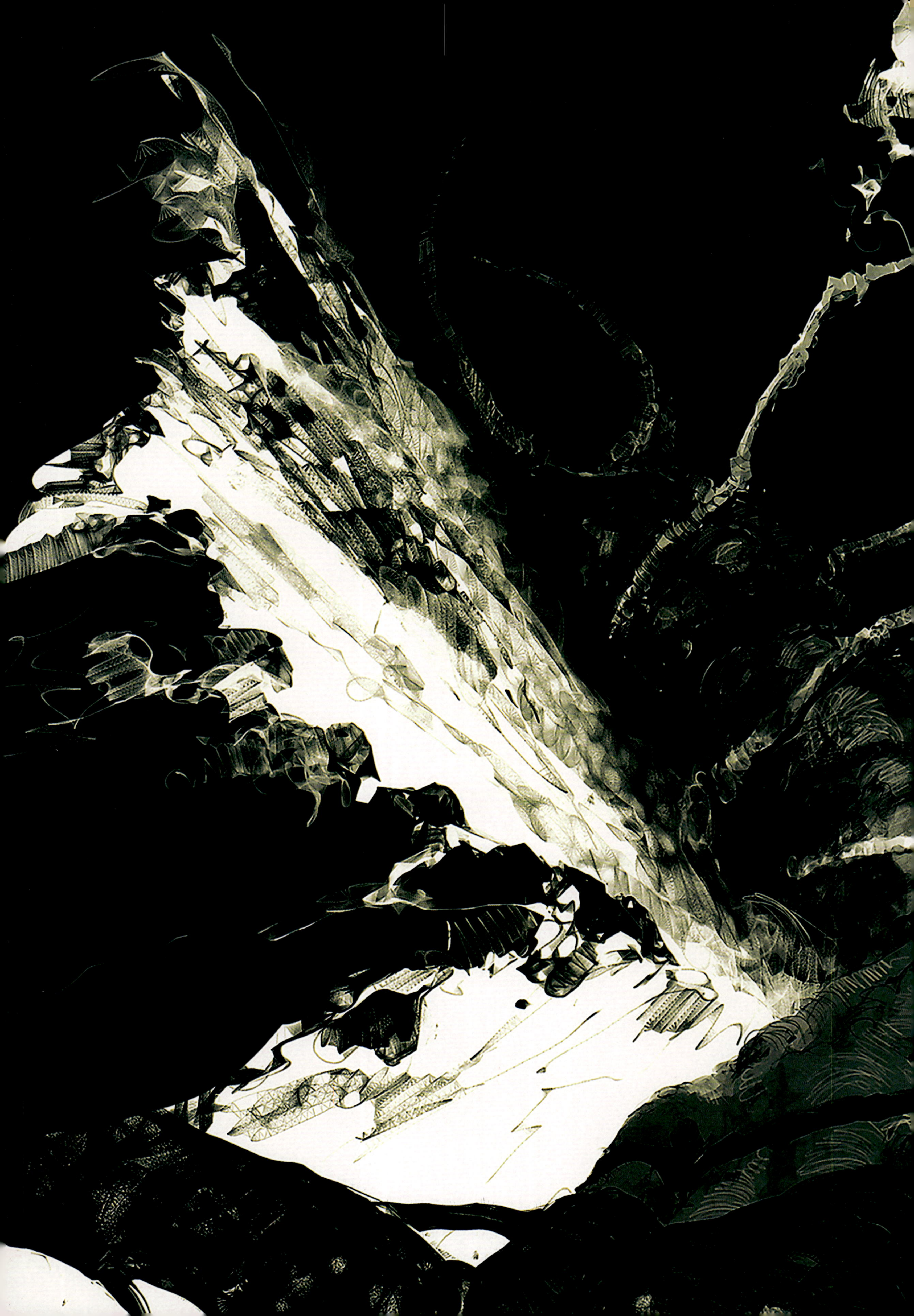

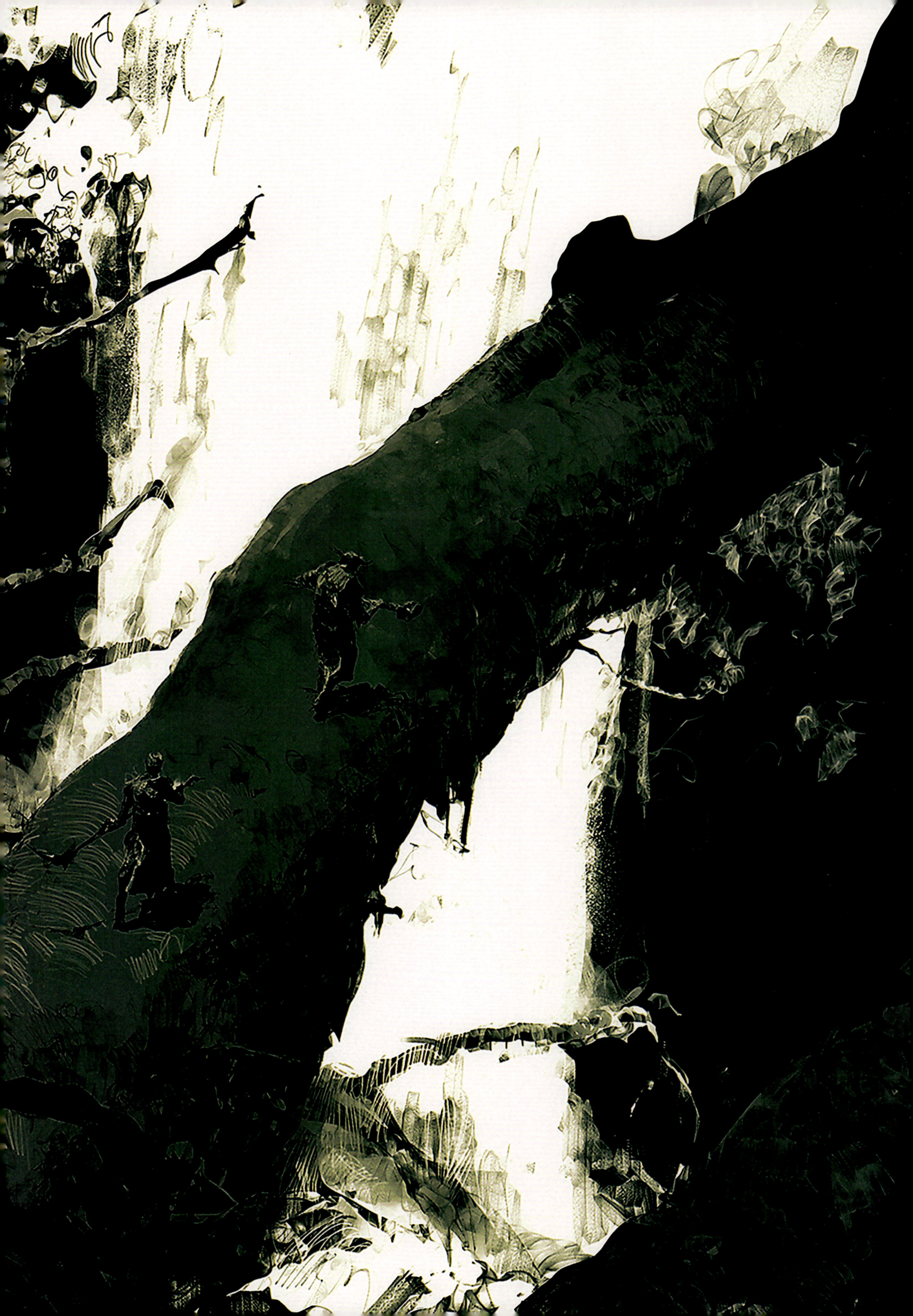

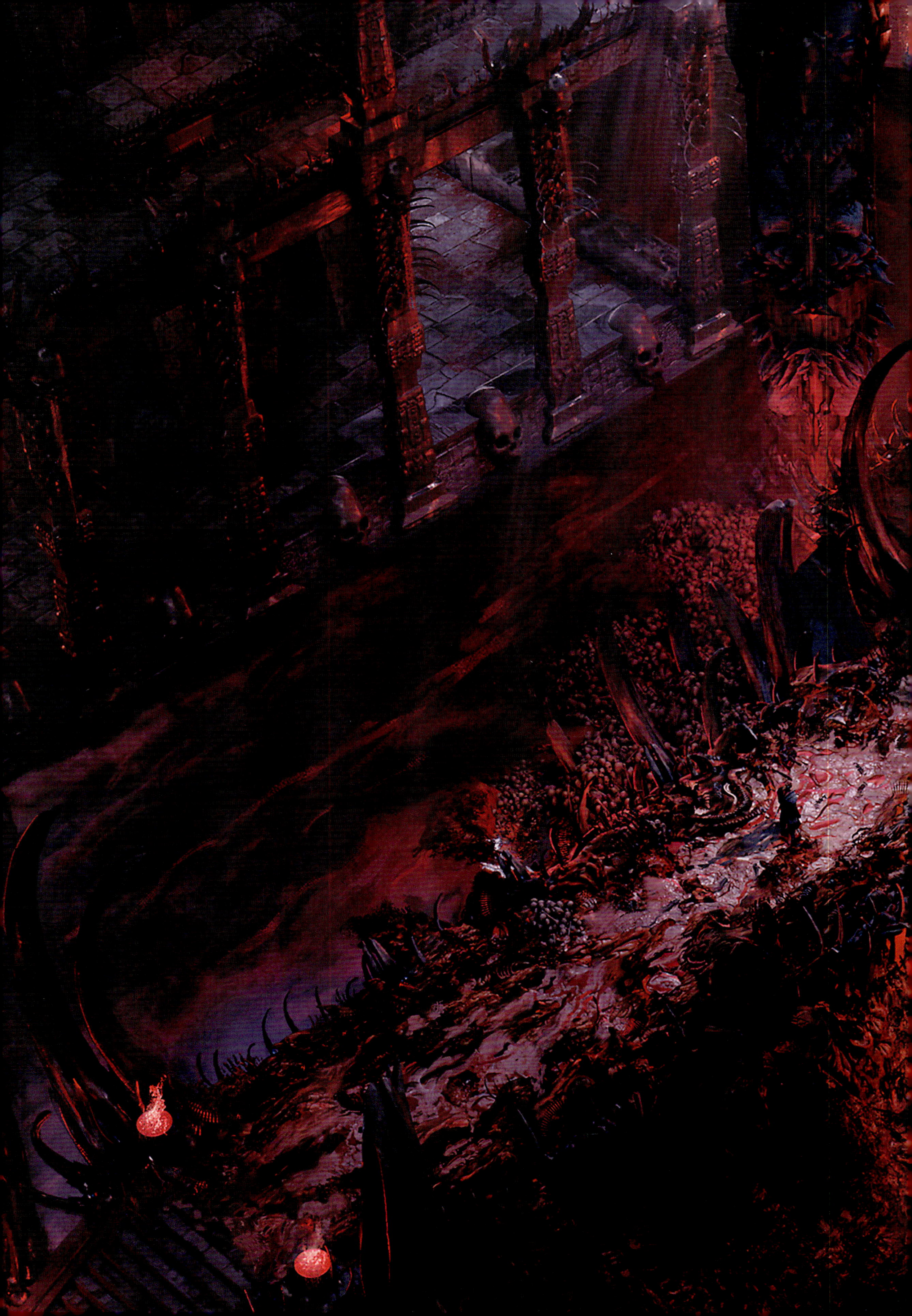

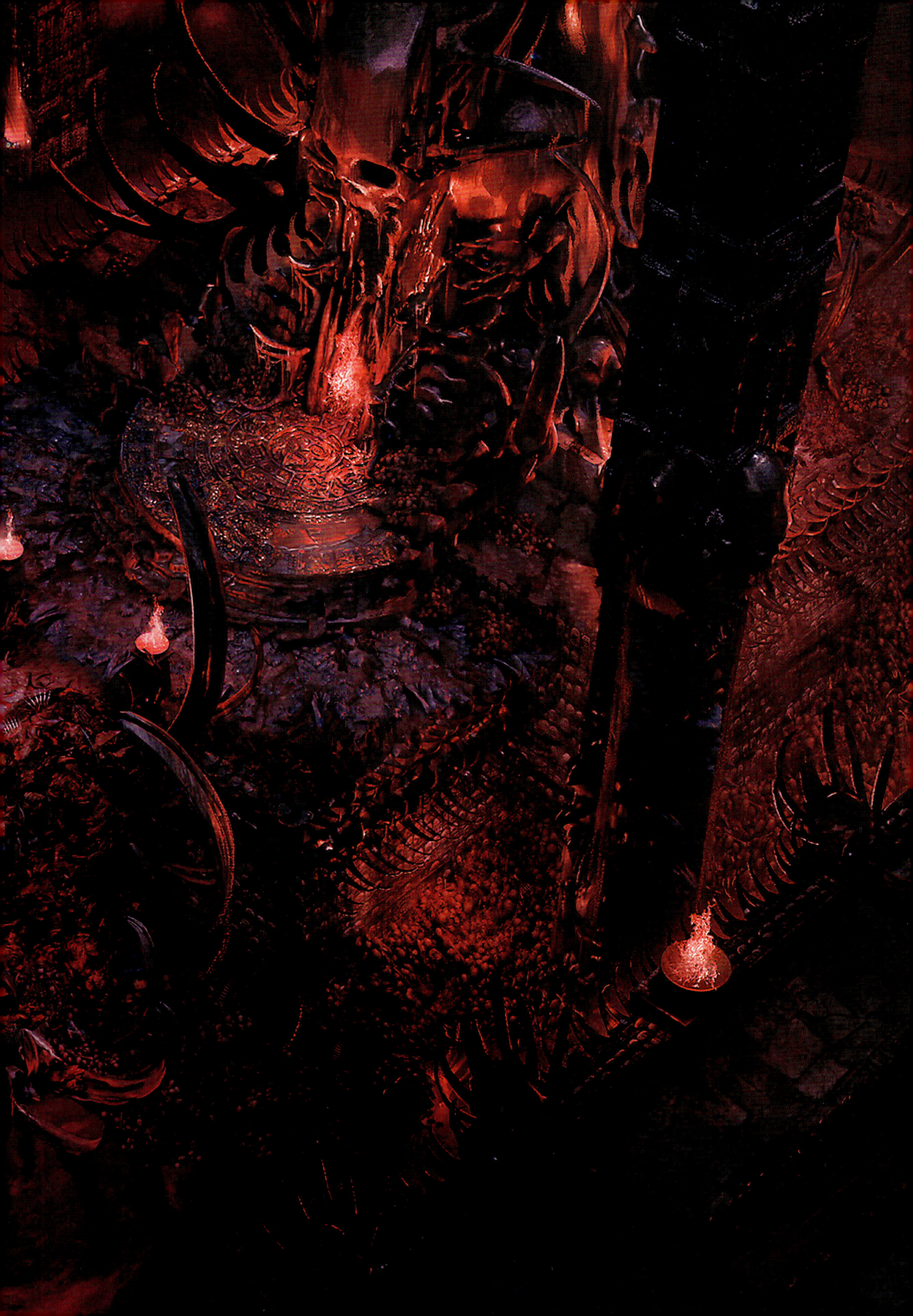

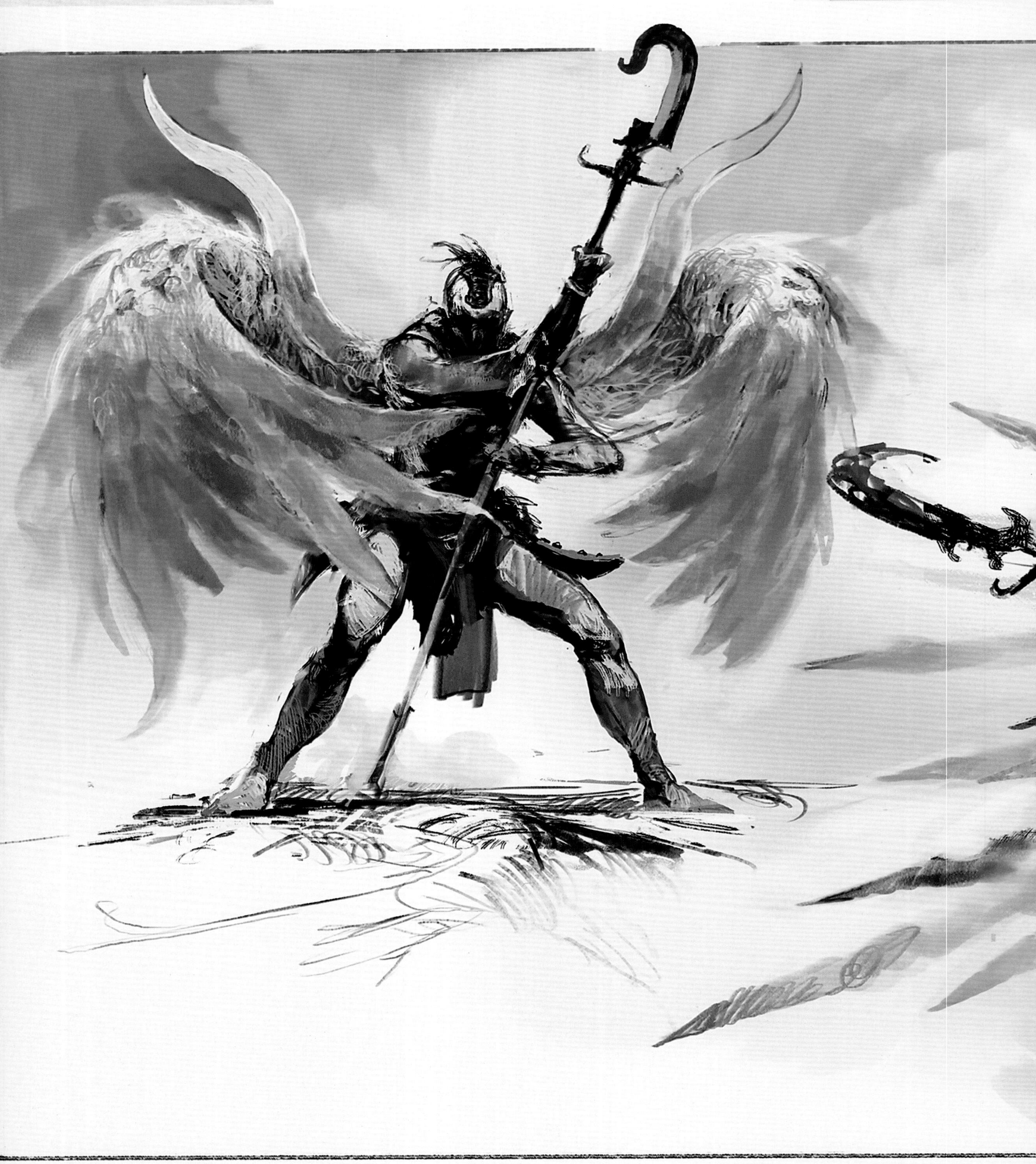

ABOVE Magic Concept + Maxim Bazhenov

PREVIOUS SPREAD Environment Concept + Karine Villette

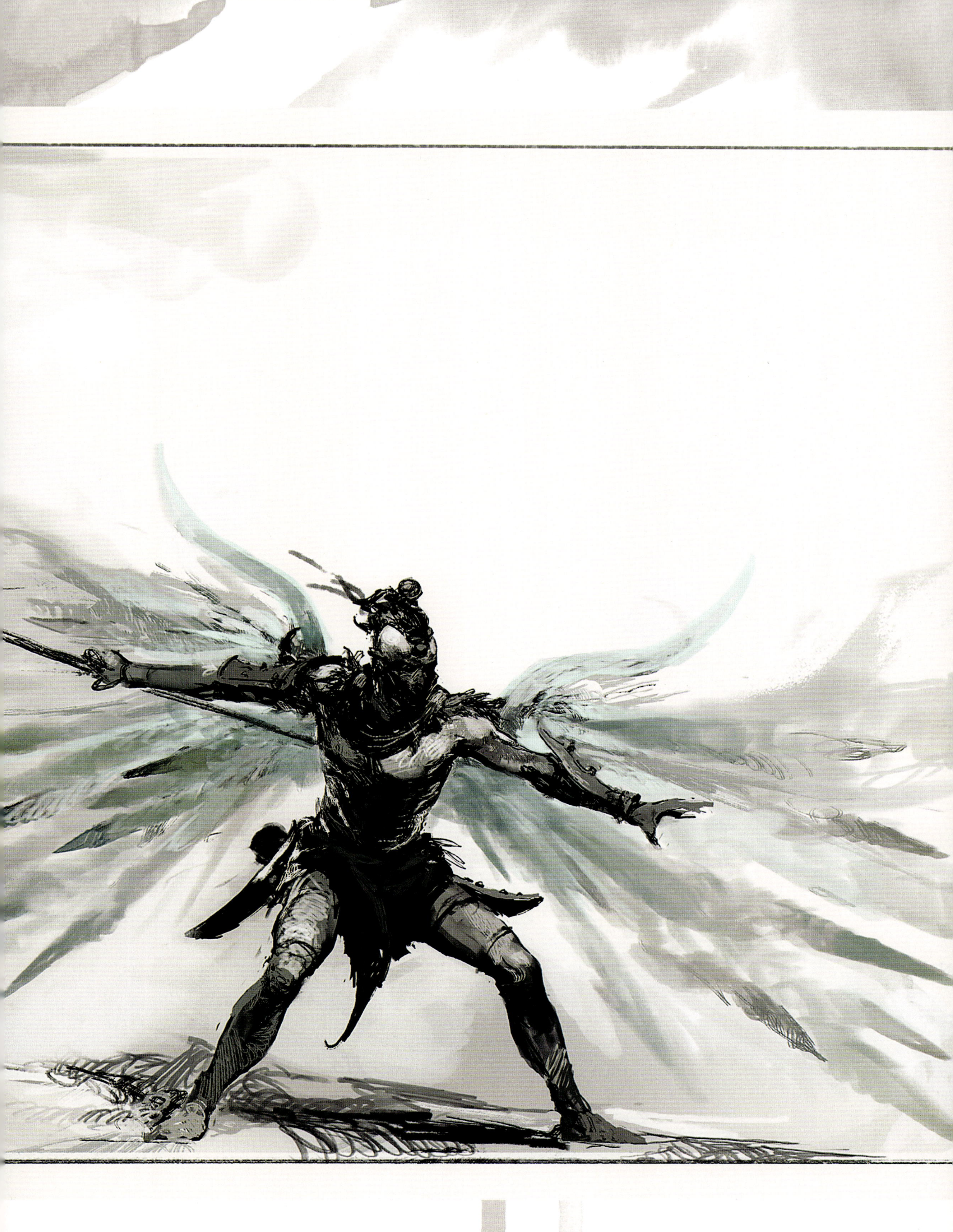

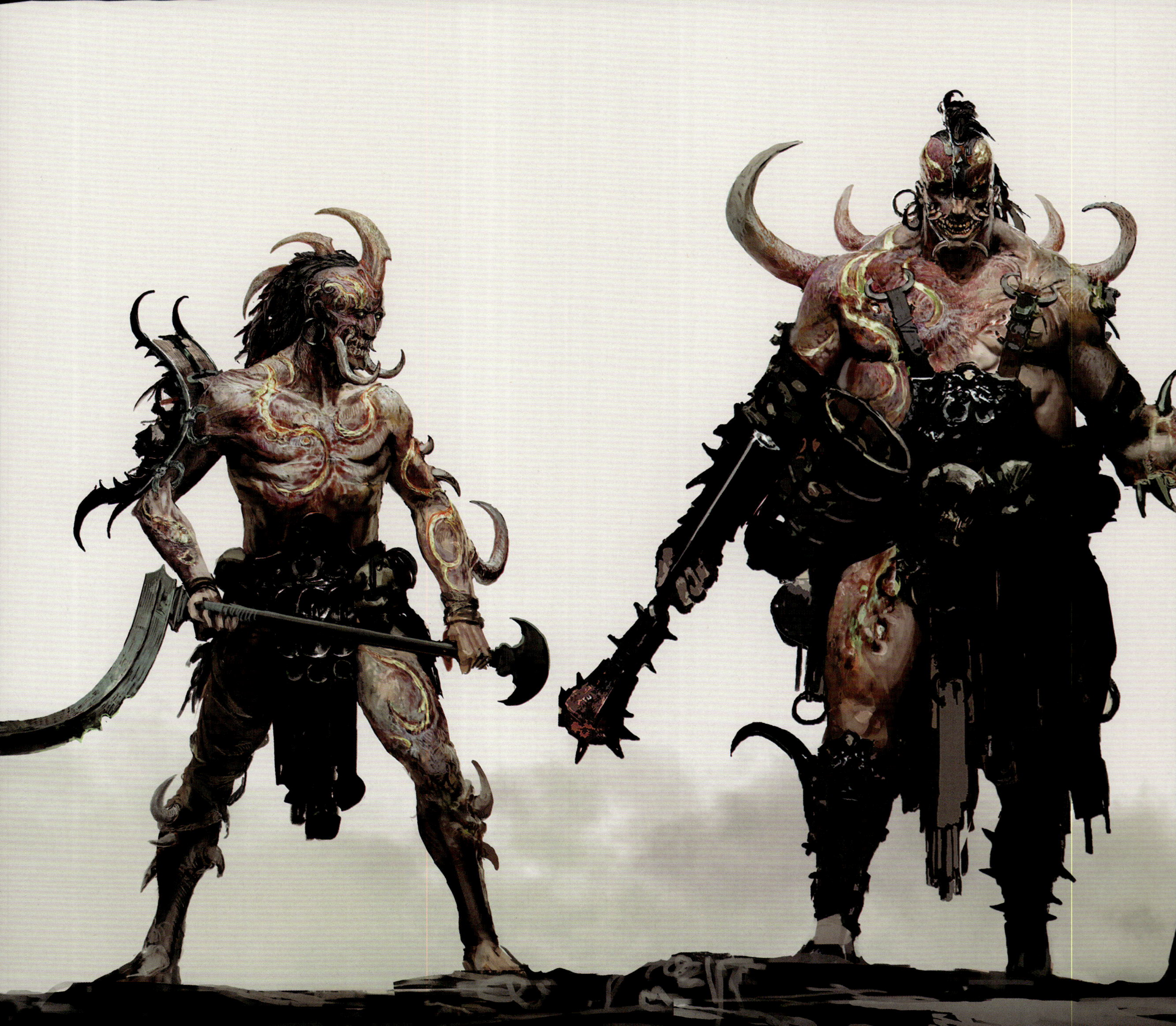

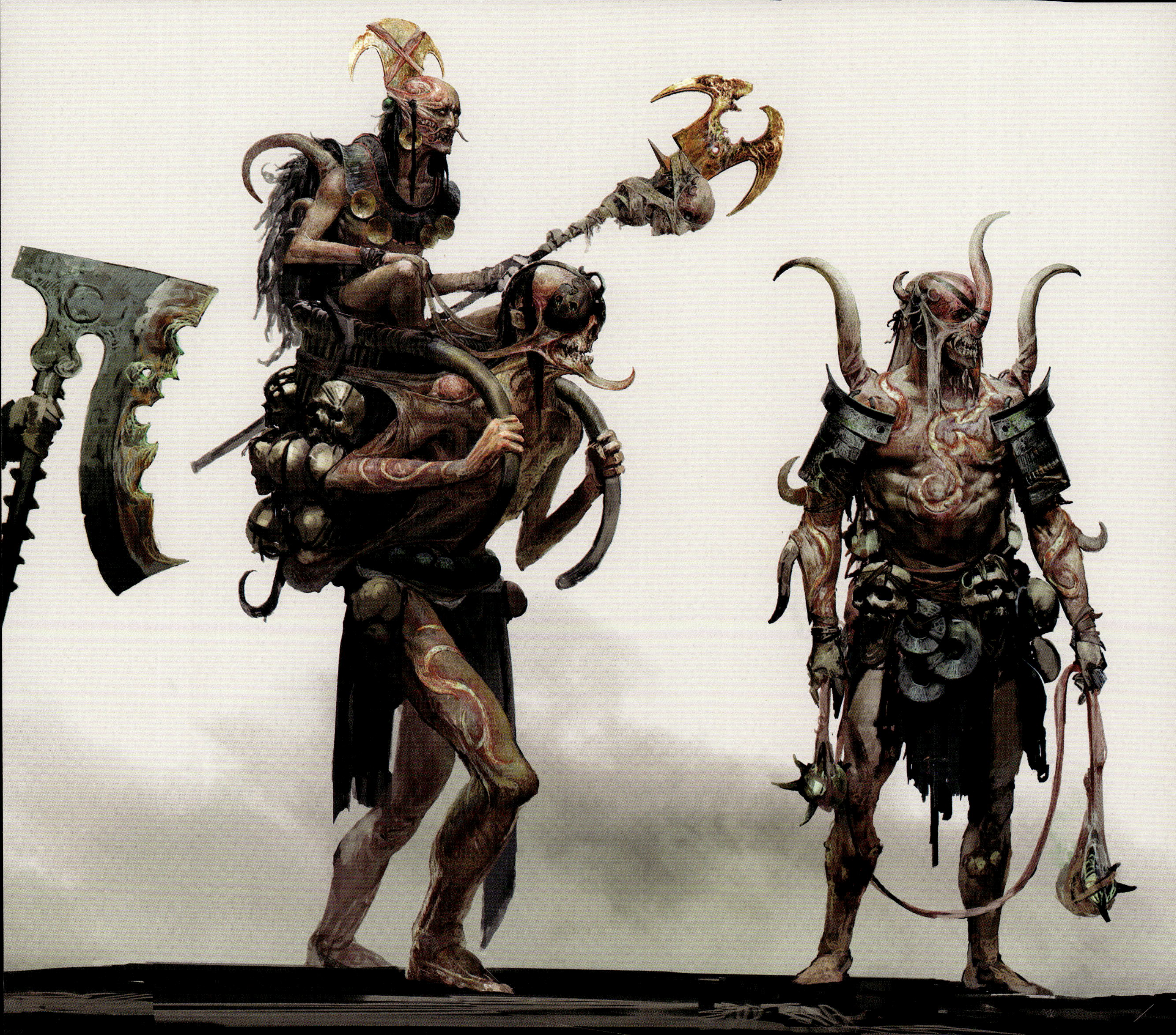

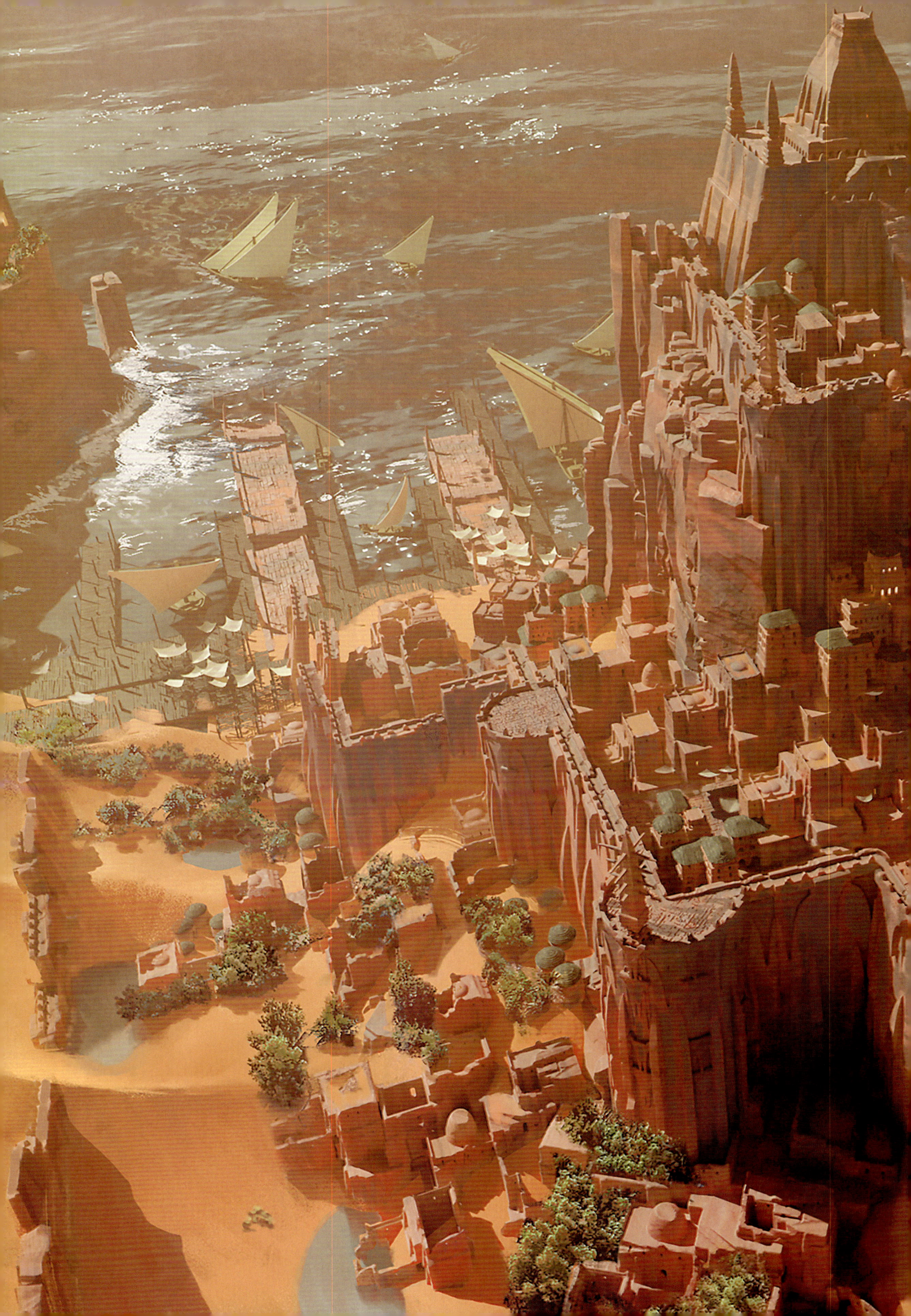

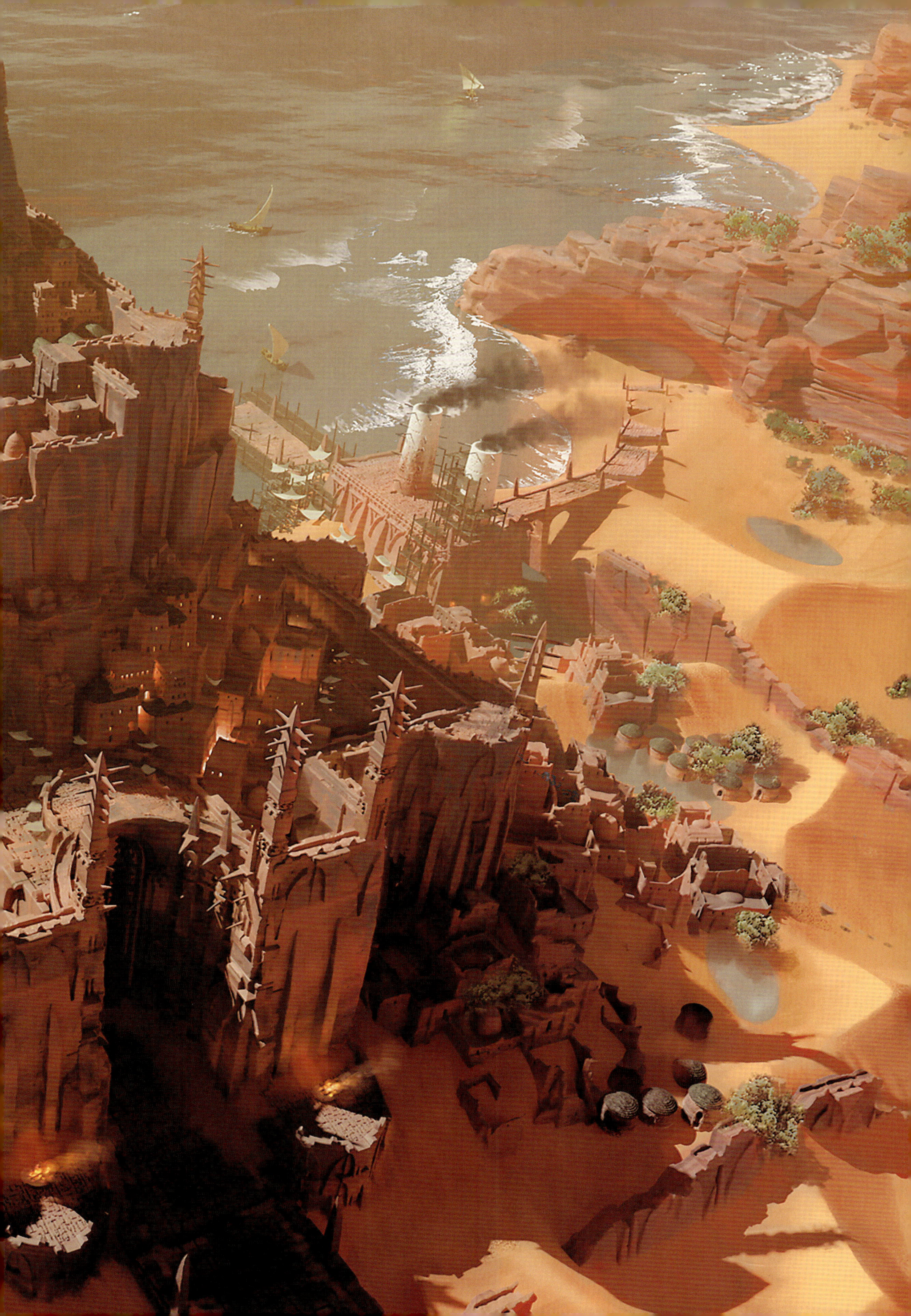

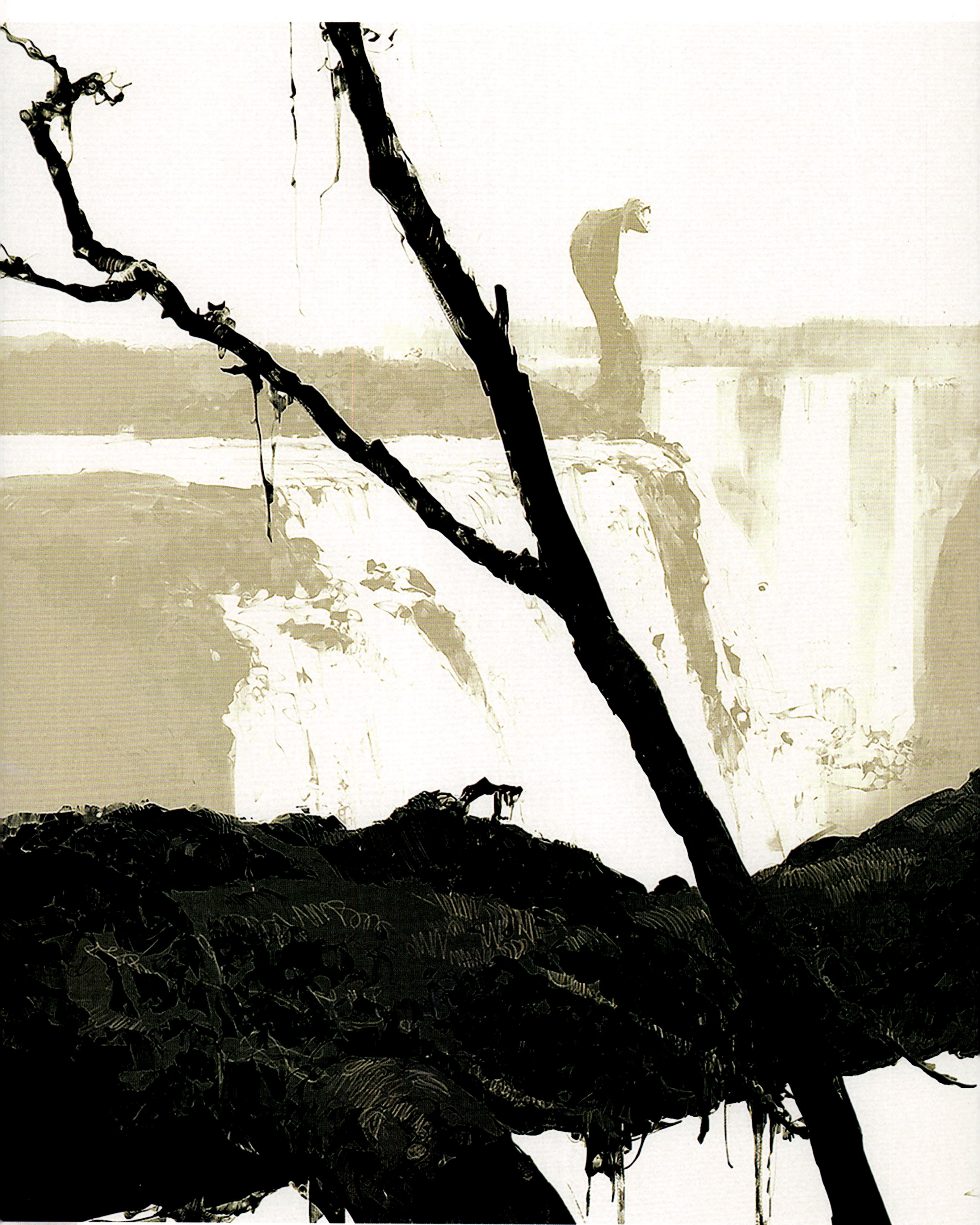

ABOVE Environment Concept + Piotr Jablonski

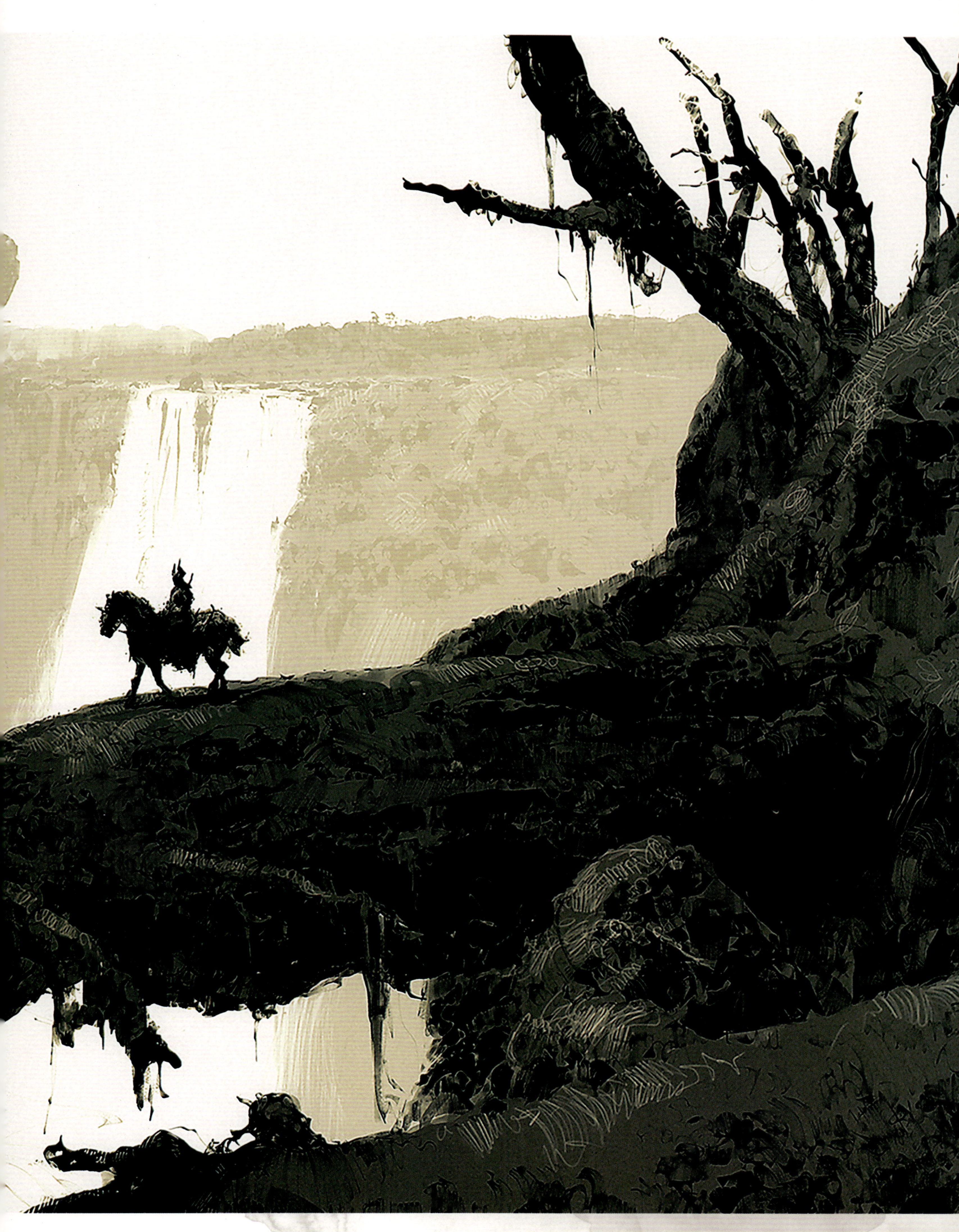

TOP Magic Concept + Maxim Bazhenov

BOTTOM Magic Concept + Maxim Bazhenov

OPPOSITE NPC Concept + Maxim Bazhenov

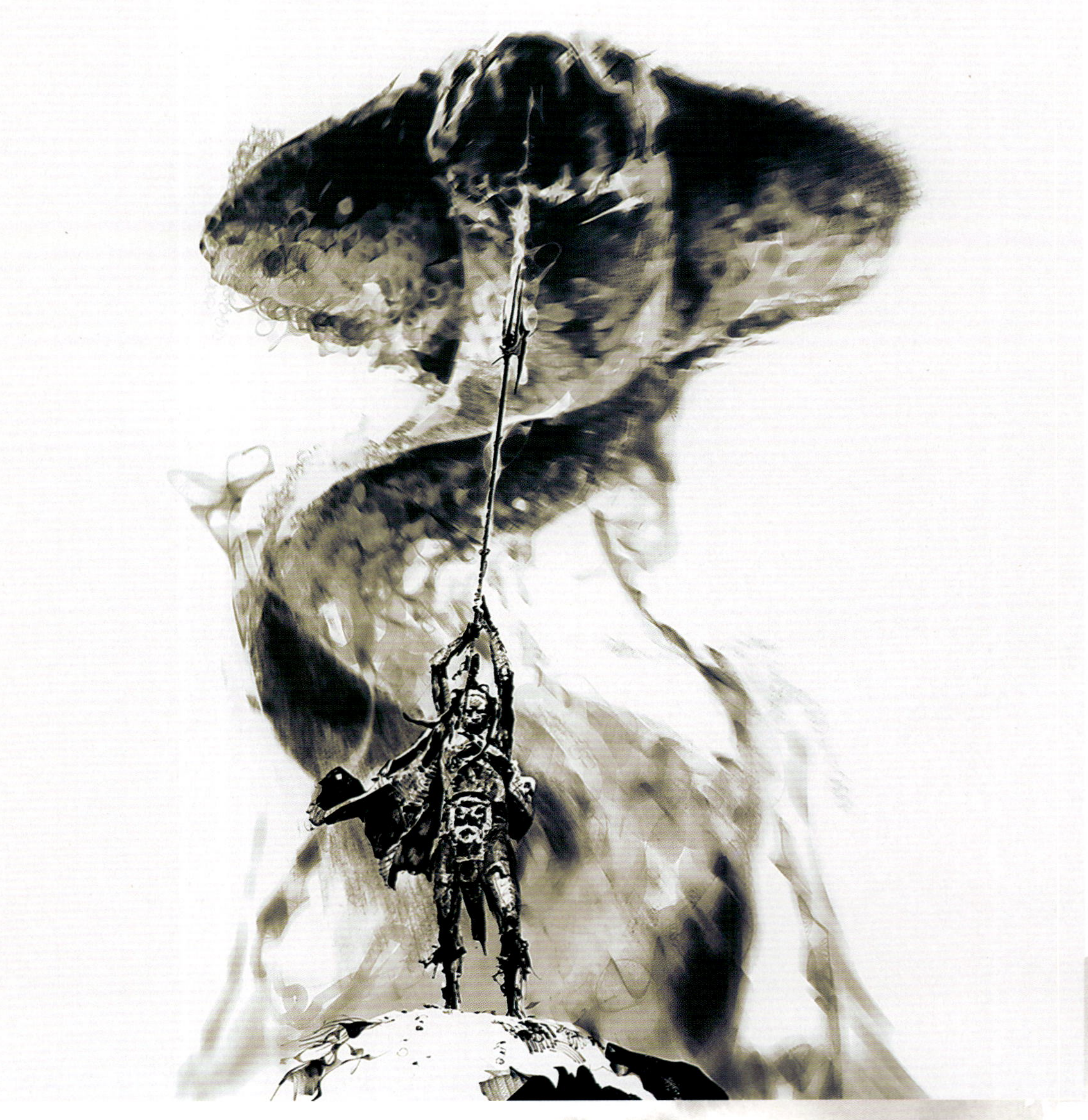

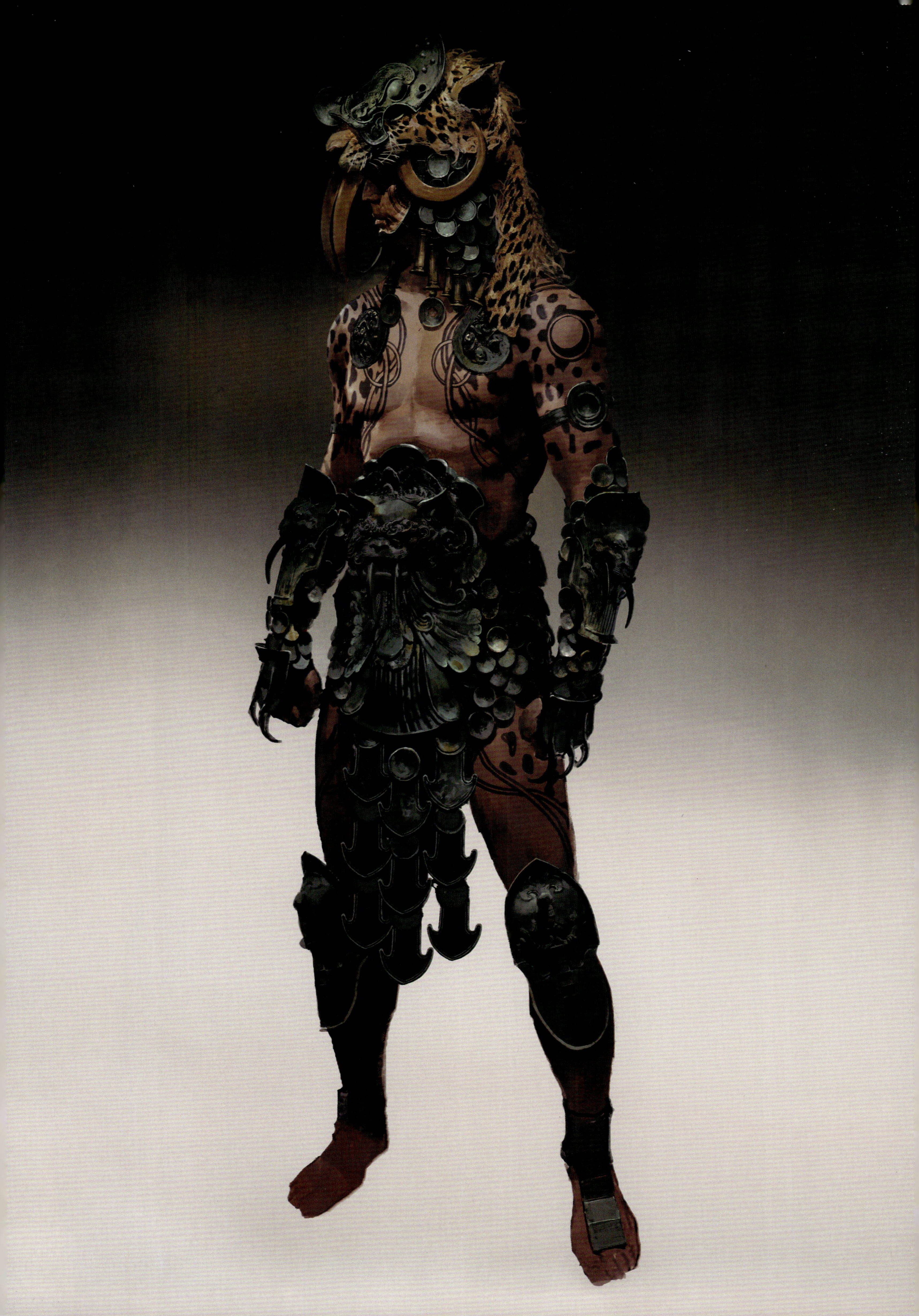

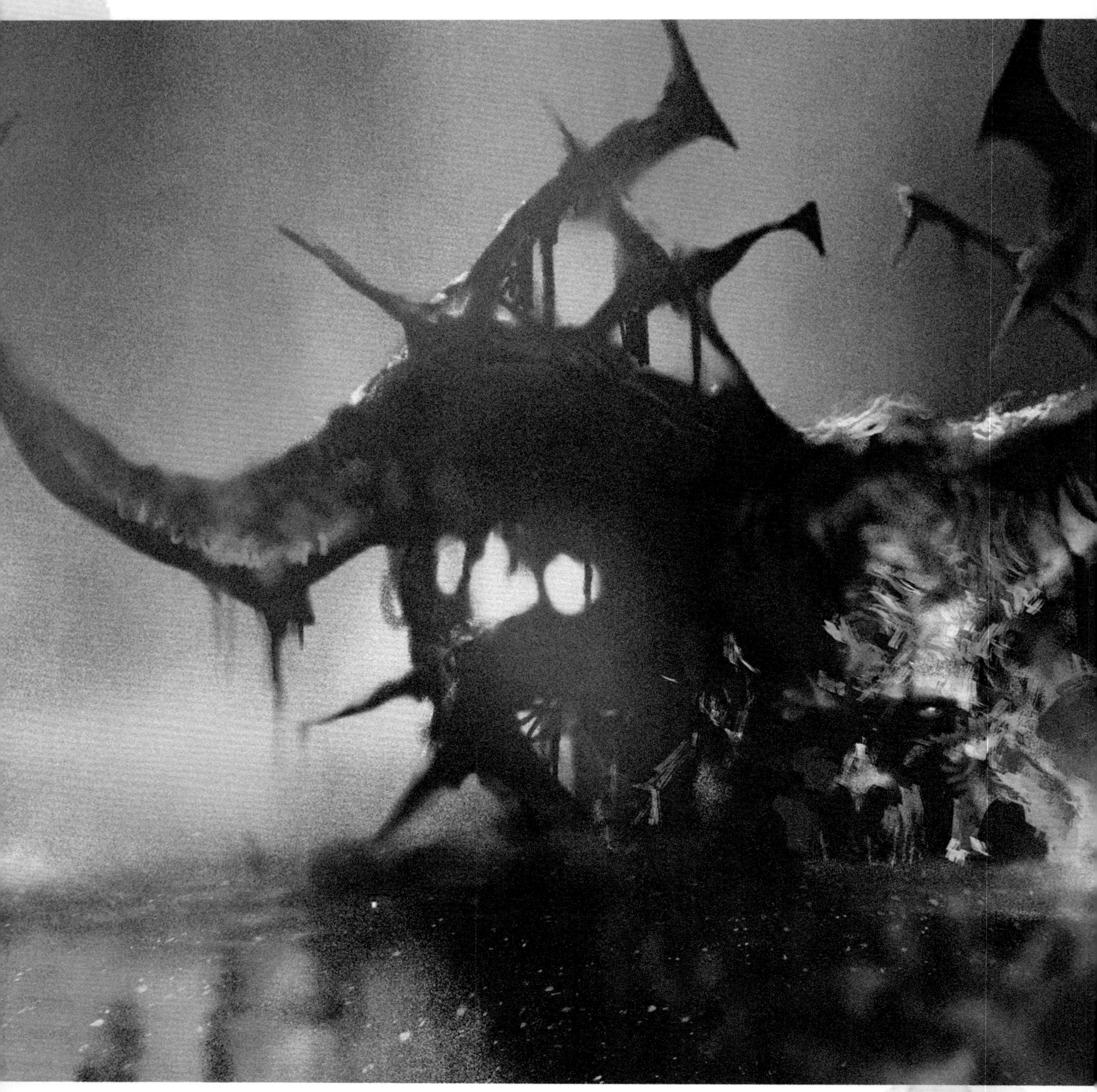

ABOVE Mephisto Concept + Piotr Jablonski

FOLLOWING SPREAD Environment Concept + Karine Villette

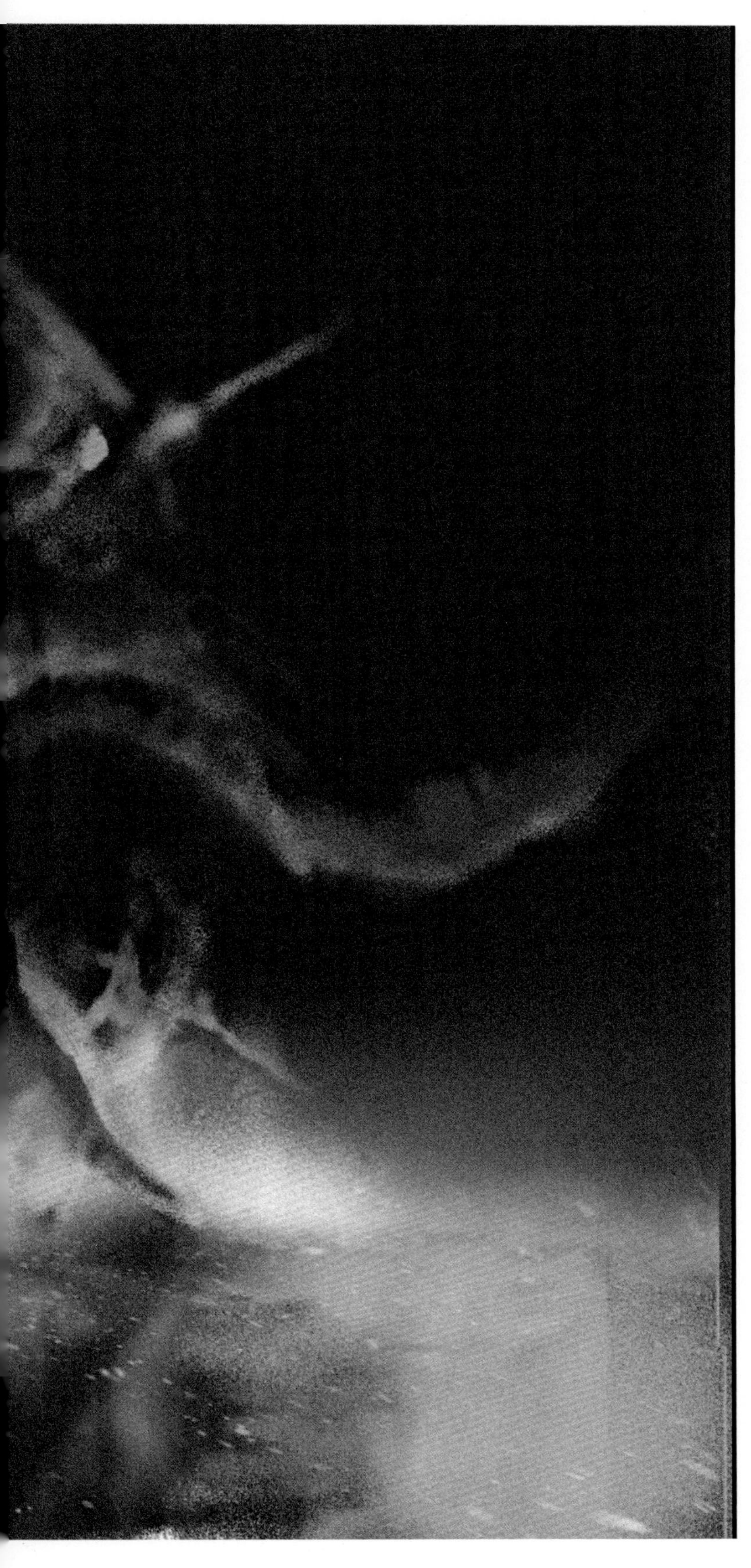

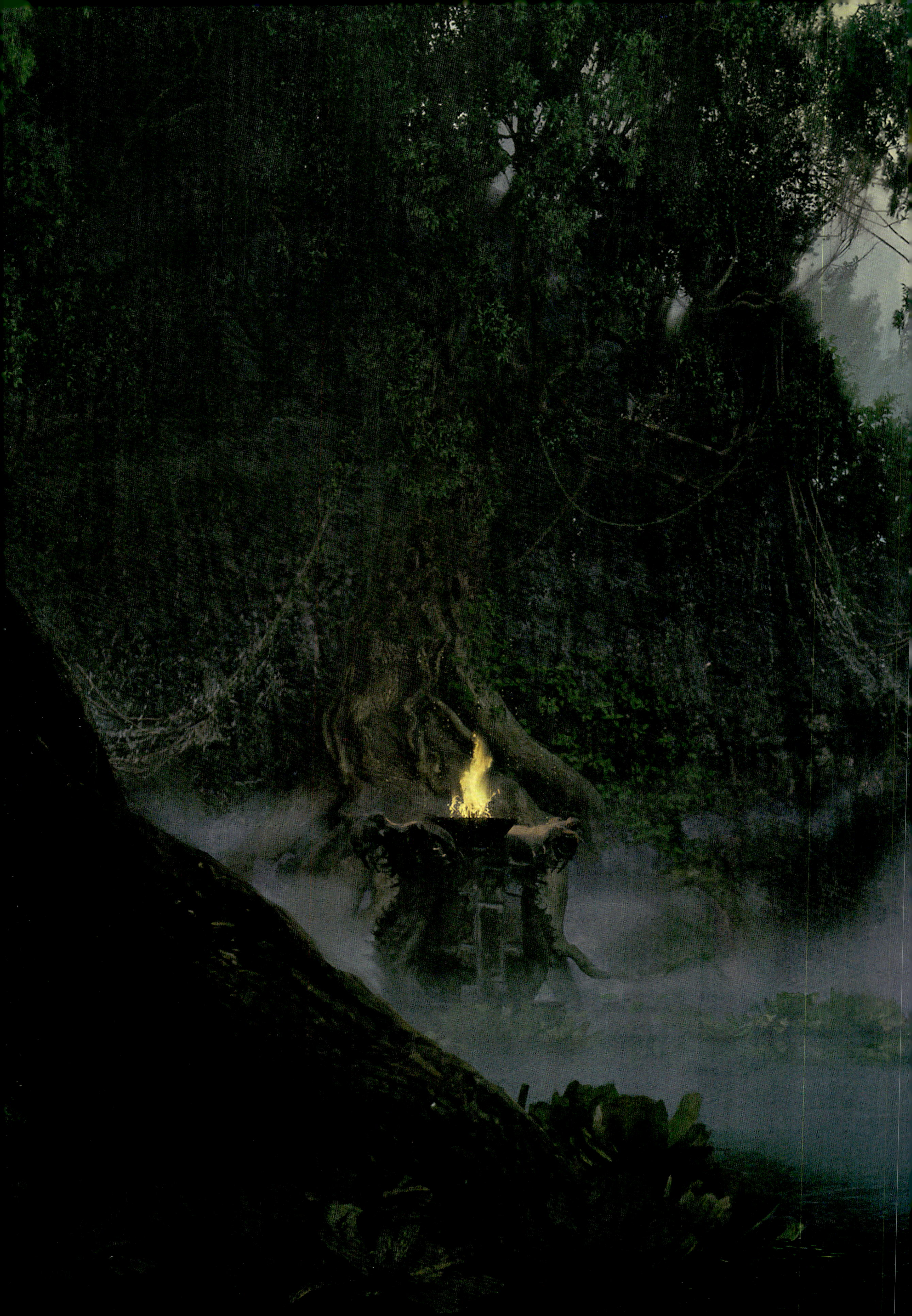

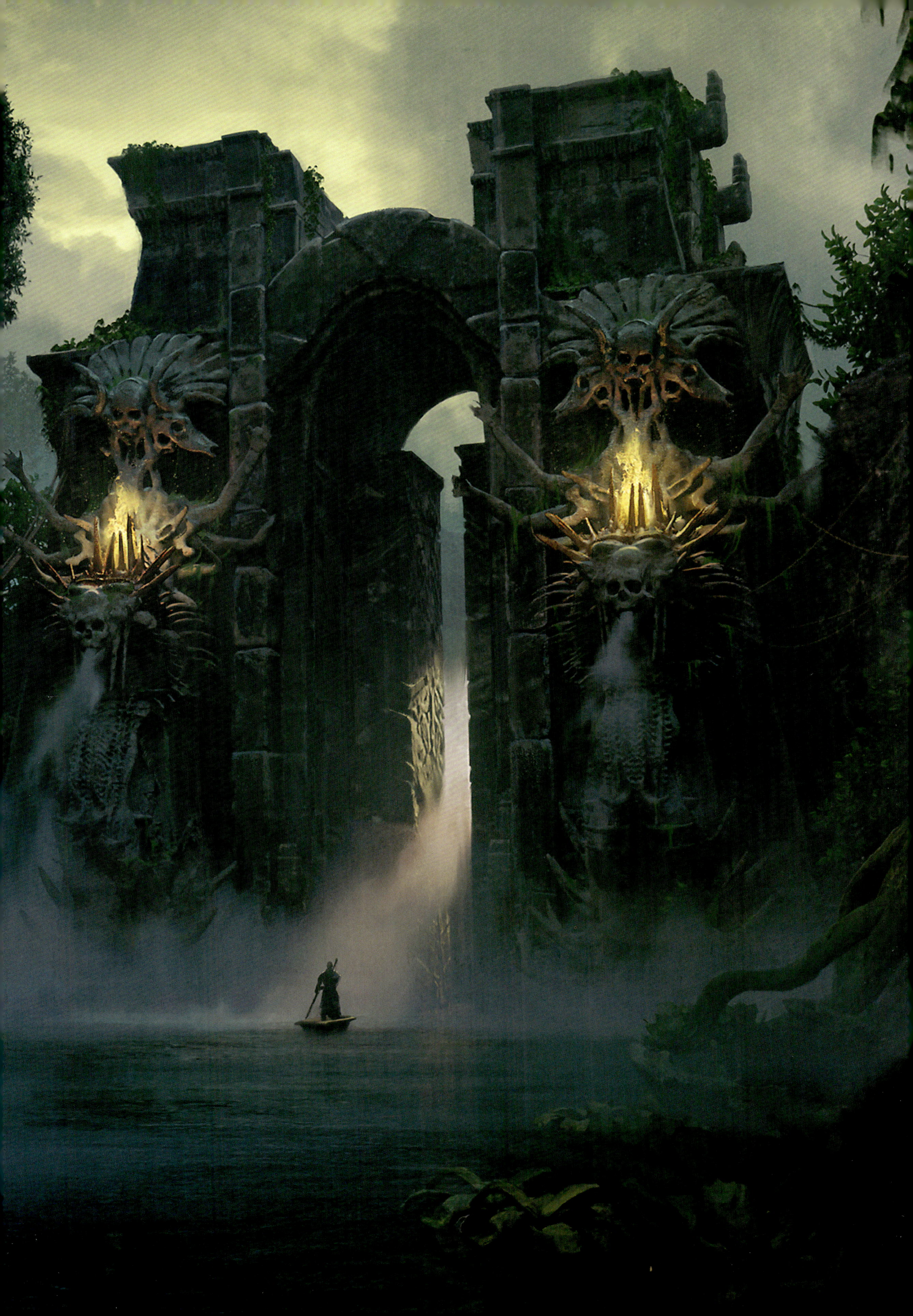

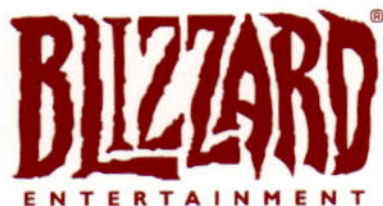

WRITTEN BY *Micky Nelson*
EDITED BY *Eric Geron, Ian Landa-Beavers*
PRODUCED BY *Brianne Messina, Amber Proue-Thibodeau*
GAME TEAM CONSULTATION *Dustin King, John Mueller, Emil Salim, Mac Smith*
LORE CONSULTATION *Madi Buckingham*
SPECIAL THANKS *Mauro Agnellini, Tania Liao, Leah Newman*
MANAGER, PUBLISHING *Peter Molinari*
ASSOCIATE MANAGER, CONSUMER PRODUCTS *Chanee' Goude*
SENIOR DIRECTOR, CREATIVE DEVELOPMENT *Venecia Duran*
SENIOR MANAGER, BOOKS & WRITING *Matthew Cohan*
SENIOR PRODUCER, BOOKS *Brianne Messina*
ASSOCIATE PRODUCER, BOOKS *Amber Proue-Thibodeau*
EDITORIAL SUPERVISOR *Chloe Fraboni*
SENIOR EDITOR *Eric Geron*
SENIOR BRAND ARTIST *Corey Peterschmidt*
SENIOR PRODUCER, LORE *Jamie Ortiz*
PRODUCER, LORE *Ed Fox*
LORE HISTORIAN LEAD *Sean Copeland*
ASSOCIATE HISTORIANS *Madi Buckingham, Courtney Chavez, Ian Landa-Beavers*

DESIGNED BY *Cameron + Company, an imprint of ABRAMS*
PUBLISHER *Chris Gruener*
CREATIVE DIRECTOR *Iain R. Morris*
DESIGNER *Suzi Hutsell*

Published by Blizzard Entertainment.

Library of Congress Cataloging-in-Publication Data available.

Trade ISBN: 978-1-956916-28-7
Limited Edition #1 ISBN: 978-1-956916-38-6
Limited Edition #2 ISBN: 978-1-956916-57-7

Manufactured in China

Print run 10 9 8 7 6 5 4 3 2 1

FRONT COVER Lilith + *Diablo IV* + Brom
BACK COVER Inarius + *Diablo IV* + Brom
PAGE 1 Inarius and Lilith Key Art + *Diablo IV* + Brom
PAGES 2–3 City of Westmarch Illustration + *Diablo Immortal* + NetEase Art Team
PAGE 4 Skarn Illustration + *Diablo Immortal* + Brom
PAGE 5 Summoning Circle Concept + *Diablo IV* + Fernando Pinilla
PAGE 6 The Skeleton King Key Art + *Diablo Immortal* + Geunjoo Baik
PAGE 7 Triune Symbol Concept + *Diablo IV* + Fernando Pinilla
RIGHT Fly Host Concept + *Diablo IV* + Victor Lee

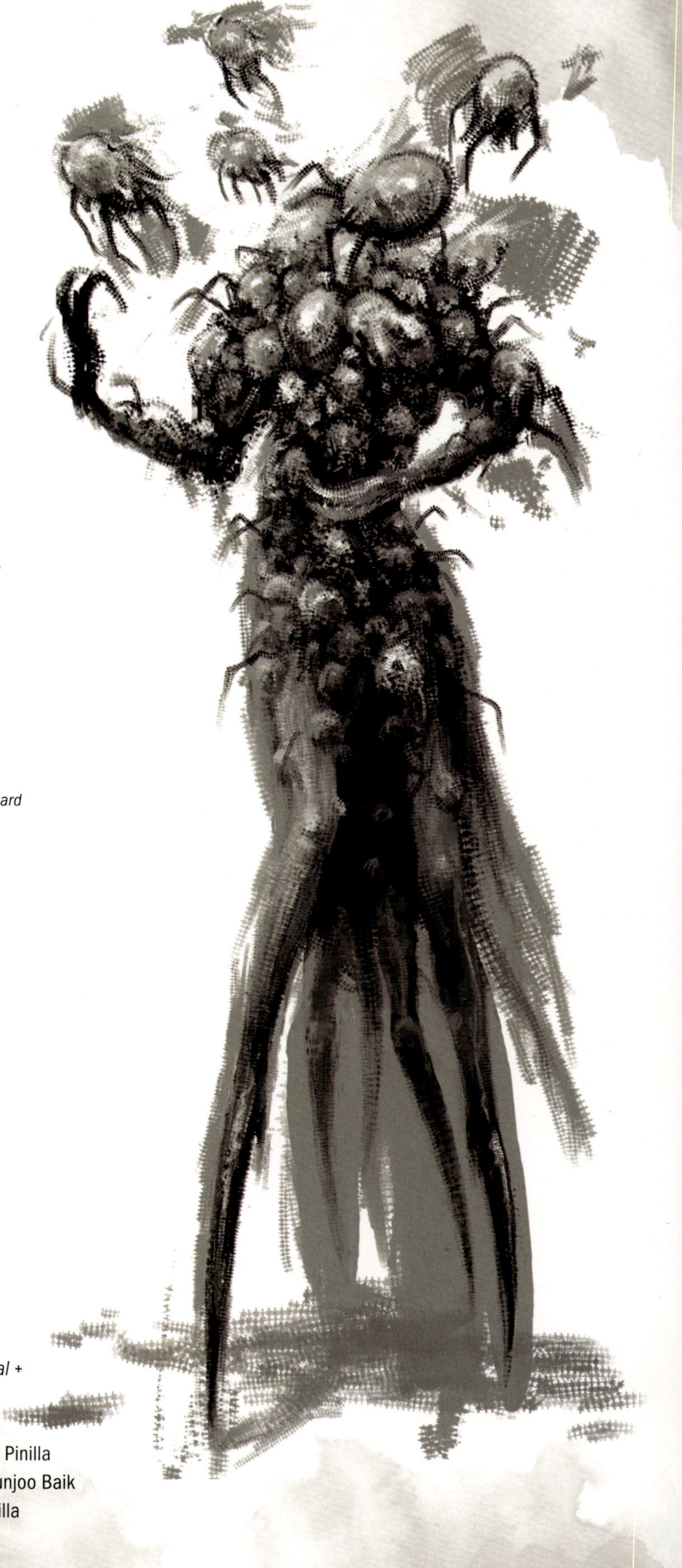

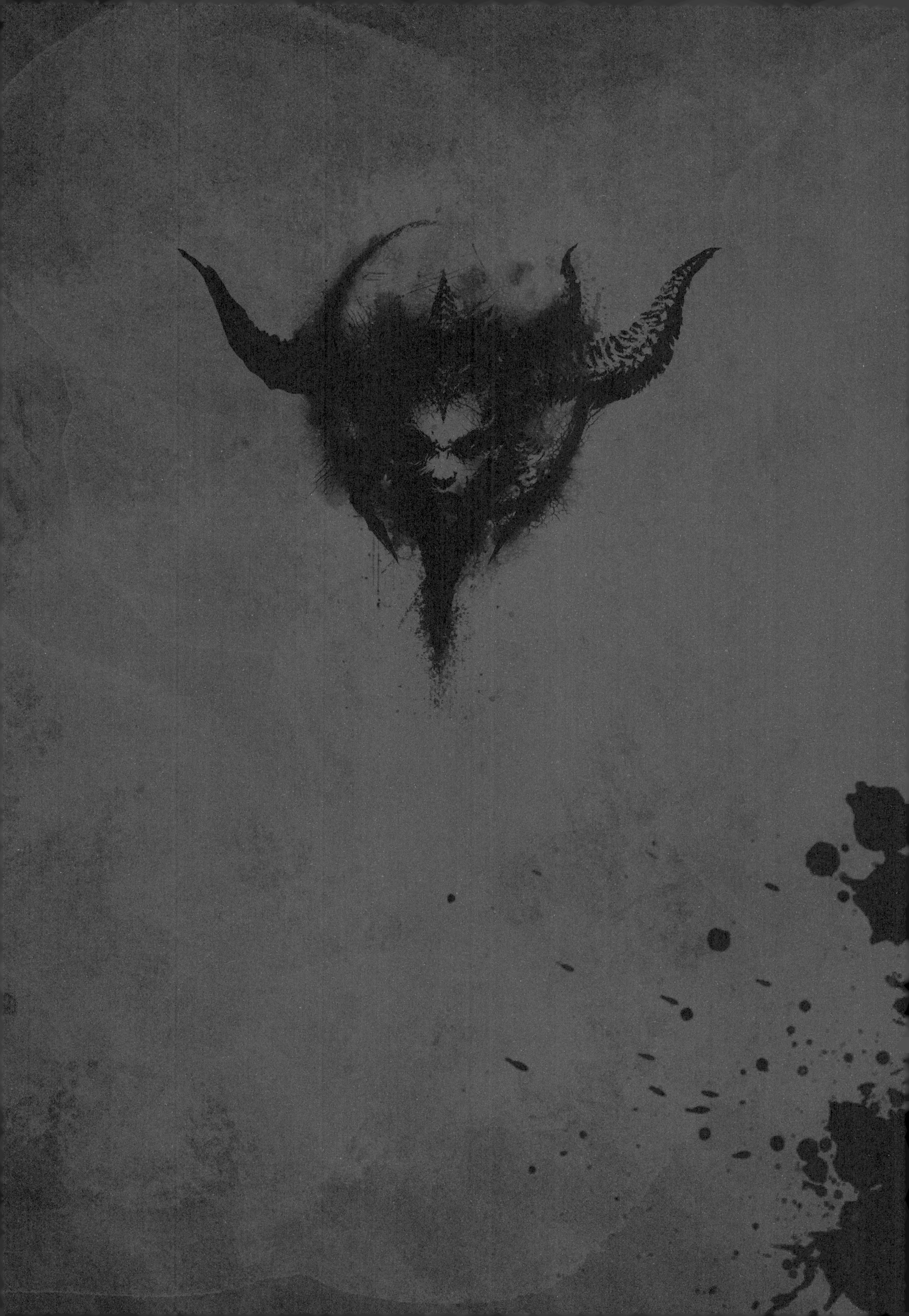

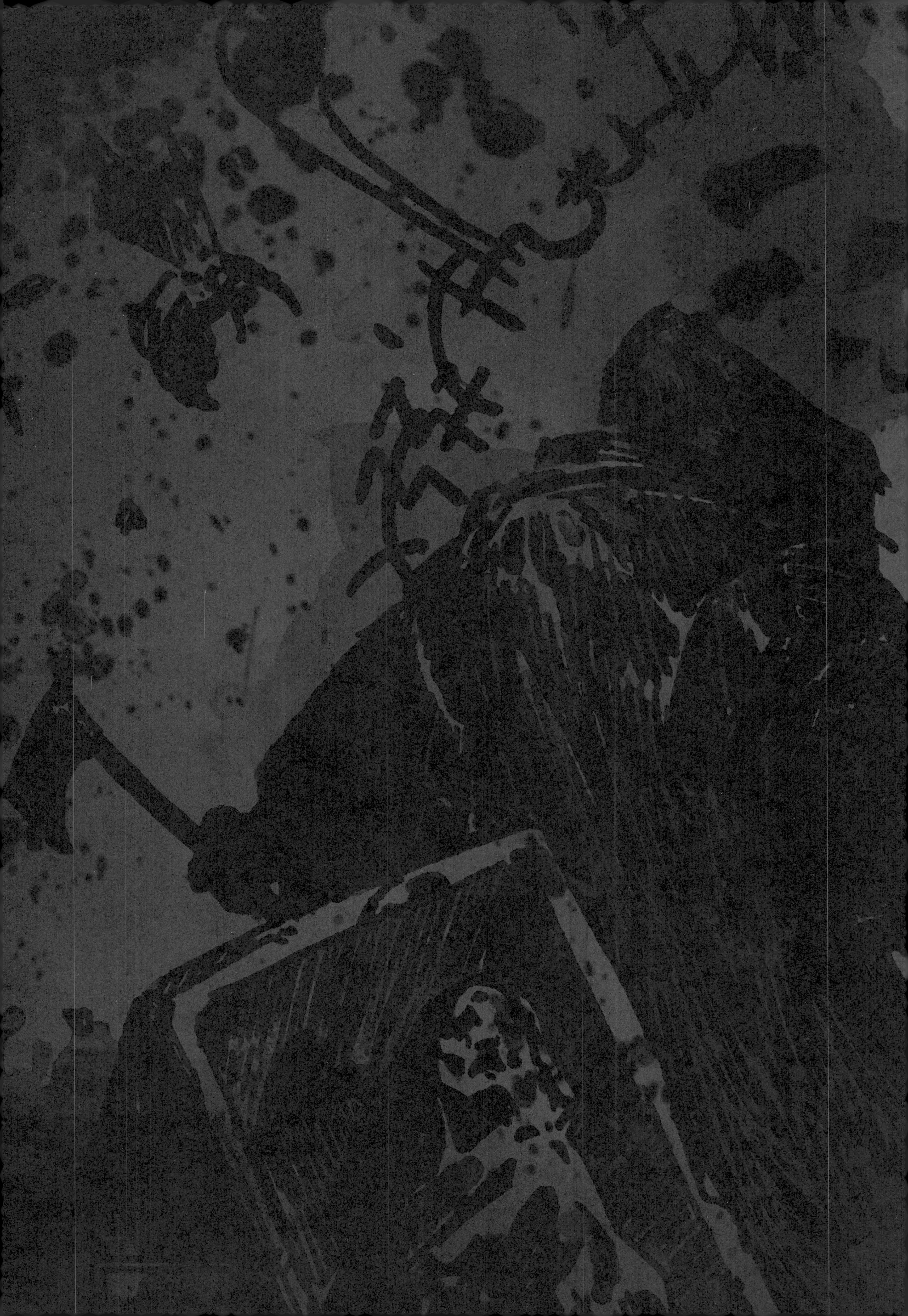